MOONRISE KINGDOM SERIES III

THE ALPHA

GOD'S LUNA

MARISSA GILBERT

I0615405

1. CAGED

"Can you believe that she was once the Teacher's favourite?" Astrea heard a female voice echoing above her head. She made an effort to open her eyes but only saw three blurry silhouettes watching her from the top of the silver pit where she had spent the last several months as the punishment for her betrayal.

She'd hoped that the Firstborn warriors were done with her, but apparently not. It was nighttime, and her ex-colleagues made time to visit her every so often to watch and enjoy her suffering. Apparently, it was at the top of this summer's to-do list.

"Was?" one of the women scoffed loudly. "If it were any of *us* that stabbed the Master in the back like that, we would have been dead months ago. Don't get it wrong, Astrea Sade was and still is very much his favourite. The Teacher has held her here for four months. Why would he keep her alive for so long if he was just going to kill her in the end?"

Now they'd grabbed her attention. Was it *four* months already? She'd stopped counting somewhere after her hundred days milestone. Simply because she had no energy to carve new tally marks on the wall anymore. Thick silver was draining her wolf's strength, making them poisoned and weaker than ever, at the same time preventing her from regeneration. She was stuck here, hurting and shocked she had lasted that long. Anyone else would have been dead by now.

There was only one plus side. Her torture would probably be over soon.

She couldn't eat or drink anymore and, frankly, saw no reason to fight for her life.

Nevertheless, she had no regrets. Maybe they'd branded her as a traitor, but if she had gone through with her last task, she would have been betraying herself. Every time she closed her eyes, she remembered the choice she made while infiltrating the Luna Trials, an event where the Northern Lycan King was choosing his Luna.

That mission was very different from all the others she'd been given before.

Usually, she was sent to make a quick kill or act as a spy somewhere for a short while. But that time... that time she had to live with those people for weeks, stay close to them, get to know them.

It didn't help that, at first, her task did not require killing anyone. So, she got to know everyone safely, weeding out the information for her Teacher but also enjoying herself in the process. At some point, pretending to be everyone's friend stopped feeling false. She quickly came to realise that she liked these people. They were kind, noble in heart, passionate, and so alive. Living her whole life on the Firstborn island, where her Teacher trained them as fierce heartless warriors, his assassins and spies, she was deprived of what the Northerners had. Seeing true love stories unwrap before her eyes and true friendships forming, she couldn't help but succumb to the charm.

That's why when she received the order to kill everyone at the Luna ceremony, she couldn't go through with it.

She was faced with a choice. To take the lives of everyone she liked and continue her path as her Teacher's favourite, his Dragonfly or... disobey him for the first time ever and give those people in the North a chance.

Astrea chose the latter. She hoped they used that chance wisely because she was the one now paying for it.

"They say that he comes to look at her every night," one of the girls whispered, but Astrea heard her. Even if he did, she personally never saw him. The last thing she felt right now was her Teacher's favour.

There was only one unbreakable rule on the island. Everyone had to obey the Teacher.

Sadly, this was the one rule she couldn't follow anymore.

"I heard they are going to execute her next week, though," the third woman muttered with an impassive face. "I personally think this long punishment was to demonstrate to all of us that no one is safe. Not even her. If you betray the Teacher and the Firstborn, you are doomed no matter who you are!"

None of the three visitors uttered another word as they watched her lying on the silver-layered ground, restrained in chains which prevented her injuries from healing, giving her the slowest death possible.

At least they were right about something. Their Teacher... that man was too heartless and too cruel to forgive anyone. At least, in all the years she'd spent by his side, she hadn't seen him show mercy to anyone.

"I say it's good that she is down there!" the first one broke the silence again. "She never deserved to be the leader of the Dragonfly squad in the first place. I still fail to understand what's so special about her! Yes, she was not a bad assassin, but she always lacked discipline!"

"Speaking of Dragonflies," one of them, a brunette, hummed as her brow quirked up, "if she dies, her spot in the Dragonfly squad would be free, right?"

Astrea watched them in amusement, not showing that she'd heard them at all. Why did everyone think that being in the Dragonfly squad was some sort of a prize? She didn't enjoy a single day in it, and technically, she was their leader. All they did was train and go on missions. Mostly alone, so it made no sense why they were called a squad. Their special dragonfly tattoos were all that they had in common.

"Probably," one of the women at the top hummed to herself. "If she dies, her place will be up for grabs."

"Imagine if she is pardoned instead, though," another one suggested, and this time, the silence between them became heavy. Astrea sensed it with her skin. This was the moment they'd decide whether to kill her now or not.

No one on the island liked her before. They sure as hell hated her now. After all, when she pretended to poison the mating ceremony in the North instead of actually poisoning them, she had to flee for her life. The Teacher sent several groups of Firstborn warriors after her, and for days, they were chasing her. Most of them were dead now because she took their lives while defending herself. She was that good. She almost managed to reach the Eastern border when they managed to overpower her. There were too many of them, and she was exhausted after days of the chase.

Astrea still remembered staring at the little strip of desert, miles away from where they caught her, and imagining what could have been if she had reached the Rogue Kingdom. She still remembered a dark creature in the distance that watched her from that free land. That was the last thing she remembered before the pit.

"It's a windy night," the second woman spoke again. "If a rock was to fall straight on her head and smash it accidentally, no one could be blamed."

"And then the Dragonflies will definitely need one more to fill the ranks.

Maybe two, considering that Astrea killed one of their own when she was on the run."

"No one would miss this traitor," the third one chimed in.

For a few seconds, everything got quiet again, and Astrea was disappointed that maybe they'd changed their minds. After months in the silver pit, death would have been mercy.

However, the three women came back with impressive boulders in their hands. Her werewolf vision was weak now, but Astrea still could feel their murderous intent. Her instincts were not dead.

She did her best not to move for them. After all, her death would be her freedom. But the first rock hit her shoulder, cracking it and bringing more pain. She cried out more out of frustration than hurt. That was nowhere near a fatal blow. Couldn't they do better?

"Oh, look, she is awake," one of her supposed killers let out an ugly laugh. "It's going to be more fun!"

"Shut up," another growled. "We need to be quick and quiet."

"Don't even think about it!" A new voice sounded on the ground above, and this time Astrea's whole body shivered at the recognition.

Niki.

Her ward, Niki. The one she trained personally and had protected since she'd gotten to the Firstborn island. Her only true friend.

No, Moon Goddess, please no! Niki was not supposed to be here! She'd begged her not to come here anymore!

"And if I think about it, what will you do?" One of the three Firstborns pivoted to glare at Niki, who had a tote bag in her hand. She probably brought food and water again in an attempt to feed her.

She shouldn't have come! Astrea had begged her not to. A lump formed in the she-wolf's throat. Niki was so close to her Ascension. It would have been best for her to break their ties and make everyone forget that there was ever a connection between them.

But this was her ward's only weakness. Niki still had too much kindness and compassion left in her. It would make it much harder for her to become a cold-blooded murderer.

It was best for Niki to dissociate herself from her traitor mentor, but she still came to see her every day.

"You are not hurting her!" Niki insisted, dropping the bag and balling her fists. Astrea felt her dry eyes burning with tears. She would get herself in trouble!

"Kid, just walk away and pretend you didn't see anything!" one of the women suggested.

"No, 'you just walk away' or rest assured that everyone will know what you were doing here today!" Niki growled, and Astrea closed her eyes, knowing it was the end of her hopes. This was the last thing she should have told those three. Now they couldn't let Niki go…

"Or we can kill you and the traitor and then pretend we caught you trying to kill her," one of the Firstborn suggested. "No one will ever know what actually happened. Not to mention that my ward will have less competition at Ascension if you are out."

"It's a win-win." The three women were circling around Niki, and Astrea couldn't see anything from where she was laying, her every muscle tense now.

The sounds of a fight reached her ears, and she knew that, although Niki was a great fighter, her chances against three fully ascended Firstborn warriors were slim. They were getting special powers and strength after Ascension. And Niki was still just a trainee.

Seconds ago Astrea wished for nothing more than a quick death, yet now she had a different purpose.

Niki was like a little sister to her. She was family, and she had a whole life ahead of her. She wasn't supposed to die defending her, and Astrea knew she would do anything in her power to stop this.

Her whole body shivered as she stood up for the first time in a while, leaning against the silver wall that burned her skin. Adrenaline rushed through her bloodstream, and she didn't feel pain anymore. She had a goal now.

This was probably the last thing she would do in this life, but if she could give Niki a chance, it would be so worth it.

Astrea's eyes fixated on a pulley system they used to lower her food. She'd thought about this trick quite a few times in the past few months but never found herself strong enough to actually try it.

Today she had no choice as she could smell the blood. Niki's blood. Two women were holding her ward while the third one was battering her.

Astrea jumped as high as she could, using her legs to push off one side of the pit and then another, swinging the long part of the chain in hopes of grasping the metallic part of the pulley with it and using it to pull herself out. An extremely unrealistic plan, but what was she to do when Niki was up there risking her life for her?

That kid should have walked away and saved herself the trouble.

The first attempt failed, and Astrea fell, hurting herself even more in the process. The bones in her ankle made an unpleasant cracking sound.

Still, the adrenaline coursed through her, so she stood up and repeated everything with a fierce growl of her wolf, Nova, escaping her as the chain finally wrapped itself over the metal track.

Astrea used her arm muscles to pull her body up, and soon, her palm reached the top of the pit. Right where three ascended Firstborn assassins were beating the crap out of Niki.

Not wasting time, with strength and dumb luck still on her side, Astrea grabbed the foot of the woman closest to her and threw her down the pit, watching her fall at an awkward angle with her head first, a pool of blood immediately forming around her.

That brought the attention of the remaining two to her. Niki winced, blood trickling down her face. One of the assassins holding her let go, moving towards Astrea.

"Look at this," she sneered. "She came to us herself—"

The woman was about to kick her when something mighty and dark swept past, grabbing her and carrying her into the dark sky. It happened so fast that none of them had time to react.

The last assailant released Niki, knowing the young girl was the last thing to worry about now. Astrea's ward fell to the ground, panting desperately.

The dark force returned, taking the last Firstborn with it as Astrea only felt the wind from the impact. Such speed... she knew only one creature capable of that.

Her Teacher.

The one who put her here.

After all, *there was only one unbreakable rule on the island. Always obey the Teacher.* And those three just tried breaking it.

Her eyes locked with Niki's, and her ward tried to crawl to her to give her a hand.

Silly girl... what was she thinking?

Before Niki could do something stupid and be the third one to be killed by the Teacher, Astrea let go, falling freely back to the bottom of the pit.

She hit the silver bottom hard, and this time it really felt like it would be the end. *She welcomed it, too tired to fight.*

It would be for the best for everyone. Especially Niki, who was now calling her name from the top as Astrea succumbed to darkness.

She was awakened by a loud thump next to her. Her eyes fluttered open and shut, having a hard time seeing the face of the man towering over her, but she recognised the tall figure with broad, muscular shoulders at once.

Joran Nathair, her Teacher and the holder of her fate, knelt beside her and gently brushed his fingers over her cheek.

She couldn't move, each bone in her body aching, her throat so dry, not a sound could leave it.

"Dragonfly," her Teacher sighed, scooping her up in his arms, "just what do I do with you?"

2. BATTLE OF WILLS

*A*s the first rays of sunlight gently streamed through the delicate curtains, Astrea stirred from her slumber and stretched in the soft satin sheets, her eyes flickering open to take in her surroundings.

For a few seconds, she was sure it was a dream, a cruel hallucination she had while slowly dying at the bottom of the silver pit.

There was no way she would be back in her old room in Teacher's mansion. However, goosebumps rushed through her skin when she sat up, and her bare feet touched the familiar soft fur rug.

It was real.

Since she was around ten-years-old, she used to call this place home. It was as if the last few months didn't happen, and only the sore bruises on her skin reminded her of what she had gone through.

I guess we are back, Nova pointed out sceptically at the back of her mind, and she didn't find a good response to that. Her wolf was one of a kind, adding a pinch of salt to everything. Sometimes it made life more flavourful, and sometimes... it was extra.

Astrea quickly scanned the room, and a beautiful black dress with a note attached to it hanging from the expensive crystal chandelier grabbed her attention at once. She was used to this. The Teacher loved surprising her with things like this. *Things she could never reject.*

She walked towards the gown on slightly shaking feet, surprised she could walk at all. A diamond-studded snake necklace collar was curling around a golden hanger and holding together a few pieces of black silk fabric that flowed freely to the floor, leaving the back bare.

She opened the note with only one sentence: The dinner is at eight p.m.

There was no doubt that the dress was for her to wear. He had always done that. Wear this, do that with your hair, use this dagger for that mission... The Teacher loved to control everything.

But she was too tired to object. He was probably still going to kill her in the end. Nothing changed. She could at least look nice and have some dignity.

Only now, Astrea realised that a soft white towel was wrapped around her body, a body that had no open wounds anymore. She walked towards a tall mirror with a golden frame and took a proper look at herself. Her silvery-white hair cascaded in soft waves down her shoulders as if she didn't spend months in a dirty hole. Her skin, however, still had red marks from where the silver chains had touched her. Those would take a while to heal. Her usually bright sky-blue eyes seemed duller now, as if there was no life in her left.

"This will not do," she sighed, clenching her fists. She refused to admit defeat.

Not like this.

If he wanted her to die, he shouldn't have got her out.

Astrea took a long shower, scrubbing every inch of her body despite having already been cleaned by someone. Then she took time to do her nails, makeup and hair to perfection.

It didn't help, and she still didn't feel like her old self.

But she could pretend...

THE DOORS to the dining hall opened, and she entered the silvery-grey marble area, her heels clicking and her head held high. If she had to meet Death itself today, she would do it with as much confidence and self-respect as she could muster. Whatever the cost.

The Teacher was sitting at the head of the long table, and just two places were set for the meal. His and the one right next to him.

He looked exactly the same as always. Tall and broad-shouldered, with perfect noble features, blonde hair brushed to one side and piercing green eyes that slowly took her in. Not a year older than thirty. And this was how he looked for over the decade she knew him.

"Finally." Joran Nathair, the mentor who taught her everything she knew, gestured at the empty seat. "Please, join me."

Astrea did not want to play this game and moved to sit in the chair opposite him, the one at the end of this very long table and with no plates and cutlery ready.

"Thanks," she offered him an unamused smile.

Joran's lips pressed into a thin line. There was one thing he hated the most.

Defiance.

Not to mention that he wasn't used to getting it from her. But she was already in deep trouble, and it couldn't possibly get any worse. *After the silver pit, what did he expect?*

"I would prefer you to sit closer," he said, voice void of emotions, but she knew he must have been fuming.

"And I would prefer to make my own decisions," she retorted. "Since I am going to die anyway."

He drummed his fingers on the surface of the table while his eyes burned holes in her skull.

"Is that what you think?" He raised his brow questioningly. "Astrea, if I wanted you dead, you would have been dead long ago."

"But you chose to torture me instead!" she huffed a dark laugh.

"To educate you. You needed a lesson in humility." As always, he saw it through a prism in his own light.

"Some lesson that was." Astrea shook her head with a disappointed smile. "How long was it? Four months? Five?"

"Four and a half," he told her, not looking guilty at all. "I aimed for half a year."

"Gee, I feel so lucky to be let out early." She glared at him.

"Take your seat," he repeated in a calm tone that did not fool her.

"I am fine here, thanks." She tried to match his tone, the two of them staring at each other across the long table in this grand room. Astrea felt it was another test, but she was too tired to play the role he wanted her to play. Something broke in her while she lay at the bottom of that silver pit, in chains with barely enough food and water to survive. It was an irreversible change, probably deeper than when she chose not to kill the Northern royal family and their friends at the Luna Trials.

"I have to say I am really disappointed in you." He took the ring off his napkin, still not looking bothered by her behaviour. "After everything I did for you, this is how you chose to repay me!"

She felt a wave of guilt wash over her. Denying that this man saved her from death early in her life and gave her a home, education, training, and purpose would be a lie. She knew she owed him, but a part of her felt like she had already repaid him for everything.

"It wasn't right." She lowered her head, not wishing to elaborate. "They were good people. They didn't deserve to die."

"Sometimes good people stand in the way of the greater good," Joran sighed heavily, back leaning over his chair. "This was the case here. They had to die so that many other people could live well."

"Doubtful!" The words left her mouth faster than she could process them.

"Just because you failed to see the bigger picture doesn't mean it's not there, Astrea. I thought I'd taught you better than that."

"You did," she admitted because it was the truth. Her training was hard, but it had impeccable results. It wasn't her training that failed her. It was the emotions she felt on that mission. The people she met at the Luna Trials had become her friends. Or at least the closest thing she had to friends.

"So, why did you defy my order? Why did you betray me?" Joran still appeared calm, cold even, but it did not fool her.

"Because I just couldn't do that! It was not right! The Queen from the Western Kingdom was pregnant, for Goddess' sake – she was the kindest person I've ever met. And her baby... I can't kill children! I told you that before!" she snapped.

"You could have poisoned everyone but her then. I would have forgiven that!" Joran's jaw tightened. "But you made me believe you completed the mission, setting me up for failure when we left the North, and everyone I thought dead suddenly appeared alive on a battlefield. Do you know I lost someone I cared about because of what you did?"

She didn't know that. She didn't even know there was someone he cared about.

Joran continued as if he had heard her thoughts, "There were just two people dear to my heart. One died, and the other is a traitor now."

For some reason, that hurt. They'd spent too many years together for her not to care. However, she didn't have any illusions either.

"So, where do we go from here?" Astrea asked quietly.

"Take your seat, and we will talk," he cut her off, still seeking to bend her to his will.

"I am *fine here*." She crossed her arms over her chest.

"So, you choose to stay stubborn," Joran sighed, and she could feel his anger rippling through the air even if nothing in his appearance gave it away.

"What now?" she asked, tired of all this. "Are you going to kill me or not?"

"Kill you?" the man scoffed, chuckling darkly. "Astrea, why would you think that? I would never hurt you. I simply can't. You are my Dragonfly."

She almost wanted to laugh at that, considering her hands and neck still had traces of the silver chains.

"We need more wine here, please!" Joran raised his voice, and Niki walked in with a tray, making Astrea's confidence fade.

Her ward poured the ruby liquid into Joran's glass and paused before the second glass at the empty seat.

"Excuse me," she asked quietly, knowing her place very well. She was still a trainee, and the Ascension was before her. "Should I take the glass to Astrea?"

"Of course not!" Joran's lips curled. "Astrea is joining me here. Aren't you, Dragonfly?"

It was a threat. A warning. Niki was here for a reason, and every cell in Astrea's body screamed that it was a new sick trap. He couldn't sway her determination, so he found leverage... She thought that no one knew they had gotten close. She tried to make it look like a regular mentor/ward relationship to avoid this exact situation.

Of course, he found out. The Teacher always knew everything. She was stupid to think she could outsmart him.

"Of course," she replied, trying to hide the venom in her voice, rising gracefully and concealing the storm of emotions inside.

As soon as she sat next to him, Joran's mood improved. Victories affected him like that, and Astrea already knew she'd lost their first battle in minutes. How stupid was she to think she could last longer? She couldn't let Niki die or get hurt in her stead. He figured out her only weakness.

Their food was served less than a minute later, but she couldn't find it in herself to touch anything. She felt trapped again. This wasn't the bottom of the silver pit, but somehow, it was just as bad.

"Eat something," Joran told her lazily. "You need to regain your strength. The steak looks especially good today. Just the way you like it."

"I haven't eaten normal food in months," she replied curtly. "If I start shoving meat into my stomach, I will only make myself sick."

Everyone was gone, and it had been just the two of them again. Joran took her hand and brought it closer to his face, examining the marks on her wrists.

"I am sorry you had to go through this. You know the rules. I am already breaking them by letting you stay alive, but you are the only one I would ever do this for." He brushed his thumb over the red welt, and she hissed as it was still too fresh. However, waves of relief rippled through her the next moment, soothing the pain and making the marks disappear. "That looks better. Now eat."

She indeed felt better, her physical strength replenishing from a single touch of his. She'd known he was not a simple shifter creature and had all kinds of abilities for years, but it was rare for him to demonstrate it like this.

They ate in silence, and she was lost. He wasn't going to kill her; he'd made that clear. But he also couldn't trust her anymore. What was this dinner for? What was his plan for her? Too many questions she couldn't ask directly because she wasn't sure she wanted to know the answers.

"You think I am too cruel," he said out of the blue when their plates were taken away. "I am disappointed you feel this way, but I feel that it's partially my fault. I still can't process that you believed I would let you die."

"I know the rules," she responded quietly, trying not to move her hands to show him how stressed she was by the whole situation. "Any Firstborn who disobeys you dies."

"But you are not just any Firstborn!" He slammed his fist on the table, making the glasses on it bounce and skitter precariously. "You are my Dragonfly! My one and only disciple. Why do you think I taught you everything I could?"

"To make me your weapon," she responded bluntly, and he threw his wine glass against the opposite wall, smashing it to pieces. Niki immediately appeared to clean the mess, and Astrea couldn't help but feel nervous. She did not like that her ward was so close when the Teacher wasn't in a good mood.

"Is that what you think?" He caught her hand, making her look at him.

"Why else would you train me?" She snatched her hand from his grasp.

His eyes gleamed with fire.

"To make you strong! To make you what you are today." His response shocked her, but she tried not to read too much into this. "Don't tell me you never knew how special you are to me, Dragonfly."

"You had four more Dragonflies," she reminded him, averting her eyes from his heavy gaze. "I wasn't that special."

"Well, it's three now, thanks to you." He reminded her that she killed one during her rebellion. "But also, they are there just to be your team when you need it. I only keep them for you and only call them that so that outsiders don't know which one of you I really care about."

Astrea didn't know what to do with this information.

Her Teacher wasn't a good man. This wasn't a healthy relationship, and if he wasn't training her to be his weapon, then she didn't want to know why she was here in the first place and why he needed her to be that strong.

"I want out," she said, knowing this was the only rational decision she could make. She couldn't pretend that everything was fine; she couldn't act as if she was his little obedient Dragonfly anymore. She had changed, and if she had to die for it, at least she would die true to herself.

He was silent for a while, and she was afraid that he would tell her off now, return her to the pit or worse - kill Niki in front of her. The latter would be the most painful, so she tried really hard not to look in her ward's direction.

"Let's make a deal then," Joran said in a calm voice which echoed through the marble halls, and her eyes darted at him, lips parted in shock.

She knew very well her Teacher's deals never ended well for the ones who took the bait. The whole Firstborn army was proof of that. They were not called Firstborns for nothing. Once upon a time, each of their parents struck a deal where they promised their firstborn children to Joran in exchange for something, and her Teacher collected without delays. Most were brought here by the age of eight.

Astrea was the only exception because he saved her when her family died. Technically, there wasn't a deal tying her to this place.

"No," she said in a tone that took no objections. "I don't want any deals with you."

"That means I taught you well." He smirked, placing his large palm over her delicate hand on the table. "However, this time, it's the deal or nothing."

"I'll take the nothing then." She gave him another defiant look, which only amused him more.

"I would like more *wine*." He accentuated the last word, and Niki appeared instantly. He clearly made a point and reminded her that she had already lost that argument.

Niki disappeared again, and Astrea shot him an irritated look.

"You know she is your best trainee, right?" The woman arched her snow-white brow. "No one's ward is better than her, and you haven't had anyone better since—"

"Since you. I am aware," Joran confirmed nonchalantly, brushing his hand through his dark blonde hair.

"She should be preparing for the Ascension and not pouring wine into glasses!" Astrea spat the words out, regretting them almost instantly. She didn't need to draw even more attention to Niki.

"And she will be. Once we are done with this nonsense." Her Teacher wasn't bothered at all. "It's all up to you."

"Then stop pretending that I have a choice!" Astrea was losing her patience fast.

"You do have a choice," he corrected. "It's just that it's not unlimited."

"What's the deal then?" She decided not to beat around the bush.

"See, that wasn't so hard, was it?" Joran let out a celebratory laugh, and when she did not react, his grin widened. "Anyway, nothing too difficult this time. Not for you, at least."

She did not buy it. He wouldn't be asking it of her if it was easy. There had to be a catch somewhere.

"I'm listening." Astrea wanted to be done with this conversation quickly.

"You already know that, thanks to you, my previous plan failed, and we did not conquer the Northern Lycan Kingdom," he informed her, and she frowned, secretly happy. In truth, she wanted to grin at him but knew better. A display of emotions could cost her. "So, now I need you to fix your mistake."

"You want me to conquer a Kingdom?" she snorted loudly. This was ridiculous.

"I want you to help me finish what I started." Joran looked as serious as ever. "Moreover, I will give you what you so desperately desire."

"Freedom?" she taunted, getting braver by the minute. He was not going to kill her, and she felt like being a brat to him. This was the only bit of joy she still had, trapped in his clutches again.

"I will give you your freedom if you succeed," he taunted back, and her arrogance faded.

"You're joking!" Astrea was sure it couldn't be true.

"I am not," he assured her, a smirk spreading over his face slowly. "Interested now?"

"Me and Niki," she said at once. It wasn't like she had a lot to lose. She could try to save her ward too.

"No," Joran replied firmly. "What do you think this is? A charity auction? This deal is for you and you alone."

She bit the inside of her cheek, trying to calm herself. The adrenaline was coursing through her. She could think of saving Niki another time. If she got out and then caught Niki on one of her future missions, she could help her ward flee.

"Don't tell me it's going to be a problem for you?" Her Teacher was enjoying this. "You've already left her behind once. What's the problem with doing it again? You abandoned us pretty easily."

Us. Not just her.

"There was nothing easy about it." Astrea locked her eyes with him, seeing an ocean of emotions in this usually cold man.

"Oh?" He tilted his head, watching her intently. "I am pleased to know that."

"When I couldn't follow your order, I knew I was doomed," she confessed honestly. "I just took the last chance I had to survive."

"You could have come to me," he interrupted, but a laugh escaped her when she heard it. He gave her a glare, and she bit her tongue. It wasn't the time to make him angry.

"What was the mission again?" She decided to return to the original topic, avoiding dangerous grounds.

"I want you to go to the East," he replied dryly. "That's where you were headed, weren't you? Well, there you go. Your wish is granted."

"Why would you need me there? That kingdom is long gone. There is nothing to conquer, nothing to gain. Only rogues live there—" She stopped talking when the realisation hit her, eyes darting at her mentor in shock.

"I see you are already on the correct path of thinking." Joran nodded at her with the corner of his lips tugging upwards. "I want to use the rogues in the upcoming war. They should fight on the side of our Southern Lycan Republic."

She stared at him in shock, speechless.

"Come on, Astrea, even you have to admit it. The plan is perfect. Rogues are expendable. They will be our perfect warriors. There is only one problem."

"What is it?" She didn't like this mission already.

"Their King is too secretive, and I want you to discover all his secrets. After all, I need to know who I am working with."

"What will they think I am doing there?" she wondered.

"Oh, that's easy. The second part of your task is to prepare those rogues to meet the Alpha Convocation in a few months. They need to know what to say and, most importantly, what not to do for us to be able to form an official alliance with them. Not every Southern Alpha agrees to this project, and I want to persuade them all."

"You want me to give etiquette lessons and play dress up with rogues?" She knitted her brows. All this still felt like a joke.

"After your experience at The Luna Trials, I think you will be perfect for the task," he taunted. "Any more questions?"

Astrea took a sip of her wine. Suddenly it felt like she needed it.

"Will you really let me go?" Their eyes locked in a silent resistance against each other.

"Once this alliance is made, I will grant you your freedom. If you would still want it, of course." Joran's lips curled.

"Why wouldn't I want it?" She finished her glass and placed it back on the table.

"Anything can happen." He looked smug for some reason, but she couldn't quite decipher him yet.

She would have never agreed to a deal with him if it was a choice. However, right now, she had to be wise. This was a game of survival, and she was still in. As long as she was alive, it wasn't over yet. And who knew, maybe Teacher would keep his word. He never broke a single promise he gave her as of yet. She had to give him that.

Not to mention that escaping from the Eastern Perished Kingdom would be easier than from this island. So, if everything went wrong, she had other options.

"Will there be any killings involved?" She wanted to clarify.

"That will depend on the kind of information you bring me." Joran smirked. "Is that a problem for you?"

"No," she replied without delay. It really wasn't. She could kill rogues if necessary. For her freedom and potentially for Niki.

"Glad we are on the same page." Joran stood up. "And now, to the important part. Your tattoo."

Astrea shivered at the thought. The people who got on the island trained for years in the camp, and then they had to undergo the ceremony of Ascension. On the auspicious date of the year, they were sent to the woods filled with deadly magical beasts and traps, and only those who came out alive were then called Firstborn and granted a special gift by Joran. This was also when they could stop calling him Master and started calling him Teacher. It was part of the privilege they shared.

The said 'gift' was a tattoo filled with divine magic. It multiplied whatever powers they had tenfold, and it could only work on the first child of shifter parents. This was the reason why Joran was only interested in those. The perfect way to build the strongest army, and since he took them away from their families quite young, they were devoted to him.

When Astrea fled after tricking everyone, she burned the dragonfly tattoo on her skin so that Joran couldn't track her by using his magic in her system. Sadly, werewolves regenerated quickly, and the tattoo was back after some time, making her repeat the burning over and over again. Even in the silver pit, it managed to heal.

"What about it?" She gulped when he was already towering over her, his fingers brushing over the tattoo on her back, eliciting a rush of goosebumps.

"You tried to destroy it, and I think you need a new one," he mused, and the blood in her veins froze.

"A new one?" She jerked away, leaving her seat. His dry chuckle followed. "Why a new one? The old one came back as a charm!"

"Because I want to ensure you can't burn it off or cut it out anymore." Joran smirked. "Come here."

He went toward his office, and she followed him, knowing she'd better not prolong this.

"Where do you want me?" she asked absentmindedly when they both were inside, and his lips curled. She decided to take it like the soldier that she was and be done with it quickly.

"Window," he told her, and she obeyed, her knees shaky.

"Hands on the glass." Joran stepped right behind. Knowing that if real tattoos hurt, the divines ones were hundreds of times worse. It was another thing some of the trainees couldn't survive.

She was different, though, and she could take it for the second time.

Joran slowly removed her long hair from her neck, lacing his fingers through it and brushing it to one side.

"When I touch your locks, it's as if I am touching the starry sky," he murmured, and she paid no attention to that. He skilfully unclasped the snake necklace on her neck, making the fabric fall. She barely caught it with one hand to stay covered and save some dignity.

"Now, where do I place it?" Joran examined her skin as a map, stopping to trace the dragonfly tattoo shining brightly on her skin. Then his fingers moved to her neck, creating more goosebumps as they went until they wrapped around it tightly, making her throw her head back.

Joran was in complete control.

"Remember that this is necessary not only for tracking you down but mostly for your protection," he whispered into her ear. "When I lost you the first time and didn't know where you were, my biggest fear was that something bad happened to you. It was so bad that I made crucial mistakes in the war. And I never make mistakes. You know it, Astrea."

"Sorry." She said it because she knew he wanted it, not because she felt it.

"That's okay now," Joran sighed, and his second hand touched the available area at the back of her neck. "We are going to fix it all together. And then... then we will see how it goes. If you want to leave me and be free, it's fine. But if you would like to return to my side at any moment during or after this task, I will always take you back. I want you to know this. You are very special to me, Astrea. So, this is the new agreement between us. Deal?" His hot breath burned her skin.

"Deal," she breathed out, and the next moment, a flash of searing hot pain pierced her whole body.

3. EAST

*A*strea was in agony, and it was worse than anything she'd ever experienced before. An invisible needle from hell itself pierced her skin, sending excruciating pain rippling down her body. Her wolf, Nova, was howling inside, and that was heart-breaking considering she hadn't recovered from their previous torture yet.

It was taking forever, and after a while, it started to feel like it would never end. She could barely keep standing, now leaning her head against her hand on the cold glass.

Soon, even the ability to scream left her. She wasn't sure what was going on anymore, concentrating on trying to keep holding her dress in place as hot tears streamed down her cheeks. This was like nothing she had ever gone through before.

Joran did not stop and did not give her a break, although she clearly needed one to come to her senses. This was a new form of punishment from him.

He enjoyed it.

The only thing she wanted now was to withstand it. Preferably with some dignity left to her, but as the darkness started to close in on her making the area she could see smaller and smaller until there was just a tiny dot left, Astrea knew she was failing miserably.

"Almost there, Dragonfly," Joran's voice rasped in her ear as he continued his torment, now touching her collarbone, and it felt like he was piercing her neck with knives. "You are doing well. As always. My brave little Dragonfly…"

She tried to breathe, but it felt like some kind of force was strangling her now and that tiny dot of vision disappeared as the darkness took over, the last of her strength leaving her.

ASTREA STRETCHED IN THE BED, the soft silk caressing her body like a cool breeze. She turned to hug the pillow the way she always did, and only then did the memories of the previous day flood her brain and make her open her eyes.

The light from a glass wall blinded her, but despite that, she knew exactly where she was. Her Teacher's bedroom. The black sheets, the golden pillows, the leather headboard, and the mirror wall next to the bed… this place was easy to recognise. She had been here just a few times when the Teacher called her late at night to give her a new task or praise her when he was in the mood for it. She felt really out of place each time, trying to leave as soon as possible. They never had the kind of relationship that would require her to stay here longer than their conversations would last.

Today was different because she was actually in his bed with no idea how much time she had spent here and what had happened. A quick check showed that her dress from yesterday was still on, though the diamond necklace was still unclasped, causing the fabric to fall down to her waist when she tried to sit up. This was the wrong time to remember that the trainees from yesterday failed to bring her any kind of underwear.

Astrea hissed as the movement brought back the pain to her neck. Her skin felt scorched and unbearable to touch.

She still wanted to get up because she had to see what he had done to her.

"Easy there." Joran strolled in, wearing nothing but a pair of loose, black silk pyjama pants, every muscle on his body carved to perfection. "You are going to need some rest after that."

She wanted to stand up, but somehow, he was right next to her faster than she anticipated and gently pushed her back to the bed.

"What did I tell you?" he asked in a reproachful tone, lacing his fingers through her hair to comb it out of his way. "Rest. You are not going anywhere today."

Astrea did not like the sound of that.

"I-I can't stay here!" she protested, and his jaw tightened.

"I am afraid you will have to," he informed her matter-of-factly. "Your new tattoo has to be looked over by me to ensure it takes on well and doesn't hurt you."

"It's fine!" She tried to brush the whole situation off, but pain subdued her whole body the moment she dared to move again.

"Do you have to be so stubborn?" he sighed and traced his fingers over her neck. She was ready to shudder from the pain, but his touch brought her soft, cooling sensations, eliciting a whimper of relief from her. This made her mentor smile. "See?" he taunted. "I am only doing what is best for you."

After he hurt her first. She still had no idea what it was on her neck.

"Thank you, Teacher." Her voice sounded so lifeless and dull, but she knew this was exactly what he wanted to hear. They'd learned each other well during the years they spent together.

"No." He shook his head, and his hand moved to caress her shoulder, making her whole body tremble, chest rising and falling at a sharp rhythm.

"No?" Astrea arched her brow, and this time, he trailed his thumb over her chin, although she could tell there was nothing there to check.

"You've disobeyed me far too many times now to call me your Teacher," he said, their gazes locking. "Use my name from now on."

"I... can't," she confessed, clutching her dress to her chest. That felt so weird. Unnatural even.

"I am afraid you will have to. It pains me to hear you call me Teacher when I know you don't mean it."

"I will try to mean it... better," she replied awkwardly, knowing that it sounded silly and he wasn't buying it.

"Astrea, just when did our relationship get this way?" He laced his fingers through her hair, playing with her long locks and clearly enjoying it.

"Somewhere between you ordering the other Firstborn to hunt and kill me and throwing me to the silver pit for months," she admitted, finally managing to sit back up, "accidentally" obstructing him from entertaining himself with her hair.

"If I issued the order to kill you, you would be dead. You know this," Joran retorted and sighed. "As for the silver pit... what choice did I have exactly? You had to die for your crime, and I... I wanted to protect you instead."

She did not respond to that. It didn't feel like protection to her, but she knew better than to say that out loud. She wanted out, and to do it... she had to play the game.

However, he wouldn't believe her if she wasn't smart about it. She had to be in her character still.

"Did it have to be so long?" she asked, turning away, and he caught her cheek into his palm, making her look at him again.

"It had to. I had the other Dragonflies petitioning me daily to kill you as I was supposed to. After all, you did kill Amber." Joran looked her straight in the eyes, and she knew that at least that part was true. Amber was the other spy sent together with her to the Northern Kingdom, another Dragonfly who hated her with a passion, and the moment she realised Astrea's plan to escape, her life was over. Leaving her alive wasn't an option.

"I didn't murder her in cold blood." Astrea swallowed uncomfortably. "We fought, and it was an honest fight."

"You know she had no chance against you, though," he sneered at her.

"I knew, but she didn't think so." The assassin met her mentor's gaze. "If there was a choice, I would never—"

"See, now you know how I feel about not being able to protect you better." Joran caressed her cheek again, and she sighed.

"Thanks," Her voice was barely a whisper, but he heard her, and his lips curled into a smirk.

"That's much better." Joran stood up from the bed and offered her his hand. "Now, come and see my new gift to you."

She followed him, now trying to keep the dress on with just one hand as he led her to the closest mirror wall. Joran loved mirrors.

Her hair was covering her neck, and once again, her Teacher gently brushed his fingers through it, pulling it back.

"Like liquid stars," he murmured, but she did not listen. Her gaze was glued to what was on her neck now.

Frozen in shock, Astrea couldn't form a single word as she watched at an intricate curling snake tattoo around her neck. It looked like a fashionable necklace pattern inked on her skin, where the head was barely touching the tail, however, that thing seemed to be alive. The stunned girl tried to touch it, and it wriggled away as if it didn't wish to be disturbed.

"Do you like it?" Joran wrapped an arm around her waist, pulling her to his chest from the back while his hand caressed the serpent on her skin. This was a touch the snake did not mind. In fact, it loved it so much that Astrea almost moaned as the two connected, throwing her head back.

"What the—" She tried to catch her breath.

"Don't worry," he chuckled softly. "It's still sore and needs to get used to you, but soon you will be inseparable."

And that was exactly the problem.

"You said you would let me go," she reminded him, and he paused.

"I did, didn't I?" His lips curved slightly. He knew exactly what she was thinking. "Astrea, this is for your protection. While it's on you, I will be calm that you are safe. If you are in trouble, I will come for you. I wish I had created such a connection between us earlier. Maybe then you would have known that I wouldn't have hurt you if you simply came to me and told me the truth. I feel like… we have misunderstood each other lately."

"Will you know everything I do?" she found herself asking, voice almost broken. This was simply another type of collar, and she had just gotten rid of the one she'd worn for months.

"Would that be a problem?" He caught her gaze in the mirror and sneered at her, still playing with the little snake. "I thought you decided to be a good girl from now on."

"Good girls love some privacy too," she almost snapped at him, but at the last moment, offered a taunting smile to cover up her frustration.

"It's for protection only," Joran assured. "It will keep you safe and on the right path. I will be able to connect with you wherever you are and feel if you are in danger."

She wasn't sure she wanted to know more now.

"All that being said," he leaned lower, and it looked like the little snake sought him because it followed his every move, "even serpents need to sleep. You will have enough privacy, but I am never losing you again. Not like the last time."

She felt his lips pressing against the wriggling tattoo and this touch made all the pain go away, the ink shining brightly until the little snake settled into its original position and froze. Astrea really preferred it that way.

"But my freedom—"

"It will be yours," Joran sighed and distanced himself away immediately as if he wanted to avoid that conversation. "All you need to do is complete your mission and return to me to claim it. Then, as I have promised, if you still want freedom, I will give it to you."

She felt like there was a catch, but it wasn't the time to annoy him any more. She was already dangerously close to his limit.

"Would you like some breakfast?" Joran asked as if they were an old married couple. Although in the past, they'd often have their meals together. She was his favourite Dragonfly, after all.

Now it felt awkward and out of place.

"I am a bit nauseous after the dinner we had." She quirked her brow up at him, pointing at her neck. "It will be a while until I can eat. So, I'd prefer to prepare for my mission instead."

He did not look pleased with her response but contemplated it none-theless.

"I wanted you to rest for tonight." His eyes travelled back to the enormous black bed, and Astrea shuddered. He had never invited her to his bed or offered her anything more than guidance before, and she wished for that same treatment again. Purely a Teacher and his Dragonfly warrior.

"You just cured me," she pointed at the tattoo with a forced grin. "No need to waste time. And I haven't been training for a while. I feel a little rusty."

"No training today," he prohibited her at once. "You may study the research I prepared for you, you may meet with Alisha in your old room and prepare your wardrobe and any gadgets you may need. But that's it until I say so. You do not leave this house, you do not meet any Firstborns who are not invited here, you eat, you sleep, you take care of yourself. And you dine with me every evening. This is an order. Are we clear?"

It was hard to hide her disappointment, but she nodded. "Of course, Teacher."

"Joran," he reminded her how he preferred to be called now and she swallowed the lump in her throat.

"Jor... an." The words tasted bitter on her tongue.

"One more time." The Serpent, however, was enjoying this.

"Joran," Astrea repeated, confident this time as their eyes locked. She was a professional, after all.

"See, it wasn't as hard, was it?" the Dragon God let out a laugh, not taking his eyes off her. "This is the evolution of our relationship, Astrea. So many great things are ahead."

Gods, she really hoped it wasn't the case.

HE ALLOWED her to return to her old room, and the moment she was there, she felt like she needed to do something. All the while knowing that, at the same time, she couldn't do much.

She looked at herself in the mirror, panting and seeing the snake collar on her neck. Astrea hated collars, and now she was a proud owner of a permanent one. Or... was she the one being owned?

Her gaze fell on her long white silver locks, and Joran's words echoed in her mind, *"Like liquid stars."*

He sure loved playing with her hair, and right now, it was the only thing she could deprive him of.

So, Astrea took the scissors and cut the first strand of hair off before she could change her mind. The snake on her neck curled angrily, and the sensation made her continue.

Snip.

The pain returned, but it only fuelled her anger.

Snip.

She could hear the sounds of footsteps.

Snip.

The last locks pooled at her feet, and the door burst open.

"What the hell is this?" Joran gritted his teeth as his gaze fell on the shining silver on the floor.

A vicious smile reached her lips. At least she took that bit of control back.

THE DAY ASTREA had to leave for the East approached quickly. Not that she minded that. She couldn't wait to escape this place.

Joran met her at the helicopter, which also reminded her of the past. He always used to send her off when she left and greet her when she returned – a privilege he only extended to her. The only time he didn't do it was when they dragged her to that pit...

"Do it quick and come back home," he said, hands in the pockets of his trousers.

"I will come back for my freedom," she reminded him of the main reason she would be returning, and his jaw twitched. At the same time, the snake on her neck wriggled slightly. She was never getting used to that.

"A deal is a deal." The Serpent smiled, but it did not reach his eyes. "As long as the mission is done and you come back safely, I am happy. I have a surprise for you, by the way."

The last words made Astrea tense, but then she saw Niki walking out of the nearest building in her black battle training uniform, and her lips parted.

"I knew you would like it." Joran leaned down to her and whispered, lips almost brushing over her earlobe. "You have one minute. Her Ascension is today, and she is kind of in a hurry."

Niki ran into her arms, and finally, Astrea could hug her ward, air whipping their hair as they allowed themselves a moment of weakness. However, she also had to be aware of time. So many things had to be said, but they had to be extra careful not to create new troubles.

"I am so glad you are alright!" Niki mumbled through tears, knowing they couldn't speak louder. "And your hair is shorter! Looks so cool!"

"Listen to me very carefully," Astrea whispered. "You need to survive the Ascension, and when you do that, wait for me to come back. When I do, we are both going to leave this wretched place. I promise."

She could feel Niki's body go stiff in her arms and noticed her eyes widening slightly.

"Stay safe and trust no one," she added, and it was exactly the time when Joran cleared his throat, which meant that they had to part again.

"Good luck on your mission." Niki offered a weak smile. It was probably the worst time to mess with her head, but there were no better options.

The helicopter's blades started spinning. It was officially time to go.

"We will wait for you right here." Joran placed a hand on Niki's shoulder, and it made Astrea's stomach churn. He knew exactly what he was doing – ensuring she did come back.

However, there was nothing she could do about it now. Her mission was waiting, and with that came the risks to her own life.

"Mission first," Nova reminded her via their mind link, her voice was soothing and reassuring. *"We deal with one problem at a time."*

"As always." Astrea took her seat in the helicopter and put her headphones on as she prepared for a long flight. There were ways to make her work in the East short and successful, and she was mentally going through them on her way there. Nova had finally recovered from everything now and could advise her properly again.

"We are almost there!" the pilot told her dryly through her headphones, and she recognised one of the werebears who had captured her during her escape attempt. This wasn't a good sign, but she tried not to show her displeasure.

Yes, she probably killed his friends during her runaway attempt. However, that could probably be said about many others, too. Other than Niki, she had no friends there.

To distract herself, she decided to look down and saw the Eastern border that was easily recognisable by the forest she once fought in and the desert that kissed it softly with its golden sands, a mix hard to find anywhere else in the world.

Astrea remembered how she saw a magnificent black creature somewhere around here. Now it was hard to know for sure if it wasn't just the product of her imagination or something that really existed. Just the memory of it made her heart beat faster.

The scenery changed again, and the first thing that drew Astrea's attention were the abandoned towns. There were so many of them... life and happiness left this kingdom a while ago. This was something that made it so attractive to the rogues now – there were no packs here, no Alphas to serve or fear.

No one wanted these lands, and the rogues were the ones to claim them.

Soon they reached another city, but this one had signs of life in it. Not too impressive, not like the buzzing polished cities of the Republic. Not like the comfortable West or cosy old-fashioned North. Astrea noticed people on the streets, shops were open, and old cars travelled the worn roads.

Gods, was this what she had to work with? The Republic would laugh at them when they saw them.

They landed next to a very spacious long mansion that was nestled in the middle of a dry mountain, the building probably serving as some kind of a fortress for protection. From here, you could see the city below and would know in advance if it was attacked.

Whoever lived here tried to preserve it the best they could, but it clearly had seen some life and needed a lot of work. The light columns and arches looked slightly shabby, which, in Astrea's opinion, only gave them more charm.

A small delegation of four people was waiting for her at the designated landing spot. The rogues were eager to meet the Southern Lycan Republic representative, and Astrea straightened her silk midi dress, preparing to make the first impression. She knew very well that those counted the most. It would be especially crucial with rogues as they would have to test her since they clearly had assumptions about her.

When the blades stopped spinning, a massive man with long black hair in dreads and a large scar crossing the brown skin on his cheek opened the door, eyes widening when he saw her.

"A girl?" He didn't even try to hide his lack of excitement and the disappointment in his bright blue eyes. "The Republic has sent us a girl?"

"As an adult, I am referred to as a woman." Astrea tilted her head, giving him a small but friendly smile. "You were in desperate need of an advisor and PR professional, and... well, here I am. You will not find anyone better."

"He won't be happy about this," the guy muttered, but she ignored it and got out on her own since it didn't look like he was going to offer her his hand.

"Who is *he*?" she asked bluntly as the guy scratched the back of his neck, watching her intently.

"The King," he responded unenthusiastically and still didn't introduce himself. But she could find his name out later.

"Oh, I'm sure we'll figure something out." She beamed. *The King would just have to deal with her presence.*

Astrea went in the direction of the other people waiting and tried to figure out which one of them was the King. If any.

There were two more men and a woman with light brown hair, which was limiting her options. However, none of them was giving her any royal vibes. Rogues did not like to listen to anyone, so their leader had to possess at least some kind of Alpha aura. One of the men was wearing a bright red suit, his long hair tied in a man-bun at the back of his head. He was the only one who eyed her curiously, but it was very unlikely that rogues would obey him.

"A girl?" The other woman raised her brow as she assessed Astrea, offering her a look of disdain in the end.

"Aren't you as well?" the Southerner taunted, reciprocating the facial expression she received and a younger guy with dark blonde hair snorted at that.

This wasn't going exactly how she expected. The rogues were the ones who needed the Republic more. Not the other way around. Yet they behaved as if she was an eyesore.

"I beg to differ!" The other woman rolled her eyes, folding her arms across her chest.

"Well, we've got what we've got," the youngest man stated plainly. "Let's go!"

None of them said another word to her as all of them simply turned on their heels and started walking. Astrea tried to keep up with their large, powerful steps in her high heels, but not too much. The weaker they thought she was, the better. They wouldn't take her as seriously as they should, and that could, potentially, give her more freedom to lurk around in the future.

"Excuse me, where are we going?" she asked after a while. This palace was long, and the inner square seemed never to end! Were they giving her a tour?

"To meet Fenrir," the man with the scar and dreads answered as if it had to mean something to her.

"Fenrir?" she chuckled. "As in the ancient Wolf God?"

"As in the King of the East!" the woman snapped. Something told Astrea that she didn't like her much. Her hair was braided in a warrior style that looked intricate and overly complicated but also... was probably there untouched for days.

"I see." Astrea forced an excited smile anyway. "That's wonderful! The sooner we meet, the sooner we can start working together!"

And there was much work to be done if they had to look presentable for the snobs of the Republic to sign the alliance. These four were typical rogues. Okay, three of them were. She wasn't sure about the Red Suit yet. All that taken into consideration, they still definitely did not have the look Joran wanted them to have at their next meeting.

Their group arrived at the bottom of a long set of stairs leading to what looked like a closed high tower.

No one said another word to Astrea and she wasn't sure if it was a good idea to start small talk now.

"Don't," Nova chuckled in her head. *"They clearly prefer actions to words and there will be time for that."*

Astrea realised that they were all talking via their mind link, and she probably knew the topic anyway. Now she had to wait for the King, who was hopefully about to make an appearance. The wait, however, turned out to be a bit too long, and she was getting frustrated, although nothing on her face showed it.

The doors at the top of the stairs slammed open without warning, and she saw the most gorgeous man she had ever laid her eyes on freeze as their gazes locked. Astrea did not expect him to be this way, feel this way... waves and waves of raw power rippling from him, filling everything around them.

His eyes were a strange mix of blue and red. As if flames of fire were burning in the centre of an iceberg. His dark brown hair was reaching his shoulders, and a carefully trimmed beard framed his masculine face with strong perfect features. The man was exceptionally tall, even for a shifter, with muscles bulging through his black unbuttoned shirt, which also gave a glimpse of his chiselled abs. The Rogue King, and she had no doubt that it was him, was made to sin, and even Astrea swallowed, realising where her thoughts went.

Damn, that wolf looked good.

Moreover, he stared at her as if she was a drop of rain in the middle of the incandescent desert, eyes travelling up and down her small frame, throat bobbing with some emotion he could not express. There was desire and longing, and it all felt oddly familiar, throwing her off her game.

He reminded her of someone, but at the moment, her brain couldn't fathom if they had met before. She didn't think so because... she would have definitely remembered him.

"Fenri—" one of the men started speaking and then coughed. "I mean, my King. This is the representative from the Southern Lycan Republic. Erm…"

She was tempted not to fill the awkward pause. After all, none of them bothered to ask her name. And it was fun to watch them suffer for it now.

However, she was on a mission here. The mission that required her to be friendly.

"Astrea Sade." She gave the King her brightest and sweetest smile. "It's my pleasure to work with you. I am sure we—"

"No!" he cut her off, eyes not leaving her for a second. "Consider the request cancelled and go back."

Her lips parted, already dry in this insanely hot climate, and she had to lick them before she spoke, making the King growl in response.

"Excuse me, Your Majesty," she said as politely as possible. "I came here to assist you and your… country with the new alliance—"

"Tell them to send someone else then!" he cut her off again and turning away, left where he came from.

4. WARM WELCOME

*H*e left just like that, leaving Astrea alone with his crew of rogues. She couldn't fathom this. Was he serious? Was this the end for him? It had to be some sick rogue joke! They needed this union more than the South!

"Well, you heard the man," the guy with dreads chuckled. "Off you go then. Too bad this alliance thing didn't work out."

He didn't sound like he was sorry about it, though.

"Maybe next time!" the woman beside him sneered and left first as if there was no more room for discussion. Others followed her. Only the man in the red suit stayed, watching her curiously with his hands in his pockets.

Astrea was speechless. Did they expect her to leave?

Every muscle in her body tensed. Was that why Joran let her go so easily on this mission, promising her freedom in return? Did he know that she didn't have a chance? Was it a test to see if she would try to run again?

Or was the intent to humiliate her? He wanted her to see that there was nothing for her in the East, taking her last hope away.

Of course, her plan was always to leave the continent. She didn't dream of living among rogues for long.

All that taken into consideration, the plan was becoming increasingly unrealistic by the minute.

She couldn't go back to her Teacher with nothing. He would make her stay by his side forever, and she would have to live with it, obeying him until the day she died. They'd made a deal. If she completed this mission, she would be free. If she did not... he would still own her. The collar snake on her neck would stay forever.

"No!" Nova growled inside her. *"We are not going back there. Not like that!"*

"Agreed." Astrea sucked in a deep breath, trying to form a new plan in her head. *"Losing is not an option."*

She turned on her heel and stared at the last remaining rogue.

"He is not serious," she stated with her brows furrowed, still hoping it was some kind of a sick joke.

"Oh, no, he is dead serious," the guy in red replied, wind whipping his long sleek hair as he observed her curiously with his amber eyes. He could promote shampoo on tv if he lived in a more civilised country. In fact, he stood out from the crowd here in his fancy fashionable suit, while his friends who'd left didn't seem to care much about their outfits. "It was a miracle he agreed to talk to your leaders at all, let alone allowing you entry here. He hates strangers. And politics. And people in general. Especially Southerners. Although, who am I kidding? Fenrir doesn't like anyone!"

"What did Southerners do to him?" Astrea asked and almost immediately regretted it. These were rogues. A wolf had to be thrown out of their pack to become a rogue. None of them had anything good to say about the other kingdoms, especially the Southern Lycan Republic, which probably had the most brutal laws and was weeding out anyone deemed weak or unworthy.

"It's a long story," the man in red admitted, shrugging with his hands still in his pockets. Seeing him wearing a perfectly tailored suit in their surroundings was odd. Everyone else dressed much more casually. "Such a shame it was a very short alliance. I have prepared a feast for us. It would have been fun."

"One question," Astrea decided to interrupt his monologue, unable to keep up with the small talk, "how strict are you guys about the rules here?"

"Depends on who is asking and what rule we are breaking." The guy smirked at her, looking intrigued.

"Let's say I follow your King for a conversation now," she suggested innocently. "Will you and others try to stop me?"

She could take them down, of course, but she needed to know first if there was a need to change into something more comfortable for the possible fight.

The rogue gawked at her for a moment before breaking into laughter that filled the space around them.

"You want to speak with Fenrir after he specifically told you to leave?" He got out a small silk handkerchief and wiped the tears that formed in his eyes. Clearly a drama lover. "Be my guest, and no, no one will obstruct you. But we will watch the show. This guy hates being contradicted. No one dares to contact him. And he absolutely loathes when anyone enters his Tower. Even I don't dare to set foot in there uninvited."

"But—" Astrea halted as her lips curled into a sly grin. "It's not exactly prohibited, is it?"

"No, but—"

"Thanks!" She was in no mood to listen to anything that could potentially ruin her very reckless plan, so she ran up the stairs, determined to make herself heard.

"My name is Devoss, by the way! Devoss Kit," the guy shouted behind her back.

"Astrea Sade!" she repeated her name and waved at him dismissively, reaching the massive doors at the top. Sadly, they were locked, and she turned to give her new acquaintance a questioning stare, hoping that he could do something about it. It looked like he was invested in them having a conversation.

"Don't look at me." He lifted his arms defensively. "Fenrir is the only one with the key."

"You are not much help, Devoss." She rolled her eyes, noticing a window above her on the wall of the Tower. Not that far from the top of the stairs where she stood. Reachable. And also her last chance.

"Take the shoes off first," Nova muttered. *"We can't break our legs. We will need them to run far and fast if this doesn't work."*

There will be nowhere to run if this doesn't work, Astrea summed their options up, throwing off her wine-red high heels.

Devoss watched how she gracefully jumped on the rails and walked them as if she was an acrobat from a circus, each movement trained to perfection.

One leap and she grabbed the edge of the open window, desperately clinging to it and trying to lift herself up. She pulled her body up and moved most of her weight on to her elbows, now resting on the windowsill.

Taking a peek, Astrea saw a spacious minimalistic room that didn't resemble a King's chambers at all. A desk with stacks of papers and folders scattered all over it, a few old bookcases, a medium-sized dining table and a wooden carved chest by a passage that led to the next floor. Not the cosiest of places.

Fenrir was standing next to the closed door, keeping one hand on it and using the other to cover his eyes.

"Excuse me!" Astrea finally managed to get in and sat on the edge of the window, placing one of her legs on top of the other to look as carefree as possible.

"What the—" The rogue was stunned to see her in his room, but he quickly regained his composure, a low warning growl leaving his chest. "What do you think you are doing?"

"Trying to create an alliance between our two countries." She raised a brow at him. "An alliance you agreed to."

"A mistake," he retorted, pushing himself off the door and stalking towards her.

She didn't flinch and held his gaze the whole time, being mesmerised by the unusual combination of his eye colour again certainly helped. Flames on ice. Something told her it was a testament to his character.

"Still, an agreement that was made." Astrea remained firm, aware that he was taking her in now: her silvery-white curly locks barely reaching her shoulders, the thin red slip dress she intentionally wore underneath her leather jacket, her bare feet, her posture. He was studying her, and she did the same.

Fenrir looked like he was in his thirties, and now that she could take a closer look, she noticed scars on his chest and face. She passed her eyes over them so as not to stare, but she was trained to detect these things.

This man was a Lycan. Lycans were one of the strongest shifters that existed… and someone managed to scar him. A little line crossed his nose and cheek, and another line was "decorating" his chin.

"The agreement I just cancelled," he reminded her dryly. "And that decision is final."

That made her smile at him, unable to let it slide. "If you've proved anything right now, you've proven that your decisions are never final."

Another growl and another warning. She couldn't afford any more of those, or he would personally throw her back into that helicopter, shipping her straight back to the Teacher.

"The more you speak, the more I am inclined not to change it again. Leave," he repeated the word he had told her before, as if her presence bothered him on a personal level. Which couldn't be the case.

"Look, I am here to help," she lied through her teeth, hopping off the windowsill. "I don't know what about me triggers you so much, but I assure you that I am the best of the best. My task is to ensure that this alliance goes smoothly, and it's all I want."

"If the South needs our help so much, and they had to be pretty desperate to ask, it will go smoothly with or without your presence." Fenrir looked at her as if she was a naïve child, which triggered *her*.

"The Southern Lycan Republic is ruled by the Alpha Convocation." She decided to give him a simple history lesson. "Which means that many Alphas decide and vote on the country's destiny. So, unless the majority votes to work with you, this alliance is not happening."

"I'll try to get over it somehow, Princess!" He exhaled a rumble of laughter that echoed through the walls.

Princess... she hated to be called that. He was pushing buttons that she didn't know she had.

"Oh, you'll be fine," Astrea filled her words with as much venom as she could, "but what about your people in that—I don't even dare to call that a city. It's a slum at best."

"We are rogues. We don't need much." Fenrir took a step forward, probably to intimidate her, but so did she. She was not new to this game of power he was playing. Only this time, her task wasn't to submit. In reality, it was unlikely that he would touch her or do anything to her. So, she was getting bolder.

"That's good because you sure as hell will not be getting any help from North or West. They are too good to deal with rogues and have too many problems of their own to send humanitarian aid here, which you so desperately need. Trust me, I've just returned from there."

"You've been to the North?" Something changed in his voice, but she still couldn't read his emotions. This rogue gave her little to work with, and she was an expert in facial expressions.

"I've been everywhere. I told you, I am the best." Astrea walked to the desk she noticed from the corner of her eye and threw her leather jacket on one of the chairs. "Let's negotiate."

"There is nothing to nego—" He stopped talking when she turned back to face him.

"What?" Her brows went up as she realised that this time, he was staring at the snake tattoo on her neck. It was probably just her imagination, but his skin became a shade paler, jaw tightening.

"How did you get this?" He pointed at the serpent that thankfully did not move now.

"Oh, this?" She traced the ink with her fingers, not knowing how to respond to the question she wasn't prepared for. The tattoo was still fresh, and she tried not to think about it as much as she could. "I just got it in the spur of the moment."

That wasn't technically a lie.

"Who sent you?" Fenrir's voice sounded like metal, the air between them thickened, making it hard to breathe.

"The Southern Lycan Republic—"

"No, who sent you from the Republic?" His lips twitched from the pressure, and she instinctively knew she'd better not lie. Especially since her Teacher wanted their real names used this time.

"Joran Nathair," Astrea replied, expecting some kind of reaction, but even as minutes flew between them, none followed.

"Then, I guess you are welcome to stay," he said. "I will send someone to show you to your room."

The change was too sudden, but Astea didn't want to question her luck.

"Thank you, Your Majesty—" she blurted out.

"Don't call me that." He shook his head. "Just Fenrir is fine."

"Great! Yeah... sure." She tried not to grin too much. "And you can call me—"

"I am not going to be calling you anything. Just do your job and leave as soon as you are done," he said, locking his eyes with hers. Something was off, and she could feel it, but for now, this was what she needed.

After all, too much depended on this task.

SHE WAITED outside the Tower until the guy with dreads returned with a sour facial expression.

"I guess you stay," he grunted.

"I guess so." She tried really hard not to beam. She came so close to failure that this felt like a kind of victory now.

Right until Dreads pushed the door to her room open.

Astrea's eyes widened with shock...

5. BUSTED

"*Y*ou are not serious!" Astrea's head snapped to her companion, who only shrugged his shoulders to demonstrate that he didn't see any problem.

"This is the Rogue Kingdom. Not a five-star hotel," Dreads reminded her, and she clenched her jaw tightly to avoid saying something she might regret.

The spartan conditions of the room were not a problem for her. The problem was that the room was tall and round, with no windows other than the glass ceiling. She was already suffocating here, and she hadn't even stepped inside.

This reminded her of the silver pit too much. The days she spent at its bottom would never be erased from her memory.

The white walls had no decorations except one dull, full-length mirror in a wooden frame. There was only a modest queen size bed and a desk with an empty clothes rack. No bathroom in sight.

"Where would I wash?" She raised a brow at her guide.

"The common bathroom is at the end of the corridor. When the hot water is gone, it's gone. And be aware that you can meet anyone there. Male, female—"

"Okay," she said calmly, knowing that this was either a test or an attempt to intimidate her. "Good to know."

If Dreads had any kind of reaction, he didn't let her see it or maybe he simply didn't care. Astrea had heard that once a wolf was banished from his or her pack, if a new pack didn't accept them, after a while they tended to grow indifferent to everything around them. This was why rogues were so dangerous. Over time, the human side was fading in them, letting their raw, feral desires and emotions take over. Less morals and remorse, more freedom to do whatever they wanted on a whim. If rogues wanted something and knew they could get it, they would. Even if they had to steal, kill or do other awful things.

Astrea didn't judge them, of course. She'd completed some very questionable missions in her life, including the one before this one. But she knew she had to be careful while living here.

"I guess I will see you around." Dreads turned on his heel, preparing to leave.

"Will my luggage be brought here?" she wondered while he didn't get far, but a derisive snort was her only response.

"I guess that's a no," Nova chuckled.

"Big scary rogues wouldn't carry our bags!" Astrea chimed in, holding back a laugh. "They sure showed us!"

"They have more in common with men of the Lycan Republic than they realise!"

Astrea took a slow stroll back to where the helicopter landed an hour or so ago, and found her bags scattered across the space like unwanted garbage. Sighing, she gathered them together, soon realising she would need a few trips to get them all into her room. She came here with all sorts of things that could be required on her mission.

It did not escape her notice that some of the bags had clearly been opened while she was gone. The rogues probably wanted to check what she brought to their space, not being as careless as they pretended to be after all. However, they didn't know that the tiny crystal on the handle of each of the zippers changed colour when used. She left them blue, and now most of them were green.

"Amateurs!" Nova stated plainly, unimpressed.

"Either that or they want us to know that they are watching," Astrea hummed as she got as many bags as she could find. So far she had three cross-body bags on her with one backpack, two luggage on wheels with smaller bags attached to them. But still about the same remained.

"I'll help," she heard a male's voice and turned to see the blonde guy from before already picking some of her luggage up. He was pretty big, so she had no doubt he would be able to help her get everything in one go.

"Thanks." She smiled as sweetly as she could. "I'm sorry, I still don't know your name."

"Bastian," he replied without sparing her as much as a glance.

"Nice to meet you, Bastian." Astrea grinned at him, fluttering her long lashes playfully just in case. "Is it Bash for short?"

"You don't need to know," he responded bluntly, and the smile on her face faded slightly. "You are here temporarily; the sooner you return to your natural habitat, the better."

She assessed his facial expression quickly, and absolutely nothing in him gave away his true emotions. As if he was trained better than her, although he looked relatively young. Did rogue life do that to him, or was there something else?

"Believe it or not, but that is exactly what I want, too," she giggled, throwing him off his game as he finally darted his sky-blue eyes at her. "If we all work hard and cooperate well, all this will end quickly and painlessly for everyone. I'll be gentle if you will."

Bastian stared at her, and she winked at him before walking away toward her room. He caught up with her only when she was already inside and dropped her bags with a thump as if to make a point, leaving abruptly.

Astrea poked her head out of her door frame to see him marching down the arched passage along the intricate white outside balcony rails that gave a view of the inner courtyard.

"Thank you, Bash!" she sang, and he stumbled at once. *This was almost too easy.*

She returned to the room and sighed, trying not to look up. She could work with this space.

Unpacking all her deadly toys, Astrea smirked to herself. Those rogues were amateurs in comparison. They could have checked her things, but it was unlikely they had noticed anything suspicious. After all, it was next to impossible to detect that some of her lipstick contained poison for different types of shifters. And that her hair accessories had thin sharp blades inside made of silver, copper and other metals. Her perfume was mixed with aconite, and some of her high heels had needles with venom or tranquilisers inside.

This had to do for now. The box with the most valuable equipment was dropped not far from here from the helicopter before they arrived at this place, and Astrea had the coordinates memorised. She would have to retrieve it in a day or two when they stopped watching her so closely.

It didn't look like they cared, but she still had to be careful. The first night always had to be the quiet one.

THE ALPHA GOD'S LUNA

So, after all the unpacking, Astrea decided to go to sleep. The instructions about the shower were clear to her, and she knew she'd better wake up around four or five o'clock in the morning to avoid unwanted company.

She closed her eyes tightly in her bed but couldn't get rid of the unending suffocating feeling. Astrea could hear her own heart pumping and tried to breathe evenly to calm down and fall asleep. No matter how long she tried though, it wasn't really working, bringing her back to the months she spent in the pit.

Opening her eyes, she saw the stars, her only companion during her silver-filled never-ending torture. She used to watch them, count them, and recognise the constellations as her only source of entertainment. They gave her peace in her most challenging moments, but today they called for action.

"Don't do this," Nova warned her, knowing her too well. *"If anyone sees you tonight, they will always suspect you. We need to keep a low profile—"*

"We do. If anyone sees me, I will tell the truth. I couldn't sleep." Astrea cut her off and stood up.

She looked at herself in the mirror and chose to stay in the provocative white lace slip she had carefully selected for the night. She didn't plan to meet anyone, but if an accident happened, her look would give her a few seconds to deal with it. Then she added a white magnolia hairpin to her hair and moved the desk to make it easier to jump and reach the glass ceiling. One of the parts of it was opened, and she got through it with ease, finding herself on the roof.

She scanned the other rooftops quickly with her shifter vision but found no one, to her relief. These rogues were too careless.

"Reminds me of someone." Nova didn't give up.

"Would you relax? I am not going on a big mission! It's just a quick, careful look around."

Astrea leapt nimbly from roof to roof, which thankfully, were all too close to each other. This building was an odd one indeed. So different from the other parts of the former Moonrise Kingdom that was now broken into four parts – the Western Lycan Kingdom, the Northern Lycan Kingdom, the South Lycan Republic and... the Perished Eastern Kingdom. The one that ceased to exist after an ongoing war between the four Lycan clans. Now it was a no man's land, and rogues from the whole continent ran here for safety. And now they wanted to create a kingdom of their own, making that infuriating Fenrir their king.

She noticed the fire in the central inner courtyard laid with white tiles and stopped, hiding behind a dome decoration. It was too dark here, and she was sure they couldn't see her.

"Her ass is all right," someone said below, and she tried to see their faces. A group of rogues sat around a fire pit with bottles of alcohol in their hands. Homemade alcohol, so it appeared.

She did not know the one talking but recognised Dreads and Bastian beside him. Devoss was there too, and so was the woman from earlier.

"This was exactly their plan." She rolled her eyes, taking a sip from her mug. She was the only one without a bottle. "Make you idiots look at her ass."

"Her tits are also nice if that's any consolation to you, Kara," Dreads told her, and Astrea was surprised that he had noticed at all. He gave the impression of being repelled by her mere presence.

"Shut up!" Kara replied, not impressed by his remark at all.

"Why are you all so negative?" Devoss chuckled, leaning back in his seat and placing one of his ankles over his knee. "It's going to be fun! Finally, something interesting is happening here!"

"Yeah, a Southern spy! How fun!" Bash splashed the rest of his drink into the fire, making the hungry flame rise in a fury.

They all got quiet, and for a moment there, Astrea wasn't sure why. Only then did she see a tall, dark shadow moving toward the group. A few rogues stood up at once; only the four she already knew remained in their respective places, unbothered by Fenrir's appearance. Which meant that they were his trusted inner circle.

He was still wearing the same dark shirt, finally buttoned adequately. The light of the flames drew his features, adding sharpness to his already majestic look. Once again, she had to admit that this man was impressive, and she grew up with a deity training her and an army of Firstborn shifters at hand. Yet... there was something about Fenrir that made her breathing hitch without her realising.

"So, we are really doing this," Dreads asked, not looking at his king. "Did the girl change your mind?"

"The girl has nothing to do with it," he responded, accepting a bottle from someone and opening it with a flick of his finger. "We continue with our plan."

"You wanted to throw her out at first," Bash reminded him.

"And should have," Kara interjected. "I don't like her."

"You don't like anyone," Devoss' laughter rumbled through the courtyard.

"And for good reason!" The woman seemed annoyed. "She reminds me of someone—"

Now, that was interesting.

"Enough!" Fenrir growled, making everyone go silent. "The South wants to use us, and we want to use the South. It's all there is, and the girl is just a bridge between us. Nothing more, nothing less."

"If you say so, my King!" Kara filled the last word with venom, and Astrea wondered if there was another kind of relationship between the two.

However, Fenrir sat far away from her, and she seemed fine with it. This was something for Astrea to explore in the future.

She had to go back. It was getting too dangerous.

Aware of the dangers of being noticed, she got to another rooftop, but Fenrir's words were not leaving her mind for some reason.

He was right, of course. She was here to use him, and obviously, they wanted to use her connections to the South to their advantage. It was normal, and she couldn't understand why it bothered her.

"Oh, no, Astrea," Nova sounded worried in her mind. *"Return to our room. Enough for today."*

But it was too late because Astrea suddenly realised Fenrir was busy. He wasn't in his suite. He was drinking outside with his friends, and that gave her an opportunity she wasn't sure she would have again.

"Return. To. Our. Room. You are not prepared!" Nova insisted, and Astrea had to shut it down.

"I'll just take one little peek," she assured her wolf, changing direction.

It was her luck that most of the windows in this fortress were open despite the low night temperatures. The window at the top of Fenrir's tower wasn't an exception, and after a bit of climbing, she was able to reach it. She carefully opened the unlocked shutters and closed them when she got in, finding herself in a different room from the one she visited earlier today. It was the Rogue King's bedroom.

"How unfortunate," Nova hissed. *"Now, let's go back."*

The massive old-fashioned bed had a transparent canopy, and the sheets were colourful, with a distinctive masculine pattern.

"Just one more minute." Astrea found a desk with piles and piles of papers.

She wondered what those could be? Rogues didn't have a government in the traditional sense of the word. What were all these documents for?

She had to be careful not to touch anything to avoid leaving any traces around, but she noticed a few odd maps at the top of the pile. A letter written in a language she didn't recognise made her furrow her brows.

Strange... all of this was so strange! She tried to memorise what she could, but she knew she'd have to get back here with a camera and be better prepared next time.

The sound of footsteps approaching the door alerted her, surprising her at the same time. Was Fenrir back so soon? She thought that he would drink for longer. Or was she the one who lost track of time?

Astrea charged for the window, thankful she had no shoes on – it made her movements soundless.

Her fingers reached the wooden shutters carved with intricate ancient eastern patterns, which was when a real shock hit her. The shutters were locked!

She tried them again and again, but nothing worked, and panic started to flood her brain. He was almost at the door!

This couldn't be real! They were open when she got here! What happened?

She could break the damn shutters, of course, but this would alert the rogue and give her away.

Cornered, Astrea did the only thing that came to her mind now and slid behind a heavy curtain.

"Great," Nova scoffed. "Now you are invisible, my dear!"

"Shut up!" Astrea bit her lip, almost drawing blood. In no way was this a good hiding place. Maybe she should have gone to the bathroom.

On the other hand, he would definitely go there sooner or later, and who knew if it had any windows to try and escape through.

"This is why you should have stayed in your room!" Nova really wasn't helpful now.

The door burst open, and Fenrir walked in, running one hand through his shiny dark hair. Astrea only saw a glimpse of him through the slit of the curtains, trying not to breathe and to mask her scent – a technique she was taught by the Teacher personally. It worked like a charm in the past, and she prayed for it not to fail her today.

The rogue still had a bottle in his hand, and he brought it to his lips, taking a few greedy gulps and then throwing it to the fireplace. He then went to it, leaning over the mantelpiece as if he was extremely tired. Flames appeared out of nowhere, a crackling fire suddenly burst out of the wood, illuminating the room with dancing shadows.

"Did he have matches there?" Astrea wondered.

"Like that is our biggest problem now!" Nova returned her to reality. The reality where she was trapped with the King of Rogues after her very unwise attempt to spy on him.

Astrea tried to think calmly. At least he looked drunk. His senses should be blunted. Maybe he would fall asleep fast or go to his bathroom and she could run in the meantime. She still couldn't believe the stupid shutters malfunctioned.

"How long are you going to stand there, Astrea?" Fenrir asked, his eyes still on the wildfire in front of him.

6. JUST A DREAM

strea cursed herself inwardly. He knew she was here the whole time! He was already onto her.

She needed an entirely new plan but, sadly, couldn't come up with anything in the spur of the moment. However, there was no time to think, and confidence was the key to everything.

Fenrir still stood by the fire, hands locked behind his back, his whole body a picture of strength and power. He was waiting for her next move.

And she decided not to disappoint. Astrea swiftly opened the curtains with both her hands, the fabric flowing around her, revealing her frame covered with a sheer expensive negligee and holding her chin high as if she wasn't caught red-handed. Fenrir slowly turned on his heels to face her, and she could swear his bright eyes got darker as he swore under his breath, jaw tightening at the same time as he took her in. The slip she had on barely hid anything from his gaze that was becoming more and more feral by the minute. The same way as the room temperature seemed to rise.

"You must be kidding me!" he growled, and the corner of her lips tugged upward slightly.

"My King," she curtsied, and he was next to her in the blink of an eye, chest heaving, but to her surprise, he didn't try to touch her.

One could say that when a woman walked into a man's bedroom late at night dressed like this, there could be only one thing she wanted. He had to assume it. Anyone would assume it.

"What do you think you are doing?" he snarled, his body emitting heat.

"What does it look like I am doing?" She gave him the most seductive smile from her arsenal. She was relatively good at flirting. Her Teacher made sure she excelled at that, but this was how far her missions went. Usually, nothing more was required. Even when she was sent to the Luna Trials, her task wasn't to seduce the Northern King. She had to stay as long as possible and report what was happening in the castle that wasn't common knowledge.

However, today she was cornered in the worst of ways. Trapped with no way out.

"It looks like you came to the wrong room." Fenrir graciously gave her a way out, which confused her more, making her brows knit together.

Why would he say that? Wasn't the most logical conclusion that she came here to offer herself to him?

His suggestion made her angry, and she wished to make him regret his words even though she didn't plan to sleep with him in the end.

"Oh, you got me!" she giggled. "I was looking for Devoss' room. Is that down the corridor on the left, then?"

She walked past this mountain of a man, but he caught her arm, pulling her closer. She bumped into his hard chest, feeling every ridge of his muscles under the shirt that separated them now.

"Devoss isn't into women," Fenrir leaned down to inform her, his breath tickling her skin, eliciting a rush of goosebumps. His unusual scent of cedarwood and smoke enveloped them both, and Astrea closed her eyes just for a second, inhaling it deep into her lungs. Smouldering cedar embers came to her mind, and when she opened her eyes, she saw the sparks of fire shimmering in his irises. As if a flame about to die was starting to burn with newfound strength.

"Bash will do too, then," she whispered, aware of their proximity far too well. Fenrir did not like her words because the flames in his eyes intensified. As if they were real and not just an optical illusion of some kind.

"None of them will touch you," Fenrir warned her, and she tilted her head playfully, arching her brow.

"Why is that?" Astrea taunted, running her fingers up his chest, which made him suck in a sharp breath. He looked like he was barely holding himself.

"Because I said so." Fenrir's voice rumbled through the room, doing something to her. Something she couldn't quite explain yet.

"Why would you say so?" She let out a chuckle, realising he was still holding her wrist hostage. "We barely know each other. Why do you care?"

She knew that it was probably due to the fact he couldn't trust her and considered her the spy that she actually was.

However, he avoided the straight reply.

"And why did you come to my room?" He raised his brow at her.

"Isn't it obvious?" she giggled, becoming more and more daring and allowing herself to brush her fingers over the tip of his carefully trimmed beard. The rough hair pricked her skin, but the sensation seemed familiar.

And pleasant.

"Elaborate on that." Fenrir did not look like he was about to release her.

"I came to get to know you better, of course!" Astrea grinned at him, thinking this would be his last straw.

"Careful what you wish for!" he warned her again, pulling her closer when it was clearly the time to push her away.

If he wanted to, of course.

"I don't limit myself when I dream," she confessed and found herself trapped in his arms when she tried to distance herself playfully. The rogue before her was watching her pathetic attempts with some kind of amusement.

"Neither do I," Fenrir admitted right before his lips crushed into hers in the most unapologetic manner. His hands roamed her body at once, only the thin silk obstructing him from caressing her bare skin.

That did not scare her, though.

It was perfect.

For the plan, of course. Not in general.

She did form a new plan after all.

Nevertheless, each swirl of his tongue in her mouth made her forget what she came here to do, and soon Astrea found herself entwining her hands around his neck, lacing her fingers in his soft hair and responding to his kiss with her whole body, some of her physiological reactions a complete surprise for her.

Like the heat that gathered at her core.

She knew the anatomy. She knew what to expect, however... Astrea had never felt like that before, despite this not being her very first kiss.

Something about this rough man she had just met awakened a part of her she did not know existed. That part did not want to play or pretend. It wanted to *experience*.

Breaking the kiss, Fenrir grabbed the hair at the back of her head and tugged it to give himself better access to her delicate neck, brushing his lips over it in a torturous caress which made her whimper softly.

"Last chance to stop," he warned her, stopping just before her collarbone, their breaths ragged and eyes fixed on each other. She could feel the fervour radiating from his body, his scent intensified for some reason, and she found herself shaking her head before the answer graced her lips.

"Where would be the fun in that?"

One innocent reply, and it undid something in Fenrir, breaking the last obstacle between them.

"As you wish." He grabbed her waist, lifting her up as if she weighed nothing. Astrea wrapped her thighs around his torso, unbuttoning his shirt as he strode to the bed. She needed the buttons intact, yet the moment she managed to pull the damn shirt off him with his help, she halted. His shoulders were covered with ancient runic tattoos in intricate patterns, but what caught her attention were the scars. Once upon a time, the man in front of her was brutally tortured and wounded by a sadist. Because... it was hard to scar a shifter. Almost impossible. The one who did this to him probably left those scars intentionally. Moreover, he had to try hard to leave them. Very hard.

"Eyes on me," Fenrir ordered, and she obeyed, leaving her trance. Her lips curled when she remembered that she was here to play a game. This wasn't personal, and none of this was real. She had to remember that.

"As you say, my King," she smiled at him, and before she could say anything else, he silenced her with a kiss, placing her on his bed and pinning her hands to the mattress.

She could feel his pulsing desire. The prominent bulge in his pants was hard to miss, but... none of this felt as horrible as she expected. In fact, she found herself enjoying being desired this much. There was something in Fenrir that called to her. It was too hard to resist him and not enjoy this.

"So long—" he muttered as his hand slid down her thigh to lift up the silky fabric. She could feel his internal growl when his fingers finally touched her skin. He moved them up to grasp her ass greedily and groaned into her mouth.

He gave her a break just for a moment when he wanted to unbuckle his belt, but at that moment Astrea took the initiative and, with one swift move of her trained thighs, rolled him next to her, straddling him to his own shock.

"I like to be on top of things." She gave him a devilish smirk and received a growl of approval in response.

"Little Menace," he snarled and cupped her ass, kneading it as he sat up, unable to tear himself off her even for a moment. There were no words anymore, no pauses to breathe, only his hands exploring her body and her moans because, despite all her training, she couldn't suppress them. Not with him.

Fenrir tugged the strap of her nightgown to make it fall to her waist and immediately took one of her hard nipples into his mouth, hungry for her flesh. Astrea arched her back for him, lost in all the new sensations.

It had to stop. She had to stop. It wasn't real. It was getting too far.

He wasn't a man. He was a mission.

Only that she didn't want to listen to this rational voice in her head. Neither did Nova. Her wolf was absolutely fine with everything that was going on, and it was strange.

She dug her nails into his skin, and he released her breast, fondling the other one with his hand

They looked at each other just for a moment...

"You shouldn't have come," he said, his voice hoarse and deeper than usual.

"I know," she replied, and their tongues collided again.

Good. It felt so good that she decided not to stop. Maybe it was a strange decision to have her first time with a complete stranger, but at least she knew that it would be good.

Astrea knew that if they stopped now, she would be the one regretting this.

He returned his attention back to her neck, sucking her delicate skin in all the right places. This was building her up quickly because she knew he was moving towards the marking spot next to her collarbone, a place so sensitive that she couldn't wait to feel him there. The anticipation was almost as good as what he was doing to her.

His tongue sent a wave of goosebumps rippling through her, and she closed her eyes, ready to enjoy everything he had to give her, but at the next moment, sharp, searing pain shot through her body, bringing her back to reality.

Astrea screamed in Fenrir's arms, her delicate frame shuddering.

He stopped at once, his darkened eyes searching for the reply to his unspoken question on her face.

Astrea wished she could have said something. When his lips left her skin, the pain stopped at once, but she could feel the snake tightening its grip around her neck now, strangling her. She couldn't breathe. This time for an entirely different reason.

Not a pleasant reason at all.

"Are you—" Fenrir looked so worried that guilt panged her heart as she pulled herself to kiss him, moving her hips to let his bulge feel it in the hope of distracting him from what was really going on.

The snake was controlling her. Her Teacher was controlling her. The Serpent.

Fenrir's hands were back on her in no time, and Astrea got the flower pin that was still holding the top of her hair out. A dainty little thing with a poisonous needle inside.

She didn't think twice, stabbing Fenrir with it in the neck. The concentrated dose could put down three huge men. It had to be enough for him to sleep until the morning. And for her to get the hell out of here.

If he felt the injection, he didn't flinch, but his hand wrapped around her throat as he looked into her eyes with that same kind of desire and longing as the whole time she had been here.

"That snake tattoo doesn't suit you!" he groaned and then pushed her back to the bed, towering over her.

"I don't like your tattoos either!" Astrea narrowed her eyes at him vengefully. She didn't like the serpent on her skin one bit, but she also wasn't in a habit of letting men criticise her for any reason.

"Liar," Fenrir chuckled and blinked, lowering his face to kiss her again.

She wanted to push him away as the game stopped being funny, but to her own disbelief, the drug finally kicked in, and the next second she found Fenrir's whole body falling on top of hers, pinning her to his bed while he was knocked out on top of her.

"Fenrir?" She called him simply to ensure that the drug worked. "Fenrir, are you okay?"

Not a sound.

The King of Rogues was so heavy that for a few minutes, she was simply wriggling under him helplessly.

He was so warm and smelled so nice that she almost regretted stopping what was happening between them.

Nevertheless, her task was clear, and this couldn't be happening. She had to leave, and she had to make it look like she had never been here.

Grasping one of the bedposts, she used all her body strength to get herself out, pushing him with her foot to turn him on his back.

Carefully, she examined him, coming to the conclusion that the drug worked just the way it was supposed to.

Next, she had to erase all of her traces here, starting with the King himself. Although she tried to control her scent, it was still all over him because of how close they were just a few seconds ago.

Astrea pulled her slip back up and looked around, her eyes landing on a cabinet filled with alcohol.

"Bingo!" She smiled to herself and took two bottles and a t-shirt she found hanging on one of the chairs. She opened the bottles and started spraying alcohol around, knowing that it would overpower any weak trace of her scent she left behind. Then she poured some on the t-shirt and returned to the King.

Swiftly and trying not to look too much, she wiped his torso with the whiskey-soaked cloth, pausing only for a second when she reached a scar right where his heart was. His wounds were strange!

She heard some noises outside and decided to hurry, spraying the rest of the bottle over the bed and then placing it in Fenrir's hand.

When he would wake up, he would be sure that he simply got drunk, and if he remembered anything about her, he would think it was a dream.

"Menace," he muttered, and she got worried that the drug wasn't strong enough for him. She had to get out of here fast.

"It's just a dream, Fenrir," she whispered into her ear. "A dream."

He did not respond, and she exhaled in relief.

Last but not least, she returned to the fireplace and threw the t-shirt into it, ensuring it all went up in flames. She checked that the hairpin was in place and then tried the window she used to get into the room again. To her surprise, this time, the shutters opened easily, and she was back onto the roof in no time, praying that she didn't leave anything behind that could give her away in Fenrir's bedroom.

She didn't stay in her room for long either, gathering shower supplies and taking the trip to the showers. After all, the middle of the night was probably the best time here.

She cleaned herself thoroughly, getting rid of the rogue's scent on her skin. Then she washed her silk slip for the same reason, and only then was she able to return and finally get the well-deserved rest. Evidence-free.

IN THE MORNING, Astrea woke up from the buzzing of her phone. The caller ID made her swallow hard, and she replied at once because she knew better than to let her Teacher wait.

"Dragonfly," the Serpent greeted her, his voice colder than usual which was a bad sign on its own.

"Teacher," she muttered, wiping her eyes.

"No," he replied, stretching the word as if it was a game. "Try again."

"Joran." She remembered their new agreement and got out of bed, looking for a robe to throw on top of her nightgown. She passed the mirror on her way to one of the luggage bags and froze when she saw her reflection in it.

"Fuck!" Astrea swore loudly, forgetting that she was still on the line…

7. LOVE BITES

*T*his couldn't be happening.

Panic rushed through Astrea's bloodstream. Her neck had a mark on it, and it wasn't the one that every shifter girl dreamed of.

It was a problem.

A big *freaking* problem for her.

Because she had a big, bright hickey where a mate's mark should go. Bright red, almost raspberry in colour.

"What is it, Astrea?" Joran sounded impatient and she received a cold shower of reality, realising he was still on the line.

"Tell him you are on your period," Nova suggested "helpfully", and Astrea was really close to blocking her wolf for a day or two. Nova knew what she was thinking, of course. *"It has always worked in the past and you know it!"* she added.

"Bye, Nova!" Astrea closed the mind link as she didn't have the mental capacity to deal with it all now and needed to be concentrating on the man who still had power over her.

"It's—" She didn't know what to say to her Teacher. For some reason, the truth seemed like a bad idea. "Sorry, it's nothing. This place is just a hell hole in general. Cockroaches are watermelon-sized here."

"You don't like the East anymore?" Joran asked with a voice void of emotions, but she knew he had to be gloating inside. He sent her here on purpose. Probably to prove to her that this wasn't the place for her. Little did he know this was never the final destination.

"There is nothing to like!" she said, grateful that this wasn't a video call. "It's a desert. We live in some ancient building. Everything is old here, and even showering is an ordeal in the East."

"Did you take a shower there, then?" the Serpent questioned, and she did not like where this was going.

"At night," she told the truth. "When no one was around."

"Are you sure about that?"

Joran's question startled her.

"Yeah, why?" She scratched the damn hickey again and noticed the snake tattoo moving on her neck.

Swearing under her breath, she rushed to the bags.

"Astrea, I want to make sure you are fine. Switch to video," Joran suddenly suggested, but luckily, she was ready.

She wasn't stupid. She realised quickly that he knew at least partially what had happened yesterday, so she threw a hoodie on to cover the evidence and only then switched the camera on, showing her Teacher an indifferent face.

"You look tired," Joran stated after observing her for a few seconds.

"Well, it's not exactly a vacation. Is it?"

"It is not," he agreed, and silence reigned once again. "Take off the hoodie."

The order was unexpected, and the Teacher had never asked anything like this from her before, so Astrea's lips parted in shock.

"Why?" she demanded, brows furrowed.

"Do you need a reason to obey an order? You are still my Dragonfly," Joran insisted. "Are you not?"

"I am," she sighed and placed the phone on the desk, using her makeup box to prop it up. She ensured he could see her and slowly pulled the hoodie off, angling her body for the camera to hide the mark on her.

"Closer," he commanded, and she took two steps forward.

Joran was silent, and she didn't like it. Astrea wanted to be done with this.

"Slowly turn for me," he said, and she sucked in a sharp breath.

"What are you searching for?" She decided to ask him bluntly and not beat around the bush.

"Hidden wounds. Yesterday I felt that someone was hurting you, and I am afraid that you would hide it from me if this was the case," Joran admitted coldly, and she couldn't hold back a chuckle.

Whatever Fenrir was doing yesterday couldn't be classified as hurting her. And the hickey on her neck was hardly a wound.

Yet she didn't find it in herself to object or share this with Joran, so she slowly spun around, hoping that he wouldn't notice anything.

She was wrong.

"What is that on your neck?"

Astrea stopped, not knowing how to respond. She suspected that he already knew everything because there was no way he saw the little spot from the crappy phone video, but of course, there was no point in confronting him.

"Show me closer!" Joran snapped and the snake on her neck tightened uncomfortably.

She did as she was told simply because it was faster and the battle was already lost.

"Is that a... love bite?" The question did not take her by surprise, but it didn't make it any easier to answer, either. Joran was far away from her, but she could feel the waves of anger he was emitting right now.

Astrea knew one thing for sure. He did not like it when anyone got too close to her.

She could never forget the time on the Firstborn Island when a young Dokkalfar elf called Steffen, one of the last of his kind and undoubtedly hard to obtain in a deal, started showing her signs of affection. He helped her on an obstacle course in front of everyone, something Firstborn never did. Astrea lied to herself for a long time that it was a coincidence that the places of their battle practices and their schedules changed so that it was practically impossible to meet one another. She tried to forget how she thought that the fact that Steffen's training became more dangerous and barely survivable was for his best, that Teacher only wanted to make him stronger.

One day Steffen found her when she was learning about poisonous herbs in the woods and took her to his favourite place in secret. He was her first kiss, and she could still remember how embarrassed she felt and how his pointy ears tinted when he leaned to capture her lips.

She also remembered how Joran tore him off her the next moment and threw him against a massive tree. His eyes were full of flames, and he shifted into his dragon form in front of her, grasping the already defeated elf with his claws and flying away...

She never saw Steffen again.

She never let any other Firstborn get close again. Not that they tried to get close to her after what happened... She was singled out. A taboo. The one not to be touched.

The Teacher's favourite.

The Teacher's Pet.

Astrea shivered remembering all this. She always hated that nickname even though no one dared to use it to her face.

"Who placed it on your skin, Dragonfly?" Joran asked again, voice menacing and demanding.

"Just some drunk rogue." She shrugged, hoping to de-escalate the situation. "I handled him."

"In what way?"

"I put him to sleep with a drugged needle," she said calmly since she didn't have to lie this time. "He would think it was all a dream."

"Do you have love bites in other places?"

Dangerous. This question was too dangerous.

"Show me," her Teacher commanded, and Astrea's eyes widened. Surely, he wasn't serious.

"There is nothing anywhere else on my body!" She stood her ground, clenching her fists.

"Show. Me." She could see him adjusting himself in his seat back in the mansion on the island.

"Teacher—Joran." She looked at him through her lashes, fixing her mistake quickly. "There is nothing. I wouldn't let—"

"You let a rogue touch you," he interjected. "He could have bitten your marking spot."

"But he didn't," Astrea insisted. "Because I know how to handle myself. Even here."

"They are rogues!"

"I know that, and so did you when you sent me here!" She was surprised by how open this conversation was turning out to be.

"You know why I sent you there." Joran leaned forward. "Don't change the subject, Astrea."

"Fine!" She gritted her teeth and removed one strap, standing straight before the camera. Her breathing was hitched, and anger was rising within. She had to control that anger because Niki would be paying the price for her if she didn't.

Astrea hated how her fingers trembled when she hooked the last strap holding her lacy nightgown in place. She raised her chin high because she refused to take this as humiliation. She had nothing to be embarrassed by here.

"Stop." Joran's voice changed, and she exhaled loudly in relief, darting her eyes back to the screen. "I'm sorry, Astrea. I trust you. I shouldn't have asked. I just hate that some dirty rogue put his hands on you."

"It's all right," she heard herself saying, still shocked that she received an apology in the first place.

"Did you meet the one they call King?" The Teacher changed the subject abruptly.

"Yes." Astrea pulled the strap back up and slipped on the hoodie to cover herself better.

"How did you find him? What is he like?"

"Rude and unwilling to communicate. He wanted me to leave and I don't think he is a big fan of the alliance," she reported, not mentioning that he was the "dirty rogue" who put his hands on her.

"Do you think you can handle him?" Joran rubbed his chin, watching her every move.

"I'm here, am I not? He obviously changed his mind." Astrea smirked and went to pick an outfit for today. She couldn't bear standing before him anymore, even if he was just on her screen.

"I want you to tell me everything you can about—" Joran wanted to continue her questioning, but a knock on the door silenced them and Astrea quickly retrieved her phone from the desk.

"Who's there?" she asked, still not hanging up.

"Just the most handsome and stylish Perished Kingdom citizen," Devoss announced with admirable confidence. "I came to take you to breakfast."

"Oh, great! I'll be just a sec!" Astrea yelled and gestured to her Teacher that the conversation had to be ended. She noticed how his jaw tightened, but he still nodded, letting her hit the disconnect button.

Finally rid of one problem, Astrea found herself with another.

The hickey seemed to get bigger since the last time she saw it in the mirror, and it just made no sense.

"No!" she whined as she assessed her skin again. "Please, Goddess, no!"

Everything was going so well, and now this could potentially ruin everything for her. Fenrir couldn't see it.

"Fuck!" she swore under her breath.

"I told you it was a stupid idea," Nova snorted in their mind. *"Now you are utterly fucked, my dear."*

She said it as if they didn't share a body.

"You know, I heard wolves are supposed to be helpful for their people," Astrea reminded her companion with a groan.

"I tried," Nova chuckled. *"It's not my fault you are helpless. One handsome rogue was enough to make you lose your mind."*

Astrea huffed a laugh. *"You were there, too, and I don't remember you objecting too much! In fact, I don't remember you objecting at all."*

"What was there to object to?" Her wolf smirked. *"He was one fine specimen and knew how to handle us well. Fenrir was simply perfect for the first time. Memories for life, you know."*

Astrea rubbed her neck in the hope that it would help the love bite disappear.

It didn't.

"How is this even possible?" She exhaled in defeat. *"It's just a hickey. It was supposed to be gone by now. Werewolves don't get hickeys for more than an hour, and it's been several."*

Nova did not reply, and Astrea sighed, realising it wasn't important. She had to deal with it anyway.

She got her makeup out and used the best waterproof concealer and foundation to mask it, working as fast as she could since she knew they were waiting for her. She put on a white jumpsuit with a plunging neckline and a massive belt, pairing it with a longline kimono-styled jacket with studs adorning its edges to keep the flowing fabric grounded.

Not thinking twice, she also added a white silk scarf to try and hide the mark on her neck in case the make-up wasn't enough.

She didn't have time to do anything with her hair, but luckily it had some natural curls in the hot and humid environment, finishing her look.

Devoss was still waiting for her when she walked out of her room and led her to the dining hall, which was simply one of the terraces of the long fortress, where all the rogues she had already met before were present.

Kara and Bastian frowned when they saw her, while Warg gave no reaction. Some Omega was serving them, and Astrea was a bit shocked by the abundance of food on the table. This wasn't how she imagined breakfast at a rogue table.

Beautiful colourful ceramic plates and bowls were full of fruit; nuts, cheeses, salads, flatbreads and some dips that Astrea didn't recognize. The impressive spread before her looked and smelled delicious. She hadn't eaten anything since she left the island and it took all of her self-control not to throw herself at what was before her.

However, she forgot about the food the moment her eyes locked with the King of Rogues.

Fenrir sat at the head of the table, wearing another black shirt and still managing to look imposing with his dark hair reaching his muscular shoulders.

"Welcome to our modest table, Astrea." He raised a brow at her, and she waited for him to say something else. Anything really...

But he did no such thing, and she took one of the seats, frustrated, choosing the one slightly away from everyone else.

"You stayed," Kara stated the obvious with no excitement in her voice. She looked both bored and annoyed beyond belief.

"Yes, and I am looking forward to our cooperation!" Astrea acted as if she didn't notice the resentment. She was good at it as she'd had a lot of practice in her past.

"So, what are your plans for us?" Devoss was the only one who seemed genuinely friendly and interested. "What are you going to do here?"

"I would like to start with exploring the East." She smiled. "I want to see the cities, meet the people, see how everything is arranged here before I can give my recommendations on what to do."

"So professional!" Devoss nodded, arranging his plate with the delicacies he liked. "Looks like you are going to need a guide here!"

"That would be very nice!" She grinned at him. "I was hoping that someone would volunteer to help me with this."

Fenrir cleared his throat, and her eyes went back to him involuntarily. It was incredibly hard not to think of what had happened between them the night before.

"Why are you wearing a scarf?" he asked, startling her. "It's a hot day, and it's only going to get hotter from here."

She stared at him for a few moments before replying, "It's there for decorative purposes."

The corners of his lips tilted upwards. "Beautiful. And now, why don't you remove it?"

8. SANDSTORM

"*N*o, thanks." Astrea gave the Rogue King her most charming smile and pretended to be focused on picking some fruit for herself.

"It goes against our traditions to wear scarves at the dining table." She heard Fenrir's mocking voice and paused. Her research of the former Eastern Kingdom had no such restrictions described anywhere. Why the rogues would have such a silly rule was beyond her. It made no sense.

"Since when?" Bash asked the reasonable question, confirming her suspicions, and she heard a distinctive sound of a kick under the table, which made Astrea straighten her back instantly.

So, Fenrir remembered something.

She prayed for her blood not to rush to her cheeks to avoid giving her away.

Luckily, she was prepared for such a turn of events, too, and immediately looked Fenrir in the eye without a shade of confusion or hesitation.

She couldn't make a big deal out of the stupid piece of fabric because she had to make his suspicions disappear.

"Oh, excuse me. I had no idea." She stood up and unwrapped the scarf, throwing it around the back of her chair as if she had nothing to hide. "Any more rules like this would be very useful to know."

The love bite was still covered with make-up, so she stretched her lips into a broader smile and sat back, meeting the Rogue King's gaze.

It was possible that he remembered something and doubted whether it was a dream or reality. Her current task was to ensure he came to the right conclusion that it was all an illusion of his drunken mind.

"Yeah, those rules would be good to know for all of us," Devoss chuckled, shooting a mocking glance at his leader.

"I will send you the list." Fenrir cocked his brow at his friend. "It starts with no bright colours in my palace."

The jab was clear because today, Devoss was wearing a bright green suit, looking even more dazzling than before. His long dark hair was gathered in a tail at the back of his head, and once again, Astrea mused that this wasn't how she imagined rogues at all. The ones she'd met before were very different from this bunch.

"Which one?" Devoss smirked, and Fenrir cast a stern gaze on him. The little interaction caught Astrea's attention.

"Do you have more than one palace?" she asked, and Bash coughed, Kara hitting him on his back as hard as she could, almost making him end up with his nose in his plate.

Something was off.

"Yeah, dozens!" Fenrir snorted, devouring his food. "The whole desert is peppered with my palaces, didn't you know?"

"How could I?" She stabbed some fruit she didn't recognize on the display before her without looking. "I am new here. I need that tour to get to know this place, remember?"

"We'll arrange that, won't we, Fenrir?" Devoss was definitely trying to smooth the edges between them.

"Sure." The King smirked, and his eyes found Astrea immediately. "Anything for our dear guest."

"That's very sweet of you." She didn't buy it. The glint in his eyes was too mischievous.

"I had a dream about you," he suddenly announced loudly, and everyone stopped doing whatever they were busy with, paying their full attention to him now.

"About me?" Devoss tried to deflect as he sat next to Astrea, but she knew very well who Fenrir was talking about.

"No, about our Southern guest." His King leaned over the back of his massive chair with a smug smile.

"Oh, really?" Astrea fluttered her eyelashes at him innocently. "Was it good? Did we make that alliance after all?"

"You came into my room late at night wearing next to nothing and offered yourself on a platter," he stated calmly, testing her, fishing for a reaction that she was not going to offer.

"Oh, my!" she giggled. "So, it was *that* kind of a dream! I am flattered. So unexpected, to be honest."

"Yeah," he chuckled. "I was shocked!"

"I would be, too!" she hummed, dipping her flatbread into some delicious-smelling paste. "So unrealistic, though!"

"Very," he agreed, not taking his piercing gaze off her. "We kissed."

"Moon Goddess!" she gasped matter-of-factly as if to let him know she wasn't impressed at all, and as soon as she said those words, he frowned.

"I marked every inch of your body with my tongue," Fenrir went on, reaching for a tall metal glass before him and taking a sip.

"I think I am done!" Kara stood up abruptly, letting her heavy wooden chair screech over the tile floor as she moved it, an expression of annoyance on her face.

"Leaving so soon?" Devoss sneered at her.

"I have a lot of training planned for today for the new arrivals," the woman brushed him off. "And I've suddenly lost my appetite."

Astrea was grateful for this distraction Kara provided because she could feel her heart drumming in her ears after Fenrir's shameless remarks. He didn't mark every inch of her body! Maybe he did dream of her after she drugged him and left? The thought alone made her feel the heat all over her body. Heat which she had to suppress.

"And then, when I relieved you of your flimsy nightgown, I spread your —" The Rogue King did not seem to be done yet.

"Kara, wait up!" Warg was next to leave, hurrying after his friend and not even bothering to finish his food. "I'll help!"

Astrea pretended to be busy with a copper coffee pot she found, pouring herself what looked like the strongest and, at the same time, most aromatic coffee of her life into a small cup.

Would he stop already with the nonsense?

Everyone was silent for a while.

"So, you tore her nightgown and spread her what?" Devoss stirred his tea with a little teaspoon, and Astrea wanted to throw something at him.

"I think I am not hungry anymore," Bastian also stood up, irritation spilling off his tone. "See you all later."

"What a touchy crowd we have here!" Devoss scoffed and put the teaspoon aside, the corners of his lips turned upwards. "So, where did we stop, Fenrir? Luckily, I am an eager listener!"

"I think we got what kind of a dream that was!" Astrea decided to intervene. Enough was enough. "Spare us the details, please."

"Of course," Fenrir chuckled, returning to his food. "It ended abruptly anyway. I bit you slightly on your marking spot, and that snake on your neck came to life and tried to bite me back."

She halted. She didn't mean to, but for just a mere second, she did.

It was one thing for him to remember bits and pieces of their little encounter and to question it. It was completely another to talk about her tattoo, which was indeed alive.

"What a cockblocking tattoo you have, Astrea!" Devoss was the one enjoying this awkward breakfast the most.

"Only in Fenrir's dreams!" she retorted with a stiff little smile, downing the remnants of her coffee.

"Is that a challenge?" the King let out a confident laugh, and she was ready to swear at herself for teasing him. She needed to dial down that tension, not escalate it more.

"Anyway," she turned to finally look at him, "I would like to see the city and possibly have a tour around. I need to know what I am working with."

"I can arrange—" Devoss started speaking, but Fenrir stopped him with a motion of his hand.

"I'll take her personally," he said, shocking them both.

A wave of goosebumps ran down Astrea's spine. That man next to her meant trouble. Especially considering his suspicions.

And also, because you are afraid of what will happen if you find yourself alone with him again, Nova jabbed her without pity, and Astrea tried to push her back in their mind to have it clear.

"There is no need for you to do it personally." She smiled. "I am sure as a King you are busy and—"

"On the contrary, you are my number one priority at the moment, Astrea," Fenrir announced, and she swallowed, the air between them getting unbearably hot.

SHE FOLLOWED him out of the fortress, once again surprised by how empty it looked. They were supposed to have people to offer to the Republic, an army. But all she saw was an empty building and endless sand behind it. A big car with huge wheels waited for them, and Astrea started to wonder where it came from because she hadn't seen any vehicles around. Too many things in this place did not add up.

To her surprise, Fenrir opened the door for her and waited the whole time while she got inside. Moreover, when she was settled, he gave her a questioning glance.

"What?" Astrea's arms almost reached for the bite mark on her neck he awarded her with last night, and it took all her willpower to control herself.

"Seat belt," he reminded her and her lips parted in disbelief.

"Seat belt?" She blinked at him, and he sighed heavily, taking the belt right next to her and leaning all the way over her to buckle it safely. He lingered on his way back, first inhaling her scent and then pausing right in front of her face, their noses almost brushing against each other. His warm breath caressed her skin, and she could almost remember how good he tasted on her tongue the other night.

"Safety first, Menace." His lips curled, and she licked her lips which were suddenly dry now. The action alone made his eyes a shade darker, while at the same time, the red in them looked ablaze.

"You... have a very unusual eye colour," she mumbled while he rested his well-trained arm on her seat right next to her head, unwilling to move away.

"So I've been told..." He studied her and his gaze alone felt like a lover's caress.

"As if someone set ice on fire," she went on, not sure where she was going with it and why she couldn't just shut up. "Not that it's possible."

"You'd be amazed to know what is possible," Fenrir said and sighed, pushing off her seat as if it pained him to do so. He closed the door and walked around the car, took the driver's seat and immediately started the car, driving into the never-ending sands drowning in the sunlight.

"I have to say, you must be a pretty adventurous person to volunteer to come here, Astrea," he praised her as she was captivated by the scenery. It looked very different from the sky, but she loved the change from her usual surroundings.

"I didn't volunteer!" She rolled her eyes at the thought alone. Who in their right mind would volunteer to go into a rogue territory?

"A punishment then," he chuckled, and she bit the inside of her cheek, shocked by how perceptive he was.

"Something like that." She decided to be honest this time.

"Was Jor the one who came up with that?"

Her head darted at him, but Fenrir seemed unfazed, his eyes behind sunglasses focused on the sands before them.

"You know him?" she gasped.

"Among others," he replied as if it was not a big deal.

When it clearly was a big deal. Very few people in the world could boast of knowing Joran Nathair other than the ones who belonged to him.

On the other hand, they had to know each other. After all, they struck the alliance somehow. Or were about to do it.

"The question is, how well do you know him?" Fenrir's lips pressed tightly the second he finished the sentence, and she noticed how the veins popped on his arms from the pressure he was now applying to the steering wheel.

"Just a working relationship." Astrea shrugged her shoulders and turned away to look out of the window. She couldn't tell him more, nor did she want to.

"If you are ever in the market for a new job…" he said all of a sudden and a smile appeared on her face.

"Are you offering me a job now?" She grinned at him.

"If you are desperate enough to work for rogues," he chuckled, his resounding laugh vibrating through the air and Astrea caught herself on the thought that she loved the sound of it.

"Not quite there yet," she giggled playfully. "But I will keep it in mind. Let's see how our collaboration works out."

"Wanna have some fun?" That question took her by surprise. It could mean anything. It could mean things she hoped it didn't mean. It probably did, considering the "dreams" Fenrir was having.

"No offence, but I think our ideas of fun are very different," she replied dryly.

"Wanna bet?" He smirked, and she didn't like that expression on his face.

As if he had something on his mind and knew she wouldn't be thrilled about it.

A sharp turn of the steering wheel and the car flew off in the air, Astrea barely managed to grasp the handle next to her head for stability.

"What are you doing!?" she squealed as he turned the wheel in the opposite direction to the maximum and held it there, making their car spin, surrounded by clouds of sand around them. For a moment, it became dark inside, and this was when he stopped, letting the dust settle.

Her heart was racing, pulse drumming in her head as she stared at the rogue beside her with an "I am going to kill you" glare.

"I told you the seat belt was a must." Fenrir adjusted the sunglasses on his nose and winked at her over them with his lips curved upwards. "Ready for more?"

"No!" she protested, but he was already pushing the life out of the gas pedal and the car drove off again, quickly getting up to speed.

She searched frantically for something to grasp on to, not quite realising it was his thigh. Although, she didn't care at this point what she was gripping as Fenrir made their car slice the air again and land on the sand that didn't seem so soft and safe anymore.

"Goddess!" Astrea panicked. Never say never. Of all the ways to die, a car accident was not very high on her list. She was used to dangerous situations but she usually had, at least, some form of control.

"The Moon Goddess is not allowed in these lands," Fenrir said in a dark, deep tone that was still calm for some reason. "You need to find other gods to worship. Or better yet, simply believe in yourself."

"Gosh, you are so deep, Fenrir!" She gritted her teeth, her words soaked in sarcasm as she wished to hit him with something heavy. "How about we discuss this calmly as soon as you stop the damn car?"

"Astrea," he gave her a knowing look through the tinted lenses, "would you relax? This is a trust-building exercise!"

"Trust?" she scoffed, worried that he wasn't looking at the road anymore. Not that there was a road to look at... but he must be crazy doing this and speaking of trust.

"I am not planning to hurt myself or to look foolish in the presence of a beautiful woman who made me dream of her after one short conversation. This is how we entertain ourselves here, and if you relax a bit, you'll be able to enjoy it too."

He had a point. Fenrir did not look tense at all, and that implied that he knew what he was doing.

"I don't like feeling trapped," she confessed suddenly, shocking herself by opening up to him this easily. She wasn't that kind of a person. However, the next moment she felt his large palm covering her hand, their fingers entwining, his grasp on her firm.

"You are not trapped," he said as they drove towards what looked like a giant sand hill. The biggest one so far. "Tell me to stop, and I will."

She knew he was telling the truth. Astrea felt it on some deep inner level and tightened her grip on him.

"Hold on tight!" he chuckled, sending the car flying again. She could feel the gravity pulling them down, but at the same time, the feeling of freedom that one could only reach during a flight, however short, filled her as well, making her forget about everything.

She squealed with joy right before they landed back into the sand, kicking up clouds and clouds of dust around them.

Astrea lost track of time entirely as he entertained her, and when they finally reached a flat dry surface with the buildings visible on the horizon, she felt a bit disappointed that it was over.

She gently tried to slip her fingers from his grasp but only heard Fenrir chuckle at her feeble attempt. The man had no intention of letting her go.

"I am fine now," she told him.

"I'm afraid I will not be fine if you let me go." He knitted his brows pitifully when he gave her a sad gaze. "And you owe me one."

She closed her eyes, exhaling sharply through her nostrils at this man and his games, turning away to stare out of her window again. As if her hand was detached from her body, and it meant nothing that he had it in his possession now.

His thumb brushed over her skin, creating all kinds of sensations she tried to block, and Astrea had to bite her lip while she was at it to suppress any reactions threatening to escape her. This was the strangest car ride of her life.

They drove into the city, if one could call it that. The car barely squeezed into the narrow, dirty streets.

It was exactly as she expected – dull, overcrowded, underdeveloped. Too sad to look at. The good things that she noticed about it were created at least a few hundred years ago. Back when the Perished Kingdom was the official Eastern stronghold of the Moonrise Kingdom, where its inhabitants mixed with the people from the continent on the other side of the sea.

She saw men and women in clothes that had seen some life – tired, unhappy, most with no hope. Others looked like the only thing they had was hope.

Astrea's heart painfully clenched for all of them.

What was life here like? It could probably be better if they started rebuilding this place. This impoverishment was what she was expecting. Rebuilding was what she would have done in their place. Not that she was going to judge.

Astrea knew very well that rogues lose their humanity over time. Was that what was happening here? Was this why Joran wanted them to join the Republic's army and fight against the West and the North? He loved heartless warriors, after all. The rogues would be expendable to him.

She shivered at her own thoughts, trying to push them away.

However bad all that was, she had to save herself first, and then Niki.

Fenrir parked the car on a central square, and she noticed a market nearby selling used goods and some fruit she didn't recognise again. Where were they taking it from?

Fenrir gave her hand one final squeeze, bringing her attention back to him, and only then did he let go of her.

"Welcome to Raja, Astrea, the Rogue City." He gave her a half-smile that did not reach his eyes.

"Is this the capital now?" she asked.

"No, we don't have a capital anymore. It's just a city."

City... she couldn't agree with calling it that, but as a professional, she didn't say a word.

"Let's explore then!" She left the car before he could do or say anything, and he watched her going toward the market, feeling how his heart was getting heavier by the minute. The white fabric of her outfit was flowing in the wind. Just like her white dress did on the day they first met.

The day that he remembered as if it was yesterday.

While she didn't remember him at all...

9. RAJA

$\mathcal{A}$ strea walked leisurely down the stalls of the market, paying close attention to everything there and trying to memorise anything that could be of use to her and her Teacher. However, she quickly had to admit that there wasn't much… worn clothes, old gadgets, questionable-looking food and broken old furniture – these were the offerings at the rogues' market.

This so-called city was barely surviving.

Precisely what she and her Teacher expected.

Rogues by the book. Just the way everyone imagined them, and this was something that didn't sit right with her.

Because Fenrir and his crew were anything but typical.

If they were forming a kingdom, surely there had to be people who strived for more than this… and she didn't see any of them here.

"Anything you are interested to see here in particular?" She didn't even notice that Fenrir was walking so closely behind her now, and when he leaned down to whisper the words, his breath was like a cool breeze to her skin in the heat of the day. It took all her willpower not to close her eyes and relax into his massive chest, especially after what had happened in the car on the way here.

Whatever that was.

"Just show me everything." She turned to face him, mainly to demonstrate that he didn't intimidate her, and that the car ride didn't affect her in the slightest.

"That *is* everything," he chuckled, removing his sunglasses and waving his hand around. "Or did you expect anything else?"

He was testing her, taunting her.

"No, Fenrir, this is exactly what I expected." She raised a brow at him and met his gaze. "You have failed to surprise me so far."

"Really?" The corners of his lips tilted upwards and she knew it was a mistake to say that. "So, our wild ride wasn't enough of a surprise? I am taking notes here, Astrea."

"So am I!" She raised her chin defiantly.

"I see I have to step up my game." He smirked at her.

"You have no idea!" she huffed in annoyance. "Tell me, Fenrir, how is it that your palace just had all that amazing food while your people live like this? Where does it come from, and why is the distribution so unfair?"

"What can I say, Astrea," the amused expression was gone from his face in an instant, "we are rogues, and it's the survival of the fittest here."

It was a reasonable response. For a rogue, of course. The island and the Southern Republic were different.

And yet something was off. She could feel it with her gut and her intuition had never failed her so far.

"Do you realise that what was on your table today could feed a few families here?" she snapped at him, all playfulness gone from both of them as they glared at one another.

"And do *you* realise that we had an important guest dining with us?" he reminded her of her own presence.

"So, it's my fault now?" She couldn't believe he was implying that.

"No, apparently, I am just a bad ruler," Fenrir scoffed, accentuating the last word.

"Your words, not mine." Astrea raised a brow and turned on her heel, picking up speed and trying to lose him, so as not to say anything else she might regret later.

She had already gone too far as it was.

"You are such a diplomat." Nova added fuel to the fire as always.

"Learning from the annoying voice in my head!" Astrea didn't ignore her wolf's little jab.

She looked completely out of place in her surroundings as she walked down the streets in her stupid expensive white outfit. She knew it. It wouldn't have been a bad idea to change before they left the fortress, but it was too late for that now. Fenrir was influencing her in the worst of ways, and she was making one mistake after another.

Astrea could feel his presence close to her but didn't let him know. Of course, he wouldn't let her wander around alone, but the less he knew of her and her training, the better. She had to gain back control.

They walked in silence for a bit, and Astrea darted into one of the narrow streets, Fenrir following closely behind, both not saying a word to each other even now.

This wasn't how she was supposed to behave with him. Her mission required otherwise, but… he threw her off her balance so easily. She needed a break.

A shabby house on a narrow street with a little girl standing right next to the entrance attracted Astrea's attention, and she found herself walking over there without even realising it. It was the first child she had seen here. A child that, for some reason, was made a rogue. Something that should have never happened in any pack or flock or wherever she came from.

And yet here they were…

"Hi sweetie." Astrea tried to smile at the girl, and the latter looked at her with bright blue eyes. For a rogue, she was pretty clean and well-dressed in jeans and a pink hoodie. The girl also had no instincts that could save her life in a place like this.

"Hi," the child whispered, a curious gaze travelling up and down the stranger.

"Emma?" Astrea heard a female's voice from inside the house and saw a woman rushing out, holding another little girl by her hand. The second girl looked identical to the first, with curly dark locks and hazelnut eyes, wearing almost the same clothes. The only difference was a stain on her hoodie.

Twins. When raising just one child in this "city" was probably challenging enough, this mother had twins to care for.

The girl in front of Astrea didn't know how to react, but her mother quickly pulled her behind her by her wrist, eyeing the she-wolf in front of her suspiciously. Astrea could tell by the look alone that this woman would fight her to death for her girl if she had to.

"I mean no harm." Astrea lifted both her hands to demonstrate her intentions. "I am just—"

"You are not from here," the woman interrupted her, hostility evident in her tone.

"No, I am not. I am a guest—"

"You'd better leave!" The mother wasn't interested in listening to her. "Emma! Ava! Inside!"

"I was just—"

"You are a disaster waiting to happen!" The woman shook her head of shiny black hair and prepared to close the door on her, the two girls darting scared gazes between both adults.

"She is with me!" Fenrir stopped the door from closing with his hand, and for a moment, the woman looked like she was about to kick him in self-defence. Her eyes travelled all over him, and Astrea noticed her lips parting in shock when her eyes lingered on the Rogue King's scars and then shot to the bead bracelets on his wrist. Something Astrea had never paid attention to before, taking it for just a part of Fenrir's look.

Now she started to question their presence. The Rogue King wasn't into fashion, and he was unlikely to follow some trend, even if they had any here. Did the bracelets mean something? No one else here had them, although she hadn't been looking for them specifically.

"It's you," the woman whispered, and Fenrir nodded in response.

"Astrea, could you give us a minute alone, please?" His tone suggested that it wasn't a request. It was an order.

She hesitated at first but soon realised she didn't mind leaving. She couldn't do anything for the family today anyway, and if there was a chance that Fenrir would help them somehow instead, she would gladly accept it.

So, she walked away, immersed in her own thoughts. Seeing the twins made her remember things she thought she had already forgotten.

She had a twin once too. She had a family.

And they all were taken away from her on one fateful night.

Astrea wasn't sure anymore if she even remembered the events correctly. Still... some of the details were etched into her memory forever.

Their car drove in the middle of the woods in the evening when it was turned upside down all of a sudden, making the world around them spin. Astrea remembered the screams of her sister, Stella, her fraternal twin who still resembled her so much.

She remembered the monsters that attacked them, breaking the window and dragging the man in the driver's seat out first. Probably her father... she couldn't remember anymore.

Only the seatbelt held her in place and her older brother, Brian, cut the straps with his claws for both her and Stella despite being seriously injured, shouting at them to run for their lives.

She remembered the fear that seized her body, preventing her from moving when it was time to flee. Brian shifted to try and protect them, but two huge dark beasts tore him apart before her eyes, ending his young life.

The sisters laced their fingers together as if this was going to help them, and then they ran. Ran, ran, ran.

Their matching white dresses were like beacons for the monsters, making them easy to spot in the darkness. Stella only had one shoe on after the accident and was slightly behind when they got to her, too, breaking the twins' hold on each other and separating them. Astrea turned to see where her sister was, only to find her twin already falling dead to the ground. Stella's dress, no longer white... She wanted to cry and scream, but for some reason, she couldn't. The dark beasts' glowing eyes watched her, their snarls letting her know she was next.

There was no way out.

She was taking step after step back until she stumbled and fell down a small slope she didn't notice, rolling all the way down to the roots of a tall old tree. Covered in scratches and bruises, she desperately crawled in between the massive roots, trying to hide. Only to see those roots crushed in a few moments, chips flying in her face.

A piercing pain in her thigh, and she was dragged for her inevitable demise.

The monster who got her decided to take its time with her and enjoy this last kill of the night.

She hadn't even had her first shift yet to have a fighting chance. There was no way to defend herself, and when the claws sliced her abdomen, there was nothing she could do but cry out as the immense pain rippled through her small body.

A guttural scream left her chest, and by some miracle, the monster was pulled away from her before she realised what was happening.

The blood was gushing from her wounds, and she felt so scared and lonely when someone's warm hands touched her skin, amber glowing eyes locking with hers.

"I've got you, little one," the Teacher said in a reassuring tone. "I am here now, and no one is going to hurt you."

Astrea didn't notice how far she managed to get on her own. She got a harsh comeback to reality when someone grabbed her wrist and pulled her into one of the dark alleys, covering her mouth with their palm at the same time.

"Easy there!" the unfamiliar man cooed into her ear as if that was supposed to calm her down.

This was, however, interesting. Just the distraction she needed to avoid drowning in her own thoughts and memories.

She was curious to see where this was going. Was this man alone, or did he have an accomplice? Were they going to commit a crime or maybe they were trying to warn her? If it was indeed a crime, how well organised was it? After all, she needed to know everything – the good and the bad.

He tried to throw her on the ground when he decided it was safe enough, but Astrea knew how to find balance fast, so she remained standing, taking a quick scan of her surroundings.

"A dead end. Two on the left, and two are blocking the way out," Nova confirmed what Astrea had already known.

It was a trap.

"There is no need to get hurt," one of the four men told her as they were surrounding her. That gang looked like proper rogues, with all the dirt and bad intentions in their eyes. They were proper criminals whom Astrea wouldn't be too sorry to kill.

"We haven't seen a pretty bird like you since we got here," the one who looked like their leader informed her with a chuckle, supported by his crew at once.

"We just want to have some fun." Another one gave her an appraising look full of lust that made her cringe.

"Boys," Astrea's lips curled involuntarily, "why didn't you just say so? I was actually looking to have some fun myself."

Her response startled them but not to the point of sending them running for the hills. Enough to stall them so they did nothing as she elegantly shook off her white longline jacket and carefully placed it on top of some boxes, stretching her neck in the process.

Moon Goddess, she needed this now.

The four of them started to close in on her slowly, and she graced them with her most dazzling smile. "Gentlemen, shall we?"

10. LET'S HAVE FUN

The first rogue charged at her, and she didn't even honour him with a blow of her own, simply dodging at the last moment and letting him meet the wooden boxes behind her.

Another was already launching a sneaky attack of his own from her back, and she found it disgraceful that he didn't have it in him to do it properly. It was like they weren't even trying. He simply attempted to grab her from behind, and that was insulting, to say the least. These guys didn't even have their claws out, completely underestimating the trouble they had just gotten themselves into.

She sent that one flying across the narrow street, pleased with how far he flew, knocking into some old crates on his way. It was impressive, considering he was a heavy fellow.

Claws elongated immediately, and the men bared their teeth at her, finally realising they hadn't chosen easy prey this time.

"Come on, guys!" she taunted, blowing a silver strand of hair off her face, and showing a savage grin. "I thought you wanted to have some fun! And so far, this has been boring!"

They leapt at her, and this time, she spared no one, catching the first one to reach her and twisting his arm, breaking it in a way that wouldn't let him regenerate quickly. She knocked another one out, stomping in the hollow of his knee until she heard a distinctive cracking sound. The third one got his head smashed against the stone wall. Before the fourth wolf could reach her, she jumped up, grabbing the metal bars of an old balcony on the nearest building and swung her legs out, grasping her opponent's neck between her thighs so hard that his ability to move and breathe were now severely restricted.

This was when Astrea noticed that the dirty rogues left muddy stains on her beautiful white outfit and frowned, thinking about what to do with them next. She would have probably just killed them if it were any other place. However, here in the East, she didn't know the boundaries and didn't want to get onto Fenrir's bad side. The King was already too hard of a nut to crack, and she didn't need any additional trouble with him.

"What is going on here?" Fenrir's voice sounded like thunder, bringing her out of her trance. *He found her too soon.*

Their eyes locked, and she saw how dark his gaze was, how his fists clenched at the sight of what she did to his disgusting men.

Nevertheless, she was in trouble.

"Some of your men wanted to get acquainted, but they forgot to ask for my consent," she tried to explain awkwardly, still holding someone's head trapped between her thighs, which, she was sure now, made Fenrir's jaw twitch. Rogues probably did not care about such things. "Sorry," she mumbled and released the rogue.

He fell to his knees, desperately gasping for air, making her roll her eyes involuntarily. She hated weak men. Those were usually the ones who gave hell to women, trying to compensate for what they themselves were lacking. Just like these four who clearly wanted to have their way with her, knowing that a regular girl wouldn't be able to stand against four men.

"Stupid bitch!" One of the guys spat blood, wiping his mouth and preparing to leave as this was officially over.

"How dare you?" Astrea chuckled with mock indignation. "I am a very clever bitch! Mind your manners!"

She hoped this would make the King of Rogues laugh, or at least not look this gloomy, but to no avail. Comic relief probably wasn't his thing.

"Move." The man with the bloody mouth tried to push Fenrir out of the way, not recognising his own King, but the latter didn't budge, closing the only possible exit with his broad chest that was going up and down at a faster rhythm than usual, eyes still on Astrea.

She expected to be scolded or reproached because the gaze cast on her was so heavy and dark. However, a gasp escaped her when, instead, Fenrir abruptly placed his large palm on top of the rogue's head and twisted it with force, breaking his neck, the breathless body of the man dropping to his feet to Astrea's shock.

"Who," Fenrir growled menacingly, catching another man who tried to flee for his life now, "do you think you are?"

"Man, it's just some girl! We didn't know anyone already had dibs on her —" The captive never finished his sentence because sharp claws sliced his torso so deep that his bowels fell out, dirtying the ground. Something that was very hard to achieve without shifting.

The King moved with speed faster than any shifter Astrea had encountered. Quick, deadly, merciless... His fist pierced the third rogue's chest, bursting out of it holding a heart that was still beating. Fenrir threw it away as if it was a piece of trash and moved on to the final offender.

The fourth man didn't even try to run, trapped between Astrea, who didn't move as she watched the scene unfolding before her eyes in awe, and Fenrir, who had his hand covered in blood. Slowly, the King approached the last rogue and grabbed his neck, yanking him up to his feet and then up in the air until his legs kicked uncontrollably... uselessly.

Fenrir's eyes found Astrea's again. "What? Are you not going to ask me to spare him?"

The words brought her out of the daze, startling her even more.

"Why would I?" She arched her brow at him. "So that he could go and hurt some other girl who can't protect herself the way I can? I will not plead for him or anyone like him for that matter."

"Good!" Fenrir scowled, and she heard another cracking noise, knowing far too well what it meant.

The Rogue King had just killed four of his own men.

Her mind was flooded with thoughts of what it could mean, but at the same time, she didn't want to read the situation wrong.

Was this planned? Or was it a coincidence? Did Fenrir care about her safety because she was an important representative from the South? Did he care about her at all?

She was a mess inside but still didn't let a single emotion slip onto her face. Exactly like she was taught.

"Are you hurt?" he asked when their silence became too awkward.

"Does it look like I am hurt?" she felt slightly offended by such a reaction. "I was handling them fine on my own, you know."

"Were you?" His lips pressed into a thin white line, a little wrinkle forming between his brows. "You were not supposed to be here at all!"

"Oh, excuse me for *your* people dragging me here without asking for my permission first!" she retorted, narrowing her eyes at him.

"You shouldn't have wandered off alone!" he persisted with his attitude, adding fuel to her fire.

"Weren't you the one who told me to get lost?" Astrea chuckled darkly, all fear and admiration for the man gone.

"No, I told you to give me a minute!" Fenrir clarified, fisting his hands so hard his knuckles became white.

"And that is what I did! It's not my fault that a gorgeous, nicely dressed woman can't take a step here without being assaulted!" she scoffed, not sure why he irked her so much. She wanted to provoke him, test him, get more emotions out of him, to see that fire in his icy eyes burn... Astrea desired it all. Not because it was her work. Not anymore. So, she added, "If only there was a King to fix that!"

"Good point!" Fenrir growled, a dangerous glint appearing in his eyes as his lips curled in a menacing smile, making her regret taunting him. "Your safety is my first priority, Menace."

He took a step forward, and she took one back, feeling the dangerous dark energy that was pouring off of him.

"Wh-what are you doing?" She knew she wasn't going to like the answer.

"See, Astrea, the problem is that I can't fix the city in one day," he sneered at her, "but I sure as hell can keep you safe."

"Fenrir!" she warned him, lifting her hand in front of her as if to ward him off.

However, he only used it to pull her closer and in less than a second, her world turned upside down.

Literally.

"Fenrir!" she yelled, realising that the rogue threw her over his shoulder and was now walking away leisurely.

"The best way to keep an esteemed guest safe is to keep you close," he explained in a matter-of-fact tone, his grip tight.

"You can't do this!" she protested.

"Really?" he chuckled. "Looks like I am already doing it."

"That's—" Astrea wanted to do and say so much, but only exhaled heavily, giving up. It wasn't like she could fight him. Not only because it would go against the mission. Mostly because she wasn't sure, after what she had just witnessed, that she would be able to take him down if she fought him. She had to admit that Fenrir was possibly too strong for her. Which meant she would avoid physical confrontation at all costs, letting the rogue feel he was the winner in this argument.

That would be the real win for her. She had to think of the long game.

Fenrir halted, not expecting her to give up so easily. His hands slid up the woman's body adjusting her position and she didn't react to that either, taking the fun out of it all. The last thing he wanted was to hurt her or make her angrier.

He was already worried he'd made a mistake by losing his temper earlier and felt he was walking on a thin line with her.

"What's the problem, Menace?" he asked.

"Problem? Here?" she chuckled darkly as she hung over his shoulder. "How did you guess?"

"I am observant like that." He smirked as he kept walking with her over his shoulder.

"Goddess, we have so much work to do!" she whimpered in response, making him huff a laugh. "You can't just do what you want!"

"Watch me."

"It's unacceptable!"

"Says who?" Fenrir chuckled. The darkness gone and the arrogance and sarcasm back.

"Everyone! A gentleman would never—"

"Gentleman?" He scoffed. "You must be kidding me! This is literally the Rogue Kingdom. I am their leader, and I am no gentleman."

"That you are not!" she agreed, still hanging upside down limply. "But maybe you should be! When you are at the Alpha Convocation, you can't behave like this, no matter what the situation!"

"Noted!" With a groan, he put her back to the ground but only to change the position, and he lifted her up again in just a few seconds. Astrea found herself in a bridal-style carry, facing the King now.

"This is not better!" She glared at Fenrir, who pretended not to notice her frustration and annoyance.

"Of course, it's better." He smirked. "Even if you don't want to admit it."

"I can walk by myself!" she insisted, nonetheless.

"I am aware," he informed her, but made no move to release her.

"How is this better again?" Astrea demanded, wriggling in his arms.

"Because when the rest of the city sees us like this, they will know that you are off-limits!" Fenrir stated.

"When they see us like what?" Astrea furrowed her brows, and their eyes met.

"Like you belong to me," Fenrir replied, placing her back on her feet next to his car. She didn't even notice that they were back, staring at him in shock. "Shall we?" He opened the door for her, ignoring how startled she was and not giving her a chance to respond to what he said.

WHEN THEY WERE BACK to the fortress after the most awkward car ride in the history of the shifter world, Astrea wanted to get out of the car with dignity but found the car door locked. Trying it over and over, she did not plan to give up.

Fenrir's shadow fell on her as he stood in front of her window. He pressed a button on his key fob, and she heard the mechanism unlocking, but before she tried again, he opened the door for her.

"There is no need for this!" she hissed, getting out without accepting the hand he offered, but the rogue was still blocking her way, keeping her trapped between him and the car.

"You implied that I should try to be a gentleman, so here you go." He was imperturbable, and it annoyed her even more. She'd had enough of him and his dominating unbreakable aura for one day. This man could wear anyone's patience thin.

"I don't know who we are kidding here!" she snapped. "Hell would freeze over before you'd be considered a gentleman!"

"And here I thought you were a professional!" He leaned lower so that his face was almost touching hers. "Teach me, master."

His hot breath tickled her skin and made her think of things she shouldn't be considering.

Heat rushed to her cheeks. Angry, uncontrollable heat.

"What happened to you two?" Devoss interrupted them, assessing the way they both looked as his brows went up. He was the only one to greet their return and had already changed into a bright yellow suit with a phoenix embroidered on it.

"A little accident," Fenrir responded without sparing his friend a glance.

"A little?" Devoss scoffed.

"Four people dead!" Astrea crossed her arms over her chest with a huff. She didn't want to let Fenrir downplay the events of today.

"Just four?" Devoss snorted, unfazed. "And I thought something big must have happened for you to have bloody handprints all over you. Did the dead people clutch you before they died?"

Astrea and Fenrir exchanged side glances.

"No," she shook her head defiantly, "a barbarian clutched me after he killed those people!"

"Did Fenrir kill them?" Devoss barely stifled a laugh, and Astrea awarded him with a dark glare. Everything was just fun and games for them.

"Four newbies attacked her, and I made sure they would never attack anyone again," Fenrir explained coldly. "That is all."

"That is not all!" Astrea protested. "When he was done, he manhandled me!"

"For all of three seconds!" The King retorted.

"And ruined my clothes!" She pointed at her jumpsuit covered in red handprints.

"It actually doesn't look that bad!" Devoss tilted his head, rubbing his chin as he took a better look. "It's edgier now and more appropriate for living in the Rogue Kingdom. Don't you think?"

"I think we have a lot of work to do if you want an alliance with the South to work out!" Astrea gritted her teeth. "From what I've seen so far, I am not impressed."

"How good it is that we have you to instruct us now!" Fenrir was clearly mocking her. "You will help us with that, won't you? Didn't you say you were the best of the best?"

She glared sharply at him. Was any of this serious for him?

"Astrea, love, the outfit is to die for, literally, but the smell... you need a bath." Devoss' nose wrinkled all of a sudden, even as he grinned.

"Yeah, thanks for reminding me!" She rolled her eyes, trying to calm herself. It was time to regroup. "I'm going to get a shower now."

She wanted to leave them both as soon as possible.

"That's probably not the best idea." Devoss stood in her way.

"Why the hell not?" Astrea had had enough of their games for one day.

"The warriors just returned from training. Unless you wish to take a shower with a few dozen naked rogues—"

A low, menacing growl escaped Fenrir, and Astrea sighed, covering her face with her hands.

"Luckily, I have a solution!" Devoss smirked, winking at her.

"You do?" She arched her brow, not even sure she wanted to hear it.

"It just so happens that I've drawn a bath for Fenrir in his tower." Devoss tried to look as innocent as he could. "I am sure, as the gentleman that he is —"

A snort escaped her.

"As the gentleman that he is," Devoss repeated, "Fenrir will allow you to take it in his stead."

Her lips parted in shock. What kind of offer was that?

"And you knew to prepare a bath for him, how again?" Astrea knitted her brows together. This whole day was bizarre. And it was just day one here.

"I am perceptive." Devoss winked at her again. "So, what do you say, Fenrir? Can our dear guest use it?"

"Sure," he replied, not taking his eyes off her. "If you are not afraid, that is."

Now she simply had to take that bath.

"That's so kind of you!" she hissed, turning on her heel. "Thanks! Offer accepted!"

Astrea marched away, Fenrir following her with his gaze until she was gone, the corners of his lips curving upwards.

However, his smile dropped when he noticed Bash walking towards him from another part of the fortress. He could tell by looking at his facial expression alone that something had happened, but he wasn't ready to deal with this now. Astrea captivated his whole mind.

"Bash, not now, please," he said wearily.

"Sorry, but I think you have to take it." The young wolf handed him a phone, and Fenrir accepted it with a low snarl.

It couldn't be anything good.

"Hello, brother," Joran's silky voice sounded from the other end of the line, bringing back the memories that Fenrir had tried to block for so many years.

11. LONG TIME NO SEE

*T*hey hadn't spoken for so long that hearing his voice still didn't feel real.

"Jor," Fenrir acknowledged his brother. After all, it would have been stupid to pretend that it wasn't him now. He was busted.

"How long has it been again?" Joran chuckled as if they did this every other weekend when in fact, it had been decades since the last time they spoke.

"Long enough." Sadly, Fenrir knew this wasn't his dream family reunion. His family was different. They were never like that…

"If I didn't know you any better, I would say that you are not happy to hear from me, Rir," Joran taunted, clearly pleased with the situation. The dragon loved to win, and this time, it looked like luck was on his side.

If only Fenrir had managed to send Astrea back the moment he saw her. Unfortunately, just a few minutes in her presence made him give up on all plans. Especially after seeing his brother's snake mark on her.

"We haven't seen each other for so long, but not much has changed since the last time we did," Fenrir brought himself to reply. "You are still your old manipulative self, brother."

"Ouch!" Joran's laugh rumbled on the other side of the line. "Tell me, Rir, was it worth it?"

"I'm not sure what you are talking about," the wolf replied, wishing to be done with this conversation as soon as possible.

"You are still so bad at lying after all these centuries," Joran said reproachfully. "Luckily for you, I am not taking it personally. I've learned that you can't think clearly when it comes to her. Although... that's not exactly her, is it? Does it make a difference? I've always wanted to know."

"What do you want, Jor?" Fenrir ignored the last question, returning to the main subject. He had only one weakness in his long life and hated when it was poked at.

"A brotherly conversation, of course!" Joran's voice was as sweet as honey on a warm summer day.

"And you are still very good at lying, but unfortunately for you, I now know when people lie."

"Ah, yes." Joran hummed. "Sure, you got me. But I insist that you answer first. Was it worth it to touch Astrea when you definitely couldn't miss my mark around her neck? If you had stayed away, I would have never discovered your location. You could have stayed hidden from me just like you wanted."

"I have no need to hide from you, Jor. Unless you have something new to tell me." Fenrir's voice was stone cold.

"It's just the way we parted—"

"That's also in the past," the wolf deity interrupted, his mood growing more sour by the minute. "Anything else?"

"So, about my Dragonfly—" Jor, on the other hand, was in the best of spirits.

"She is the past," Fenrir interjected roughly. "I don't like to be reminded of the past, and you know it."

"Are you trying to tell me that you don't care anymore?" the Serpent scoffed, the mocking in his tone too evident to miss.

"I am trying to tell you that the past is in the past, and I would like to leave it there."

"Hmm," Joran stretched the word, contemplating what was next. "So, are you telling me that I saved my Dragonfly for nothing?"

Fenrir hated how his brother repeatedly called Astrea his, using her old nickname. This was another test, another game, and he was failing at it badly. He failed the moment he kissed her, the moment he let himself trail his tongue down her silky skin, tasting what could have been...

What could he say now to downplay it in front of his sibling to keep her safe? Sadly, Joran knew what Astrea meant to him. What she would always mean to him, even if *she* didn't remember.

"I don't know what you were expecting, but as I have told you, Astrea is in the past for me," he insisted dryly, hoping that his brother would buy the deflection, but knowing deep inside that he probably wouldn't.

"I expected that I would keep an eye on her for you, for old times' sake." Fenrir could practically see his brother smirking as he said that. "I met her when she was a damsel in distress and saved her knowing how much she meant to you. Sadly, you were nowhere around, and she was an orphan. I *had* to raise her and take care of her."

Fenrir closed his eyes in despair. He knew that Astrea was connected to Jor somehow, but he had hoped it was a recent and meaningless connection. His brother's words proved otherwise.

"Naturally, we grew very close, her and I," Joran went on, notes of delight in his voice. "One can say we are practically inseparable, and I have to tell you – I finally see what you saw. All that being said, you should be proud of how far she has come."

Fenrir wasn't proud at all. He was fuming, feeling his insides burning with flames from hell itself. Hearing his brother make all these claims brought him more pain than he could have imagined.

"Cut the crap, Jor. What do you want?" He had to ask bluntly because it was the only way with the tricksters like Joran.

"I want world peace," the Serpent chuckled, but after he got no reaction to his joke, he cleared his throat. "No, seriously. This is all I want and all I strive for."

"Sure! I'm convinced that your intentions are pure." Now it was Fenrir's turn to mock his sibling.

"I am offended that no one ever believes this, but this is what I've always wanted!" Joran insisted. "The world needs a better order because, at the moment, people who live in it do not appreciate it."

"So, it's world domination you want!" A laugh rumbled through Fenrir's chest.

"I want you to fight on my side again," the dragon's tone finally became serious, "the way we were always meant to be. Two divine brothers, showing mortals the way."

"Because it ended so well for us the last time," Fenrir chuckled darkly.

"Don't be like that," Joran reproached him. "I could feel your energy the last time I was in the North. You blessed many people back there and made me lose an important battle. At the worst time possible, might I add."

Fenrir knew this would come into play sooner or later. The Dragon God would never forgive him or something like that.

"You broke the balance first," he reminded his younger brother.

"On the contrary, I was about to bring the balance back, but you stood in my way!"

"Those people did not deserve to die. Not like that."

"Don't you think I know that?" Joran finally snapped. "But it's not about them! What are their insignificant lives in the grand course of history? They were the sacrifices that had to be made for the sake of many!"

"See, and that's the problem for me right there." Fenrir closed his eyes and rubbed the bridge of his nose. This conversation was going nowhere. "I see it differently."

"Rir, if you'd just talked to me and let me explain," the Serpent sighed. "I have proof that what I am doing is right. I have numbers, statistics, and research. The Moonrise Kingdom was once what we loved, and if we managed to restore it, then people would actually stop dying in such quantities. This division they have now is bad for everyone. The North, the West, the South and the East have to become one again; only then would peace be possible. But I need your help, brother. I need you to side with me now."

Fenrir contemplated, remembering why he interfered the last time. He was in the North by accident and never planned to meddle in anything. When he saw the other shifters of the North fighting the bear shifters, their army blessed and enhanced by Joran, knowing that they didn't stand a chance against them, something changed. Fenrir always believed that everyone should build their own destiny, but at the same time, he knew how it felt to fight a power above and beyond you. So, he made a decision to help the ones who had prayed to him for centuries and blessed their army, too, giving them the much-needed boost to even the field. That action alone weakened him significantly, and only one thing made him happy. At least Joran's powers were also running low now.

That boost ruined all of Joran's plans; naturally, he wanted revenge. His brother wasn't one to give up.

However, Fenrir knew that it couldn't be this simple. It couldn't be just kinship that Joran sought. His brother didn't exactly need him that much and was fine on his own for so long. Fenrir chose a life of solitude, and the Serpent was fine with it for a very long time.

"What else do you want?" he asked plainly, tired of all the games already. While Joran took after his father with his trickster nature, Fenrir was more like their mother, who preferred deeds over words and was a power to be reckoned with.

"You know me too well!" Joran snickered over the phone. "I miss this—"

"I am sure you do," Fenrir cut him off. "So?"

"You know what I want," the Serpent sneered. Fenrir didn't hear him, but he could feel it with his skin.

"No." That could be the one and only answer.

"Think of it, brother," Joran knew how to be persistent. "Give it to me and join me. Then you could finally get the life you've always wanted. I will be the one to give it to you."

"No!" Fenrir exhaled heavily. "You know I can't."

"I know you do not want to. That's what I know." With each new sentence, Jor's tone was getting icier, all the playfulness finally gone.

"I have my reasons," the wolf confirmed and they remained silent for a few minutes.

"Think about it for a week," Joran suggested finally. "Think while Astrea can still stay with you because after one week—"

A growl escaped Fenrir which only made his brother chuckle.

"Jor!" He was about to tell him what he thought about those hidden threats and ultimatums but only heard another fit of laughter over the phone.

"I knew you couldn't hide it for long!" Joran sounded pleased with himself. "Don't say anything now. Think on it, my brother, the Rogue King."

He hung up, and Fenrir threw the phone at the stone wall of the room he was in, breaking it and only then realising that it wasn't his phone. Bash would be so angry.

He was cornered again, but for the first time in years, he knew exactly what he had to do. The only problem was that he didn't know how to get there.

"So?" Devoss and Bash waited for him outside and darted their eyes at him the moment he walked out.

"He knows," Fenrir reported and kept walking, the other two men following close behind as he tried to form a new plan in his head.

"Everything?" Bash's jaw twitched.

"Not everything," the King reassured him. "But he knows more than we need him to know."

"Bastian, call Kara and Warg. We need to discuss it." Devoss went into his strategizing mode, which was so different from his usual self.

"Not right now," Fenrir shook his head. "I need to calm down first and think straight. See you in a few hours."

He left his friends behind and went up the stairs to his Tower, fully settled into his gloomy thoughts.

The wolf entered his room and took off his shirt, wishing for nothing more than a shower to wash away all the blood he still had on his hands and body.

"What the hell is wrong with you?" Astrea's voice brought him back to reality the moment he entered his own bathroom and saw her in the bronze tub, staring at him with her blue eyes that shone now like stars in the night sky.

Her presence alone made him both agitated and calm, and he didn't know how that was possible.

He knew he should apologise for the interruption and leave her be. He knew it very well. A decent guy would do it, but...

"What surprises you so much?" The corners of Fenrir's lips turned upwards slightly. "It is my bathroom, is it not?"

The tint on her cheeks and the anger that made her delicate wet body shudder were too good to resist, so he closed the door behind him and went further inside, knowing she wouldn't make him leave.

She may not remember him, but deep inside, she had to feel it too...

12. MENACE

*A*strea didn't know what she expected from him. Did she really think a rogue would leave a naked woman alone in the bathroom? She knew better than that. And he... he knew exactly what he was doing, waltzing in here shirtless and covered in his stupid tattoos, knowing that she would have to look at him one way or another. She glanced at the King and found him staring shamelessly, eyes greedily devouring every inch of her exposed wet skin.

"How dare you?" she demanded, her whole body shaking from anger.

"It's my space," Fenrir replied calmly and strolled inside.

"So?" She arched her brow.

"So, I want a bath too."

"Wait for your turn then!" The Dragonfly was appalled.

"It's the desert, Astrea. Water supplies are limited, and we have to economise the little we've got."

"Isn't the point of being the King that you can have two baths during a day if you wish to?" she taunted, overwhelmed with his proximity.

"You've met the wrong kind of King if that's what you're thinking." Fenrir sat at the other end of the bronze bathtub, eyes locked with hers as if he wasn't interested in anything else but her gaze. As if she wasn't naked and vulnerable before him.

"I've actually met two outstanding ones." Astrea decided not to be intimidated and moved through the water, closer to him, resting her head on her arms on the bathtub's edge.

"Menace, are you taunting me?" he asked bluntly, and her lips curled into a smile.

"Are you taunting *me?*" She tilted her head a bit more, and his eyes grazed over her delicate neck.

"What if I am?" Fenrir leaned lower so that his hot breath tickled her wet skin as their scents intertwined together, creating something else, something entirely new.

He wanted to touch her, taste her, take her. Right here. Right now. Until she begged him to stop, but he knew better than to push her. She was the love of his life, but he was practically a stranger to her.

"Then you are playing with the wrong girl!" Her sweet smile turned into a vicious one as she rose from the bath, water droplets rolling down her silky skin like shimmering falling stars.

He took her in, afraid to move. Knowing that when he did, she would find a way to escape him again, and he wouldn't stop her.

"If you think you scare me or intimidate me, think again, Fenrir!" she dared him, her chin raised high. "And if you want your bath back, be my guest!"

She stepped out of it as gracefully as she could, but her wet feet betrayed her causing her to slip and almost fall, bringing Fenrir out of his daze.

Astrea felt him getting closer and was ready to fight him if she had to. However, a soft white towel was wrapped around her, to her surprise.

"So that you don't tempt my men by walking naked around the fortress," he explained with a chuckle, making the blood rush to her cheeks. "If they touch you, they die. Don't cause unnecessary deaths, Astrea. Have some mercy on us rogues."

He was mocking her, and she turned to glare at him, unable to come up with a snarky response as he carefully adjusted the towel to cover her. After he barged in on her bathing and she stood before his eyes wearing nothing, this wasn't the outcome she'd expected.

"Oh, my, Astrea, you seem so shocked." The corners of Fenrir's lips turned upwards as he was enjoying the moment. "It's almost as if you thought I was some kind of animal that was going to devour you!"

Moon Goddess, she hated him right now.

"Just because you didn't devour me doesn't mean that—"

A laugh rumbled in his chest.

"Make no mistake, I would be happy to." He gave her a knowing grin. "I'd make you cum on my fingers in that bath first, and then after getting you out, my tongue would make you scream my name so loudly that they would hear you back in the South. Then I'd take you against every fucking surface in this tower as many times as you could take, which I assume would be many. You seem like a strong one—"

She released a shaking breath, and that made him chuckle.

"But…" He furrowed his brows, his facial expression getting darker.

She wanted to ask, "But what?" yet didn't do it, so as not to seem desperate to him. She would hate that. She hated him because none of this was logical or according to her plan. He broke her every mould.

"It may come as a shock to you, but I only sleep with women who have feelings for me," he announced, making her lips part once again.

He wasn't serious, was he?

"Are you for real?" A snort escaped her.

"Yes, Astrea, I am." He brushed a strand of silver locks behind her ear, creating a wave of goosebumps. "The moment I see it in your eyes, you are mine."

She shivered. Not because it was cold, but because his words reached something deep inside her, and that was a completely new and undefined emotion that she wasn't sure how to decipher yet.

"*Leave before we embarrass ourselves further!*" Nova insisted, breaking the train of her disarrayed thoughts.

"*Escape it is!*" Astrea confirmed and tried to push the rogue, who was too close to her, away.

"In your dreams, Fenrir!" she hissed.

"Speaking about dreams!" He pulled her closer by her waist, dipping his face into her wet hair, and trailing his nose over her collarbone. "That love bite looks exactly like the one I left on you in my dream."

She gasped, her hand instantly reaching for her marking spot. So much had happened that it completely slipped her mind.

Astrea's eyes darted to the mirror on the opposite wall, and to her relief, no hickey was gracing her skin anymore.

However…

"Yeah," Fenrir scoffed, "nothing there. It's funny, though, that you knew exactly where it was supposed to be."

"Don't feel so special. We are not sharing dreams." She knew she had fallen for his trap, but she wasn't going to admit it. "This is where you were staring!"

"If you say so." He was unable to hide his grin, and it annoyed her even more.

"I am too tired for this!" Astrea muttered and rushed to leave the room, not bothering to pick up the clothes she had left in there. The towel was big enough to cover her, and she needed to leave as soon as possible.

Never in her whole career was she so close to failure on every single level. Fenrir was out-playing her, and she had to regroup.

"Astrea?" Devoss greeted her at the exit, but she brushed past him, storming toward her room.

Devoss, who had changed again and was wearing purple now, went up, knowing that Fenrir wouldn't be too happy with another visitor. His privacy was already invaded beyond belief, and he was surprised that the Rogue King was still tolerating them all.

He found his friend still in the bathroom, sitting on the edge of the bathtub that Devoss had personally filled in an effort to bring the couple closer.

"That bad?" he asked and was immediately pinned to the wall with Fenrir's large hand wrapped against his neck.

"Do this again, and I will make you regret our deal!"

The deity released him, and Devoss coughed, grasping his throat.

"A simple thank you would do next time!" he grunted and watched the Wolf God breathing heavily next to the only window in the room. "I'm sorry, okay? Bash told me who she is to you, and I wanted to help."

"This is not how it works," Fenrir exhaled loudly. "It—I should have stayed away."

"Let's agree to disagree," Devoss commented. "I can see you two working out just fine. You just need to—"

"Dev, seriously, leave me alone!" Fenrir interrupted, not in the mood for the fox's lecture. What could he know about any of this?

"Fine," Devoss sighed in defeat. "Sorry if I overstepped. Let's talk later."

He left just as he was asked, leaving Fenrir in solitude.

Only it didn't give him the peace he sought anymore. Not like it used to.

Astrea's presence changed everything, taking this peace he managed to find after so long and crushing it.

The memories were now flooding his brain, invading his mind. He wouldn't be able to have peace anymore now that the box he had hidden them all in was opened again.

Thousands of years have passed, but he remembered the first day he met her as if it was yesterday.

THE SKIES of Asgard were the perfect shade of azure when Tyr threw Fenrir to the ground, raising a large cloud of dust around them. Letting the young wolf regain his breath and the remnants of his dignity, he circled him with a smile curving his lips.

Fenrir groaned, and his mentor chuckled in response.

"You are off of your game today, boy! It's as if I've taught you nothing!"

Fenrir clenched his jaw, feeling his ribs falling back into place, regeneration still in progress. He didn't let another sound escape, so as not to humiliate himself in front of his one and only friend. Especially since he wasn't going to let it end this way.

"Are you sure?" he chuckled and kicked his mentor in the knee, making him trip and fall right next to him, suddenly feeling better about himself. "I remember that the battle is not over until the opponent is dead or has admitted his defeat. Maybe I am just waiting for the right moment!"

The smile dropped from Tyr's face, and the change did not escape Fenrir. He'd learned to read the room early on, knowing that he was not loved here in Asgard. Just tolerated on the good days.

"You are upset. Is it because of our guests? The ones who are arriving today? Do you know what all this is about?" he asked, curious and hoping to find out at least a little something. It was rare for Asgard to have visitors from outside of their realm.

No one was telling him anything as usual, which only spiked his interest. It must have been kept a secret for a very good reason.

Tyr sat up, dusting himself off, still panting slightly after sparring.

"Yeah, I don't think it's a good idea," Tyr confessed.

"Why not?" Fenrir taunted, eager to learn what he could.

His mentor studied his face briefly and then forced a careless empty laugh.

"Don't get these things into your head, boy." Tyr slapped his back. "Trust me, it's going to be long and boring, and you are lucky—"

"I know." Fenrir stood up. He was lucky he wasn't invited. This was how it worked for him.

The thunder rumbled despite not a single cloud present in the sky.

"I think that means it's time for me to go," Tyr mused, giving him that look he hated. A mixture of pity, worry and regret.

"Yeah, I have business to attend to tonight too." The wolf grinned, to which his friend huffed a small laugh.

"Good." Tyr nodded, probably thinking he would spend the night with some maiden in his bedroom. "Tomorrow. Here. Same time."

His friend left him in a rush, and Fenrir had to return to his chambers to clean up and be ready before night fell. His little secret was probably what excited him the most lately.

His home was at the very top of the mountain, close to the main palace, but slightly lower and much less pompous. However, the position came with its perks, giving him the best view of the realm all the way to the gates.

He was on his way out when the portal arch in the central garden started glowing, and he heard screams and cheers of excitement as Asgardians surrounded their guests who had just arrived. Fenrir couldn't see them clearly because of the crowds greeting them, leaving him to wonder again what the whole deal was about. They usually despised everyone who wasn't from here.

He was about to give up and leave when he noticed something shimmering in between the heads of his family members.

Shimmering like stars themselves...

13. ASGARD PART I

*A*SGARD

Fenrir was late to the meeting for the first time in the last decade or two. Worried that his brother had already left, he blamed his own curiosity for the unfortunate occurrence.

The rules had been simple since they were taken away from their mother. His brother and sister were prohibited from entering Asgard. He was the only one with the privilege to reside among the other gods. And with his sister locked in Niflheim's underworld realm, he could only see Jormungandr from time to time. Once per month on the first day of the Full Moon. In secret, just as they agreed.

Tonight was the night, and he was unforgivably late because he'd tried to catch a glimpse of the guests from the other divine realm. An event to which he wasn't invited, so he couldn't actually march in there and see everything he wanted to see.

It was so stupid, but he couldn't help himself. The Olympian group was small, yet he'd managed to see almost everyone who arrived. Just three deities and he had only been able to see two, Selene and her brother Helios in their silver and golden attire, respectively. Two perfect gods, probably the most beautiful people he had ever seen.

But there was one more in their party. The one whose name was on everyone's lips the moment her small foot stepped through the portal. She was so popular that he couldn't catch sight of her because a crowd of Asgardians surrounded her constantly, making it impossible for Fenrir to see anything but her silvery-white hair, shining like threads of starlight.

He'd tried to change his location or wait for people to give her some space, just step aside for a moment, but that never happened. Whatever he did, he couldn't see her face.

Astrea, the one they called the new goddess of stars, remained a mystery to him.

Fenrir didn't notice how and when it got dark and when he remembered he had more important things to do tonight, he was already running late.

Joran wasn't in their meeting spot when he got there, and Fenrir was angry with himself. He'd missed meeting the one and only person who cared about him, because he was trying to see some... girl.

He settled in to wait in the secret cave he had discovered years ago, with the perfect view of the river that fell into the sea. This was where Joran used to sneak into Asgard for them to meet.

Still angry, Fenrir kicked a rock on the ground, realising he had missed his brother, and now he would have to wait another month to see him. Other than lessons with Tyr, it was the only thing that brought him joy, and he always looked forward to this day.

Tonight, he'd deprived himself of the opportunity. Jormungandr had to be careful in these lands.

The sky was clear tonight, and Fenrir gazed at the blanket of stars stretched above his head, glimmering like diamonds, one more beautiful than the other. The full moon glowed, kissing the surface of the calm river. He noticed movement in the water, a smile curling on his lips instantly.

"Jor!" The young wolf breathed out in relief, seeing the Serpent's scales glide through the water. A wave crashed over a massive boulder in front of him. A familiar broad-shouldered figure walked out of it, wearing his usual tunic, embroidered by their mother back in the day, with pants and boots, only the moonlight illuminating his features in the darkness.

"Rir!" Jormungandr smiled as they gave each other a warm brotherly hug. "I thought you forgot about me!"

"Never!" Fenrir chuckled. "I was distracted today, but——Never mind! We are both here, and that's all that matters now."

"True," Joran agreed and hit his shoulder in a friendly manner.

Fenrir was excited to see his sibling. Jor was the only one who could travel between the nine realms and meet both him and their sister if he was careful enough. When Odin tore them away from their home, he threw Hel into Niflheim, the underworld realm, and released Jor into the sea, binding him in his serpent form. Only Fenrir was accepted to live with the rest of the deities in Asgard but was never told why.

His life was... tolerable. Living in Asgard had many perks, but his father was rarely there, his mother and siblings weren't allowed inside, and the other gods weren't his biggest fans. He was different. This was something undeniable, something he'd learned to live with and accept.

He didn't look like them, he didn't behave like them, he didn't have the same powers they had. He couldn't wield any kind of magic and was therefore considered a lesser god.

The only thing he could offer them was his physical strength. This was his domain, where he had no rivals.

However, that didn't exactly help him find friends. Tyr was the only one who paid him any mind, because he respected strength and was initially curious about the young wolf. In many ways, he was Fenrir's one and only friend.

That being said, Fenrir was working on fixing that.

"Father told me about the guests." Jor mentioned the matter casually as they walked inside the cave to hide in case anyone passed by. No one was supposed to know about these meetings. "Who could have thought that our realms would finally find something in common!"

An unexpected wave of jealousy rippled through Fenrir. Their father barely spoke to him. Especially in public. He travelled a lot and, thanks to that, could see Jor more often than anyone else; the Serpent loved to follow him on his many quests. While Fenrir had to stay behind and behave, representing their family branch.

He suppressed the ugly feeling quickly. All of that wasn't important. The important thing was that no matter how far they travelled together, Jor made an effort every month to come back to Asgard and meet him. This was more than anyone else ever did for him and he appreciated it.

In return, Fenrir always made sure to bring his brother Asgardian mead. The drink of the gods and the only thing that could help the dragon to sustain his power and grow. Each time they saw each other, his serpent dragon form was getting bigger and bigger.

"I wonder why they let them in," Joran muttered as he sat on a rock with the flask his brother brought for him, taking his first gulp and enjoying the taste.

"I heard they want some kind of alliance with us." Fenrir shrugged. "You know what happened to them, right? Most of their pantheon was wiped out."

"Not much of a loss if you ask me!" Jor huffed a laugh. "More world and power for us!"

"Not everything is about power." Fenrir leaned against the same boulder, chuckling.

"Yeah, sure!" Jor scoffed. "Easy for you to say. Living here takes your fighting spirit away."

"My fighting spirit is fine, in case you want to test it!" the wolf deity teased with a snarl. They loved friendly sparring.

They stared at each other for a few seconds before bursting out laughing.

Fenrir missed this. His biggest hope was that one day he would prove to Asgardians, he was one of them, and they would let their family reunite.

"They still didn't notice you stealing this?" Jor sneered, shaking the flask. The mead didn't have much effect on him, although a regular Asgardian would be properly drunk after a full flask.

"It's not like they are looking. No one expects this," Fenrir confessed, averting his gaze.

"You know what they expect." Joran's playful tone was gone. This was a topic that never ended well.

"They are just... worried," Fenrir sighed heavily, a familiar unpleasant feeling building in the pit of his stomach. "And for good reason."

"Of course," Joran sneered, "when the end of days come, they will have to go, and we will stay and rule. I'd be afraid of that day, too, if I was in their place."

"You still talk about this—"

"It's not like I have a choice, do I? No one invited me to live in Asgard with the gods and their faithful servants. They threw me into the sea, hoping never to see me again. Just shifting back into human form took me decades!"

"Yet here you are—"

"Here I am." Jor smirked, locking eyes with his brother. "Together with you. Same blood. Same essence. Maybe you like your life in Asgard, but deep inside, you know it will never be... it. You are not one of them, Fenrir; you will never be one of them. But you will always be one of us."

"You know very well there is no one I care about more than you and Hel. I am doing my best to fix everything," Fenrir tried to explain. "If I earn their trust, they will let you back in and then—"

"It will never happen, brother." Joran placed his palm on his shoulder and squeezed it tightly. "The only way for us to move forward is to destroy them. Think of it when they shun you again and deprive you, me, Hel and Father of the respect and life we deserve."

Fenrir wanted to retort, to make his brother see reason, but a strange glow filled the space outside the cave, and both of their heads snapped in its direction.

Someone was approaching them, and Fenrir recognised the ethereal shimmering almost instantly.

14. ASGARD PART II

*A*SGARD

"What's that?" Joran hopped off the rock, finishing his flask in a hurry, ready to shift back and run. Or worse – fight. "Were you followed today?" he demanded.

"Wait!" Fenrir stopped him, stepping forward and poking his head out of the cave to confirm his suspicions. "I think I know who that is."

"Can we kill him?" was the first thing Jormungandr asked, and his brother elbowed him as they tried to see what was happening outside.

Fenrir couldn't believe his own eyes. Of all people, it had to be her. What was she even doing here?

A slender figure of a woman in an elaborate white dress with long sleeves blown by the wind stood by the riverbank, watching the water flow before her eyes. Her silvery hair glowed like the stars in the night sky, each curl dancing to its own rhythm in the breeze, but what shocked him the most were the glowing dragonflies fluttering around her. Those belonged to another goddess and never liked anyone else. Yet tonight, they had a different favourite...

He still couldn't see her face, but even from this angle, she was mesmerising.

"Who is that?" Joran asked, his voice gruffer than usual. "She is—"

For the first time ever, his brother couldn't find the right words, and Fenrir didn't care enough to mock him about it.

"Dragonfly," Fenrir muttered, unable to take his eyes off the magnificent woman.

"Who?" Jor repeated with more interest and enthusiasm in his voice, which for some reason, irked his sibling.

"Someone we can't let see us together," the wolf responded, and after a long pause, added, "Or touch."

"She is one of the guests, isn't she?" Jormungandr was excited. He rarely got to see Asgardians, let alone deities from other pantheons.

"Yes, but remember—" Fenrir didn't get to finish his words as the woman in question shrugged her shoulders and slipped her dress off in one swift move, letting it pool at her feet and stepping out of it.

They both forgot how to breathe. Her long silky hair covered everything, but at the same time, the outlines of her soft curves made their imaginations go places.

It was probably the most enticing thing they both had ever witnessed.

The beauty jumped into the water, and before Fenrir realised it, Joran left their hideout, storming towards where the woman just stood.

"What the hell, Jor?" He barely managed to catch up with him, pulling him behind a massive moss-covered rock to avoid her noticing them. "What do you think you are doing?"

"Don't get me wrong, it's a lovely family reunion, Rir, but there is a gorgeous naked woman in that river, and that happens to be my speciality. Nature calls, so to speak. I just have to introduce myself. You and I can speak next month, all right?"

He was serious, and that made Fenrir angry.

"Of course not! No one is supposed to see you, remember?" His words were laced with fury and frustration, but they didn't have much effect on the dragon.

"She would never even know it was me. I can introduce myself as... anyone, really. What seems to be the problem? I can be any Asgardian who decides to swim at night. She would never know the difference."

"Because so many people swim in the Gopul River at night!" Fenrir ran his hand over his face. This was ridiculous, and he wasn't sure what frustrated and annoyed him more – how easily Jor planned to abandon him or how confident he was that he could meet and woo Astrea.

"Who cares!" Joran grinned at him, untying the top of his tunic as if this wasn't up for negotiation. "I saw her first!"

"Well, actually, I saw her first," Fenrir reasoned, trying to cool his brother down.

"Maybe, but unlike me, you aren't interested, right?" Jor snorted, throwing a quick glance at him.

"Wrong!" Fenrir snarled, and his brother's grin faded. The boulder was hiding them from the river well, and from the corner of his eye, Joran noticed that the girl swam back to the surface. Only to dive back in again in seconds.

"Would you just look at her?" he sighed, admiring her. "No women love to dive that deep! She was made for me to—"

"No!" Fenrir growled louder this time. "It's dangerous for you to come here! Who knows what your next punishment will be if they find out."

"And yours," Jor reminded him that his position wasn't much better.

"And mine," he had to agree with this. "Hell, even Father could suffer for this, and who knows what his wrath would look like this time."

Joran groaned, throwing one last look at the beautiful maiden. He was closer to their father than his siblings and believed in his cause. That was why mentioning the impact on the God of Mischief was a safe bet.

Joran knew that one night with a woman wasn't worth the risks. He shouldn't have been here. The rulers of Asgard couldn't find out that he came here every month to find out their secrets and drink their mead to grow stronger. He may have hated it, but Fenrir was right.

Nevertheless, it didn't mean he couldn't have any fun.

He ran as fast as a flash to where the starry maiden stood moments ago and returned back to his astonished brother with her clothes in his hands.

"If I can't touch, I can at least look!" He smirked, and Fenrir got furious for some reason.

"What is wrong with you?" he demanded, snapping the white fabric out of his hands. "We can't afford mistakes like this—"

"Correction," Jor chuckled, "*you* can't afford mistakes like this. I can afford all the mistakes in the world. What are they going to do? Throw me into the sea?"

His brother had a point. However, Fenrir calmed down, knowing that this was just his way of letting off some steam. Jor wasn't going to risk their little arrangement coming to light. He literally needed it to survive. This was just a tantrum, and he would get over it eventually.

Now all he needed to do was return the clothes and lead Joran as far away from here as quickly as possible. Just why did this woman have to come and swim here? And where were her guards? She had to have at least a few.

"Who's there?" Fenrir heard a sweet but confident voice and realised they'd been caught red-handed, and there was no more time for extra manoeuvres.

He was ready to throw the clothes back to the goddess and thought they could escape while she pulled them back on. Jormungandr could get back into the river and swim all the way into the sea while he himself could shift, and she wouldn't even notice his black fur in the darkness, thanks to his speed. Nor would she be able to catch up with him in his wolf form if she decided to try.

Yet in the next moment, his brother, his own flesh and blood, pushed him from behind the boulder that was their refuge, with the white dress still in his hands. Fenrir glared at his sibling and only received an apologetic smirk in return as Jor lifted his arms to show him he was giving up. He was their father's son, after all. And now Fenrir had to face the music because of that.

He finally looked directly at the woman, who stood waist-deep in water, giving him the iciest gaze he had ever seen, and he had seen a fair share of those. The dragonflies still hovered around her as if they tried to defend her from him. And that was a miracle all on its own...

She was undoubtedly the most beautiful woman he had ever laid his eyes on, shimmering like a star. Her beauty was otherworldly, almost ethereal, but at the same time... she held her heavy gaze on him with the whole universe enclosed in it. For a second, it seemed to him that she controlled a raw and ancient power. But it couldn't be since everyone knew that Astrea was practically brand new.

There was something about her that he had never seen or felt before. Some kind of inexplicable power that kept him drawn to her.

"What is the meaning of this?" she demanded sternly, not afraid of him in the slightest. If anything, she seemed annoyed and rightfully so. However, he admired how calmly she handled it.

"I... didn't notice you," Fenrir lied, and he could swear he heard Joran chuckling just a few steps away from him, still leaning against the giant boulder.

"Didn't you?" She tilted her head, piercing him with her starry eyes. "I know I am practically invisible with all that glow around me, and you—" she paused to arch her brow at him. "You must be into pretty dresses then."

The last phrase made his jaw clench, and he gave his brother, who had a hard time suppressing his laughter now, an annoyed glare. After all, this was all his fault.

Fenrir had wanted to be introduced to the divine guest, but this wasn't quite how he wanted it to happen.

However, he wasn't exactly unhappy about the whole situation because it allowed him to speak to her while they were alone. Something he couldn't count on in the city.

"Oh, this?" His lips curled slightly as he weighed the fabric in his hand. "Is this yours?"

She furrowed her white brows, and the silver glow intensified, spiking his curiosity again.

"You know it's mine! You stole it!" she accused him bluntly, a frown on her perfect face.

"I did no such thing!" Fenrir insisted, and it wasn't even a lie.

"Then give it back!" She gritted her teeth.

"Of course," he teased, not being able to help himself. She was so... not what he imagined she would be. "It's yours. Come here and take it!"

He stretched his arm, and she pursed her lips, offering him another withering glance.

Fenrir waited a few seconds, knowing that in the end, he would give up and do the decent thing, but teasing her had woken up some feral part of him that had rarely been awakened since he'd moved here.

"What is your name?" she asked him, still not moving in the water where she stood, her skin glistening in the moonlight.

"Fenrir." He genuinely smiled at her for the first time, prepared to tell her that her dress would be where she left it and offer to escort her back later.

"Never heard of you." She shattered his plans with some kind of spite in her tone, and a little growl escaped him against his will. She was pushing buttons he didn't even know he had.

"Well, you've heard of me now, Astrea." He smirked, and she rolled her eyes at him as if to tell him how insignificant that was, although a slight tint appeared on her cheeks.

"And you are going to see me." Her lips stretched into a sneer, something he didn't expect from such a sweet and innocent creature. He was coming up with a good reply to that when everything changed.

Her glow went from subtle to blinding within seconds and disoriented him completely. He shielded his eyes with his arm, knowing that trying to see anything was useless. Moreover, the temperature around him became unbearably hot, and Fenrir was ready to shift to defend himself when he felt the dress pulled out of his other hand.

She was so close, and she wasn't doing anything other than putting her clothes back on.

"Impressive," he chuckled, using the opportunity to take in her scent. It was composed of floral notes that were accented with hints of shimmering stardust, her divine magic evoking images of glittering galaxies and twinkling constellations in his mind. He tried to recognise the floral notes and smiled when he distinctively smelled moonflowers. All the details of her scent intertwined in her, connecting both the natural world that was so close to him and her own cosmic realm.

"You smell like a spring night right before the dawn, Goddess of Stars," he told her, and he could feel her close again.

"Stars burn, Fenrir," she whispered in his ear, brushing her delicate fingers over his cheek to demonstrate to him that she was in control now. "Never forget this."

"Don't worry, Astrea," he caught her hand, bringing it to his lips for a quick kiss, which he knew startled her, "you are unforgettable."

He released her and felt her leave immediately, to his own disappointment. He desired so much more than this, but when the light dissipated and he was able to see again, he found himself alone on the shore.

Astrea was gone, and so was Joran.

Fenrir looked around and saw the Serpent back in his domain, his scales glistening in the water as he waved him goodbye with his long tail.

Their time was up, but he wasn't regretting it today.

His cheek still felt warm where she had touched him, and he rubbed his calloused hand over it, realising that something was on it.

Taking a closer look, the young wolf noticed that his skin had shimmering dust on it.

"Stardust," he muttered, not quite believing his own eyes.

She was made of stars, this Astrea...

AFTER JORAN HAD FINISHED the conversation with his brother over the phone, he gulped the whole glass of whiskey in his hand in one go and placed it back on the glass table, almost breaking it. He should have been happy because everything was falling into place just as he wanted. Still, for some reason, that familiar feeling of satisfaction he usually experienced when his plans worked wasn't there now.

He'd kept Astrea close to lure his brother out of his hiding. He knew that the moment Fenrir saw her, he would be in his hands. The one thing he needed from him now wouldn't be a problem. Sooner or later, he would give in.

For her.

So, why wasn't he happy?

Joran restlessly tapped his fingers on the armrest of his chair and closed his eyes. He had to go through with this. Fenrir would give him what he wanted, and it would all be over.

"She is here," one of his trusted Firstborns announced, and Joran nodded with his eyes closed, still, trying to keep his dragon nature suppressed. Today it was a struggle. No matter how hard he tried to avoid it, his Dragonfly didn't leave his mind.

"Master," Niki's voice was confident, making the corners of his lips turn upwards. She was still too young to not be afraid of him but managed to hide it well. She would be perfect...

"Please, Nikiah, take a seat. I have a special task for you and would like to explain its importance to you, along with some of the details of what is required of you."

Niki swallowed the lump that had formed in her throat and nodded curtly. Who knew that Astrea had trained her so well?

This girl would help him to get everything that he needed.

15. NIGHTMARE

*A*strea paced around her room, too agitated to fall asleep after the events of today.

She decided to skip dinner after her quick stroll around the fortress, where she noticed that the warriors were, indeed, stationed in the building now. She counted at least a hundred. That fact made her uneasy since they all were still technically rogues. Their Kingdom wasn't acknowledged. Their packs were just groups of wolves without the connection of a real pack and its binding hierarchy that helped control the beasts inside them.

To become a pack, they needed to perform a ritual, swearing their loyalties to the Alpha and getting their blessing from Moon Goddess priestesses. Only then would they be able to mind link each other and work as one when necessary. The Moon Goddess' intention was to give her children a family they could count on. Their very nature required it, which is why pack connections were so sacred.

Rogues were deprived of that sacred connection. Their wolves were slowly going insane in their minds, leading to all kinds of trouble which Astrea didn't want to face.

She doubted any Moon Goddess priestesses were living here to help them build proper packs. Especially considering how rare forming a completely new pack was. Usually, they were created from existing ones by uniting them or… conquering them. All that plus needing an Alpha with Alpha blood in his or her veins to lead them.

Her phone buzzed, and Astrea groaned, knowing that only one person could be calling her. A part of her wished she didn't have to reply, but the snake tattoo on her neck moved again, and she sighed as she brought the phone to her ear to answer it.

"Dragonfly," Joran practically purred, not even bothering to check if it was really her. It was like he knew, and her hand instinctively touched the tingling tattoo. The connection that was forced on her.

"Yes," she replied calmly, still unable to use his name but knowing that if she called him 'Teacher' again, he would get angry. Something she couldn't afford, so she chose not to call him anything at all.

"Any news for me?" he asked, his voice unnervingly tranquil.

"I've been to the city. It's nothing special. Very underdeveloped," she reported curtly. "Got attacked while there."

"Hmm," he hummed to himself, and she wasn't sure how to read it without seeing his face. "I know you are not hurt. So, how did it go?"

"I defended myself and then—" Astrea stopped talking, almost biting her tongue.

"Then what?" Joran's tone became sharper.

"The King arrived," she confessed dryly, not knowing why she didn't want to speak about it. It was literally her job.

"Did he?" The Teacher's words were slow and deliberate, each dripping with malice, causing Astrea to feel a deep unease. She knew him too well not to pick up on the passive-aggressive notes in his speech.

"Yeah," she cleared her throat, choosing her words carefully. "He is—"

She halted halfway, suddenly realising she didn't know whom she was protecting, herself or... Fenrir? Why the hell would she be protecting him?

"What did he do?" Joran insisted.

"He killed everyone," she admitted, thinking that the Big Bad Wolf could take care of himself. She had to think of herself and Niki. "It was quick."

"What did you think when he did this?" The next question surprised her.

Did it really matter what she thought? He'd never asked her similar questions before.

"That he is an animal! A barbarian just as we expected," she informed her mentor dryly, knowing that it wasn't quite what she really thought, but it was a safe thing to say.

"Do you hate him?"

Again, a strange question.

"Hate is a strong word." Astrea shrugged. "I simply don't care."

"Good," Joran chuckled finally, and she secretly breathed out. Whatever test that was, she had just passed it. "Then you will have no problem with a change to your task."

A knot formed in Astrea's stomach, and her free hand instinctively balled into a fist. *This couldn't be good.*

"Don't!" her wolf warned her, knowing how quickly she could get herself in trouble again.

"What has changed in such a short period of time?" she asked, knowing she could regret this.

"The Rogue King has something precious in his possession, and I want it," Joran admitted, and a snort escaped her.

"That guy?" She scoffed. "His most priceless possession is his leather jacket, and trust me, that thing is as old as time."

"He can keep that." The Serpent was unimpressed. "I heard that there is a bracelet on his hand. With beads."

Astrea furrowed her brows. There was indeed a bracelet on Fenrir at all times. Quite old from the looks of it, with natural crystal beads.

"What about it?" Surely that couldn't be anything significant.

"I want it. You need to bring it to me."

She pondered for a few moments before deciding to test her luck.

"It will be hard," she sighed heavily.

"Careful there, Asti," Nova growled at her.

"I know what I am doing," she assured her.

"That's why you are the one there and not anyone else. You can do it." Joran either didn't take the hint or completely ignored it.

"He will kill me! Have you seen the guy? He crushed a skull in his hand today! I've never seen anything like it!" Astrea decided to thicken the colours of her story.

"Then find a way to kill him first," Joran cut her off, and she almost gasped but covered her mouth with her palm in time.

"Kill him?" Killing the King wasn't mentioned once during her preparation. "But what about the alliance?"

"When he is dead, they will need a new leader, and I would be happy to assist them with that. Why bother with an alliance when we can simply take the army? So, there is no need for buttering up the King anymore. Kill him and bring me his bracelet."

"Niki," she heard herself saying her ward's name before she realised it.

"What about her?" Joran asked dryly.

"Free her together with me if I succeed." A sense of disbelief washed over

Astrea at her own boldness. She was making demands now, something she couldn't imagine before.

"Is that what you want?" Joran didn't sound too happy about that.

"Yes. I want a peaceful life somewhere far away," she confessed.

"You do not. I know you," the Serpent retorted with a chuckle and for some reason, it infuriated her. Why did he think he knew what she wanted?

"It doesn't matter what you think you know. Let Niki leave with me," Astrea insisted, biting her lip and almost drawing blood from it. "She deserves a peaceful life too."

"Only if she wants to, "Joran added. "It may come as a shock to you, but some people don't want to leave the Firstborn island. Niki has a talent, and I see a great future for her within our ranks. I don't want to kick her out if it's your dream and not hers."

"Fine," she agreed. "If Niki wants to leave, she leaves with me."

"Only if you succeed in both killing him and delivering that bracelet to me," the Teacher clarified.

"Deal." She bit her lip, realising she didn't want to do it.

She didn't want to kill Fenrir.

And yet, she now had to. It was either him or her freedom.

"I will send you some help to help you escape when you are done. You know what to do," her mentor said.

"Okay, speak to you later." She was ready to end the call.

"Astrea," Joran's voice trembled for a moment, but it didn't escape her. "Just remember that if you want to come back home and stay here, you are always welcome."

This was new. This tone and this... attitude.

"Someone is at the door," she lied. "I need to go!"

ASTREA prepared for her little night outing quickly. It was time to retrieve her weapons and other gadgets and, although she would have been done faster in her wolf form, she decided against it because, in that way, she would be more noticeable. Not to mention that she had to check the coordinates with her phone while she was at it.

Running in the sand was a nightmare, even for someone as well-trained as her. It shifted under her feet as she ran, sinking and rising like the ocean tide, slowing her down. However, she reached the place in less than an hour.

Two bags were waiting for her, and she kneeled next to them to check if everything was in place. Meanwhile, the sounds of a rhythmic thudding distracted her.

It couldn't have been a wolf, a fox or a bear, and for a moment, she wasn't sure what she was hearing until the realisation hit her. A horse!

This was probably the last thing that she expected to see here.

"A horse? I get that they are underdeveloped here, but horses? Really?" she snorted in her mind and expected Nova to support her.

"Stay alert." There wasn't even a trace of laughter in her wolf's voice. *"Something is off here."*

She could feel it, too, now. The air shifted, becoming thicker and heavier. Astrea looked around, and it seemed as if the night had gotten darker despite the stars and the crescent moon shining brightly.

The sounds of the hooves were more distinct now, and she was ready for anything, letting her claws out. She was ready to fight if she had to.

However, only a single dark horse appeared on the horizon, its coat shimmering in the moonlight like polished obsidian. Its muscled form was sleek and graceful, gliding through the sand towards her, its mane and tail whipped by the wind.

A magnificent sight!

Right until the moment, she noticed its eyes glowing purple.

"What is this? Don't get too close to it!" Nova snarled, her instincts inflamed.

"I don't feel danger coming from it," Astrea told her, mesmerised. *"Isn't it beautiful?"*

"Is that a horn on its head?" The wolf bristled, not liking any of it.

Astrea couldn't believe her eyes. A spiralled horn was indeed growing out of the creature's head, a subtle purple glow radiating from it as well.

It slowed down when it saw her. As if it was afraid to scare her off.

Not that she was going anywhere. She couldn't leave this wonder without exploring it first.

"Where did you come from?" Astrea smiled at it, still not feeling any danger from the beast despite its heavy and dark aura. "A unicorn! Who would have thought!"

She stepped closer, stretching her hand forward and trying to create some kind of bond with the ethereal creature.

"Don't touch it!" Fenrir's voice cut through the stillness of the night, sending shivers down her spine.

She was so busted! Two bags full of weapons and gadgets were right behind her, and she was unlikely to frame the unicorn for hiding them here.

She could, however, use the creature as a distraction.

"How could I not touch this beauty?" she giggled, continuing her way and thinking, hectically, of what to do next. Between the unicorn and Fenrir, the horse seemed like the safe option. This was now officially one big mess!

"Astrea!" the wolf growled behind her back, but she was only looking at the beast before her, their eyes locked. She could tell it liked her, and when her hand was finally close, it brushed its head against her. Its coat was as soft as silk, and she could feel the energy coursing through the creature, knowing it wouldn't hurt her.

"What are you so worked up about, Fenrir? It's just a unicorn!" she scoffed, thinking if the creature could help her escape. Her mission had officially failed. Unless...

Unless she tried to kill him here and now. Just the thought of it made her nauseous, but it wasn't a choice anymore. When he found out about her bags, he would kill her himself. And if she returned to the Firstborn island, not completing her mission, she would have to stay with the Serpent forever.

And yet she didn't want to do it, prolonging the inevitable as long as possible.

"It's not a unicorn!" Fenrir informed her, folding his arms over his chest. He clearly saw the bags already but mainly looked annoyed with her not obeying him. She wondered why he was so hard to read while she thought of reaching for her knife. One quick throw and...

It had to be done.

Quick. She would do it quickly and forget about it.

"It's not?" She smirked at the Rogue King and slowly brushed her finger over the horse's horn, playing with fire. It felt cool to the touch. As if it was made of glass.

Fenrir watched her intently, and when the corners of his lips went upwards slightly, she knew there was a problem she didn't figure out yet.

"No." He shook his head with a chuckle. "It's not a unicorn. It's a Nightmare. And you really shouldn't have touched its horn."

"Why not?" Astrea tried smiling, but her vision suddenly got blurry, alarming her. Did she just miscalculate who was the biggest danger?

"Because it's poisonous!" Fenrir replied, confirming her suspicions and watching how her legs gave up on her.

Panic rippled through her body as she was losing control over it. Her eyelids were getting heavier and heavier as she watched the Nightmare staring at her with its deep purple eyes.

One second later, the demon, or whatever it was, galloped away into the night, sprinkling her with sand in the process.

Fenrir towered over her, and she tried squeezing the knife in her hand harder, knowing that he would probably kill her.

The King was saying something, his eyes sad for some reason, but she couldn't decipher the words anymore, regretting only that her end was this… unimpressive. She always knew she would die young but hoped to go out with a bang.

"Do it… fast!" She managed to form her last words before her mind switched off, and she lost the battle to the darkness.

"How could you bring her here?" The witch was furious. "She is going to be the end of this place!"

"Salome, I don't think I need your permission," Fenrir snarled at her. "I only need a detoxifying potion from you, and you may go."

"Tell me why I shouldn't leave her like that?" the brunette hissed, narrowing her eyes at him, her bright red kaftan flowing as she walked back and forth to calm herself down.

"Because that would make me very angry, that's why! And because next time you need a favour, I will be the one hesitating."

That seemed to work, and the woman clenched her jaw tightly as she considered her options.

"Fine!" she finally agreed. "I'll be back in half an hour. She can wait that long."

The witch stormed out of the bedroom, and he knew this wasn't the end of it.

He knew and, yet he didn't care.

"I should have sent you away," he sighed, brushing a lock of silvery-white hair off Astrea's forehead. He should have known that horrible thing would get to her sooner or later. It found her every time!

He took her hand to check her pulse and… didn't find it in himself to let go. The thoughts of Asgard invaded his mind again.

Especially that night…

16. ONE DANCE

A SGARD

"They want me to attend?" Fenrir asked, words laced with distrust.

"Yes," Tyr chuckled, adjusting his gauntlets.

It was rare for Fenrir to be invited to big events and, although he was concerned, he couldn't contain the excitement that was building inside him against his will.

For the first time ever, the stars aligned for him. The invitation came right when the young wolf wanted to be present at the feast because there was someone he wanted to see.

He had seen her a few times during the past weeks, but Astraea was always surrounded by other people and, on top of that, awarded him with such a glare every time she noticed him that he avoided approaching her to let her cool off after their first encounter.

He liked it, though. He liked the way her cheeks flushed each time their eyes locked. He loved getting any kind of reaction from her because, after observing her for a while from a distance, he could tell that no other man aroused such emotions in her.

Fenrir craved her attention, and he was going to get it tonight.

"Rir, you are not going to cause trouble, are you?" Tyr asked him, narrowing his eyes.

"When have I ever caused trouble?" Fenrir adjusted his golden pauldrons and received a reproachful gaze from his mentor. Which wasn't fair because he wasn't the troublemaker. His father – yes, his brother – definitely, his sister – probably, but Fenrir's life goal prevented him from having fun. All he wanted was for the ruler of Asgard to allow his siblings to live with him here and for that, he was ready to behave.

"I will pay my respects to the guests, eat, and leave," he promised and noticed Tyr sighing, a flicker of sadness in his eyes.

"I'm sorry." The God of War and Justice could never pretend he didn't see how his pupil was treated. "Just a bit longer—" He stopped talking because this was something he had promised Fenrir many times, but there had been no changes for centuries. "Just a little longer" wasn't cutting it anymore.

"Never mind," Fenrir friendly nudged his shoulder, "let's drink mead and have fun tonight."

"After you!" Tyr grinned, happy to enjoy this rare opportunity together.

THE LIGHTS BLINDED him when he entered the feasting hall in the Asgardian palace. The white columns with the carvings of Asgard's rich history were gleaming brighter than usual. The best golden thread tapestries were on display, and Fenrir noted that there were more beautifully crafted statues of gods here today than usual.

The Golden Hall didn't inspire awe in Fenrir anymore. It was a place that demanded reverence and respect, a place where he had to kneel and not say a word until he was spoken to.

He knew very well that he was the strongest warrior in the room, yet he had no power. He couldn't embrace the same lifestyle as everyone else.

One day it would be worth it, though. When Jor and Hel could join him in here to eat, drink, and dance together. When he would be able to see his sister and not hide his brother. He was working towards that day.

"Astrea, I think my dragonflies love you," Freyja's giggle and the sound of her name made him snap his head in its direction.

He hadn't seen the little goddess for days, and finally, she was here right before his eyes. She was seated at the main table, of course. He hadn't expected anything less. The men and women around her looked mesmerised by her presence, while Freyja laughed at something she said with the warmest glint in her eyes. At the same time, Vidar, *that silent prick*, stood right behind Astrea with his hands clasped behind his back and his eyes not leaving her slender frame.

A growl escaped Fenrir against his will, and everyone grew still, acknowledging his arrival.

Hostile... their looks were so hostile, but he focused on the All-Father, and bowed only to Odin, feigning as much respect in the gesture as possible.

"There he is!" the ruler of Asgard chuckled and gestured for him to come closer. The siblings from the other realm sat beside him, both Helios and Selene observing him with interest.

"Is this the wolf you were talking about?" the Moon Goddess asked.

"Yes, and trust me when I tell you he is the biggest one you'll ever see," Odin boasted, his golden eye patch glinting.

"That's unlikely." Selene smiled gently. "Wolves are my creatures. They obey the Moon Cycle, and their souls are connected to me. I think I have seen everything there is to see in this kind."

"But our Fenrir is different." Someone huffed a laugh, a sound that was more derisive than amused. To which the young wolf only lifted his head higher, not giving any other reaction and getting a quick glance of approval from Tyr, who had already left him to join the main deities at their table.

He was on his own now.

"Now you've piqued my interest." Selene's smile was gentle, her pale blue hair glowing slightly. "What is the difference from my wolves? I thought you said he could shift the same way."

"Shift, yes, but I never said it was the same way!" Odin smirked at his guest. "It's a shame you are missing my brother. You would have liked him. He has this... desire to experiment and, well, let's say his children are something else!"

More laughter erupted, and for the first time, Fenrir allowed himself to glance at Astrea. Her luscious lips didn't curl; in fact, she looked around with disapproval in her gaze, which lifted Fenrir's spirits almost instantly.

"Would you like to see our Fenrir shift?" Frigg, Odin's wife, asked the young Star Goddess, and something told him the latter wasn't pleased with it.

"No." She shook her head firmly. "As my mother mentioned, wolf shifting is not new to us. Let's allow Fenrir to have a peaceful night."

"But he would love to!" Vidar interjected, his scornful gaze meeting Fenrir's. "It's his honour to entertain the esteemed guests. Isn't it?"

All eyes were on the young wolf again. For the first time, he couldn't stand it. He couldn't take the insult and swallow it. Something was different today, and he couldn't explain it.

His lips curled into a provocative smile. "If the starry maiden wishes me to entertain her, it would indeed be my honour and pleasure to do so. I would gladly indulge her every desire all night long."

Astrea's lips parted at the audacity of his remark, but she quickly pressed them back together, pretending to ignore the insolent remark.

"How dare you?" Vidar scowled, ready to start a fight, but a simple touch of Freyja's hand on his arm calmed him.

"Please," the Goddess of Fertility offered a dazzling smile, "let's not ruin our guests' impression of us. We were doing so well."

Vidar turned his attention back to Astrea, who was busy playing with one of the glowing dragonflies instead, and Fenrir wanted to smack his head against the wall.

"Excuse my brother," Heimdall, another son of Odin, spoke. "He doesn't know how to behave. Or have fun."

Fenrir took the chance to escape and bowed to Odin, wishing to leave to get some mead when he was stopped.

"But our wolf is indeed like no one else." Heimdall didn't want to let it go. "How about a little demonstration?"

Fenrir glared at him, knowing that it wasn't, in fact, a request. The other deities observed him with rabid interest as if their lives depended on it.

"Sure," he agreed dryly, knowing that whatever it was, he wouldn't like it.

"Allow me to demonstrate how strong our friend here is!" Heimdall continued.

They were family, but he still referred to him as a friend.

They weren't friends. Not even close.

Heim produced what looked like a thick golden chain out of thin air and Fenrir wanted to snarl at him, knowing where this was going.

"This again?" He arched his brow at Odin's son and noticed how quiet everyone around them became.

"I call her Dromi!" Heimdall taunted, wriggling his brows. "It's twice as strong as the last one. I bet you cannot break this one."

Fenrir frowned. He hated how eagerly they wanted to see him chained by this new creation. The last time they offered the same entertainment, he didn't think of it much when he agreed, but when he saw how carefully they'd wrapped the chain to bind him and how disappointed they looked when he broke it, doubt crept into his mind.

His eyes met with Astrea's again, but she didn't say a word.

"Come on! One time for the guests!" Heimdall insisted, and Odin gave a curt nod, meaning it was in his best interest not to refuse.

"Fine," he agreed, emptying a new goblet of mead first.

Heimdall was already wrapping the chain around his feet, and Fenrir felt the magic in it trying to subdue him. It was unpleasant, as if a poisoned spider with long legs crawled over his skin, trying to get inside.

He couldn't wield magic himself, but his tolerance was a different question. The young wolf offered his hands with a sneer on his face, knowing that it would never hold him.

In the worst-case scenario, the bead bracelet was still on him.

However, he wanted to test something first. Slowly and patiently, he looked into the eyes of each Asgardian present, noting every visible hint of emotions. Some were good at hiding their feelings or were simply not involved in this. But some, like Freyja, couldn't handle it. She may have been one of the most powerful deities, but she turned away the moment he stared at her, pretending to say something to Astrea instead.

The little Goddess of Stars did not react, the corners of her lips tilted downward slightly. Fenrir wanted to believe that his ordeal was the reason for it.

He also tried to look at Tyr, but his mentor was busy talking to Helios, who wasn't too impressed by "the show".

"So?" Heimdall asked eagerly. "Can you break it?"

He smiled, but it seemed empty, making Fenrir wary. What was the point of all this? To laugh at him? To put him in his place? To prove that he would never truly belong here?

He decided to give them a little show and feigned struggling with the chain he could easily break, observing everyone around him.

"Come on!" someone drunk cheered him on, while others looked tense. Odin drank from his cup, his jaw tight the whole time, not taking his healthy eye from him.

It was time to be done with the farce.

A growl emerged from Fenrir's chest, echoing through the high ivory walls of the hall. Flexing his muscles as if it required some effort, he glanced at Astrea, who rolled her eyes discreetly, almost making him lose his serious expression and smirk.

He freed his feet first, and only then did the gods start cheering him on as if they meant it. He was their source of entertainment tonight, after all, so he slowly walked around, demonstrating his chained wrists, the magical metal still trying to subdue him.

He stopped before the Star Goddess and noticed how tight her lips were pressed together. Fenrir wanted to believe this was because she didn't like how he was treated, but he knew better than to hope.

However, he didn't find it in himself to move any further, so he raised his hands and pulled the chain apart, breaking it into several pieces that fell to his feet.

The gods cheered him on as if they were friends; someone brought him another goblet of divine mead. In this chaos, only Astrea did not display any emotions. She didn't flinch or blink, staying like a statue and staring at him while he refused to leave his spot.

The world around them spun and moved, but the two of them remained the same.

Fenrir bowed and stretched his hand to her.

"Astrea, the Goddess of Stars, the Lady of Justice, will you do me the honour of a dance?" he asked in the most confident tone.

All sounds died down and Fenrir knew he was overstepping.

"Know your place, mutt!" Vidar gritted his teeth, ready to charge at him, but Freyja touched his arm again.

"Don't forget we have guests," she purred with a sweet smile. "This is for Astraea to decide."

"Like she'd ever agree to dance with a dog!" someone said, not bothering to lower his voice.

Fenrir grew tired of standing with his head bowed and hand held out, waiting for acceptance. He was about to retract it and laugh it off, saying it was a joke, when a delicate palm touched his skin, sending all kinds of emotions rippling through his body.

Astrea circled the table and was now so close to him that he was caught completely off guard.

"Don't tell me you've changed your mind, Fenrir," she said and he loved the sound of his name on her lips.

She was wearing a beautiful shimmering white gown, almost translucent and flowing like the Milky Way when she moved. The gauzy material was light and airy, hugging her curves perfectly and trailing behind her in a mesmerising cascade of glowing fabric.

Fenrir found himself in an awkward position because he had never actually danced with another goddess, quickly realising that he had set himself up for failure. Women who usually graced him with their company were of lower ranks, thus his dancing skills were lacking.

The music played divine sounds surrounding them as he noticed her lips curling.

"Don't tell me you didn't expect this?" She tilted her head, enjoying herself already.

"I didn't," he admitted, and she giggled discreetly.

"Well, now the joke is on you." Astrea let out a laugh and that sound made him forget about everything.

His free hand found her waist, pulling her closer as he towered over her. Astrea sighed, biting her lip, but didn't try to distance herself from him, although it was what he expected. His powerful steps were matched with her graceful ones as they started to move together in perfect harmony.

He guided her around the hall as their movements grew more intense, drawing attention from everyone watching the unlikely pair.

Some were in awe, some intrigued and some furious.

Fenrir did not care. He enjoyed the proximity to Astrea and their dance. He enjoyed it when their eyes found each other after a twirl or a spin. He enjoyed her scent and when her silky hair touched his exposed skin.

The final chords of the melody sounded, and he managed to pull her close again, both breathing heavily but not because they were tired.

"Thank you, my goddess," he murmured so that only she could hear him.

Astrea looked at him and the whole universe was locked in her gaze, stirring something inside him. Something new.

"They shouldn't have done it," she whispered, stunning him as his lips parted in shock. The world had faded away, leaving them alone and drawing them closer.

"Astrea, can I ask you to join me for a moment," Selene's voice brought them out of their daze.

"Of course, Mother." She forced herself to take her hands off of his chest, making the world seem cold and empty again. "Excuse me," she apologised, her voice barely a whisper as her cheeks gained that delicious pink tint again.

"No worries." Fenrir smiled at her, bowing respectfully. "I will find you again."

He could swear her breathing hitched, but she hid this fact and rushed to join her mother and uncle beside Odin.

A smug smile spread over Fenrir's face. This night had turned out to be not so bad after all.

"What the hell are you doing?" Tyr grabbed his arm and practically dragged him out of the feasting hall. The wolf did not resist, chuckling as they went.

"What? This is what feasts are for, are they not?" He clapped his mentor's back with his hand.

"Fenrir!" Tyr hissed, shoving him into a dark corner behind one of the biggest columns. "What were you thinking?"

"I danced with a beautiful woman right now. I think it's pretty clear what I was thinking."

"Is this a joke to you?" His mentor ran his hand over his face. "Why did you have to pick her out of everyone?"

"Because I like her," Fenrir answered honestly. "Why else? And what is the problem here exactly?"

"The problem?" Tyr scowled at him. "The problem, Fenrir, is that you don't understand why our guests are here and why we accept them with open arms."

"Of course, I don't. No one, including you, have bothered explaining anything to me!" Fenrir retorted.

"More than half of their pantheon is dead. They need help, and so do we," Tyr sighed. "Everyone came to the conclusion that we should join forces."

"So?" Fenrir quivered his brow up. "Astraea and I will gladly join forces."

"And that is exactly the problem!" Tyr grunted. "Astrea was brought here to marry another. They are about to be betrothed!"

That news didn't sit right with Fenrir.

"Who?" he growled, feeling like he knew the answer already.

"You are not going to like it."

17. SOLACE

*F*enrir's lips were softer than she'd imagined. He brushed them over hers, sliding his tongue gently along her bottom lip, begging for entrance which she granted with a gasp.

She shouldn't have done it... but she couldn't resist anymore either.

The moment their tongues collided, his strong hands pulled her closer so that she could feel all the heat radiating from him.

A growl rumbled through his chest, followed by her moan as he found the ties of her dress and pulled at them roughly, breaking them in the middle. The sheer fabric pooled at her feet, exposing her skin. The cold air made her shiver, but Fenrir's large, calloused fingers explored every inch of her body, not letting her get cold.

"You are so beautiful," he whispered as they broke their kiss to gasp for air, his voice hoarse for some reason. "So... ethereal—"

Her lips curled into a smile. "That couldn't be further away from the truth!"

"I am afraid you will just have to trust me on this one." He smirked, making her giggle. That laughter, however, changed something in him. His eyes got a shade darker, his breathing became ragged, as if he was barely restraining himself.

"Fenrir," she called his name, awakening something else in him, and he pressed her closer against his warm, broad chest.

"Say that you are mine," he whispered, his chest rising and falling.

"Are you mine then?" she taunted, biting her pink lip and sliding her delicate hand up his arm to wrap it around his strong shoulder.

"If you will have me." He didn't break eye contact when the words left his mouth, surprising her.

"Are you offering?" She arched her brow at him.

"I am begging, Astraea," he confessed, exhaling loudly and pressing her naked body against the temple wall. The moonstone was cold to the touch, but it couldn't cool the flames between them.

There was so much pain in his eyes that she couldn't bear it anymore, cupping his cheek and smiling at him.

"Then it's a deal. You are mine and I am yours. Remember that these words are binding, Fenrir."

"You are mine and I am yours," he repeated, sending tingles down her spine.

She stood on her tiptoes to try and reach his lips, but he still had to lean down for her to do it. Her featherlike kiss was met with him capturing her lips completely, greedily thrusting his tongue into her mouth as if he couldn't wait anymore.

He lifted her as if she weighed nothing and took her to the altar, placing her on top of it and towering over her.

They chose the worst place in the world to do it...

She pulled his tunic up, revealing his immaculate physique and throwing the unwanted piece of fabric away. Their gazes locked once again, and she ran her nails over the chiselled lines of his abdomen, leaving a trail of shimmering magic all the way to his chest, which looked as if it was carved from stone, desperately restraining herself from begging him to take her quickly.

This wasn't like her at all, but she'd never desired a man like this before.

Fenrir trailed his tongue over her neck, eliciting a rush of goosebumps over her flesh as she laced her fingers into his hair. When his mouth inhaled one of her nipples, she arched her back, unable to hold back a loud moan.

Fenrir chuckled, sliding his free hand between her thighs and dragging his fingers over her wetness, teasing her.

She was untouched and so pure.

And now she was his. He couldn't believe his own luck.

"Please," she whimpered when he drove her too close to the edge and stopped.

"Anything for you," Fenrir replied, parting her thighs and taking her beauty in. Her naked body was at full display for him, silvery hair scattered over the moonstone table, her body glittering with the magic she couldn't control anymore.

She was trembling from his every touch, her body made for him.

"What are you waiting for?" she asked, not taking her eyes off him.

"You once said stars burn," he reminded her, and her smile dropped as she wasn't sure where he was going with it at a moment like this. "I will gladly burn forever if I get to be with you."

She rose to him to pull him in for a kiss, unable to find words to match this confession but wishing for him to know how she felt about it. The motion undid him, his desire almost painful. He peppered her with kisses, swirling his tongue over her breast's peak and drawing a gasp from her, pushing her to lay back again. His caresses went lower and lower until he felt her shiver in his hands when his lips descended to her core.

Fenrir's body quivered with restraint, the need to possess her overwhelming him, but not before he could hear her screaming his name in pleasure. So he kept teasing her glistening flesh over and over, driving inside her with his tongue and then getting back to the little sensitive bundle of nerves which made her moan every time he touched her.

Astrea arched her back, screaming when her release pulsed through her...

Astrea screamed, panting as she sat up in the bed, the dream still haunting her as if she was indeed in Fenrir's arms moments ago. Luckily, it was just an illusion, and she was in bed with grey satin sheets in the bedroom... she didn't recognise.

"What the—" There was something in her palm, and when she unclenched her fingers, she saw a little dark crystal she didn't recognize.

"Morning," Fenrir greeted her, taking a sip of his coffee at a little table next to a glass wall.

A glass wall she didn't recognise.

In the room, she was seeing for the first time in her life.

A beautiful luxurious room decorated with beautiful expensive things.

"Wh-where are we?" she asked meekly, frantically assessing the situation and thinking of what to do next. The memory of the previous evening made her heart race because there was no chance in hell Fenrir didn't notice her bag full of weapons. She did not manage to run away, so the only way to leave now would be to try and kill him right now, then figure out where she was and how to escape this place later.

Maybe the Teacher was already looking for her. After all, wasn't this why he put that snake tattoo on her. Her hand instinctively went for her neck, and Fenrir furrowed his brows as if he didn't like that motion.

"That thing won't work here," he informed her matter-of-factly, and she gulped.

Not only did he know that the tattoo had to be "working", but he also managed to block it somehow. If this was the case, how would the other Firstborn find her? The Teacher relied on that stupid snake.

Their eyes met, and her stomach churned.

He knew. Fenrir knew everything.

"Listen…" She got up, realising she was wearing just a thin black lace slip. Not something she went into the desert wearing. "Who changed my clothes?" she yelled, forgetting what was important.

"Really?" the Rogue King chuckled. "This is what worries you the most now? Not anything else?"

"Many things worry me," she admitted. "But I have the right—"

She lost her voice when she noticed all her weapons neatly arranged on a different table behind Fenrir. Her knives, her little grenades, the gun she hated but brought anyway and everything else she'd packed for this mission. It was all there.

"They were all sandy, so I cleaned them for you," Fenrir chuckled, angering her. He was mocking her failure and she didn't find it funny at all. Although he did have a right to it. She had to give him that.

"Well, I couldn't come to the Rogue Kingdom unarmed." She defiantly crossed her arms over her chest.

"No one expected you to," he retorted, standing up. "Why hide them, though?"

She didn't have a good reply to that, but she had to come up with something.

"Oh, excuse me for not revealing all of my tricks to my potential attackers! How silly of me!"

"No one will touch you here," he growled, towering over her, and for a moment, it reminded her of what happened in the dream, heating up her cheeks. That dream was… intense.

"Well, someone already did, remember?" Astrea reminded him, desperately trying to change the subject and get herself off the hook.

"And you remember what happened to them." Fenrir raised his chin higher, giving her a warning glance. He turned away and walked past the table with weapons. "Interesting collection. Do all Southern women carry grenades in their purses?"

"Depends on where they work," she retorted, not wishing to give up. "It's a must for me and those are for self-defence only!"

"Really?" Fenrir chuckled and picked up a small black ball, making every muscle in Astrea's body tense. "So, you are telling me this little thing here would not blow-up half of my building?"

"You are so clever, Fenrir," she sneered at him, "you tell me."

"Why don't we try and see?" He arched his brow, and she knew he wasn't serious.

He couldn't be serious.

That would be nuts.

"*He knows it's explosive, he is bluffing!*" she said to Nova.

"*He doesn't look like he is bluffing,*" her wolf replied. "*I don't feel anything from him.*"

She clenched her jaw, not wishing to lose this staring contest.

"Do it!" she approved with a curt nod, squeezing the crystal in her hand tighter. She still didn't know what it was.

"Fine!" The man smirked and crushed the ball in his hand, stopping the whole world around them.

"No!" Astrea screamed, feeling time around them freeze. She threw herself at him, not even knowing why. He couldn't be this stupid; he couldn't risk and end his life just like that!

He couldn't—

She found herself holding his fist with the tiny grenade, her fingers digging into his skin. Astrea stared at it in horror, not able to say a word. She could sense it exploding in his palm; she could feel how heated his skin became, only for it to return to its normal temperature almost instantly.

"Got you," Fenrir scoffed, pulling her closer by her waist and enjoying her shocked expression.

"You—" She couldn't find the words to express herself. Which was a first.

What was going on? Did he trick her and it wasn't a real grenade from the island?

"Relax, Astrea," the King chuckled. "I knew you were a spy the moment I saw you. It's not a big deal for me."

Slowly, she returned to her senses, processing the new information. It had to be a trap! There was no other reasonable explanation for it.

"I am not—I don't know what you're talking about!" She put her best innocent face on, knitting her brows together as if she was offended. "And take this back" —she shoved the dark crystal into his hand— "whatever that is!"

It was probably safer to just get rid of it.

"I am afraid you need it more than I do now." Fenrir took her hand and placed the crystal back into it. "After all, I am not the one with a crazy deity's tattoo on my neck the day after I touched a Nightmare's horn."

Her lips parted, remembering the events of the previous night with more clarity now. The majestic black unicorn... and how she'd touched its horn. That creature mesmerised her enough for her to be that careless.

"Was that real?" She locked her gaze with the wolf. "A Nightmare! What was that thing? I... I've never read about them in books!"

"That's because this one is the last one," Fenrir responded, watching her closely, afraid to miss even a flicker of emotions in her. "And you're lucky he likes you or you would be long dead. Although you can still end up that way if you don't keep that."

Astrea looked at the crystal again.

"What is it?"

"A fragment of a Nightmare's horn," he replied calmly, and she almost dropped the thing to the floor.

"Didn't you say they were poisonous?" she panicked.

"I did," he chuckled, still holding her wrist. "But not this one. This one was dropped a long time ago. Nightmares shed their horns like deer do with their antlers. After the horn is dropped, it can be used for many things, including healing. So, you're welcome."

"Th-thanks," she muttered, still lost.

He was too calm for someone who had discovered a spy.

Unless... he wasn't afraid of her at all. He knew she was powerless here. Didn't he tell her that her tattoo didn't work anymore? That meant that help wouldn't be arriving for her anytime soon. He had all her weapons, and she didn't even have footwear.

The Rogue King took precautions.

"Where are we?" she repeated her question from before, realising that this was the most important one out of them all.

"Ah this," Fenrir's lips curled into a smirk as he led her to the room's glass wall, "this is the real East, Astrea. Welcome to the city of Solace, the place where everyone is free."

"Except for you!" a female voice sounded as the door behind them opened.

18. OLD FOES

*A*strea did her best to keep her expression neutral when she saw who entered the room. She was utterly surprised to find herself face-to-face with the dark-haired woman.

"Fenrir, she can't walk freely in here!" Salome pierced her with her brown eyes, crossing her arms over her chest in a defiant manner. She looked like she owned the place, taking Astrea off guard. This was the last thing she needed.

She knew Salome. This beautiful delicate woman was one of the contenders at the Luna Trials – her previous failed mission. Salome was a strong witch and one of the first to leave the event. Back then, Astrea didn't pay her much attention for that reason alone, regretting it now. Otherwise, she would have at least some kind of insight on that woman.

"Well, everything officially sucks now!" Nova announced. *"She knows us."*

"I have a feeling they already know all about us," Astrea hissed at her wolf. *"Can you keep up with it, please? Fenrir just exploded one of my grenades in his hand and didn't even feel it! He knew I was a spy from day one! We are in some city that's not on the map! And the Teacher cannot reach us here!"*

"That last part is not so bad, though," Nova noted, and she had to agree with that.

"Maybe she doesn't recognise us," Astrea suggested, trying to sound optimistic.

"Astrid," the witch sneered, dashing her hopes on the spot, "nice to see you here. You should have stayed where you belong, though. In the South!"

Not only did she recognise her, but she even remembered her alias.

"Just call me Astrea." She cleared her throat. "Astrid is what my father used to call me—"

"Save it, dear!" Salome raised her hand to demonstrate how unimpressed she was. The witch looked dazzling today in a red silk kaftan dress with her shiny long black hair. She did not look this gorgeous back at the Trials, although her beauty was undeniable. Astrea took a quick glance at herself, realising that she hadn't had a chance to brush her messy, wavy hair and was trying to ignore the fact she was wearing nothing but a flimsy nightgown. A nightgown that wasn't hers.

Could it be Salome's?

The thought alone made her shiver in disgust, but the question that bothered her the most, though, was why the witch felt so at ease with Fenrir.

"Yeah, I don't like it," Nova snarled, not helping her rising anxiety.

"You were sent here to spy on us!" Salome's words were laced with an accusatory tone and directed at Astrea with a sharpness that couldn't be ignored. "You want to bring all the information to your masters in the Southern Republic!"

The she-wolf cast a quick side-glance at Fenrir, who was watching her reaction the whole time, making Astrea wonder how much she gave away.

"Excuse me, since when is it a surprise?" Astrea straightened her back, folding her arms over her chest. "That's literally what you agreed on. I come here, spend a few months learning everything there is to learn about you and help you prepare for your presentation at the Alpha Convocation. 'Spy' is the wrong word for it, though. I prefer the term 'mediator'."

"We should put her in a cell and forget she ever came here!" Salome suggested, and the words alone made Astrea shiver as the memories of the silver pit flooded her mind. That was the one and only thing she wasn't sure she could take again.

"Then I demand to be sent back to the South!" she declared as if she had any rights in this strange kingdom.

"No," Fenrir cut her off, and Salome's mouth twisted into a smirk, making a chill run down her spine. Were they seriously going to lock her in a cell?

She eyed the other grenades, instantly thinking of possible escape routes.

"Don't you even think about it," Fenrir warned her, and she pretended to stare at the wall instead, not sure if it was convincing.

"I'll tell Warg to take her to the dungeons," Salome suggested eagerly, and Astrea couldn't help rolling her eyes.

"No," Fenrir said firmly, making both women snap their heads at him.

"Fenrir, please!" Salome knitted her brows.

"What can I say? He wouldn't like seeing me behind bars!" Astrea shrugged, unable to feign indifference. "He likes to keep me close."

"Shut your mouth!" the witch hissed, bringing her some satisfaction. This was almost too easy.

"Salome, did you want anything other than to harass my guest?" The Rogue King arched his brow at the woman in red, and she balled her fists involuntarily.

"Fenrir, you know that Solace's safety is my first priority." Salome attempted to rectify the situation.

"Good," he nodded at her, "then go back there and patrol it."

The reply didn't sit well with the witch, and Astrea could tell by just one glance at her. Their eyes fixed on each other and she felt hatred vibrating from the other woman. Nevertheless, Salome turned on her heel and left.

"You are going regret keeping her here!" she blurted out before she was gone from their sight.

"So, *she's* nice!" Astrea cleared her throat and glanced at the man next to her, watching his lips curve slightly at her words.

"Where were we?" He took a step in her direction and she took one back because she still wasn't sure how to handle him.

"In Solace, everyone is free," she reminded him. "I have to say I really dig the whole freedom idea."

His small smile turned into a wicked grin.

"Do you?" Fenrir took another step, backing her into the wall. He braced himself against the glass, trapping her between his arms.

"As long as it includes me." She tilted her head up.

"Oh, it includes everyone who has good intentions, Astrea," he breathed out. "Are your intentions good, Astrea?"

She felt a twinge of pain in her heart, knowing that she was here to learn everything there was to learn and kill him when she was done. It was as far from good intentions as possible.

"My intentions are crystal clear, and the most honourable," she lied through her teeth and noticed a glint of sadness in his eyes as his grin faded slightly.

"Very well then." He pushed himself off the wall, making her feel unexpectedly disappointed. "Dress up."

"Into what?" she replied, trying to understand why she had these exact emotions now. "All my things are in the Fortress."

"They were brought here hours ago," he informed her. "The East has decided to extend its welcome to you and show you its true face."

"I am honoured," Astrea hesitated slightly. "Does that mean I'm a hostage here?"

This made him chuckle.

"Of course not, you are my guest. Didn't I tell you this before?"

He did, but she was sceptical about the whole idea of a city where everyone was free. Let alone a confirmed spy, like her.

Fenrir was already at the door when she realised he was leaving her alone in this room.

"Is it wise to leave me with all the weapons?" She pointed out and he stopped in the doorway, shifting his head to glance at her.

"Didn't you say your intentions were honourable and pure?" He didn't take his gaze off her, and she realised that this was a test. Which was a good thing because she'd never failed one in her life.

"I am going to take a silver knife with me," she informed him. If he knew then she wasn't being sneaky about it.

"Whatever makes you feel better." He shrugged as if he didn't care. "Take the crystal I gave you as well. You will probably faint without it and I am not carrying you."

"I wouldn't expect you to be that gallant," she retorted with a raised brow, which made him look at her again, eyes grazing over her well-trained frame.

"I'll be waiting downstairs," he said and walked away, leaving her alone at last.

Astrea got ready in a record amount of time, forming a new plan in her head.

Find out where we are first, kill Fenrir and run later, she repeated over and over in her head, trying to convince herself that it was for the best.

"And what if we are far away from everything?" Nova wasn't excited.

"Find out where we are first, find a car, kill Fenrir and run later," she corrected herself.

"What could go wrong?" the wolf snorted.

"Everything has already gone wrong," Astrea sighed. *"And now we are improvising, trying to survive. You are not really buying the 'everyone is free' fairytale, are you?"*

"Please!" Nova rolled her eyes. *"We grew up among Firstborn. I stopped believing in anything a long time ago."*

132

"Likewise." Astrea felt better knowing that they were on the same page. *"I mean, the North was great... The way King Kai and Savvy fell in love. I could write a song about it."*

"Dumb luck," her wolf scoffed. *"How many other happy couples have you seen?"*

"Queen Riannon and King Gideon seemed happy as well..."

"So, that makes it... two," Nova summed up.

"Yeah, just two," Astrea agreed. *"Sometimes I think of my parents. I wonder if they loved each other."*

"Even if they did, they died," Nova reminded her. *"Still not a happy ending. That's unrealistic."*

"You're right," the woman agreed, chasing away the thoughts. *"But Niki is real, and she deserves better. Just a calm life away with her by our side would be enough for me. I wonder how she is—"*

"She is tough," Nova tried to console her. *"I'm sure she is doing her best and waiting for us. Her Ascension must be done by now and she probably got her gift already."*

"Probably—"

She had to stop worrying and daydreaming. *One problem at a time.*

Astrea took one last glance in the mirror, happy with her choice for today. She had to throw Fenrir off his game and she was ready for the challenge.

The mansion she was in was modern and minimalistic. It was a stunning display of contemporary design, with sleek lines and an abundance of glass elements throughout its structure. Greenery was everywhere, unlike what she was used to back at the Fortress, which was dull and lifeless. The windows were only on one side, making her believe the building was built on a cliff or a mountain.

She found no one else here; every decor element gave strong masculine vibes. Mostly practical things were on display. She caught herself on the thought that she hoped Fenrir lived here alone.

"At least if Salome lived here, it would have some witchy stuff," Nova gloated, lifting up her mood.

A whistle broke her train of thought as she descended a black and green marble staircase. Two men, Fenrir and Devoss, stood in the middle of a spacious living room, staring at her.

"You take no prisoners, Astrea, I see!" Devoss let out a laugh.

"Thanks." She beamed at him, happy that her plan was working.

"What do you think you're wearing?" Fenrir growled, and her lips curled instinctively. This was just what the reaction she was hoping for.

NIKI'S FOOTSTEPS faltered as she walked into the room shrouded with darkness, her eyes struggling to adjust for a few moments.

"Hello," she tried to sound confident, but her voice quivered, betraying her.

No one responded, but her task was clear and it wasn't exactly a choice. She still couldn't believe that, after all her work and training with Astrea, this was what she ended up doing.

Niki was finally able to see, so she walked inside, noticing that the room was minimalistic, with just a bed, a desk and a chair next to the window that was heavily curtained not to let any light in. She saw the outline of a man in that same chair, her pulse quickening with a mix of fear and curiosity.

"I was sent to—" She was about to introduce herself when a roar interrupted her.

"Go away!" the man in the chair said, and she could feel it was a warning.

"I'm sorry, but I can't," she tried to explain but only received another roar as a response. The man grabbed the curtains to help himself up, ripping them off and filling the space with the light that didn't even make him flinch, his silver hair shining brightly.

However, what astonished Niki the most were the sunglasses on his face, as she realised that the man she was so scared of was completely blind.

19. CHAINS

"You are not wearing that," Fenrir growled, and Astrea brushed her fingers over the golden chains that covered her chest. They gave minimal coverage to her breasts and were getting under the King's skin by the looks of it.

"Excuse me?" She tilted her head questioningly. "Since when do I need your permission? Remind me."

"Since—" He closed his eyes and exhaled sharply through his nostrils, knowing she had a point. "Since you are in my territory and have to respect the East and its traditions."

"So much for 'everyone is free' here!" She rolled her eyes, not making another move but shifting her gaze to Devoss. "Is this offending you?"

"As a true Easterner, I have to say that I do not feel offended!" Devoss interjected and received an angry glare from Fenrir.

"That's not a top!" The King insisted, his jaw clenched.

"It is!" Astrea placed her hands on her hips, provoking him more and not quite knowing why she was enjoying all this so much.

It wasn't a top, of course. It was an embellishment on one of her dresses that she'd ripped off in her haste to cause a distraction. She had to throw Fenrir off his game and had to think on the go. It was clearly working, so she had no regrets.

"Seriously, I don't see what all the fuss is about!" Devos went on, and Fenrir gave him a menacing glare.

"Isn't it time for you to go?" Fenrir's tone was also a warning.

"Nah," Devoss replied and got elbowed immediately, which made him cough.

"Are you sure?" The King repeated his question.

"Now that you mention it," Devos rubbed his neck, giving a sly grin to Astrea, "I have this thing—It's very urgent!"

"Sure." The woman waved goodbye to him. "I am sure that... *thing* has to be dealt with as soon as possible."

"Not only does our guest have a great fashion sense, but she's also so understanding. Don't you think so, Fenrir? This one is a keeper."

Astea's smile faded as she wasn't sure if the comment was a joke or a threat.

She exchanged glances with Fenrir, who snarled at Devoss in response.

"Bye, Dev."

They watched him leave in silence, and their eyes met again, bolts of lightning flashing between them as the tension rose.

"Shall we?" Astrea's lips curled as she maintained control of the situation.

"Not until you are properly dressed." He stood his ground, and she grazed her eyes over him.

"Oh fine!" she sighed and descended, walking as close to him as possible. He watched her every move like a predator, ready for anything she might do to him. Astrea slid her hands up his torso to his shoulders, making them tense, but disappointing him when she simply pulled on a light black scarf he had on.

"What are you—" Fenrir's voice caught in his throat.

"Can I borrow this?" She giggled as she was already draping the thin fabric around herself to form a loose top. "How is this? Better?"

The woman twirled for him, demonstrating her new look where everything was covered properly, yet the chains remained on her delicate flesh, giving him ideas that he did not wish to have in his head right now.

He clenched his jaw when he realised she was playing with him. Again.

"You heartless little minx," he muttered under his breath.

"And I will smell like you now." She pretended not to hear.

"Next time, if you want to smell like me, Menace, just ask. I assure you, there are other, more pleasurable ways, to do that which we will both enjoy."

Now Astrea was the one who was lost for words, but the Rogue King took her hand and led her out of the building.

"So, what are our plans?" she wondered, throwing a quick glance up at the man next to her.

"I am giving you a tour of Solace," he informed her dryly, their fingers lacing together. Astrea's heart fluttered, but she tried to kill the feeling on the spot. Fenrir was playing his game, and she was playing hers. It was purely business; she couldn't let it become anything more. Not when her own and Niki's lives were on the line.

FENRIR'S MANSION overlooked the entire city as it was mounted into a big rocky mountain like the ancient shrines of the East that she'd studied for her research. The design, however, was modern, rivalling the best mansions of the South, with lots of greenery growing over the glassy walls to give it a fresh look.

There was a pond in front of the house and an abundant garden on either side. Things that shouldn't have existed in a desert, yet here they were.

A long staircase led from the house to the actual city, and Astrea wondered if it was annoying to go up and down it every day.

She tried to study the city's structure while she saw it from this vantage point, noting that the glassy modern buildings were all equipped with solar panels, which probably helped to sustain the city's need for electricity. Quite a few wind turbines were on the outskirts, which also made a lot of sense.

This was clearly a hidden city no one knew of. They had to be independent and self-sustainable to pull off a scheme of this magnitude.

For a city in a desert, Solace was unexpectedly a lush green and brightly polished at the same time, a rare mix of nature and high-tech marvels. The buildings were not tall, but each had its unique features. However, they all blended nicely together in style. Astrea hated to admit it, but she loved it.

It felt like Solace was alive, people buzzing everywhere, buildings connected by intricate walkways and bridges to allow inhabitants to move freely between destinations.

Nevertheless, the most beautiful sight for Astrea was the river that ran right in the centre of it all, glimmering in the sunshine and disappearing into the sandy horizon.

A river that was not supposed to be there.

They were walking down the stairs for quite a while, and she lost her patience quickly.

"That river is not on the map." She pointed at the water.

"Nope," Fenrir confirmed, but didn't add another word to it.

"Then how?" She tried not to sound too eager, unwilling to demonstrate how intrigued she was. A smile curled onto his lips, letting her know he was already aware anyway.

"All in due time," he promised, showing her to the car.

THIS TIME WAS DIFFERENT. Not like her tour of Raja at all. This place lived differently, breathed differently. The people they met on the streets were happy. Solace was beautiful with its long alleys and narrow streets bustling with everything one could imagine – from green parks full of trees and flowers to shops and galleries. Astrea spotted a few museums that caught her attention, but Fenrir didn't let her linger anywhere until they got to the riverbank.

"Will this tour become audible at any point?" She mocked him lightly because he'd hardly said a word to her. She leaned against a stone rail with her back, watching her silent tour guide.

"Your eyes will tell you more than my words," he retorted, and she was about to annoy him more when something drew her attention away.

"No way!" she gasped and went to a tall silver wolf statue that was a short distance from them.

"Astrea, please!" He tried to stop her, but she ignored him, marching straight to the majestic monument.

"Fenrir." She read the letters on a silver plaque at the wolf's feet and bit her lip so not to make a sound.

"It's—" The man next to her was looking for words to explain why there was a giant statue of him in his city.

"What a size!" Astrea whistled. "Are you compensating for something, my King?"

The words made him grunt. "It's not a statue of me. It's the Wolf God," he tried to explain, and she glanced at the beautiful monument again.

"Strange, I thought they only believed in Fenrir in the North," she admitted, remembering her days during the Luna Trials.

"Do they?" He smiled. "And you believe in—"

"Myself," she replied without hesitation.

"So, you don't believe that gods exist?" He smirked.

"I do." Astrea shrugged, continuing her way alongside the river. "How could I not when my wolf claims the Moon Goddess chose her spirit for me personally? It's just—"

"It's just what?"

"I don't worship them." She gave him a stern look, holding his gaze as if she expected him to challenge her beliefs. Wolves were usually very protective of their gods because they were so tightly connected to them.

"How so?" He surprised her with the question, and she contemplated a moment before responding.

"Deities are selfish and power hungry. They have it all but still want more, not caring who might get in their way. We are just tools for them to achieve what they desire." She was surprised she'd said this much. She hadn't intended to have a heart-to-heart conversation with Fenrir, and she'd already deviated from her plan.

"Deities…" Fenrir tasted the word on his tongue. "Or maybe just the one who sent you here?"

Her eyes darted at him. This knowledge… he wasn't supposed to know this. Joran hid who he was from everyone. Even his buddies in the Alpha Convocation had no idea who they were dealing with. Not every Firstborn knew his true identity.

"I don't know what you are talking about," she muttered, still taken aback. This just further complicated things. If Fenrir knew about this, then he wasn't easy prey. Her task had just become a tad more complicated. She had to stop underestimating the rogue.

"As you wish," he turned away from her, "but he shouldn't have put that tattoo mark on your neck."

She shivered, remembering the day it happened.

"What would you even know about it?" The words escaped her again. She wasn't usually this careless, but today, she sang like a bird for this man.

"I know that as long as you are here in the city, it won't work. Especially if you keep that crystal." Fenrir looked at her as if he expected something, but she wasn't sure what.

"Did Salome tell you this?" She was surprised the witch's name came to her mind.

"No, but I love that jealous tint on your cheeks," Fenrir chuckled, and she inhaled deeply. She was supposed to be the one throwing him off the game, not the other way around. Why was she reacting to him so much?

"Nice try on changing the subject. Why does the snake tattoo bother you so much, but you are fine with the dragonfly one? The same person gave me both." She narrowed her eyes at the Rogue King.

Fenrir tried to stifle the laugh that threatened to escape him but failed miserably.

"What's so funny?" The woman furrowed her brows.

"It's funny that you don't know a damned thing about your own tattoos." He started walking again, and she was forced to follow him, feeling that she was so close to getting an essential piece of information.

He knew something she didn't, and now she was dying to find out what that was.

"Care to elaborate?" she asked as she caught up with him.

"Why should I?" He offered her a wide grin. "You seem like such a strong and independent woman. I am sure you'll figure it out without me all on your own. Besides, it's lunchtime, and I'm hungry."

"So, you got me to take your bait, and now you are changing the subject," Astrea summed up, following him.

"Why would you say that? I really am hungry." Fenrir let out a small laugh. "Solace has the best cuisine in the world, I assure you. Though… it may be a bit spicy for you."

"I can handle any amount of spice!" she insisted, still annoyed with him and willing to prove him wrong anywhere she could.

"I am not joking, Astrea, it's very—"

"I said I can handle it!" she growled, and it was the first time she'd lost her cool while working. "And what about you? Can you handle giving me an honest answer?"

She glared at him with such intensity that memories from the past started circling in his mind. That stubbornness stayed with her through every rebirth.

And it still worked the same on him, igniting his inner fire.

"Let's make a deal." He gave a slight quirk to the corner of his mouth as she greedily traced his every move, eager to get what she wanted from him – information.

"What kind of a deal?" Astrea folded her arms over her chest.

"I will order lunch for you and, if you last through each course, you can ask me any question you like and I will answer to the best of my abilities."

"Another trap," Nova hissed in her mind.

"Deal," Astrea agreed on the spot.

20. HOT

Fenrir took her to his favourite place. Ironically, he almost never was here in person, preferring the solitude of his "cave". So, the owner almost fainted when he saw him and Astrea walk into his small family restaurant, hidden in the depths of Solace's streets.

"My--" He bowed his head respectfully, but the wolf waved him off immediately.

"No need for formalities. I am just Fenrir today, and this is my guest, Astrea. Astrea, this is Dylar, the owner of the best restaurant in Solace," he briefly introduced everyone and marched to the table in the corner.

Astrea quickly scanned the place and hummed to herself. It wasn't much to be called the best, but she was ready to give it the benefit of the doubt.

When the old man heard Fenrir's order, his eyes widened slightly, which warned her that their bet was no joke. The Dragonfly regretted she didn't take one of her potions. She had one for almost any occasion, although it was probably risky now to use anything after Fenrir and his people went through her stuff.

"Sir, are you sure?" Dylar asked, giving Astrea a side glance as if he tried to warn Fenrir that those dishes were not for everyone. In fact, barely anyone could handle those.

"Sure," Fenrir's grin widened. "Astrea here likes it hot."

"Smoking hot," she corrected, narrowing her eyes at him and tilting her head. He wasn't going to intimidate her.

The rogue gave her a questioning look, and she knew it was her last chance to get out of this. Which only made her laugh. If he thought that some spicy food would stop her or make her change her mind, he thought wrong. She wanted answers and was ready to fight for them. Having dinner wasn't scaring her off.

"One course, one question." Fenrir leaned back in his chair, crossing his large hands over his chest, impressed by her stubbornness.

"Perfect." Astrea stretched her neck as if she was preparing for a fight. In a way… she was.

Dylar returned with a tray and placed two bowls in front of them, pausing slightly to see if one of them would change their mind.

"Last chance," Fenrir taunted.

"Smells delicious." She ignored him and took the spoon.

It was a soup, clearly just taken off the stove as the substance still seethed and bubbled like liquid lava. That still wasn't enough to stop her.

Astrea took a whole spoonful and blew on it to make it cooler. Then, under the watchful eye of Fenrir, she took it into her mouth, letting out a loud moan. It was exaggerated, of course, but it still managed to elicit a guttural growl from the man in front of her.

"Ambrosial." She closed her eyes and threw her head back to tease him more, chains dangling on her chest.

"Wait for it." His lips curled into a knowing smile as he started eating, and she quickly took a few more spoons just to prove him wrong.

"You know, Fenrir, it's so typical for a man to think that a woman can't handle a bowl of spicy soup. What's next? You'll decide that walking is too hard for me and carry me in your arms?"

"If you don't mind, I am in," he scoffed, enjoying his meal but not taking his eyes off her.

"In the South, we have equal roles for males and females because, in reality, the difference is not that—" She stopped talking because a whole inferno exploded in her mouth and throat, burning out the rest of her insides inch by inch.

"There it is!" Fenrir commented, keenly observing her.

Astrea's face contorted as tears started welling in her eyes, forcing her to recoil slightly and put the spoon back into the bowl. She felt like she could breathe fire if she wanted to. She needed a few seconds to regain her composure.

"It's fine," the rogue next to her cooed. "Even Warg and Kara can't take—"

She slammed her fist over the table to silence him and grasped the spoon again, bending it slightly from the force she applied. He had no idea what she had been through. After Joran's training for poison resistance, she could take the stupid soup in exchange for a valuable piece of information.

Astrea sped up, knowing there was no point in prolonging the torture. The sooner she ate, the sooner she would be done with it. When the soup was gone, she took only one sip of water, trying to rinse her throat from the damn spice but failing, so she ended up drinking it all.

"Come on, Astrea, we don't have to continue." Fenrir cleared his throat, putting his bowl aside.

"Ice, please!" the woman ordered, her voice unnaturally hoarse. She raised her empty glass and sent a begging gaze at Dylar, who was happy to obey. One look at him was enough to see how scared he was that something might go wrong.

"So," now it was Astrea's turn to smirk, "tell me what you know about my tattoos."

Fenrir took a gulp of his drink and gestured to Dylar to bring him another one.

"That's not exactly a question." He tapped his fingers over the table's surface, locking their eyes.

"Don't be shy, Fenrir," she giggled, finally able to speak again. "You know you want to tell me everything yourself, or you would have never mentioned it."

It was the truth with which he couldn't argue.

"The snake around your neck," he gritted his teeth, "I am sure you already know what it does. At least partially."

"And yet I want to hear it from you. A deal is a deal," Astrea insisted.

"It's a mark," Fenrir turned away because he didn't want to look at that thing again. "It tracks your every movement, lets its owner know what you are feeling and how you are doing, as well as where you are and who you are with."

She gulped. Of course, that wasn't big news, but hearing it confirmed was still unpleasant. Her privacy was gone.

"It also means that you belong to the one who gave you this mark," the rogue continued, each word hard for him to pronounce.

"You mean metaphorically?" she decided to clarify.

"I mean that it's a claim." Finally, Fenrir's heavy gaze landed on her face. "But I am far from done."

The woman's brow quirked up.

"It is also blocking the other tattoo," Fenrir said, and now she was confused.

"This doesn't make any sense," she admitted. "Why on Earth would he block—" She bit her tongue before she was the one revealing information to the – even in her thoughts, she couldn't call Fenrir her enemy – to the rogue.

"Why would he block a *Firstborn* tattoo?" A laugh rumbled through Fenrir's chest as he accentuated the secret title, and she clenched her lips tighter. He indeed knew too much.

"Maybe because you aren't exactly a Firstborn?"

He waited for her to give him any reaction, and she sighed, giving up.

"I guess I am not. I remember I had an older brother once."

Fenrir nodded understandingly, a glint of something she couldn't decipher in his eyes.

It still wasn't the answer to her question. The Firstborn tattoos were given after a successful Ascension. Those things were making the shifters stronger and faster. Sometimes, depending on Joran's wishes, those came with special powers and since she was one of the strongest, so was the tattoo given to her.

"So, you are not a Firstborn. Did you just assume that you were special and somehow the Ascension worked on you when it's only for the Firstborn children of powerful shifters?" he asked, a challenge in his voice.

She didn't say anything because it was exactly what she thought. Prior to this moment.

Fenrir gave her a second and then continued, "In a way, you weren't wrong, of course. You are special. But that dragonfly tattoo of yours has nothing to do with Firstborns."

Once again, Astrea remained silent, processing the information. Things did not add up.

"But there are other people with dragonfly tattoos, and they are Firstborns for sure."

"Let me guess," Fenrir chuckled darkly, "they appeared after your Ascension?"

They did. Astrea remembered clearly how Emma was announced the second Dragonfly by the Teacher and how hurt she felt because of that, not feeling that unique anymore. Back then, no one could compare to her, and she felt threatened. Emma also didn't make it easy on her, wishing to push Astrea from the first place and take it for herself. The remaining four Dragonflies wanted the same, adding stress to her life instead being the team Joran promised they would be. This was why it was always so hard to unite with them for a monthly Dragonfly Circle where they were connecting their powers on a spiritual level. They spent about an hour each week holding hands and meditating, and Astrea always hated that practice, feeling drained afterwards.

"Wait!" Nova gasped as they suddenly came to the same conclusion. The conclusion none of them was ready to sound.

"Wh-why would the second tattoo block the first one?" Astrea asked again, forming the question better.

"Because he doesn't want you at your full power." Their eyes met again, and she instinctively knew that he wasn't lying to her now.

She wanted to ask what her power was but stopped herself before she did. She could find out without his help if it was something within her. She didn't before because she didn't know she was supposed to be looking for something. Now that she was aware, it would be different.

At the same time, here and now, she had to choose the right questions and the opportunities were limited.

"Try to trick him into giving us more info," Nova suggested, and Astrea cleared her throat.

"You know my Teacher," she said, hoping to start a conversation. "You know what he is."

"Very nice try," Fenrir praised her with a chuckle. "But that's not a question."

Dylar returned with more food. This time there were flatbreads and dips. After the soup, that could have been a slightly easier option.

"Very well." She took a deep breath and broke the bread, dipping it and placing the piece into her mouth. There was no point in delaying the inevitable.

The dip was far spicier than she had anticipated, worse than the soup by a mile. Her taste buds screamed in agony, overwhelmed with the intense burn. Her face flushed with colour, and a sheen of sweat appeared on her brow as she tried to remain composed in front of her watcher. She reached for a glass of water, taking a long sip before trying again, hoping to acclimate to the heat. But every bite only intensified the burn, causing her to tear off the scarf she had wrapped around herself.

A growl emerged from the Rogue King's chest. She would have laughed if she wasn't crying already.

"Just stop." Fenrir ran his palm over his face. "You don't have to—"

"Stop distracting me!" she growled, Nova was healing her as fast as she could, but it was still too intense.

Nevertheless, with each new bite, Astrea felt the rush of endorphins, pushing her limits. Regardless, it was much harder this time because the insides of her throat were still sore after the first course.

"We are done with this stupid bet!" Fenrir growled.

"You don't get to stop!" she hissed at him, searching for a drink. He quickly moved a cup toward her, and she was happy to realise it was cold milk.

The flatbread and the dip were done, the drink bringing her the relief she needed. Even if it was temporary. At least, she got another question.

"I have to say I am surprised you managed to sneak a few cows in here," she said before taking another greedy gulp to ease the burning.

"Who says it's from the cows," Fenrir scoffed, and her eyes widened as she spat the liquid out to her left, too afraid to ask where it came from.

"Would you relax?" The rogue handed her a napkin. "It's camel milk. Nutritious and delicious. Just drink the rest!"

She did as she was told. After all, it was helping.

"Tell me what's so special about your bracelet." She pointed at the lines of colourful beads on his wrist, each different from the other, and noticed how his brows went up. He didn't expect that question.

21. PLAN C

"*T*his?" He touched a few beads, and a little smirk curled his lips. "My father gave this to me. It was a long time ago."

"But that's not why Teacher wants it," Nova hummed.

"Nope," Astrea agreed. *"But I can't tell him that."*

"That's not the only thing that makes it special, though," she tried another approach. "Fenrir, I am not eating coals here for vague answers."

"No, you are not," he agreed with a grin. "You are eating them out of stubbornness."

"Why is this bracelet special?" she repeated.

"It… stores things," Fenrir replied after a few seconds of contemplation. "Each bead is unique and priceless."

That was more like it.

"What exactly does it store?" She leaned forward, and so did he.

"That's a new question." The rogue smirked, and she groaned, returning to her seat.

"Third dish, please!" she called for Dylar.

"No." Fenrir shook his head. "We are done here."

"You don't get to—" She was about to reprimand him when the air in the room shifted and got thicker.

"This is it for today," he announced. "Your stomach must be on fire as it is! Sometimes I forget how—"

He stopped talking, and she rolled her eyes at him. She knew it was too good to be true, but she still couldn't hide her disappointment.

"Then I am done too!" the Dragonfly declared, standing up.

She didn't wait for him to respond this time and charged for the exit. It was the golden hour, and everything around seemed even more beautiful now.

"Astrea!" His resounding voice made her shudder, but she wasn't in the mood to talk if he wasn't going to give her new information. She already got some and needed to process it.

From the corner of her eye, Astrea noticed an ice cream cart and grabbed the cone prepared for another woman, pointing at Fenrir.

"He will pay!" she sneered and kept walking fast, knowing that the rogue would take care of it.

She tried to get lost in the narrow streets, devouring the delicious vanilla ice cream that helped her tongue and throat heal faster from the spice.

"You behave like a bratty child!" Fenrir caught up with her when she was on the bridge that went over the river. It was one of the smaller ones, and no one was there at this hour. She licked her ice cream as slowly as she could, winking at him. Letting out a low snarl, Fenrir wrapped the scarf back around her, fingers lingering on the shiny chains on her chest for a few moments before he came back to reality.

Their eyes locked, and the cheerful expression she forced onto her face faded away.

"Well, what did you expect? I am trapped here! Should I have cried somewhere in the corner like a proper damsel in distress?" Astrea wondered.

They stood like that for a few minutes, glaring and not saying another word.

"You are safe here," Fenrir sighed. "Moreover, you are not trapped."

"Oh really?" She let out a humourless laugh.

"Yes. You can leave now if you want – the border of the city is right there." Fenrir pointed to their left, and she tensed. "If you follow that road for about an hour, you will find yourself at the Solace's border."

"Is he serious?" she asked Nova, and her wolf hummed in response.

"No way. This is some kind of test. What was the point of bringing us here if we were really free the whole time?"

"Right," Astrea agreed. They knew far too well that nothing could be this simple. The Firstborn island taught them everything they needed to know about how life worked.

"This must be another test," she suggested.

"*Most definitely!*" Nova was on the same page with her.

"Will you give me a car?" Astrea glanced at Fenrir with a raised brow.

"No." He shook his head. "We have a limited supply, so if you want to leave, you must shift and run."

That was still reasonable. She could do it in her wolf form, of that she was sure.

Thoughts were racing through her mind under the pressure of making this very important decision. Her task wasn't complete, and she couldn't exactly return to Joran empty-handed. This would make her his slave forever, and she would rather return to the silver pit.

However, staying here for longer would be problematic too. Nobody was covering for her, and her story was falling apart more and more with each passing day.

Her main task didn't change. She had to kill him and get his bracelet. And they were alone now... The silver knife was safely strapped to her belt, and he was too relaxed in her company, underestimating her like many before him.

She could try it now, and no one would stop her. He was strong, stronger than her. She remembered how he killed four people without as much as straining himself. So, she would need to distract him. For example, if she kissed him...

She had to kiss him.

That was the best idea that came to her mind now.

"Goodbye then." She took a step in his direction, and he didn't take his eyes off her. A part of her was disappointed that he didn't try to stop her, and she didn't know why.

"Goodbye, Astrea." His words sounded dull and lifeless, and she took another step.

One kiss, one quick stab into the artery on his neck. Easy. She could do it. She was trained to kill; this wasn't anything special.

Just. One. Kiss.

"Don't miss me too much." She brushed her palm over his cheek, his beard prickling her fingers, creating goosebumps all over her for some reason.

"No promises." Fenrir's voice rasped in his chest, and she halted abruptly. Why would he say something like this?

"Thank you for your hospitality." Astrea stood on her tiptoes, and he lowered himself gently. Initially, her plan was to pretend that she was going to kiss his cheek and then ambush him the next moment. The Dragonfly was about to do this when she decided to back away at the last moment. That didn't work. Fenrir caught her waist and pulled her closer, crashing his lips into hers.

His lips moved against hers with hunger as old as time, one hand pressing her tighter against his chest while the other tangled in her hair. Fenrir snarled into her mouth, deepening the kiss, their breathing ragged.

It was the perfect moment, and Astrea's hand rested on the belt where she secured her dagger, fingers brushing over the cold metal that could take the rogue's life in less than a second.

She could do it.

She had to do it.

For Niki...

"Mine!" The word left his mouth, and she gasped for air, pushing him away because... because he wasn't supposed to say this!

The perfect assassination moment was gone.

Fenrir nodded understandingly, trying to catch his breath and kill the glow in his eyes. Nova was going crazy inside. They never felt anything like this before, and Astrea couldn't explain this.

"I should leave!" she blurted out and noticed how quickly Fenrir clenched his jaw, his eyes full of anticipation just a moment ago turned cold and distant.

"As you say," he said dryly, not trying to stop her.

Anger washed over her. He couldn't kiss her like that and then wave her goodbye.

She wouldn't be begging him to stay, either. If he was fine with it, so be it. The Dragonfly wished she had those emotions moments ago when she had the dagger in her hand. That would have been so helpful.

Instead, she turned on her heels and started walking.

"Plan C," she announced to Nova. *"We leave the city, regroup, call help, wait for Fenrir to be alone again and then—"*

"Wait!" the rogue growled, and her treacherous heart skipped a beat.

"I knew you missed me already." She angled her head to give him a taunting smile. "What do you want now?"

"You see, Astrea," the corners of Fenrir's lips turned upwards, "if you leave Solace, there is a catch—"

22. THE GLOWING GARDEN

~*A*SGARD~

It was just one stupid dance, but Fenrir couldn't get her out of his head for the past two days. Tyr's words were also coursing through his mind, and although no announcements had been made as of yet… the possibility bothered him.

So, he went to the only place that brought him peace – the cliff above the cave where he usually met with his brother. No one ever went there because there wasn't anything particularly interesting near that river. However, when he reached his destination today, everything looked different.

He paused at the gates that definitely weren't there the last time he checked, but when he sensed the familiar energy, his instincts compelled him to enter what looked like a garden.

Fenrir was greeted by moonstone arches and columns, sparkling with a silver light that glinted off the surrounding rocks.

Glowing flowers lined the winding paths, shimmering with iridescent hues of blue, purple and gold, interspersed with exotic plants that seemed to swirl and dance playfully in the night breeze.

Pure magic.

Foreign magic.

"You are not supposed to be here!" Astraea tried to sound reproachful, but her voice betrayed her as she couldn't hide a little note of excitement.

Fenrir froze, transfixed at the sight before him. She wore a delicate silver and white dress that seemed to shimmer with the light of the stars. Nothing like women wore here in Asgard. Her hair, a cascade of gleaming silver locks, hung down her back like a gentle waterfall of starlight.

Astraea was mesmerising as she stepped out of the shadows to meet his gaze.

"Me?" Fenrir scoffed, leaning against a nearby column as if he was leisurely passing by. "How about you? What do you think you are doing in a realm that isn't yours? Alone and at night... Exploiting our land."

Unlike her, he didn't have trouble pretending. He spent most of his life playing a role that wasn't really his. So, when he furrowed his brows, a shadow of doubt ran across the woman's beautiful face.

Astraea regained her composure quickly, though.

"This is my gift for Asgard." She lifted her chin, sending him a daring glance. "And I have official permission from the ruler to do whatever I like here."

"That doesn't sound like good old Odin at all," Fenrir chuckled. "He is very territorial about everything that belongs to him."

"Maybe he just likes me more!" she suggested with a giggle that died down at once when she realised what she had just said. "I'm sorry—" She covered her lips with her fingers quickly, and something warm spread across Fenrir's chest.

Because she cared. And no one else in his life did.

"You have nothing to apologise for." He cleared his throat, not sure what to say next.

"It's good that you are here!" Astraea said suddenly and grasped his hand, breaking down the walls he had built up over his lifetime, tearing them down in less than a second. "Come with me! You can help me test it."

"Test what?" he asked, although he didn't really care. She was pulling him deep into the garden, and he was more than happy to oblige. There probably wouldn't be another chance like this during the day, and he wanted as much time with this unpredictable young goddess as he could get.

"You know everything about this place and what they like. I am worried that my gift is not good enough." She bit her lower lip, probably not realising what kind of effect it had on him. "So, I will show you everything first, and you can tell me what you think."

"I am afraid you will owe me more than a dance after this," he let out a low laugh.

"I think you are mistaken." Astraea arched her brow at him. "You are the one who owes me now."

Their gazes locked, and he noticed how a pink tint crept up her cheeks.

"Is that how you see it?" Fenrir's lips curled into a smirk, and her smile faded. She still held his hand, and he felt how she squeezed it tighter.

"They shouldn't treat you that way," she whispered as if she was afraid that someone would hear them.

His whole body stiffened because he knew that she meant it. It was the first time someone said it out loud. Someone other than his father or Jor.

"Lead the way." He changed the subject swiftly, and that pretty smile curved her lips again.

She walked him through the labyrinth she'd created here and explained every turn, arch, and sculpture. Everything had meaning and he was amazed by how her mind worked.

"The garden's true power lies in its bloom, which only occurs at night," Astrea explained. "These are not just regular flowers. I sprayed each with my personal magic, and because of that, every time the moon rises and the stars appear in the sky—"

"They will glow," Fenrir finished her thought.

He looked around again, seeing how the flowers erupted in a chorus of luminescence, illuminating the whole garden and casting everything in a soft and mystical glow. It was then that the garden truly came alive, blossoming into a riot of colour and magic. Her magic. A particle of her soul.

Something Asgardians would never appreciate. She poured her heart and soul into this place, but they would never see it or even if they did... they would never care. It pained him to know that all her effort would be in vain.

"So, what do you think?" She caught him off-guard. "Is it beautiful enough?"

"It's the most beautiful thing I have ever seen," he replied, not taking his eyes off her.

"Do you think Freyja would like it?" Astrea smiled, and his treacherous heart began racing again in his chest.

"She loves nature and flowers," he said. "She will love it."

Astraea's smile became brighter, and he realised he wanted to see more of that.

"You know what may be a good touch here," he casually suggested, rubbing the back of his neck.

"What?" She looked at him through her long lashes.

"Runes." He crossed his arms over his chest to look more serious while he was spouting nonsense.

"Runes?" She looked puzzled.

"Yeah, runes. Freyja created quite a few magical ones for luck, prosperity, fertility and so on. If it's her approval you seek—"

"But I... don't know any runes." Their eyes locked, and the corner of his lips tilted upwards.

"Well then," he sighed, "you are in luck, because I know every single one."

She sucked in a breath, and he knew that everything would depend on her response now.

"Are you suggesting that you'd help me?" she asked.

"And absolutely free of charge." He nodded, trying to hold back that smirk that threatened to escape him.

"Chivalry in Asgard is blooming." She gave him a look that implied she knew what he was doing, and for a second, he was sure she was going to decline his offer. "How long do you think it will take us?"

"At least a week," he blurted out, and she tried to suppress a giggle. "Maybe two or three if we want to do all of them."

"Wouldn't it be too much?" she taunted.

"No, sounds about right." He stepped closer. He was planning to make those two weeks count.

~SOLACE~

"I knew there would be a catch!" Astrea narrowed her eyes at him, and Fenrir shrugged.

"Depends on how you look at it, really," he said nonchalantly.

"What is it?" she snapped, lips still burning from his kiss. A kiss she wouldn't mind repeating even though she'd sooner die than admit it.

"If you cross the border of Solace, you will forget everything about this place and what happened here," he informed her, knowing this changed everything.

"Big deal," she scoffed, tensing on the inside. There was no way she could return to Joran without Fenrir dead or at least some kind of valuable information. "So, I'd forget the tour of the city and a very questionable dinner." She still tried to pretend it didn't matter.

"And the kiss of your life!" A laugh rumbled through Fenrir's chest.

"Don't flatter yourself!" she hissed, wondering if any kind of magic could erase that from her mind. She doubted it. "I've already forgotten it."

"I don't know how you've lasted so long at your job." Fenrir stepped closer, towering over her. "You are a terrible liar."

"Or maybe you are a terrible kisser!" she retorted defiantly, knowing it sounded stupid. "Overestimating yourself mu—"

He leaned lower as if he was about to kiss her again, and she lost her train of thought completely, their breaths mingling as one.

"You were saying?" he chuckled, his beard barely brushing over her skin.

"I am leaving!" she seethed through her teeth, balling her fists.

"Bye then." Fenrir's lips curved.

"Just so that you know, it's not freedom if people *have* to stay here!" Astrea tilted her head, locking their eyes once again.

"No one has to *stay* here. That's the whole point. Everyone who wants to leave is free to do so. Yourself included. Wanna leave? Be my guest!"

"And if someone here decides to leave, do they forget their family?" Astrea furrowed her brows. "Don't you think that it's cruel? Is there anything worse than not remembering the ones you love?"

His throat bobbed. If only she knew what she was talking about.

"Trust me, it's more painful for the ones who *do* remember!" he told her, and her lips parted when she noticed the look in his eyes.

"Did... did someone forget you?" Her voice was barely a whisper.

"Anyway," he decided to return to the original topic, "are you leaving or staying?"

She wanted to reply but quickly realised that she hadn't made the decision and had no clue what to do now. She wasn't prepared to leave. If she did now, Joran would own her for the rest of her life.

They stared at each other for a few more seconds when she realised something.

"But you can leave," she pointed out.

"I can," he confirmed.

"And so can Devoss and Salome," Astrea continued.

"The trusted circle can leave and return as they please." Fenrir watched her intensely.

"Nova, I think I know what to do next!" Astrea mentally grinned at her wolf.

"Stay and find out how the others leave," Nova sneered. *"Then leave the same way and use Solace as the bargaining chip for trading ours and Niki's freedom."*

"Yeah, exactly," she agreed, but for some reason, she didn't feel happiness or excitement. It didn't feel like a victory at all.

"I will still remember that Unicorn thing," she suddenly said, although there was no reason to remind him of that. What if he changed his mind about letting her leave based on that?

"The question is if you want to leave," Nova said in a strange tone. *"I am getting mixed signals here."*

"You will forget." He nodded, eyes on her at all times.

"Didn't you bring me here so that I couldn't tell anyone?" Astrea reminded him.

"That wasn't the only reason. And I don't think you will tell anyone about that."

"What makes you so sure?" Now she was genuinely interested. He couldn't possibly trust her with this kind of information.

"It's the last Nightmare," Fenrir disclosed what had to be a secret. "If you tell Joran about it, he will hunt it and kill it."

"And you decided that I would care about it... why exactly?" Her brows went up. "That thing poisoned me!"

"But right before that, it bonded to you." The rogue's words stunned her. He gave her a few seconds to process this information and went on with a chuckle. "What? You didn't think a Nightmare lets just anyone touch it? Besides, if anyone else wrapped their hands around his horn, they would be dead instantly. He softened the blow for you."

"Wh-why?" Astrea looked at him with wide eyes.

"That's a question for another day." The man smirked at her, dimples on his cheeks deepening. She hated how handsome he was. "That's, of course, if you're staying."

She gave him a withering glance. It's not like she was going to leave anyway, but he still had the upper hand.

"All right," she sighed dramatically. "I'll give this place a few more days before deciding. I'm free to do so, right?"

"Of course you are!" Fenrir's tone let her know that he knew she was faking it, but he was letting it slide. "I think it's time for us to head back."

"Fine!" she agreed. "But I'm going to need more of that ice cream. My mouth is still on fire."

"How much are we talking?" he asked.

"A whole cart, at least!" She let out infectious laugh that made him grin at her against his will as he laced his fingers with hers just like back then...

***

"Is that a whole cart of ice cream?" Bash gaped at them when he saw the couple approaching Fenrir's house. The blonde man was sitting on the steps next to the entrance, with Salome standing beside him and watching the whole thing in awe.

"It is!" Astrea smirked as she licked the one in her hands, casting a playful glance at Fenrir. "Be my guest and treat yourself!"

She giggled and ran up the stairs, Fenrir following her with a low snarl escaping him.

The duo watched them with their jaws clenched tightly.

"Do you see what I'm talking about now?" The witch folded her arms over her chest. "I'm telling you, she's a problem and a liability!"

"Fine!" the man snarled. "I'll talk to him."

"I think we're past the point of talking." Salome shook her head, rubbing the bridge of her nose.

"What do you have in mind then?" Bash asked, and her lips twitched as she tried to suppress a sneer.

23. BEST CHANCE

A SGARD

"LIKE THIS?" Astraea asked, bouncing at the top of a ladder and furrowing her silver brows as she finished yet another set of runes. As always, Fenrir's gaze was fixed on her after he was done drawing the signs on the ground for her to copy.

It was perfect. Astraea loved working in her glowing garden at night, and it was the only time when he could approach her alone. It was worth it, despite Tyr wiping the floor with him due to his tiredness during their battle training.

Time with Astraea was worth every struggle.

He knew it wasn't meant to be. He wasn't naïve. Tyr prohibited him from seeing her because she was meant for another. At least those were the rumours.

But days passed, and nothing happened. No announcement, no proposals.

Maybe Tyr was wrong about this.

"No, there should be another line on the left." He pointed to where it should be, but she placed her finger on a different spot.

"Here?"

"No, not—"

"Here?" The Goddess of Stars was impatient, her starry magic glowing at the top of her finger.

"No!" he chuckled and decided to use the chance to get closer to her. "I'll show you. Just wait a second."

"What? No!" she gasped as she saw him climbing up the ladder. "Fenrir, no offence, but you are huge. This thing is going to break!"

"It's going to be fine!" He was behind her in no time, and they both froze from the sudden closeness.

"Here!" He pointed at the correct spot, placing his palm over her tiny hand and moved it gently following the rune. His cheek barely brushed over her silky hair, but he felt as if he'd been struck by lightning, while heat radiated from his body.

Astraea angled her head to look at him, their gazes locking together. The attraction was undeniable. Especially now that she was trapped here with his strong arms around her.

It would have been the right thing for him to move away, but Fenrir did no such thing, inhaling her scent so that it filled his lungs instead. Her lips parted as she watched him and he leaned lower, somehow knowing that she wouldn't push him away. Her breath was already burning his skin as he was about to claim her first kiss when a snapping sound echoed through the garden. Before they realised what was happening, the ladder suddenly gave way beneath them, sending the couple tumbling towards the ground. Astraea gasped and reached out to him, while he managed to twist his body and catch her in his arms, hoping to save her from the fall.

What he didn't expect was that the impact never happened as the air around them became thicker, allowing them to float instead. It took him a few seconds to realise that she was the one doing it.

"Astraea?" Her name escaped from his lips as he realised how tightly he held her in his arms.

"I-I've got you," she whispered, cheeks flushing from their proximity and their hair intertwining in the air.

Their gazes locked, and the world around them slipped away. They were caught up in the heat of the moment, unable to resist the pull that brought them closer. Astraea's long white hair seemed to dance in the light, and Fenrir was drawn to the shimmering strands as if they were a manifestation of pure magic. There were no Asgardians and no Olympians anymore. No cursed wolf deity and no new goddess of stars. They were just Fenrir and Astraea and they couldn't fight their attraction anymore.

One of his arms wrapped around her waist while his other hand slipped all the way up to the back of her head, fingers entangling themselves in her silvery locks.

Fenrir pulled her closer, covering her lips with his, greedily thrusting his tongue into her mouth the moment she granted him access. She tasted so sweet that he couldn't possibly have enough of her. Astraea moaned into him and the sound alone undid something inside him, something feral... something he couldn't control anymore.

"Mine!" Fenrir growled and her fingers dug into his flesh, letting him know that she loved this as much as he did.

They gasped for air, Astraea's heart racing in her chest.

"Oh my—" Her eyes met his again as if she realised for the first time what they had been doing and whatever power kept them floating in the air dispersed instantly.

They landed in a heap on the soft glowing grass, Fenrir taking the brunt of the impact as he shielded her from harm.

Astraea lay on top of him, trying to catch her breath and find the words to thank him for protecting her.

"Th-thank you," she mumbled, realising she needed to add something else not to look like she was thanking him for kissing her, but in the next moment he rolled on top of her, pinning her hands to the ground.

"I've got you too, Astraea." He smirked, leaning lower. "I want to kiss you again. Tell me if you want me to stop."

He was looking her straight in the eye and she... didn't say a thing.

"Thanks to all the gods!" Fenrir muttered and crashed his lips against the lips of the woman he craved more than anything in this world.

Fenrir returned to his chambers, but no matter how hard he tried to keep his excellent mood up, it was fading away with every passing second.

Now that he'd kissed her and held her in his arms, he couldn't lie to himself anymore. It wasn't curiosity or a simple infatuation. He wanted that woman on every level imaginable. He wanted to claim her, make her happy, make her his wife and give her everything she could ever want. This was something he'd never thought about with anyone else. He wished to be the reason that her wonderful smile blossomed on her beautiful lips. He desired to take her, to worship her the way she deserved. Fenrir wanted it all.

Sadly, he knew that every single Asgardian would stand in his way if he so much as dared to speak his claim on that woman out loud.

"Long time no see, son!" The familiar voice made every muscle in his body strain.

Was it that month of the year again already? The last time he checked, it wasn't. So, what the hell was this man doing here?

"Father," Fenrir greeted his unexpected guest dryly.

All the illusions about this man were long dead. Although usually, Fenrir longed to see his father, today, his heart didn't jump in his chest at the sight of him. Loki could have tricked anyone into giving him anything. Yet one thing he'd never attempted was to bring his children back together again. He'd never begged Odin to change his decision. He'd never asked other gods to support him. All he was doing was living his life as if he had produced no offspring.

"Look at you!" The trickster deity hugged his son, gracing him with a wide smile that meant nothing because he offered it to anyone. "A true warrior! A leader!"

Fenrir would have rolled his eyes, but it wasn't worth the effort.

"Good to see you, Father; I hope you had a nice journey," he muttered, walking past the man to his desk and wishing for nothing more than to be left alone. "Can't wait to hear all about it at the next feast."

That was how he usually found out about his father's adventures – at celebrations where he wasn't really welcome. Or from Jor, who followed the old man when it was possible.

"Your words are like an arrow through my heart, son," Loki chuckled, trailing him deeper into his chambers.

Fenrir dropped into a large wooden armchair, and his father sat on the armrest, observing him with a curious eye.

"Nothing like that," Fenrir tried to brush him off. "Just a long day."

His father was not to be trusted with any secrets, unless he wanted everyone to find out about them the next day and not in the best light. Sometimes Loki's desire to have fun outweighed his fatherly feelings, and it made Fenrir feel even lonelier here. For now, only his secret about seeing Jormungandr each month was safe for very obvious reasons.

"I'd say the day is long gone!" Loki smirked and leaned closer. "Maybe that young, starry goddess made you lose track of time?"

So, he already knew everything. That explained the visit.

Usually, Fenrir couldn't wait to spend time with his father, but not today. For the first time in his life, getting Loki's attention or approval didn't mean much. He had more important things to worry about.

"Did you want something?" the young wolf snapped, regretting it almost instantly.

"You do know why she is here?" The playfulness was gone from the trickster's face, and their eyes locked in a heavy, unspoken confrontation.

"I do," Fenrir admitted coldly. He didn't want to think about it if he could help it.

"And still, you pursue her," Loki said. Not asked. It wasn't a question, but a statement.

"She deserves better than that—" Fenrir forced himself to stop talking. He knew he was heading down a dangerous road.

"And you consider yourself a better option?" His father cocked a brow up.

"We have… something—" Speaking about his feelings was new to Fenrir, and his father was the last one he wanted to open up his soul to. Yet… he had no better options.

"Something." Loki rolled the word on his tongue, tasting it. "*Something* isn't going to cut it, son, when you aim that high."

A growl escaped his chest. He tried to suppress it, but his nature was overpowering him at moments like this.

Loki stood up and paced back and forth with his hands behind his back for a while.

"We don't have to talk about it," Fenrir said, tired of this… whatever that was.

His father sighed, a few wrinkles gathering between the brows on his still youthful face.

"She is a prize, son," he sighed, giving him another pitying look. "A priceless prize from a dying realm. The Olympians are on the brink of death, and she is their last chance. The previous goddess of stars is dead, and now this young child is wielding that huge cosmic power without understanding what it really means. They will only give her to one they think can save them."

Fenrir turned away to look out the window and into the dark, night sky. The silence was deafening, and the only sound to be heard was the gentle rustling of leaves in the wind. In the distance, he could see the stars twinkling and shimmering against the midnight blue canvas. But as he gazed out into the expanse, something caught his eye. A shooting star streaked across the sky, leaving a trail of shimmering light in its wake. He watched in awe as it disappeared beyond the horizon, making a wish before he realised it.

"This is why I think it's not impossible," Loki said, and it took a few moments for his words to register.

"What?" Fenrir's head snapped in his direction.

"Don't get me wrong," Loki sighed and walked back towards him. "If it was any other goddess, I would reprimand you now and make you lay low, but... Astraea is Selene's daughter. If the Moon Goddess loves anything, it's her daughter and her wolves. She was already interested to see you, and I bet she wasn't disappointed."

"Do you really think so?" Fenrir tried to suppress the excitement building up inside him.

"I think you have a shot if you play it right, son." Loki nodded, finally getting his son's full attention.

"Care to elaborate?" Fenrir attempted to conceal his curiosity, but apparently, he failed miserably because a familiar, knowing smile curled his father's lips.

"Of course." Loki rested his hand upon his son's shoulder, giving him hope. "Join me and your brother when the time comes and help us overthrow the current rulers of—"

"Not this again!" Fenrir let out a growl of frustration. He'd heard all that before.

"This is the best solution!" Loki protested. "Just think about it. The Olympians will be happy to give you any goddess you want when they know your true power!"

"Ideas like that made them separate me and my siblings in the first place!" Fenrir retorted angrily.

"It's ideas like this that can bring us back together," Loki insisted, but seeing his son's reluctant face, he sighed heavily and gave up. "Fine, there is another way," he groaned, rolling his eyes.

"I am all ears." Fenrir poured himself some mead and gulped it down, all in one go.

"Go to the Moon Goddess, and ask for Astraea's hand before any announcements are made." His father laid on him a heavy gaze. "This is your best chance. Now or never. After she is promised to another, it will be done. And remember that you will only have a shot if you remind her of your wolf side. Also, your chances will increase if that conversation happens when no Asgardians are present."

"Like that's ever going to happen," Fenrir scoffed, knowing how the guests were always surrounded by people.

"What can I say? You are in luck that Selene is a night goddess. If you ask for an audience before dawn, you may be lucky enough to see her alone as she never sleeps."

Fenrir tapped his fingers over the armrest of his chair and then stood up in one sharp move.

"So be it!" he announced, storming out of his chambers and leaving the God of Trickery behind.

Loki decided not to wait for him and went to the place he knew Fenrir would end up tonight.

"Did you do it?" Jor walked out of the cave the moment he saw his father arrive. "Will he—"

"He will try." Loki nodded, sadness lacing his words.

"I can't believe it's this serious. He is going to make a fool out of himself for some girl!" The young dragon hit the huge boulder next to him with his fist.

"It may be for the best," Loki admitted. "Fenrir is naïve, thinking that if he behaves, he will get what he wants from Asgardians. They will never care about any of us. Each of you is alive only because they couldn't kill you. They would rather die themselves, than accept you."

"Do you think there is a chance they will let him marry that girl?" Jormungandr calmed down, seeing how reserved his parent was.

"No, I don't think he stands a chance. They want royalty for her, not a villain. No one would care that they love each other."

"Why did you send him there then?" Jor furrowed his blonde brows.

"Because he has to learn that lesson, he has to experience the pain. Then, when he is down and abandoned, he will realise that only you, Hel, and me are his family. Soon he will know that his plan will never work, and there is no hope other than taking what's ours by force. On that day, Fenrir will join our cause, and the gods of Asgard will die."

WHEN ASTREA DISAPPEARED on the first day from his radar, Joran did not panic. He knew that this was to be expected when his brother was involved.

But then she did not reappear on the second and third days, causing different emotions to reign inside his soul.

"She couldn't have remembered him so soon!" He knocked the desk over and sent it flying against the wall, watching it break into myriads of pieces. "And she couldn't disappear with my mark around her neck!"

Without warning, he lashed out at the nearest object, a delicate porcelain vase perched on a mahogany side table. With a guttural growl, he grabbed it and hurled it at one of the onyx columns, shattering it into hundreds of glittering shards. The sound of breaking glass echoed through the room like a war cry, fuelling the man's anger further.

He tried to summon the little snake again and again, but there was no response. He couldn't feel it; he didn't control it anymore.

Joran couldn't do anything about it, and this was something he hadn't felt for centuries. He did not get what he wanted, and his little Dragonfly had slipped from his grasp.

He closed his eyes and tried to get through again, to no avail. However, this time he tried to think clearly. Fenrir couldn't hide her from him. Their powers didn't work like that. Which only meant he needed more information.

"Call her!" he snapped at one of the Firstborn, and the latter immediately realised who his Master was talking about.

24. THE DAWN

"*Touch me," Astraea whispered. She never had to ask Fenrir twice, and his hands immediately slid down her silky skin, one grasping her ass and the other kneading her breast, eliciting a moan from her.*

Fenrir's tongue swirled against her soft flesh, torturously slow and taunting. She had to reach for his hair, lacing her fingers in it to give him a tug, demanding for him to stop the games. The delightful pressure was already building inside her with every stroke he made, her thighs resting on his shoulders.

"Mine!" he growled, devouring her, and that word alone tipped her over the edge.

"Please!" Astraea hissed her plea, which unleashed the beast in him, and he lapped and sucked at her sensitive bundle of nerves. "Fenrir!" she screamed his name, arching her back...

Astrea jolted upright in bed, her breathing ragged and with beads of sweat already formed all over her body. Her heart was racing after yet another mind-splitting orgasm she'd endured within these walls.

On her own.

While sleeping.

This was the fifth night in a row. No matter what she did, she couldn't stop dreaming about herself and Fenrir doing all sorts of things to each other. Some of those she'd learned from those dreams, and now she was sure it wasn't normal.

"*Nova!*" she called out in the hope that her wolf could help her.

"It's out of my control!" The wolf was already tired of her complaining. *"I can't control dreams, Astrea. It doesn't work like that. Besides— is it that bad?"*

Waking up from extensive climaxing wasn't actually the worst thing in the world, but at the same time, it was torture. Everything in regards to the Rogue King was.

Nothing changed. He was still her target. She would have to kill him sooner or later. It didn't matter how incredibly hot he was or how he made her laugh with just one word or that smirk of his. It was wrong to be that invested in thinking about him. She was a professional.

Her last mission was just an emotional slip. This won't happen again. Not when her freedom and Niki's life were both on the line.

"Fenrir, what do I do with you?" she groaned, falling back to bed.

"Anything." The Rogue King's voice rumbled through the room, and she jumped up again, gasping. "Especially when you look like this."

Astrea found his glowing eyes in the darkness instantly.

"What are you doing here? How dare you!" She tried to find something to cover herself, which only made him chuckle as he strolled in without permission. She stopped her search, realising that he had already seen her wearing less than her silk lace slip from the time he'd found her in his room.

Each day he took her on a city tour, and each day she tried to test his patience in one way or another. However, they never spoke about the kiss that happened on the bridge in Solace, and he had never tried to get a second one out of her. Which made her feel... puzzled. Frustrated, even.

Why wasn't he trying anything? He'd behaved as if he was a mere tour guide for almost a week, distancing himself from her emotionally and making her question her sanity. She provoked him many times, not because it was required for her mission, but because she simply couldn't help herself. He'd ignored every attempt, acting like the perfect gentleman and annoying the hell out of her.

And now he pranced into her room in the middle of the night? She wanted to make him regret it!

"How dare I?" Fenrir raised a brow at her, not at all bothered by the glares she shot his way. "First of all, it's my house. Second, I feel obliged to check on you when you call my name."

"I didn't call you—" she started, but stopped talking the moment she realised that it was possible.

"Oh, you did!" he insisted with a cocky grin. "Loud and clear. 'Please, Fenrir! Please!' and other similar niceties." The rogue imitated the tone just as she remembered it from her dream, and now Astrea was happy that it was still dark in the room.

"I was sleeping." She gritted her teeth and stood up, walking towards him.

"So, you were dreaming about me?" The corner of his lips tilted upwards slightly, and she wanted to wipe that smirk off his handsome face once and for all.

"Who says it was you? Fenrir is a popular name as far as I know." She pursed her lips. "I know of at least ten guys with that name!"

"Liar!" He snorted and stepped closer.

"I never lie!" she lied through her teeth, backing away. "And it wasn't the type of dream that your sick mind is imagining!"

Another lie.

"Sure, Menace, I believe you." Fenrir, however, didn't plan to retreat, advancing towards her. He was now so close that she could feel the heat radiating from his body.

Just like in the dream…

Astrea didn't realise how close to her bed she was until she stumbled on the edge and fell back onto the softness of her sheets, with Fenrir chuckling, watching her struggle. Breathing ragged, she looked left and right in search of anything to save her from embarrassment.

Her gaze caught on the gleam created by the moonlight falling onto the crystal on her bedside table. The one she kept close since she got here because Fenrir told her to…

"Oh, shimmering goddess!" She gritted her teeth in realisation and snapped her eyes back at the Rogue King, whose smirk was now gone. "You didn't!"

"I have no idea what you are talking about!" He shook his head. "I just came to check on you, and you seem fine! Good night!"

He was already at her door when she screamed at him, "Fenrir! Does this damn crystal have anything to do with the dreams I've been having?"

"No," he stretched the word in an unusually high-pitched, for him, tone, "of course not!"

She grabbed the crystal and stormed his way, shaking it in his face. "Did you give me some kind of… weird sex crystal?"

"That's a Nightmare's horn! I told you that!" He tried to keep his face straight. "It suppresses the foreign magic on you."

"And…?" She arched her brow expectantly. There had to be more.

"It may or may not have some… side effects," he finally admitted.

"So, it makes me see you fucking me every damned night?" she hissed. "In every way imaginable! You sick Eastern—"

"Whoa! It's not supposed to do that!" Now his face was straight, and she choked on her own words. "Is that what you've been seeing?"

He furrowed his brows, and she realised that if he was still messing with her, he had to be the best actor in the world. Much better than she was.

"No!" Now her voice was high-pitched, and she swallowed hard, licking her dry lips.

Fenrir's gaze traced her every move, and a heavy sigh escaped him right before he pinned her to the wall, looming over her with his imposing stature.

"Let me make this clear, once and for all," his voice was low and husky, "I don't need to make you have dreams about me to get you into my bed. It's not as hard as you think for an experienced man to seduce a virgin, even if she is a big bad assassin like you are. It just so happens that I know everything there is to know about you, and you don't have a clue about who I really am, so this will never work unless—"

His voice broke, and her breath wavered unsteadily. The world around them stopped spinning, the wind stopped blowing, and even the shimmering stars froze, expecting his next words to change everything.

"Unless what?" she whispered her question, looking straight into his eyes and seeing flames in them. It wasn't the usual glow she knew from other shifters. The flames flickered and danced like a mesmerising inferno, enchanting Astrea and making her unable to break free from the pull of this man.

"Unless you choose to stay with me forever. Here. In Solace." Fenrir's face maintained an unwavering composure.

"Is that a joke?" It had to be.

"No." He didn't hesitate one bit, his eyes still locked with hers. "Stay here with me, and I am yours. I will do all those things you saw in your dreams and more. I will protect you, fight for you, kill for you, do whatever you want me to do. But it has to be your choice."

"Fenrir—" She was lost for words. She expected anything but this.

He was so close, so warm, so alive, so god-damn good-looking, but all of this came absolutely out of nowhere. They'd known each other for barely a week. And she had never met a man she could trust before. Not like this. Not with everything.

"I—"

She was about to say that she couldn't before he stopped her.

"Get dressed. I need to show you something today." He stepped back slowly as if it was painful for him to distance himself from her, and she still didn't know if it was in jest or if he was serious. He did, however, pause at the door again. "I will wait for you in the car."

Despite not knowing how serious he was, she dressed in record time, choosing an appropriate outfit for once – a white flowing dress and a scarf.

It was still dark when she left the mansion and saw him waiting for her, just as he'd promised. He drove her to the rocky part of the desert, where a chain of mountains was decorating the scenery.

Fenrir didn't talk much, just like the last five days, only answering yes, no or dry, boring facts to her questions.

A part of her wanted to explode. He couldn't drop a bomb like that on her and then play the silent game. This wasn't right.

Another part of her, however, didn't want to raise the subject.

She couldn't stay. There was Niki. And all those plans to travel the world, tasting her freedom for the first time. She couldn't.

Not for a man she barely knew.

It was stupid. So stupid.

But why was her heart racing so much that her breathing got heavier and heavier by the minute?

When the car suddenly stopped, and he opened the door for her, she got out without saying a word herself. Two could play this game.

Fenrir motioned for her to follow him, and she did, sensing that the sunrise was close.

The Rogue King placed a blanket on the ground and gestured for her to sit down. She did just that, and he joined her. It was always the praying time for the Easterners who believed in the old gods. One thing that she'd quickly learned was that, although Solace accepted everyone who wanted to live here and could prove themselves worthy, the majority of the people were still the Easterners who survived the Kingdom that Perished, which was once composed of several cultures and religions, a reflection of its location. They still prayed to the gods they believed in, and the ruler did not object to any of it.

Now that Astrea was thinking about it, she didn't feel that one religion was above another here. She saw people with Moon Goddess crescents on them; she saw that hideous statue of the Northern god Fenrir; she knew about fox deities of the past and many others. Fenrir's tour introduced her to all that. It looked like a religion here was a personal matter for everyone to cherish on their own and without frowning upon others. She liked that part.

The first light of dawn began to pierce the velvety darkness, awakening something deep in Astrea's soul as she stole a glance at Fenrir. The majesty of the towering peaks, with their rugged contours and deep shadows, illuminate under a palette of warm hues. From deep reds and oranges to golden yellows and light pinks, the vibrant sky created a breathtaking backdrop against the mountains and the desert below, spread like a golden carpet.

It was a beautiful spot, perfect for a romantic date, but Fenrir was not making a move, keeping his distance.

Astrea watched him, trying to push the eagerness and disappointment at his lack of action deep down.

He was a target. Just a target. Nothing more than a target. A target. She didn't need to get involved with him.

"Wait for it," he said, keeping his composure as always, but this was enough to pique her interest.

"Wait for what?" she asked and turned back, her lips parting in surprise.

She could have never anticipated it, but she noticed two colourful hot air balloons flying up into the sky. She was about to comment on them when three more appeared from behind the sandy peaks. Then more and more and more of them until a whole rainbow of colours painted the sky, a stark contrast against the desert's beige hues.

"Fenrir!" She grasped his hand without realising it, lacing their fingers together. "It's so beautiful!"

"Mesmerising," he agreed, looking only at her.

"What is this?" She didn't notice his focus on her as she was too busy looking at what was unfolding before her eyes.

"Yesterday was the night of the New Moon," the Rogue King sighed as if it was explaining everything.

"What does it mean?" She couldn't tear her gaze away from the colourful display. She had seen many things but nothing quite like that. The balloons soared and bobbed gracefully, harmonious in their dance with the wind.

"It's a tradition here." Fenrir tightened his grip on her hand. "There are only couples in those baskets now."

"Really?" Her lips curled into a smile. "What are they doing?"

"They're trying to find their mates," he said, immediately getting her attention.

"A weird way to try to look for your mate." She shrugged with a chuckle, shaking her silvery white locks. "Not that I am an expert, but there are easier ways."

"Not here." Fenrir's expression became darker. "The protection of Solace blocks the mate bond. It doesn't let anyone find their mates."

25. LOVE VS MATES

"Is this a joke?" Astrea's brows went up.

"No." The Rogue King shook his head, not offering her any explanation.

"Fenrir, come on!" She jabbed him gently with her elbow. "You dropped a bomb on me, and now you are leaving me hanging? I don't think so!"

"Ask whatever you want to know," The King suggested as if he really didn't mind.

She wanted to know a lot. Starting from his story with her Teacher to the specifics of what his bracelet was holding, but that was probably off the table. So, she stuck to the subject at hand instead.

"What do you mean Solace's protection prevents people from finding mates?"

"Exactly that. When we were building Solace, I had only one condition. No mates will be found on this land," he stated nonchalantly, and Astrea's lips parted in shock. "That's why they are up in the air now. One day per month, on the morning after the New Moon, is the day when they can feel the bond if they are up there."

"How is that even possible?" She tried to see the couples in the wicker baskets, but they were too far away.

"Magic, of course," Fenrir said, and his fingers drifted over the beads of his bracelet.

"That has to be a clue," Nova whispered, and Astrea had to agree.

Were those beads holding magic inside? That would explain why Joran wanted the bracelet.

"No offence, it's romantic and all that, but what happens when they go down?" Astrea was still processing the information.

"Nothing." He shrugged. "They just know now."

"Will they still feel the bond?"

"No." Again, his tone suggested that it wasn't a big deal and that didn't sit right with the Dragonfly.

"But why can't they feel it again?" She tried to understand if she missed some crucial piece of information. Who wouldn't want to feel their mate?

"Why would they need to feel it?" He offered her a questioning glance. "I don't even understand why they want to know in the first place. If they love each other, that should be enough."

"But we are talking about mates!" Astrea inhaled sharply, trying to hold back her fiery temper. "Who wouldn't want to know?"

"Anyone with common sense." Fenrir's laugh rumbled through his chest.

"And that was *your* idea? What on Earth do you have against mates?" she gasped and noticed a momentary flicker of pain in the man's eyes, wondering if she had overstepped.

"Everything." He cut her off as if it wasn't a big deal. "What's so special about mates?"

"Everything!" she repeated his word to prove her point. "The mate bond is a divine connection that transcends time and space, forging an unbreakable link between two souls. Everyone strives to find it. It's an honour to feel it at least once in your lifetime. Nothing else can compare to it."

Astrea could see his spirits dampening at first, but then something else appeared in his gaze. An unyielding flame she recognised from somewhere.

"Nothing can compare to it? How about love? Real love!" His voice became darker, and she didn't know if he was angry or simply passionate about the topic.

"The mate bond *is* love!" she insisted, but a growl escaped his chest in response.

"Is it, though? So, you're telling me that two people need the Moon Goddess to tell them they are in love? How is that real love? If they need her to tell them, then they aren't in love at all!"

"I mean… she sees the souls perfect for each other and binds them." Astrea had never heard of such an argument against mate bonds, although she had to admit that he had a point.

"Are we just assuming she knows everything about everyone to make such decisions? The last time I checked, she was the Goddess of the Moon, not of people's destinies. Do you know how many couples she got wrong?"

It seemed as if he'd had this conversation before.

"A few." Astrea couldn't deny this. She knew it, too. Everyone did. The Moon Goddess indeed made mistakes from time to time. Queen Savannah of the North had a terrible first mate. Astrea had to work with him for a while, and even she could tell the two were wrong for each other. Then why would the goddess do it? A part of her believed that their pairing was part of a bigger plan. But... what if it wasn't?

"But that doesn't mean the whole mate system is bad," she pointed out. More often, the bond did work as intended, and it was beautiful to watch.

"Doesn't it?" He glared at her as if she insulted him. "Imagine spending your whole life bound to a man who is not the one for you."

"This is why mates can reject each other!" she argued, not knowing why she bothered with all this at all. It's not like she had a mate. But like any girl, she did sometimes imagine what it would be like if there was someone out there for her. She usually quickly erased those thoughts from her mind because, due to her line of work, she didn't consider herself worthy of such a gift.

"What's the point of this cosmic connection if they can break it any moment?" Fenrir clearly had been thinking about all this before, which almost made her giggle, but she suppressed the urge.

"They say it enhances the... experience!" She winked at him, watching how a little wrinkle deepened between his brows.

Taken aback at first, Fenrir's lips soon curled into a menacing smirk.

"Menace, if you are with the right man, there is no need to enhance the experience. You'd be barely managing it anyway."

"Oh, please." She rolled her eyes, but before she could retort further, Fenrir's hands snaked around her waist and pulled her against him roughly, their lips crashing against each other in a kiss she didn't expect. The best kind. Her dreams surfaced in her mind, making her forget the clever and snarky response she came up with as she returned his passion. Her body was shaking with desire for this man; his firm dominance did things to her that she'd never admit to out loud. The feverish kiss left her wanting more, and she almost winced when the rogue finally broke it and made her look at him, holding her face in his rough hands gently.

"Listen to me, Astrea," he said, his eyes filled with fire and determination. "From the moment I saw you for the first time, I knew you were the one for me. Maybe I didn't know how to express it or what to do with you, but I sure as hell didn't need some goddess telling me if this was right or not. I knew it, and deep inside, you know it too."

Her heart skipped a beat, a familiar pain rising inside her chest.

"N-no, I don't," she muttered, but that only deepened his smirk.

"Then why won't you leave?" He arched his brow, and she didn't find how to respond. It was rare for her to be lost for words when she needed them, yet with Fenrir, it happened more often than she liked.

Of course, she couldn't tell him that she couldn't leave empty-handed. She couldn't tell him he was her mark, and she didn't have any relevant information for Joran yet.

And these were the only reasons why she was still here. Nothing else. He was her target. Her target, her target, her target, her target. Maybe if she repeated it enough times, she would believe in it.

"Anyway, it's time to go." Fenrir stood up and offered her a hand. "We'll get breakfast in the city today. There is something else you need to see."

"Oh, really? What is it?" She smiled, happy to finally get off that awkward subject that made her breathing ragged. This mission would be the end of her.

"You'll see." He chose to remain mysterious. "We need to get out of here fast."

"Why?" Astrea blinked. The dawn was beautiful, and the hot air balloons peacefully soared in the skies, creating a picture of perfection.

"Because some of those couples up there will come down soon, and those breakups will be ugly," he scoffed. "The idea of mates is so deep in shifters' heads that they are going to ruin the good relationships they already have for the illusion that one day they would find someone more perfect for them."

"You really hate the mating system," she giggled, not realising how easily and naturally their fingers laced together as they walked.

"I do," he confessed with ease. "I already told you I don't need a mate bond to know what woman I want by my side."

"Well, maybe you want me because I *am* your mate." She let out a little laugh, teasing him and felt her cheeks heat. *What was that nonsense?*

"You are not," Fenrir replied as he kept walking, and it felt like a lightning bolt hit her. Why was he dismissing that idea so quickly? Almost as if it was impossible.

She slipped her hand out of his grip immediately.

"You already had a mate," she whispered, and he stopped.

"I did." He sighed almost painfully without looking at her. "It didn't end well."

This made her mood sour, but to her own surprise, she didn't remain silent when they returned to the car.

"Is she dead?" Her voice quivered, and she hated that she was demonstrating her weakness.

"They are dead, yes." Fenrir was clearly regretting sharing this information with her, but she couldn't stop. For some reason, it was painful. More painful than it was supposed to be with a target.

"They?" she breathed out. "As in more than one? You had several mates?"

"Yes." He looked like he was concentrating on driving, but she noticed how his hand muscles flexed while he grasped the steering wheel.

"Did you… love them?" This was a stupid question. Of course, he loved his mates. Everybody loved their mates.

"No." His response startled her. As always, he wasn't giving her any details. She wanted to smack the back of his head for that.

"Have you… loved anyone in your life?" she heard herself asking. Just when did she become such an emotional mess? It wasn't like her at all.

"I will answer that question when you make your decision." Fenrir avoided looking at her, and she was glad. Because even though she knew very well that the right decision for her mission would be to tell him what she thought he wanted to hear, she couldn't bring herself to lie and say she was going to stay here with him.

That treacherous thought of what her life here would be if she could stay revisited her, and she tried to mentally strangle it and shove it deep, deep down her mind where no one would ever find it.

⁂

THE BREAKFAST TURNED out to be two flatbreads filled with eggs, cheese and vegetables, brought from a line of colourful little kiosks in the central square. Astrea didn't mind, especially since it tasted delicious, and they could keep walking around the city together.

After spending most of her conscious life on an island with the same people around her, Astrea loved it here. Not to mention that Fenrir was always good company. Even though she'd rather die than admit it out loud.

She couldn't help but notice that today was especially busy, though. Energetic bustle filled the space as if the city anticipated something.

"Fenrir! You're here at last!" Salome moved her hand, surrounded by a crowd of warriors. Astrea's recognised some of them, and her body stiffened. There was something she didn't like about the witch. Salome always tried to demonstrate to her that she was only temporary here in Solace and in Fenrir's life. The worst thing about it was that she was never openly aggressive, but her words and actions always had a hidden meaning. And to top it off – most people were buying the act. Here in Solace, Salome was practically a saint.

The witch made her way to them and almost instantly draped her arm around Fenrir's, which made Astrea curse inwardly.

"I am sure Astrea will find her way back to the house; we have work to do today, remember?" She glanced at the King through her thick lashes, which would have been perfect for a mascara ad. The Dragonfly loathed that fact.

"Hey, Sal," she said just to annoy the witch. "I just got here and have no plans of going back but thank you for being so considerate."

"Considerate my ass," Nova growled.

"Astrea," Salome acknowledged her but quickly returned to what she was really interested in. "Fenrir, Bash can entertain her today. We are about to start."

The Dragonfly tensed. Was Salome trying to get rid of her?

"I brought Astrea here so that she could see everything and draw her own conclusions later," Fenrir retorted as Astrea continued to eat the rest of her delicious wrap to keep her mouth busy because quite a few swear words threatened to spill from her tongue right now.

"How... wonderful." The witch frowned. "So, you were serious about the 'no secrets' part? Is it wise, though?"

She fluttered those lashes again, but to Astrea's satisfaction, it had zero effect on the Rogue King.

"If you don't like it, you don't have to participate this month," he said to the woman, and her red lips pressed tightly into a thin line.

"No, that's fine." Salome shook her head. "How can I be missing when I am one of the Founders?"

Astrea rolled her eyes. The founder word, or the f-card as she called it in her mind, was thrown out by the witch a lot.

"I've never asked, but what exactly does that mean?" She decided that it was as good a time as any to finally find that part out. "So, you founded this city together? What about Raja?"

"I've founded nothing," Fenrir grunted, and Salome sighed.

"Then why—" Astrea could tell that the subject was annoying to him, and this was exactly why she wanted to poke it again.

"Of course you did!" The witch smiled at him. "Don't be shy, Fenrir. All these people are here because of you!"

"Yeah, Fenrir, don't be shy!" Astrea nudged him with her elbow as he gave her a menacing gaze, which she enjoyed to her heart's content.

"I am not the best storyteller out there," he said, nodding at Devoss, who stood next to the crowd and waved for him to join them. "Will you excuse me? Astrea, I will be back in a minute or so, and then we can start."

"Sure, coward," she whispered into his ear as she stood on her tiptoes, eliciting a low growl from him. Another thing she enjoyed doing. "Don't think that I will forget about this topic."

"Fenrir!" Devoss shouted, waving vigorously at his King. "Just a second, please."

"Excuse me." Fenrir left, leaving the two women alone.

"So, no Solace foundation story then!" Astrea chuckled, smirking at the witch. "Unless you are willing to fill the gap, of course." She winked at the woman, knowing that the mighty founder never spared her even a minute of her time to show her how insignificant she was.

"I'm sorry." Salome shrugged. "It's a very busy day for the Founders. I need to be over there with my people."

"Isn't your tribe your people?" Astrea pointed out, arching a brow.

"They are," the witch wasn't even looking at her anymore, "but the people of Solace are my family now."

"I regret you asked her." Nova imitated a gagging sound.

"That makes two of us," Astrea scoffed.

"But if you want to find out about the founding of Solace, hurry in there!" Salome sneered, and the Dragonfly didn't like that expression on her pretty face as she pointed behind her. "Old Magda is about to start her retelling. She was one of the first we took in and knows everything about us."

Astrea's gaze followed a crowd of children on the square near what looked like a mini stage. An old woman was arranging something behind the curtains, and very soon, Astrea realised that she was about to start a puppet show.

"That's a first for us," Nova snorted. *"Let's watch."*

Astrea bought herself a cup of coffee from a nearby kiosk and stood at the back, leaning against an arch and watched the kids getting quiet. The old woman put a hat next to her improvised platform, and a few people immediately threw a few coins and banknotes inside.

A navy-blue fabric with silver stars was used as a backdrop, and Astrea found it pretty.

Pleasant Eastern music started playing from an old stereo on the ground as the old woman expertly manipulated the strings of the puppet show, bringing her two first characters to life, a Lycan doll and a woman in a red dress.

"It's quite possible that we are going to hate this show," Nova pointed out.

"No shit!" Astrea inhaled through her nostrils but still decided to stay. Any information could be useful.

"Welcome, dear guests!" she said in a surprisingly resounding voice, grabbing the attention of everyone around. "It is the time of the month when we remember how this city was built. The place where even the loneliest of rejected souls can find peace and happiness. It all started when a special wolf and the kindest witch fell in love!"

"Say what?" Astrea spit her coffee back into the cup.

26. PUPPETS

*A*strea watched the show with a frown on her face.

"What in the witch's hallucinations is this?" Nova snarled.

"The best puppet show in town," the Dragonfly commented. *"Enjoy what that...bi—I mean, witch Salome wants us to see."*

"Long ago, deep in the desert, there lived a beautiful maiden unlike any other. For she was not only gifted with prominent beauty but also with great magical powers." The woman's eyes sparkled with mischief as she leaned into the puppetry, coaxing the children's imagination to new heights. There was no doubt that the doll in the red dress looked almost identical to Salome.

Astrea felt a twinge of revulsion rising in the pit of her stomach.

"Everyone in her tribe loved her, for she was the kindest and purest of souls."

"Oh, gods!" Nova snickered as Magda went on.

"However, one fateful night, a marauding group of rogues descended upon her home, burning it to the ground and forcing the beautiful maiden to flee. The maiden ran with all her might, tears streaming down her face, as the men relentlessly pursued her, eager to inflict their cruel intentions and mercilessly take her in turns right in the middle of the desert. For every one of them wanted a piece of this beauty."

"Someone should probably tell them that this children's show is not actually PG13," Nova commented dryly, and it took all Astrea's willpower not to roll her eyes.

In the meantime, the doll in the red dress was running away from men in black who were screaming about how gorgeous she was to her fleeing back.

"*Typical rogue behaviour,*" the wolf scoffed again.

"Just when the maiden was about to surrender," Magda continued in a grim voice, "a large wolf leapt out of the shadows, fiercely protecting her from imminent danger."

A doll that was supposed to represent Fenrir appeared, and Astrea giggled for noticing how poorly it was made.

"*Is that an old sock? I bet he hates this show,*" she commented while Nova chuckled profusely.

"As the morning sun emerged, the maiden gasped in shock as the wolf turned into a tall and handsome man before her eyes!"

"*She's probably the first witch who had never seen a werewolf before,*" Nova huffed another laugh. "*At least this is funny.*"

"But he was far from the kind gentleman she expected." Old Magda raised her index finger into the sky.

"*There is our Fenrir!*" Astrea cheered. Finally, there was a part of the story that looked believable.

"Rather, he was a lone wolf shifter with incredible magical powers who lived in solitary confinement in a cave and did not wish to see anyone. Only three brave warriors were guarding him day and night."

The blue backdrop with silver stars was pulled away, replaced by an embroidered cave on a piece of canvas fabric.

"Despite his reluctance to allow her to stay, the maiden persisted, refusing to leave his side. She stayed by the cave together with the warriors, waiting for the wolf to accept them. Day and night, they slept in tents by the entrance until one day, in gratitude for their steadfast love and persistence, the wolf rewarded them by using his magical abilities, creating new homes with great haste to house his friends. And guess who got the house first?"

"Salome!" children screamed in delight as Astrea rolled her eyes so hard it was almost painful. Did they listen to this piece of local folklore daily?

"Of course!" Magda grinned at her spectators. "Since he loved her the most, the maiden's house was built first, and it also was the biggest one. It still stands to this day, watching over the entrance to Solace."

"So, you're saying it's the furthest away from Fenrir's mansion?" Astrea couldn't help saying it out loud.

"Shh!" Some boy gave her a reproachful glare.

"What?" She looked at him innocently, quickly replacing that glance with a menacing grin. "He wanted to get rid of her so much that he was ready to build her house. Just saying."

The child's face contorted in confusion, and she almost felt guilty about her words. Almost.

"Word quickly travelled that a new city was established in the middle of a kingdom that perished, and its name was Solace. New people arrived, accepted by the maiden, the wolf and the three warriors. The community soon grew, melting the cold wolf's heart with their love and generosity, making him the protector of all the people who were once rejected. As the city grows in prosperity and graciousness, the wolf still protects it to this day. And the beautiful maiden, together with the three warriors, are always by his side."

The crowd burst into applause, and Astrea clapped a few times too. Simply out of respect for the elderly.

"Magda," one girl raised a hand, "is that story about Fenrir and Salome?"

"What do you think?" The old lady winked at her, implying that, of course, it was, and a wave of giggles erupted.

"Yes!"

"Of course!"

"They are perfect together!"

More and more praise of the happy couple sounded from every corner.

"*I am going to throw up!*" Astrea announced, ready to leave. Enough was enough.

"Are you done ruining the dreams of children?" Devoss appeared by her side wearing a dazzling emerald-green suit.

"Oh, one of the three great warriors, I assume?" She raised a brow at him, and the man's smile faded.

"Actually no," he shot an angry look at Magda, who reciprocated with narrowing her eyes, "the old hag doesn't like me and she cut me out of the story."

"Oh, I didn't cut you out!" Magda let out an annoyed sigh. "Here you are."

She pointed somewhere near the Fenrir doll's leg, and Astrea had to look closer to see a little dirty black fox sewn to it.

"I am not even gracing that with a response!" A frustrated sigh escaped Devoss' chest, punctuating his displeasure with the situation.

"I am just concentrating on what was important!" The old woman was already packing her little theatre in a box as kids dispersed in the crowds.

Devoss mimicked her as he draped his hand around Astrea's and pulled her away.

"Seriously, what are you even doing here?"

"I was just—" She couldn't find the right words to explain, still feeling the bitter aftertaste of Magda's story. "Learning the history of Solace's founding."

"That?" He almost choked. "Please, tell me you are not taking this seriously!"

"Okay," she arched her brow, "so, tell me then, is there anything between Fenrir and Salome? Were they ever together?"

"Why do you want to know?" Devoss' lips stretched in a sly smile. She was about to tell him to forget it when a familiar scent enveloped her.

"Yeah, why do you want to know?" Fenrir's breath burned the skin on her neck and next to her ear, making her whole body shudder with excitement.

"I—" Astrea was looking for the right words when the Rogue King laced their fingers together and tugged her gently to follow him.

"I'll take it from here, Dev." Fenrir led her back to the line of people on the other end of the square as she was cursing at herself inwardly.

He stopped before they reached the crowd and said, without looking at her.

"Nothing ever happened. She is a friend just like Kara. I have no other women in my life except for—"

His mates. Or that other woman he said he loved. He did love someone, after all.

"Except for you." His grip tightened, and her heart skipped a beat.

Target, target, target. Just a target.

"So, what is this?" Astrea asked, clearing her throat and pointing at the people. Warg and Kara were checking something on their wrists and then typing something on their tablets. After this check or whatever that was, they were greeted by the warriors Astrea remembered from the Fortress and given a red box.

"This is what I brought you here to see today," Fenrir replied, the corners of his lips rising slightly. "The newcomers."

"Newcomers?" Now that she was looking at the people with interest, she noticed three familiar faces almost instantly. The woman she saw back at Raja with twin girls. Fenrir spoke to them privately back then, and now they were here with red bracelets on their wrists. Just like everyone else in that line. "Is that—"

"I see you recognise them," the rogue chuckled.

"Back then you—"

"Gave them the passes." He nodded with a smug smile on their face. "Raja means border, Astrea. People who live there need to prove that they aren't rogues in the traditional sense. We keep watch over them and choose the worthy ones to live in Solace."

"What are the criteria?" she wondered, feeling warmth spreading over her chest. She was happy to know that the woman and the twins would live here now. Solace was a good place. She had to admit that.

"Basically, not to be a criminal or a psychotic murderer," Devoss snorted to her left, appearing behind her back with a cardboard box, full of the red smaller boxes they were distributing. "Wanna help?"

"Sure," she smiled, "what can I do, though?"

It was rare for her to be able to do anything that didn't require either killing or spying, so she was really happy to join them today.

"Each red box has a number corresponding to newcomers' bracelets. They tell you their number, and you find their box," Fenrir explained. "Be careful as their new life is in it. New documents, the keys from their new home, information they need for their new job. We try to think of everything."

"That's very kind of you." She had to admit that. "Not everyone would bother with such things."

"But someone should, and here we are," Fenrir replied, as if it was the simplest of matters.

They stood in front of tables with the red boxes, distributing them, and Astrea found peace in this little task. The people were thanking her as if she did more than just hand them something that others had prepared, but thanks to that she could tell how much this new life meant to them.

Deep inside, she could understand. After all, a new life was what she craved. Like a stealthy intruder, a treacherous thought slithered into the depths of her mind. What if she could have a new life right here in Solace? Next to Fenrir…

Astrea swallowed hard, chasing it away. It wouldn't work. The Teacher would search the whole desert for her. It would never be safe here.

"Thank you so much! I don't know how to thank you!" The woman she met in Raja was accepting her box from Fenrir, her eyes glistening with tears.

"I chose the perfect place for you." He smiled at them, and Astrea felt an unmistakable pang that tugged her heartstrings. Did he have to be this sweet?

"Anything would do!" The mother clutched the box and pressed it against her chest. "You have no idea how much it means."

"It's very close to the school," Fenrir added, and Astrea closed her eyes. This was too much. "There is a little garden attached to the house and a big playground within walking distance. You are going to love it here."

"Damn it," Astrea swore under her breath, pretending to look for something underneath the table. Anything to take her eyes off that man.

He was changing lives here while she plotted to kill him.

He was her target and usually she wouldn't think twice. Especially not when Niki's life was also on the line. But this... this was different. Fenrir wasn't a criminal mastermind or a corrupt politician.

She came here thinking that he was just a rogue, but in reality, this couldn't be further from the truth. Fenrir was anything but. The people of Solace relied on him. They loved him.

The whisper of doubt echoed in her mind, planting seeds of uncertainty deep inside her soul.

She couldn't do it.

She wouldn't be able to kill Fenrir.

"My number is 4837." A familiar voice brought her back to reality and, to her credit, Astrea didn't flinch when she saw the woman who was not supposed to be here.

27. OLD FRIENDS

*a*strea stiffened, carefully observing the woman in front of her.

The unexpected arrival triggered her, and now her brain was frantically trying to find an explanation as to why this person was here in Solace. The city was a secret no one knew about, after all.

Unless the secret was out...

"It's 4837," the Dragonfly repeated the number from her bracelet with a hopeful smile curling on her dry lips. A fake smile.

Astrea had to give it to her. Lenora was always one of the best at acting. Even now, she looked nothing like her usual bright self. Her long, medium-length ginger hair was dull and braided to one side, with a linen cloth thrown over to cover her face that looked sunburnt and sweaty. As if she had made it here on foot, which she definitely hadn't. All new arrivals were brought here by Fenrir's men on buses and in other cars.

The square brimmed with warriors and sentinels, indicating a high level of security, and Astrea wondered how on Earth Lenora managed to get in.

It was time to return to her real job from this wonderful hazy reality Fenrir almost made her believe in. She diligently went through all the boxes in front of her, starting with number four and finding the correct container. She really hoped that Lenora didn't kill anyone to get the place.

"Here." Astrea smiled as she had with anyone else in the long line and handed the red box to the woman, only now noticing that she had a big round stomach… as if she was pregnant.

"Thank you," Lenora accepted the box with trembling fingers. *Damn, she was good.*

"You are welcome. Everything you might need should be in there, including contact details in case we did miss something." Astrea dryly gave her the same line they gave to everyone.

"You have no idea how much it means to me." The Dragonfly tilted her head as if she was truly grateful for the help.

"How far along are you?" Astrea decided to keep up the façade.

"Almost seven months now." Lenora smiled again and then suddenly her face contorted, and the red box fell to the ground as she hissed from pain, which was imaginary for sure.

"Let me help!" Astrea charged to her, knowing that it was a signal. They had to talk one way or another.

"Is everything okay?" Fenrir asked as she knelt on the ground, and she waved him off with a little chuckle while her heart was pierced with needles of guilt.

"Yeah, just helping this lady. Maybe I can take her to her new house? Considering her condition—" The words felt like crushed glass in her mouth. It wasn't the first time she lied to Fenrir, but the taste was somehow bitter now.

"No need," he brushed her off, handing another red box to someone, "just get her to the cars over there and tell one of my men to take her. They were instructed to do what you say."

"Like a knife to the heart," Nova admitted. *"Does he have to be so sweet?"*

"Thanks." A strained, painful smile tugged at the corners of Astrea's mouth, and she took Lenora's box from her, playing along with the narrative of her being really pregnant and struggling. "Nice cover," she whispered so that only the two of them could hear. "You blend in impeccably here."

"That makes two of us," Lenora said sarcastically, but her face still transmitted exhaustion. "Look at you. We thought you failed the task and were a captive here, but here you are with the Rogue King ordering his men to obey you. Bravo, A."

"We?" Astrea's stomach churned. *Were the others here as well?*

"They are waiting near the border, where it's safer." Lenora confirmed her worst suspicions. "We have to meet tonight to talk about how to proceed. Not to mention that it's time for the Dragonfly Circle already."

"Yeah." Astrea nodded as her blood turned to ice. That damned ritual was what she hated the most. Not to mention that she couldn't forget what she learned during her spicy dinner with Fenrir. Nothing was what it seemed, but right now wasn't the moment to confront anyone.

"Meet us behind the North gate, but do not cross the barrier," Lenora went on, "I think I don't have to explain to you what would happen if you do."

"Have a safe delivery!" Astrea smiled at her as they reached the cars, and the other assassin grabbed her hand.

"I will never forget what you did." She beamed, but considering their circumstances, it sounded like a threat. Astrea knew very well that the other Dragonflies weren't her biggest fans. Especially now, when she had been deemed a traitor.

Back when she was held in the pit, they used to visit her from time to time to watch her torturous demise and humiliation. Or to perform the stupid ritual because while she was alive, they were bound together. Their laughs and harsh words after they were done still rang in her ears from time to time.

Astrea shoved those memories down and walked away without saying anything else. She couldn't waste time now, knowing she had hours to decide what to do.

Fenrir watched her as she returned to the tables, but Astrea pretended to be busy with the work.

Kara brought the next batch of red boxes, and Astrea threw herself into helping her. She was ready to do anything to avoid being close to Fenrir. Looking into his eyes and lying through her teeth was too much now.

This task... was different from everything else she had done before. She had a sense of deja vu. It was as if she was back in the North when she decided not to commit mass murder at a mating ceremony because the people she was supposed to kill deserved better.

Fenrir deserved better too.

"If you break his heart, I will break your neck," Kara said calmly as they both arranged the boxes in a specific order, and Astrea cast a questioning gaze at her.

"Excuse me?" She thought it might be a joke, but the grim expression on the other woman's face told her otherwise.

"You heard me." Kara didn't spare her a glance, continuing her work. "As my personal gift to you, I promise to make it quick."

Astrea needed a few seconds to process that.

"Okay. That's... generous," she snorted. "I'll keep that in mind for the future."

"Not the future," Kara shook her head, and the brown curls cascaded around her face, "I am talking about now. Think twice about what you are doing. I don't think—I don't think he can go through this again."

"You know what, I can't even get angry at that," the Dragonfly giggled. "Fenrir is lucky to have such friends as you. But let's not get carried away. We just met and—

"No," Kara stopped her. "I am not going to stay silent this time and do nothing. If you are not ready for him, it's best if you walk over that border and forget about everything."

"And if I don't?" Astrea didn't know why she asked that. Kara's words were reasonable.

"Then lives will get broken if you are not ready to fight for him," the woman said. "And not only yours."

"Got it." Astrea placed her hand on Kara's and squeezed it firmly.

SHE AVOIDED SEEING Fenrir for the rest of the day and excused herself from the dinner, getting ready in her room.

A plan was brewing in her head. A decent plan. A plan that would let her not kill him, and somehow, that felt like a win on its own.

"Are you sure about that?" Nova asked with a hint of sarcasm in her voice.

"It's the best shot I have," Astrea admitted bluntly, massaging her skin with one of the oils they provided for her. It smelled like a starry sky and sin, and there was some poetry in that, considering her plans for the night.

She had to look radiant for this.

"If he catches you, you are screwed," Nova pointed out, and Astrea's cheeks heated, making the wolf realise that this wasn't the worst-case scenario for them.

"I mean... if I absolutely have to, I am ready to take one for the team." The woman cleared her throat, making her wolf chuckle.

"Your sacrifice will not be forgotten!" Nova scoffed.

"You are saying it as if you are not going to be a part of it." Astrea rolled her eyes.

She knew one thing – under absolutely no circumstances would she kill Fenrir. However, the Teacher wouldn't be happy about it.

So, in an attempt to keep Joran satisfied, she knew she had to give him at least something. A sob story would be one thing, but to prove her so-called loyalty, she needed more.

"All we need is one bracelet off his wrist, and then we are good to go," she sighed.

Today she would get one of the bead bracelets whatever it cost her, and when she met with the other Dragonflies later, she would give it to them with a letter for the Teacher. As soon as that was done, she would throw them out of Solace through its border, making them forget everything. They will have a note to deliver the bracelet to Joran and no memories of what happened, which would give her some time to flee.

Hypothetically.

Hopefully.

She would have to leave a letter for Fenrir too, and then she had to think of how to get Niki out. Maybe if she got two bracelets, she could use one as a bargaining chip.

"It's time," Nova announced, and she exhaled heavily, the pressure of the situation getting to her.

Thankfully, this wasn't her first time. She was a professional. She could do this. She could pretend… although, with Fenrir, she wouldn't have to.

This would be their goodbye.

She was wearing a thin red backless dress, the luxurious silk fabric flowing like a whisper of desire against her skin. She hoped that the vibrant colour would be enough of a hint for Fenrir. She hoped that he would do the hard part for her because she didn't know if she could get through this on her own.

Her silvery hair was barely touching her shoulders, and she couldn't help curling it around her fingers as she walked, hoping that she didn't overdo it with the makeup.

At this time of the night, Fenrir was supposed to be in his greenhouse. That was a little habit of his she noticed during her time here. He spent hours there, tending to plants. And this was something she particularly enjoyed watching as she spied on him, learning everything there was to learn.

Tonight, however, she visited his office first, placing the letter in his top drawer. There was no chance he wouldn't find it there in the morning.

He was right where she expected him to be, watering some of the plants with a thoughtful expression on his face. She still couldn't believe that this was how the mighty Rogue King was spending his evenings.

"Knock-knock." Astrea smiled at him as she stepped inside, pretending to be slightly cold. After all, the temperatures were falling significantly during the night.

"Hey," Fenrir greeted her warmly and was about to turn his attention back to the greenery when he stopped in his tracks, taking her in.

28. THE GREENHOUSE

"*A*m I interrupting?" Her slender fingers traced along the delicate neckline of the dress.

"Looking like that, you can interrupt my funeral. I would surely rise from the dead just to have a better look." Fenrir's voice got huskier than usual as his gaze traced her every curve.

"Oh, you mean this old thing?" she giggled, curling her lips and stepping closer.

Fenrir threw the hose he had in his hand away, and it began curling and twisting, spraying glimmering droplets of water in all directions. Under the dull light of the lamps inside the greenhouse, they seemed like cascades of diamonds falling on their heads.

Laughter erupted from Astrea, but Fenrir remained calm, his eyes not leaving the beautiful woman in front of him, even for a fraction of a second.

"You totally did this on purpose!" she giggled and lifted her hands up, dancing in the improvised rain, her silk dress soaked and clinging to her skin.

In two abrupt steps, he was next to her, catching her by her waist and pulling her closer, their breathing ragged as her fingers ran up his chest and to his cheek.

"Why did you come here tonight, Astrea?" he asked her bluntly, but she knew she was not going to verbally answer that question. She simply couldn't.

"Kiss me," she ordered him firmly, and a low growl escaped his chest.

"Why are you here now?" he repeated the question.

"Fenrir," she cupped his face, "if you don't kiss me now, I will die."

Technically, it wasn't even a lie.

The words changed something in him. For a moment, she could swear she saw fear, but she brushed it off, not quite believing he cared about her that much already. It was a crazy infatuation, an illusion. What they had here was special but absolutely impossible. He had to know that.

She was repeating it to herself every day.

Impossible, impossible, impossible.

"I wouldn't allow that to happen," he whispered and greedily covered her lips with his.

For a moment, they were the only two people on the planet, finding themselves at a place where their hearts could no longer resist the pull towards one another as the rest of the world faded away. With every droplet that touched their skin, their tongues sought each other as if their lives depended on it. They needed each other like air, the unspoken energy drawing them closer and closer.

Astrea wasn't sure at first if it was the droplets that caressed her skin or Fenrir's hands; too many new sensations at once made her question if she was dreaming again. After all, this did remind her of her previous dreams about him. Passion overwhelmed them both as she heard his heart racing and her fingers laced into his hair to close the last tiny gaps between their heated bodies. She wanted to be one with him more than anything.

Their lips parted briefly to gulp some air, and his tongue trailed down her neck as his hands grasped her ass, lifting her up and sliding underneath the wet fabric clinging to her silky skin.

"Touch me," she begged, and although everything inside him told him not to, he hadn't been with her for too long. He wanted her, needed her, he waited for her, and she was finally here again, almost begging for him to do everything he wanted to do with her.

Fenrir brought her to a wooden table with new empty pots he had received a few days ago, and with one sweep of his arm, they all found themselves broken on the ground.

He placed her on the wooden surface gently because she was the most precious thing in the whole world. His eyes glowed red as he watched his beloved woman arch her back for him, hard nipples poking through wet silk, teasing him.

"Fenrir!" His name on her lips was always his weakness, and he captured them once again as his hand slid between her thighs, searching for the underwear... which wasn't there.

"Menace, you little minx!" he snarled into her mouth, knowing that he wouldn't be able to restrain himself for long.

"Please." She tugged at his shirt, ripping the buttons away to touch his skin, too. His scars radiated with a heat she couldn't explain. "Fenrir—"

His fingers slipped across her core, one finding its way inside while the other expertly circled around her clit, creating exquisitely torturous friction.

She tried to push her hips against him, but he held her in place, letting her know that he was now in control.

Astrea bit her lip painfully, trying not to scream from frustration, but when her nails dug into his skin, he was the one who lost control first, and a loud growl echoed through the space surrounding them.

Fenrir pulled the straps of her dress down, yearning for more of her flesh. His lips found her breasts, teasing them, caressing them, devouring them... all while his fingers found the rhythm which made Astrea's body respond to him.

She clenched around him, unable to form words now that the pleasure built up at the bottom of her stomach.

"Fen... rir—" she panted, not knowing what to expect next.

"Let go for me," he told her in a calm but commanding tone, which tipped her over the edge, and she screamed as he worked her through her release, watching her come undone as the droplets of water still sprayed over her exposed body.

"You are the most fucking beautiful thing in this world, Astrea," he stated as if there couldn't be any objections to it.

She watched him towering over her. So strong, so beautiful... with eyes full of love.

"More," she whispered, although it wasn't exactly what she wanted to say.

She felt that there had to be something else. Something familiar and something that would make those eyes full of desire and sadness lose the latter part.

But she couldn't say it.

The bracelets glimmered in the lights of the greenhouse and she came back to her senses. This... whatever this was, was the most wonderful experience of her life, but this wasn't why she was here today.

Although she was happy that she would have this memory of him in the future, her plan had to be executed today. For her own life and for Niki's.

However, it wasn't the time to stop yet.

"More." She curled her arms around his neck, claiming his lips again. His whole body was as hard as stone and almost unbearably hot...

"Sorry, Astrea," he exhaled heavily and distanced himself from her, his hardness evident through the fabric of his jeans. "Not like this—"

That unexpectedly hurt her. More than she could have imagined.

He wanted her, she could tell this much, but then why was he rejecting her?

Fenrir turned away, and she jumped off the table, quickly adjusting her dress to cover herself again as he caught the hose and switched the water off.

The greenhouse lost its magic as she stood in a puddle, not sure where her shoes were.

"Why?" she asked him straight because she needed to know his reasons more than anything.

"Because you didn't say you would stay with me." He turned to look at her, wet hair to his shoulders framing his beautiful masculine face. "You didn't say that you chose me."

Astrea pursed her lips. There were already enough lies and secrets between them. She didn't want the lies to be his last memory of her, so she said nothing, and a sad smile graced his face as his eyes seemed to lose their colour.

"See you tomorrow, Astrea," he said and turned away to leave when she caught up with him.

"Fenrir, wait!" she gasped desperately as she cut one of the strands on his wrist with her sharp claw that she managed to hide almost instantly. Beads scattered around the room as she managed to slide one more strand off and hide it in the secret pocket of her dress without him noticing.

He didn't say anything, and she swallowed uncomfortably.

"I am so sorry," she whispered.

"It's all right," he brushed his large palm over her cheek, cupping it gently. "I'd never hold it against you."

His words felt like a knife through her heart.

"Fenrir," she called his name again, not sure why. What could she say now? It was time to go to that meeting already.

"Go, Astrea." He turned away and she couldn't find it in herself to torture him further.

She ran to her room as fast as she could, squeezing the damn bracelet in her palm and hoping that it was worth what she had just done.

It was for him, too. And for Niki. She had to do it for them both. It was for the greater good...

But why was it so hard to convince herself?

"Let's go," Nova suggested dryly. *"It's best not to be late."*

Her wolf was right, and although Astrea felt like her heart was breaking with every step she made, she kept on walking.

The days she stayed here were enough to learn this place and know how to avoid the guards, Warg being the toughest of them all. He circled around the gardens day and night, so Astrea had to choose to climb the mountain that served as one of the walls instead. Many would find that impossible, but she managed to do it just fine. Though it made her way to the Northern border longer, it was safer.

There weren't too many buildings next to the border, and the ones that stood here were mostly empty as they were to be used in case the city was under attack. With the secrecy of the location and the protective barrier, this wasn't much of a problem, so when Astrea saw four figures on one of the rooftops, she knew that they were her colleagues.

"It's past 3 a.m. already," Lenora scolded her when she got upstairs to meet them. "You are late."

"And you have already delivered the baby, I see! Congrats! Motherhood suits you," Astrea retorted with a smirk.

"Seriously, you have no shame, Astrea!" Adisa growled, crossing her arms over her chest. "How quickly you forget the months you spent in the pit below our feet. You're already talking back to us again."

"Excuse me?" Astrea arched her brow up. "Should I talk differently to you after how you acted during those months?"

"You killed Emma!" Dominica snapped, her full lips trembling. Astrea had no snappy retort for her. Dominica used to be Emma's ward. They had a connection similar to what she shared with Niki. She was probably the only one Astrea didn't expect different behaviour from. The youngest Dragonfly had her reasons to hate her.

"She tried to kill me first," Astrea admitted dryly.

"And we should believe you because... what?" Adisa let out a snort, brushing her hand through her short curly hair as her ebony skin glowed, reflecting the moonlight.

"Of course, she wanted to kill you! She probably realised you were a traitor! She had to at least try and stop you!" Dominica narrowed her brown eyes, her black outfit unapologetically embracing her generous curves. If she could kill Astrea here and now, she absolutely would.

"Ladies, we can leave all this for later." Lenora took the role of the leader.

The role that was always Astrea's. They were letting her know the new place she had here.

"Yes, I have some news you should pass to the Teacher." Astrea prepared to distract them, but the redhead raised her hand, motioning for her to stop.

"Later," she said in a strange tone, and they all exchanged discreet looks. As if they couldn't wait for something important.

"I think we should—" Astrea was testing her luck again.

"Dragonfly Circle first!" Lenora interrupted her. "What if we are attacked soon? We need to recharge our powers."

Astrea hated this. Recharge wasn't the word she would use for the ritual.

The snake tattoo on her neck tingled for the first time in a while, making her shiver. She was probably too close to the border.

Just then, she remembered Fenrir's words again...

29. MOON GODDESS

*A*SGARD

Fenrir had been waiting at least two hours since the guards announced his arrival in the wing designated for the Moon Goddess.

He wasn't going to rush it, though. It was nighttime, and she was probably busy with her work. Once again, he couldn't believe his own luck. No Asgardian would be in his way to speak to Selene. Most were probably drunk or asleep by now, his own father included.

"Please, follow me." A warrior in golden armour bowed to him and led the way through the white marble halls, sheer curtains swaying gracefully in the breeze. It was funny how the guests made this familiar place seem so foreign and ethereal.

She was standing on a large balcony, looking at the moon in the sky, her pale blue hair cascading down her silver open-back dress. Selene didn't look any older than her daughter, yet when she turned to meet his gaze, Fenrir saw countless memories etched across the expanse of time. The Moon Goddess was an old soul. There were no doubts about that.

"My apologies for interrupting your evening." He bowed his head in respect, and the woman's lips curved slightly. To his relief, she radiated warmth.

"No need for formalities, my boy." Selene stepped closer. "You know I have a soft spot for you. Why did you want to see me?"

This was a good start, yet still, Fenrir couldn't help but swallow nervously. One wrong word, and he could ruin it all, losing Astraea forever.

"I don't want to seem disrespectful," he started, immediately cursing himself inwardly. He didn't want to look like a barbarian to her, but it wasn't like he was taught how to handle such matters. Most of his education came from Tyr, and Tyr only knew war.

"You are not. Come in." Selene walked to a long table, gesturing for Fenrir to join her. A servant moved a silver chair for her and then helped to arrange the fabric of her dress so that she looked regal. Something deities here in Asgard didn't bother to do.

The Asgardian took his seat in front of her, and immediately goblets of wine and all kinds of snacks appeared on the table before them out of nowhere.

"Thank you." He took one of the goblets and tasted the drink that was as sweet as mead yet so different.

"It's my and Astraea's favourite." Selene also took a sip, closing her eyes just for a moment, enjoying herself. When she opened them, her interested gaze fell on her guest. "I am glad that you visited. This is a safe space for you, my boy. Actually, I wanted to speak to you too."

This was a pleasant surprise. Maybe his father was right after all, and he had a shot because of who he was. For once, being a wolf shifter was playing in his favour. Rumours had it that Selene not only loved wolves, she was creating shifters similar to him, sending them into Midgard, the human realm. Of course, he didn't know which of the rumours were true.

"You probably know that I was helping Astraea with her garden." Fenrir was choosing each word carefully, not wishing for the woman in front of him to misunderstand what they were doing. He teased Astraea and was crazy about her but didn't want his actions to taint her gleaming reputation. He wanted her to become his wife and had nothing but respect for her.

"I had no idea." The Moon Goddess looked slightly surprised, but then the corners of her lips tilted upwards. "Well, it may be for the best. After all, I wanted to ask you to spend more time with my daughter."

Fenrir's heart skipped a beat. Maybe this was all a dream, and he was about to wake up. He hated to lift his hopes up for nothing, but his dream was now so close.

"It would be my honour." He cleared his throat, unable to hold back a smile. "Astraea and I—"

"She will need help once she lives here," the Moon Goddess continued, sadness lacing her words. "I hate to be separated from her. I've already lost so many people dear to me—" she hesitated briefly, lost in thought.

"Never mind. After Astraea gets married, she will stay here in Asgard, and she will need a friend on her side. You can be that friend, Fenrir."

The realisation hit him so hard that it felt like a dagger pierced his heart and was twisting, twisting, twisting in his chest, enveloping him in agony.

Friend. The Moon Goddess wanted him to be Astraea's friend.

Which also meant she had someone else in mind as her husband.

"I will always be her friend," he said dryly, but Selene was not in a hurry to grace him with a smile. She could feel that something was wrong.

"I am glad—" Her discerning gaze studied him cautiously.

"But her and I, we are more than friends," he announced boldly, his resounding voice echoing through the marble room.

There was a hint of puzzlement written over the goddess' face.

"I—" He was about to explain, but she lifted her hand to stop him, all pleasantness drained from her features.

"How dare you imply such things!" She stood up from her seat and clenched her fists tight. Like any deity, she was a warrior, and now he saw it.

He knew that this was the most important moment of his life. Here and now, his fate was about to be decided.

"I know why you brought Astraea here," he started, confidence growing with each second. *He would fight for her if he had to.* "Your realm is dying, and you hope to unite with Asgard to prevent it."

The goddess watched him for a few moments, not saying a word to confirm it but not denying it either.

"This is the reason you want her to marry an Asgardian." Fenrir did not allow his voice to tremble. It was all or nothing. "You need a powerful alliance to defend yourselves. I-I can be that Asgardian for you."

"Oh, you foolish boy." She sighed and massaged the bridge of her nose. "If this is how you see this, you will not bring her anything good. Just forget what we talked about. Let's pretend this meeting never happened. And don't go to see her in that garden ever again."

She was about to walk away when he gave her a reply she didn't ask for.

"No." His voice was like steel. Unyielding. Almost a threat.

And Selene felt that because now she was glaring at him.

"No?" She let out a little cruel laugh. "Boy, I think you are forgetting who you are talking to. This is not up for negotiation."

"I am sorry if I come across as rude." Fenrir stood up too. "This is not my intention. But Astraea and I have something special. I—We are in love. I want only the best for her, and I am ready to fight to the death for her if I have to. Her light awakened something in me that I had no idea was even there and—"

"This is a nightmare!" The Moon Goddess covered her face with her hands.

"At least think about it," Fenrir offered, ready to drop to his knees and beg her. "I know I'm not the perfect candidate for—"

"Do you?" Now Selene was mocking him, an icy smile stretching her lips. "I don't think you understand what you're doing at all! You don't understand what kind of place you have here."

"I fully understand," he said, knowing far too well how the others treated him. "But you love wolves, and I happen to be a wolf deity myself. There will never be anyone bigger or stronger than me. I thought that maybe—"

"Stop it!" the goddess screamed, stomping her foot. The moonlight that illuminated everything inside became duller. "Even talking to you about it can bring us trouble!"

"I am ready to give any oath to prove my intentions are pure!" he insisted, not ready to give up.

"An oath is not going to help here!" Selene was getting angrier. "Who do you think you are to ask for her hand? She is the Goddess of Stars, for goodness sake! Do you know how pure her blood is? How strong is she going to be when she reaches her full potential? She will control the stars, Fenrir! And *everything* is made out of stars! Even you and me. What do you think someone like you can offer my daughter?"

"Protection, love, happiness." He stated what was most important in his opinion, but it only made her laugh.

"Protection?" She threw her head back laughing, while exhaustion and anger pulsed through her. "If she is with you, you will only put a target on her back!"

"Didn't you want me to be her friend just now?" he growled, anger surging through him.

"I wanted you to be her guard!" Selene snapped. "It's an honour for someone like you!"

"Someone like me? Am I not the same as your favourite creations?"

"The same?" The Moon Goddess let out a cold, heartless laugh, not caring that her words would stab him in the heart. "Don't compare yourself to my wolves, boy! I created my werewolves, carefully selecting humans to be rewarded with the honour of hosting an immortal soul and a beast to go with it to allow them to protect themselves. Yes, they are wolves, but they are also my fallen brothers and sisters, my loyal comrades who went to war on our side. While you… you are an abomination created by your father for fun! You call yourself a god? I doubt that even your father is one! What does that make you? A self-proclaimed deity! A demon! A monster! Never compare yourself to my werewolves ever again!"

It felt as if she had slapped him in the face over and over, but at the same time, it also explained a lot. The important piece of information finally sunk in and explained something Fenrir couldn't understand before. For weeks he thought about why Asgardians treated these deities from the other realm like dear guests and not potential rivals. Just a couple of hundred years back, they would wipe them out and then laugh about it at a feast. Asgardians were killing their own with ease, let alone outlanders. Now he finally knew what could cause such a change.

If Selene found a way to preserve the souls of falling Olympians, even in such a questionable way, this could be her bargaining chip here. This was why she was the one to come here. This was why Odin did not destroy these rivals, using their weakness. It became clear that he would want to know such an invaluable secret and pay for it with whatever Selene wanted.

After all, despite being the most powerful divine creatures, the gods of Asgard could still be killed. Even Odin was familiar with the pain of losing the ones he loved.

This complicated everything because there was no place for him in that plan of theirs.

"Tell me what to do!" For the first time, emotions slipped into his tone, betraying him. "Name your price. I will do whatever you need from me. I will fight for your realm; I will kill—"

"Just leave!" Selene replied, exhaustion overtaking her. "They hate you here. You can scare them, but she will never be safe with you; she will never be respected if she is your wife. It's not what I want for my daughter."

"But she will be happy," he argued his case, knowing deep in his heart that it was true. He often watched Astraea while she was with the others and could tell she was only at ease beside him. When they were together, she was funny and relaxed, a real alive woman and not the beautiful perfect statuette she was during the day while performing her duties in front of other deities. He was the only one who saw the real her.

"She will be happy with the one I chose for her," the Moon Goddess said, but for the first time, she did not sound so sure anymore.

"You were in love before," he decided to use his one and only leverage, "you know how precious that is. Not everyone gets to experience it! Will you take this away from her? No matter how safe and powerful she is, she would despise you forever if you broke us up!"

The silence between them grew heavy, and he was afraid to ruin the fragile success of his words.

"Just… just think about it," he offered. "You don't have to make the decision now. Deep in your heart, you will know what is right."

"Fine," the woman muttered. "You can leave now."

He decided to take this little win and, with a curt bow, turned on his heel and rushed to the Glowing Garden, where he knew Astraea was waiting for him.

AFTER A SLEEPLESS NIGHT he spent with Astraea, holding her in his arms and kissing under a blossoming glowing tree for what seemed like hours, Fenrir refused to change anything in his schedule. He had to act as he usually did so as not to draw unwanted attention.

He had made only one exception which was a strategic choice.

"I am surprised I don't have to drag you to the feast this time!" Tyr clapped his shoulder warmly and gestured for the servants to bring them mead. "And you even dressed for the occasion!"

"Father said I need to make an effort," he lied, searching for the Goddess of Stars with his eyes and finding her in the same company as usual. Freyja, Vidar and other bright stars of Asgard were surrounding her.

He wanted to join them and was already on his way when his gaze met Freyja's, and she immediately stood up with a goblet in her hand.

"I think it's about time for a gift exchange!" she announced loudly, and the others grew quiet.

30. GIFTS

*F*reyja was the most respected deity after Odin, so when she spoke, no one dared to say a word, giving her their full attention.

"I have prepared something for you, sweet child." She beamed at Astraea, eliciting a nervous smile from her.

"I have to apologise," the starry goddess blushed slightly, "my present for you is not yet finished—"

"Nonsense, my dear!" Freyja smiled at her. "I visited your garden this morning, and it is lovely. My dragonflies only want to live there now. Speaking of which—"

The goddess lifted her hand, and her fingers emanated a golden glow which slowly materialised into a beautiful golden dragonfly. The delicate creature shimmered with ethereal radiance as it fluttered its wings.

Freyja pivoted to face Astraea, and the magical insect flew off her fingers, gliding elegantly through the air. As if drawn by an unseen connection, it lingered in the air next to the Goddess of Stars as if waiting for something.

Fenrir stiffened, watching Astraea offer the magical creature her palm, the dragonfly landing gracefully at once. The colour of its glow changed almost instantly to a silvery one, and the wolf's breathing hitched, recognising Astraea's star magic.

"I didn't have to think too long for my gift to you, child." Freyja's face radiated joy. "My dragonflies chose you themselves, because you are so similar. They belong to two worlds, and so will you, child, starting today."

Astraea looked at him, aching sorrow reflecting in her eyes as Freyja continued her speech. They never spoke of why she was in Asgard. This was the one and only topic off-limits when they were together.

"They are born in water but live in air. Their souls are with me in Asgard while their lives are in the human realm. They are hunters and symbols of power in their delicate bodies. Just like you, Astraea." A kind smile graced Freyja's lips. "And just like you, they can fly against any storm. The dragonfly I gave you today will be your protection and strength for as long as your soul exists. It's my pledge to you and a symbol of a new beginning as I am sharing my magic with you. Here in Asgard, you will be loved and accepted by all. May my gift always accompany you in your new life."

"Thank you." Astraea's eyes filled with tears as she bowed her head in a grateful gesture, not adding anything to it. The new kind of magic was surging through her, but Fenrir wondered if it would be of any use to her, considering that her future power was predicted to be greater than Freyja's.

The Asgardians erupted in jubilant cheers, and he hoped it would be the end of this, but when the Moon Goddess rose from her seat, slowly walking to the centre of the hall, an unsettling sensation crept up his spine.

"Sharing magic is very generous." Selene smiled at Freyja, who was now taking her seat. "I have a gift too. Although I am no Goddess of Love, I know a thing or two about it."

Approving murmurs echoed through the room.

"You already know what I have been busy with lately." She smiled, her voice carrying a celestial melody to it. "My fallen brothers and sisters of Olympus, as well as my loyal subjects, have received a new life in the human realm. This is something I am offering to the Asgardian deities. But there is more."

No one dared to speak or make any noise, and Fenrir realised how important this was to everyone present today.

Gods were dying. Asgardian gods were prophesied to be wiped out at the end of days, and a hint of desperation lingered in the air for as long as he had lived here. They would do anything to get a second chance.

"My werewolves have proven to be of pure hearts, and I found the best reward possible for their loyalty," Selene went on. "An ultimate gift of a mate bond." She accentuated the words.

A wave of gasps erupted, and Fenrir's heart started racing like crazy. A sense of foreboding washed over him, his instincts suddenly on high alert.

"I have to say," Freyja interjected, "at first, I was reluctant about this. After all, love is love. You either feel it, or you don't. You cannot fake it. But when Selene showed it to me, even I had to admit it was perfect."

"The mate bond is given to two souls perfect for each other, two souls that can work as one. When they find each other in what you call Midgard, they will recognise each other at once," Selene explained. "No mistakes will be made; they will know they belong together because they will experience a pull like no other. When mates find each other, they still have a choice, though. If they choose to embrace the bond and mark each other, it will become more than just a physical attraction. Together they will grow stronger, the emotional connection and understanding between true mates will transcend time and space. They will feel each other's pain and joy, understand each other's feelings and emotions. They will be able to trust unconditionally, knowing the other person will always be on their side. When nourished, the mate bond strengthens them, making them and their heirs more powerful."

"I don't know about the rest of you, but I am sold!" someone joked in the crowd, and approving chuckles rippled through the room.

"Two mates can always rely on one another." Selene raised her hand, and moonglow appeared on her palm. "Together, they can achieve anything. This is why I think there is no better gift to my daughter, who is to be wed here in Asgard, than this sacred connection."

For a second, Fenrir hoped that the Moon Goddess would give the mate bond she talked about to them, but when his eyes locked with Astraea's, he saw the colour drain from her face as panic surged through her.

"Vidar and Astraea, accept my gift to you," Selene said, and Fenrir felt a thousand blades piercing his heart. He wanted to scream, but no sound came out.

Before he could do anything, the moon magic coalesced and flew to the woman he desperately loved– and to her betrothed.

The glow reached the couple, enveloping them in its warm embrace of celestial energy, making Astraea's lips part from the shocking realisation that she was now bound to another. She cast an accusatory glare at her mother, but at the same time, two strong arms possessively wrapped around her shoulders.

Vidar seemed pleased with the situation, and Fenrir had never seen him like this before. The way he looked at her, the way he touched her. The wolf in him couldn't stand that silent prick.

"We thank you for such a generous gift," he spoke for the two of them, and Astraea visibly shuddered as his thumb drew circles on her bare flesh.

"This requires more mead," Odin let out a laugh, which everyone gladly supported.

A loud growl escaped Fenrir, immediately drawing everyone's attention. Tyr appeared by his side at once, shoving a goblet into his hand with a nervous false smile playing on his lips.

"Skol!" The God of War shouted as loud as he could, and others joined him, roaring in a cheer that muffled another growl from Fenrir. Asgardians did not spare any more attention on him.

Music filled the air with enchanting melodies, and the truce celebration began, with dozens of deities surrounding Astraea and Vidar to congratulate them.

He couldn't even see her, his whole body shaking with anger.

"Don't look in her direction," Selene told him as she passed him, heading for the exit. For some reason, the woman that had just crushed his heart and laid ruin to his life didn't want to stay and celebrate her success. "She knows her role; she will play it well. It's done. Whatever you had—it is over now."

"You just made her the unhappiest woman in all the realms." Fenrir gritted his teeth, clenching his fists so hard that his knuckles turned white. "And she will never forgive you for that."

"What would you know?" the Moon Goddess sighed heavily and turned away. "You are just a couple of hundred years old. That is nothing compared to the millennia I have existed. Time cures any pain. One day, Astraea will forget you and forgive me. One day, all this will just be stardust scattered under her feet. Unimportant and forgotten."

The words stung him, but he wouldn't show it.

"Go, Fenrir." Tyr squeezed his shoulder painfully, trying to bring him back to reality. "Don't create trouble for anyone. It will not end well."

Their eyes met, and Fenrir wondered how many Asgardians knew about all this because Tyr seemed informed enough. And so did Freyja. They were the main players, and he couldn't help but wonder if everyone knew but him.

After he left the hall, he walked for a long time until he found himself right next to what in his mind was their place now, an agonising tightness gripping his chest.

He couldn't enter the Star Garden anymore. That magical place made him believe in fairy tales, and now he was back to his harsh reality.

He would never have someone like her.

He had to leave.

"Fenrir!" His breath caught in his throat as he heard the familiar timbre of his beloved's voice, unexpected but so desperately longed for. He turned to look at her on his shaky legs, just the sight of her instantly bringing his strength back.

"Astraea," he muttered, lost for words. What could they tell each other now?

She was so beautiful today in her intricate shimmering gown. So mesmerising that it was almost painful to look at her.

The dream that could have been...

"I begged her to stop this," she said after the silence between them went on too long, tears streaming down her divine face. "I-I can't do this! Not with him, not with anyone but you!"

"What about the mate bond?" he asked, hating how weak he sounded.

"It's just some tingles from a man I do not know and do not wish to know!" She let out a desperate sob, and more tears, glistening like stars in the sky, rolled down her cheeks and fell to the ground, giving the grass under her feet a slight glow. "Fenrir... my heart is already taken by another!"

She looked at him with pain and guilt in her eyes, and he couldn't take it anymore. If she still wanted him, he wouldn't be saying no to that. He would fight for her over and over, as many battles as it took. Anything for them to be together.

"Don't cry." He stepped forward and pulled her against his chest, gently wiping her cheeks with his fingers. "You will not cry because of this. No one makes this choice for us! I choose you! I love you! And no one in any of the realms can tell me that I don't have a right to feel that! You are the only one who can reject me—"

His voice broke. It was the first time he couldn't control his emotions like that.

"I will never reject you!" She shook her head, her fingers digging into his tunic. "I love you too."

He could hear her heart pounding in her chest as relief washed over him. This wasn't one-sided; he hadn't imagined everything in his head.

Their emotions intertwined and mirrored in each other's gazes, the air between them crackling with tension. Fenrir laced his hand into her luminescent hair, bringing her closer and covering her lips with his. Gentle at first, it grew into a whirlwind of passion in seconds. The need to possess her, to hide her from everyone else, was so immense that he couldn't fight it anymore.

He broke the kiss, looking around and searching for where to take her. They needed privacy which was so hard to obtain.

"There is a temple nearby," he told her hoarsely. "We can speak there—"

He shifted into a wolf, making himself as small as possible so that she could climb on his back. She did so without him urging her, as if she could read his mind. He raced to the hill where an abandoned temple of Frigg stood. Years ago, Odin built her a new one close to the palace, so Fenrir knew this one would be empty.

Astraea had to grasp his fur to stay atop of him, but it felt amazing for both of them. By the time they got there, it had started raining, and when he shifted back, catching her in his strong arms, Astraea was trembling from the cold.

"I'll get you warm, and we will talk," he promised as they entered the building. He carefully placed the woman on her feet and clicked his fingers to make every candle and fire pit burn to illuminate and heat the room. Fire was his second nature.

He wanted to search for something dry for her to wear when she grasped his wrist, stopping him from walking away and making him look at her with surprise.

"I only need you to get warm," she said, her eyes searching for his approval. "And... I don't want us to talk. I want you, Fenrir."

"Your wish is my command." He lowered his head and kissed her again.

FENRIR WAS LYING on the altar after they made love for hours, caressing her soft, warm body on top of his and still not believing how happy he was.

She was his. She had chosen him and belonged to him now.

"I love you," he repeated their new favourite phrase again and kissed the top of her head, watching how her lips curled happily in response and listening to her fluttering heart.

Astraea lifted her head to meet his gaze and was about to say something when the doors to the shrine burst open...

PRESENT

Astrea watched the three women cautiously. The anticipation and excitement they tried to suppress was building on their faces. It was undeniable, and something was fundamentally wrong with that. Mostly because now they looked as if they were happy to see her, and that couldn't be further from the truth.

"We need to form the Dragonfly Circle now because danger lurks every-where here," Lenora insisted as they took their usual positions.

"It's been a while." Adisa stretched her neck and offered Astrea her hand, already holding Dominica's. "Don't look at me like that. Out of all of us, you probably need it the most, A."

The corners of Dominica's lips tilted upwards, and a sense of unease welled up within Astrea, causing a knot to form in her chest.

Something was off.

"I heard Fenrir telling his witch Salome that they could sense magic used here in Solace," she lied through her teeth, making it sound like she didn't care much. "I think it's best if we do nothing and just discuss the job we have."

"Nonsense!" Lenora growled, baring her teeth slightly. Almost a threat...

"Ladies, let's just do it and be done with it," Adisa purred, her eyes shifting to its cat-like vertical pupils.

"Fine." Astrea shrugged, pretending to give up. "Let's do it since you all need it so much."

31. RITUAL

*A*strea took their hands, preparing herself for what was to come. She never liked that ritual but standing in a circle with these women was simply revolting.

The plan formed in her mind very quickly, but at the same time, she couldn't help but slightly shiver at the thought that they were using her all these years.

Fenrir told her that the snake tattoo was suppressing the other one.

Well, she only had two of those. And why the hell would her dragonfly tattoo need suppressing if it always needed recharging?

Unless it didn't… unless everything she knew about it was a lie.

But why would the Teacher lie to her?

"Many reasons, actually," Nova had to admit.

"Maybe because you aren't exactly a Firstborn?" Fenrir asked her once, and this should have been her best clue. Too bad she was always too busy with other things. He tried to tell her, but she didn't listen. Was Fenrir the only one who was honest with her?

Now that she was thinking about it, all the other Dragonflies were always eager to have the joining ritual. At the same time, this wasn't something she enjoyed. Not once. Not ever.

It made her feel so weak afterwards, but she hated to admit it in front of others because back when she was just a lost kid, Joran insisted it was because she was intoxicated with the power that surged through them. She didn't want to appear struggling with what the new Dragonflies thrived on, trying not to look bad.

She was an idiot.

Lenora's fingers laced with hers, and Astrea began to feel the tiny sparks as their connection started forming. They didn't need to say any particular words or perform any actions other than creating an unbreakable circle. Their dragonfly tattoos were doing most of the job from the moment they were tied and in the correct positions. The glow illuminated the rooftop they stood on with its soft silvery light. The glow that was spreading out from her. Not them.

Before today, Astrea was convinced that it was because she was their leader.

She knew better now.

From the corner of her eye, she could see the bliss on the other women's faces. However, the pure ecstasy of their connection was only on their side. She felt weaker with each passing second. Like leeches, they drained her, drowning in the power that wasn't theirs.

Astrea could feel something warm and vital slipping out of her through her bloodstream and to her fingertips, entering the Dragonflies who held her hands, clenching to her as if she was their air.

Was this why she always felt nauseous while everyone else was invigorated? Did they drink her energy and make her weak?

Memories started surfacing in Astrea's mind. There were so many things that she saw in a different light now! Emma, Lenora, Adissa and Dominica were always ready for the joining ritual as if it was their drug of choice.

Meanwhile, the best Astrea ever felt was during the Luna Trials when she had a break from them. And then Emma appeared to "charge" her, which only resulted in headaches and little help.

Afterwards, when she tried to flee from the Firstborn following her betrayal, knowing they would want to kill her, she burnt her tattoo, trying to prevent Joran from tracking her with its help. That slowed her down significantly and eventually resulted in her being caught.

However, when she was thrown into the silver pit, she lasted there for longer than she was supposed to. And although some of her wounds couldn't heal because she was surrounded by silver, her dragonfly tattoo did. Was this what helped her last there for months? Was the dragonfly tattoo giving her strength?

All the signs were always there!

Astrea's whole body went rigid. They called her a traitor, but who was the first to betray their trust?

Did they know? She observed them all, absorbing her energy, not a tint of shame on any of their faces. They loved it.

Of course, they knew. She was the only one in the dark. They probably thought she was a fool, and she couldn't disagree with it now. They all played her well.

Anger made her blood boil, obscuring her vision as she clenched her "teammates" hands tighter.

"Stars burn—" a voice echoed in her head. Her own voice.

She never said these words before, but they sounded so familiar.

It was so hard to breathe; her anger was overwhelming. They wanted power? She would give them power! So much that they wouldn't be able to handle it!

Light coursed through her and was released in a blinding wave that distorted the air and made everything around them shimmer.

The screams brought her back to reality, though. Loud, piercing screams.

"What are you doing?" Lenora was now desperately trying to free her hand from Astrea's grasp, the dark fabric of her sleeve on fire. The pure white and silver flames engulfed everything around them, setting the rooftop ablaze.

Astrea was sure she had never seen anything like it, but not a single cell in her body was afraid now.

Adissa was in agony on her right, and it took Astrea a few extra seconds to realise what was happening and unclench her fingers, letting them both go.

This wasn't her plan. Not exactly.

Originally, she wanted to create a distraction and manage to get them all out of the border with Fenrir's bracelet and a letter to herself with coded instructions on what to do next. The bracelet would have to be enough for Joran, and maybe she could lie that Fenrir was dead, winning a day or two to flee with Niki. This was her plan A.

The perfect plan because, in that way, the Dragonflies would forget about Solace. And Fenrir would have a chance too. He had her other letter to read.

"What did you do?" Dominica cast a glare full of raw hatred on her, kneeling on the rooftop with her hand, trying to reach her back of all places.

"Why do you think I did anything?" Astrea arched her brow, watching the three women panting and disoriented.

"We only have one traitor!" Adissa announced spitefully, unzipping her black leather jacket to Astrea's surprise.

"And yet you were so willing to form the circle with me," Astrea pointed out, carefully assessing the situation. There were three of them against her, but they were hurt. Moreover, they were fake.

Among them all, she was the only real Dragonfly. Whatever that meant.

There was only one question: did they recharge from her? Judging by how she felt weaker than usual now, she could tell that they did.

She should have stopped that sooner.

Nevertheless, they were panicking for some reason, and Astrea wondered if she could summon more of that white fire. However, no matter how hard she tried, it seemed out of her control again.

Another shriek brought her attention to Adisa and Lenora, who were hectically checking each other's backs.

"It's gone!" Lenora whispered, astonished by her discovery.

"What are you talking about?" Adissa gasped, reaching out for Dominica and forcefully removing her jacket to check the girl's back. This was where the dragonfly tattoos were supposed to be.

Astrea's eyes lingered on them. The once vibrant and mesmerising dragonfly tattoos that had graced their skin were now gone, leaving a few ugly scars in their wake. These three women built their whole identities on being the Dragonflies, and she had just taken it from them.

"It's you!" Dominica bared her teeth, ready to attack any moment. "Once a traitor, always a traitor!"

"If they were real, they would have stayed!" Astrea pointed out the truth calmly, knowing that they wouldn't like hearing the truth. "Anyway, there is no time for that now. We should go back to the Teacher. I have what he wants and some urgent information too. We need to rush."

"Oh really?" Lenora raised her brow, crossing her hands over her chest. "Tell us what the information is."

"This information is not for your ears." Astrea took a few test steps, noticing the trio mirroring her movements. They were about to perform the dance of death, and she was ready.

Despite what had just happened, they still wanted to fight her.

"Don't we share everything?" Dominica sneered, growing her sharp claws out.

"I have my mission, and you have yours—" Astrea tried to figure out which one of them would be the first to attack.

The dark silhouettes contrasted against the silver of the desert landscape as each woman moved with calculated precision. After all, their skills were honed through years of training, pain and determination. None of them was ready to lose today. This was the problem of all Firstborns. They did not know a better life and usually fought until their death. This was what Joran raised them for.

"You're right about that," Lenora ran her hand through her short ginger hair. "We do have our own task. The Teacher ordered us not to bother listening to you and just to bring you home."

This was exactly what she was worried about. Now it was obvious that Joran did not trust her, and the whole mission might have been just one big test she had already failed. Still, she had to try, even if this was the case.

"I don't know how you did this, but I will make you pay." Dominica still moved awkwardly, as if her back was causing her pain. That little fact made Astrea a little bit happier about the whole thing. They had been stealing from her for years. She hoped it hurt them, at least for now.

"Ladies," she tilted her head, trying to hold back a laugh that threatened to escape her. "Let's think about our next move carefully here. You have just lost your precious advantage, and I'm not even tired yet. If you turn away now and cross that border willingly, forgetting about Solace and everything that happened here, I promise not to follow you and let you go."

"You think you're so generous," Adissa scoffed, rolling her eyes. "We're not in the same position as you, Astrea. We never were. If we ever fail the Teacher, there will be no silver pit for a few months for us. I'm even afraid to think what he would come up with to punish us for not bringing him the desired results. Let alone betrayal! Unlike you, we aren't his favourite golden girls!"

"Golden girl?" Now it was Astrea's turn to chuckle bitterly as they circled her, each assassin choosing the perfect position to start their first real fight. This wasn't the training combat they were used to anymore. "Don't you ever forget that I spent more years on this island than any of you!"

"What does it matter?" Lenora shook her head, elongating her red claws to make a point. "We are all going to die for that island and for him! But something tells me you would outlive us all! He'll make sure of that."

"Aren't you going to kill me?" Astrea lifted her chin defiantly, and Dominica rolled her eyes, letting out an ugly laugh.

"You aren't paying attention." Adissa's eyes glowed amber. "If we kill you, we die. If we could do it without harsh consequences, you would have died years ago, bitch!"

"What's stopping you?" She desperately wanted them to lose their cool and go into a chaotic panic attack, but they didn't give her the pleasure.

"Simply because we like what we are about to do instead," Lenora informed her with a slight smirk. "We are going to knock you out and put those silver chains you spent months in back on you. Yes, we made an effort to bring those exact ones. Then, after you are subdued, we will call Fenrir and tell him where you are. He will be instructed to come alone to the coordinates we provide, and when he does, we will kill him in front of your eyes. This is probably my favourite part."

"Yeah," Dominica smirked. "I like that version more as well."

"Please, do just that," Astrea bluffed, feeling the chill creeping down her spine at the thought alone that it was possible. "He would never come alone for me. You will just get yourself caught, and I will play an innocent victim when Fenrir arrives here with his army—"

"He will come alone," Lenora interrupted her. "You know it. I know it. We all know it. I saw the way he looked at you. And the way you looked at him." She paused briefly to let it sink in and added, "He will come for you. I have no doubts."

"And it will be the last thing he does," Adissa chimed in, gloating as if they had already won.

32. MIDNIGHT

A sharp wind blew straight into Astrea's face as Dominica charged at her first without warning, wielding her twin daggers with deadly accuracy. For someone with generous curves, she always moved unexpectedly fast, making Astrea work to remain in one piece. When Lenora and Adissa joined her with their own weapons of choice, Astrea could barely manage to dodge their group attacks. They worked as one sleek, perfect machine. It did not help that she had charged them while they drained her of her strength. It may have been the last time they ever did it, but she could still feel the consequences of their deception. Her instincts were duller, her movements not as sharp as she needed them against these opponents.

Lenora was armed with a slender sword, each move carefully choreographed to perfection just as she practised it for many, many years. Her stands were fluid and precise, each swing of her blade a testament to the years of discipline and mastery. Adissa was using a whip trying to capture Astrea's arms or feet, or at least slash her skin open, but luckily they weren't the only ones who had trained for many years.

This was probably the first time Astrea was happy that she was indeed Joran's favourite, because thanks to that she learned from him personally, mastering every technique her opponents were using today, even before they arrived on the Firstborn island.

The three women she fought were fuelled by jealousy and hatred.

Well, she was fighting for something much better.

From the moment they mentioned their plan regarding killing Fenrir, Astrea knew she would die before she would let that happen.

She did not tell him she chose him, but she was certainly choosing him now over everything else. Although she knew she had to leave, at least she could ensure his and Solace's safety first.

Astrea quickly knelt and extracted her twin blades from her boots, cutting Dominica's heel tendon just before she jumped off the roof.

The border was very close, and she wanted to get them there. Technically, her plan could still work if she got them out. They would forget everything that happened in Solace, and she could lie to them that they escaped an attack. If she remembered what to tell them, of course. This was a problem for later, though.

Lenora's blade cut air right next to her ear, but Astrea managed to block the next swing of the sword. However, this time the whip managed to lash her wrist, knocking one of her knives out of it and wrapping around it tightly, pulling her back.

She blocked another attack, but this time Lenora managed to kick her in the stomach, forcing her to kneel. Dominica was already on her way, her foot only half healed but enough to continue the battle.

Astrea grasped the whip and pulled it roughly towards herself, making Adissa land face down on the sand. Another swing of Lenora's sword came way too close, and she grabbed her arm, losing another one of her daggers in the process.

This wasn't going well. Astrea wished she could set them on fire again, but counting on the miracle repeating itself so shortly was silly.

She tried to free her wrist from the whip while Adissa was standing up, at the same time grasping Lenora's right hand to prevent her from new attacks. She noticed a thin black thread with a single bead on Lenora's wrist, and it made her furrow her brows in confusion.

This was definitely new. And she hadn't noticed it before.

The confusion cost her a few priceless seconds, and a sharp pain pierced her left side, causing her to let out a soundless pant. Ruby drops of blood fell on the golden sand next to her feet, and this was when the whip hit her, preventing her from defending her again with her arm.

"A little slice here and there wouldn't hurt!" Dominica offered her a cruel cold smile as she twisted the dagger in her flesh, forcing her to scream.

Lenora was already behind her, kicking her down on her knees and ready to wound her more. They all knew that it was better to be safe than sorry.

"Agreed." The redhead was about to stab her thighs where it would hurt the most and have to heal the longest.

Astrea cursed at herself inwardly. She shouldn't have let them form the Dragonfly Circle at all. This was her biggest mistake today.

After not telling Fenrir how she felt to his face.

Breathing ragged, she needed at least a few seconds to regain her strength. A few seconds that none of them planned to give her.

"Cut the tendons in both her arms and legs!" Adissa pulled the whip higher to make sure she couldn't do anything with the captured hand.

Astrea heard her own heart racing in her ears… and a rhythm of hooves on sand joining it.

Disoriented, she was sure it was just an illusion at first. Yet the whip holding her trembled, meaning that Adissa lost her composure.

"What the fuck is this?" Lenora snapped her hand in the direction of the dark sand cloud.

"Relax, it's not a wolf or anything dangerous." Dominica twisted the blade again, and Astrea whimpered. The desert was illuminated with a soft teal and purple glow. Not bright at all, and for some reason menacing…

"It's a—" Adissa was lost for words as the Nightmare unicorn finally galloped out of the darkness.

Even Astrea gasped when she saw it, because today it looked nothing like the last time. Its ebony coat shimmered with hues of teal, purple and black as if the shadows themselves had been woven into its majestic form. Eyes the colour of smouldering amethysts glowed with an intensity that mirrored the inferno of its dark soul. It was the night itself.

Nightmare Incarnate. And its horn was pointed straight at Adissa.

The girl didn't manage to scream or move before she found herself pierced by the deadly unicorn's horn and thrown away, breathless. Lifeless.

Lenora hesitated, but Astrea did not. It's not like she saw a Nightmare for the first time. She twisted her arm, ignoring the pain in her side and grasped some sand, throwing it in Dominica's eyes. That finally had her let go of the dagger.

"What the hell?" The redhead was about to raise her sword, but Astrea took the dagger out of her side and plunged it right into Lenora's chest. Mere seconds passed, and she could feel the vibrations of her heart beating… once, twice…

Dominica scrambled to her feet, panic written all over her face.

One would have to do, Astrea thought to herself, but the Nightmare was coming back. Its horn still glistened with Adissa's blood, sharp teeth ready to destroy.

They were right next to the border; Astrea could feel it with her skin and bones. And despite all the hatred Dominica had for her, she couldn't find it in herself to kill her. Not like that.

Before she could change her mind, Astrea got the bracelet out with a note to Joran in case of a major force like this one and put it onto the startled girl's wrist.

"Run!" she commanded. "Shift and run!"

Dominica's lips parted, but the Nightmare's neighing brought her to her senses. She couldn't fight that... not without the dragonfly power.

"Go!" Astrea pushed her, and this time, she obeyed, running away as fast as she could.

Astrea wasn't sure how this memory barrier of Solace worked, but she hoped she didn't just make the biggest mistake of her life.

Dominica would forget everything and return to the Firstborn island, alone and confused, giving her at least a few days to think of what to do next.

She could only hope she didn't blow it for Niki and her...

The Nightmare stopped right next to her, and she flinched when she saw it, not a trace of the beauty from their first meeting.

As if reading her mind, the creature shifted back to its more presentable form, his long hair turned from clouds of darkness to pure silk in just an instant, and it tucked its nose into Astrea's chest.

"You like me indeed." She hissed in pain as she laced her fingers through his mane. The Nightmare's eyes locked with her, and she could tell this had happened before. "Midnight," she said, and the unicorn bowed its head to her.

Blood was gushing out of her, and that took her attention away from the fact that she somehow knew the name. There were more pressing matters now.

What was she to do with all this mess?

"Astrea?" Fenrir's voice cut through the air and she turned, eliciting more pain from her wounds than she expected, Midnight giving her something to lean on.

"Fen... rir—" She didn't know whether to cry or smile. Devoss, Bash, Salome and Kara appeared right behind him, taking in the scene with shocked expressions.

"What happened?" He wanted to walk towards her, but Bash and Salome grasped both his arms, trying to prevent him from doing so,

"Fenrir, what does it look like?" Salome said, knitting her dark brows together. "Look around. She betrayed us! Isn't this the woman she was helping yesterday?"

Astrea's lips twitched with the realisation that all of this didn't look good. Would he ever believe her if she told him the truth?

His eyes went to the blood pouring down her waist and hips, and he ran over, catching her in his arms before she fell.

"Fenrir, you can't ignore it!" Bash insisted, lifting Lenora's arm to show something to him. "This is how she used the beads she stole from you."

Astrea watched in horror how the situation developed. She did no such thing. They had beads, but she wasn't the one to give them to these women.

Their eyes locked, and there was so much pain in his.

"What did you do?" She couldn't tell if Fenrir was angry or worried.

"I chose you," she whispered before the darkness finally overpowered her.

33. DARIUS

*F*IRSTBORN ISLAND

When Niki was told she was going to be a Firstborn warrior and risk her life on a daily basis, this wasn't quite what she imagined. Being stuck between two controlling men with fiery tempers wasn't a walk in the park.

All day that man – who didn't even bother introducing himself to her – was throwing things at her and telling her to leave as if she could. As if, at any point, the choice to be there was hers.

Although she was initially sympathetic to his situation, he started to get on her nerves quickly. Being fully blind did not excuse his awful behaviour. And, frankly, he was lucky she still hadn't put a dagger through his throat and blamed it on his clumsiness. After all, he couldn't see, which meant he could trip and fall on a knife... *accidentally*. A few times. A dozen, at least.

"This is disgusting!" He threw the cup of hot coffee at her, and she barely managed to dodge it, her own anger reaching a boiling point. He'd made her roast the coffee beans and then grind them manually. And now this was the third cup he'd rejected after she followed his own instructions carefully. It was as if he was setting her up to fail just to entertain himself.

"Maybe coffee is not for you anymore," she said, her words laced with venom she could no longer hide, and his head snapped in her direction.

Astrea had taught her not to object to orders and not to speak when there was no point, so she took everything like the soldier she was. And yet, this colourless bastard was getting on her nerves.

It seemed like he loathed her as much as she did him. However, she was the one stuck here with him. Not the other way around.

"You speak too much." He gritted his teeth.

"I was sent here to take care of you, and coffee makes you grumpy," Niki retorted. "Since I was told to pay special care to your health, you will have herbal tea from now."

"That is not going to fly!" His hands were moving, and she realised quickly that he was searching for something to throw at her again.

Asshole.

"You know, nettle tea will do," she couldn't help the grin stretching on her face, "it will be so good for your nerves. I'll get it and some toast. Gluten-free, of course."

So that maybe you would choke on it! She gloated on the inside.

She was about to leave for the kitchen when she heard the sound of claws tearing the leather of the chair's armrest.

"You think you are so clever?" He smirked, and she didn't like it. There was something menacing in the way his lips curled.

"Me?" she gasped, slightly overdoing the innocence. "No, of course not."

"I can fall through the glass window in front of me and say that you pushed me," he informed her, making a chill crawl down her spine. "I can throw myself at the glass cabinet on my left and say that you tripped me. The next drink might scorch my skin, and I'd say you did it on purpose. I can do many things and blame them on you. Would you like that?"

She definitely wouldn't like that, but she wasn't going to give him that power over her.

"You would regenerate faster than you can shout for help," she reminded him, trying to persuade herself before him.

"Shall we test your theory?" he taunted her, smiling genuinely for the first time since she met him. The colourless bastard was enjoying this.

Niki didn't say anything. He looked crazy enough to do it, and she didn't want trouble with the Teacher. She already had enough on her hands since Astrea's punishment. If they were lucky, her mentor would return soon, and everything would go back to normal. At least, she would have a better idea of what to do next. She just needed to hold on until then.

"I see we understand each other," the man said in a smug tone, and she wanted to remind him that two could play this game.

"You do realise that I can spit into your coffee, and you would never know?" Her voice was sweet as honey, but she did not get the reaction she wanted from the patient in question.

"Sweetheart, I would know." He turned away from her as if it made a difference. He couldn't see anything anyway. "Your delicious wild strawberry scent would be way more intense if you did that."

Niki stumbled, unsure how to react to that. It was probably normal that he paid attention to her scent, considering this was the only sense he could rely on. Her cheeks still heated slightly, and she rushed to the kitchen to keep herself busy and stop thinking about it.

She returned a few minutes later, handing him the cup, and to her surprise, he did not complain and just drank it, trying to pretend he was not enjoying his little win.

"Did you bring it?" he asked all of a sudden, and she groaned, hoping he would forget. From the moment he asked, she wasn't sure it was such a good idea to obey that order. But the Teacher was too busy to ask, and no one else could know about her new task.

"I guess so," she muttered under her breath. A few days ago, he requested that she get an issue of The Northern Star, one of the most popular newspapers in the Northern Lycan Kingdom. She had no idea why he would want to read that, but then again... if this would keep him quiet and help the day pass more quickly, then it probably wasn't such a bad idea after all.

"Read it to me," he ordered, a slight tremor in his usually firm voice.

"Fine." She took a seat in front of him. "What would you like to start with? Politics, entertainment—"

"There is a column about the royals—" He tapped his fingers nervously over where he ripped the leather on the armrest just minutes ago.

Niki didn't take him for a gossip lover, but who was she to judge?

"Okay," she mumbled, looking for the correct page. "Oh, it's not a column. It's a whole spread."

"Read," he rushed her impatiently.

"Fine." Niki rolled her eyes, slightly annoyed by him. "Princess Elene is accepting the role as Ambassador—"

"Next," he stopped her at once. "Anything about the... Queen?"

"Hmm, let me see." She searched for the titles and finally found something. "Yeah, here is something. King Kai and Queen Savannah are about to welcome their firstborn child into this world. The couple appeared together at the Bookathon Charity Auction in a dazzling display of elegance and grace, wearing shades of Northern blue. The royal beauty, who is expecting the first heir to the throne, donned a stunning maxi dress with Northern quartz natural beads created by a local designer Anne Gilmore, especially for the occasion. While the royal couple has remained tight-lipped about the gender of their baby, their enchanting appearances together in the past few months has stoked the excitement and anticipation among the Northerners. Royal enthusiasts and well-wishers eagerly await the official announcement, while bookmakers accept bets on whether we will have a Prince or a Princess, the King and Queen look as in love as they did on—"

"Enough." The man in front stopped her, running his hand through his white hair. "You can go now."

"I can't leave you this early," Niki objected, noticing how the corners of his lips tilted down, a little wrinkle forming between his eyebrows.

"I said go!" he growled, and she stood up immediately, knowing well enough by now what was to follow.

She closed the door to his room as the sounds of broken glass and furniture followed.

"Just go," her wolf urged her. *"He will be done in an hour or two, as usual. There is nothing for us here until then."*

Yet something stopped her this time. She couldn't move, clenching the latest edition of the Northern Star available on the island. Niki did not tell him that there was a beautiful picture of Queen Savannah and King Kai on the page she read to him. She decided not to describe how happy they looked together and how he gently held her by the waist. They looked like they were each other's everything, and she chose not to tell this strange blind man about that. Something told her he wouldn't be able to bear it.

He was done sooner than she'd expected, and Niki gave him a few extra minutes after the sounds of things breaking stopped.

His room was minimalistic for a reason. She understood that on the second day of her new post.

Now, the space looked like it had been through a couple of rogue attacks on the same day and then got run over by a train. Pieces of glass and furniture were scattered around, marks of claws decorating the walls.

Usually, she was met with this picture of chaos in the morning when the trainees were already cleaning the mess tup, and all she had to do was pretend that everything was A-okay.

It was the first time she'd found him breathing heavily on the floor, scratches on his skin still not healed, and his white hair a mess. His black glasses were missing, broken pieces in different corners of the room while the daylight sun traced the lines of his face.

Niki shuddered when she saw the scars etched into his flesh. Those were the wounds that made him lose both his eyes. They were a testament to the darkness he had faced and the price he had paid for whatever sins he had committed. Some of those scars were at least a decade old, some were still fresh and not healing properly. He was probably in pain, and for the first time in a long time, Niki felt sorry for him.

She started cleaning up without saying a word, and nothing in him acknowledged her presence.

"You know, you could at least let me know your name," she grunted when she noticed one of his hands was bleeding and went for the first aid kid.

He stayed silent, and she was sure this was it for today. She knelt next to him and took his arm to examine it, blowing on it gently before removing a piece of glass stuck in it. He didn't even flinch.

"I don't think you'll need a plaster or anything else," she informed him. "The cut is clean, and it's already healing. A few minutes and it will be gone."

Just like all the other wounds he had inflicted on himself since she'd started working here.

"I'll go tell them you need some more furniture," she announced, standing up.

When she was already at the door, she heard a heavy sigh.

"Darius." His voice was so low and lifeless that, at first, she thought she imagined it.

"What?" She glanced at him curiously.

"My name is Darius," he repeated, making her smile awkwardly at this sudden progress.

"Nice to meet you, Darius." She did her best not to chuckle. "I'm Nikiah, but you can call me Niki."

34. TELL ME

Fenrir knocked the entrance door out with his foot, Astrea's bleeding body in his hands, his heart racing the way it didn't for the past century. If he lost her this lifetime like this, he wouldn't be able to go on anymore...

She was so tiny. Every time he was forgetting how small she was in comparison to him, how fragile...

A mortal, not a deity.

Her life was slipping away, and he couldn't take it.

"Fenrir, she is a traitor!" Salome insisted. "Heal her if you are so kind, but—"

A loud growl was his response to her, and the witch shuddered, exchanging glances with Warg and Bash.

"Fenrir!" She let out a frustrated sound when they followed him upstairs, and she realised he was taking Astrea to his bedroom. "Doesn't she have her own room?"

"Does it look like I give a damn?" the man growled at her, and Kara moved the witch aside, coming forward.

"What can I do?" she asked.

"Investigate," he practically snarled at her, seething, but the woman did not get offended at all. Luckily, Kara was a woman of action.

"What do you mean investigate?" Salome pursed her lips. "Isn't it clear what she was doing? She allowed intruders into Solace! We have laws for that!"

"I wonder how she let them in?" Fenrir finally offered her a glance, and she almost instantly regretted it because the storm of emotions inside didn't promise her anything good. "She had no contact with anyone and spent most of the time with me. Everything she had with her was inspected when we brought her here, and she still doesn't know most of our secrets."

"We found her with the intruders! She escaped and looked like she was ready to flee!" Salome crossed her hands over her chest. "And that's on top of what we already know about her! She is not to be trusted! Whatever your plan with her was—"

"Stop testing my patience," the wolf warned her.

"Then, at least let me investigate!" she begged, clenching her fists. "With my magic, I can—"

"I think the last Valkyrie would be a better fit for the job this time," Fenrir waved her off. "Just leave. All of you!"

They knew better than question him. After all, he was a god, and it was his territory.

Salome lingered at the door and threw one last glance at the man who had her heart for the last decade. He never looked at her the way he looked at that spy. Not once.

The familiar ugly cobweb was spreading over the witch's chest again, casting a shadow on her confidence. That dark feeling first appeared when Fenrir brought Astrea to his house and didn't listen to her advice to get rid of that girl as soon as possible. And then, every time she had to meet them on the streets of Solace together, that cobweb was growing, obstructing her from seeing things clearly.

She watched him touch one of the beads on his bracelet, the magic responding instantly and letting him take it off. Another prickle of jealousy as the witch realised he was going to waste something so precious on that traitor.

"Come on." Warg wrapped his large hand around her shoulders, moving her away, but Salome couldn't stop looking until the door closed right before her eyes.

"What was that all about?" She scanned her friends' faces for a reply. "Why is he like that? Why does he ignore the obvious?"

"Does he?" Devoss appeared out of nowhere, an indifferent expression on his face which never fooled her. The fox could always see through her. On this dark night, he was dressed in a golden suit with elaborate embroidery, standing out as always.

"Of course he does!" she insisted, feeling how Warg's embrace became tighter. "It's so obvious what she was doing! He said it himself; she stole his bracelet! And then we realised she fled. We found her with intruder assassins and—"

"And she killed all of them." Kara gave her a heavy glance. "Why would she if she was the one to invite them?"

"How would I know?" Salome shrugged, grateful that Warg still held her, providing her with the needed balance. "I wouldn't know how these people without honour interact."

"Ah, isn't it great to be noble?" Devoss let out a heavy sigh and then clapped his hands as if it was a done deal. "Well, anyway! If everything is so… *obvious*, then you have nothing to worry about. Kara will fly around and bring Fenrir the same old news. Problem solved."

They all exchanged glances, admitting that there was nothing else to say.

"Every time she appears, it's a mess!" Bash growled. "Look at us! A few months, and we are back to square one."

"What?" Salome's head snapped in his direction. "What do you mean every time?"

She already knew the answer, but her brain still needed confirmation from the ones who knew Fenrir best. However, none of them said a word, avoiding her gaze.

Which was answer enough.

FENRIR'S LIPS brushed softly over Astraea's as he pressed her against a tree, the glowing willow branches tickling their skin. "They really shouldn't let you wander alone at night," he whispered, claiming her mouth, thirsty for her taste.

Astraea giggled, lacing her fingers into his hair. She did not want to talk, she wanted to kiss, but he was asking for it.

"Who says that I am ever alone?"

Her eyes shone as a devilish grin curled her lips.

"You are always alone," he chuckled, but his smile dropped when he saw her whistle, and a huge Nightmare unicorn materialised out of the night mist in its battle form with glowing eyes and sharp teeth, ready to destroy whoever touched his mistress. The creature instantly recognised Fenrir as his enemy since his hands were all over the starry goddess and went into full-blown attack, which the wolf barely

dodged. The man fell to the ground, and Astraea waved her hand to stop her protector at the last minute, giggling uncontrollably.

"Fenrir, meet Midnight. My guard." She beamed, offering him her hand. He pretended to take it just for a moment, pulling her onto the ground the next. In seconds he rolled to appear on top of her, and the ugly thing pointed his horn at him again.

"Midnight!" Astrea let out the most beautiful laugh again. "Don't! It's Fenrir! He is... ours." The unicorn huffed as if telling her she could do better, but that made her giggle even more, and Fenrir couldn't help but kiss her again...

ASTREA OPENED her eyes with a gasp, and it took her a few good minutes to process her surroundings. Her fingers clenched around something cold, and she brought it closer to her face recognising the crystal Fenrir gave her a while ago. The one made of a Nightmare's horn.

The Dragonflies, the black unicorn whose name was Midnight... Fenrir catching her red-handed while killing her ex-colleagues... it all seemed like a dream now.

She would give anything for it to be a dream.

Yet Astrea bounced up in bed the moment she recognised the Rogue King's bedroom. The Dragonfly quickly assessed herself, realising she was surprisingly clean and suspiciously well for someone pierced with a silver dagger twisted a few times inside her. On top of that, she was only wearing Fenrir's enormous black shirt embroidered with Eastern motives. There was nothing else underneath.

Someone had to put that on her... and take off what was there before.

She checked her side for any scars but found absolutely nothing, which was bizarre. Injuries like this usually require more time to heal.

However, questioning luck wasn't in her nature.

Astrea found Fenrir sitting in a tall rattan chair on the balcony in front of the bed. Astrea couldn't believe her eyes because the sun was setting down on the horizon, which meant she was asleep for almost twenty-four hours. Remembering how serious her wounds were, that made slightly more sense. Especially since she wasn't supposed to make it at all. Lenora, Dominica and Adissa may not have been real Dragonflies, but they were still trained too well to make blows that weren't fatal.

Fenrir's eyes were closed, and she wondered if he had stayed with her the whole time without any sleep, finally dozing off now.

He sure looked tired.

She tiptoed to him over the cold marble with her bare feet, unsure what to do.

Was he angry at her for everything, or could he possibly forgive her?

Astrea stretched her hand to touch his cheek, and his beard prickled her fingers, letting warmth spread over her chest. His blue eyes with tiny specks of red locked with hers, making her try to pull the hand away. Fenrir captured it, leaning into her palm as if this was all he needed from life.

"You were going to leave," he stated, surprising her with the question and the cold contrast of his voice.

"I was," she had to admit.

"And you were not going to come back—" His grasp on her tightened.

"No, I wasn't—" She couldn't bring herself to lie or look at him again, so she averted her gaze.

"Why do you want to go back to him so much?" Fenrir's words were filled with pain. "Would it have been so terrible to stay with me?"

"No." She shook her head, astonished by his reaction. "Of course not. That's not what it's about at all."

"Then why?" Fenrir exhaled sharply, barely restraining himself.

It pained her to see him like this.

"I still chose you," she reminded him. "I killed my friends for you."

"They were not your friends," the rogue retorted. "You know that much."

She had nothing to say to that, and he pulled her onto his lap, cupping her face with his large palm to make her look at him.

"They were harming you for years, lying to you and yet you were ready to go back with them to the man who orchestrated all this. It's the only thing I want to know. Why, Astrea?" His gaze was so intense she wanted to hide, but at the same time, she felt safe enough to tell him the truth.

"Because of my ward," she confessed, and this changed everything for Fenrir, who wrapped his hands tighter around her.

"Your ward?" He furrowed his brows.

"Yes, it's a girl I trained. A friend of mine... she is like a little sister to me," Astrea explained. "For the past few years, she was the only family I had, and she stayed behind. I can't leave her there."

He was thinking for a few seconds before nodding for her to go on.

"Tell me everything and start from the very beginning." Fenrir gently stroked her hair, and she felt like there was nothing to lose. With him, she felt secure, and words poured out of her with ease. She started with the first memory of her family, followed by how Joran saved her and her life on the Firstborn island ever since.

At first, Fenrir was calm, but when her story reached the silver pit, she felt his whole body turn to stone, and she could swear that the red specs in his eyes were shifting to real flames from time to time. Like smouldering embers.

"I am going to kill him," he announced. "I am going to kill my brother."

"Your... brother?" Astrea's breathing hitched from the shock as her world turned upside down.

35. ANOTHER FIRST

"Oh, goddess!" Astrea found it difficult to breathe because, for a moment there, she thought it was all a product of her inflamed imagination.

Did Fenrir just call Joran his brother?

How was this even possible? This couldn't be real!

"You are brothers," she said aloud to try and make the words real. So many thoughts circled through her mind that she didn't notice how she grasped his hand and squeezed it tight.

As if it could help her.

"Yes." Fenrir was ready to curse himself for the slip-up. It was so dangerous. Too dangerous. He had experience with this and knew that any information had to be revealed carefully; otherwise, the consequences could be brutal.

"This means—" Her sky-blue eyes met his, and he felt a prickle of guilt. "This means he knew precisely where he was sending me."

"Not exactly," Fenrir shook his head, "we lost touch decades ago. He found out I was in the East when you arrived here."

"Decades," she muttered to herself while staring at him.

She knew for quite some time that her Teacher was more than just a shifter. He was something else entirely. He did not get old, and his powers didn't match any species. He was a dragon, yet he was too different from any other known dragon shifter in history.

Which could only mean that Fenrir was the same. Different from any other wolf.

"Fen... rir—" She tasted his name on her tongue again, getting a completely new flavour this time. "Oh, my god—"

Astrea was lost for words as the realisation finally sunk in.

"You are the Wolf God Fenrir!" she gasped, letting go of his hand.

This changed everything!

He lowered his gaze before answering her in a low voice. "Yes."

"Why didn't you... tell me?"

Partially she knew why. Who was she to be informed of such things?

And yet... he chose her. He wanted her. He told this to her time after time.

A whirlwind of emotions struck her. All the puzzle pieces were falling in their places.

It finally made sense. Of course... only a deity could keep Solace protected like this. No witches were ever able to do anything of this magnitude.

He had immense powers...

"Astrea, I couldn't." He found her hand again, lacing their fingers together. "It's not that simple."

"Are you serious? This is all you are going to give me?" She raised her brow at him but not a muscle flinched on his face.

"All in due time, Astrea. You are too fragile to—"

"Oh," she huffed a laugh, "that's a first for me! Do you really think I am that fragile to handle a grown-up conversation after everything I've been through?"

"Of course not." He shook his head. "It's more complicated than that."

"I bet it is! You are a freaking *god*, Fenrir!" she chuckled darkly. "And so is the man who trained me! Is this a coincidence?"

"I highly doubt it," Fenrir responded honestly, but it still wasn't enough.

"Tell me everything I need to know!" she demanded.

"Astrea, I can't! Not like this. You need to remember everything yourself," he said sternly, running his hand through his hair. "Just trust me on this one, okay? If we rush, you can pay a high price for this. And I can't—I can't lose you. Not again."

She stared at him, searching his face for the answers she so desperately needed. She could already feel the truth, but deep inside, she was afraid even to assume it was possible.

"You need to get some rest." He cupped her cheek, stroking his thumb over her delicate skin. "We will talk more in the morning, okay?"

Astrea didn't like this "solution" but nodded at him nonetheless. After all, she did need time to think of what was happening. She had to process it all.

FENRIR FOUND himself back in the greenhouse in no time, his heart racing like crazy. Pacing back and forth between the plants, he couldn't forget the disappointment on her face.

He hated that he couldn't just pour all the memories into her in one go. He hated this waiting game. He hated to feel this powerless. Just like back then...

Not thinking twice, Fenrir swung his arms, shattering glass panes and sending shards flying in all directions. Pot after pot, stand after stand, he ruined them all one by one to appease the anger rising inside him. The once vibrant and meticulously arranged plants were now crushed under his relentless fury, their delicate leaves and blossoms reduced to debris.

He was breathing heavily when he noticed her.

Astrea was watching him quietly from the doorframe.

"You—How long have you been here?" His voice broke in the middle of the sentence.

It couldn't have gotten any worse. Now she saw him in such a state.

"Long enough." Astrea stepped carefully between the shards, and only now Fenrir noticed that her feet were bare as she only had his shirt on. He sprinted towards her, picking her up as if she weighed nothing and looking around for a safe place to put her on.

Ironically, he destroyed them all.

"I am fine," she whispered while he held her with just one arm, lifting a table he knocked over with another. After carefully inspecting it, he sat her on the top of it, eyes searching all over her body for cuts.

"Are you sure?" he asked, avoiding her gaze.

"Fenrir—" Astrea tilted her head, realising what he was doing.

"The glass was everywhere—" he muttered as she caught his hand and pointed at a long cut on his wrists.

"Look at this." She glided her fingers over his skin, watching how the wound healed faster than it should have.

"It's nothing." He tried to hide his hand from her, and she placed her hand on his chest instead, arousing all kinds of emotions in him.

"I remember you, Fenrir," she said, catching him off-guard.

He thought he was ready for this, but he was mistaken.

"You... remember?" His discerning gaze was searching for answers.

Astrea was still watching his wound disappearing, and when it was done leaving no trace, she placed something cold into his hand.

"That's not to suppress my tattoo, is it?" She offered a reproachful look as he found Midnight's old crystal horn in his palm, swallowing hard.

"You caught me." Fenrir let out a low chuckle, meeting her gaze.

"That Nightmare helps to jog my memories." She furrowed her brows, the tension between them rising. "And you knew exactly what you were doing when you gave it to me."

"Maybe." A smirk curled his lips. "The question is, Astrea, did it help?"

"I remember that I loved you," she said bluntly, and it made his heart clench painfully. It's been so long since he heard these words from her.

"Anything else?" It was too early to be agitated. He knew better than raise his hopes up.

"You loved me too." Astrea's lips trembled. "And Midnight was there."

He waited for more, only to realise that she didn't remember anything else, the disappointment almost breaking him.

"That's good." He smiled, cupping her cheek. "Very good. Hopefully, soon you will remember more."

He wanted to walk away, when she caught his arm, pulling him back.

"Astrea, I am sorry—" He was about to apologise and find a way to escape when their eyes locked, and he saw determination in hers.

"You said that all I need to do is choose you," she reminded him. "Well, guess what, I did. I chose you before my mission and before my friend."

"I swear, I will find a way to—" He was about to explain that he would find a way to negotiate Niki's release with Joran in one way or another, but she interrupted him.

"I know." Astrea placed his palm on her heart. "I can feel it, Fenrir. I trust you."

"Good." He nodded, knowing that he had to pull away but doing no such thing.

"I don't need the crystal anymore," she breathed out, "but I need something from you."

"What is it?" Fenrir couldn't control the heat building up in him.

"Remind me," she whispered, lacing her hands around his neck. "Make me remember—"

She covered his lips with hers slowly, sliding her hot little tongue into his mouth and exploring it gently. Like only she was able to, probably not aware of what exactly she was awakening within him with her actions.

"Astrea," he snarled when they broke the kiss to take greedy gulps of air, "I will not be able to decline this invitation."

"Good!" She kissed him again, and this time something in him snapped as his hands pulled her into him greedily, roughly even. He deepened the kiss, the world around them fading into insignificance as he laced his fingers in her hair as if he was afraid that she would disappear any moment.

"You are mine, Astrea!" A growl escaped him in between kisses. "No matter how much time passes, no matter who thinks they have a claim on you, you only belong to me!"

"Yours," she confirmed, her elegant fingers working on the buttons of his shirt. He did the same with the ones on her shirt, tearing some of them off because they were too stubborn, and he couldn't wait anymore.

At last, he was able to free her from the fabric, gently lowering her on the table, his hands all over her, kneading, grasping, stroking.

His tongue traced her jawline, getting all the way down to her collarbone. She trembled under him, eager for more, encouraging him.

"Please!" she whimpered as his fingers found her core, probing it gently.

"I barely touched you, and you are so wet already—" His eyes locked with hers, breathing ragged.

"You said it yourself; it's easy for a man like you to seduce a virgin—" she panted, and he paused, circling his fingers over and over her sensitive bundle of nerves.

"Don't worry, Astrea, I had your first time many times," he confessed, "You are safe with me."

"Fenrir!" The woman arched her back because the first release of the night rippled through her body, making her forget everything...

36. SURPRISE, WITCH

Fenrir watched her trying to come to her senses after what he had just done to her, and a part of him was afraid that he wouldn't be able to remember to control his strength with her. He desired her too much, and it had been too long since the last time he had her. His whole body was burning just at the mere sight of her, uncontrollable flames coursing through his veins.

Astrea's naked chest rose and fell as he brushed his fingers from her core to her navel and up to between her perfect perky breasts, finally resting on her neck.

"Look at me," he commanded, and she tried to focus her gaze on him. "Eyes on me at all times, Astrea."

This was the only way. He needed it. He had to have those eyes to trace his every movement because he would remember how fragile she was as long as she did that. His monstrous nature would not harm her.

"Tell me what you want," he taunted her, and she bit her lip, making it a more intense shade of pink.

"I want you to take me," she whispered. She wasn't shy about her desires, though. He knew that much. Astrea had a hard time restraining herself too. He recognised that primal hunger in her because it matched his own.

He missed this.

Fenrir leaned over her, their lips colliding at once. They couldn't get enough of each other.

"Mine," he growled again because he was never tired of repeating this word when he was with her. He could hear her heart beating faster each time he did this, and there was a different kind of satisfaction in that.

He left a wet trail of kisses down her neck, shoulder and chest, inhaling one of her nipples, swirling his tongue around it until it hardened in his mouth. When he reached the other, it was already firm, so he bit on it gently, eliciting a moan from Astrea, who entwined her fingers in his hair, encouraging him to do more.

He teased her, played with her, bringing her as high as he could and stopping at the last moment to watch her helpless protests and frustration. The game he knew how to play with her. She had no chance to win this one.

"Please!" she groaned, arching her back when he kneeled before her, placing her thigh on his shoulder and tracing his fingers all the way down her sleek sex, parting it slightly.

"Anything for you." Fenrir ran his tongue along her folds, making her body shudder in his grasp. "I am going to worship every inch of you tonight."

The words made her centre clench against her will. He loved getting this reaction, so he made another torturous slide, and then another, and another, until he drove his tongue in her, drawing a beautiful scream. She was still so new to this, so innocent… so when he inserted a digit in her, it almost tipped her over the edge.

Fenrir pleasured her, adding one more finger to thrust in and out as he teased her sensitive bundle of nerves at the same time.

Astrea couldn't control herself anymore, the heat was building up quickly inside her. He knew exactly what he was doing. She had to admit now that he knew her body way better than she did. Probably the benefit of having his memories of her.

Fenrir added a third finger, and she lost it, trying to ride them, craving more than he was giving her, finally ready to take all of him. The need inside her was so overwhelming that she did not care how it looked. He curled his fingers, hitting a sensitive spot inside her over and over, and she gripped the table she lay on, almost breaking it as the earth-shuttering climax surged through her while he watched her come undone.

Fenrir let her ride her pleasure, not stopping until her body became limp. He placed one last kiss on her core, sending a wave of tingles all over her.

She was so beautiful now, and he was barely holding back. He took his shirt off, throwing it away somewhere in the dark corner. Just as promised, Astrea watched his every move, not missing the moment when his pants fell to the ground, and he stepped out of them, crushing grass under his feet. His body was pulsing with strength and desire, hard as stone. Nothing could hurt him now.

Astrea licked her lips when she noticed a tiny drop of precum glistening at his tip. She was about to touch it when her eyes were drawn to the scars on his body instead.

Fenrir shivered slightly, noticing her interest, and she rose to trace his scars with her fingers.

"Will I remember where you got those?" She arched a brow at him, and he brushed his palm over her cheek in return.

"These ugly things?" He hummed. "One day—"

"Fenrir," she shook her head with a heavy sigh, "no part of you is ugly."

To prove her words, she traced every scar she found with her mouth, making him tremble with restraint as tingles erupted every time she touched him. He knew she didn't lie to him. Those exact words left her lips every single time... many things could change between them, but never this.

"Astrea," he growled, throwing his head back. "This—"

"Yes." She looked at him innocently, wrapping her hand around his length and stroking it just as torturously as he caressed her earlier that night.

He entwined his fingers into her hair, pulling her closer and claiming her lips with a snarl, then carefully laid her back on the table, positioning himself at her entrance.

"I'll be careful," he promised, nudging the tip to probe her and soak it in her arousal.

"I know," Astrea whispered. "I am ready."

He pushed in, watching her breath come in sharp pants despite her confidence. So, he took his time with her, letting her adjust despite his whole body shaking with the need to take her faster. Inch after inch, soon his hips met hers, and Astrea let out a moan of pleasure.

Fenrir withdrew slowly, swearing under his breath. This felt too good, and he thrust back in faster this time.

"More," she pleaded, and he grasped her thighs, bringing them up slightly to give himself better access.

"As you wish," he groaned, feeling his cock pulsating inside her as he plunged it to the hilt. She let out another moan, urging him to go on, and he was happy to comply.

He pounded into her again and again, watching her breasts bounce in unison with his movements and finding his growls matching her screams of pleasure.

"Mine!" he snarled when he felt her inner muscles clenching around him, knowing she was at her edge again. Astrea didn't find how to respond, her nails digging into his flesh. She was too lost in the sensations because, right now, they were the most intense she had ever felt.

He grasped her breast as he drove into her with force, tugging her nipple between his fingers and lowering himself to capture her lips. She was too undone to respond to the kiss, and her new moan greeted the orgasm that ripped through him as he filled her with his seed, both of them climaxing together.

This felt like heaven. Just the way he remembered it. Her sweet scent enveloped them, mixing up with his. As it should be.

"I love you, Astrea," he whispered. "I've never loved anyone else but you, and I never will. You are mine, and I am yours."

She looked at him, eyes still slightly hazy after what she experienced.

"You are mine and I am yours," she repeated with a smile, getting used to his closeness. She loved to feel his heavy chiselled body covering hers. She loved the way he looked at her. She loved the way he made her feel like the most desirable woman in the world.

She loved that she felt whole again. As if he had returned to her a piece she didn't know she was missing.

This was hers. They belonged together, and there were no doubts about that.

Her heart barely stopped racing when he scooped her up and walked away from the greenhouse.

"Wh-what are you doing?" she asked, wrapping her hands around his neck.

"Giving you time to regenerate." He smirked, marching straight up the stairs leading to his bedroom. "I am afraid this is just the beginning. I was deprived of you for so long, and there is no way we can catch up. But it doesn't mean that I will stop trying."

She rested her head on his chest, grinning.

"You want to continue?" Astrea giggled.

"Menace, we barely started—" He offered her a devilish grin, already bursting the door to his bedroom open and throwing her onto his soft bed. "If you want to stop, just tell me."

Astrea crawled deeper onto the bed, liking the soft satin sheets more than the firm old table. "And what if I don't want to?"

He flipped her on the mattress and lifted her hips, adjusting his already hard cock back at her core while grasping her waist with one hand and her bottom with another. *He could do this forever.*

"Then I will not have to painfully restrain myself." He smirked and thrust back into her, making her hips quiver.

THEY MANAGED to fall asleep only in the morning when the sun was already rising, but none of them cared, their bodies entwined around each other, and happy smiles etched on both their faces.

Fenrir watched her falling asleep in his arms, still not able to take his hands off her. He knew how precious moments like these were. He knew the price they had to pay for them.

And he refused to waste even a second.

SALOME TRIED to get into Fenrir's mansion as early as possible every day, even though he repeatedly told her there was no need. Ever since Astrea moved in, she felt that their connection with Fenrir was slipping away, and the witch was ready to do anything to try and restore it.

She often found him in his greenhouse when she arrived, suspecting that the Alpha God rarely slept like a normal person, but today she gasped when she saw the building's state. It looked like it went through a gruesome battle, but no one was alerted, and the house was slowly waking up when she arrived, so she decided that it was one of Fenrir's angry episodes.

Sadly, sometimes his anger was taking over him, and this was the result. He destroyed something he built to avoid hurting people.

Salome spent at least half an hour restoring the place with her magic, saving any plant she could, knowing that Fenrir would be sorry about destroying them later. The little task put a smile on her face because, finally, there was a problem for her to solve. To remind him why they worked so well together.

Her next stop was the kitchen, where she brewed fresh coffee for him, knowing that it was the best way to appease his cranky mood. A part of her hoped that his disappointment with that traitor caused him to wreck his favourite greenhouse, but as long as she would be the one to bring peace to him, she was fine.

She opened the door without knocking since he never scolded her for her boldness and expected to find him on his balcony or in his favourite chair at this hour. However, what she saw caused her to drop the tray she carried, and black coffee spilt all over the floor.

Astrea was the first to wake up, sitting up in bed on instinct and meeting the witch's frustrated gaze as she pulled the sheets to cover herself. Fenrir followed soon after, arms wrapping around the woman next to him defensively. His eyes filled with flames, ready to destroy the intruder before realising who stood on his doorstep.

"What the hell, Salome?" he growled at her, and her heart sank. Watching the two of them together was too painful. More painful than she could ever imagine.

Astrea squeezed his hand discreetly, but the motion did not escape the witch's gaze. She also noticed how relaxed Fenrir became after such a little gesture. She had never seen him calm down so fast.

"I-I am sorry," she muttered, waving for the cups to go back on the tray, but it didn't work since they were shattered in myriads of little pieces and she couldn't concentrate enough to make it work.

"It's okay." Astrea was next to her in no time. She was wrapped in nothing but sheets. Fenrir's sheets Salome personally picked for him.

The pain was choking her. This was too much for anyone.

"I am fine!" she snapped when Astrea tried to gather the pieces, pushing her hand away angrily. She was embarrassed for her actions immediately, knowing Fenrir was watching her.

Salome swore at all her ancestors in her mind for allowing this to happen.

She was about to say something when the silver spear on the wall next to the bed began to glow, blinding them all.

"Fucking hell!" Fenrir swore under his breath. "Not now!"

37. THE SILVER SPEAR

*A*strea was sure she'd never felt this happy in her entire life, yet somehow this was all so familiar. It was nice to know this wasn't just another dream as she curled up in bed with Fenrir's arms pulling her possessively against his chest. He had a peculiar scent that she couldn't quite decipher. There was a distinct note of cedar wood, but at the same time, he smelled a little bit like smoke. Or *smouldering embers*. However bizarre, she would be happy to breathe it in all day, everyday.

It suited him.

They were still naked and still entangled together, and neither of them wished for this to end.

He looked so relaxed now. As if he slept for the first time in years, and Astrea loved that she was the one to bring this peace to him.

The door opened all of a sudden, and before Astrea had time to react, she heard clanking and breaking sounds.

When she saw Salome's eyes full of pain, she wanted to help her. She knew that look in the witch's gaze. So many women on the Firstborn island looked that way at the Teacher. Some were ready to do anything just to end up in his bed.

"I-I'm sorry," Salome muttered, waving for the cups to go back on the tray, but it didn't work for some reason.

"It's okay." Astrea was next to her in no time, wrapped in nothing but sheets.

"I am fine!" the witch snapped when Astrea tried to gather the pieces, pushing her hand away angrily, which brought Astrea back to reality. She didn't owe anything to Salome.

She was about to say something when the silver spear on the wall next to the bed began to glow, blinding them all.

"Fucking hell!" Fenrir swore under his breath, causing everyone to look at him. "Not now!"

"What is this?" Astrea felt a sense of foreboding looming over her.

"It's—" Fenrir was looking for the right words, getting out of bed absolutely naked as if it was nothing. Salome's cheeks flushed, and Astrea cleared her throat, overdoing it slightly to get the man's attention. He swore under his breath again, and clothes appeared on him out of nowhere, which, she had to repeat to herself, was perfectly normal.

"His baby is born!" Salome spat the words out, making Astrea's lips part.

"Your what?" she gasped in shock at him.

"It's not what you think," Fenrir raised his hands defensively. "It's just—"

"A firstborn he has to collect for a favour he provided!" Salome announced bitterly, trying to blink away the tears that formed in her eyes.

That didn't bother Astrea as she sat down on the floor, ignoring the shards of glass around her.

A million thoughts swirled in her mind.

A firstborn baby... A favour... A deity who was Joran's brother.

She felt physically sick just thinking about it. She thought Fenrir was so different from his sibling but...was he? Her memories were not back yet to make a fair judgement. She was crazy about the man, but at the end of the day, she didn't know him that well yet.

"Astrea," Fenrir rushed towards her "You cut yourself!"

Only now she noticed the aching of her palm and brought it closer to her face to see blood on it. It was nothing compared to the pain in her chest.

"You collect firstborns?" Her voice was barely a whisper as the colour drained from her face.

Fenrir knew what she meant at once, taking her hand to heal it.

"He—" The witch was about to say something else when he glared at her.

"You've helped enough, Salome, thank you." He gritted his teeth, and the witch pressed her lips together so hard they turned white.

"I was just—" She was desperately looking for an excuse for her behaviour to fix all this mess, but nothing good came to mind, so she decided to change the subject. "If it glows, it probably means the baby is born. You have to go."

Now that Salome was thinking about it, it was actually good. Thanks to Savannah Fionnlagh, she just got a chance to regroup.

"I'll deal with it," Fenrir growled. "Could you give us a moment in private, please?"

"Excuse me." The witch tried to make an indifferent face. This time she waved her hand, and all the little shards and liquid from the floor got back onto her tray. One of the biggest pieces flew out of Astrea's palm, cutting more of her skin, making her wince.

She left before Fenrir had time to react, avoiding the confrontation.

Although furious with his friend, Fenrir was more preoccupied with his woman. He was panicking because he knew exactly what was on Astrea's mind now. She may have fallen for him, but she didn't remember anything about his character to not be upset now.

He was healing her hand, and she couldn't bring herself to look at him.

"Astrea," he brought her palm to his lips and kissed it gently. "I know how it looks but—"

"It's fine!" She stood up, yanking her wrist back. "Who am I to judge the gods? Go collect your baby!"

"I am not going to," he said, and finally, she spared him a distrustful glance. "Not until she is eighteen."

Astrea gave him the eye roll of her life.

"No, Fenrir." She shook her head, searching the room for something to wear. "Don't do this to a child! Don't let her grow up in a loving family and then rip her away from them to turn her into a Firstborn warrior! I saw kids like that! They don't do well! If you are going to do this, it's best if she is taken young and brought up in the environment that—"

"I am not planning on turning her into a warrior!" Fenrir closed the distance between them. "I am not planning on turning her into anything."

"Then why did you—" Her voice broke in the middle of the sentence and he couldn't take it anymore, pulling her into a tight hug.

"It was an accident!" he assured her. "I came to the North to claim that spear, and it was buried in some dead guy's body. I hadn't used it for so long that I forgot that property existed... When I grasped the spear to remove it from his body, a jolt of electricity burst forth from it and revived the corpse. I lost my composure for a moment when he started to beg me for help, and I —"

He stopped, not knowing how to tell her.

"You what?" Astrea furrowed her brows.

"I kind of... joked that it would cost him his firstborn." Fenrir barely squeezed the words out of himself.

"You JOKED about it?" Astrea tried to push him away, but he held her tight regardless, hoping to wait out her wrath.

"I know, I know! Trust me, if I could turn back time, I would! I was frustrated and tired. And usually people never give up their firstborn kids like that! But it turned out that this guy was pretty desperate... his beloved woman had been abducted and—"

"Wait!" Astrea's head snapped back to the spear. No wonder it looked so familiar. "Oh, goddess, Fenrir! Are you talking about King Kai Fionnlagh?!"

"Yeah." He offered her an awkward smile.

"So, you are the one who performed that miracle and saved him." She finally allowed herself to relax in his hands, and he breathed out in relief, knowing that she didn't hate him after all.

"I guess so—"

"And their daughter is the price—" She bit her lip painfully.

"I didn't want this," he said, "but words given to the gods are binding."

"It still feels so wrong. She is their baby!" Astrea knew the King and his wife. She liked them. They were the ones she risked her life for.

"I know, Astrea, this is why I want to give them time until she is eighteen. It's time for me too. Time to think of what to do with her. I don't need another woman bound to me. It's not like I am planning on keeping her as a concubine or anything."

"A concubine?" She scoffed with a raised brow. "Was that ever an option?"

"No," Fenrir chuckled, placing a soft kiss on the top of her head. "There is only one woman for me, and that's you. I had all the chances in the world to be with someone else, but I know that my heart will only desire you. So, no. Concubines were never an option."

The spear started glowing again and Astrea groaned in frustration. It wasn't like they didn't have problems, but now there was also a baby. Savvy's baby. Astrea loved Savvy. It was quite possible that Savvy hated her now. Their last conversation wasn't great, and Astrea had to run away right after, but to her... to her, Savannah was a dear friend. Someone she'd grown to cherish. She'd risked everything for her and her family once.

And now Fenrir practically owned her child. It was weird, wrong, and absolutely unbelievable. Not to mention that none of them knew what to do now. Even Fenrir looked puzzled.

"You have to go." She sighed, imagining how unhappy Savvy and Kai probably were about this. "Tell them."

"You are upset." He cupped her chin and made her look at him.

"It's not exactly something to be happy about." She tried to smile.

"We will have eighteen years to think of how to break the bond between that girl and me," he leaned down to kiss her nose, "but today will not be a bad day for us. We finally found each other. It's a great day, Astrea. And I will return to you as soon as possible."

She couldn't hold back a smile because his words meant everything to her, but that smile dropped when he took her hand and put one of his bracelets into her palm.

"I wish I had a ring, but I hope this will do until I get one." Fenrir smiled at her, waiting for an answer.

"Are you sure?" She glanced at him, realising that she still didn't confess she stole from him or that one of the Dragonflies escaped with the beads. Neither did she mention that they came to Solace already wearing similar beads.

"I am." He took the bracelet back and then slid it onto her wrist. "This is so that everyone knows that you are mine. And also, if the need arises, you can protect yourself with these. Each bead contains magic and can give you a specific power or ability. I have been collecting these for years. They are temporary, and it will depend on the bead size how long they last. If you touch them with the intention of using them, you will feel what they do first. The power will be yours when you crush a bead. But, Astrea, do be careful and only use in case of an emergency."

"Is that what you meant when you said they store things?" Astrea's eyes widened. "Fenrir, I—"

"Don't worry, Astrea," he cupped her cheek, "there wasn't anything useful on the bracelet you took for my brother."

She didn't know how to respond to that, and Fenrir chuckled, seeing her confusion.

"You knew?" She felt so stupid now, thinking she could trick him so easily. He had been playing her this whole time.

"Remember that I know you and the way you think." He smirked. "And this is exactly why I don't hold anything against you. I-I understand your motivation."

"I am sorry," she muttered.

"You are not the one to be sorry for this," he kissed her forehead, "neither are you going to be the one paying for this."

"Out of interest, what beads did you give him?" Astrea's lips curled.

"The ones he would need the most," Fenrir chuckled. "Calming and wound healing."

Astrea couldn't stifle a laugh, and Fenrir captured her lips, kissing her gently at first but quickly turning into a wolf and an intoxicating storm. They were nowhere near done with each other, and soon their hands were roaming each others bodies again.

The spear glowed persistently, more intensely this time.

"Damn it!" Fenrir swore under his breath.

"I will wait for you," Astrea said, her breathing ragged and heart racing.

"Even if you don't, I will turn the whole world upside down to find you," he promised, eliciting another smile from her. "You are so beautiful—and mine."

"Go," she giggled. "This is more important now. I'll be good."

ASTREA HAD A LONG MORNING, taking a bath and thinking about everything that happened. She missed Fenrir and still had so many questions, but it had been hours since he left. It worried her, considering all he had to do was tell the parents that he wouldn't be taking their child. Each passing hour made her more agitated because she sensed that something went wrong on the other end.

She couldn't sit and wait even though she technically promised to do exactly that. But it wasn't who she was as a person, and Fenrir claimed to know her well, so she decided to go out into the city and see if she could help in any way. Or, at the very least, simply distract herself.

"Hey!" Kara met her on her way out.

"The last Valkyrie in the flesh!" Astrea smirked at the woman.

"You know what, I am honoured that you had time to chat about me while actively reuniting all night long!" Kara offered her a sly glance. "In fact, I am surprised you managed to have a full-blown conversation."

"We didn't," the Dragonfly had to admit. "It kinda came out in between—"

"Ew, gross. Spare me the details," the Valkyrie snorted.

"By any chance, do you have a way to contact Fenrir?" Astrea asked bluntly, not able to contain her anxiety anymore.

"Not really." Kara shrugged.

"I am just worried because he was supposed to be back by now but there is no sign of him." The confession wasn't easy. She wasn't used to pouring her heart out to anyone.

"He'll be fine," the woman chuckled. "What can happen to him? He is Fenrir, the mighty Wolf God, an immortal who will, quite literally, outlive us all."

They went into the city together, having a somewhat nice conversation for the first time. Finally, Astrea felt like Kara could open up to her, telling her more and more about Fenrir's work in Solace. She was like a completely new person now.

"You don't have to try and sell him to me this hard." Astrea laughed as they entered the central street in search of a coffee house. "He will have a hard time getting rid of me now."

From the corner of her eye, Astrea noticed a group of people watching them and whispering. She tried not to pay too much attention to it, but soon two women pointed at her and that simply couldn't be a coincidence.

As someone who was taught to stay invisible when needed, Astrea knew when she was the centre of attention.

And right now, it felt uncomfortable.

"Do you feel that something is a little bit off today?" She side-eyed Kara, but the Valkyrie only shook her head in response.

A huge green car stopped right in front of them and Devoss jumped out of it in a matching salad green suit, hair slightly dishevelled.

"Oh, there you are!" he chuckled nervously. "Why don't I give you a lift back home?"

"I'm fine." Astrea noticed a few more people watching her and pointing their fingers. "We just arrived."

"Yeah, but it's so hot out here! Let's get back!" Devoss insisted, giving a glare at Kara.

"You know what, he is right," the Valkyrie changed her mind all of a sudden. "It is crazy hot today."

"We are in the desert," Astrea reminded them. "What is happening? Why are you both acting so weird?"

"Weird?" Devoss' voice reached an unusually high-pitched tone. "I don't know what you are talking about! But Fenrir is probably back and you have so many things to talk about judging by how the night went—"

Astrea prepared to reply something snarky to the man when a cold splash of water distracted her from the conversation. She saw an angry woman with an empty cup in her hand, pushing a stroller with a baby in it, her chest rising and falling sharply and her face red with anger.

"How dare you remain here after what you've done!" the woman growled at her, her eyes glowing blue.

"What have I done?" Astrea gasped, still shocked.

"You ask?" A few people surrounded them now, all looking furious.

"Shameless!"

"Traitor!"

The words stung, and Astrea's breathing hitched. Not this again...

"Call her that again and you will die!" Kara snarled, giving her slightly more confidence.

"How can you protect her?" A man stepped forward, throwing accusatory looks at them. "You know she is responsible for the breach yesterday, and now Raja is under attack by the Southern Republic! They say no one made it out of there alive!"

Astrea's lips parted in shock as the world stopped spinning.

38. NORTHERN PRINCESS

NORTHERN LYCAN KINGDOM
Fenrir wanted to be done with his North business as soon as possible. Just the thought that Astrea was waiting for him back at home in his bed made his whole body shiver with anticipation.

However, he had to deal with the baby first.

He always had a soft spot for the North. This place was his home once.

However, he did not expect a warm welcome this time. It was his mistake and he hoped to fix it one day.

It just so happened that he was right, as always, because the moment he stepped into the room where the firstborn child, who now technically belonged to him was, he felt binding magic crawling up his feet.

A dirty trick. A trick that would never work on him, yet the worst news was that he recognised the pentagram on the floor. The runes, the style, the magic... everything looked like Salome's work.

He noticed more protective circles and signs around. The King and Queen of the North prepared to meet him.

It didn't help that he felt like the villain in this situation.

Just seeing Kai, his chosen Champion, trying to reassure his young and beautiful wife with a baby in her arms made his heart clench painfully. He wasn't a monster. He didn't want to take the child. It was a mistake, but... *the words given to the gods were binding.*

He gave them a few more minutes before making himself visible, but he could tell that it was of no help. The new parents were aware of what was to come. The best event of their lives was darkened by the pain of inevitable separation.

Thunder rumbled behind the windows, thick dark clouds gathered fast, and the lamps in the room of the Northern castle blinked again. Lightning sliced the sky.

Nothing else was happening, though.

"Maybe... it's not today," Savannah suggested hopefully, and the look in her eyes almost broke her husband's heart. Fenrir felt sorry for him. Kai had similar luck to his own, always getting the shorter end of the stick.

"Maybe—" The Northerner offered her a weak smile that did not reach his eyes.

None of them believed it. They could sense the power rippling in the air with their skin.

"Sorry to disappoint," Fenrir sighed as he stepped out of the darkness, his voice deep and unearthly.

Queen Savannah clenched the child to her chest with one hand, treacherous tears streaming down her face at the inevitable encounter. However, she did not let the hormones cloud her judgement and grew sharp claws on her free hand. She wouldn't give up her baby without a fight.

Fenrir would have probably smiled if it was appropriate. She reminded him too much of Astrea, and he could see why his Champion was ready to give anything for her.

King Kai was now watching his movements, probably hoping that the trap they set up with the witches' help was enough to subdue a god.

Fenrir decided to play along and stepped just in the right place on the carpet, allowing the couple to feel more at ease while they talked. Kai breathed out when he saw magical lines forming in the air.

The cage, weaved with ancient magic appeared, locking him inside. It was a good one and he would have praised Salome later if he didn't feel she went overboard with all this. What was she doing exactly? They never spoke of this.

The worst part of this was that this magic was not new to Fenrir since he had already spent many years in a similar cage, trapped by the ones he trusted the most.

"Rude much?" He arched his dark brow at the royal couple as his eyes traced the glowing bars of their trap.

"It's not like we had a choice." Kai still couldn't relax. This was far from being over.

"On the contrary, you always have a choice," the deity countered, rubbing his well-trimmed beard. He was dressed in a black shirt and pants, looking like a regular modern man. An insanely handsome, very tall, perfectly built modern man.

"The last time we met, I made a mistake." Kai decided to cut straight to the point.

"You think?" The god let out a humourless chuckle. At least they could agree on something.

"I was desperate." The Northern King gritted his teeth. "And I agreed to what you asked!"

Fenrir exhaled heavily, rubbing the bridge of his nose. If anything, he looked tired.

"See, I didn't actually ask you, did I? I was joking!" he confessed, bringing the royal couple into a state of shock.

A heavy silence hung in the room as Kai and Savannah processed what they had just heard.

"You—you joked about the life of our child?" Savvy looked as if she wished to rip Fenrir's head off, but didn't move. Wise girl.

"I didn't joke about your child! I joked in general, and your husband here was the one to spit the promise in my face without any warning!" Fenrir rolled his eyes. He was so tired of everyone villainising him. They didn't even say thank you for him saving them twice in the length of one week. "While touching a divine weapon, may I add! Didn't you hear that the words you give to the gods are binding, Amarok?"

Kai lowered his head. Fenrir made him an Amarok, a giant ice wolf who was much stronger than regular Lycans and werewolves. The child was the price for the miracle.

Their eyes locked and Fenrir knew that they both wished they could turn back time. Sadly, he didn't have a bead like that.

"So, you don't want to take our child?" The Queen cleared her throat, her voice hopeful but at the same time distrustful.

"I don't want to," Fenrir confirmed, not knowing how to approach this better, "but I will have to."

The hope drained from their eyes, and Kai squeezed his wife's hand, trying to give her strength.

"I am ready to do anything to fix this." His voice was confident as he met Fenrir's glare. "Let's make a new deal. I will pay any price you want. Take my life instead. Take me. I will do whatever you want! I will serve you forever."

"Did it ever occur to you that maybe I don't need anyone to serve me?"

Fenrir threw his head back in exasperation. "All I wanted was to live peacefully away from humans."

"Then walk away and have your wish!" Kai insisted. "None of us would ever bother you! I swear!"

Fenrir snorted. "If only it worked like that."

"But you don't want her, and we don't want to give her up!" Savannah tried to sit up higher and reason with the god before her. "What is the problem?"

"This is the problem!" Fenrir waved his fingers, and the cage around him dissipated while the familiar silver spear appeared in his hand, making the Queen gasp and the King bare his teeth at him, ready to shift any moment.

The air in the room became chilly at once, windows covering with frost. Amarok was unable to sustain his power, but Fenrir tapped the spear on the floor, and everything returned to normal.

A power move on his side. He had definitely just proven them his might, so that they didn't test him anymore.

"Gungnir," the deity clarified the name of the divine weapon. "Your daughter is now bound to it forever. I cannot release her from that oath of yours until the spear releases her. And knowing how these things work, it's probably forever."

"No!" Savvy whispered, clenching the child tighter. She couldn't bear the thought of separating from her.

"Listen," Fenrir was already tired from this conversation, "I don't need a child. Or anyone, for that matter. I will not be taking her today. Or ever."

To his credit, the King and Queen didn't smile. They knew better than believe it was that easy.

"But..." Fenrir pressed his lips together tightly, his knuckles white from grasping the spear too tight.

There it was... the but that was going to ruin everything.

"But what?" Kai snarled.

"But the oath will not go away," Fenrir admitted. "It's not up to any of us, the fates will do their work, and when the time comes, everything in the world will be pushing your daughter towards me and the spear. None of us will be able to do anything about it, and if we fight it, she'll be the one to suffer."

"Where does that leave us?" Kai asked, still trying to figure out how to process the new information.

"That leaves you with your daughter. For now." Fenrir grazed his eyes over the child. Her place was with her parents. He really wasn't thrilled about the whole thing. "Bring her up as you wish. I think the fates will give her time until adulthood at least, but once you start seeing the signs, you will need to surrender her to me."

"No!" Savannah protested. "Callista will choose her own fate!"

"That she will." Fenrir didn't argue. "She will have to live next to me, but I will not restrict her in any way. As I have already told you, I have no interest in her. She will find her place in my realm, and that will be it."

He really hoped that the Northern Princess would be open-minded enough to enjoy the desert life.

"But—" Kai wanted to counter, to say something that would change things, to strike a bargain… anything to free his daughter from this unknown fate.

"That's enough!" Fenrir raised his hand, and they heard thunder rumbling behind the window again. "I came here to inform you so that you don't spend every day of your life drawing witch traps for me. Tell Salome that it's not funny, by the way. And keep the trinket she gave you. It will be useful one day."

He sensed they had one of the witch's old amulets.

Their gazes snapped back to him, confused and frustrated.

"When the time comes, bring Callista to my cave in the mountains. I am sure you know which one." Fenrir turned on his heels and started walking away. "She will be safe, but this is all I can promise you."

He felt like they had enough for one day. There was nothing to speak of for now, as he needed them to process the information. Not to mention, that he desperately wanted to return to Astrea.

For now, this matter was done.

Fenrir closed his eyes and thought of his little dragonfly, transporting back to his bedroom.

However, when he opened his eyes, he was surrounded by darkness, swearing loudly because this time the trap was a bit better.

"Fucking Gleipnir!" he muttered, realising that he was now stuck in this void of a place, locked inside his own portal until he can break the chain that caught him the second he left the King and Queen of the North.

39. GLEIPNIR

*A*SGARD

"How dare you, Scum?" Vidar's roar echoed through the golden halls of the Asgardian palace. "She is mine! You took what belongs to me!"

Fenrir did not want to grace that nonsense with a response. Astraea wasn't a property for anyone to own.

He was worried for her, remembering how scared and startled she looked when this monster stormed into the temple where they made love, devouring her with his greedy eyes while trying to kill him. It was an ugly fight, and Fenrir would have probably killed that annoying son of Odin if other gods didn't interfere and if the Moon Goddess didn't appear to take Astraea away.

"What have you done?" Tyr whispered, trying to subdue and bring him back to his senses. However, that day wasn't when Fenrir wanted to lay low. He didn't know if a day like this would grace this world again. He was done with quiet submission.

Hearing Vidar spouting Astraea's name made him want to wipe the damned Asgardian from the face of all nine realms. Enough was enough!

They called the Divine Council to decide what to do with all this. They would judge him, and he had no doubts that they wanted to get his apologies, including an oath never to approach Astraea again.

An oath they were not going to get.

Over his dead body.

The All-Father was sitting on his throne and watching the scandal unfold with a stern expression.

"Selene gave Astraea to me! She is my bride, and now she is my fated mate. He had no right to—" Vidar's voice faltered.

"Defile the goddess?" Heimdall scoffed, offering the end of the sentence.

The words made Fenrir even more furious, flames filling his insides, ready to burst out at any moment. It was so hard to control the hellfire coursing through his bloodstream, and the Asgardians weren't helping.

"Do you even need her now, brother?" Heimdall continued with a sneer. "She was supposed to be a virgin goddess, after all. And now she is spoilt goods—"

"Enough!" Freyja walked inside with her entourage, passing Fenrir without sparing him a glance. She was a kind goddess, he always knew that, but for some reason, she was never kind to him and he could never understand why.

"Thank you for joining us, Freyja," Odin welcomed her as she took her grand seat not far from him.

"I would ask everyone to choose their words!" she warned them, her eyes glowing just for a second, reminding them she wasn't just a goddess of love and fertility. She could quickly turn into a warrior who almost won the war between the gods. Who knew if she wouldn't be the one to sit on the throne if they didn't agree to a peace treaty.

That finally made Heimdall close his mouth and bow in respect.

"Astraea was given to me!" Vidar stepped forward again. "She is mine. And I don't plan to refuse such a gift! I am only demanding what is just."

For a silent prick, he was talkative today.

"She is not a thing to be given!" Fenrir retorted, letting them know that he had an opinion too. "She didn't choose you! She chose me, and I—"

"How dare you interrupt my son?" Odin's voice rumbled through the room. He was imposing when he wanted to be, but Fenrir was not going to back down.

"It's irrelevant who he is!" the young wolf thundered, shocking everyone with his resistance. They were not used to seeing this side of him. "It's about her and her choice! She is a goddess too! Just like you all. She doesn't need anyone's permission!"

"Is that why you are speaking on her behalf?" Freyja seemed angry. "She doesn't need our permission, but she needs your useless claim? Tell me, Fenrir, what are you going to offer her?"

That was a low blow because, unlike Vidar, Odin's son and one of his heirs, Fenrir had nothing to boast but his strength.

"I already offered her my love and protection," he announced, raising his head high. "And she accepted."

"Too bad she is my mate now!" Vidar gritted his teeth. "She did not object when her mother bound us for life! Which tells me that she must have been deceived by you!"

If looks could kill, Fenrir would probably be already beheaded by now.

"That was her mother's decision! Not hers! It doesn't count!" he argued, clenching his fists. If Vidar wanted to fight, he was ready to give him that. "Take her mother then if you like this mate bond thing so much—"

"Shut up!" Odin bellowed the words in a fit of rage. "Is this all a joke for you?"

"On the contrary," Fenrir growled. "This is the first time ever I asked for anything! Astraea and I—"

"You ask for my bride!" Vidar charged at him, and this time Heimdall had to hold him back from a physical confrontation.

"She doesn't even love you! Why are you so—"

"She will never be with a dog like you!" one of the other gods spat. He didn't even know who, but it didn't matter much. They were all the same.

Fenrir was about to send them all to his sister, Hel, when the tall doors behind him opened, filling the room with a serene glow. He could feel her with his bones, his heart racing with anticipation.

Selene and Helios entered the Golden Hall first. Astraea followed right after, the attention of every Asgardian on her. She was as beautiful as ever, with her long glowing hair adorned with diamonds and silver threads. Their eyes locked, and he could finally breathe out because he could tell that nothing had changed for her. She loved him today the same as she did yesterday.

And he would burn Asgard for her if he had to. Especially if they were asking for it.

The silence was unbearable as the three Olympians stood soaking in everyone's attention.

"Welcome," Odin greeted them. For once, even the All-Father didn't know what to say. They all needed the alliance, but the situation was tricky.

"Thank you for accepting us here today once again." Helios flashed his blinding smile, but the tension was too strong for anyone to reciprocate it.

"We want to say that—" Selene spoke, but Astraea stepped forward.

"My apologies. I am the one at fault here," she announced loud enough for everyone to hear.

Gasps and whispers filled the Golden Hall. Everyone was astonished by the brazen little goddess.

"What are you talking about, child." Freyja smiled. "We have all been young once. There is nothing to apologise for. Having a lover is not a crime for a god. In your lifetime, you will have many."

A growl escaped Fenrir's chest, and Odin sent him a warning glare. At the same time, Vidar frowned, folding his hands over his chest. His eyes did not leave Astraea, and Fenrir wanted to gauge them.

"I only want one," the goddess of stars replied politely, and a few chuckles followed. They thought she was too young to understand what she was talking about, sure that they knew better.

"That's good to hear, considering—" Odin spoke, but he was bluntly interrupted.

"I am happy to provide an alliance for our realms." Astraea looked the ruler of Asgard straight in the eyes. "It's my honour. I ask only for one thing. I want to choose my future husband myself!"

Another wave of astonished gasps ripped through the room as Fenrir felt warmth spreading over his chest. She was fighting for him just as he fought for her minutes ago, alone against everyone.

"Astraea!" Selene took her daughter's hand. "But you already have a fated mate! My gift—"

"It would have been nice if you asked me first, Mother," the starry goddess sighed. "We could have avoided all this mess."

"Niece," Helios tried to interfere but Astraea shook her head.

"It should be my decision and—"

"Very well!" Odin stood up from his throne. "We want a happy union, don't we?"

This was probably the one and only thing everyone agreed on.

"So be it, Astraea." the All-Father nodded, the golden eye patch in his eye reflecting her glow. "Any Asgardian would be honoured to have you as his wife. And in three days, we will have a feast in your honour. You will be free to choose any eligible god."

"Even Fenrir?" she asked, ensuring that there were no tricks.

"Yes," Odin confirmed. "Whoever you see fit for yourself on that day. The choice is yours."

"That's—Thank you." A smile curled her lips.

"Forgive my niece for being so... *difficult.*" Helios also produced a charming smile despite his ugly words.

Fenrir wanted to get to her, but Tyr stepped in his way.

"Not now," he whispered, offering his friend a new cup of wine. "Too many witnesses, and Vidar is still here."

Fenrir caught another gaze from Astraea, and she didn't walk to him either, realising that keeping her distance for three days wasn't such a bad idea. They have offended enough people today to display their affections publicly.

All they had to do was just wait three days.

"Can I speak with you in private?" Selene asked Odin and the latter nodded in response.

"Everyone dismissed!" The ruler waved them off, and although Fenrir didn't like that those two wanted to speak without anyone present, he could also understand why they had to.

On top of that, he wanted to see Astraea, and he knew there would be only one way to do it.

FENRIR USED every hidden path he knew to avoid being seen as he went straight to the Starry Garden.

It stood empty, and he waited for quite some time in their usual spot before he realised she probably couldn't get out. Although disappointing, the day ended very well, and he couldn't complain.

The desire to see Astraea and claim her again was clouding his mind, but he knew that after years he spent here alone, three days were nothing.

He was about to leave when her voice stopped him.

"Fenrir!" Astraea appeared with her elegant skirt in her hands, ankles visible to his sight, evoking all kinds of sinful thoughts in his head. He knew she was running here by the way her chest rose and fell, and he opened his arms for her as she closed the distance between them, pulling her as close as he could without hurting her.

"What do you do with me, my little star?" He kissed the tip of her head while she tucked her face in his chest.

"Tell me it's going to be alright," she whispered.

"Astraea," he cupped her chin and made her look at him, "I will die before I let them separate us."

"You aren't exactly helping the case!" She shook her head.

"Forgive me, my love." He leaned down to claim her lips in a gentle kiss, feeling how agitated she was. He wanted to reassure her and give her strength. After all, didn't he promise to protect her?

"Give me your hand," the wolf signed, watching her eyes widen.

"What are you doing?" The little goddess gasped when she saw him slide his bracelet onto her. Both rows of precious beads were given to him by his father and collected personally when opportunities presented themselves. "Fenrir, no," she tried to protest. "These mean so much to you."

"And you mean everything to me," he countered. "I want you to have it. That way, you always have a piece of me with you."

She brightened a bit and he knew he did the right thing.

"Fenrir," Astraea whispered so that he could barely hear her. "I love you."

"I love you too." He kissed the tip of her nose.

"I can't say I trust any of them," she confessed, unwilling to distance herself from him.

"Out of everyone here, I only trust Tyr," Fenrir admitted. "He is the only one who I can call a friend."

"Do you think he would help us if the worst happened?"

He didn't know what to answer, because deep inside, he wasn't so sure.

"I can speak to him about it first," Fenrir suggested, and his beloved nodded.

"Try that. We need any help we can get."

"THAT'S QUITE a mess you've caused." Tyr leaned over the doorframe to his study.

"That's one way of looking at it," Fenrir replied with a chuckle, putting aside the book he was reading. It didn't help to distract him anyway. "How can I help you?"

"I am afraid I am the one who has to help you." Tyr smirked, waving for Fenrir to join him. "It's best if no one sees you these three days. Everyone is fuming, and anything can happen."

"What are you offering exactly?" The wolf arched his brow lazily.

"Help me test my new invention." Tyr smiled, but for some reason, that smile didn't reach his eyes. "It's in a nearby cave, and no one can see it until it's done."

"Another one?" Fenrir rolled his eyes, but deep inside, he was happy that the God of War needed his assistance. It was a perfect opportunity for that conversation, away from this place where even the walls had ears.

"If I am correct, this chain will be enough to subdue Odin himself." Tyr shrugged. "But I need someone like you to tell me for sure before I present it to him. Maybe such a gift would lift his mood up."

"One can hope," Fenrir snorted, standing up. "Show me the way!"

THEY WALKED DEEP into the mountains, and the further they went, the less Fenrir liked the idea.

"How far away is this exactly?" he asked his friend.

"We are almost there," Tyr replied without looking into his eyes. He tried not to read too much into this. They were always doing things like this, yet something felt off today.

"Is everything fine?" He wanted to hear the confirmation. He needed it.

"Yeah, sure," Tyr insisted, letting out a laugh just like usual. "If anything is wrong, you can take my arm off."

"What would I do with your arm?" Fenrir burst out laughing. "Only to scratch my ass, but that's too good for your hands."

They joked some more on their way to the cave's entrance, and Fenrir was relieved that all his worry was just his imagination.

Until something heavy bound his feet without any forewarning, and then his thighs, getting his hands too before he could do anything about it.

"Tyr, what the fuck?" he growled, trying to free himself, but it proved impossible. He tried to reach his wrist to get the beads... only to realise his mistake.

"Tyr?" he roared, the sound echoing through the tall walls of the cave.

"I am sorry, Rir." The God of War was unusually quiet. "I had no choice—"

"What did you think?" Vidar walked out of the darkness, and Fenrir realised the gravity of the situation. "That Tyr is really your friend? He was just watching you because it was an order! You have no friends!"

"Release me!" Fenrir demanded, struggling against the strange chain that was so thin and yet prevented him from moving.

Vidar's boot landed harshly on his face.

"Do you even realise how much work that was to subdue you finally? So many creatures had to take part. We had to repeat it on werewolves and create werecats, werebirds, werebears... all just for you. So that Gleipnir could be made."

"Gleipnir?" Fenrir met his rival's gaze and got hit in the stomach.

"The chain that bound the monstrous wolf," Vidar explained. "The sound of a cat's footfall, the roots of a mountain, the claws of the bear, the breath of the siren, the feather of the birds and a maiden's hair. As a special courtesy to you, we used Astraea's strand to bring you down. I hope you can find some solace in it because nothing else will ever happen to you. This is where you stay to rot forever. Forever!"

PRESENT TIME

This was so clever that if he weren't absolutely furious, he would probably complement Salome on the idea.

Gleipnir, the chain that held him prisoner once, was the only thing able to contain him. Temporarily because he already broke it once, and he would do it again. And yet it would hold him here for quite some time.

Anger coursing through his veins, he tried to concentrate on reaching the state just like back then.

It seemed like hours had passed, but he still had no results.

This was when an ethereal glow illuminated the void, and he saw an elegant figure appearing right before him.

"Long time no see, Fenrir."

40. SACRIFICE

SOLACE

Astrea watched the people surrounding her with anger written all over their faces. Their fury was palpable, and the worst part was that she couldn't even blame them for it. She was the one at fault; she knew it very well. Maybe not directly, but she was the reason for what was happening, and it was eating her from the inside out.

Yet it did break her heart a little that, once again, she was an outsider, the odd one out. She allowed herself to live in happy bliss, thinking she had finally found a place she could call home for just a few hours.

Now, the heavy reality of her situation sunk in.

She would never belong anywhere.

Astrea was thinking of what to do when her eyes met a pair of dark ones, and everything became clear instantly.

Salome was smirking. SMIRKING!

"Shall we kill her as a farewell gift to Solace?" Nova suggested sarcastically. *"They would do so much better without her! Just saying."*

"When did murder solve any troubles?" Astrea tried not to let emotions take over her.

"I can't stand when such people win," the wolf grunted.

"There is no world where we allow ourselves to be set up like that and let the person at fault get away with it," Astrea assured her.

This was the main thing she learned on the Firstborn island. You let them walk over you once, and it would never end.

"It's her fault!" someone shouted, pointing at the newcomer again. "Everyone in Raja died because of her!"

"We should kill her for this!" some man insisted. "My son is dead thanks to her! She ruined our lives!"

"Kill her, and you will join him!" Kara crossed her hands over her chest, stepping before Astrea as if to shield her. Her unnervingly calm voice was not mistaken for a sign of weakness, so a few people took a few steps back.

"Let's remember the rules of Solace for a moment." Devoss tried to calm everyone down with his usual carefree expression. "No murders allowed! No physical fights! You know what the punishment is!"

A wave of disapproval rippled through the crowd. They really wanted her blood.

Astrea noticed Warg and Bash running from another corner of the square towards them, but she couldn't tell yet if this was good or bad. If Kara and Devoss were on her side and Salome was clearly against her, both Warg and Bash remained a mystery.

"She deceived Fenrir!" someone suggested bitterly. "We need to throw her out of Solace!"

"Good riddance!" another supported the idea. "Let her join her people!"

Astrea's patience was growing thinner by the minute. They didn't know what they were talking about.

"I did not deceive Fenrir!" she announced loudly, making everyone quiet as she raised her hand to draw attention. "I came from the South, yes, but Fenrir knew everything there was to know about me. Who do you think your King is?"

That was a powerful argument. They may not have trusted her, but they had no doubts about their King. That gave Astrea the confidence to go on.

"On top of that, I had no idea Solace existed, and I didn't ask to be brought here. Fenrir did it because of an accident on the border of Raja, and I was not aware until I woke up here. But I don't regret anything. I am happy I ended up in this place and got to meet you all. This was a life-changing experience. All that being said, I have no part in what happened in Raja. I didn't know about it and—"

"Shut up!" an older woman growled at her. "We all know that there was a breach here in Solace! For the first time ever! And we know that you were there! You brought the enemy here! You are at fault!"

"Now the Southern army is probably marching here!" someone from the back added.

Astrea clenched her fists.

"It's true that I knew the people who breached Solace, and I was there when it happened!" She breathed out and prospered to tell them everything. It couldn't get worse anyway. "But I didn't invite them. I didn't help them! I didn't know it would happen, and when I found out... I chose to fight for Solace! I killed two spies out of three with my own hands and almost died in the process! This was why Fenrir believed me! He saw it with his own eyes!"

She could tell that people were not so sure anymore, but most were far from convinced. After all, words were just words.

"It's true!" Kara confirmed, and they seemed to believe her more. "I was there as well."

"Not to mention that I couldn't help anyone to get in!" Astrea decided to give them some harsh facts. "All the intruders had bead bracelets on, and before this morning, I didn't have one. It could be literally anyone but me!"

She raised her wrist to demonstrate the beads Fenrir gave her just a few hours ago, and finally, everyone got quiet.

"See?" Kara pointed at the jewellery piece. "Fenrir trusts her, and he knows everything! Why are you still questioning her?"

"This—" Salome became pale as she pushed through the crowd. "Who gave it to you? So many—"

The witch's lips trembled uncontrollably, but Astrea did not feel sorry for her. Not anymore.

"The question is," Devoss was smirking, "who *did* have access to those other beads? Salome, dear, do you have any idea?"

The witch's head snapped to him defiantly as she regained her composure.

"For starters, you did, Dev," she replied unemotionally, rolling her eyes to demonstrate how unbothered she was by the subtle accusations.

"And who else?" The fox's lips curled.

"Look," Bash stepped forward, "that's not important right now. We have an army moving towards us, and Fenrir is missing."

"And whose fault is that?" Devoss arched his brow, making the blonde guy frown.

They all knew more than they were telling her.

"Their leader would stop at nothing to get what he wants!" the witch interrupted him again. "We need to work on the problems at hand!"

"How would you know how their leader works?" Astrea decided to jab her one last time. "I thought South and East never communicated before I arrived."

"It's my job to know these things!" Salome gritted her teeth. "I am the protector of the East! I've been doing this job perfectly for years until you arrived!"

"Maybe you shouldn't have lost your focus then." Astrea couldn't hide her amusement.

However, her excitement died down fast when she saw the faces of the people around her, who seemed utterly lost now. They didn't know what to do or think, and this public conversation wasn't helping.

This was when the citizens of Solace needed reassurance, but their leader was gone, and his team they trusted so much was falling apart before their eyes. They were losing trust in everything, devoured by panic, fear and pain. And worst of all – they didn't know what to do with the army on their doorsteps.

"It's going to be alright!" Astrea raised her hand again, attracting everyone's attention. "We can't change what happened in Raja, but you are right, I know these people. I know these people and I-I think I have something that can stop them."

"You shouldn't do it!" Kara grasped Astrea's hand, and the two women crossed gazes briefly.

"Kara, I could feel that there is a story between you and me," Astrea told her as she slipped her hand away. "A story you are not telling me."

The Valkyrie sighed heavily, which was a subtle confirmation of her suspicions.

"I owe you a debt that can never be repaid," Kara admitted, and Astrea nodded understandingly. That explained it.

"Well, it's good that I want to collect," the Dragonfly snorted. "Kara, I want you to take care of Fenrir when I am gone and always stay loyal to him. Gods know he needs loyal people by his side. Especially now."

"He will never forgive us for this." Kara shook her head, running her palm over her face. "If he was here, he would never have allowed this to happen."

"But he is not here." Astrea smiled sincerely, adjusting her weapons on her battle suit. "And we are. It's up to us to try and defend this place, don't you think?"

"When he is back, heads will roll," Devoss commented as they all watched her getting ready. She had to look a certain way for what she was going to do.

"And our task is to keep the right heads intact for now." Astrea let out a dark chuckle, but no one joined her.

Salome lowered her eyes, while Warg swore under his breath.

"It's not right!" The tall warrior punched the wall, indenting it permanently.

"Aww," Astrea grinned, "I had no idea you liked me that much! Good to know for the future."

Once again, no one joined her fake fun and this time Bash was the one who pushed off the wall, walking towards her firmly.

She expected something snarky as usual, but instead, the young wolf took her hand and placed something cold into her palm.

"Fenrir forgot to add this one to your bracelet," he said dryly when Astrea looked at what he gave her.

A little red crystal bead was gleaming in her palm, and she raised her brow questioningly.

"What is this for?"

"This will help you not to forget everything again when you cross the border," Bash informed her, and she noticed that his bracelet didn't have a red bead anymore. "And when you come back, it will allow you to see and enter the city. Just remember to destroy it if the wrong person tries using it. Keep it safe."

She was surprised by this sudden change, but Devoss and Kara were calm about it, meaning it was safe to accept the gift.

"Wait!" She tried to stop him. "What about you?"

He turned to look at her, the corners of his lips tilting upward.

"Let's just say I owe you one."

Astrea decided not to waste the time and leave that conversation for later. The closer the Teacher got to Solace, the fewer chances they had to save it.

She could see the dust gathering at the horizon and knew it would take the Firstborn less than an hour to get to the border. They had the coordinates. Back when she fought the other Dragonflies, she helped Dominica escape Midnight's wrath and leave Solace. Now it looked like this was the price, and the beads on their hands back then were identical to the one Bash gave her now. They helped to cross the border of Solace without forgetting everything that happened here. They also helped them see it.

A sad smile played on Astrea's lips when she stepped to the border, feeling the magic rippling through her body. Fenrir's magic.

The people of Solace were right. It was her fault, after all. Her mistake. And now she would have to fix it.

JORAN WAS FURIOUS.

It had been hours since he destroyed that dirty city, leaving it in flames. It helped him to appease his anger just a bit, but he still couldn't feel his Dragonfly no matter how hard he tried. Cursing himself every time for his stupid decision to let her go, he knew she had to be somewhere near.

The desert was vast, but it wasn't endless, and he was ready to turn it upside down just to get her back.

Ever since the day she left him again, he couldn't eat or sleep properly, confirming his worst suspicions. He needed her now. Needed her more than ever.

His plan seemed to be so perfect at first. Originally, when he didn't know that Fenrir was acting as the Rogue King, he knew that Astrea would fail her mission of arranging an alliance between the rogues and the republic. There was no way the South would ever want to work with rogues, no matter how well she groomed them. The idea was to learn everything about them and conquer them fast, getting spare access to the North from the side they didn't expect an attack, and recruiting any leftover rogue warriors as his spare chess pieces in the end. After all, what the South didn't know couldn't hurt them. They would die distracting the North and the West while the South conquered the continent in a clean swipe.

But he had to adjust when it became evident that he had made a mistake and Astrea met his brother again. He ordered his Dragonfly to kill Fenrir, knowing very well that in no lifetime, under no circumstances, she would be able to do it, which would, in turn, give him what he wanted. Her failure.

If she lost, she could never leave him again. She would have to stay by his side.

Maybe she thought otherwise, but Astrea wasn't aware she was giving a word to a god.

And the words given to the gods are binding.

Now, she would have to stay with him forever no matter what plans she had before that.

His father taught him well, after all. Each deal always came to one little technicality in the end.

There was only one problem, though. He couldn't find her.

He chose to drive in a car, not to be a target in the air. His little personal army was by his side, and they were moving towards the location Dominica specified.

A part of him was wondering what kind of city Fenrir built and how he created a protection so good that no one could detect it for years. Not even him.

The little red bead was on his wrist now. He had never seen anything like that one before. His brother, whom he considered broken and useless now, turned out to not be wasting all that time they spent apart.

First, his tricks cost him the North. And now, he tried to take the Dragonfly away.

Just the thought of the false Dragonflies made him cringe. Three dead, one useless now. And Astrea slowly regaining her full power.

He had to find her fast.

The wolves that ran before his car stopped, and so did his driver, making him get out and see what all the fuss was about.

One of his men pointed somewhere far in the desert, and he noticed her.

Astrea was walking towards them...

41. SCARS

*A*SGARD

Almost every god in Asgard loved Vidar. Or, at the very least, considered him nice simply because he never spoke much.

Fenrir always knew that it wasn't the case. While the others could afford not to pay attention, he didn't have that luxury. He had to learn each and every one of them in ways they probably never knew themselves. By observing them when they thought no one was watching, he came to learn a great deal.

He always knew there was nothing nice about Vidar. He noticed how he looked at his older, more popular brothers loved by everyone. There was nothing "nice" about it.

And now Vidar proved he was right about him all along.

Initially, Fenrir thought that the son of Odin would grow tired of beating him up every day, but days turned into weeks and weeks turned into months. Every night the bastard left Fenrir bruised and bleeding on the ground, with Gleipnir still wrapped all over him. Then, when he healed from his wounds, Vidar would be back to inflict his revenge all over again.

Until one day, he returned with more than just his fists. Vidar's lips curled in a cruel smirk when Fenrir noticed the gleaming sword in his hand.

A divine weapon.

Divine weapons could leave permanent scars. Divine weapons could kill.

Although Fenrir was not new to torture by now, he was not ready to die. He still knew nothing about Astrea. They didn't get to spend at least a lifetime together. His sister was still locked in hell and his brother was still an outcast everywhere. He couldn't leave things like this. He wasn't done yet.

"Let's try something new today." Vidar stepped closer, his finger tracing the sharp blade of his blade. "I think our games are ready for the next step."

"Fuck you!" Fenrir growled, emitting defiance as Gleipnir tightened, raising his hands in the air to make him an easier target for his tormentor. That chain had a cruel mind of its own.

A chuckle was his response.

"Don't be so boring!" Vidar methodically glided the sharp edge of his sword across the prisoner's face, exerting controlled force. He did not take his eyes off his captor as the blade traced a menacing path, leaving behind a faint, searing mark.

The drops of Fenrir's blood fell to the rocky ground, but he was not going to give that prick any kind of satisfaction.

"Out of the two of us, I'm not the boring one," the wolf commented, voice void of emotions. "You are the one who apparently has nothing better to do than come here. And here I thought I was the lonely one in Asgard. It seems that this crown is yours, after all. Even your brothers don't want to spend time with you. How is Thor, by the way? Any new conquests? I bet he brought another big fat victory while you were beating the crap out of a tied up man. It's been a while since the last one."

Fenrir's head snapped to the side as Vidar's boot connected solidly with his face, the sheer force of the blow kicking the air out of his lungs.

"Choose your words, mutt!" The next savage blow came to his abdomen. And then again and again until it forced Fenrir to wince, curling on the ground from the pain. If there were enough chains, he would have strangled Vidar with those. Gods knew he had nothing to lose.

"Fine!" Fenrir growled, seething with anger. "I'll choose some words for you. Pathetic—"

Kick.

"Slimy!"

Kick.

"Weakling!"

Vidar swung his sword, slicing it through one of Fenrir's hands, finally getting the guttural scream he desired so much.

His face contorted into a mask of rage as he brandished his sword, his intentions clear. With swift movements, he unleashed a barrage of calculated strikes upon his defenceless arrival.

The sharp steel bit into the prisoner's flesh, leaving shallow cuts that oozed blood all over his body. Each blow was carefully aimed at inflicting pain rather than causing fatal harm. Vidar wanted to break him, not kill him.

"I will stop if you beg me," he taunted with a cruel sneer. "Plead with me, apologise, beg for my forgiveness, tell me she is mine!"

"Never!" Fenrir snarled. Something very dark and dangerous was waking up inside him. Something new.

Vidar swore under his breath, making his attacks more brutal and dangerous.

Gods could live forever, but divine weapons could end their lives.

"I will marry her in a month!" Vidar shouted, kick after kick landing on Fenrir's battered body. "By the time I am done taking her on every surface in my palace, she won't even remember your name!"

"Is that what you are telling yourself?" The corners of Fenrir's lips quirked up despite the pain it caused.

It drove Vidar mad. A new series of blows and cuts unleashed, and this time, Fenrir didn't believe his enemy would stop. This was probably the end. He tried to shield himself, but the chains didn't let him move much.

"What are you doing?" A familiar voice made him flinch as the assault ended abruptly.

Tyr ran towards them, pushing Vidar away. Eyes filled with guilt, his rage filled the air quickly.

"Don't fucking touch him! This wasn't the agreement! You had your revenge. Now leave him alone!" The God of War was fuming, his hand on the hilt of his own sword, ready to pounce anytime.

Vidar spat, wiping away the beads of sweat that formed on his forehead from all the "work" he had done.

"It's not worth it!" he muttered, storming out of the cave and leaving the old mentor alone with his student.

Fenrir hated to be seen like this, bleeding and humiliated. Not to mention that it was the first time they had met after Tyr's betrayal. His old friend didn't visit him, probably unable to face him without shame.

The God of War silently kneeled next to him, taking off his cloak and using it to pat his many wounds.

"It's going to be alright," he promised, as if his words could be trusted.

"Are you going to release me, then?" Fenrir raised his brow questioningly, knowing the answer too damn well.

"You know I can't," Tyr grunted. "But I swear to you, he will never hurt you like this again."

A deep dark laugh echoed through the walls of the cave. It took Fenrir some time to realise that he was the one laughing.

"How sweet of you," he told his once best friend. "Too bad that you are the one who hurt me way more than Vidar ever could."

Tyr's fingers twitched at the words.

"I'll ease the chains a bit." He ignored the topic. Neither did he apologise for his betrayal. "Fenrir, I know it's bad now, but at least you are alive. A century or two, and Odin will change his mind. I think—"

The moment his binding loosened enough, Fenrir jumped onto his feet, blinded by rage, and wrapped it around Tyr's hand, pulling them tight around his joint. Gleipnir was very thin, with a goddess's hair strand as a part of it, making it a divine weapon too. So it sliced through his mentor's flesh fast as he put all his strength in it. One last sharp pull, and he managed to tear the hand off, eliciting am ear-shuttering scream from Tyr.

The moment it was done, they both fell to their knees in agony.

"You did owe me a hand," Fenrir reminded as Tyr watched him in horror. "Don't worry. In a century or two, you will have learnt to live without it."

Tyr scrambled to his feet, still in disbelief at what happened.

Fenrir threw the blooded cloak at him. "Here, pat your wounds with it. After all, I'm not a monster."

His ex-friend's lips trembled as the irony sunk in.

"I'll send Valkyries to guard you," the God of War informed him. "Vidar will not bother you anymore."

Tyr winced from the pain as he walked towards the exit and Fenrir hated himself for asking, but there was no other way to get the information he needed.

"Is it true that they're getting married, after all?"

His mentor stopped in his tracks, panting and not turning to face him.

"Really? You still care about her after everything that relationship cost you?"

"I'm not surprised you have to ask—" Fenrir sprawled on the ground, looking at the little opening in the cave's ceiling that allowed him to see the stars each night. It was literally the best thing he could experience in the last months. Each time he looked at them, he could imagine talking to Astraea. Sometimes it even seemed like she was talking back to him, whispering words of love and encouragement in his ears.

"I love her," Fenrir said, knowing he didn't need to explain himself, but he had nothing to hide. "I will love her until the day the last star dies in the sky, and even when the darkness consumes everything, my love for her will still be there to bring her back."

"You will die for her," Tyr stated dryly.

"In a heartbeat. As many times as she needs me."

Fenrir closed his eyes, his injuries finally catching up to him. He lost too much blood, and Gleipnir was still sucking the life out of him.

THE NEXT TIME he opened them, a woman with long brown hair with golden wings stood before him. He recognised the Valkyrie who observed him with concern written all over her face.

"My name is Kara, I am in charge of—"

"—my prison," he finished for her, his voice unusually gruff.

"The food will be over there." She pointed at a nearby rock. "Don't try to escape or break any rules again. There will be punishment if you do."

She was ready to leave when he spoke again.

"And here I thought the Valkyries were on the side of justice, honour and best warriors."

The words made Kara turn on her heels to glare at him.

"We are!" She gritted her teeth.

"Then remind me again what crime I have committed other than being born different from everyone here in Asgard?" He locked eyes with her, knowing that the Valkyrie wouldn't be able to look away.

"You seduced someone's betrothed." The woman didn't let a single emotion cripple onto her face.

"I did no such thing," he countered, trying to sit up, his face contorting from pain. "We fell in love long before that deal of a marriage was struck. We begged not to do this to us, but no one cared to listen. Everyone wanted the union we could have given them in a heartbeat if they simply allowed us to be happy together—"

Kara said nothing, but it didn't escape Fenrir how her fingers clenched around the hilt of the sword she was carrying.

"The water is next to the food," she said before spreading her wings and flying into the opening of the cave. Not that he expected anyone to regret their actions. That would have been too good to be true.

Fenrir didn't need food. He needed something else.

His whole body was sore, bringing waves of excruciating pain every time he moved. Those wounds would leave ugly scars.

The night fell, and the stars appeared before him once again. He tried concentrating on them, thinking of Astrea, remembering her scent and how her silky hair felt between his fingers.

He closed his eyes just for a moment, allowing himself to drift off to sleep and hoping to see her in one of those dreams. He loved dreaming now. In his dreams, he could meet her again.

"I missed you," Astrea whispered, peppering his chest with kisses. Waves of tingles rippled through him when she did it, and it was a very pleasant feeling.

"I will get to you one day. I promise," he muttered, barely able to open his eyes. He wanted to see her better, to take her in, to slide his hands all over her body. Sadly, his eyes couldn't open from the bruises while his joints were too weak to even grasp her flesh the way he loved to.

"Fenrir, I want you so much," she breathed out, undoing his pants.

His member was already hard for her when her fingers wrapped around it, stroking it up and down. Fenrir threw his head back when her lips touched his tip, making it moist.

It felt good but… he couldn't quite enjoy it the way he thought he would.

Astraea took him in, letting him hit the back of her throat. Then, when he was so hard for her he couldn't take it anymore, she released him with a pop and climbed on top of him.

She was so beautiful on top of him, untying the top of her dress to let it fall to her waist. He groaned at the sight and she smirked, taking his hand and placing it on her bare breast to help him feel more of her.

"Like that," she teased, guiding his cock to her entrance with her free hand and sliding it all the way in.

It felt good, but… at the same time, he couldn't help but feel that this was so wrong.

And yet. It was her, and she was here. It was everything he had hoped for…

"Gods, you are so big!" she moaned, riding him as fast as she could. There was no love in those movements, no warmth he always felt when they were together. She pounded her own flesh into him, screaming as the release ripped through her body, knowing that his followed right after.

Fenrir grunted as he came inside her and she finally stopped, panting.

"You are as good as they say," she muttered and his whole body went rigid.

It was her voice, her face but... it wasn't her behaviour. Astraea would never say these words.

She was about to slip out when he finally found the strength to grasp her hand and yank her towards him with force.

"Who are you?" he growled so loudly that the mountains surrounding the cave shook.

42. SHATTERED STARDUST

$\mathcal{A}$SGARD

"Who are you?" Fenrir snarled as the realisation hit him hard.

There was only one woman for him, and now someone violated his body by pretending to be her. A sinking feeling settled in the pit of his stomach. He felt so dirty and… used.

"Who sent you?" he demanded loudly, fire rising inside him. That fire burned away the pain in his exhausted body and dulled down the shame. The flames wanted to punish those who dared to deceive him in the most horrible way, whispering words of destruction in his ears.

"It's time for me to go, my love." The woman who looked identical to Astraea now tried to crawl away from him. Her foot got trapped in the grip of Gleipnir, stalling her and allowing Fenrir to grasp and pull her closer.

"Who. The Fuck. Are. You?!" he growled, his fury causing the cave walls to stagger.

"I am—Astr—" He was about to snap her neck when three Valkyries descended from the sky in the blink of an eye, pointing their sharp swords at him.

"Release her!" one of them ordered him, and Fenrir contemplated snapping the fake Astraea's neck just to spite them. They deserved it. They deserved so much more than that.

"No one dares to put her face on!" He raised his voice again, and one sword pierced his skin enough for blood to trickle down his chest. It was meant to intimidate him but had the opposite effect, simply making him angry.

"Enough!" Kara was the last one to appear, her golden wings blinding him temporarily as she landed, creating a cloud of dust around her. "Take your swords away!"

Her sisters didn't rush to obey the order at first, but meeting her withering glare, they quickly changed their minds.

"Now you, Fenrir," the Valkyrie said calmly. "Release the girl."

"Why should I?" He chuckled darkly, and she shuddered slightly, seeing him in such a state. "I am a criminal, remember? If I kill her, at least I would feel like I committed some sort of crime for the abundance of punishment I am getting."

"She simply follows orders like the rest of us," Kara informed him, and although he hoped she would shed some light on what was happening, she did no such thing.

And yet... he knew she was right. It was unlikely that the woman came here on her own, considering how heavily he was guarded. He hated her for what she did to him, and yet... he knew very well that not everyone in Asgard was a god. Hence, not everyone in Asgard had a choice. The stars were shimmering in the sky above his head, and he looked at them, remembering that the real Astraea was out there somewhere. What would she think of him now?

Disgusted, he pushed the woman away, and she quickly crawled to hide behind the Valkyries in a rush, trembling like a leaf in the strong wind.

"If this repeats, the next one will die instantly, and her blood will be on your hands!" he warned the women, and Kara nodded curtly. She was the last one to leave, and before she did, she turned to have a look at him one more time. It looked like she wanted to say something but did not find the right words.

TYR KEPT HIS WORD, and Vidar did not visit him anymore. Day after day was passing, and Fenrir refused to eat or drink because trusting anyone around him was impossible now.

Neither his brother nor his father came to free him, and hope was fading away each day. When it started raining, no one cared that he was bound under the open sky. His body, which usually radiated heat, was now trembling from the cold. He had a hard time remembering what day it was, and it seemed that the sky wouldn't stop crying along with his heart and soul.

Fenrir was now sure that being a god was a curse. However miserable and drained he was, this wouldn't kill him. He would endure an eternity of suffering and despair within the confines of this cave. Forgotten by the Asgardians, *he* couldn't forget what they had done to him.

His mind was slipping away, and only one thing kept him going.

The desire for the clouds to disappear and to see the stars again. The closest he could get to her in his stone cage—

He didn't even know if she would want him now. He wasn't the man she fell in love with anymore. What would she tell if she knew? Would she ever want him again?

Or maybe she knew already? After all, what was the purpose of such atrocities if not to use them against him?

Maybe Astraea already hated him like the rest of the gods.

Maybe they were done, and she was preparing for a wedding with her mate…

He drifted in and out of consciousness, trying to stay alert but too weak to do so. Gleipnir was slowly sucking the life out of him.

"Fenrir!" Warm hands cupped his face, and for a moment, he leaned into them, a familiar scent enveloping him. Gods knew he needed that warmth after such a long time alone in the darkness. "What did they do to you?"

Her voice was so sweet that he wanted to soak in that sound until… The memories rushed back, and his whole body shivered with fear.

"Get away from me!" He shook the hands off him.

Astraea's eyes widened as she looked at him, tears stinging her eyes. She was more beautiful than ever today in a flowing white dress with silver vines entwining around her slender frame. She had a white cloak on to cover her glowing hair, and a gleaming star necklace adorned her neck.

Fenrir closed his eyes, muttering, "It's not her. It's not her. It can't be her."

It pained her to see him like this. She hadn't seen him for months, and he looked at her as if she was a stranger now.

"Fenrir, please!" she begged him, brushing her palm over his cheek. "It's me. I came to free you. Tell me what to do."

"Lies," he mumbled quietly under his breath. "Not real—"

"How do I take this off?" Astraea tried to remove the chain, noticing how deep it went into his skin, leaving red lines. Tears rolled up in her eyes as she searched for a flaw or a loophole but found nothing.

"Go away," Fenrir stuttered. "Not—her—"

"It's me!" Astraea insisted, taking his face into her hands again. She simply couldn't take no for an answer. Not like that. "Fenrir, I love you! I came for you! It's me! I swear it's me! I am yours, and you are mine, remember? Those words bound us forever. Stronger than any chain!"

He finally looked at her, allowing himself to doubt that she was an illusion for the first time. Then his eyes lowered to her hands on the chains, and he saw his bead bracelet still on her wrist.

"It's you—" he breathed out, his heart clenching painfully.

She nodded and continued to check the chains, searching for a way to free him.

"We will go far away," she promised him, trying to hold back a sob that threatened to escape her. "To a place where no one will find us! We'll go to the human realm if we have to!"

"Will you—drop everything for me?" He was watching her in disbelief.

"Of course I will." Astraea wiped the tears off her cheeks. "I came back here just for you. I am not leaving without you! Not if I can help it!"

"Did you—marry him?"

"No, Fenrir, I didn't. Damn it, you have scars all over you. What have they done?"

"You didn't marry him!" A smile curled his lips despite the situation they were in. At this moment in time, nothing mattered to him more than Astraea being there for him and avoiding the marriage everyone else tried to force on her.

"My mother took me back to our realm at first and only agreed to let me return here when I promised to go through with the marriage and mating bond. So, I had to pretend," she explained hastily, "but I was searching for you. Fenrir, no one was saying a word until that one Valkyrie—"

She didn't get to finish her words when a sharp blade poked out of her abdomen.

Shock coursed through Fenrir's veins, rendering him momentarily numb as their eyes met in the understanding of what happened. He tried to scream, but no sound came out. His body jerked against the restraints in an attempt to intervene and save her, but Gleipnir held him well.

Astraea grasped his shoulder for support as the sword disappeared again. Blood gushed over both of them as she leaned into him, and he held her with his free hand.

"Pretend?" Vidar gritted his teeth, glaring at the red stain growing over the once-white dress of his fated mate. A woman who dared to be in love with another.

He couldn't let them humiliate him like that. There and now, Vidar knew what kind of god he was. She made him that.

The God of Vengeance.

"You think you can humiliate Asgard like that?" he shouted as Valkyries started to appear, trying to separate him from Astraea and Fenrir. "You think you can humiliate me?!"

"You are prohibited from entering this cave!" Kara bared her sword, ready to fight the deity who was much stronger than her. "Leave!"

The air in the cave thickened as a portal opened, and Tyr ran out of it, shocked by the scene unfolding before his eyes.

"Vidar!" he shouted, charging towards him and taking the sword away from Odin's son.

Another portal opened just a few seconds later, and Freyja walked out of it together with Selene. The Moon Goddess searched for her daughter and gasped in disbelief when she finally found her, colour draining from her beautiful face.

Fenrir did not care if they all killed each other. Life was slipping away from the woman he loved, and he couldn't help her. All he cared about was slipping away before his eyes.

His knees buckled, and he lowered her to the ground. For some reason, the chains loosened enough to allow him that.

"No!" His voice was hoarse as he watched Astraea trying to say something, too. "No, my love. You cannot leave me. Not like this. Not ever. Please—"

For the first time in his adult life, tears burned his eyes, rolling down his cheeks.

Astraea's gentle fingers brushed them away as she tried to smile at him.

Vidar pierced her with a divine weapon. Life was draining away from her, and yet she was the one who tried to console him.

"If we ever were to be married—" she whispered so that he was the only one who could hear her, "I'd want it to be in the Glowing Garden. This is where I fell in love with you, Fenrir—"

"Then this is where I will always be waiting for you. Do you hear me, Astraea? I'll wait for you in the Glowing Garden." He kissed her forehead, unable to stop the tears when he felt her hand slipping down his cheek. He caught it and kissed it too, kissed her palm and every finger. As if it could help him to hold her here for longer...

He tried to take her in – the hair, the face, the way she looked at him, the way her lips curved, yet at the same time, he knew too well none of this would ever be nearly enough if she wouldn't be with him.

She was watching him with glassy eyes when he leaned down to claim her lips one last time. The bittersweet feeling only brought him more pain.

"I am not losing you—" All the hurt was slowly turning into something else. Something dark and hollow.

"Don't give up—" Astraea's lips barely moved when she squeezed his palm as strongly as she could. "Fight—Be free—"

"What have you done?" Selene screamed at the two gods, looking at the bloodied sword in Tyr's hand. "How could you? Why?!"

"It was an accident!" Vidar replied dryly, and the Moon Goddess created a sphere of energy on her band, ready to erase them both from existence. "No one was supposed to be here. We thought it was an intruder! We realised that it was Astraea when it was too late."

Fenrir heard the lie, but he couldn't bring himself to react. Not with a dying Astraea in his arms.

However, Vidar didn't stay calm for long, grasping his heart just a few moments later and falling to the ground.

"What is this?" His face was contorted with pain.

"The mate bond!" Selene replied coldly. "When she is in pain, you feel it, remember?"

Vidar groaned on the ground, but he wasn't the main concern for anyone now.

"What, did you think that I would give my daughter away without precautions? You two are connected by a thread woven by Fates themselves."

"Let's calm down." Freyja touched Selene's shoulder. "We can fix this."

"My daughter is dying!" The goddess pushed her friend away. "Stabbed by a divine weapon! How do you imagine fixing that? It's impossible!"

"It is possible," Freyja replied confidently but slightly quieter than usual. "I saw Astraea in the future. More than once."

Selene wasn't listening, her attention on her daughter in the arms of that... animal.

"I can't imagine what kind of power is needed to save her," she mumbled, biting her lips. "She is the only one who potentially has that kind of divine power, but now it is disappearing before our eyes. She can't save herself because her power had never reached its prime. There is no deity who can—"

"We can save her but—" Freyja stumbled on her words. "But not her divine power. Just her soul."

Selene looked at the other woman in horror, but Freyja went on.

"I am sorry. I cannot think of anything better, but the gift I gave her protects her soul and connects her to the human realm—"

"No!" Selene protested. "It's the same as losing her if not worse!"

"Is it, though?" The Asgardian goddess took her hand and squeezed it lightly. "This is a way to keep her. She can live a thousand lives with that dragonfly mark. You can give her one of your wolves to protect her and—"

"How long will something like this last?" Selene knitted her brows together.

"Hopefully, long enough for us to find a solution on how to bring her back." Freyja turned to look at the starry goddess still in Fenrir's embrace. "After all, we all need Astraea—"

"You will not touch her again!" Fenrir growled as they neared them.

"It's not for you to decide!" Vidar spoke, words laced with venom. "She is my—"

Just then, Fenrir felt tingling on his fingertips and noticed Astrea's skin glowing. Little glimmering specs were forming on her skin and floating into the air.

"No," he whispered, clenching her tighter. "Don't go!"

Tiny partials of brilliance slipped through his fingers until she turned into a cascade of shimmering stardust that danced, flying into the sky and leaving him alone.

He thought he was alone for so long. Gods, he had no idea what real loneliness was until this moment.

His body and soul were aching. Everything around turned into a blur.

Fenrir woke up when it was dark, and only a few glittering specs on his hands were a reminder of what had happened here today.

That and the bracelet in his hand. The bracelet that still had her blood on it.

Fenrir looked at it, sensing something he didn't expect. A new bead.

One of the empty ones was glowing as if it had a star concealed inside. Astraea's power.

Anguish consumed him. They destroyed him. Killed her. And now they all were probably feasting together in the Golden Halls. He couldn't bear the thought of any of them getting away with their sins. He wanted to take just as much from them as they have taken from him.

Not thinking twice, Fenrir crushed the glowing bead between his fingers along with the rest of them, summoning all the powers he had been carefully collecting over centuries.

One after one, his bones were breaking as he chose to shift into the form that was now closer to his heart. They wanted a monster? He would give them the worst monster they had ever seen.

Gleipnir tried to sustain him, but the bigger he got, the thinner the chain became. And when hell flames kindled all over his fur, the binding fell to his feet.

The exit of the cave was too small for him, so he broke it, finally getting the freedom he wanted so much just a day ago. Now he wanted other things. Things he wouldn't get.

"Brother!" Joran greeted him at the foot of the mountain, with his father walking out of the darkness. "We've been waiting for you!"

"I am so sorry for what happened to you, son." Loki was about to touch his firefur, but withdrew his hand at the last moment. "We tried to get to you so many times. Luckily, you got out. Now—the time has come to start Ragnarok."

~SOLACE~

Astrea took her time on the way to her Teacher, and he also waited patiently for her to arrive.

She stopped just a few feet away from him, expecting an instruction on what to do next.

Joran quickly closed the distance between them, placing his hands on her shoulders.

"Dragonfly." He smiled, and for a moment, she thought it was genuine.

"I couldn't kill him," she admitted bluntly, and he clenched his lips. It wasn't that he expected her to, but this wasn't the first words he wanted to hear from her after so long.

"That's okay. We talked about this before. You know what it means."

She nodded because, of course, she knew. She did not fulfil her end of the deal, and now she had to stay with him for as long as he wished.

Astrea lowered her eyes, trying to hide her disappointment and anger. That man played her as if she was a child.

"Don't get sad," Joran chuckled. "It wouldn't be so bad. We are going home now."

He leaned down and planted a chaste kiss on her forehead, taking her hand and leading her away to his car.

"The city—" She wanted to tell him the lie she prepared, but he gestured for her to stop.

"Retract!" Joran ordered the warriors and then informed her cheerfully, "Niki will be happy to see you. She misses you every day."

Astrea tried to smile, but it was so hard to fake it.

"We are leaving?" she asked.

"I don't know about you, but I don't find deserts amusing. That's not my kind of thing."

They were already in the car when his phone rang, and he answered.

"Forrest," Jor greeted his colleague from the Southern Lycan Republic. Then after about a minute of listening, he added, "Fine. Sure. We'll pop by. Prepare my wings."

The car drove off, and Astrea couldn't help looking at all that sand in the window with a sense of longing she had never experienced before.

"What was that about?" she asked apathetically.

"Something came up in the Republic," her Teacher confessed.

"So, are you going there?"

"No, Astrea, *we* are going there. From now on, you will stay by my side at all times." Joran broke the news, and her heart sank.

That was new.

43. GOING SOUTH

*A*strea had been to the South a few times. In fact, this was where most of her past missions took place.

Joran was a member of the Alpha Convocation in the Southern Republic, and he didn't exactly get there by playing nice. Quite a few people had to disappear or be threatened for the Serpent to gain access to such a high position.

As a result, she didn't have any good memories of this place. This dirty job was never to her taste, even though she was considered one of the best in the field.

Joran watched her all the way to the Southern capital, New Verum, feeling more and more frustrated every minute.

She did not look at him once. Didn't even engage when he mentioned Niki. It was as if he was giving a ride to a statue of his Dragonfly and not the real person.

Astrea did not say a word when they switched to a helicopter; just a tiny tear blinked in her eye when she saw the remnants of Raja, the city he destroyed for her.

They were supposed to land soon, but he still couldn't get a word out of her pretty mouth. He had never been disrespected this much. Not since his Asgardian days.

"There will be some changes now," he informed her, making the snake on her neck tighten its grip. That made her touch the tattoo he gave her. At least they had some kind of contact now.

"Fine," she said quietly. "Whatever."

"I don't need you as an assassin anymore," he said, and she turned away to look at the window, not acknowledging his words. "You will live with me. I will take care of you."

She visibly shivered, but of course, it was new for her. This was officially unchartered territory for the two of them.

Ever since that day years ago when he found her terrified, alone in the woods and crying, he knew she would give him everything he ever desired. Now, he was starting to think that she could give him even more than that. Now, he began to want things he never considered before.

"I am going to run for the High Chancellor in two years." He continued explaining his plan as if she had shown some interest in the matter. Which she did not. Yet he knew her too well to know she was listening. "I will need to present myself as a good family man."

A snort escaped her, which she didn't try to hide from him, causing him to grow his claws and pierce the expensive leather of his seat.

"Do you want me to find you a bride?" She finally gave him an unimpressed glance, knowing she would get away with her reckless provocation.

"No need." His lips curled into a smirk. He was happy to repay her. "I already have a perfect candidate. I can only tolerate one person in the entire world."

He watched the colour drain from her face, painting it with utter shock. She knew what he meant without him having to say it out loud, and he was wondering why he announced it like that.

This wasn't his plan, but the words left his mouth as if he had no control over them.

"That would be a horrible political move," Astrea tried to reason with him.

"Good that it's not all about politics then." Joran chuckled, taking his turn to look away. He was completely off his game, and that rarely happened to him.

"You are not serious!"

Now they were finally having a conversation, but he didn't like it.

"I am dead serious. We will conquer the world together, Dragonfly. Just you wait."

"I have no interest in that!" she gasped, annoying him more. Couldn't she just play along for once? It's not like she could leave him. What did she expect to do?

"Astrea, you are bound to spend your entire life with me. This is the perfect place for you." He offered her his best argument. "You used to tell me that you want to change the world for the better, and this is exactly the chance I am giving you."

"I am not exactly marriage material," she countered, hopelessly looking for something more. As if she could change his mind.

"And I am not exactly High Chancellor material according to the South, but when did stuff like that ever stop us?"

She stared at him without saying a word, eyes full of fury.

"Take the snake off me." The Dragonfly gritted her teeth.

"No." He shook his head. "You need it for protection and—"

"Lies!" she exploded. "This is control! It's not a protection! And what you offer here is not a marriage. It's—"

"Don't confuse the situation," Joran had, had enough of it all, "I am not offering anything. I am telling you how it's going to be from now on so that you can get used to it sooner. Your role is changing, and that is all. I am not planning to force you to sleep with me if that's what you are afraid of, but you will forever be on my team, and you know it. Might as well make it pleasant for yourself and stop fighting me on every corner. I am trying, Astrea! I am really trying to make you happy the way only I can."

Deep inside, he really believed in this. He did so much for that stubborn girl, and she had no idea.

"If you really wanted me happy, you would have never done everything you've done to me!" she hissed, tears burning her eyes. "I am not some—"

"Niki is already waiting for us in the Verum residence," he interjected to make this stop. He did not want to hear about her cruel training, silver pit and Fenrir all over again. Everything he did had its purpose, and one day she would see that.

Joran knew he lost her trust very well when she grew up, but he also knew he would have it back someday. The day she would see the whole picture. Luckily, he was a very patient man.

"Just let her go," Astrea exhaled with some kind of desperation in her tired voice. "You know I can't leave you because I failed my mission, and now I am at your service forever. You can let Niki go."

"Why are you so sure she even wants to leave?" The Serpent raised his brow. "She is pretty happy where she is now. She has a great job and—"

"What kind of job?" Astrea's head snapped in his direction, but no muscle flinched on his face.

"A job that would allow her to live with us when we restore the Moonrise Kingdom to its former glory."

She ignored the crazy plan that had already caused too many wars and deaths because she knew he was distracting her.

"Joran," Astrea did her best to say his name and not call him Teacher, which seemed to please him a bit, "where is Niki? What is she doing? You said before that her Ascension went well, but she didn't have a mission yet."

"Her Ascension went well indeed." The man nodded, the corners of his lips tilting upwards slightly. "I am still thinking what gift to give her, which makes her a perfect candidate to look after my Champion."

A thousand thoughts went through Astrea's head.

"You have a new Champion?" she asked, remembering that according to what she had heard, the white bear he used to favour before died in the Northern War.

"Still the same," Joran admitted dryly. "Darius Bjorn. He lost—"

"Bjorn?" the Dragonfly gasped. "You made Niki look after Bjorn? That psychopath?"

She despised that man. Everything she knew about him was horrible. He was the one who wanted to kill all those people back at the Luna Trials. He represented everything she despised.

Just the thought that Niki had to spend time with him was driving her insane.

"They have a good relationship," he told her and placed his large palm on top of hers. "I want to keep him close, and she is the only one who managed to tame his temper a bit."

"She is an innocent girl!" Astrea couldn't find the right words to express her disgust. "And he—"

"He is blind. He will not touch her." Joran said it as if it was supposed to be the end of the conversation.

"Being blind doesn't make him a nice person!" She slipped her hand from under his.

"No, it's not, but she does." Joran had no intention of giving up. "Just like you make a better person out of me."

She was lost for words once again.

"You just slaughtered a city!" she reminded him.

"And spared another." He smirked, causing her to stiffen beside him. "You didn't think I wasn't aware of that secret city built under everyone's noses. I knew it was there. All I had to do was knock, and it would have had the same fate as Raja."

Astrea put all imaginable effort into not letting any emotion slip onto her face.

"I spared that city because I knew you liked it. So, you are welcome."

She turned away once again before she did something she'd regret later.

"We don't have to discuss everything and make all decisions today." Finally, Joran felt like he had won again.

They were about to land, and he wanted their visit to the capital to be as pleasant as possible. Astrea would need a lot of time to adjust to the new reality, and he would have to keep her busy for it to go smoothly. After all, no one knew her in this lifetime like he did. Not even Fenrir.

Someone was already waiting for them on the landing ground at the top of the central government skyscraper, and he frowned, noticing that it was his old frenemy, Forrest Romero.

His fellow chairman was true to himself, wearing his usual strict navy coat with a high collar, his dark brown curls whipped by the unyielding force of the helicopter rotors. Hands in pockets, he waited as if it didn't bother him in the slightest, and just the fact that he was there told Joran that it was indeed an urgent matter.

The Serpent gestured for Astrea to follow him, and, to his relief, she obeyed, knowing that causing a tantrum here would not help her with anything.

If Forrest was surprised to see him accompanied by her, he didn't let it show.

"Whatever caused you to rush me here?" Joran went straight to the point, his hand brushing briefly over Astrea's just to check she was there. "And why the hell couldn't you tell me this over the phone?"

"One would think it's obvious," the prick commented as if it was a plain fact. "It's not a phone matter."

He waved for them to go with him, and after locking eyes briefly, they did. They reached a long, glassy conference room just after a few flights of stairs.

The South loved everything made of glass. Or plastic. Which spoke volumes to Astrea. Her heart belonged in countries like the Northern Lycan Kingdom with its old-fashioned charm and the East, which gave her peace she never knew before.

"Forrest, seriously, cut the crap. What do you want?" The Serpent was losing patience. Forrest was one of the few who knew his true identity, and he didn't like to play around with him.

"We need to call an urgent vote," Romero said in a lower-than-usual voice. "Alpha Lothgar, the High Chancellor, is dead."

Astrea watched her Teacher go pale and a part of her enjoyed it. However, she wasn't clueless. She knew exactly what they were talking about.

The High Chancellor was basically the ruler of the Southern Republic. Although most questions were decided on during the Convocation meetings, the High Chancellor was ruling the country in their absence. He was also the one capable of vetoing any decision.

Not to mention that this was the position Joran expressed he wanted for himself just a few minutes ago.

"How did that happen?" Joran snarled. "I put the best protection in place for him. He was guarded by my Firstborn warriors!"

"A heart attack." Forrest rolled his eyes. "You can't foresee everything."

"I need two more years to prep the South for me taking this position." The dragon deity closed his eyes, trying to contain his fury.

He needed people to elect him for his plan to go well. This ruined it because he failed to bring the North to their feet. His ratings were mediocre at best, and despite being a deity, he couldn't just conquer the city. He needed at least one country truly on his side for his grand plans to work the way he intended.

The South was perfect for that.

"That's not the worst part," Forrest said, and Astrea noticed he was enjoying this just a little bit.

"What else?" Joran tilted his head to the side.

"His son is on the way here," the other man informed him, rolling his eyes, "and he wants to take his place until we have a proper vote."

Astrea didn't think this terrible day could get better. However, at the very least, it was getting entertaining.

Seeing Joran's plans crumble was very satisfying, even though her mind wandered to Fenrir every time she got a spare second. She could only hope he was back in Solace by now and had no idea what any of them would be doing next.

She was entranced by her thoughts when a strong scent of blue spruce brought her back to reality. It was incredibly pleasant and so strong she was surprised its owner wasn't in the room still.

"What the hell," Joran swore under his breath, and at the same moment, the tall doors opened, revealing a tall man with long brown hair looking directly at her with some sort of familiar longing.

Nova became restless inside of her, agitated with the sudden revelation.

"Mate," Astrea whispered before she realised what she was saying.

"Mine," the man's resounding reply echoed through the glassy room.

44. BORROWED TIME

enrir hated that this was the exact moment she had to make an appearance.

Selene, the Moon Goddess, was watching him struggle against the remnants of Gleipnir, the only chain in the world capable of binding him. Someone went to the trouble of getting it and reconnecting the links just to stall him here.

Someone powerful.

There was a list of people he despised, and Selene was definitely at the top of it.

"Came to gloat?" He raised his chin, offering her a defiant glare and trying to channel his anger into breaking the damn binding. "Happy?"

"I haven't been happy for a while." The woman before him sighed, and for some incomprehensible reason, he knew it was true.

It's been a while since they last saw each other. Just one look at her was enough to believe her. Selene seemed young, and her skin had that celestial moon glow, yet small wrinkles gathered around her eyes and above the bridge of her nose. They didn't ruin her beauty but gave her that tired look she never had before. Her eyes lacked their usual magical gleam. They were dull now, nothing ethereal in them anymore.

"Who ran a bus over you, and can I buy them a drink?" The wolf chuckled, not sparing the goddess's feelings. *She never spared his.*

"Sure, you can." The woman shrugged nonchalantly. This was the relationship they had. "He is your brother, after all."

"Ah, Joran!" Fenrir nodded understandingly. "I thought you two could work together this time, considering where Astrea was brought up."

"Work isn't the word I'd choose." Selene frowned.

"This is probably killing you." A hearty laugh rumbled through Fenrir's chest. "You have to cooperate with another—what was the word? Abomination."

"Do we have to do this?" The Moon Goddess rolled her eyes.

"No, we don't. So, off you go," he grunted, wishing for her to leave him alone as soon as possible.

"We have to speak," Selene insisted, giving up first.

"We really don't." Fenrir tried to stifle a scoff. "We had many conversations, and none of them ended well. Remember?"

"It's about Astraea—"

"It is always about Astrea! And one thing we can always agree on is that we will never agree on anything!" He pulled the chains again, but the concentration wasn't there. It was a useless move, and once again, he loathed the fact she was witnessing his failure.

"I was wrong," she said so quietly that he could barely hear her voice.

Yet it made him stop in his tracks. Never in a million years, he thought he would be able to hear anything like this from her lips.

"I didn't hear you," Fenrir stated bluntly. Not to be a jerk. He was sure he imagined that. Surely, she wasn't—

"I was *wrong!*" Selene repeated louder this time, furrowing her brows. "I thought I was right, I thought sooner or later she would forget you and move on. And I was *wrong.*"

He couldn't find what to say to her. Centuries ago, he allowed himself to imagine this moment sometimes. He never thought it would happen in a portal void with him in chains, but he did think that when Selene finally admitted her mistakes, he would be able to gloat or say something smug to her.

Sadly, that wasn't the case.

He did not care for the Moon Goddess anymore. He didn't count on her. All he thought of was Astrea, who was waiting for him back in Solace, and that someone close to him betrayed him. What if she was their goal?

He was too happy and too distracted by the birth of the promised baby. He rushed, and this was the result.

"What do you want, Selene?" he asked her, tired of their usual banter already. If she could admit her faults, he could skip that part.

"I want my last daughter to be happy." The woman blinked away a single tear that formed on her long lashes. "I had many children once upon a time, but they all died. Astraea is the last one."

He knew that much, but it still never helped him to see her side of things.

"I only sought for a way to protect her." She turned away, unable to face him. "An eternity with a son of Odin seemed like a good idea once. She would have ruled all the divine realms together with him. He could give her anything she wanted – protect her – it was a good plan."

"Well, that worked out great!" He let out a heavy breath. "All those lives wasted on being miserable!"

"If she could accept her mate—"

"It could only happen if I was her mate!" A growl escaped his chest, but for the first time, she didn't comment that he was an uncivilised animal. That was the most progress they had made in centuries.

"That's impossible," Selene admitted dryly. "You know that much."

"I know you ruined all of our lives!" The familiar flames ignited inside. A little more, and he could escape. For once, that woman was helping.

"I am sorry," she whispered, and his lips parted. Shock coursed through his veins. It was one thing to admit some of her mistakes, it was another to apologise properly. For a moment, he wondered if it was really Selene, but her aura was unmistakable.

"Did someone poison you or something?" Fenrir decided to clarify and saw her letting out a nervous laugh.

"Everything's changed, Fenrir." Selene couldn't hold back tears anymore. "Astraea has no more lives to waste."

Every muscle in his body got tense hearing that.

"What do you mean?" He could feel the fire burning through his skin, anticipating the answer and hoping he was wrong about it.

"Because—it's Astraea's last life," the Moon Goddess confessed, causing him to fall to his knees, pain engulfing every cell of his body.

"No." He shook his head, not accepting the news. "She is a celestial. She is supposed to live forever."

"Fenrir!" Selene covered her face with her hands. "She already died. She hasn't reached her celestial powers once in millennia. Astraea—she lived on borrowed time thanks to Freyja's gift. Unfortunately, her time is over. This is her last life in a werewolf's body."

"I fucking hate you!" He said the words with a note of despair in them, not sparing her a glance. "I hate what you did to us! I hate everything you represent! I hate how you feel you are better than anyone and that you know better. You ruined her! You ruined the best, the purest creature in the entire universe and never paid the price for what you have done!"

"I know!" she shouted, bursting out crying, unable to control her emotions.

Fenrir observed her in utter shock. They had known each other so long, and yet he never saw her like that.

A mess.

"I know—" she repeated after a while in a much weaker voice. The whole time, he was watching her, not knowing what to think and sadly realising it did not bring him joy to witness her falling apart. "But don't think I paid no price. I have been paying it for so long. Watching her suffer like that—it wasn't a walk in the park for me either."

"You could have stopped it!" he growled.

"I wish I could!" she countered. "Fenrir, the more time that passed, the less control I had over anything. Vidar has forged the threads that bind them to each other, sacrificing the divine weapons of his deceased family for it to happen. I had nothing to counter it with. I asked him to consider letting her go, but he—"

For once, Fenrir was glad he was chained. Just listening to this made him want to destroy everything around it. This void was a good place to get the news.

"He still wants his revenge." Fenrir gritted his teeth, clenching his hands around the chains. "Hasn't he had enough?"

"You know him as well as I do," Selene sighed, pacing back and forth. "He claims he loves her, but the mate bond is driving him crazy."

"And who do we have to thank for that?"

"Look, I came here for a reason." The Moon Goddess stopped him. "In this world, you are the only one who would do anything for her, and so am I."

"Are you?" he scoffed. "You let so many of her lives be destroyed by that monster!"

"That monster is the only one who can save her," Selene reasoned, and he became anxious hearing this.

"Save her? Do you even remember how many times he was the reason for her death? Each time Astraea and I got together, he was throwing hell at us until he got us apart!"

"I remember very well. I had to watch this. Over and over and over again! Each wolf I gave her perished as a result."

There was the Selene he remembered, her face once again lacking emotions.

"I was the one who pitched him the deal you two made. You steer clear of Astraea, and he lets her be as long as you two don't meet."

Every muscle in Fenrir's body stiffened.

That deal gave Astraea a few calm lives, but he wasn't allowed to be with her or help her in any way.

"That was you?" He always thought it was weird Vidar even considered offering him something like that.

He hated it, but it was better than watching her be tormented and killed. Ironically, she never was completely happy in those lives, but she lived. And there were good days in those lives. Knowing what bad days could look like, he wanted to give her at least that.

"Yes." Selene nodded. "It was better than nothing. I hoped that maybe he would calm down and leave her alone, but—"

"But he is too obsessed to forget," Fenrir chuckled darkly. The silent prick was a sadist. "So, if you solved the problem and everything was amazing, what is all this?"

"He broke your deal," the Moon Goddess informed him, and he pulled the chains harder.

"What do you mean? Astrea didn't meet him. She knows nothing of him."

"He tried to kill her when she was a child." Selene frowned, fisting her hands. "If not for your brother, her last life would be over—"

45. KEEPER OF MY HEART

*A*SGARD

Fenrir watched his brother fighting Thor in the sea next to Asgard. The bloody battle took longer than it took him to kill Odin, but he knew he couldn't interfere. It was Jor's destiny to kill his nemesis.

His own fight exhausted him, but also finally gave him some closure.

Odin destroyed his life. The All-Father was the reason for his suffering, and now he finally paid the price. If the ruler of Asgard didn't treat him like an unwanted pet, none of this would have happened. And Astraea would have been alive.

The gods were dying like flies around him, and he needed to find one more man. The man who took Astraea away from him.

A deep slash left by Odin on his abdomen was bleeding and he tried to heal it, but the power and strength were slipping away from him.

A stomp of water rose to the skies, and somehow Fenrir knew it meant the end of his brother's battle. He saw Thor walking out of the sea on shaky feet, black liquid oozing from his wounds. Jor's venom. This would be Thor's end.

Fenrir turned away from the dying son of Odin. He did not feel sorry for him. Strangely, he felt nothing. Somehow, all his emotions had been blocked since the last shimmering star of Astraea dissipated in his arms.

He searched for his brother, not knowing what he would do without him and found his human body washed up on the shore. An ominous sign for sure.

It took him a while to get there, but he dragged Joran, barely breathing, to safety, collapsing next to him.

"He got me!" His brother was trying to close his gushing wound, but judging by its placement, it was useless. The two gods killed each other. This wasn't the end they counted on.

"Hold on just a little!" Fenrir begged him. He had already lost Astraea. He wasn't losing Jormungandr, too. His brother did not deserve it. He didn't have the long and fulfilling life that Thor had. He wasn't everyone's favourite; he never knew what home or love was. It wasn't fair!

"Damn, that's one embarrassing death!" Jor could barely focus his eyes.

"For what it's worth, his wounds look more embarrassing to me." Fenrir tried to keep a brave face. "A slow death from poison is not that heroic if you ask me. And lucky for you, you have a far better brother than all of his put together. You are not going anywhere."

"I probably lost most of my dragon form—"

"You'll grow a new one. Remember you wanted large wings to be able to fly?"

Joran smiled at the thought. Flying was one of his biggest dreams, but he needed to slay another dragon and steal that ability from him. Dragons were hard to come by.

"We can get you wings, too," he muttered.

"I'll pass," Fenrir chuckled.

He ripped his bracelet off, searching for suitable beads. It was hard to concentrate now, but even if he simply gave Jor more time to regenerate, it could work.

Finally, he found what he was looking for and crushed it, seeing instant relief on his brother's face.

His joy was short-lived because a sword went right through his back and all the way to his chin and nose at a sharp angle.

Such an unexpected and brutal attack...

No Asgardian hit from the back. They were all too honourable—

All but one.

"You didn't think you were getting away with it all, did you?" Vidar spat, disgust clear on his face.

Joran watched blood trickle down Fenrir's neck, eyes wide as he grasped his wrist with the bracelet, knowing that there had to be more than one healing bead.

Vidar drew his sword back, and Fenrir towered over his sibling, disbelief surging through him. It wasn't supposed to go this way... his father and brother planned Ragnarok for years.

Fenrir was supposed to have an honest battle with Vidar. Just like he did with his father. And he would have ripped the silent prick apart—

"Coward!" Joran hissed, trying to get up, yet they were both too weak to fight.

"Call me whatever the fuck you want!" Vidar chuckled darkly. "I am the last man standing. All the heroes die today like the fools they are! I have to say thank you to you both and your father whom I just killed. If not for your nasty plans, I would have never risen to rule Asgard!"

"You rule nothing, you bastard!" Fenrir gathered his strength to face his enemy. "We fight and—"

"Fenrir, I already won a long time ago," Vidar announced. "When everyone you loved betrayed you. Asgardians, Tyr, your father and even your brother—"

"What are you talking about?" The wolf narrowed his eyes.

"Who do you think was bringing all these women to you while you were imprisoned in that cave? Who made them look like her? Who could change someone's appearance so that the glamour can fool even the gods? Who do you think drugged you?"

Fenrir swallowed his own blood, regeneration not working as fast as he had hoped.

"No!" he whispered as the realisation settled in his head.

"Have you not noticed your own children fighting today?" Vidar burst out laughing. "They grew those mutts so fast! You are an incredibly disgusting family."

"Are we?" Joran's lips curled into a smirk. "Aren't you the one celebrating the death of your father and brothers now?"

"At least I didn't use them for breeding to create chess pieces for myself!" Vidar pointed out, and Fenrir's blood boiled. Vidar could be lying but—his father and brother never came to his rescue. They waited under the cave and were ready as soon as he was out. And he did notice other wolves fighting. He just didn't care who was on the battlefield because he sought Odin and Vidar.

From the corner of his eye, he already saw a familiar Valkyrie flying towards him with the body of a white wolf in her hands. Five seconds ago he would have no idea who that was, but now his heart clenched when he saw a blood stain on the fur. His stomach churned as a whirlwind of emotions stormed through his soul. He hated what had happened to him, but if the acts resulted in women giving birth to his children, those kids were not to be blamed.

Vidar did not see Kara and it was doubtful she could kill him, but there was one thing Valkyrie's were particularly good at – opening portals between the realms.

A swirling vortex opened right next to him, and before he could do anything, Kara flew right into him, pushing him and his brother into the portal.

The kaleidoscope of colours caught them in the middle of a storm as they fell, fell, fell… landing in the middle of ice mountains. Fluffy snow caught them in its soft embrace.

"Where are we?" Joran tried to stand up, but landed back into the snow. His bleeding had stopped but he needed days of regeneration to feel better.

"Midgard." Kara carefully placed the white wolf on the ground, hissing as she tried to open her broken wings.

"Midgard?" Joran looked at her with wide eyes. "Don't tell me—"

"Yeah, I brought you to the mortal realm. The only one I had access to." The woman did not look apologetic. If anything, she looked concerned.

"Thank you." Fenrir stood up. Talking was painful due to his injuries, but he had to know. "Is that—"

Kara couldn't bring herself to look him in the eyes. She was the guard in his prison. All the terrible things that were done to him were done on her watch.

"One of your sons—Skoll."

"Let me guess, my father named him." Fenrir shook his head, still in disbelief. "If he survives, I will give him a better name."

The Valkyrie glanced at him, surprised beyond belief.

"You are—" Kara swallowed her pride and kneeled before him. "I owe you a debt that I will never be able to repay. Please accept my service as the payment."

She offered her sword to him, and Fenrir looked around.

What was he to do? A young dying wolf who was apparently his child from one of the women he hated. A Valkyrie with a tarnished humour, who has just betrayed Asgard for him and begged him to accept her sword. And his brother, who watched all this without saying a word.

Fenrir slowly turned to see him.

"Rir." Joran understood at once what was about to happen. "If there was any other choice, I would gladly—"

He did not get to finish because a powerful punch landed on his face, knocking him off his feet.

FENRIR PULLED THE CHAINS AGAIN, his powers still lacking, but they would soon be enough. Just a little more…

"Vidar wanted to kill her?" he growled, fire coursing through his veins.

"I don't know what exactly his plan was, but he attacked her car when she was just a child in this life. He killed her guards, older brother and her twin sister. He sent demons from Hel's realm after them, Fenrir. If Joran didn't feel the divine presence next to him and interfered, she would have been out of our reach forever."

"And Joran was there by accident, of course," the wolf groaned, not buying it.

"He was helping his Champion's interests in the area," Selene informed him. "It's a long story, and most of it doesn't matter anymore, but I checked, and it looks like he was not lying. We were lucky that Freyja told me this life would be Astrea's last, so I gave her a twin when she was reborn. A girl who was identical to her in looks. It's probably cruel, but—"

"Cruelty was never a problem for you," the man chuckled.

"No, it wasn't. Not when it's about protecting my daughter."

"This way of thinking really helps you sleep at night, right?" He scoffed. "I can't believe you let her live her life by my brother's side."

"It was the best choice at that moment," she reasoned. "You were nowhere to be found, and he was… there."

The words stung him. If only he knew the truce was broken, he would have taken Astrea away that very day and hidden her in Solace. He built the city with her in his thoughts. It was a place for those who wanted to disappear and feel safe. A home that was impossible for the outsiders to find.

And yet, it was his brother who ruined everything for him again.

Joran. That selfish bastard.

"I guess this is the abomination you can tolerate." He couldn't help but throw a jab her way.

"It's not about us anymore! Joran promised to keep her away from Vidar, to keep her safe. Vidar thought she was dead because he saw Astrea's twin's body, however—"

She stopped talking, and he knew that something was up.

"However, what?"

"I think deep inside, he knew it wasn't her. He kept looking, kept watching us, kept searching for her." The Moon Goddess looked anxious, hugging herself, and he knew she wasn't acting. "I think… he senses her through their mate bond. He feels she is alive."

"That psychopath!" Fenrir gritted his teeth. "He could have rejected her years ago, but he kept the bond to torture her."

"Fenrir, you don't get it. Barely anyone would break a mate bond." The woman sighed. "It's a life-changing experience—"

"The Western Princess and the Northern King would have broken any mate bond just to be together," Fenrir reminded her. "The bonds shouldn't serve an agenda. You never even considered them as mates, and their love is stronger than any mated couple's."

"It's an exception to the otherwise perfect rule." Selene ran her hand over her face. "As for Vidar, I think he loves her in his own way—"

That thought alone was so disgusting that the anger rolled over him in waves, finding the exit at the tips of his fingers as his claws grew.

"He." Fenrir pulled Gleipnir to its limits.

"Doesn't." His claws went in between the links, cutting through them.

"Know." The first link was broken.

"What." The second was crushed into pieces.

"Love." Pulling the chain by his other hand, he broke it in two.

"Is!" Gleipnir fell to the deity's feet as his chest heaved with fury.

The Moon Goddess didn't flinch, watching him rise before her. It was as if she expected it, wanted it.

"It took you a while," she commented calmly.

"Thanks for being as unhelpful as always." He raised a brow at her.

"Fenrir, our old grudges are not important anymore. I am here, and I want to help," Selene assured him, but he took it with a grain of salt. He would have killed for her help years ago, but what good was it doing to him now?

"I don't need you," he told her bluntly, without sparing her feelings.

"I guess you know Vidar's plan then." The Moon Goddess pursed her lips.

"I don't need to know it." He brushed her off, gathering the chains he had just broken. "I'm going to kill him and end this once and for all."

"And how exactly would you do this?" The woman looked at him questioningly.

"That's none of your business." He let out a dry laugh. "You don't think I will share my secrets with you, do you?"

"Fenrir, whatever Vidar is doing, he's been planning it for years!" she reminded him.

"And I wasn't sitting on my ass without thinking of our situation daily either," he snapped at her. "He is going down this time."

"Fenrir, he is a god in his prime power and you—"

"I know very well what I am, Selene." His response was firm as he wrapped Gleipnir around his hand. "But if this is really Astrea's last life, I am not leaving anything up to a chance. She is all that matters to me. If she dies, I die as well. Maybe in that way, we will finally be together without all of you meddling."

"Is that all you want to offer to my daughter?" The Moon Goddess called him out, but he did not stop. This was nothing new to him.

"See you in another millennia, Selene!" He raised his hand to wave her a goodbye without turning to face her.

"Her divinity can be returned!" the woman shouted into his back, making him pause for a second.

He didn't say anything, but she did not want to waste her chance, so she continued.

"One god can give his or her divinity to another as a sacrifice—"

Resounding laughter erupted and Selene bit her lip.

"There it is!" He threw his head back, unable to control himself. "Now, this whole conversation finally makes sense! You want me to sacrifice my divinity and immortality for Astrea!"

"Didn't you say you love her?" The woman crossed her hands over her chest.

"Didn't you?" He turned on his heels to meet her gaze. "What was that about motherly love and all?"

"Do you think I didn't consider doing it myself?" She sounded as if she was appalled. "Unfortunately, Fenrir, no one can replace me! I am the Goddess of the Moon! I help to keep two races from slaughtering each other or maybe you have forgotten how you begged me once to give mates to your Lycans, too, because they were losing their minds otherwise?"

"How can I forget when you constantly remind me of that. You have to give mates to everyone now, don't you? After all, werecats, werebirds and other creatures created to help destroy me needed them, too."

"I hate doing this again." She closed her eyes, exhaling sharply. "If Astrea will take the burden of—"

"Selene, so many centuries, and you still know nothing about me," he reproached her. "You don't need to trick me to help Astrea, you don't need to ask me, you will never have to beg me. She is in my heart, and no one will ever take her place. All I do is always in her best interest, and if I need to give up my divinity for her, it's not a question. She can take it all – my immortality, my soul and my life. She has them even if she doesn't need them. She will always be the only keeper of my heart."

"I am sorry," Selene said as sincerely as she could. "Then—then, if you can do this, she could be saved. Everything will be restored to its place!"

"Really?" a scoff escaped him. "If I sacrifice my divinity, I will die, and you know it. Astrea will stay alone. It may come as a shock to you, but for the two of us it's worse than death. At least in my case, I knew she would be reborn again and again. I had something to look forward to before you and Vidar broke me. When I am gone, Astrea will have nothing. And I am not sure she will be grateful to any of us for that decision."

Fenrir raised his hand, creating a portal back home. He was done here.

"Wait!" Selene said, rushing to stop him, grasping him by his shoulder. Shock pulsed through the Wolf God. That woman never touched him in all those years, considering it beneath her.

"What do you want?" he grunted. The wind of the portal was whipping both their hair.

"You are right about me. I don't know you," Selene admitted. "I never gave you the benefit of a doubt. I have long forgotten what being in love feels like. Ever since my husband died, I have been alone, our children were my only source of joy. And when my realm started to crumble, I lost them too. I was one of the last ones standing and I thought I knew what I was doing. You two proved me wrong."

He was glad she finally understood, but here and now it was irrelevant.

"Your confession is too late," he told her, locking their eyes. "It will change nothing now, but if you need forgiveness, you have to ask for it from your daughter."

"I don't need forgiveness." The goddess lowered her head. "I need—I need to see her happy."

"That makes two of us."

She let go of him, and they stood like that for a few seconds before he exhaled heavily and prepared to leave.

"And what if... there is another way?"

"To hell with it, Selene! Why won't you start with it then?"

She hesitated.

"Because I am not sure you are going to like it."

46. SHADOWS OF THE PAST

strea stared at the man who had just announced his claim on her, and he couldn't take his eyes off her either, mesmerised by her presence. Her body was reacting to him in a way she never imagined reacting to a stranger, waves and waves of emotions mixed with desire coursing through her. These waves, she had to shut them down as soon as possible.

"He is... mate," Nova couldn't calm down, restless beyond belief. "I lost hope we would ever get one."

"Don't get used to him," Astrea commanded. "We are not keeping him. You know very well that nothing is that simple in our life, and a mate appearing now, at this time, is suspicious."

"Maybe he can save us," Nova suggested.

"Or maybe he is the one we need saving from," Astrea reasoned. "Besides, I'd rather we saved ourselves."

"But it's mate!" Nova became agitated. "He was destined for us—"

"And what about Fenrir?" the woman reminded her wolf. "Or maybe you forgot we love him and that it's not the first time we met?"

"Of course not." Now Nova was lost for thoughts, her excitement finally wearing off. "Fenrir is... everything, but—"

"No buts," Astrea insisted. "Fenrir is everything. It's in our nature to be enchanted by a mate, but we have to think straight. We are stronger than that."

"Got you," her wolf agreed, trying to build a wall around them quickly to avoid showing weakness or falling deeper.

"Did I hear what I think I heard just now?" Alpha Forrest whistled, watching the scene.

"Mine!" the stranger repeated, bringing Astrea out of her trance. Joran stepped in front of her, covering her with his body, and for the first time, she was grateful for his presence.

"Excuse me, you must be mistaken." He smirked.

"Talk about starting with the wrong foot," Forrest commented. "Gentlemen, allow me to introduce yourselves before you say anything else. Chairman Joran Nathair, Alpha Vincent Lothgar, son of the deceased High Chancellor."

Astrea almost whistled herself. So, the stranger was the one who wanted the position of the High Chancellor, also known as the Head of the Southern Lycan Republic. Although they had a system built on equality, there was still one person who could veto the decisions of the Alpha Convocation and act as the person in charge in case of emergencies. Joran had wanted this position for years. The Dragonfly always wondered why he couldn't take it by force, and now she began to realise he simply couldn't. Something was preventing him from it, or that man in front of them would have lost his head here and now.

"Last time I met Alpha Lothgar's son, he was just a teen pup." Joran did not seem happy with his new acquaintance. "That was just one year ago. Now, you either take some serious growth hormones or—"

"You met my younger brother," Vincent sneered. "Sadly, he had an unfortunate accident right before father's death."

"Unfortunate indeed," Joran sighed, although it sounded like a scoff. "And what a coincidence. But it still doesn't explain where you have been all this time?"

"Banished," Vincent explained without a care in the world. "My mother was my father's first mate, but it didn't go well after she betrayed him with another man. It took me years to prove my worth to my father, and he finally reinstated me just before his death."

That story sounded so cliché that it was hard to believe. Alpha Lothgar didn't seem to try in the least to make it believable, either, and that told Astrea a lot. He did not care whether two of the most influential people in the Southern Republic, as well as his own newly found mate, believed in him or not. He did not need them to.

"Fascinating! And how convenient!" Joran rolled his eyes. "About the vote—"

"We can discuss this later at the Convocation," Vincent shrugged and brushed his hand through his perfect hair, "right now, I have more pressing matters at hand. I didn't expect to meet my mate here, and I would like to—"

"I am afraid you will have to let it go. She is already taken." The Serpent didn't let him finish, marking his territory at once.

Astrea observed both men with keen interest, not saying a word and thinking of how she could use the situation to her advantage. It helped that they both were busy glaring at each other now, and none of them bothered to ask her for an opinion.

She was taught to observe and learn, which greatly helped her. Be invisible but know everything – this is how she usually worked. So, it didn't escape her eye that a new vibe was coming from her Teacher – he was intimidated by her mate.

And if he wasn't intimidated by Fenrir, who was his equal, it meant that he knew something about Vincent Lothgar that prevented him from acting rashly around the man.

"I don't see a mark on her neck," her mate commented, and Astrea shivered as the snake tattoo started moving. She still loathed that feeling.

"Look closer then." Joran clenched his jaw tightly.

"What is that?" Vincent furrowed his brows and pushed Joran away as if he was nothing. He was next to Astrea in no time, his fingers digging into her shoulders as he pushed the jacket down her arms and saw the moving snake that tried to bite him the second he was about to touch it.

"The mark you were looking for." Joran smirked, celebrating his momentary dominance.

"It's not a mark!" Alpha Lothgar growled. "It's not a real mark!"

"It's the only one I need!" A low growl escaped the Serpent. "Why don't you take your hands off her now?"

The snake moved again, demonstrating it was ready to defend its property, and Astrea decided to test the situation a little. This was interesting.

"It hurts," she whispered, rubbing her neck. Vincent's expression became darker at once.

"Take that thing off her!" he ordered and only received a mocking smile in return.

"I choose to decline that offer. Come here, Astrea." Joran seemed impatient as he stretched his hand to her, escalating the situation.

She looked sheepishly at Vincent and added quietly, "It's probably best if we reject each other here and now. I hope you will find your happiness—"

His anger became palpable as electricity filled the air.

"Never!" Vincent's eyes glowed blue.

"O-kay," Alpha Forrest cleared his throat. "We all need to take a deep breath and step back. This has been a long day. We don't have to discuss everything tonight. It's best to put off important life decisions for later."

"Well said," Joran agreed. "Let's go, Astrea. Our rooms should be ready by now."

Her eyes locked with her mate again, and she offered an apologetic smile. Alpha Lothgar's lips pressed into a thin white line. He took her hand, sending waves of tingles down her skin and pressed his lips against her fingers.

He knew exactly what he was doing.

"I will see you around, my mate," he promised right before her Teacher lost his patience and yanked her other hand to get her away from the man.

He opened the doors for her, and Astrea noted she could definitely work with the situation. It was almost as if they did the work for her.

The elevator ride through the Convocation building was unnervingly silent. That is, until Joran finally broke it.

"It changes nothing!" he announced dryly, and Astrea decided to play along. After all, her plan wasn't fully formed yet.

"I understand." She shrugged, startling him with her emotionless response.

For one-hundredth time, Joran regretted he had no power to read her mind. It would have been so helpful now.

"What did you feel when he walked in?" he asked.

"So many things!" she gasped, purposely avoiding his gaze. "He is—you know, my mate. His scent, the tingles... I could barely stay in the same room as him and wanted—"

"He is dangerous, Astrea!" Joran interrupted her.

"Isn't he just a werewolf?" She knitted her brows, hugging herself.

"Stay away from him. That's all you need to know. It's not like you can leave me anyway. A deal is a deal."

She clenched her lips tightly, trying not to snap at him.

"I understand," she nodded, "but what about the whole mate bond thing? I don't see him backing away from it."

"Leave it to me," Joran sneered. "All you need to do is to reject him when I tell you. At that precise moment."

"Sure," Astrea agreed, sensing that things would get interesting pretty soon.

The elevator stopped on one of the top floors, and they walked out into a lavish hall with several doors. Private apartments of the most notorious Alphas of the Convocation.

"I have a surprise for you." A smile curled onto the Serpent's lips.

"I feel like there has been enough surprises for a lifetime!" Astrea let out a chuckle, biting her lower lip when he shot an angry gaze at her. A motion that softened him.

Joran exhaled heavily and said, his voice laced with confidence, "You are going to love this one."

He pushed the heavy door, and they entered a spacious, light-filled room. It was a comfortable modern living room in an expensive yet minimalistic style, with one of the walls made of glass to observe the city.

Astrea's eyes immediately went to a person standing before it, but before she could react, she heard a familiar voice.

"Astrea!" Niki threw herself into her embrace, the sweet scent of magnolia enveloping her.

Her ward, her one and only friend, was here.

Her looks had not changed, yet somehow, it felt as if everything about her changed. She felt... grown up.

Astrea relaxed a bit, relief washing over her. Niki was fine. When they distanced from each other, she carefully studied her face and noticed that her ward was visibly happy. She didn't expect this; however, it could have been easily explained by their reunion.

"I will leave you," Joran interjected, and she nodded, not too sad to see him leave.

"You look amazing!" Niki finally distanced herself with a wide grin. "How have you been?"

"Been better." Astrea shrugged, her eyes travelling back to the man next to the window wall as memories coursed through her mind again.

She recognised him at once.

Darius Bjorn.

The Rebel Bear King of the North. The cold-blooded murderer. The manipulator.

The last time they met, the circumstances were very different. He had just abducted her friend, and Astrea pretended she had poisoned a few dozen people for his cause. By now, she knew that the war had ended with his defeat, and he probably was still holding a grudge against her for deceiving him since her lies were the main reasons for his failure.

"You are too noisy," he complained, and Astrea thought of how satisfying it would have been to throw him through that glass wall. It would take him at least a few minutes to fly to the ground...

She had prepared a snarky remark when the man turned to face them; the words refused to form on her tongue.

Bjorn was wearing a blindfold, and it was doubtful that anything kinky was happening there. So, that piece of black fabric had to have a different purpose.

"What happened to you?" she gasped, but found her answer watching the way he moved, searching for the direction her voice came from.

"It's none of your business, traitor!" Bjorn recognised her, and for a moment there, it made her proud. She almost thought he had forgotten her.

"Still the heartthrob I remember!" Astrea rolled her eyes.

"You betrayed me, and you stole from me!" he growled, his claws growing longer.

"I was never on your side to begin with to betray you," she reminded him. "And technically, the ring I took did not belong to you anymore, so—"

Bjorn moved towards them and almost fell because of a step near the window.

Niki caught him, moving as fast as the wind.

"Careful!" She clicked her tongue. "And be nice to Astrea! She is my friend."

Bjorn swore under his breath as she led him to the sofa and helped him down.

"Just more reason not to be nice," he groaned, crossing his hands over his chest.

"Excuse him," Niki giggled. "We are working on his motor skills now and haven't started on his manners!"

Astrea expected an outburst of anger from the white werebear, but nothing followed, to her surprise.

It wasn't good.

"Hey, Nik," she smiled at her ward. "Is there coffee here by any chance?"

"Sure." The girl nodded. "I'll make you a cup."

Niki disappeared, and Astrea did not waste time.

Bjorn was about to stand up and leave for his bedroom when he felt cold metal pressed against his neck.

"If you hurt her, I will skin you alive!" the Dragonfly assassin promised, pressing the blade deeper into his skin.

His throat bobbed, which made her smile and regret that he couldn't see that.

But his reply startled her.

"I would never hurt Niki!"

She pierced his skin to draw a little blood.

"Don't lie to me! It may be the last thing that you do!" she hissed. "And don't think I bought your little stumbling trick! I know very well you trained to fight blind because you already had one eye and knew this may happen to you if your enemies were clever enough."

Bjorn pressed his lips together.

"I will never hurt her! Ever!" Astrea listened to his heartbeat and knew he meant it.

"What is going on?" Niki walked in with a tray and three cups, which alerted her mentor since Bjorn didn't ask for anything. Just what was happening between the two?

"Nothing much." She smiled and fell on the sofa next to Bjorn, to ensure the seat was taken. "We were just reminiscing about the old times."

"You know each other?" Niki put the tray on the little table between them.

"Yeah, we do!" Astrea sneered. "Bjorn here is partially responsible for me spending months in the silver pit. He was the one who had this great idea to unalive dozens of people at the Northern Luna ceremony."

"What?" Colour drained from Niki's face, and Bjorn clenched the sofa's armrest harder. "Darius did that?"

"Not even his worst deed," the Dragonfly chuckled, getting her cup and sipping the coffee. "Amongst others, we have abducting a woman, chaining her and parading her on his back as a trophy, killing another and discarding her as if she was garbage, multiple innocent unnecessary people's deaths—"

"I am bored!" Bjorn stood up, and Niki was about to assist him, but he stormed out of the room before she could do that.

"Leave him be." Astrea stopped her ward. "He doesn't deserve your help."

"It's my... job." Niki lowered her gaze.

"You don't have to be that diligent. Just stay with me. We can finally talk."

JORAN WANTED to find Forrest and strategize for the upcoming vote when he noticed the door to the High Chancellor's office was opened.

He walked inside, knowing very well who and what he would see there.

Vidar stood with his hands behind his back, watching the mesmerising view in the glass wall.

"Verum is more beautiful than I remember," he stated without turning to greet him.

"And now that you've seen it, off to the New Asgard you go!" Joran clenched his fists. "This is my territory, Vincent." He said the name with so much venom that it made his opponent curl his lips.

"Luckily for you, I don't care about that territory." The God of Vengeance turned on his heels to face him.

"I am not letting her go if that's what you want." Jor stood his ground, ready to fight if he had to.

"And what if I can offer you something you wanted for so long but could never get?" Vidar smirked. "What if I offer you the deal of your life?"

47. SELF-MADE

*J*oran considered spitting in the other deity's face and leaving, but... he knew far too well he couldn't afford it.

Vidar was a god in the prime of his power. He resided in the divine realm and got all the nourishment his immortal soul needed.

Joran's story was different. He wasn't born a full god, to begin with. And since then, he had to evolve on his own. From a Serpent who could only roam the Earth and the sea, he had to slay one of the mightiest dragons out there to get his wings and fire, which allowed him to fly.

He was the definition of self-made, and that made him resent golden boys like Vidar, who had everything handed to them since birth. Vidar did not know the struggles he faced. Even so, he was currently more powerful.

Currently being the keyword. It could have been fixed if Joran got the entrance to the New Asgard, the divine realm he was thrown out of right after they lost Ragnarok.

For years, his and Fenrir's life was that of survival. They had to gain magic, gain powers, gain abilities. Then, they had to avoid Vidar whenever possible because every fight with him would take their gains away and waste the accumulated power and energy. Joran was so tired of this, tired of being a god and still having to hide.

He had been hiding as long as he had existed and absolutely loathed it.

Meanwhile, Vidar led the perfect life in the realm of gods. He would only come down when Astrea was close to adulthood during one of her new lives.

If Fenrir was near, he would tear them apart, destroy them, make them miserable, and when he was done, he would go back to enjoying himself as the ruler of New Asgard.

At first, Joran sought his brother's forgiveness. Their bond had to be deeper than what happened between them. He was sure that one day, he would be forgiven for bringing those women to the cave and for lying to him. After all, Fenrir grew to love and take care of his one and only surviving son, so it wasn't all bad.

Yet that day never arrived. No matter how many times he tried to get back into his brother's good graces, Fenrir only pushed him away or tolerated him when necessary.

When the dragon came back with a plan to return to the divine realm, Fenrir laughed in his face.

"You are still trying to be something that you are not, Jor!" he told him. "I lived in Asgard for centuries. And trust me, that place will not make you happy if you don't have the right person by your side."

"That's why I want to go with you!" Joran reasoned. "Together we are unstoppable."

"Forgive me, brother, but I have more important things to do. And I will never trust you enough to go on a battlefield with you again. I will never let you guard my back after what you did."

Those words hurt him. Their father was dead, and their sister Hel locked herself in her realm... Fenrir was everything he had left. Unfortunately, the wolf sibling did not consider him family anymore.

Over time, Joran accepted this and realised he was alone in his fight to go back home. However, now he wanted to take Astrea with him, too, which wasn't the original plan. He hated changes, and yet he was so close to achieving everything he ever wanted despite how complicated that was.

Shame, one more obstacle was in his way now.

Vidar sat in the High Chancellor's chair, which did not belong to him, and placed his feet on the long desk, glaring at him as if he was a disobedient servant. As always, the silent bastard had the most expensive shoes with tiny golden buckles and rare-looking leather. He loved his ridiculous footwear.

"Crocodile?" Joran raised his brow, pointing at the brogues and casually taking a seat in front of the man.

"Wild dragon," Vidar responded, knowing how disrespectful it was to say out loud.

"Goodness gracious, the universe is in good hands if you are ready to kill rare creatures for shoes." Joran did not plan to give that asshole the satisfaction of seeing him agitated, so not a muscle flinched on his face.

"It was not for shoes," the God of Vengeance chuckled. "You really made me hate your kind, and wild dragons are the easiest to find where I come from. Not to mention that I managed to finally change the old-fashioned upholstery in one of my reception rooms. Was worth it, if you ask me."

"Okay, I was under the impression you wanted to discuss more than your questionable fashion choices. Did I hear the word deal correctly?"

"You know you did, or you wouldn't be here," Vidar pointed out with a sneer and finally took his feet down, taking a less insulting posture.

"I know we are immortal, but I would greatly appreciate it if you cut to the point this century." Joran tapped his fingers on the wooden desk expectantly. "I have plans for the evening."

"Oh, it's easy." Vidar's lips stretched, but the smile did not look nice. "You know what I want, I am sure of it."

"My lovely fiancée is not for sale," Jor stated bluntly. "To be honest, I don't think you could offer me anything worthy of giving her up. You and my brother have been torturing my Dragonfly for centuries. I think she deserves a break, and I am happy to provide her one."

"She is not *your* Dragonfly." Vidar's thin lips twitched slightly, and that was like an ointment to the dragon's soul. He broke him first.

Perfect.

"She doesn't look too thrilled to be by your side. Besides, you do know that if you don't give her to me, I will find other ways to get what I want," Vidar warned him as his eyes darkened.

"And yet here we are in a situation you probably couldn't imagine. Ever." Joran pretended to enjoy the view through the glass wall. "If you don't have to bargain with me, why waste your precious divine time if you have everything figured out?"

Vidar contemplated whether to grace this abomination with a response, giving up in the end.

"Because it's important for me to make her choose me."

The words lingered between them as both men tasted them.

"Believe it or not, I can understand," Joran chuckled. He could understand indeed. He had been thinking about it, too. Fenrir was staking his claim on Astraea for so long, and yet it was he who appreciated her first. Joran had been pondering on that so many times. Would the story be different if he didn't hide behind that huge rock back then? What would have happened if he hadn't pushed Fenrir to talk to Astraea and take the blame for her missing clothes? What if he walked her back then and became her lover instead of his brother?

A part of him was always sure that she wouldn't have such a tragic ending by his side. He was selfish enough to steal her away from Asgard the moment she fell for him and keep her safe, away from that psychopath Vidar, who was now glaring at him.

"Let me guess"— the God of Vengeance lost his patience— "you took her in with your ulterior motives to use her to blackmail your brother or the Moon Goddess, or, possibly, both. However, the more time you spent with her, the more she got under your skin. You close your eyes, and you think of her. You give an order to your people, and you realise it benefits her. You see her as your Queen, the mother of your kids. She is the only woman you can imagine spending eternity with because there is no other like her. You've tried and tasted many, but it's her you desire the most. I understand. I really do."

"Funny you should think so after how many times you hurt her in the past," Joran reminded him, disgusted by that prick comparing the two of them.

"I have the worst temper, and I know it, but guess what, making her suffer never made me happy. She is my mate, and I want her to be happy with me. I can feel everything she feels, and I am most happy with her by my side."

"If only she didn't hate your guts!" the dragon snorted.

"She remembers nothing, and to be honest, it's not important."

"That's one way of looking at it," Joran scoffed.

"Do not pretend to be a saint – silver pit. I did my research this lifetime." Vidar sent him a withering glance as they scowled at each other.

"What I am trying to say," Vidar breathed out in annoyance, "you probably already know it's her last life. Unless you are ready to sacrifice your divinity for her, you can't help her."

"I am working on it!" Joran hated to be told he couldn't do anything.

"And, by now, you can also probably tell how impossible that is. You can't enter the New Asgard, and she doesn't have her divinity to survive. Maybe you can achieve one with all the little tricks you've been doing, but not both."

Joran pursed his lips, knowing well it was the truth. Falling for Astrea was never the plan. He wasn't supposed to take her with him to the divine realm when he was done here. Then again, he would need many more years to achieve that alone. He would have to unite the Moonrise Kingdom to get that kind of power as was promised in the prophecy he read many years ago – if that thing was true at all.

Unfortunately, his every attempt at uniting East, West, North and South failed, placing him back to square one. It would take more schemes and more generations to weave his vision into the minds of the people. Astrea did not have that much time.

"Out of us all, only I can have her and everything else." Vidar was as arrogant as ever, annoying him. "You'd have to choose because you can have only one at best. Not to mention there are no guarantees you'd be able to achieve anything. Especially if I am against you."

"You've been against me for years. And don't forget about Fenrir."

The deity sneered, resting his chin on his fist.

"As for your brother, it wouldn't be the first time you betrayed him. So, what's the big deal?"

"I don't hear what I get out of it all." Joran pretended to be bored.

"Everything but her," Vidar announced, his tone as serious as it could get. "I will grant you entrance to the New Asgard personally. I will give you your own palace. You will finally be able to live like a real god and have everything you ever wanted. I will even make Asgardians accept you. In return, you will take that serpent off her neck and renounce your claim on her, freeing her for me."

"What will you do then?" This was too good to be true, but at the same time, the new opportunity was not making him happy.

"I will bring her back to Asgard too. The moment she chooses me."

There it was. The catch.

"And if she doesn't?" If Joran knew one thing, Astrea had never chosen that monster in all her lifetimes. If there was a choice, she always went with Fenrir and died for it each time. This was one of the reasons he placed that snake around her delicate neck. He did not want to give her the choice that would undoubtedly kill her. Enough was enough.

His plan was to save her. To change the course of events. Something that both his brother and Vidar could never do.

"She will," the new ruler of Asgard cut him off. "Regardless of what happens to her, you will get what is promised to you. Think of it, snake, this is your best chance. The gates of Asgard will not open to you otherwise."

"Unless I kill you." The words slipped off his tongue involuntarily, but he did not regret them. He didn't want that prick to know what kind of effect that deal had on him.

"There, there—" A deep laugh rumbled through the God of Vengeance's chest. "If you could, we wouldn't be having this conversation."

He wanted to say something else, but the doors opened, and Alpha Forrest entered the room, eyeing them both suspiciously.

"Finally, I found you both!" he muttered, walking in without invitation. "We have a situation."

"What is it?" Joran was happy about the interruption. He needed more time to think about everything.

"The Delegation from the Western Lycan Kingdom arrived," Forrest informed them.

"Excuse me?" The dragon's brow went up. "We are not expecting any delegations from the West."

"Exactly!"

48. GAME CHANGER

Salome couldn't hold back her tears as she escaped to the front garden and sat next to Fenrir's favourite fountain. The plan was so simple, but everything went wrong. Ever since Astrea left with the Serpent, she couldn't find a place for herself. Getting rid of her rival was never supposed to feel like this.

She was miserable. It did not feel like a victory at all.

It did not help that all her friends seemed to know what she had done. And none of them approved.

Bash, who was initially on her side, couldn't look at her anymore. Kara pretended she did not exist. Devoss stopped making jokes, which was probably the worst sign of all.

Of course, they all guessed what she had done.

A heavy hand lay on her shoulder, and she didn't flinch, knowing it could only be one person.

"There is no use in crying now. What's done is done," Warg told her, taking a seat next to her on the stone bench. The witch couldn't face him, so she only glanced at the water's reflection.

"I only wanted to protect Solace and Fenrir," she whispered, knowing that only a part of it was true.

"I'll tell you something," Warg said, taking her tiny hand into his large one, squeezing it gently. "I know what he means to you. And don't think I do not know how it feels to see him looking at Astrea the way he never looked at you. I get it."

She swallowed nervously as a needle of jealousy pierced her heart again.

"Sal, I am old enough to know a thing or two. So, listen to the words of the first Lycan ever to exist: He will never love you the way you want him to, but don't let that pain turn you into a monster. It's an ugly feeling to want something another person has, and you have to fight it. Maybe one day you will stop loving him. Maybe you will love him forever—"

She sucked in a sharp breath, shuddering at the thought.

"But one thing is for sure," Warg continued, "he doesn't deserve all the horrible things that keep happening to him. You know it, and so do I. Fenrir is a good man. He is a better man than most, even when he is not trying, and when he does... he builds civilisations. He has sacrificed himself so many times, and in this regard, even you must agree they are similar. She left so that the Solace stood untouched. We could have defended ourselves here for at least a couple of days, but she decided not to take any chances. She believed in him enough to step away from the safety into his brother's arms. He will be back, and he will find her again. He always does. This is one constant I will always count on, but you know what?"

She avoided his gaze because he was right about everything; it was a hard pill to swallow.

Warg cupped her chin and made her look at him, wiping her tears away with his free hand.

"You are a good person, too, Salome," he insisted.

"Not anymore!" She tried to turn away, but he didn't let her.

"You've made a wrong choice, but it was just one day in your life. No one is perfect," Warg said, and she finally brought herself up to meet his gaze. "Remember this day forever. Remember what you feel now. And make it count. Work every day to fix this until you do, and never repeat it afterwards."

"Warg," another tear rolled down her cheek, "he will never forgive me—"

"This is where you are wrong. Fenrir is all about second chances." The Lycan smiled at her, and this was so rare for him that it made the corners of her lips tilt upwards, too.

"Warg, you are the only one who—" She wanted to tell him so much, but the air thickened, and she felt powerful energy swirling right next to them. The portal became visible in just a few moments, and Fenrir walked out of it with a chain wrapped around his hand.

"Tell him the truth," Warg whispered while the wind settled down. "And know that I am here for you, no matter what."

Fenrir looked around expectantly, and Salome knew who he was looking for as the disappointment painted itself all over his face. The guilt settled at the pit of her stomach.

"She is not here," the witch said quietly as their eyes locked.

"You've got some nerve to speak to me after all your tricks," the Rogue King snarled at her.

"Fenrir, I'm so sorry," she muttered, seeing how he clenched his fists and pursed his lips. "Astrea left with your brother. He burned down Raja and—"

"And you betrayed me," he interrupted her, watching the colour drain from her cheeks. She could see fire coursing through his veins.

"I thought—"

"I don't have time for this!" The man ignored her, walking past her. She knew it was probably better than him lashing out at her, but on the other hand, it made her feel so… insignificant.

Kara and Devoss greeted him in the house with the latest reports of the recent event, which only made Fenrir angrier. His lips twitched while he listened to how Astrea sacrificed herself to ensure Solace's safety and how the people remaining in Raja were slaughtered.

"Where is my son?" he asked dryly.

"Bash went to mobilise the army," Devoss replied. "Rir, I am so sorry we failed you—"

"Only one person failed me—" He frowned, going straight into his office, where his friends followed him.

"At least we accepted everyone who made the cut before the breach," Devoss tried to reassure him, seeing how he was barely holding back. "And now your brother thinks he broke all our army when it was just a fraction."

"It's still a loss." Fenrir threw Gleipnir on his desk.

"Is that what I think it is?" Kara furrowed her brows, and he nodded in response, checking the beads on his bracelet. He was going to need all of them for this. A plan was already forming in his head, but he needed to review all the details before acting.

"We are going to get her back," Devoss promised. "Rir, she is a tough cookie. You should have seen her—"

"If I saw her, she would be here with me now." The wolf gritted his teeth.

"Listen," Warg stepped forward, wearing his usual calm expression, "Salome—"

"Salome will have to search for a way to redeem herself before she shows herself before my eyes again," Fenrir growled. "I banish her from Solace, and I am not punishing her harder out of my respect for you and for her previous achievements. But let's not forget that a place in Solace should be earned. She just lost hers."

Warg knew when not to push his creator, so he bowed his head and left.

Neither Kara nor Devoss argued the decision, knowing there was no point.

"We are going to the South, aren't we?" The Valkyrie crossed her arms over her chest, sighing heavily.

"Yes, we are," Fenrir confirmed. "They paid us a visit and took something of ours. We have to repay the favour and get Astrea back."

"Sounds reasonable to me!" Devoss smirked. "This old fox needs new suits."

"I doubt there will be any left after I am done with them," Fenrir chuckled menacingly.

They started strategizing, thinking of different case scenarios and trying to predict every possible situation, knowing this wouldn't be a simple mission. They wouldn't be playing on their turf.

Hours passed, and Fenrir opened the top drawer of his desk in search of an old map, noticing an envelope that definitely did not belong there.

His hand flexed before he touched it as a familiar scent engulfed him – Astrea's scent.

"When did she—" His voice broke in the middle of a sentence. His friends looked at him with concern, seeing the letter and realising what happened.

"You know what," Devoss' voice sounded very high-pitched, "we will leave you alone to read it. We have to make the necessary arrangements, anyway."

She always had this effect on him and his life. She was there with him, even if they were apart, her presence undeniable.

There was only one piece of paper inside with handwriting he would recognise anywhere making him clench it tighter.

Dear Fenrir,

Though our paths crossed only recently, I feel as though we have known each other for eternity. I have no mate, but my soul is bound to you. I wish I could do as you asked, choose you and live in Solace forever, but I would do you and your life's work a disservice. Everything I touch dies, and I want you to live.

I want you to be happy, Fenrir.

Promise me you will be happy whatever happens.

I never said those words to anyone, and you deserved to hear them from me, but here they are in writing so that you know how I felt on the day I knew I couldn't stay.

I think I love you.

She crossed out those words, replacing them with new ones.

I love you so much it hurts to think about it.

Thank you for being you and for making me experience emotions I wasn't sure I was capable of.

Forever yours,

Astrea.

P.S. I left something for you on the Northern border. Find a dead oak tree, and you will find my little gift in its roots. I didn't know what to do with this, but something tells me you will. 23.4162 N, 25.6628 E.

He wanted to crumple the letter, but as always, destroying anything of Astraea's was too much for him. Let alone a love confession. He wasn't even sure when she wrote that letter. Not that it mattered. Now that he was thinking about it, she probably left it when she went to meet the other Dragonflies. What mattered the most, however, was to check what kind of farewell gift she had prepared for him this time. She wouldn't have sent him to the border if she didn't think it was important. She also hadn't gone there on his watch, so it meant she left that thing there before they met and only disclosed the location to him now.

"My hands are too pretty for this!" Devoss complained while digging in the roots of a dried oak tree, just like the letter instructed. "There are so many bugs in here. Why are there so many?"

"They like you." Fenrir rolled his eyes. "What takes you so long?"

"So many things!" the fox muttered under his breath. "For instance, we have no idea what we are looking for."

Fenrir exhaled heavily, not gracing him with a response as he searched on the other side. They were there for a while but still found nothing, making him wonder if it was a good idea to waste their time here, when they needed to be preparing to go to the Southern Lycan Republic.

He almost gave up when he felt a powerful source of energy not so far away. Fenrir closed his eyes not to be distracted and relied on what he felt instead of what he saw, inserting his hand deeply under the tree, and finally, he touched it, feeling the familiar energy. He grabbed the dirt and dried grass around the object and pulled his hand out, unclenching his fingers to see what all the fuss was about.

"It can't be," he muttered, shocked by his discovery.

"What is it?" Devoss leaned lower to see Astrea's gift better.

"It's just what I needed, Dev. A game changer!"

WHEN JORAN CAME to his penthouse, he found Astrea chatting with Niki and no Bjorn in sight. She was in a far better mood than he expected, and he caught himself in the thought that this was how he wanted to come back home every day.

However, the moment she noticed him, the smile dropped from her pretty face, replacing the warmth in her eyes she had for her ward with the coldness she had prepared for him.

"Teacher," she greeted him, knowing how much that title annoyed him now, but after his conversation with Vidar, he knew better than to be unhappy about it. He had to treasure every moment he got.

"Where is Darius?" He arched a brow at Niki, who stood up and lowered her head immediately.

"He is in his room minding his own business as he should be!" Astrea stood between him and his ward. "That bear is not a baby, you know. He'll manage."

Joran decided to ignore that attitude, too.

"Tomorrow, we are all going to an event to celebrate the late High Chancellor Lothgar," he informed them.

"You are throwing him a party instead of a funeral?" Astrea scoffed.

"His achievements should be celebrated." Joran went straight to the bar and poured himself a glass of his strongest whiskey. "Niki, you will go with Darius."

"Does she have to?" The Dragonfly stood up, fisting her hands.

"Yes, she has to because this is her work!" He took a sip without looking at her. "And you have to go to because—"

He stopped before he said something wrong again.

"Because otherwise, you will strangle me. I know." She smirked, narrowing her eyes. He hated it.

"Go check on Darius, Niki," he ordered to the girl and, luckily, she was clever enough to obey, leaving them alone and in silence.

Joran finished his glass and poured himself another one.

"Astrea, it doesn't have to be like this. I don't want to fight you and will not force you to do anything."

"Anything other than staying forcefully by your side!" she chuckled darkly.

"This is where you will be safe," he assured her, knowing it wouldn't make an impression on her. "Over time, you will understand what I am doing and why."

"I gave up on that a long time ago," the woman confessed, rubbing her forehead as if she was tired. It was a long day for her.

"Eventually, you will see what I did for you and why. You may think I was harsh with you, but everything I did made you the woman you are today. It made you strong! You are the strongest you've ever been."

He finished speaking and waited for her reaction. He needed at least something. Anything.

Astrea folded her arms over her chest, licking her dry lips and making his heart race.

"Thank you for that," she said in a huskier voice than usual. Relief surged through him. "Now, if you will excuse me, I am tired and would like to retire for the night."

He nodded and watched her going into the main bedroom. The one that they were sharing tonight.

Joran poured himself another glass and gulped it hastily, unbuttoning the top of his shirt. He knew it would be a while until she fully accepted him, but it would be progress even if he got just to sleep next to her in bed tonight.

He imagined his fingers stroking her delicate skin as she drifted to sleep, teaching her to get used to his presence.

His mood improved, and he followed her. It would be a hard night to control his urges next to her, but it still made him excited.

Joran breathed out as he placed his hand on the door handle... only to find it... locked.

49. UNFASHIONABLY LATE

"*W*hat is taking her so long?" Joran gobbled another glass of whiskey and placed the glass back on the bar table. Bjorn stood still next to him while Niki was adjusting his tie.

"She is probably doing her makeup," Niki mumbled apologetically, and he poured himself another glass.

"That's your fourth," Bjorn pointed out flatly.

"Your point?" The dragon still wasn't in the mood after last night, having to spend the night on the sofa. Never in his life had he ever been this humiliated, but he knew his limits with Astrea now that she had met his brother and Vidar, who was still technically her mate. Thanks to their history, he was the one she was not drawn to. He had no advantages over those two other than her word that bound them. So, he had to play nice.

"My point is that if you didn't get any yesterday when you were sober, you aren't getting it when you are drunk—" The bear cut off, and it took all Niki's willpower to suppress her laugh. She had never imagined anyone talking to the Teacher in that way.

"Talking from your experience with Savvy?" Joran snorted, but put the glass down.

Bjorn wasn't smiling or showing any emotions to her, but Niki could feel how tense he became.

So, the woman he was in love with was this Savvy...

Warm skin on her wrist brought her out of her trance.

"It's too tight, Strawberry," Darius told her, and she was happy he couldn't see her blushing.

"Sorry." She cleared her throat and loosened the tie a little, sliding her hands up and down his neck to check if it was comfortable.

"It's ok," the werebear said and touched her shoulder. It was something he did a lot lately, and not once did she distance herself from him, freezing every time it happened until he let her go. "Go check on your friend. I need to speak to Jor."

Since the Teacher did not object, Niki rushed to escape his company.

The corners of Bjorn's eyes tilted upwards when he heard the long train of her dress rustling over the floor, mixed with the clicking of her heels. He imagined how she looked, knowing her height and size from the times she helped him. He also already checked that her long silky hair was down today and wondered what colour it was. No one ever told him.

Joran, clearing his throat, brought his attention back to the deity.

"I am glad you like her," he told him, and Bjorn frowned in response.

"I tolerate her," he lied.

"Sure," the dragon chuckled. "Should I kill her then? I have no other use for her since you don't need her."

"Do as you wish." The bear turned away.

"It's a done deal, then." Joran shrugged. "She knows too much, and I can't risk it."

Joran watched his Champion and was honestly impressed how not a single muscle on his face flinched. He had chosen the right candidate back then. It may be that he could still rise to power if he played his cards right.

"Now that I think of it," Joran went on, "I should probably make it quick before the party."

Bjorn used his cane confidently to walk back to the window wall. He couldn't see the view, but he could feel the sun kissing his face, and it was better than nothing.

He shouldn't have said a word.

And yet he heard himself saying, "Astrea will hate you forever when she finds out. And she will. She is not dumb."

They both got silent. Joran's lips stretched into a wicked grin.

"There is no shame in admitting you like the Firstborn girl." The Serpent's mood went up.

"I don't," Bjorn brushed him off coldly. "She is no one to me."

"She is no one now, but she could be someone in the future. Don't you think so?"

"I already have a mate. One is more than enough."

"I am afraid that ship has sailed. My brother connected her and the Northern King, and you—"

"I know that very well and don't need a reminder," Bjorn cut him off. "This is exactly why I don't want anyone else. You can't replace a mate with just anyone."

"And I know that," the dragon deity retorted. "That's why I want to make her your mate. A mate can only be replaced by a second-chance mate. Or a third one in your case."

Bjorn's lips pressed into a thin white line.

"And how exactly would you do that?"

"I'll figure this out," Joran promised. "I just need a bit more time and—"

"No." The bear raised his hand to stop him. "Don't. Let Niki be."

"So, she is Niki to you now?" the Serpent smirked.

"You heard me. Leave her alone. She may meet her real mate and then—"

"And then she will have to kill him," Joran interjected. "One of the rules of the Firstborn island – no mates."

Bjorn clenched the silver bear handle of his cane so tight he left indents.

"Come on!" Joran tapped his shoulder as he suddenly appeared right next to him. "Just imagine it."

"Imagine what?"

"What I am offering here. We can be one big happy family," the Serpent teased him. "Astrea will stay with me, she loves Niki like a sister. As my Champion, I will give you more powers to compensate for the lost sight. She will be proud to be yours. And then we will think of what to do with our Northern predicament. We can still put them to their knees."

Bjorn tensed, realising that this was tempting and repelling at the same time. Luckily, he didn't have to respond because Niki was back. He could feel her before she opened the door of her mentor's room and walked out of it.

"Astrea said to go without her. She will join us shortly," she informed them, slightly scared. It was a tiny vibration in her sweet voice, but Darius could tell. He learned to feel what others couldn't see. She tried to be brave, but her mentor was too cocky to send her with a message like that for the crazy god.

"Is that what she said?" Joran's words were filled with venom, and Bjorn knew this intonation very well.

"What's the big deal?" he found himself saying as he stood between the Serpent and Niki, taking away the attention from her. "The Dragonfly is bound to you and will not go far away even if she tried. In the meantime, you are almost one hour late to an important political party. I am sure that Lothgar guy is already the centre of everyone's attention."

"Fine!" Joran had to agree, reminded that he was playing more than one game at once, and all of them were equally important. He wanted to walk into the event with Astrea, but they would have many events like that in the future.

Bjorn heard his angry, receding steps and the slamming of the door, but he forgot about all that the second a little hand draped itself around his arm.

"I guess we have to follow, too," Niki whispered awkwardly. "Thanks for your help, by the way."

"It wasn't free," the bear grunted, stumbling to ensure they didn't have to be in the elevator with Joran. He felt the woman tensing, cursing himself inwardly for the stupid joke.

"Wasn't it?" The girl let out a shaky laugh, which was not typical. "What do you want, then?"

He paused with the reply until she led him out of the penthouse and pressed the elevator button.

"Tell me what you are wearing," he said, the first thing that came to his mind.

"Excuse me?" Niki gasped as the door opened, and she roughly shoved him inside. That was more like her. "Why the hell would I tell you that?"

He chuckled the moment he found his balance. By now, he was adept enough with his blindness not to fall on the straight surface.

"Why?" He smirked, knowing she was watching him. "What if some other woman that smells like strawberries attempts to lead me away? I'd have to check if it's you or not, and I need to know what I am looking for."

"Oh, you poor teddy bear," she cooed sarcastically. "Don't worry, I don't think it would tempt anyone to lead you away!"

He knew she was fuming as the heat was radiating from her body. He knew it, and he liked it.

"You never know," he said, and sadly, the elevator door opened again. She led him out into a spacious room full of people, the buzz of many conversations filling his ears at once.

"I'll take that chance!" she hissed and added, "There! We are at the party, and we came together. Mission done. They say we have to mingle as not to be rude, so off you go. I know you can manage that much!"

She left abruptly, and he felt the disappointment settling in his chest. For some reason, he expected it to be different now, but it was the same as always – yet another woman did not care about him.

He checked the space before him and exhaled heavily, realising he was standing before a descending staircase. Worst-case scenario.

VIDAR WATCHED the entrance like a hawk despite talking to more people than he cared to remember. The annoying ants always wanted something from him. It was as if they could feel the power he emitted.

Jormungandr was already here, trying to sabotage his position and claims. As if he cared about that! He truly only cared about one thing here, and she was unfashionably late.

New guests stopped appearing from the main entrance a while ago, but Vidar kept watching, knowing she would arrive sooner or later. His little mate was too curious to pass up the opportunity. He knew her well enough to be sure of that. Thousands of years of observing the woman gave him an advantage. It was unlikely she could surprise him now.

He noticed some blind guy in dark glasses searching for the rails as everyone at the party ignored him. At least it was some kind of entertainment. His chances of falling down grew as his cane found the second step rather than the first. He was about to trip when a delicate arm caught his elbow, helping him, and Vidar's jaw tightened as he saw the Goddess of Stars in person.

She looked like a vision in a silvery chiffon dress with shimmering sequins adorning her bodice and the single long off-shoulder sleeve. The delicate fabric was draped around her toned body, reminding him of the outfits she wore when he first met her, with the ornaments imitating fallen stars. The diamond and silver clasp on her shoulder seemed to hold the whole thing together, allowing a sheer cape to flow freely behind her.

She was the goddess he remembered. Even when she did not.

Her hair in this life barely reached her shoulders, but it was still arranged in an intricate hairdo with a delicate star halo crown holding it all together.

Astrea let go of the blind guy the moment they were down, and Vidar moved in her direction like a shark chasing his prey.

But before he could get there, Joran stepped before her and wrapped his dirty hand around her waist.

"Ladies and gentlemen," he announced loudly. "Allow me to introduce Astrea Sade. My future wife."

A round of applause erupted, and Vidar knew it was his time for a speech.

50. POETIC JUSTICE

*A*strea walked into the banquet hall with an agenda of her own, hoping to make the grand entrance of her life.

It had to be done if she wanted to play her cards right, and she wanted it badly.

No one was telling her what was going on, but she was not a fool. She could see through schemes and secrets because Joran raised her that way. He taught her not to trust anyone, including him, and for the first time ever, she was grateful for the lessons.

She knew Fenrir couldn't tell her the truth, but maybe one of those two could spill the secrets, ending this mystery game once and for all.

Dragonfly simply knew better than to believe that her mate appeared out of the blue at the worst moment possible. Considering Vincent and Joran definitely knew each other despite pretending otherwise, she came to the conclusion he was someone powerful too, and not just a Lycan from a prominent family. The fact that even though her Teacher didn't like him, the Southerner was still alive and with all his limbs intact meant that he wasn't someone to dispose of easily.

So, she chose the prettiest dress that would certainly glimmer in the evening lights. Just enough to attract attention, but not over the top.

However, the entire plan went to waste when she walked in, ready to slay suitors, but that damn bear was in her way again. She stopped, giving him time to disappear. Yet it took Bjorn forever to check the stairs with his cane. On top of that, he was clearly about to fall and break his nose.

Although he deserved that, considering his past actions, gloating at the man who was already down and paying for his sins was not fun.

To add to the pain, she noticed Niki rushing towards him through the crowd.

Astrea grasped Bjorn's arm before her ward reached him, not letting him plaster all over the floor, and helped him down with a forced smile on her face.

"Be a good little bear, Bjorn," she hissed at him. "Find a dark corner and hide there. Don't think about looking for Niki. Don't look for her. Don't act all pitiful. She knows exactly what kind of monster you are."

She felt his whole body tensing under her grasp and knew she hit the bullseye with her words.

"I don't want her, and I don't need her," the werebear cut her off, freeing his hand and fixing his dark glasses. "If I could get rid of her, I would. I thought that you, Astrid, of all people, know very well that we aren't free. My life belongs to Joran now, just like yours, and until it remains so, I am stuck with that girl!"

He sucked in a sharp, angry breath and his lungs filled with the scent of strawberries. Bjorn's lips parted as he realised she was near and heard it all.

Astrea felt horrible seeing Niki's face during that conversation, and although she had done many questionable things in the past, for some reason, to allow her to hear all that felt the lowest of the low.

"Sorry," she mouthed to her ward, and Niki pretended she wasn't offended at all. Even though her lips quivered slightly, and her eyes glistened with tears. The tears she'd never allow to fall because she was trained better than that.

The girl walked away, and Bjorn stayed as if he was carved of unmovable stone.

"You and I may be stuck here," Astrea whispered to the man, "but Niki has a chance of getting her freedom back. Stay away from her. I will not say this again."

He did not respond, and she felt worse. If he said something snarky, she could convince herself that she was right. But now...

"There you are!" Joran appeared out of nowhere and wrapped his hand around her waist as his political buddies surrounded them, studying her with interest. Astrea turned back to search for the werebear, but he disappeared into the crowd without a trace.

The Dragonfly was a novelty to these men and women who supported her Teacher's political career in the Southern Lycan Republic, but she knew all of them very well. She had to study each of their files Joran had so carefully prepared at one time or another during her work for him. Little did they know they were all his pawns.

"Who is this beauty?" one of the Southerners asked, devouring her with his eyes as if he had never seen a woman before. Astrea hated cringy men like that.

A smile curled onto Joran's lips as he pulled her closer. "Ladies and gentlemen! Allow me to introduce Astrea Sade! My future wife."

The words almost made her ears bleed, but she still managed to suppress her frown, forcing a little smile as people around them started congratulating them. Just a moment ago, she was some pretty thing without a name, and now her importance grew in an instant, making everyone eager to get closer.

"Joran is a lucky man. You look absolutely divine, my dear," a woman with bright red hair said as she gave her a handshake. Astrea recognised her as one of the key Chairwomen in the country. She was someone Joran wouldn't mess with for some reason. He had to be elected for the position he wanted. Otherwise, he would have taken it a while ago, but here he was, buttering them all up.

"You two are such a beautiful and happy couple!" someone chimed in from the back.

"Oh, trust me," Astrea giggled, "we aren't *that* happy!"

Joran's grip on her tightened, only making her grin wider. He hated defiance, and she was going to drown him in it.

"Can I see the ring?" someone's trophy wife wondered, and Astrea waved her empty hands at her.

"He didn't put a ring on it! Can you believe it?" she huffed. "I guess technically, I am still single and up for grabs."

The grasp around her became even tighter, and so did the snake tattoo on her neck. She was ready for that trick, though, and started coughing, forcing him to back down.

"Are you all right?" One man seemed really concerned.

"Peachy!" Astrea gritted her teeth, slipping out of her so-called fiancé's arms. "Darling, it seems like I need some fresh air, but please, don't mind me. I'd hate to bother you at such an important event."

"Beautiful and understanding," another Southerner praised her. "Jor, you hit the jackpot with this one."

"You have no idea!" Joran clenched his jaw, angry but unable to object. Their eyes locked in a silent battle, and she knew she won that one.

Maybe she couldn't leave him because of their deal, but Joran wasn't exactly free, either. Something was holding him back. She never thought of that before. Why would a deity need a Firstborn army of assassins? Why was it so important for him to make deals when he could take whatever he wanted?

Maybe it was simply because he couldn't?

Her lips stretched into a cold smirk as she turned on her heels and sauntered out of the hall to the main balcony that, luckily, was empty now.

Hundreds of thoughts were circling through her mind. She could tell she was so close. However, there was something constantly in her way of remembering everything.

She was ready to swear, but then the familiar scent reached her nose.

Astrea had to admit that a mate had an appeal. If this were before Fenrir, she would have been interested in knowing him better. She could feel him with her skin, each cell calling to her to embrace the bond.

It was her heart and soul that told her otherwise.

"It's cold," Vincent sighed as he wrapped his blazer around her without asking if she needed it, his fingers lingering around her shoulders.

"The view here is beautiful." She did not turn to look at him, and he had to step forward to stand next to her.

"I've seen better," her mate admitted. "But I can't say I had better company."

"Well, I like it here," she stated firmly. "I always loved the South, and being here makes me happy. I don't think I see myself living anywhere else in the world."

"If you love it so much, then—"

"I think it will be poetic to do it here." She angled her head at him, and their gazes met at last. He leaned lower, their breaths mingling.

"Whatever you say—" His lips almost brushed hers.

"I reject you, Alpha Vincent Loth—" she started saying the words, but he grasped her and shook her almost violently.

"What are you doing?" he demanded angrily as she gazed at him with big eyes, forcing tears.

"It has to be done," Astrea's voice was barely a whisper. "We could never —"

"You are my mate," he seethed, desperately trying to calm down, but she could tell he didn't hear "no" often.

"And therefore I am doing this." She placed her palm on his chest as the first tear rolled down her cheek. "You'll be free of me, and the Moon Goddess will find someone better for you."

The mention of Selene caused a shadow to cross his face.

He caught her arm, pulling her closer. "I don't want anyone else. I want my mate. You."

Vincent looked at her as if he was waiting for something, but she only bit her lip, which had a stronger effect on him than she expected, his eyes glowing red just for a moment before he suppressed it.

"Astrea—" He brushed his fingers over her cheeks, creating tingles, and she closed her eyes just for a moment. "Don't fight this. We are meant to be together."

"He will never let us," she whispered. "Just trust me on this one, okay? Joran will never allow us to be happy."

"He is nothing to me. He can't do anything!" Vincent narrowed his eyes, clenching her wrist tighter. "You belong to me."

"You have no idea who he is!" she started whispering in panic, checking to see if anyone was listening. "He—he is not a regular Lycan. He has powers beyond anyone's imagination, and he can be so cruel. Please, don't make it hard for me. We can just reject each other and pretend it never happened. It will be safer for us both."

"He can't do anything to me," Vincent assured her, giving her shoulders in his blazer a squeeze. "And to you."

"He can! Once he made me spend six months in a silver pit—"

"I'll kill him for you!" The man was fuming with rage.

"You don't know what you are talking about." She lowered her head, and he had to cup her chin to make her look at him.

"I know no one can stop me on the way to my mate. And if you like the South so much, I'll lay it at your feet."

"Preposterous promises to someone else's fiancée!" Joran seethed, leaning over the balcony entrance.

If looks could kill…

Astrea rushed to push Vincent away, and that only made the man angrier.

"You have no rights to her!" he growled to her Teacher's face.

"Oh, and you do?" Joran scoffed, not intimidated in the slightest.

"She is my mate, given to me by the Moon Goddess!"

"Big deal!" The dragon rolled his eyes. "I don't get the fuss with that mate bond thing."

"It's the strongest connection to exist!" Vincent scowled and lifted his chin to demonstrate his superiority.

"Is it, though? You, of all people, should know." Joran's lips curled into a menacing smirk. "Surely it can't be that strong if just a couple of words can break it."

"I can say the same about your neck! Just one snap can end it all!" Vincent clenched his fists, and it took all Astrea's willpower not to smile, seeing them exactly in the positions she wanted them to be. It took her just one night.

"Gentlemen," a calm but confident female voice interrupted them and made everyone look at the beautiful woman at the entrance. "You are making a scene."

51. BLAZING SUNSET

*A*strea didn't know how to react. She did not expect to meet the Queen of the Western Lycan Kingdom ever again, yet here she was. Riannon Stormhold in the flesh.

It wasn't like they were great friends during her brief visit to the Luna Trials in the North, but a few simple interactions made a lasting impression on Astrea. For some reason, she thought of Riannon often.

She knew at once that the woman recognised her too, but at the same time, it was hard to tell whether it was a good thing. The Queen was heavily pregnant the last time they saw each other. Now, her stomach was flat, hugged by a tight dress.

On the day they met, Joran ordered her to kill everyone, including Riannon and her unborn baby. This was probably the tipping point for Astrea. She took life before, but it had never been someone so pure-hearted as the people she met in the North.

It was never a child.

However, there was something else she was constantly worried about. To save everyone, she had to fake their death without them realising it. Sadly, she knew only one way to do it – with a potion from a witch, who made it using rare berries that grew only on the outskirts of the North and South. This potion was often used to fake death during assassins' missions if things went wrong and an unlucky Firstborn needed a last resort. They hoped their persecutor would take them for a dead person and leave them alone.

The problem was that the poison could harm the ones who took it.

Astrea figured it was better than dying back then, but now she couldn't stop thinking about it.

What if the baby was harmed because of what she had done? In that case, she wouldn't be able to live with herself.

"Gentlemen, you are making a scene." Riannon managed to stop the two angry men with just one phrase, the two of them looking at her in shock. However, what surprised Astrea the most was that Forrest stood beside her.

"Vincent, allow me to introduce Queen Riannon Stormhold." The Southerner pursed his lips, his facial expression clearly judging by the mess they created. "And King Gideon wants to speak to you, too."

"Your Majesty," Vincent acknowledged the guest. "Forgive us for this ugly scene."

"Apology accepted." The Luna arched her brow at him. "And my husband can't wait to talk to you. I think the photographers want to take a few pictures, too."

"We will finish this later." Vincent gave Joran a withering glance.

"Don't forget your jacket!" The dragon gritted his teeth as he was already next to Astrea, helping her to get rid of the garment and throwing it back at his rival with force.

Vincent clenched his jaw and offered him a fiery glare right before he stormed out, followed by Forrest, who surprisingly did not seem confused by all of this at all.

Astrea was afraid to breathe, knowing Riannon recognised her.

"So, we meet again." The Queen smiled as if she wasn't on the balcony with two of her potential murderers. She acted as if she was well-versed in handling such situations. "You look great, Astrid."

Astrid... the name she used at the Luna Trials.

"You look wonderful too, Your Majesty—"

"Please," the woman shook her head as the corners of her lips turned upwards, "Just call me Ria. After all, you are the one who saved my life."

Astrea was not sure how to react. The Queen was not supposed to know anything but said it confidently, taking no objections.

"And your child?" the Dragonfly heard herself asking before she realised it.

"He is fine too." The Luna nodded with a sweet smile, bringing her instant relief.

"It's a sweet little reunion, but I am afraid we have to go," Joran interjected. "Good to see you, Riannon."

"It's 'Your Majesty' to you!" The woman's demeanour changed when she shifted her gaze to him.

"We need to go!" The Serpent cut her off, grasping Astrea's hand and trying to lead her away, but the Luna stood in his way.

"Last time, you were more eager to speak to me!" She smirked, blocking their exit and knowing very well there wasn't a damn thing he could do about it. "Why leave so fast now?"

He definitely couldn't cause another scene with so many people around. Pushing the Queen of the neighbouring country would cross the line for someone who wanted to be elected as a High Chancellor.

"You've met?" Colour drained from Astrea's face. This couldn't be good.

"Oh, we did!" Riannon chuckled, and Joran's grasp tightened so much it became painful.

"I don't recall it!" he lied.

"Well!" Ria huffed a laugh. "I guess shoving a pregnant woman against a wall to make her perform seidr wasn't that memorable for you! Just another Monday, right?"

Astrea yanked her hand back, shocked by the revelation.

"What?" Her head snapped to her Teacher, and only then she realised she knew exactly what seidr was, although no one ever explained it to her. It was an old form of premonition magic. Ancient as can be.

"He was looking for you, by the way," the Queen added. "I am sorry he found you. I really am—"

"We have no time for this!" Joran bristled and grabbed her wrist again. "This is some petty revenge plot!"

"On the contrary," Riannon's smile deepened, "I don't have to do anything."

Joran froze. "What's that supposed to mean?"

"Exactly what you think." Ria calmly smoothed the creases on her dress. "There is no need for me to do anything. I did perform seidr, and I saw your ending. I am good."

"I see the game that you are playing." Joran was at a tipping point, and Astrea decided to de-escalate the situation. She didn't want Riannon in harm's way.

"Maybe we should go, indeed." She placed her free hand on his shoulder, and bringing him out of this state.

"It was good to see you... Astrea," Riannon said as they walked past her, and the Dragonfly smiled at her. "You've changed, but it's for the best."

"Th-thanks. I am glad you are all right," the Dragonfly said, stalling slightly. "I swear."

"I know." Ria touched her arm briefly, a tiny bolt of electricity going between them. "By the way, there is nothing wrong with solving some of your troubles with weapons. Even though sometimes it can be a Nightmare."

The words puzzled Astrea for a moment, but Joran pulled her roughly behind himself.

"Enough of this!"

He navigated her through the crowd of people who still wanted to congratulate them. However, this time, all her Teacher wanted was to leave the event.

Astrea did not object. It was best to leave and keep the others safe.

The elevator was painfully slow, but the moment it stopped on their floor, Joran yanked her out of it, his chest heaving rapidly.

"You have to reject him!" he commanded, and she realised that, even after everything, he was most worried about her mate. Not the fact that one of his victims practically called him out a few minutes ago.

"It's easier said than done," she sighed, deciding to play some more.

"What's that supposed to mean?" He narrowed his eyes at her, clenching his fists.

"He is—" Astrea turned away and walked towards the glass wall, leaning over it. "He is my mate, Joran. I have never felt anything like the connection we have. Those tingles—"

"Don't tell me that those tingles mean so much to you. Remember that no one knows you as well as I do!" the dragon insisted.

"What do you want me to say?" She glanced at him over her shoulder. "I am afraid that rejecting him will break me. We talked just once, but Vincent—"

"That's not even his real name!" he snapped, and she did her best not to demonstrate her excitement. This was exactly what she needed – information.

"You know him, don't you?" She furrowed her brows. "You knew him before all this!"

"I do," he finally admitted. "And I know that a mate like that will not bring you anything good!"

"And you know better." She rolled her eyes. "You always do!"

"Believe it or not, but yes, I do! I've spent years gathering power and learning everything there is to learn. I am the one who kept you safe all those years! I am the one who made you this strong! I am the reason you are standing here today because he is the one who sent monsters to kill your family! Everything I did! Everything I taught you, was to prepare you for what had to inevitably happen to you! And I am the only one who can help you go through this!"

She couldn't agree with him.

"You threw me into the silver pit!" Astrea reminded him. "What were the months I spent in there supposed to do to me?"

"Anyone else would have killed you for the betrayal!" Joran reasoned, stepping closer and towering over her. "I only taught you a lesson that there is a price for good deeds. Riannon, Savannah and their friends were enjoying life while you were suffering, and not one of them cared to look for you—their saviour."

"I didn't do it for praise!" Astrea's face contorted into a frown. "I did it because it was the only thing I could do alone for them, and it was the right thing to do! I knew it back then, and I sure as hell know it now!"

The Serpent roughly cupped her chin and crashed his lips against hers, brazenly demanding entrance with his tongue. His fingers laced into her hair, not letting her pull away as he stole her breath and when she inevitably gasped for it, he finally got what he wanted, devouring her greedily and hastily.

"Too... late," he muttered, "you belong to me now!"

Everything inside her rose against this, and she pushed him away with as much force as she could muster.

"This is where you are wrong!" Astrea hissed. "Our deal was that I will stay with you if I lose. It said nothing about me belonging to you. I am not an object to possess! So, I will be by your side as promised, but don't expect it to be anything more than that!"

He brushed his fingers over his red, swollen lips, realising she managed to bite him, drawing blood. Joran assessed the ruby red drop on his finger before licking it away.

She expected another burst of outrage at her defiance, but it did not follow.

"I did save you," her Teacher said as he exhaled heavily. "If I wasn't there that day, you would have died."

"And then you turned me into your puppet!" she added bitterly.

"No, then I hid you away from everyone," Joran explained without looking at her. "And I trained you to protect yourself when the need arises."

"In the meantime, you made the other Dragonflies feed on my power!" Her voice dripped with fury.

"It's not exactly like that—" The dragon locked his gaze with her, pressing his lips into a thin white line.

"It's exactly like that because I witnessed it myself! I can't believe how stupid I was to believe everything you said when you only lied to me from the very beginning!"

"I did it for you!" The man did not give up, trying to persuade her.

"You used me! You were never honest with me, and now you only want to own me!"

"No, Astrea, no!" He rubbed his forehead. "It's—it was never the plan to fall in love with you."

Her lips parted upon hearing this. She knew he wanted her, but the confession was too unexpected.

The sound of alarms in the distance pierced their ears, and they both turned to look at where it was coming from. The horizon of the Southern capital transformed into a mesmerising canvas of vibrant hues as the sun was setting down, blending deep crimson and fiery orange. The city's silhouette was painted against the backdrop of the blazing sky, and Astrea knitted her brows together when she noticed several helicopters flying in the same direction.

"What is this?" she gasped, placing her hands on the glass to have a better look.

Joran did not respond, so she kept looking... until a large dark shadow became visible in the flames. Taller than the buildings and more menacing than death itself.

Only now, Astrea realised it wasn't a colourful sunset before her. It was an enormous black fire wolf walking down the streets of the Southern capital.

"Fenrir—" she whispered, still finding it hard to believe her eyes.

She recognised him at once; no doubt crossed her mind even once.

"What the hell!" Joran growled, balling his fists. "Is he out of his mind?"

"See?" Astrea pointed at the smouldering silhouette before them. "You are not the only one to care about me. And this is how a selfless act is done."

Joran clenched his jaw.

"This changes nothing!" he warned her, to which she replied nothing. "Stay here until I come back for you!"

Joran waited for a response, but Astrea didn't say or do anything, simply staring at the scene unfolding before her eyes.

The giant fire wolf mesmerised her, and she was impressed by what he was doing for her, but mostly, she was surprised by how confident she felt it was Fenrir. There were no doubts about that.

Joran's phone rang, and he switched it on, barking angrily, "What is it? I am busy."

Astrea listened carefully, knowing that no device could overcome a were-wolf's hearing.

"Master," Dominica's shaky voice sounded. A few seconds passed, but she added nothing else.

"What do you want?" Joran grew increasingly furious. "I told you I have no time for—"

"Th-the Firstborn island... it is... destroyed," the last false Dragonfly told him, barely holding back from crying.

52. THE EAST HAS ARRIVED

a mixture of emotions coursed through Astrea. The Firstborn island was hardly a place she could call home after everything that was done to her, but she still grew up on it and knew pretty much everyone who lived there.

"What do you mean, destroyed?" Joran said through gritted teeth as Astrea's eyes went back to the fire wolf on the horizon. Surely Fenrir wouldn't... some of them were just kids.

"It's... b-burned to the ground," Dominica stuttered. "Most of our best warriors were on missions. It was just me, a few guards, and the trainees. The battle was very short. In the end, they gave us a boat and took the kids on a different one."

"What?" The Teacher clenched his phone so hard the expensive glass cracked, and he swore under his breath.

"They burned down every building on the island," Dominica went on. "We were lucky to survive. That wolf—"

"I'll call you back later!" Joran snapped and hung up, turning back to face his Dragonfly. "Do you see what he did?" His voice was filled with venom.

"Freed the kids you stole from their parents?" She raised a brow at him while crossing her arms over her chest.

"They. Belong. To. Me." He took a step with each claim, cornering her into a column. "Same as you."

The snake tattoo on her neck became tighter.

"Do you even realise that all of the people in your life right now are there only because this is what you do to them?" she growled, scratching at her throat. "You strangle us, suffocate us and keep us on a leash! Or in a silver pit! It depends on how lucky we are and your current mood!"

Joran pressed his lips tightly, both hands behind his back as he watched her struggle. So beautiful and so defiant.

"At least I have *you*," he replied.

"Joran," she scowled through the tears forming in her eyes, "you don't even have Bjorn!"

Something changed in his face. He barely showed it, but she knew she finally managed to hurt him back.

"Don't come out until I say it's safe," Joran ordered.

"You wish!" she snarled back, and the hold on her became tighter, causing her to fall to her knees in her fight for air.

"I mean it, Astrea! I didn't protect you for so many years to lose everything now! Stay here where you are safe!"

The world around her began to fade into a blur, making the window she saw smaller and smaller with each passing second. Astrea scratched the marble floor with her elongated claws as her heart raced in a feeble attempt to fight the inevitable. Yet her body succumbed to the lack of air, a soft whimper leaving her lips before she collapsed to the ground and closed her eyes, her mind slipping into an unconscious state.

Joran sighed, knowing he had to urgently deal with his brother's arrival. However, he couldn't leave her like that, not on the ground, not after causing this state.

Everything was wrong, and he didn't have time to fix it.

He carefully picked her up and walked to the settee next to the glass wall, carefully placing her there. Knowing her strength, she would be up soon, and he had to deal with everything before that.

JORAN RUSHED to the Alpha Convocation office and found everyone already there, watching Fenrir marching through their city as if he owned it, proving all their modern defences to be useless against him.

The flames on his fur seemed to have a life of their own, moving and shifting with each step, painting the sky red. A display of power like no other.

Joran forgot when the last time was that he saw his brother using that form. *It had been ages.*

Two helicopters flew close to him, their rotor blades melting before they could approach him, causing both to crash land.

"Should we prepare the rockets?" someone asked, with a note of hesitation in the voice. The hesitation they all felt now.

"Not in the city," Forrest commanded. "Maybe if we can lure it outside."

"Do we know what it wants?" one of the Alphas wondered, and a heavy silence coated the room.

Joran knew. And so did Vidar. Forrest suspected, at the very least. He always knew more than he let others believe.

"Do we know what it is?" one of the youngest Alphas voiced the question on everyone's minds.

"Could it be—" One of the oldest men looked at Joran. "One of the changed ones from the Avalanche Battle in the North?"

"You know the rumours. Everyone returned differently from there," someone added, and Vidar sent a warning glance to Joran. During that battle, Joran and Fenrir blessed thousands of warriors, giving them gifts and powers they shouldn't have possessed. Gods were not supposed to do that. Their actions could have had serious consequences according to the divine laws. There were reasons why gods did not bless everyone left and right.

Then again, Fenrir and Joran were never typical gods.

"Why don't we ask him?" Forrest suggested all of a sudden, drawing everyone's attention to himself.

"Ask him?" someone let out a nervous laugh. "Are you out of your mind?"

"I don't see him attacking us," Forrest commented, rubbing his chin and nodding at the screen. "Just look at him. He clearly can wipe the city away from the face of the Earth if he wants, but instead, he only destroys vehicles that attack him, moving firmly but slowly. As if he gives people time to escape."

"So, who is going to talk to him then? You?" an Alpha from the opposing party chuckled, making Forrest sneer.

"This is a task for those who want to represent the Southern Lycan Republic as our High Chancellor, don't you think? As far as I know, we already have two candidates for the role."

Now, all eyes were on Joran and Vincent, causing them both to frown, knowing they got trapped but not sure yet what the game was. The move from Fenrir was too unexpected.

"I'll do it," Joran agreed hastily. No time could be wasted. Maybe he could talk some sense into Fenrir.

"I can do it myself," Vidar insisted, unwilling to lose points.

"Why won't you both do it?" Forrest suggested helpfully. "And I will go as well to mediate if necessary."

The rest agreed with this decision eagerly, letting their most dangerous rivals risk their lives for the country while preparing the rest of the military in the background in case negotiations failed. The fire wolf was too close to the centre of Verum already.

"Your brother is nuts!" Vidar seethed as they walked outside, watching the panic unfold as people tried to flee. Fenrir took his time, although he had definitely already seen and recognised them, but for some reason, he wanted to make a show of this.

Gods didn't act that way for a reason. It could cost them. Meddling in the mortal realm could drain one's divinity, and once the process started, it couldn't be undone. Too many gods died because the repercussions of their actions weakened them.

However, it looked like Fenrir did not care about the price anymore. Something changed.

"And whose fault is that!" Joran rolled his eyes.

"Have you thought of my deal?" the God of Vengeance asked flatly.

"I have." Jor shrugged. "And now I want to hear if my brother has anything to offer me as well."

That answer annoyed the other deity, and Joran felt better. It was annoying how confident Vidar was the whole time. Yes, he had his advantages, but they destroyed his beloved Asgard once and deserved respect for that alone.

"Really?" Vidar let out a dark chuckle after regaining composure. "He would never forgive you, and you know it. There is nothing you can do to earn his forgiveness. Even giving up Astrea wouldn't help."

"Then you have absolutely nothing to worry about, right?" the dragon retorted with a scoff.

Forrest caught up with them, and they had to stop talking.

"So, if things go wrong, can we count on you shifting into your flying form to deal with this for us?" the Southerner whispered, adding, "The South needs you."

"If I fight him here, there will be no South," Joran informed him, furrowing his brows. People had no idea how devastating the consequences of a battle between the two brothers and Vidar could be.

They were lucky Fenrir simply entered the city and wasn't actually attacking it. There was no time to evacuate anyone. If Fenrir really wanted to destroy Verum, it would take him minutes. If they engaged in a fight, it would be even more devastating, and the reunion of the Moonrise Kingdom would be postponed again.

"Just give him what he wants, then!" Forrest suggested, the muscles on his face tensing at the realisation there weren't too many options. "And make him leave."

Joran was about to reply when something gleamed high in the sky, making everyone snap their heads up. Golden wings flashed just for one second, and she was down on the ground the next, landing with a thud which shattered the ground and created a cloud of dust around her. A Valkyrie in golden armour stretched her wings as she proudly raised her chin. Things were becoming more and more serious.

A giant Lycan in the third form walked from the shadows to join her, bigger than any royal they had ever seen and with no visible signs of trouble to control himself. Followed by a white fox with red markings on its snowy fur right between its eyes. It was an unusual colour for the fox shifters, but the creature initially seemed the most harmless out of the three. Right until nine sharp elongated tails appeared behind his back, all ready to be used as weapons.

Finally, a young man in a brown leather jacket walked out with an axe relaxed against his shoulder, and his appearance made both deities uneasy.

"Who is this?" Forrest could feel that shift of power.

"My dear nephew," Joran replied dryly, clenching his fists. Skoll's arrival could definitely change today's scenario, and he hadn't even picked a side yet.

Fenrir didn't let them wait long, and the giant wolf burst out in flames, a human walking out of the inferno in its stead, shocking the observers. Several news crews were already there, filming the events from different locations.

"Greetings!" Fenrir waved as he approached the three Southerners, a confident smile playing on his lips. "I apologise we are late. Your invitation came months ago."

"Invitation?" Forrest arched his brow questioningly while his colleagues were speechless at the audacity.

"Yes, Alpha Joran Nathair was very persistent, and we decided to give our collaboration with the South a chance. So, here we are to see what the Southern Lycan Republic is really about." Fenrir's little speech astonished pretty much everyone.

Vidar was the first one to speak.

"No," he stated bluntly, not adding anything to it.

"No?" Fenrir tilted his head. "Are you revoking the invitation?"

"Of course not," Forrest interjected. "Alpha Vincent has a sick sense of humour. Matters like this are for the Alpha Convocation to decide. And we will vote as soon as possible since you made it here. Of course, while that happens, you can consider yourselves our esteemed guests."

"Very well." Fenrir nodded respectfully, holding back a smirk. "I think we can give you three days to decide, and, in the meantime, we would like to ensure the children's safety."

"What children?" Joran asked through clenched teeth, knowing very well they were his Firstborns.

"Ah, you know, on the way here, we got our location wrong and ended up on some island. It looked like a criminal organisation was running there, which abducted and enslaved children, making them believe they were there for a greater purpose." Fenrir sighed heavily. "Like a cult. Of course, we couldn't let it continue. After we... rescued them, it turned out that most were from the South. So, we would like them to reunite with their families. Most of them are teens and remember very well where they came from."

"Well, we will certainly deal with this." Joran stretched his arm to him. "Thanks for bringing them here."

Fenrir shook his hand. Hard. And then pulled him closer without letting it go.

"I am glad we are on the same page with this. May I have your word that every child I brought will be reunited with their family and sent home?" A smirk curled onto the wolf's lips.

He knew he had set his brother up for failure. *The words given to the gods and by the gods were binding.*

"I'll see what I can do," Joran tried to escape it. Losing his future Firstborn warriors wasn't in his plans. They were talking about a whole generation of trainees.

"I think you can do better than that." Fenrir's grin deepened as he pointed at the cameras by his eyes. What candidate for the highest position in the country wouldn't agree to help the kids?

"I'll do anything in my power to bring those kids back to their homes and loved ones." Joran gave up, and his brother let go of his hand, satisfied with winning this round.

"Why don't we go and talk in private?" Vidar understood the rules of the game.

"I like that you are all business," Fenrir finally locked eyes with his nemesis, "but we are all tired after the long road. And also, there is someone I would like to see."

"We can discuss it later," Vidar insisted, anger rippling through each cell in this mortal body.

"No, we shall discuss it now because I want to see the ambassador you sent to the East. Astrea Sade. And I want to see her now."

Joran knew he couldn't say the words. He had to keep them apart for as long as possible.

He shot an angry gaze at Forrest, hoping he would take the lead.

"Oh, don't look at me." The Southerner raised his arm defensively. "Astrea Sade is Alpha Nathair's fiancé and... Alpha Lothgar's mate. I am the last person to speak on her behalf."

Vidar was ready to explode. He didn't care about this city. Not really. Fenrir could burn it for all he cared. He was about to announce that when Joran stopped him, standing in his way.

"Very well," he said. "You can see her."

"Today." Fenrir pushed further. "I want to see and speak to her today."

"Fine!" his brother exhaled and nodded. "I will escort you to her, but after you talk, we have to talk as well."

"All of us!" Vidar interjected.

"This would be my pleasure." Fenrir scowled. "Lead the way."

He gestured for his team to shift, and the next second, four humans followed him with their heads held high.

The East had arrived.

JORAN WAS grim on the way to the penthouse, and, ironically, they didn't say a word to Fenrir. That was the hugest step back for him, and the last thing he wanted to see now would be Astrea running into his brother's arms.

Yet he was trapped by giving his word. Breaking it could make him powerless, and since Fenrir was here, they would see each other anyway.

It changed nothing. Astrea belonged to him. It was his mark on her neck, and Fenrir couldn't pressure him into removing it. And then there was Vidar...

The elevator door opened, and Joran walked out into the hall, strolling to where he left Astrea sleeping on the settee.

However, Astrea was not there. The room, settee, however, was occupied.

53. BLIND LOVE

"*There* is a giant fire wolf attacking the capital!" Some woman showed her phone to her husband. "We need to go!"

Confusion quickly turned into panic as fear painted people's faces, turning them pale. In a matter of seconds, a once jubilant crowd erupted into chaos, scattering in all directions. Frantic screams filled the air as people desperately tried to escape while Niki stayed, searching for Bjorn. One person accidentally hit her on his way out, and then another one, almost knocking the Firstborn off her feet, but she had to search for that man because … he was her responsibility.

If something happened to him—She wasn't sure what she'd feel if something happened to him, but something was telling her she wouldn't be happy.

Niki was stuck in the middle of the crowd when someone grasped her and pressed her against his chest, wrapping large arms around her. The scent of wintergreen enveloped her as she looked up to see Darius's emotionless face. He engulfed her in his giant embrace, placing his back against the fleeting crowd, and it took Niki a few good moments to realise he was trying to protect her.

She tried to move, but he held her in place, his tall form serving as a shield for her.

"Easy, Strawberry!" he said, leaning slightly towards her ear. "The best course of action is to wait it out."

"Let me go!" Niki hissed. "It's your chance to finally get rid of me! Use it!"

She could handle herself. Astrea trained her well enough not to be afraid of a mad crowd. Moreover, she was the one who was supposed to protect him.

And yet he was doing this for her, despite his earlier claims.

The blind bear found her in this mess and now did everything to protect every inch of her as his fingers brushed her bare back.

"At least I get to see what you are wearing, after all," he whispered, her cheeks flushing at his words. She was happy he couldn't really see her now.

"W-why are you doing this?" Niki's breathing hitched.

"It would be a shame if something happened to you," he replied nonchalantly. As if it wasn't a big deal. As if they didn't spend months hating each other. And as if he didn't say all those hurtful words to Astrea earlier today.

She lifted her head to look at him and realised they were finally alone in the hall.

How long had it been? She couldn't tell.

"We need to go," Niki heard herself saying.

"Do we?" Bjorn held her as tight as before.

"Absolutely." The assassin knew she had to push him away, but despite that, she didn't.

"Fine," the bear sighed. "Lead the way but remember, you owe me one."

Her breathing hitched, but she took his hand firmly and led him out of this place and into the safety of the Teacher's penthouse. But when the elevator doors opened, and she saw the view behind the glass wall, she froze from shock.

A giant wolf with flames all over his black fur was clearly marching in their direction, setting the sky ablaze with shades of crimson and vermillion.

"What is it?" Bjorn asked. "I feel the heat. I smell the smoke, but it's hard to tell."

"Frankly speaking, it looks like we all may die if we stay here," Niki confessed. "I probably should—"

"—Leave me and escape," he finished the sentence for her.

"That's not what I was saying!" Nikiah protested, but Bjorn caught her arm and pressed her fingers against his chest. She could tell his heart was racing inside, and that did something to her. Something she couldn't quite explain.

"That's what *I* am telling *you* to do," he said. "Run away like your friend did. You are not her. He will not look for you. Leave me and save yourself. No one would blame you."

She needed a few seconds to process what he was saying.

"I—"

"Please, go," he whispered. "That's all I can do for you."

Darius let go of her hand, and she felt colder and... lonelier.

Tears welled up in her eyes.

"I can't go," Niki sighed heavily and touched his cheek, making him flinch because he didn't expect it. "I still owe you one, remember?"

He wanted to say something and stopped before the words left his mouth.

"If it's bad, you really need to go." His voice rasped in his chest.

Niki glanced at the window again, noticing the wolf was already gone and wondering if it was an illusion. Unexplainable things were happening today.

"I think we have a few minutes," she whispered, and his lips trembled just for a second. "How can I repay you?"

He sucked in a sharp breath, and that sound held so many unspoken words that Niki was sure he would push her away. Yet the werebear surprised her.

"I want to see you," Darius confessed, startling her.

"I-I—Sorry but—"

"Like this." He stretched his hand, searching for her face. For a second there, she doubted if this was a good idea. Too intimate. Too close. "It's okay if you don't want to—"

Niki leaned into his palm, and Bjorn shuddered because he did not expect this. Yet she did not pull away, so neither did he.

Her skin was soft like a rose petal – just like he imagined. He brushed it with his thumb to remember how it felt. Not wishing to stop, Bjorn traced his fingertips gently over the contours of her face, noticing the curve of her lovely cheekbones. She probably looked insanely cute when she smiled.

Slowly, he drew his fingers over her forehead, then explored her eyes, noting how long and thick her eyelashes were. Then, he traced her little perky nose. Right until he got to her lips. So soft and full. They probably tasted like strawberries, too...

Bjorn brushed his fingers through her silky hair, and after that, he couldn't resist leaning a little lower to inhale her scent.

He shouldn't have done it.

"You need to go," he whispered into her ear and heard how her heart began to beat faster. *Faster for him.*

"No." She touched his cheek, and he froze, too afraid to scare her off.

"It's dangerous!" he told her, his voice dark and heavy.

"I think the danger is over," she said, not even glancing outside anymore.

"It's wrong!" he warned her.

"That we can agree on." Niki stood on the tips of her toes, pulling his face lower. He obeyed, and she brushed his lips with hers, gently, like a feather.

"Stop—" His breathing was ragged, and his grasp on her became tighter.

"I don't want to," the girl stated firmly, and he crashed his lips onto hers, demanding entrance that she granted without delay.

The world of sensations unfolded. Now that he couldn't see, everything felt so much more intense. Her sweet strawberry scent intensified, making him want to devour her.

His hands glided over her bare back, allowing him to feel more of her flesh. He wanted it all. Desperately. Greedily.

Selfishly.

The bear beast in him was awakening.

Niki pressed herself against him. It was her first kiss ever, and had she known it would feel so good, she would have initiated it sooner.

Darius laced his fingers in her hair at the back of her head, not letting her distance herself. Not that she tried.

She wanted to be closer, wanted to be one.

Nikiah pushed him onto the settee right behind him, enjoying his confused expression for a few seconds before she inched closer, and he caught her wrist on pure instinct, pulling her onto his lap.

Their lips collided again, and a soft whimper left Niki when Bjorn dipped his head in the crook of her neck, leaving a wet trail of kisses.

"Darius!" she whispered, digging her fingers in his hair.

Bjorn froze.

He couldn't do it. Sure, she knew who he was, but she didn't *really* know. She didn't see him commit his crimes. This beautiful little creature had no idea she placed herself in the hands of a predator.

He could tell it was her first kiss. Of course, it was. The Firstborns didn't lead a normal life. That girl saw nothing, knew nothing. It was the only reason she was remotely interested in him.

He couldn't take her innocence. He couldn't do that to her.

"Darius?" Her heart was about to burst out of her chest, leaving her panting breathlessly.

"Strawberry," he sighed and cupped her cheek. "We should stop. You don't need this."

"The only thing I don't need is you telling me what to do!" she insisted, angry as hell itself.

He sensed it and tried to smile apologetically, but his lips quivered and curled downwards instead.

"You will understand why I do this one day," Bjorn promised. "You deserve so much better than me... than this—"

"It's not for you to decide!" Niki's eyes were already burning with tears. He was doing it again – leading her on and then hurting her feelings. She had never felt this way for anyone before. He was the first one who had awakened this side of her.

"I am a... horrible man," he tried to reason with the girl who was still sitting on top of him, arousing desire like no other.

Niki may not have been experienced, but she knew what that meant. He wanted her just as much as she wanted him.

"Maybe you are," she agreed, her fingers digging into his skin. "Or maybe you were. Who am I to judge? After you, they will send me on a new mission, and I will have to kill someone. And then again, and again, and again. Until one of those missions becomes my last one."

His whole body shuddered at the thought. She was not wrong. This was how the Firstborns lived. This was how they died.

The same destiny awaited Niki.

"This is why you should run. Now!" An internal growl left him.

"They found Astrea, and she is ten times more prepared for anything than I am. If I run, I am as good as dead. Because he keeps me to control her. If I run, he will lose her and I will be the one to pay the price."

Bjorn clenched his jaw, thinking of what she said and knowing it was the truth.

"You still deserve better—"

"You are right," she finally agreed. "I deserve so much better than this! I deserve to be loved and wanted. I deserved to have my body worshipped and cherished. And I definitely deserve not to have to beg the man I like to take me because this may as well be the only good memory I have this year!"

Niki's voice broke, and she tried to stand up when he held her in place.

"I just—I don't want to hurt you."

"Then don't." She claimed his lips again, and this time, he couldn't resist.

Bjorn checked the settee with one hand, and in the next moment, he flipped Niki over, pinning her arms above her head.

"Tell me you want this."

"I want this," she murmured, and that was all he needed to unleash him.

The werebear traced his tongue across her delicate neck while one of his hands lifted her skirt, sliding up her smooth, toned thigh.

"Strawberry, you... drive me crazy," he rasped out as she arched her back for him.

It was quite possible that the world around them was falling apart, but in this moment, there were only the two of them in the entire universe.

When his fingers reached her core, a sweet moan escaped her lips, and Bjorn gave her a smug half-smile. He drew his finger along her ruined underwear, ready to hook it and rip it off, when Niki reached for him and... took his sunglasses away.

Bjorn stopped in his tracks, knowing that what she saw could only be ugly. He used to wear an eyepatch over the eye he lost first or cover it with his hair after his late mate, Ingrid, told him she couldn't stand to look at the scars. And he was no fool to know that his second eye hardly looked any better after a divine weapon went through it. He didn't even have his long locks to cover it anymore.

"What's wrong?" Niki asked, seeing his frustration.

"The glasses—"

"Weren't they in the way?" She blinked, afraid she just ruined the moment.

"Maybe we can use a ribbon or something instead?" he suggested.

"For what?" Niki furrowed her brows.

"So that... you don't have to look at it."

"Why would—" She stopped mid-sentence, realising how insecure the man on top of her was about his scars. He was worried they would scare her off, and that made the young assassin bite her lip.

He tried to pull away, but she took his face in her hands.

"It's fine," she breathed. "I like you this way. Scars are normal to me."

Bjorn leaned down, searching her lips, and she helped him find them, entwining her hands around his neck to get him closer.

"What the hell is this?" Joran's voice broke their bliss, and Bjorn instinctively pressed Niki to his chest, ready to pounce at the intruder before them. Right then, he smelled a new yet somehow familiar scent.

"Goddess!" Niki gasped and urged him to stand up. Luckily, they were both still fully dressed.

"Is this a joke to you?" Fenrir shot his brow up at his brother. "May I remind you it's your clock that is ticking, Jor?"

Niki still tried to fix her dress, even though it was perfect. She was sure her hair was dishevelled, though, and she couldn't help but notice her lipstick on Bjorn's chin. She never realised it could stain like that.

"It's a private matter," Bjorn responded calmly and searched for her hand, gripping her fingers the moment they touched. She was amazed at how composed he remained despite the circumstances, which gave her confidence, too.

"I'll deal with you both later." Joran gave them both a withering glance. "Where is Astrea?"

"But…— she was with you." Niki's brows went up. She wasn't sure if this was a joke or a test, but then her eyes went to the man she had never met before. Tall, strong and handsome, he had flames burning in his eyes, and she instinctively knew who or what he was.

"I left her right here!" Joran pointed at the settee. "Use common sense! Would I be asking if she was with me?"

"No one was here when we came," Bjorn interjected. "We were alone the whole time."

The Teacher looked surprised, and Niki had a gut feeling that something was wrong.

"I'll look for her," she said and rushed to check every available room in the penthouse, finding all of them empty.

Her thoughts were racing. Astrea would never leave her. Joran would never let her go. Yet there were no signs of a fight.

Just what was happening?

"And?" Joran growled when she returned to the main area, and she shook her head, confused. "What the fuck?!" the Teacher swore under his breath, and the man next to him clenched his fists.

"Where is she, Jor?" he demanded.

"I—" Joran looked at his brother with knitted brows. "I don't know, Rir. But I will find her!"

ASTREA FELT NAUSEOUS, her whole body contorting, forcing her to open her eyes. She tried to move her arms, but found them bound by a golden chain to a tree. The chain was wrapped around her body several times. So thin, yet she couldn't break it when she tried because she noticed how stiff all her muscles felt.

She had been here for a while.

"Wakey-wakey, bitch!" A familiar voice made her shudder.

54. QUEEN'S GAMBIT

*J*oran banged his fist on the door, awaiting a reply, while his brother burned a hole at the back of his head with his eyes. He could feel Fenrir's patience growing thin, and this was not how he planned for everything to go between the four of them. He was supposed to be the one in power since he practically owned Astrea.

You don't even have Bjorn! Her words rang in his mind repeatedly since the moment he left her.

The words that stung him.

"If this is another trick of yours, I swear I will find a way to replace Hel with you in the underworld realm!" Fenrir promised, his voice dark and unyielding.

"That's not it!" the dragon said through clenched teeth. "I cannot sense the tattoo, which means that a divine weapon was used on her! And that could mean that Vidar has her!"

"If he has her, I'll kill him, but your destiny will still remain the same. You ruined our lives!"

"I saved her!" Jor exploded, breathing in sharp pants. He was tired of hearing the same thing over and over. Why couldn't they see it his way? "I did what none of you could do! She is the strongest she's ever been!"

"You make others feed from her power!" Fenrir threw the accusation his way.

"And how do you think I managed to hide her from Vidar for so many years?" Joran scowled. "That stupid glowing dragonfly on her skin is like a beacon for him. Wherever she is, he'll find her. The only way I could prevent him from doing so was to dull it down. Four, Fenrir, I needed four people draining her power to make her invisible! And you ruined it all in a matter of months! She could have had a calm life for once!"

"With you?" The wolf let out a chuckle.

"And why not? If I could—"

"You made her obey you like you owned her. You turned her into a killer when it goes against her nature. Don't give me crap about making her happy. If you wanted that, you would have never come to retrieve her from Solace and set the whole city on fire searching for her."

"It was working just fine until I sent her to you!"

"She ran away from you long before we met in this life!" Fenrir gave him an eye roll. "But whatever helps you sleep at night!"

Joran clenched his fists. Why couldn't that wolf admit this woman was not for him? Life proved that to him time after time. Did it have to be this way? Fenrir and Astrea ruined each other time after time for centuries, almost destroying what was left of them. Just why were they still drawn to each other? She'd be better off with him, and Fenrir could be happy for them for once. If he loved her so much, he could learn to be happy for them!

You don't even have Bjorn...

That boy hiding Niki from him stood before his eyes. He was covering her behind his back as if Joran would hurt her when everything he did was to draw them both together and give that bear his second chance after his past mishaps. Something he didn't have to do but did out of his good will.

Why did everyone ignore that?

They finally heard sounds from behind the door, and in a few seconds, it swung open, a tall, imposing man glaring at them both.

"Is this how the South greets their guests?" King Gideon Stormhold raised his dark brow at them. "First, you can't guarantee safety to anyone in your own capital, and now you take away our privacy as well? Considering you call yourselves the most advanced country of our continent, it's laughable!"

"I am pretty sure you know why we are here!" Joran stopped him, not wishing to prolong this humiliation. Mortals did not dare speak to him this way, but right now, he had to take it because he needed something from the royal couple of the West.

"I do, but I really want to hear you beg." Gideon smirked, leaning over his doorframe. Expectantly.

"Do you realise I can burn your country to the ground?" Joran flared his nostrils at the cocky man.

"No, he can't," Fenrir pointed out from behind his back. "He needs it for his grand, evil plan. But we really have no time for this."

"And who would you be?" Gideon lazily shifted his gaze to the other deity. *That mutt had some balls.*

"You know who I am," Fenrir said, and just for a second, the King's lips parted. "You've heard my voice before, and you responded to my call. I gave something to you. A gift of sorts."

Now Joran saw something the King did not give him but was offering freely to his brother – respect.

"Come in." Gideon stepped inside, and both men followed him.

Joran hated the situation. He knew what Fenrir did. In the battle where they were on opposing sides, they both blessed two different armies of shifters, changing the world as they knew it. That meant Gideon Stormhold was now Fenrir's Champion. That complicated matters for the dragon. He didn't really have a pressure point here, but Fenrir did.

They walked into a spacious room and saw the Queen of the West sitting in a comfortable white chair with a high back and golden studs adorning the edges. She was still wearing the same elegant white dress and looked serene.

"Long time no see!" Riannon beamed at Joran. She was about to stand up, noticing Fenrir, but he shook his head, and she stayed in place.

"You know why we are here!" Impatience was getting the better of the dragon.

"I do!" Riannon smirked, leaning over the armrest and relaxing her head on her palm.

She didn't say another word, provoking him.

"Where is she?" Joran growled.

"Who are you asking about?" The insolent woman shrugged.

"No games! Is she in danger?" The dragon decided to try a different approach.

"She is," the Queen responded calmly. "Then again, that's nothing new for her. Is it? She is always in danger when she is with you. Just earlier today—"

"Who took her?" Joran interrupted her before any unwanted information was spilt in front of his sibling.

"Someone you know," Riannon replied, pursing her lips.

"Do I have to drag each word out of you?" Joran gritted his teeth, seething. "Because I will. To be honest, I thought you cared about her, and I wouldn't have to—"

"Funny you should say that." The Queen stood up. "Caring is a word with such vast meaning. It really depends on whoever interprets it, don't you think?"

"I know you hate me." Joran exhaled sharply through his nostrils, barely holding himself back from killing this woman on the spot. He knew Fenrir would stop him, though. Moreover, Riannon had the gift that none of them could lay their hands on. A gift that couldn't have been stolen. Not even after her death. They all needed her now.

"That's... an understatement," the Queen's lips curled in a half-smile.

"But will you really let her die for your revenge?" Joran tried to manipulate her feelings. Surely, Riannon cared about Astrea enough not to want her dead. She had to know who they were to each other by now.

"Of course, not!" the woman chuckled. "According to my predictions, we still have some time, though."

"And what happens when this time is over?"

"I take your brother aside and tell him where she is," the Western Queen sighed nonchalantly. "Just him, though. Not you."

The dragon deity clenched his fists so hard his knuckles turned white.

"And what do I need to do for you to include me?" He knew he lost this game already.

"You want that, don't you?" Riannon finally locked eyes with him, knowing she had him under her heel now. He wouldn't want his brother to find Astrea without him present and be the hero of the day. He wouldn't want to risk the wolf taking her away and hiding her forever. Getting Astrea out of Solace worked because of how unexpected it was, and also... he had some help. If Fenrir took her away from him now, finding them would be hard even for Vidar. And Joran would be left aside.

"What. Do. You. Want?" he repeated, anger coursing through his veins.

Fenrir watched the entire show, growing tired of it. He was ready to accuse the Queen of playing games with Astrea's life when he heard something that shook him to the core.

"I want your word," the woman said calmly but with so much confidence that it seemed she could move mountains.

"My word?" Joran furrowed his brows. This couldn't be good. "What—"

"I'll give you the information on where she is, and when you find her, and she is safe," Riannon's eyes became as cold as ice, "you will remove your mark from her. Forever. No tricks."

Now it was Fenrir's turn to part his lips in shock. Never in a million years had he expected that a mortal would solve this little problem for him.

He knew he'd find a way to make Joran do it eventually, but what happened just now was a surprise.

"No!" Joran ground out the word through clenched teeth.

This would mean he'd lose power over Astrea. He'd lose his leverage over Fenrir and Vidar. This would be his end, and it couldn't be, not after centuries of getting to this point.

"Fine!" Riannon shrugged. "Leave then. We are done here."

"Don't think for one moment I wouldn't fly to the West and get your son to—"

Gideon snarled, his eyes glowing golden and claws elongating.

"I know for a fact you wouldn't." His wife's voice calmed down the King instantly, but he left the sharp claws, ready to use them any moment if needed.

"So, what's it going to be?" Riannon tilted her head. "Tick tock."

Joran peered at his brother.

"Yeah, Jor, what is it going to be?" Fenrir crossed his arms over his chest.

"What's in it for me?" The dragon turned to face his brother. "Do you have any idea what Vidar is offering? What is your offer, Rir?"

"I offer you to do the right thing for once," the wolf replied. "You know you owe me a debt that cannot be repaid. But you owe one to Astrea, too. Whatever you choose, it will not change anything for me. I know what I have to do. Your choice is for you."

A laugh escaped Joran.

"Not much of an offer, is it?"

"Suit yourself." Fenrir shrugged and turned to the Luna. "Riannon Stormhold, I think it's time for us to have that conversation."

"It will be my honour." The Western Queen stood up finally.

"Fine!" Joran raised his hand. He had to go to Astrea. He had to try to save the situation somehow.

The divine mark on Astrea's neck meant a lot, but not everything. This was already proven.

Besides, it was a preventative measure for when he sent her away. The real power over her was Niki. And Niki, as every Firstborn, belonged to him.

Still, it wasn't ideal.

"Fine what?" Ria knew the rules of the game by now. He had to say it.

"Tell me where she is, and I will take my mark off today." He gave up, knowing it would cost him.

"Of course." Riannon smiled genuinely at him for the first time. "A deal is a deal."

55. STROKE OF MIDNIGHT

a strea couldn't believe her eyes.

She was back in that forsaken place after its destruction, witnessing the charred remains of what was once a bustling training ground. The island, once filled with the echoes of swords clashing and the whispers of Firstborn in training, lay in ruins. The buildings that once stood tall were now reduced to ashes, smoke still lingering in the air.

She had a pretty good idea of what had happened here, and her thoughts went to the many kids who lived and trained in this very place. However, knowing Fenrir, she knew he'd never hurt the innocent and trusted his process, whatever that was. This had to be a message for her Teacher, and she didn't feel sorry for him. After all, this island only brought her and others pain.

The real trouble, though, stood before her.

Dominica crossed her arms over her chest as she watched her with a sneer, dressed in her usual black leathers.

"You sleep like a log!" she commented.

"That wasn't sleep," Astrea retorted, checking what limbs she could still move. "I was strangled until I fainted. There is a difference."

"If that's an attempt to make me feel sorry for you, then you are delusional!" the Dragonfly scoffed.

"You? Sorry for anyone?" Astrea rolled her eyes. "Please! You are a leech who fed off me for years and still was ready to put a knife in my back! I don't remember hearing a nice word from you once."

"Like I had a choice!" Dominica growled. "He didn't ask me! He didn't ask any of us! Do you think we liked this? Do you think any of us wanted to experience this? Craving the power you had was no joke to any of us! It changed us in unimaginable ways."

Astrea tried slipping her wrist from under the chain, but it held her in place tight. As if by magic...

"You seemed to enjoy it! You guys always wanted to do the Joining Ritual. Even if I was sick for days after," Astrea reminded her.

"With the power you had, that was hardly a challenge," Dominica brushed her off. "Do you even realise what you are capable of when the four of us were turned into super strong warriors just by taking a few sips of power from you?"

"Didn't feel like a few sips to me!" Astrea frowned.

"Cry me a river!" The woman curled the strands of her long brown pony-tail around her finger. "You always had it all and appreciated it the least."

"Dom, you have no idea what you are talking about!" Astrea sighed, still trying her luck around the chains. The luck, sadly, was not on her side.

"Don't call me that!" The girl closed the distance between them in seconds and slapped her face so hard Astrea tasted blood. "Only Emma could call me that!"

Damn it. Astrea knew this would come up.

"It was self-defence," she repeated the words she had already told Dominica many times.

"Shut up!" the brunette screamed, her eyes glowing as a warning. "Do you think I care why you killed the love of my life? She is gone, and nothing can fix this!"

Astrea's heart skipped a beat. She did not want anyone to experience this kind of loss. This was never her goal. She would find another way to escape if she could turn back time.

"I am so—"

Another slap prevented her from talking.

"Shut up! Shut up! Shut up!" Dominica's scream pierced her ears. "I don't need your petty words and apologies! You can't give her back to me!"

This was true, and Astrea regretted it like no one else. Would things be different if Emma survived? Would they leave her alone?

"Right now, the only thing I want is my freedom, and there is only one way to get it!" Dominica grabbed her hair, and Astrea thought she'd hit her again. She was ready for it, but instead, her ex-teammate grasped her shoulder, ripping the fabric of her dress to reveal the dragonfly tattoo on her back.

"What are you—" Astrea didn't get to finish her sentence because sharp claws pierced her skin right where the dragonfly tattoo was. The sensation was painful at first, but quickly, it changed to something else.

Something way worse.

Astrea could feel strength slipping away through her wounds as Dominica rolled her eyes back in ecstasy, lost to the sensations of draining the life and energy out of the woman she hated the most.

Unable to fight her, Astrea finally realised why she was brought here. It wasn't just to kill her. Her ex-colleague wanted to bleed her dry, stripping her of power.

The Joining Ritual for one.

Looking at Dominica now, Astrea saw how the process consumed her, glowing magic flowing through them both while blood trickled down Astrea's back. Despite that, the woman deepened her claws into her flesh, making Astrea hiss from the pain.

"It's too much!" she tried to explain, but the assassin didn't even spare her a glance.

She did not care.

Insatiable hunger took over Dominica. She wanted it all. All that Astrea had to offer – her power and her life.

"There is only one way to be free," she leaned forward to whisper in her helpless victim's ear. "Emma knew it, and she told me. We were supposed to do it together. You have enough for two—"

"You want to drain me!" Astrea gritted her teeth, thrashing against the chains.

"I want to do worse things to you!" Dominica sneered. "If it was a choice, I would have given you the most horrible death I could imagine. But this will have to do!"

"You don't have to do this! You said it yourself: I have enough for two. You can just—"

"I know, but I really want to." The false Dragonfly's full lips curled into a cruel smirk. "I want to see your eyes when life leaves you! I want you to know I took it all from you! I want you to be this helpless and pathetic! This is something I can finally enjoy! Because you deserve it, you fucking bitch!"

Astrea felt claws going deeper again. A bit more, and Dominica would reach her heart.

Her strength began to wane, a deep fatigue settling in her bones. Just a few seconds ago, she was ready to fight, but now, each movement was laborious.

Her mind became clouded, but when Astrea's eyes locked with her attacker's, she saw how full of life and energy Dominica was.

If she didn't stop her now, it would be too late. A few more minutes and she wouldn't be able to fight her, even if the chain disappeared. It was a race against time.

Astrea tried to think about what she could do, but her mind was now a mixture of abrupt, unconnected thoughts. What *could* she do?

"When you die, I will throw your body into the silver pit where you belong! It was so satisfying to see you there before!" Dominica was gloating, getting intoxicated by the dragonfly energy. "And now you will rot in there forever!"

Astrea looked at her with pity because she knew the woman was addicted. The ecstasy she felt now was temporary. Regardless of how everything ended today, Dominica would eventually come down from her high and feel her life empty with double strength.

However, she had no luxury to delve into pity. She had to fight for her life in any way imaginable.

"I dropped Emma's body in a pit, too," Astrea said in a hoarse voice, and the woman's blissful expression faded as she tried to focus her vision on her face.

"What—what did you say?"

"It wasn't silver, though. Just some dirt and dried leaves in the forest." Astrea waited for her to process the information, and she felt the claws ripping her flesh when Dominica removed them roughly.

"Repeat this!" she hissed, leaning closer.

"I said—" Astrea did not plan to finish that sentence. Instead, she lured her enemy closer and thrust her head forward, hitting her as hard as possible.

The plan proved successful, disorienting Dominica long enough as her broken nose caused blood to gush over her face while Astrea tried to manipulate the chain.

What the hell was this? Why couldn't she break it?

Astrea knew she needed help. Urgently. Desperately.

But no one even knew she was here.

She needed a miracle. Just like the last time she fought the other Dragonflies...

The last drops of life were leaving her when she heard distinct neighing coming from the ruins behind them, and her breathing hitched, realising that maybe her prayers had been heard.

It was absolutely impossible, and maybe all this was just a product of her inflamed, dying imagination. Still she saw a dark cloud gathering behind Dominica, who really wasn't paying attention to anything now other than herself. The Firstborn finally regained her control and charged at Astrea.

At the same time, against the backdrop of charred buildings, a Nightmare with a glistening ebony coat strode in their direction, emanating darkness.

He came to help her, answering her inner call, and the corners of Astrea's lips tilted upwards despite Dominica stalking towards her, wielding a long blade she was ready to use. The fake Dragonfly was close enough for the real one to kick her on the knee, dislocating it and winning a few more seconds—the seconds she so desperately needed.

"The chain!" she screamed at the Nightmare, hoping he could understand her now, too. The creature lowered its head, its horn gleaming in the shadows. It hooked up the chain and easily tore it in half, letting it fall to Astrea's feet and freeing her.

Their eyes met, and once again, she felt they were close. She knew that black unicorn as if it was a part of her.

A gut-wrenching sound left the Nightmare's chest and at first, Astrea did not understand what was happening. Time stood still while the world around them shattered at the realisation of what was happening. A few seconds later, she noticed Dominica retrieving her bloody daggers from the creature's back.

She wanted to scream, but no sound came out of her as the majestic black unicorn fell to the ground.

He came to save her, only to be killed.

He saved her so many times.

He looked at her with so much hope, and there she was... useless.

"Oops!" Dominica chuckled darkly. "I guess it's my lucky day because I wanted to find that thing too."

The last Nightmare... Astrea swallowed her pain, seeing that her opponent was now charging at her.

She was still weak in a torn evening dress and with bare feet, but she had no intention of letting it go. Fury was coursing through her every cell now.

Dominica had an advantage. She just drank Astrea's power and strength, weakening her. She seemed to be as angry as her opponent, and yet, unlike her, Astrea had something to fight for.

"I guess you are going to get that gruesome death after all," the brunette spat while stretching her neck.

"I am offering this to you once," Astrea warned her, not yielding. "Walk away and be free of all of this. Joran wouldn't care."

"It's Joran to you now, is it?" the woman sneered. "I guess he finally got what he wanted. I hope it hurts when he fucks you!"

The ex-Dragonfly said nothing else and, fuelled by raw power, launched forward, her strikes imbued with almost primal force. Each swing of her blades created a whirlwind of high precision. Still, Astrea's nimble footwork allowed her to effortlessly dodge and parry, the silver dress swirling around her like a protective cloak to mask her movements.

She had to explore every opening with calculated accuracy. The mesmerising dance of death went on for a while, and soon Astrea realised she would have to create an opportunity herself.

Dominica lunged forward, and Astrea screamed, falling to the sand, her ruby-red blood spraying over the light silk of her garment.

"It's your end, bitch!" The dark-haired woman prepared to make a lethal blow when Astrea threw sand in her face and ripped her skirt with lightning speed, wrapping it around Dominica's neck to block her airflow.

"Yield!" she grounded out, struggling to keep the bigger woman in place. Her muscles still ached after all the draining.

"Fuck you!" The girl tried to cut her again, but Astrea dodge. She smashed her opponent over the tree with the chain and finally knocked the blades out of her hands.

"Yield!" Astrea ordered. "We don't have to—"

Dominica grew her claws and tried to thrust them into her, but the true Dragonfly caught her hand and twisted it with force, making her enemy scream in pain.

"I don't want to kill you!" she yelled at her, breathing ragged.

"Then you will have to sleep with one eye open!" Dominica roared, tears streaming down her face. "I hate you! I hate you so much, and it will never change!"

The woman tried to hurt her with her free hand, and Astrea was tired of it. She tied her hands at the back with piece of her dress, knowing it would not hold the assassin for long, but also not wishing to slaughter her like that.

She wrapped the chain around the defeated warrior, rushing to check on the Nightmare.

"Midnight!" She wanted to cry, but there were no tears left. She assessed the creature's wounds and used the remnant of her skirt to stop the blood. "You are going to be okay. It's going to be alright!"

Her lips trembled as she repeated the lies, looking into Midnight's eyes.

He knew. He knew that this was it.

"I am so sorry!" She lowered herself and hugged him, finally able to let out an internal desperate sob. "It's all my fault! I am so sorry!"

Midnight tried to neigh, but the sound from him was unnatural. It was as if he was trying to tell her something.

She stroked his coat, crying, brushed her fingers through his silky mane, but still had that feeling inside that he wanted more.

"What can I—" she whispered and gasped when she realised what the magical creature was trying to tell her.

The horn.

The memories of the last time she touched it circled in her mind. She couldn't faint now.

"Should I... touch it?" she asked and saw the relief in the Nightmare's gaze. This was what it wanted from her.

In no way that sounded like a good idea, but each time she called, he arrived to save her.

If anything, she owed him one.

"Fine!" Astrea nodded and wiped away her tears, checking that Dominica was still struggling with her bounds.

She exhaled heavily, preparing for what was yet to come.

"Fenrir," she whispered, praying that he would hear her too, "I hope I am doing the right thing."

And with those words, she wrapped her fingers around the Nightmare's horn...

56. NIGHTMARE'S TALE

*A*strea's body told her to let go of the horn, but she couldn't let Midnight down, not after the sacrifice he made for her.

She felt dizzy and slightly scared as dark clouds began surrounding her, her fingers prickling as if bolts of electricity were hitting her. It was hard to tell if the darkness enveloping her was real, but she knew one thing… she felt it with her bones – she had to hold the horn as long as she was physically capable. Everything depended on it now.

"I'll call you Midnight," she said, stroking the creature's iridescent mane. "It suits you, and you can keep me company at night when I am working."

The creature looked at her with his wide violet eyes and ticked its wet nose in her chest, eliciting a chuckle from her.

"They told me to create a divine weapon, but you are no weapon! You are gorgeous!" The goddess laughed. "I am going to take good care of you, and you will do the same for me, all right?"

"What kind of Nightmare is this?" her mother gasped, walking into the Moonlight Garden in their home, and Astraea smirked in response.

"Nightmare?" she smiled at the black unicorn in front of her, caressing him more. "He will only be a Nightmare to my enemies—"

Astrea desperately sucked in the air as a kaleidoscope of memories flashed before her mind's eye. One of them lingered ever so slightly, and she saw Fenrir standing on a beach next to a huge rock. His hair was much longer than she was used to now, and eyes locked with hers.

"*Stars burn,*" she told him and marvelled at the stunned expression that painted his face just for a second before he gained composure.

Astrea's lips curled involuntarily, reliving their first-ever meeting.

"*Can I kiss you?*" Fenrir asked under a glowing willow tree.

"*You don't have to ask—*" She could barely finish the sentence before his lips crashed into hers, mighty hands pressing her delicate body against his.

"*You once said stars burn. I will gladly burn forever if I get to be with you.*" His words rang in her ears.

"*Astraea, the Goddess of Stars, the Lady of Justice, will you do me the honour of a dance?*" Fenrir bowed before her, and deities around laughed, not trying to hide their smug expressions and igniting something new inside her. She had never been a rebellious daughter, but that night, she couldn't ignore injustice.

Her hand touched his, and his whole body shuddered momentarily because he didn't expect this.

"*Don't tell me you changed your mind, Fenrir,*" she teased him and felt his fingers closing around hers.

There were so many memories she could barely breathe. A whole lifetime she couldn't remember before. Now, Astrea was greedy to get every single piece of the puzzle back and kept holding the horn as if her life depended on it.

"*Say that you are mine,*" he whispered, his chest rising and falling.

"*Are you mine, then?*" she taunted, biting her pink lip and sliding her delicate hand up his arm to wrap it around his strong shoulder.

"*If you will have me.*"

"*Are you offering?*"

"*I am begging, Astraea!*" His confession changed everything.

There was so much pain in his eyes that she couldn't bear it anymore.

"*Then it's a deal. You are mine, and I am yours. Remember that these words are binding, Fenrir.*"

A tear rolled down Astrea's cheek.

She was walking down the beach in Asgard, loyal Midnight by her side. Another wasted day. The Goddess of Stars was back in Asgard after so long, but she couldn't find even a trace of Fenrir, and the date of her wedding was getting closer and closer. Vidar tried to kiss her again earlier today, and she wasn't sure she'd be able to hold him back any longer, considering the colours he was beginning to show her.

"*I can help you.*" *Joran walked out from behind the large stone where she had met Fenrir for the first time, startling her.*

Instinctively, she felt he was trouble, so she raised her hand, igniting her starry magic at the tips of her fingers as Midnight lowered his head, his horn ready to kill another deity. Waves of cosmic energy made him raise his hands in defence.

"Easy there!" The Serpent let out a chuckle. "I am just trying to help. My name is Jormungandr and I am Fenrir's—"

"I know who you are." She dissipated her magic immediately. Fenrir told her about him, so the goddess chose to cut straight to the chase. "Where is he?"

"They... hurt him." He avoided looking into her eyes.

Her heart ached hearing his words. She suspected it, but knowing this was different. Fenrir didn't run away like everyone claimed. They tortured him somewhere for what they had done together.

"Where is he?" Her voice was getting louder, and she could feel her power near, almost reaching her this time.

"Listen, it's dangerous. He wouldn't want you to risk—" Joran ran his hand through his long blonde hair.

"I asked where he was!" she yelled at him, a warning pulsating in her tone.

"In the sacred mountain, there is a passage. I can take you there, but I tried to get him out many times. It's useless. You cannot do anything." Joran finally met her gaze, and she still wasn't sure if she could trust him, but it wasn't like she had much choice now.

"We'll see about that!" Astraea said through clenched teeth. "Lead the way."

"Fine." The young dragon nodded and pointed at the Nightmare. "You'll have to leave that behind."

Astraea bit her lip, considering whether or not that was a good idea. The black unicorn protested, shaking his head and urging her to reconsider.

But Fenrir needed her, so she had to agree.

"There is a Valkyrie who I think can help us." Joran tried to force a smile on his face, but it seemed too hard for him to do at the moment.

"Valkyries serve Odin. Can she be trusted?" Astraea furrowed her brows.

He paused, exhaling heavily and saying, "No one can be trusted. So, are you in?"

She nodded quietly.

"Are you sure about it?" He tested her once more.

"I've never been so sure about anything in my life!" the goddess responded. "Take me to Fenrir!"

Astrea had to gasp for air, again and again, as memories were hitting her one after another. There were too many and her head felt like exploding already, but she didn't want to miss one single thing. This was her past. It belonged to her!

Fenrir in chains... He looked so tired, barely any clothes left on him. They didn't even bother to create any kind of acceptable conditions to keep him here. As if they indeed considered him just an unwanted pet.

She rushed towards him, stepping into puddles on her way.

"Fenrir! What did they do to you?" It was painful to see him like this.

"It's not her, it's not her, it's not her!" he repeated over and over, startling her. She had never been so scared in her life because that muttering was so not like the man she loved.

SHE GRASPED HIS CHAINS, *trying to remove them—*

Until a sword pierced her chest, and she saw the pain in the eyes of her beloved.

Astrea screamed, waking up back in the present, beads of sweat trickling down her spine as she panted.

The Nightmare looked at her through hooded eyes; his horn had no effect on her anymore, and he finally allowed himself to collapse to the ground fully.

"Oh, Midnight!" Tears sprayed down her cheeks as Astrea wrapped her arms around her oldest friend. "You knew your poison would not harm me, but help me remember. You always knew that!"

The sounds of the creature's laboured breathing filled the air, but it still let out an approving noise as a reply.

A strong wind blew right into her face, and she lifted her gaze to see a portal opening right before her and two tall masculine figures walking out of it.

Fenrir saw her first, and his fists clenched at the sight, but the moment their eyes locked, he knew.

He knew that gaze.

She recognised him. Not the him she got to meet in this lifetime.

Him. The real one. The one only she knew.

"Fenrir—" Her voice was barely a whisper, but for him, it moved mountains.

"Astr—" His eyes shifted to what was right behind her. A woman in black leather stood up, grabbed a charred metal rod from the ground and charged at Astrea.

No! He couldn't let it happen! It was her last lifetime, and he had just found her. He couldn't lose her again.

But before he managed to wield his prime gift of fire and stop that girl, her neck snapped at an awkward angle before she could reach Astrea.

"How dare you!" Joran gritted his teeth. "A Firstborn disobeying my order is a breach that has to be paid with one's life!"

Dominica's body fell on the sand, and the dragon's attention returned to his Dragonfly. Yet she did not look back at him. She did not see him.

In fact, Astrea probably hadn't noticed that she almost got killed by her ex-colleague. Her eyes were only on Fenrir, and Joran knew that this was when he officially lost her.

If chances were slim before, now they were completely gone.

"Astraea!" Fenrir rushed towards her, falling to his feet next to her, and she wrapped her arms around him, sobbing.

She didn't say a single word, but her cries told them everything. She cried for what had happened to them, for the things she lost and for what was taken from her over and over. She cried for her love and for finally knowing that not one day passed when he didn't think about her.

Fenrir pressed her against his chest, a rare tear rolling down his cheek. He almost thought this would never happen again. He loved her either way. Each new life, whatever she was like, whatever their story was, he was falling for her without a doubt. When he promised to stay away, he still loved her, watching her from afar and trying to protect her by any means available to him.

But nothing could compare to when she knew who he was. When she remembered their first encounters and their tragic story. Only then were they able to share the pain and happiness of being together at last.

"Fenrir!" she whispered when her little body stopped shuddering from all the crying in his arms. She lifted her face to look at him, and he wiped away her tears with his thumbs.

"I know." He kissed her forehead gently, lacing his fingers into her hair. "I know—Gods, Astrea, I love you so much! I—"

She wrapped her hands around his neck and pulled him closer, their breaths mingling in a kiss they both had been longing for years. Slow and torturous at first, it quickly turned into something else.

A whirlwind of emotions consuming them both until she finally broke it, fear written all over her face.

"Fenrir, Midnight is hurt!" She distanced herself and returned her hands to her oldest friend. "We need to help him!"

"Damn it!" Fenrir swore under his breath and tried to assess the black unicorn's condition, finding out instantly how bad it was.

"Astrea, he is a part of you. Do you have any of your powers back?" the wolf asked, and she shook her head, biting her lip.

"Only the memories—" she confessed.

"Shit," he muttered. "He is dying."

"He saved me." Astrea stroked Midnight to try and reassure him, even though she was aware that the Nightmare knew this was his end. "And he helped me to get my memories from my first life back."

"We can't save him, I am afraid," Fenrir told her. "He is your divine weapon, but because he was a living being, it's different for him. If you got your powers back, you could replenish him, but without them, whatever I have is irrelevant—"

"Make him shed his horn. It can still be used even after his death," Joran interjected, and Astrea shot him a withering glare.

"Is this what you are worried about now?" Her words were filled with so much venom that it made him flinch.

"He is right!" Fenrir agreed, shocking his beloved.

"I refuse to do it!" she said, holding back another sob that threatened to escape her.

"No, Astrea, you don't understand," he placed his hand on top of hers, "we can try to preserve him until you get your powers back."

She paused, hearing this had hope blooming in her chest.

Fenrir took a bead out of his bracelet.

"This one is empty," he said. "It can hold his spirit while—"

He didn't finish because he could see she was barely holding it together. Too much had happened in one day.

"Do it!" Astrea agreed and cupped Midnight's chest. "My dear friend," she sucked in a deep breath, tears burning her eyes, "trust me one more time, please. This is for the best. I'll do anything to bring you back. I swear—"

Midnight let out a pained sound and closed his eyes, barely able to open them again – a sign of approval.

She wrapped her fingers around his horn once again. At the same time, Fenrir prepared his magical bead, placing his large hand where Midnight's heart was barely beating now.

"I am here with you." Astrea lowered herself to kiss her Nightmare's forehead and as she did, the horn fell off right into her palm. At the same time, Fenrir concentrated on getting the last sparks of Midnight's soul. Like little stars, they flew from the creature, dancing in the air before they reached the bead, causing it to glow just as the colour of Midnight's eyes in the past.

Astrea was afraid to distance herself, afraid to move, feeling how heavy the unicorn's head became.

"Until we meet again, my friend," she whispered, unwilling to move. She cried until she couldn't anymore and Fenrir only caressed her back, unwilling to leave her even for a second.

"We'll get him back," he swore. "I promise. We'll get him back."

"WE NEED TO GO," Joran spoke at last, pain rippling all over him as he watched Astrea being cradled in Fenrir's arms. It was as if he didn't exist.

"We?" She arched a brow at him, the corners of her lips tilted downwards. "I am not going anywhere with the likes of you!"

"Really?" The dragon furrowed his brows. "After everything I have done for you?"

"Like enslaving me from childhood?" Astrea finally stood up, Fenrir helping her.

"I. Saved. You," Joran said through clenched teeth.

"Bullshit!" she threw back in his direction, unwilling to spare him another glance.

"You are standing here right now because I managed to hide you from Vidar for so long! You are trained to fight and, more importantly, trained to survive! All thanks to ME!"

"How generous!" she chuckled darkly.

"No, the two of you are the generous ones!" he bellowed. "Not a single thank you for everything I have done! You are literally standing in my home, burned to the ground! By one of you!"

"Then I guess we are even!" Astrea announced and took Fenrir's hand.

"Let's go." He pulled her in the opposite direction, and she followed.

Joran was before them in seconds, standing in their way.

"You've got some nerve!" Astrea snarled at him, her eyes glowing with fury. "Mark my words! One day, my powers will be back, and I will make you regret everything you did to me and others too!"

He searched her eyes for remorse or any emotions for him, but she was indifferent to him. This was a promise she intended to keep, and an unfamiliar pain appeared in his chest. It was something new to him. New and heart-breaking.

"I will personally ensure you know exactly the pain we suffered thanks to you!" Astrea promised and flinched when he placed his hand on her shoulder. It was as if his touch revolted her whole body, and he couldn't bear it any longer.

"I know," Joran breathed out, the ink from her neck slowly returning to where it originally came from – his skin.

Her lips parted when she realised what he was doing as the serpent tattoo finally disappeared from her neck. She touched it when he was done, as if she couldn't believe that he would actually go through with this.

"Thanks for keeping your word, Jor." Fenrir waved his hand and opened another portal. "I am glad you are still capable of that."

He had nothing to respond to that because he was starting to feel a void forming inside. The familiar sense of emptiness was finally back.

VIDAR STOOD in the empty Alpha Convocation room, observing the city through the wide glass wall and processing the news he had just gotten from his trusted people.

Not everything went perfectly, but at least now he finally knew why the divine realm was dying and who was behind it.

This changed his plans drastically as he had to ensure Astraea's fast return to where she belonged. Not only did he desperately desire to see her by his side, but he also knew he needed her powers to restore what was stolen from the gods. There was no time to play games anymore, as he had to stop the process. No matter what the cost was.

Luckily, he had just the perfect plan...

57. LUNA RISING

enrir walked out of the portal with Astrea in his arms, Joran following them into his penthouse, not surprised to find everyone already there. Years had passed, but no one had acquired manners.

"Finally!" Kara ran towards them, eyes on Astrea. "Are you okay? Are you hurt?" Then, she awarded the Serpent with a withering glare, which he ignored. He did not question how and why they were here. Nothing mattered anymore.

"I'll live," Astrea replied as a smile curled onto her lips. It was nice to know her new friends were worried about her. Warg and Bash exchanged glances with her and Fenrir, not saying much as usual, but she noticed relief on their faces, which warmed her chest. When she said goodbye to them last time, she wasn't sure they'd ever see each other again. However, reuniting with these people now made her happy.

"Astrea!" Niki pushed through the men and got to her mentor, grasping and squeezing her hand so tight she almost broke the bones in her wrist. "I was so worried! Who was it? How—"

"Let her get some rest!" Joran grunted, and the woman froze.

"Your tattoo—" Niki noticed her empty neck, and Astrea smiled at her.

"I am free now," she whispered.

Her ward gave her an awkward smile, not knowing if it was appropriate to congratulate her in front of their Teacher. Luckily, she was saved by the elevator doors opening, and Forrest, who seemed confused to see this kind of crowd here, walked out.

He did not look lost for long, though, finding the man he came looking for.

"Joran, what the hell? I couldn't reach you! Where were you again?" He furrowed his brows, glaring at the Serpent.

"None of your business," the dragon muttered, but the Southerner grasped his shoulder to make him face his annoyed expression.

"Do you have any idea what is going on lately?" he demanded.

"No, but you are about to tell me!" Joran rolled his eyes, and Forrest exhaled sharply, running his hand through his rich brown hair.

"Vincent wanted to gather the Alpha Convocation while you were gone!" the man announced, expecting a loud reaction that did not follow, stunning him.

Joran felt empty. Just a few hours ago, that would have made him furious. Vidar probably wanted to push his own agenda and ruin his plans, but now... now all his plans had been already ruined, and he felt so empty inside he could barely shrug his shoulders in response.

"Let him," he said, and Forrest's lips parted as he let go of his old frenemy.

"Let him?" the Alpha seethed. "*Let him*?! Nathair, we are lucky that this Southern clown entered the scene and distracted everyone with the help of the Western royal couple. But I don't know how long they can go on like this. Not to mention they probably have their own agenda."

"Devoss?" Fenrir arched a questioning brow, and Bash nodded.

"We have only one man for the job." His son smirked.

"And the army?"

"Ready when needed on the border," Bash whispered, but Forrest still heard him.

"I hope you are talking about the Eastern border! And whatever you call an army better stay there!" he warned them, making Fenrir chuckle.

"That would solely depend on the actions of the South," the King replied.

"Is that a threat?" The Alpha clenched his fists.

"Not at all." Fenrir shook his head. "It's a fact that I hope you take into account while making decisions."

"Enough." Joran stepped between them. "Believe me or not, but you two are not the problem here. Only Vi—Vincent is. So why don't we go there and listen to what he has to say?"

They quietly agreed.

"Astrea, go and get some rest. I'll be back as soon as I can." Fenrir turned his attention to the woman next to him, and she was slightly disappointed they were separating so soon after their reunion. But she knew him. Now she *really* knew him and was aware that he wouldn't leave her if it wasn't absolutely necessary.

So, she nodded and watched the men walk out of the room, leaving her alone with Niki and Bjorn.

The white bear shifter stood right by the window again. As if he could see what was outside.

"Come." Niki touched her gently and smiled. "I will help you take a bath. You are hurt."

"It's fine." She shrugged, not knowing what that feeling inside her was. Something was off, something important.

They were almost to her bedroom when she heard that damn bear saying.

"Free my ass."

She froze, and Niki glared at the man on her behalf.

"Don't be mean," her ward hissed, fingers clenching tighter around her. They were always this defensive of each other.

"How is stating the facts mean?" He didn't turn to them. "She said she was free, yet she had just taken an order without so much as questioning it."

"He wasn't exactly... ordering," Niki argued, and Astrea realised what that odd feeling inside her was.

She was furious.

Furious to get left behind.

Her Firstborn upbringing taught her not to question such things, not to take the lead. She rebelled against that, of course, but only in extreme situations. And right now, she was confident Fenrir could handle everything without her.

But it was Vidar who was waiting for him in that Alpha Convocation conference hall right now. It was Vidar who was clearly plotting against them.

Vidar was the current ruler of Asgard, and he was the man who broke them apart time after time. She had to be there. She had to oppose him, and she had to fight him with all she had.

She had to be a part of this.

"He is right," she said, and her ward knitted her brows together.

"Don't listen to him!" she said through clenched teeth. "He is just being an asshole."

Astrea glanced at herself in the decorative mirror on the wall. Her dress was dirty and torn, her hair a mess, and dried blood was where she had wounds before. She really needed that bath.

"Excuse me!" She straightened her back. "There is an urgent matter to attend to!"

She sauntered into the elevator and pressed the button.

"See what you have done?" Niki snarled and bit her lips when she realised what she said.

A little smile curled on Bjorn's lips, but he did not comment.

The elevator doors opened, and Astrea rushed inside, leaving them alone.

"Sometimes we need to hear what we do not want to," Bjorn added and finally turned towards where he thought Niki stood. "I learned that lesson the hard way."

"What the hell is she going to do there?" the Firstborn sighed, finding herself already close to him.

"Nikiah." Bjorn stretched his hand, searching for her face, and she let him find it, blush tinting her cheeks. "Your friend is the key to everything. Don't you get it?"

"In my humble opinion, the further she is away from all that, the better," Niki hummed sarcastically and felt his thumb stroking her cheek.

"That's something I want for you," he confessed. "Freedom, far away from this place and these people. It's the only way for you to stay safe."

She was stunned by his words.

"You know it's not going to happen, Darius." She lowered her eyes and was happy he couldn't see how ashamed she was right now by her response. Unfortunately, she knew too well how dangerous conversations like these were.

"On the contrary." Bjorn shook his head. "I think it's happening this very moment."

WARG PUSHED the doors open for them. Fenrir, Joran and Forrest walked inside the Alpha Convocation conference room, a strong Eastern fragrance hitting their nostrils at once.

Everyone important in the South was present, and two special seats were prepared for King Gideon and Queen Riannon, who eyed the newcomers curiously.

Devoss stood in the centre of the room with a thin metal stick in one hand and what looked like a brass lid in the other.

"Ah, more guests for the *incense ceremony!*" He grinned at them, and Fenrir noted how annoyed almost every single Alpha in the room was. That sly fox knew how to evoke this emotion in people.

"How long—" someone tried to ask, but Devoss was next to him in seconds.

"Shh." He touched his lips and shook his head like a teacher scolding his naughty student. "We don't talk during the incense ceremony. Unless you guess what incense is burned. But we have burned none yet, right?"

With these words, he hit the metal stick over the lid, creating a bell-like sound with the most serious expression.

"This is a vital tradition in our Eastern Kingdom. No important meeting is done without it."

Lie.

"If you break the ritual, misfortunes will follow everyone involved, and according to our laws, we have to kill the one at fault to prevent this from happening."

Another lie.

It worked, though, because after the fire show they pulled, no one wanted to provoke them.

Fenrir took a seat at the head of the table, ignoring the one next to Gideon and Riannon, clearly designated for him.

"This seat is meant for the High Chancellor," a female Alpha in her fifties whispered to him.

"Well, you don't have one yet, do you?" He raised a brow at her. "In the East, we give the best seat to the guests."

"This is—" one of the older Alphas wanted to protest, but Devoss was next to him in the blink of an eye, hitting the stick over the lid again right next to his ear, creating another loud sound. A pure torture for any shifter, considering their hearing.

"So," the fox could finally speed up the process, "we levelled the ash and used the seal for the incense. Now, all that is left is to light up its edge. All I need is to get some fire and—"

Fenrir clicked his fingers, and the powder sparkled, starting the burning process and helping him to remind everyone in the room what kind of power he held. They would have to listen to him.

Devoss closed the little incense burner, watching a thin stream of smoke rise to the ceiling.

"At the end of the ceremony, guess the scent." He grinned at his exhausted audience.

"Cherry blossom and white sage." Astrea's voice made all eyes dart in her direction as she stood before them in her destroyed dress. "Excuse me, ladies and gentlemen. I am late."

"Dear, are you all right?" one female Alpha asked, eyes assessing her look.

"It was a long night!" Astrea shrugged and raised her chin.

"You can't be here." A man with silver hair rolled his eyes. "This is the Alpha Convocation, for crying out loud! We let the Kings and the Queen in, but you—"

"She is here as a Luna." Riannon Stormhold tried to suppress a smile, but for the first time ever, she was failing. Her husband laced his fingers with hers, watching the show.

"Nathair," one of the men glared at Joran, who had already taken his usual seat. "How about you tell your fiancée to wait outside with the other Lunas —"

Fenrir cleared his throat loudly and smirked.

"She is here as *my* Luna."

While everyone else in the room was in awe, he stood up and offered her his chair. "I warmed it up for you, my love."

Astrea walked towards him, finally feeling like she was in the right place.

Joran and Vidar traced each movement with their eyes.

She sat down, and Fenrir remained standing next to her, his hand resting on her bare shoulder.

"The dress from last night, all in blood and with a new Alpha by her side?" one of the younger men scoffed. "It was a long night indeed!"

A group of Alphas next to him exchanged knowing smiles.

Warg growled loudly, making them all flinch.

"Excuse my friend," Devoss sneered at the offenders. "In the East, remarks like this get people killed. But we will *try* to restrain him."

He punctuated the word try.

"Okay, I think it's safe to say we are done with introductions." Vidar took the word, not sparing another glance at Astrea. "Obviously, we have guests here today, and maybe they will share their perspective on the situation we found ourselves in. The South has nothing to hide. We are a very transparent nation."

Fenrir did not like how confident that prick was.

"And what is this situation again?" Forrest asked, tapping his fingers over the cold surface of the long table.

"The Northern army is on our border," Vidar announced, making everyone gasp. "I just received a report an hour ago."

Gasps, whispers and growls filled the room as a wave of first reactions rippled through it. Astrea stiffened in her seat. Knowing King Kai and Queen Savannah, that didn't sound right.

"Moreover," Vidar continued, "they say they are led by a witch from the East."

Once again, all eyes were on them.

58. FOUND

"What exactly are you implying here?" King Gideon furrowed his dark brows while his wife gently drew circles on the back of his palm with her thumb. "You know Queen Savannah of the Northern Lycan Kingdom is my sister! Neither she nor her husband would ever attack a neighbouring country! This goes against everything they believe in!"

"Or maybe you don't know them that well anymore?" Vidar smirked, folding his arms over his chest as every Alpha in the room watched him.

"Or maybe your lack of political experience shows," Riannon pointed out calmly and met the deity's stern gaze with a little smile. "We all know your story. Your father didn't train you well, did he? You aren't exactly prepared to deal with matters like this, so maybe it's best you sit this one out? This isn't similar to ruling a small pack, but I think by watching, you will get the necessary experience for your future endeavours."

Joran snorted loudly, finding the conversation amusing, and all eyes in the room darted at him. This wasn't his usual behaviour, but he did not care anymore, so he just leaned against the back of his seat to get a better view of the show.

"Right," Forrest cleared his throat, trying to distract everyone. "Right now, it's all simple speculation. We are not at war with them, and there is no reason for them to attack us."

"The reason is sitting right there!" Vidar pointed his index finger at

Fenrir. "Or is it a coincidence that it all happened during your spectacular arrival and that it's the witch from the East that leads them?"

"What is the name of the witch?" Astrea asked innocently, and Vidar sent her a withering glare, which she pretended not to notice. He always wanted her to be his silent accessory, and she wasn't going to give him that.

"Salome Gray," one of the older men read the report before him.

"Then why do you say she is an Eastern witch?" Astrea knitted her brows together. "Salome Gray was not born in the East. Moreover, she was banished from the Eastern Kingdom. I think you need to get your facts straight before accusing anyone. I honestly thought the Southern Republic had better intel than that."

"Are you implying the North is the only one at fault?" someone demanded.

"My Luna is not implying anything," Fenrir interfered. "She just tells the truth. Salome left our country, and although it is quite possible she's now working in the North because she's a very talented witch, I highly doubt that she is leading their army. Not to mention that I don't believe the North is about to attack."

"Then how would you explain an army on our border?" another Alpha asked.

"Actually, I am afraid this can be my fault indeed." Fenrir shrugged. "My... arrival was a bit... let's say flashy. Maybe they got worried I would attack them next and just prepare to defend themselves if the need arises."

Vidar did not like that response because it did make sense and was ruining the narrative he weaved so carefully.

"The bottom line is they didn't attack," Forrest interjected. "And we are not going to attack first, considering our values. So, in my opinion, as the acting general and member of the Alpha Convocation, we should seek comments on what is going on from the Northerners and assess the threat level, but at the same time our army mobilisation is a must."

A few men in the room nodded.

"Any comments, Nathair?" an older woman asked, and the dragon lazily shifted his gaze to her.

"I think Forrest pretty much got it under control. Are we done here?" The man in question stretched his neck.

The silence in the room became heavy.

"Unless we are going to discuss our military strategy in front of strangers, of course." Joran stood up. "We heard what they have to say. We know what we have to do. Forrest is our acting chief general. This is the end of the story for me until we know what the North has to say about it."

He left the room before anyone could say anything else.

"We will give the Alpha Convocation the privacy it needs." Gideon stood up as well and offered his wife a hand. His Queen accepted it with a subtle smile, and they were about to leave when Astrea gave a quick signal to Fenrir that she was going to follow them.

"Queen Riannon, I would like to have a minute of your time, if possible," she said, suddenly remembering how she looked. Maybe she had to let it go and take that shower first.

Soft, silky fabric touched her shoulders, and she angled her head to see Devoss bowing his head to her. "My Luna."

The bright purple blazer wasn't exactly her style, but it did feel nice to be cared for and respected. Fenrir gave his friend a thankful gaze. He only had a shirt on and had nothing to offer Astrea at this moment, so his friend's gesture was appreciated.

"Thank you," the Dragonfly nodded politely and turned back to look at the Western royal couple.

"It would be my honour, Luna." Ria nodded subtly as Gideon opened the door for them both. "I wanted to speak to you too."

Outside, Gideon kissed his wife's hand.

"I have an urgent matter to attend to," he said and nodded at Astrea. "I hope to see you again soon, Luna of the East."

"Me too," the girl replied nervously.

The Western King was gone and the two women took a stroll down the long corridors of the building, searching for a quiet place to speak. Finally, they saw a passage that led them to a hidden gem of the building – a spacious balcony with the city sprawling below. Green plants adorned it on all sides, creating a relaxing atmosphere.

Taking a deep breath of fresh air, Astrea felt a little better and slightly more confident about what she was going to do.

Her memories were back, as in the memories of her first life ever.

However, at the same time, she started to see glimpses of her childhood in this lifetime. They were mere fleeting moments, but each one resonated in her heart. Sometimes it was the memory of bare feet on the grass; sometimes it was children's laughter. She saw wolves running and distinctly remembered hugging one. She remembered how soft it was and what a wonderful scent it had. Still, it was hard to tell what she saw.

Until she remembered a woman. Her shiny blond hair cascaded to her waist, her warm smile and eyes that looked through her soul. It wasn't the Queen of the Western Lycan Kingdom. Astrea was sure of it, but the woman she saw resembled Riannon a lot. Same features, same elegance. It couldn't be a coincidence.

They stood on this balcony for a while, and none of them said a word.

Astrea didn't know why it was so hard for her. She wasn't usually the shy type.

"So, what did you want to talk about?" Riannon asked, leaning over the rails and touching one of the green leaves with her long fingers.

"I—" Once again, Astrea lost her words. "I wanted to make sure you are fine. And to thank you for not holding what I did against me."

"You saved us all." The corners of Ria's lips tilted upwards. "I have to thank you. None of us would have survived if you hadn't betrayed your Teacher."

Astrea tried to form her question, but the words were not reaching her tongue. What if she was wrong about it?

"You know," Riannon sighed, "family is the most important thing in the world for me."

"I can tell that." Astrea nodded.

"Maybe it's because prior to meeting Gideon, I had lost everyone I loved," Ria confessed, and her voice trembled.

"Your parents?" Something in the Dragonfly's chest stirred. She hoped at least someone was still alive.

"Died right after my marriage. My first marriage." Tears glistened in the Western Queen's eyes. "This wasn't the first time I lost someone. When I was still a teen, my brother and two twin sisters were killed in a rogue attack."

"Wh-what were their names?" It suddenly became much harder to breathe, and she clenched the rails so hard that the metal bent under her grip.

"Brian," Riannon's voice was barely a whisper, "Stella and—"

The woman turned to face her, tears now streaming freely down her beautiful, perfect face.

"And Astrea." Ria took her hand and gave it a light squeeze.

"You know," the Dragonfly muttered under her breath. "How long have you known?"

"For a while." The Western Queen tried to force a smile, but it wasn't working. "I knew after I woke up in that Northern Hall. I knew who you were and what sacrifice you made for us all. I wanted to go look for you as soon as the battles were over, but—"

"But she sold you out to me!" Joran leaned over the balcony frame with a bottle of whiskey in his hand, taking a long sip as the two startled women watched him.

"I am pretty sure that's a lie!" Astrea gritted her teeth, lacing her fingers with Ria's to reassure her, but noticing how she lowered her head.

"I did not want to—" Her older sister was fighting a sob that threatened to escape her. "He—"

"Come on!" Joran chuckled coldly, enjoying the moment. "I didn't even have to torture her. The whole thing took me like a minute or two. She sold you out because she did not care about you. The only person who really cared about you is me!"

"Is that so?" Astrea snapped her head in his direction. "Is that what you caring about me looks like?"

He frowned, taking another gulp of the liquid that failed to burn his throat the way he wanted it to. He wished for it to burn away all the pain from his chest, but it wasn't working. She still couldn't see what he saw.

"It's true," Riannon admitted. "I don't want there to be lies between us, Astrea. He asked me about your location and I told him. Maybe if I didn't, you could have escaped to the East and be safe there with Fenrir."

"Or maybe he would have found me anyway." The girl shook her head. "He is a god and a freaking dragon! It was naïve to think I could escape that easily."

"It's still my fault—" Riannon exhaled painfully, and Joran let out a bitter laugh.

"Let me guess," his Dragonfly gave him a contemptuous glance, "you were pregnant, and he threatened to hurt your child?"

"And she chose the brat that wasn't even born yet!" he "reasoned" and she rolled her eyes at him.

"As she should! This is her child and my nephew! I would have been appalled if she chose otherwise! But that's something you wouldn't understand!"

"If she really loved you—" The dragon got angrier and threw the whiskey bottle against the wall right next to Riannon, myriads of shards flying in all directions, cutting the Western Queen's skin in several places.

Ria hissed in pain, and Astrea was next to her in seconds.

"Are you out of your mind?" she yelled at the god before her and then concentrated on her sister. "Are you okay?"

"I am fine." Riannon cupped her cheek and smiled through tears. "It's just a scratch, and I am already regenerating. And to be honest, nothing can ruin this day for me. Not when I finally found you, Asti."

The word sent a rush of goosebumps down her spine, evoking more childhood memories that were now flooding her mind.

Astrea took off the blazer Devoss gave her and tried to use the fabric to soak the blood from her sister's wounds, while the latter assured her she was fine.

"Ria, we will talk again soon!" Astrea pulled her into a tight hug and whispered into her ear, "Right now, I need you to find Gideon. Take him and leave back to the West. It's not safe here at the moment and you have a kid to worry about."

"I am not leaving you!" Riannon embraced her back. "Not again!"

"You are not leaving me." The Dragonfly smiled. "You are helping me and Fenrir do what is right. In the meantime, you need to take care of your country and your people. You know that."

The Queen of the West pursed her lips. It wasn't what she wanted to hear or how they wished for this conversation to go, but they both knew that at this given moment in time, it was the best course of action.

"Just know that me, Gideon and the West are always with you." Riannon gave her one last hug. "Whatever you need. Any time."

"I know." Astrea smiled and embraced her tighter. "Go, Ria. We will catch up another time."

Riannon was about to leave, when she stopped right next to Joran.

"Remember what I told you," she said through clenched teeth. "I don't even have to do anything. Your end has already been written!"

"Bye, witch!" He ignored her and stepped onto the balcony, crushing the glass under his boots.

He waited for the sounds of receding steps to disappear before he spoke up again.

"Is it finally my turn?"

"What do you want?" the woman snapped, throwing the blazer over the rail and meeting his gaze.

"Really, Astrea? Is that all you have to tell me after everything?" He ran his hand through his blonde hair.

"I just know you better," she retorted. "You always want something."

"I saved you!" he bellowed.

"And turned me into your slave! You are sad now because I am not wearing my collar anymore. Or am I wrong?"

"Everything I did was for your protection." He threw his head back, trying not to look at her because it was too painful for his liking.

"You know it's a lie just as well as I do." Astrea shook her head. "Get over it."

She turned on her heels to leave, but he caught her arm, fingers digging into her flesh.

"Why?" A fire she hadn't seen before burned in his eyes. "Why, after all these years, couldn't you fall for me?"

59. FIRST TIME OFFER

*J*oran held her tight, and she glared at him so fiercely that his heart clenched painfully. He did not even realise before that moment how much she meant to him and how much she hated him.

Not like that.

"Why?" he repeated. "Why couldn't you fall for me? I was always there, doing everything for you!"

Astrea stared at him for a few minutes, shocked he had to ask her that.

"Because I was already taken!" she replied, making him flinch at her words. "Because I never saw you that way. You never acted like a man who knew how to love, a man with whom I could feel safe with, and to be absolutely honest, I still think you don't know what actual love is."

Those words were like a slap to him, and his first instinct was to pull her closer.

"I have lived for thousands of years. Do you think I have never been in love before? I know very well what love is!"

"You had women in your life, no doubt there." Astrea tilted her head, meeting his gaze. "But would you sacrifice yourself for any of them? You are an immortal, and where are all those women now?"

His fingers unclenched, letting her go, and she straightened her dress, distancing herself as far as the balcony would allow it.

"I cared for you. I cherished you. I didn't push you. Don't think for one second I couldn't have done whatever the hell I wanted to you." The bitter words left him while the pain was still spreading through his chest.

"You don't get a medal for not forcing me," she cut him off and turned away. "It's not how it works, Joran."

Joran wanted to spin her around so that she faced him again and yell at her, but something told him it would only make matters worse, so he stormed out of the balcony to find more alcohol. It was annoying how much fiery liquid was required to make him stop feeling anything. Sometimes his divine status seemed like a curse.

He bumped into someone at the end of the corridor and swore under his breath.

"Don't stop on my account." The God of Vengeance measured him from head to toe with his gaze. "It's not like we have anything to talk about."

"What, no deals then?" Joran let out a dark chuckle.

"No deals for you, that is." Vidar's lips curled into a merciless smile. "I don't think I need you anymore. Someone else took advantage of my offer, and they will reap the benefits."

"Some benefits!" Joran scoffed, rolling his eyes. "To be locked away as your subject in Asgard forever?"

"Nothing you will have to worry about anymore." Vidar kept walking, demonstrating that he was done with this conversation.

Joran was happy to get rid of him, and although initially, he wanted to be left alone, his legs somehow brought him back somewhere else while he processed what he had just heard.

He saw his brother talking to his team next to the Convocation Hall.

"May I have a word?" he interrupted them, and Fenrir raised a brow questioningly but still followed him to an empty corner of the grand corridor.

"I thought I wouldn't see you for another century or two," the wolf chuckled. "What do you want?"

"I just spoke to Vidar," Joran cut straight to the chase, frowning. "And I think one of your inner circle has betrayed you."

Astrea took a gulp of the evening air, trying to calm herself down after the nightmare of a conversation with her ex-Teacher when warm fingers touched the bare skin on her shoulders.

Vidar knew what kind of effect his touch would have on her as goosebumps rippled over both their bodies, awakening their mate bond whether she wanted it to or not. Any physical contact between them always promised so much pleasure...

"Don't do that." She shivered, hoping he would take his hands away, but his fingers only pressed harder into her flesh.

"I wish I could," he breathed out.

"A sorry excuse!" Astrea shook her head with a sigh.

"I have been waiting for you for so long. The wait almost killed me, and I don't know if I can do it anymore. Don't you see I am the only one who can make you happy? The only one who truly cares about you?"

"And how many times in the past did I hear that speech?" She turned to face him, staring him straight in the eye.

The corners of his lips twisted into a smirk.

"I see your memories are back!" Vidar leaned lower and captured her lips before she could do anything about it, startling her and pressing her against the balcony. His fingers dug into her hair, making it impossible to distance herself even though she tried to wriggle away from him.

Tingles erupted, making his breathing ragged. Even a god had his limits. That woman was driving him crazy from the first moment he saw her. Moreover, she belonged to him. She was given to him and tied with a forever kind of bond. He was only taking what was rightfully his, which was why her slap stung like no other.

Astrea glared at him as he rubbed his cheek, tasting the bitter rejection once again.

"How long are you going to fight this?" he sneered, changing his tone to a much colder one. "You know it's true as much as I do."

"What is true?" She shook her head.

"That you can fight me as long as you want, but it will change nothing. You are mine, and it's not a coincidence that even after all this time, I am the only one who can save you now. The universe is trying to restore everything to where it belongs."

"Save me?" She huffed, pushing him against the wall before he could realise it and pressing a cold blade to his neck, shocking him. She clearly had never been an assassin before in her previous lives. "Who says I need saving at all? What does saving me even mean to you?" Astrea wrinkled her forehead. "You are the one I need saving from! So I guess I have to save myself."

"Easy there." Vidar raised his eyes to demonstrate he was giving up. "It's not like anyone but me has divinity to spare to save your soul from perishing."

She did her best not to let her lips flinch, holding his gaze.

"Oh, your hero did not tell you, did he?" A smug smile stretched over the God of Vengeance's face. "Last lifetime, deary. You have no more lives to spare on your little tantrum."

"Little tantrum?" A laugh escaped her as she released him. A simple knife wouldn't kill him, anyway. Who was she kidding? "Is that how you are calling millennia of my defiance?"

"What's a few thousand years for gods?" Vidar's eyes glowed red, and she clenched her fingers around the hilt of her dagger, thanking herself for taking it from the sand on the Firstborn island when she had a chance and regretting leaving Midnight's horn with Fenrir instead. That could have been scarier for this prick.

"We have an eternity to spend together," Vidar continued, regardless of their position. "Let's stop playing these games, Astraea. Come with me, and I'll make you the Queen and goddess you were always supposed to be."

"No, thank you." She shook her head. "Even if it's my last life—especially if it's my last life, I want to spend it with Fenrir. Our mate bond is just a mista —"

"It can be a much shorter lifetime than you think!" Vidar gritted his teeth. "Why do you think I am here?"

"To cut my life short because I dared to say no? Again," she suggested, playing with her blade.

"I found the problem, Astraea. I know why gods are still dying."

The announcement made her pause in her tracks. It all happened so long ago, but the pain in her chest was so real. She had lost so much. All her divine sisters died, her aunts and uncles, cousins… the gods were dying like flies. As if their divinity meant nothing and no one could stop that process.

"Finally, I got to the real you." Vidar tilted his head to look at her. "The one who has the *responsibility* to save her kind on her shoulders."

"What's causing the divine realm to crumble?" she asked bluntly, wishing to stop the game they were playing.

He smirked, walking back to the balcony rail and waving his arm around the city landscape lit by the setting sun.

"This," he said.

"The Southern capital?" She really hoped that was it, but his chuckle proved her worst suspicions.

"No, Astraea, no, it's not the capital. It's all of it. The whole mortal realm!" he announced, as if mocking her. "All this time, we were thinking about why we were growing weaker and why it became possible to kill us. Well, now we know! It's the vermin under our feet sucking the life out of our realm! The one we took pity on and cared for almost caused our demise."

Astrea swallowed uncomfortably.

"What are you going to do?"

"I'll tell you what I am *not* going to do." Vidar straightened his back. "I will not let the mortals feed from our divine power anymore. This has to end."

"What do you mean?" Every muscle in Astrea's body went rigid as her heart palpitated with a sense of impending dread. "There is a balance to be kept—"

"You are the one to talk about balance!" A laugh rumbled through his chest. Not a warm and joyous one. When Vidar laughed, she felt colder and lonelier than ever before. "Your two boyfriends went on a spree, blessing armies and rewarding them with gifts just because they could! How do you think that affected the so-called balance?"

"It can be evened out over time." She hugged her shoulders, not liking where this conversation was going.

"I am afraid I don't want to wait and see," the ruler of New Asgard exhaled heavily. "I am not risking the divine realm for... this."

"What are you planning to do?" she whispered, knowing the answer.

"If this world is a problem for us, then I will have to erase it," he responded calmly, as if it wasn't a big deal.

"You are going to destroy this world?" Astrea was barely able to form the words. "This is madness!"

He turned on his heels to face her again. "This brings me back to our original topic of discussion, Astraea. Join me and avoid all this. Live in luxury, feel the power that was always supposed to be yours. You need divinity to become a goddess again, and I have plenty after the fall of my brothers and sisters. You will need nothing. And as a special courtesy to you, I will postpone destroying this realm for another century. So that the people you care about can live their lives as planned. One century, though, no more and no less."

"Have these threats worked before?" She folded her arms over her chest, coming to her senses after the initial shock of the revelations.

"It's the first time I am offering," Vidar admitted. "And the clock is ticking, Astraea. Each extra hour you think takes a year away from my offer."

The God of Vengeance assessed her once again, his eyes roaming her frame as if he had already won.

"I will wait for your decision." He passed her and paused near the door.

"But not too long. I am still getting everything I want. The question is, what are you getting out of it?"

He left her standing there, angry and lost. And scared.

No matter how she looked at it, this conversation did not go well. If Vidar wanted to destroy this realm, could he really do it?

60. LET THEM LISTEN

"*There* you are." Fenrir's voice brought her back, and her heart skipped a beat when she saw him standing in the doorway, watching her with that gaze of his that made her forget about everything.

He didn't say anything else, clenching and unclenching his fists a few times, and she realised he didn't know *what* to say. It was the first time they were finally alone and the first time she remembered who he was to her.

Now, she looked at him differently, noticing the changes the years that passed had made on him. Now she knew how he got the scars on his face and body. She noticed a few new wrinkles here and there, but most of all, she couldn't ignore the longing in his eyes.

"Here I am." She tried to curl her lips, but her smile faltered.

Too long. It's been too long since they were able to be together, touch each other... It didn't feel like centuries, it felt like forever.

Astrea did not remember her other lives, but right now, even though she had been with him just a few days ago, it seemed like he hadn't touched her in years.

She needed him like air. Needed to feel him, to belong to him, and from the flames burning in his eyes, she could tell he felt the same way.

Just this once. This once, she would be selfish and let them forget the world outside this balcony existed. They could save everyone later. Together. Not now...

She did not have to tell him a word because they both were clearly thinking the same thing as their bodies magnetically pulled towards each other – lips crashing, breathing mingled, hands grasping.

Fenrir pinned her against the wall in one swift move, his hot tongue descending on her delicate neck that was finally free from another man's mark.

A whimper left her mouth because it felt so good. Her so-called mate touched her just a few minutes ago, but the primal physical reaction she had to Fenrir's caresses couldn't be compared to anything. This was the man she loved, the one whose touch she craved.

Tonight, they would reign in their desires.

And they would enjoy it.

She wrapped her arms around his neck, ripping off the top button of his shirt. A long scar ran up from his chest and she traced it with her tongue, eliciting a growl of approval from him. His erection was pressing into her stomach, and she slid her hands to unbuckle his pants.

This was probably the worst place to do this, but they couldn't postpone this even for a second.

Not to mention, they were used to expressing their love in the worst places.

Fenrir lifted her up and placed her on top of the balcony rail, securing her with just one hand as if she weighed nothing. It was one of the top floors, and she felt gravity pulling her down, yet at the same time, she knew that with this man, she was safe.

He dipped his head at the crook of her neck, brushing off the fabric of her dress and draping her leg around his waist as she reached for his hard cock and wrapped her fingers around it, stroking it in torturous moves that made him snarl into her.

"You are mine," he stated. Not asked.

"Always and forever," she confirmed, feeling his hand pulling her lacy thong aside, two fingers probing her wetness, followed by a growl of approval. She clenched his shaft tighter, guiding it to her entrance as Fenrir slipped the fabric of her dress down to reveal her breast and almost instantly sucked on one of her nipples, making it hard.

She arched her back for him, wanting to feel him more. Everywhere. All the time.

Anyone could walk in here. Anyone could see them if they knew where to look.

Yet none of them cared as he thrust into her, filling her and making her feel whole again.

"Damn it, Astrea," he groaned against her as he started moving. Those were not gentle caresses anymore. Raw primal need overwhelmed them both as he withdrew and slammed back into her to the hilt, watching her breasts echo his movement, only arousing him more.

She was divine. Radiating desire as he watched her beautiful body spread for him against the canvas of the city below. So gorgeous and all his.

Only one thing in the entire world was ever his, but it was the one he couldn't live without.

Her fingers dug into his flesh, not to hold herself. She knew he took care of that. This was the only way she could express the pleasure she was getting from him now.

He shoved into her roughly again, watching her scream as the wind whipped her silvery-white hair. Again and again, he pounded into her with all his might, and she moaned his name just the way he liked it.

He was unleashed. After years and years of waiting, he could finally have her again.

"More!" she begged. "Don't stop!"

"Not... going to!" he groaned, grasping her ass to bring her even closer to him. "All mine!"

Beads of sweat formed on both their bodies as she screamed her release, not caring if the whole world heard them.

Let them listen.

Fenrir watched her, not being able to stop and letting her ride her climax before he finally tipped over the edge and came into her, his seed overflowing as he desperately tried to seal it deeper within her.

He finally stopped, the world around them spinning as he held her in his arms as if she was the most precious thing.

She wrapped her arms around his neck, her face pressed against his chest, and tears silently falling from her eyes.

"I love you," she whispered to him.

"I love you too." He placed a kiss on the top of her head, knowing what she was going through now. The mix of happiness and pain was their constant companion.

"We lost so much time!" she said, not able to look at him.

"I know," he sighed, covering her from the cruel reality in his enormous arms. "But I'd do it all over again, even for a fleeting moment of love with you."

A chuckle escaped her, which turned into a sob.

They lost so much.

They still could lose each other again.

"Vidar wants to destroy this realm." The words left her against her will. She did not want to talk about this. Not really. She wanted to enjoy her moment with the love of her life.

But she couldn't be selfish any longer. He had to know this.

"Whatever for?" Fenrir furrowed his brows and looked at her, searching her face for answers.

"He thinks this realm is the reason the gods are dying," she told him the truth. "And he believes you and Joran are to blame for this because you blessed too many mortals."

"Gods were dying long before that." He sighed and pulled her dress back up to cover her breast, throwing his head back so as not to look at her still hard nipples.

"I know!" she agreed with him as he gently took her off the railing. "But he insists this realm ruins the balance. He wants to destroy it to strengthen the divine one."

"He is... something!" Fenrir growled. "Someone was killing off the gods. Some power. It's not like they were dying from sickness. There is something else."

"Do you know what?" She glanced at him, and he brushed his fingers through her silky hair simply because he couldn't help himself.

"I met them just once. A long time ago," he said. "They call themselves Hunters."

"Who are they?" she asked.

"Who knows?" Fenrir shook his head. "They wanted to kill the gods, and I had nothing against it. Maybe that was why they left me alone. But it was so many centuries ago. Now I wish I knew more."

"Maybe if we tell this to Vidar—"

"That prick would never listen," the wolf exhaled heavily. "Besides, he may have a point. Blessing a Champion takes away from the divine source. Despite being banished from Asgard and not able to enter it, we are still both connected to the source by blood. When we blessed all those mortals, it definitely took its toll."

"Still, we can't let him do that!" She looked up at him with her beautiful starry eyes, the whole universe trapped in them.

"We won't." Fenrir pulled her closer. "He has to be dealt with, anyway. I can't stand him anywhere near you, and you still need a divinity, which, trust me, I am getting you."

She knew he meant it, and her lips curled into a smile as she allowed herself to close her eyes and enjoy this moment with him.

"Mark me," she whispered, making him flinch.

Fenrir stopped and distanced her slightly from him, so that he could see her face and the determination written all over it.

"Are you… sure?" he asked, his voice so different from his usual tone.

The question stung her a bit. Did he really have to ask?

"It's just"— the wolf cleared his throat— "we are gods, and gods don't mark each other that way. Technically—"

Astrea cupped his cheek gently, making him lock his eyes with hers.

"I love you more than life," she smiled at him through tears forming in her eyes, "I loved you in every lifetime, every scenario, every time we met. I loved you when the whole universe was against us, and every power that ever existed wished to tear us apart. I will love you whether this world stands or perishes into oblivion. Through the chaos and destruction, I always hold on to you, and you never disappoint. So, yes, Fenrir, I really want it. I want to bear your mark wherever you are willing to place it, because I want everyone to see who I belong to. Because it was *my* choice!"

He sucked in a sharp breath and wanted to reply, but her soft fingers touched his lips. She wasn't done yet.

"And I want to mark you too. Would you let me?"

She bit her lip, waiting for his reply, and Fenrir brushed his palm over her cheek, the last golden rays of the setting sun drawing their features, almost making them feel ethereal.

"You can do anything to me, Astrea."

Any other god would have been afraid to even pronounce such words because of their binding effect. But not Fenrir. And not with her.

It was a confession in itself, and she stood on the tips of her toes to try to reach his lips. He met her halfway, claiming what was rightfully his.

The kiss was quickly growing into something else again.

"We need to find a better place to continue this," he growled into her mouth as she giggled, agreeing with him.

Sudden light blinded them, and a deafening sound followed. The world around them seemed to shake and an unexpected wave of heat washed over them, carrying with it the acrid scent of smoke and burning debris.

Fenrir locked her in his arms, trying to protect her from whatever it was, but she still pushed away a little to be able to see what was going on.

The air filled with the sounds of sirens blaring, mingling with the distant cries of people below as an enormous stomp of fire was dying down in the centre of this sovereign capital.

The flickering flames danced in the sky, casting an eerie glow over the city. It became almost impossible to breathe from all the dust and the heat.

"Explosion," Astrea gasped. "But how—Who?"

They looked at each other, concern and realisation painting their faces. The weight of uncertainty and fear settled upon them, causing both their hearts to race.

"Those people," she whispered. "This is terrible!"

She looked at Fenrir, trying to find some consolation in him, but only saw the wrinkle between his eyes deepen as he loudly swore under his breath.

"Fuck! We are royally screwed!" he grunted, his grip on her tightening.

She followed his gaze, and her lips parted in shock as she watched a huge blue flag with a white wolf and a Northern star projected onto one of the still-standing buildings.

A flag of the Northern Lycan Kingdom.

61. VANISHED

*a*strea tried to distract a group of people while Fenrir discreetly lifted a heavy block to let Gideon save a child who survived the explosion from piles of rubble. Sadly, his parents didn't make it; she couldn't take this anymore. They had been working here for hours, trying to help along with the Southern fire and rescue crews, who were overwhelmed by the scale of the disaster.

It was the middle of the night and still too dangerous here, but they couldn't give up and leave these people alone. Fenrir had to think twice about using anything divine; this was clearly a response from Vidar. The first payment for the disrupted balance.

Astrea wiped the sheen of sweat from her forehead when she thought her werewolf hearing picked up another sound from a mountain of debris.

"I think I have another one," she screamed, alerting people next to her and went to it. Her movements had to be deliberate and focused as she assessed the situation, searching for any signs of the trapped person after each removed stone. She remained cautious, aware of the potential risks for her own safety.

Unfortunately, it wasn't the best place to be stuck as a huge half-destroyed wall towered over the exact place she was at, threatening to collapse at any moment.

"You only have one chance at this," Nova warned her.

Each minute mattered. Too many people died today, and quite a few were on her watch. She was not ready to lose anyone else.

The closer she got, the more convinced she became; someone was moaning beneath the remnants of a once-tall office building, so she sped up her work, finally reaching a hand covered in dust.

"Do you hear me?" she called and gently grasped the fingers, happy to find them somewhat warm and trembling. Now she could tell that it was a woman, but all she heard from her was a little whimper. She probably couldn't talk.

There was quite a heavy piece of concrete on top of her with a few broken wooden planks, pipes and wire, which she cleared first.

"Astrea!" She heard Fenrir's worried voice. He was clearly searching for her, worried beyond belief. Considering how many dead bodies were around them, it was understandable.

"Here!" she yelled as loud as she could, ready to lift the reinforced concrete, but the moment she did, the light around her disappeared, and she felt a deep sense of dread welling up in her stomach. Turning her head, she noticed cracks spreading fast at the base of that massive wall. *A terrible sign!*

She could choose to abandon the woman, but if she did, the latter would never make it. If she didn't, it was quite possible they both would die here and now.

"Astrea!" Fenrir was running towards her, but they both knew he wouldn't be there in time.

"Nova, help me!" Astrea prepared for a final push.

"I am trying!" her wolf growled, lending her the strength she needed.

Yet it was too late. She could hear the wall cracking at the base. She would die under it. It would simply smash her on top of the woman she tried to save.

She closed her eyes, ready for the impact. There was no way to avoid it—

Astrea held her breath as the cloud of dust enveloped her. Something pressed against her back, and she sensed the boulders falling around her, not causing her any harm.

She was fine.

"Astrea!" Fenrir roared, and for a split second, she was shocked to hear him so far away because someone had just covered her, saving her life from imminent death. Her first thought was that it was him, but apparently, she was wrong.

"Are you going to stand like this for a long time?" Joran seethed, holding the biggest piece of the broken wall over them and not letting it hammer her.

Her lips parted in shock. He was the last man she expected to see here.

"Dragonfly!" he groaned as one of his knees budged a bit, showcasing she wasn't safe yet. "I thought I trained you better than that."

"You did!" she muttered, pushing the concrete away, revealing a woman underneath who couldn't speak but tried to open her eyes.

Responsive. And with a distinct werewolf scent. All good signs.

Astrea knew she just needed to drag her out and not break anything vital in the process. This was the benefit of working with shifters – if they were not dead, they could recover from pretty much anything over time. She simply needed to get the woman to safety.

"Hurry up, will you?" Joran rushed her, and she obeyed him, swearing under her breath. If anyone had told her they would work together just hours ago, she would have laughed in their faces.

She was out right before the wall collapsed completely, clouds of dust chasing her as she ran into a furious Fenrir.

"Astrea, what the hell?" he growled loudly, his terrified gaze scanning her. "If anything happened to you—"

"I am fine!" She tried to force a smile onto her lips, although it was hard considering the circumstances. A group of medics ran up to them with a stretcher and took the woman under their care, allowing Astrea to breathe out in relief. One more life saved.

"Please, leave these things to me." He pulled her into his embrace. "If he had been a few seconds late, I would have lost you again—"

Astrea bit her lips, guilt washing over her.

"Sorry." She raised her head to look at her beloved, but noticed his eyes were elsewhere.

Joran walked past them, trying to brush the dust off his jacket.

"You are welcome!" His words were filled with venom despite his selfless act, and he did not stop to talk to them, carrying on as if nothing had happened.

"You couldn't let literally anyone else save you?" Fenrir raised his brow at her, brushing his fingers over her cheek.

"It may come as a shock to you, but I don't want anyone to save me at all." Her shoulders drooped. "In this lifetime, I have always felt so strong and able to go through anything, but ever since I remembered who I am...— I can't stop thinking about it, Fenrir. I am literally a goddess trapped in a dying body. Powerless. Useless."

"Don't say that!" He cupped her chin, lifting it up so that she looked at him. "You are the most precious—"

"I know, I know… but hear me out." She glanced at the stars. "Vidar is at the peak of his power. Joran hates us both; you are still banished from the divine realm and unable to replenish your power the normal way, and I have nothing to offer in this fight. All I know is how to cut throats discretely or how to slip poison into someone's cup. But all my battle skills are worth nothing when I am a mortal fighting gods."

"I don't want you to fight at all," he confessed, and she placed her palms on his chest.

"Fenrir, I know, but I can't simply watch you fighting alone!" She rolled her eyes, which only caused his lips to curl.

"I am not done talking, Astrea." Fenrir gave her shoulders a light squeeze. "I don't want you to fight, but it was always your destiny. Don't you see? Every event was connected to you, and I am afraid you will be the one to end all this."

He pulled her into his chest and locked his arms around her, kissing the top of her head.

"And when you are there, I will be by your side," he assured her.

"I just hope no one I love suffers in the process." Astrea gave him a half-smile, which faded almost instantly.

She lifted her head to the sky peppered with stars, and closed her eyes for just a moment, opening them almost instantly in shock.

"Gideon!" she screamed, searching for the King of the Western Lycan Kingdom. "Gideon!"

She found him next to the ambulance, helping people when their eyes locked, and he dropped everything, marching towards her.

"What is it?" His brows were knitted together.

"Where is Ria now?" she asked bluntly. "Can you check?"

Gideon's eyes lost focus for a moment as he tried to mind-link his wife, but very soon, they were back to normal, a shadow running over his eyes as he couldn't reach her.

"Can you call her over the phone?" Astrea suggested.

Gideon did not question her even for a moment. Riannon had to stay behind to help at the improvised first aid centre in the main Convocation building. In the first minutes, they all fell into chaos, and she helped them to organise everything effectively to accept the first wounded survivors. After all, the closest hospital was also destroyed. On top of that, the Queen of the West was supposed to watch over the members of the Convocation and alert the group if they had to return urgently.

Gideon waited for her to reply, but the call went unanswered. He dialled again, the wrinkle between his brows deepening as he waited.

"I am returning!" he announced, placing his phone back in his pants. "Even if we are suddenly too far from each other for a mind link, it's not like Riannon to not pick up her phone when I call."

Astrea cast an anxious look at Fenrir.

"We will go with you," she announced, and he nodded in agreement.

THEY DID NOT FIND Riannon in the emergency medical centre she created just hours ago to help the Southerners. Gideon's roar shuttered the walls when their designated room also appeared to be empty.

Astrea felt her stomach churn.

"It cannot be good," she muttered to Fenrir, hoping the Western King did not hear her.

"We need to confront Vidar and Joran." Her beloved laced their fingers together. "If she is missing, it's definitely one of them."

"If one hair falls from my wife's head, the explosion would be the least of their problems!" Gideon growled, his eyes glowing golden.

"Listen," Astrea stepped forward to reason with him, "I understand your feelings. I really do, but this is exactly what they want. This is all a game for them. They already made the North look bad, and I am afraid this may be the West's turn. Don't fall into this trap and support their narrative. We will get her back. I promise."

"And if they hurt her?" The King bared his teeth, barely able to hold his wolf back.

"If they hurt her, you will have no time to do anything because I will kill them first. Whatever that costs me!" She felt bloodthirsty as fury rose in her chest after she locked her eyes with her brother-in-law. "No one touches my sister and stays alive!"

"It's a deal then." Gideon clenched his jaw, offering her his hand, which she shook firmly.

"O-kay." Fenrir watched them both with concern. "How about I speak when we get in there?"

"You can speak as much as you like," Gideon cut him off, "but I am getting my wife back today."

THEY ENTERED the Alpha Convocation Hall and found them all in the same places at the long table, discussing something vigorously. Vidar stood near a large interactive screen and sneered when they walked in.

"Welcome," he greeted the group. "We were about to invite you in any way."

"Excuse us." Fenrir strolled in, offering Astrea the seat at the head of the table just like the last time. The seat that was supposed to belong to the High Chancellor. "We were busy getting your people from under the rubble of destroyed buildings while you were... here."

Astrea glanced around quickly, noticing that Joran was missing.

"The Southern Lycan Republic thanks you for your help in this time of need." Vidar smirked, bowing his head respectfully. "However, a few things were brought to our attention that we would like to discuss."

"Where is my wife?" Gideon gritted his teeth, clenching his fists so tight his knuckles turned white.

"The last time I checked, she was helping the survivors." Vidar shrugged his shoulders as if it wasn't a big deal.

"Well, she is not there anymore," Astrea chimed in, hoping Gideon could hold it together. "Her room is also empty."

"It's a bit chaotic right now because we were under a terrorist attack," Vidar tried to downplay it, "but I am sure she is safe and sound. After all, the Queen of the West has so many people who care about her. I assure you, no one disappears in the South without a trace."

It wasn't really a threat, but it sure sounded like one to Astrea. Vidar knew about their connection.

Forrest cleared his throat, typing something on his phone. "I am sending my people to look for her right now."

"Now, if you will allow me to continue." Vidar changed the image on the interactive screen to showcase the projected Northern flag on one of the buildings in the capital. "Since it's a direct attack of the North on the Republic, I suggest—"

"One picture doesn't prove that the North was behind the attack!" Astrea interrupted his undoubtedly well-prepared speech. "They are obviously being set up!"

"I have to agree here," one of the women at the table interjected. "It's not enough to accuse them."

"They literally have an army on our doorstep!" a councilman with grey hair added, rubbing his thick silver moustache. "We can't ignore that."

"But they didn't attack, did they?" Fenrir leaned over the back of his chair.

"Now would have been the perfect moment to attack, when the country is already devastated by this... disaster. Yet the North army didn't move."

"Well, this is simply because we took countermeasures!" Vidar said in a smug tone, adjusting the lapels of his jacket. "And thanks to those measures, I have concrete proof that we are under a deliberate attack of the North."

Astrea tensed in her seat. This couldn't be good.

"What do you mean, Vincent?" Forrest furrowed his brows.

"Let me demonstrate!" He clicked his fingers, and the side door swung open, letting in two men dragging a woman dressed in red. They threw her to the ground in front of everyone, her ebony black hair covering her face.

Every muscle in Astrea's body strained because she did not need to see that face. She knew exactly who that was.

"Meet the witch behind the atrocities performed by the Northern Lycan Kingdom!" Vidar lifted his chin, smug at his little victory. "Salome Gray."

62. HOLD MY HAND

*J*oran was so empty inside, yet his chest felt heavy. As if that wall was still on his shoulders, obstructing his airways.

He couldn't even remember if Astrea thanked him for saving her life. That girl always took everything he did for her for granted, and he was getting fed up with it.

He closed his eyes, and immediately, the image of Fenrir holding her painted itself in his mind. The way she looked at him. The way he touched her... these things repulsed him and hurt him more than anything before. Just why did he let himself be that attached to her? Wasn't losing a brother enough? Did he have to create even more pain for himself?

He used to imagine how he would live with Astrea and how Fenrir one day would accept them for her sake. He used to believe he was the remedy to their curse, imagining the picture-perfect family.

Now they will have this picture, but cut him out of it. He was alone again.

Joran rubbed his forehead. He needed a swim. Or at least a shower. Water was the first element he ever mastered, and it still managed to bring him peace. Not to mention that he wanted to get rid of Astrea's lingering scent. It was driving him crazy, more than he cared to admit.

The elevator doors opened, and his heart sank at the sight before him. The once luxurious and pristine space he was so proud to call his was now a scene of chaos and destruction. The doors were broken, furniture upturned, glass shattered, and debris scattered across the floor. It was as if a tempest had turned through the room, leaving nothing unscathed. And bodies... several dead bodies lay in awkward positions around, some missing limbs.

Joran was too physically tired and too emotionally exhausted to process it all, so it took him a few seconds to notice that amidst the wreckage, there was a figure lying on the ground in a pool of ruby-red blood.

"Bjorn!" He rushed to the bear's side, falling to his knees and trying to assess the wounds.

It looked bad. So bad that scales began to emerge from beneath his skin. It had been years since the last time that happened uncontrollably.

His Champion looked like he went through one hell of a fight. Joran knew that blindness did not make him defenceless, but he could smell the blood of his enemies everywhere in the living room and wondered if he had underestimated the guy's abilities after all. The warrior in Bjorn did not go anywhere.

"Th-they took her," he muttered, desperately clenching the deity's arm as if to urge him.

"It's okay, it doesn't matter!" Joran tried to reassure him, seeing how much blood he had lost. "I am just glad you are still alive and—"

"No!" Bjorn bared his teeth, fingers digging into his flesh. "You don't get it! Niki... they came for her—"

"Irrelevant! I don't care where she is, and you should—"

"But I do," the bear seethed, his chest constricting as he coughed blood. It wasn't the time for him to start caring about that girl. He had to think of what was best for him!

"I'll send someone after her," the dragon tried to distract him, his priorities elsewhere. He had already lost his brother and Astrea. Losing his favourite Champion would be too much.

"No!" Bjorn's claws grew longer. If Jormungandr weren't a god, they would have pierced his skin. "I need... Strawberry... she is—I'll go!"

"You will go nowhere." The dragon let out an aggravated sigh. Why was everyone in his life so stubborn?

"I can't... leave her—"

"You are in no state to go anywhere!" Joran warned him. "I will need to perform a miracle to heal you, and you know I have already surpassed my limits for you and Astrea."

"I'll give you anything!" Bjorn's grip tightened. "Whatever the hell you want from me! My soul! My firstborn! *Anything!*"

Joran's lips parted.

Bjorn did not take these words lightly. He knew who he was dealing with, but he was still offering...

If he accepted the plea now, he could bind him to—No, that wasn't right.

"You don't mean that," he tried to brush it off. The bear must have been delusional because of his injuries. "No woman is worth it, Bjorn."

"This is why Astrea will never be yours!" the bear retorted, letting out a bitter chuckle. "Why do you think she never trusted you? You only take what conveniently falls into your arms or what you can manipulate. You—you don't fight for her, don't make sacrifices, don't see her the way he sees her... a person. You wouldn't walk through fire for her."

"You were ready to walk through fire for Savannah a little less than a year ago," Joran reminded him. "And look how that ended."

"And I still would. She was my mate even if she didn't love me. You'd never understand!"

"You are lucky you are already hurt," Jor muttered, watching his Champion struggle with his breathing laboured.

"Anything!" Bjorn repeated himself. "I'll be your slave for life. For eternity, if you want it."

This was too tempting. After all, today, it looked like he would spend the eternity alone.

"Please," the bear was now ready to beg him, "Niki—She deserves everything good in this life. She went through the training of the Firstborn island and remained so pure-hearted."

"If you think she loves you—"

"She hates me." A sad smile curled onto Bjorn's lips as he remembered the little she-wolf. "It... doesn't matter. I-I don't hate her, you know—"

Joran knew exactly what he meant. No matter how he tried, he couldn't hate Astrea either.

He also knew that they had seconds until the decision had to be made.

"If you want to go after her, I'll have to turn you into something else." His words were cold and quiet, but the bear heard him well. "You'll be... *something else.*"

"I am already a monster, am I not?" Bjorn chuckled and ended up coughing more blood. "Just do it! Whatever it is!"

"It'll hurt like hell, and you may die in the process." This was the last attempt to bring him back to his senses. "Or I can just heal you and—"

"Do it!" the man roared, the pool of blood under him growing bigger.

"Before we begin, is there anything else you want to tell me?" Joran asked, still hesitant about the whole thing.

"The warriors who came here—Apart from their scents, there was one

more on them. I wouldn't have noticed before, but in my current condition
—"

"What's the scent?" the dragon rushed him. They couldn't waste a second
more.

"Peppermint with a hint of grapefruit." Bjorn's face tensed after he said
that, which meant he knew whom the scent belonged to. Joran knew as well.
This changed everything.

"That's all I know," the bear admitted. "Use it as you will, *friend.*"

"Here." Joran pretended he did not feel the single treacherous tear that was
now rolling down his cheek. Just like Bjorn pretended he didn't know what it
was when it landed on the scars of his long-gone eye. "Hold my hand, *Darius.*"

Bjorn's fingers wrapped around his, and the dragon took three beads off
his bracelet, hoping it would work.

"Try to be still," the Dragon God said, clenching his lips into a thin white
line and crushing all the beads simultaneously.

A resounding roar pierced the silence in the room, reverberating through
the entire building.

AFTER WHAT SEEMED LIKE HOURS, Joran stood up on shaky legs as his stomach
was about to empty itself. He was done. Done with the pain. Done with
loving anyone. Done with people betraying him.

He didn't trust too many people, and now he had remembered why.

Partially, it was his fault. He was too busy to notice what was happening
under his nose, and now this was the result.

Peppermint and grapefruit... the bearer of this scent had to pay for the
betrayal, for what was taken from him today.

Thanks to the traitor, Darius Bjorn was dead.

"SPEAK, WITCH!" Vidar commanded, but Salome did not move. "You will tell
us everything one way or another. There's no need to make this hard on
yourself."

"Threatening a witness is a sure way to get false results." Astrea was hectically thinking of ways to throw her so-called mate off his game.

"Sadly, we don't have time to dance around her." The God of Vengeance acted as if she was a silly child passing by and not a Luna of a whole country. "There is an army on our doorstep, and we need answers now. If anything, I find it suspicious that you want to stall us. It makes more sense, though, when I remember you recently swapped sides and joined the East."

"I don't know what you are implying. I lived my whole life in the South, and it will always be my home. I have its best interest in my heart no matter where I live." Astrea sent a withering glance down his way. "I am sensing a bad energy here. Yes, I had to reject you as my mate, but I hoped we could deal with it privately as two adults."

A wave of whispers erupted, and the Dragonfly knew she had made him look like a bitter fool now.

"No offence taken." Vidar inhaled through his nostril, clenching a little remote in his hand so hard it let out a cracking noise. "I have many candidates for the role of my Queen."

"Luna," Fenrir interjected, lips curved into a slight smirk.

"Excuse me?" Vidar raised his brow at him, annoyed by them both and barely holding back his anger.

"As far as I remember, you are not a King, *Vincent*. Why would you have a Queen? Unless there is something we all don't know about your plans?"

Another wave of whispers rippled. The newcomer already looked power-hungry, but this little slip-up made it worse.

"We are not here to discuss my personal life," Vidar reasoned. "My Luna will be treated like a Queen. That's all."

"Good for her." The Councilwoman with silver hair tapped her fingers over the desk. "Now, can we get back to the witch? You seemed to have a point about something there, and we are all ears."

"Yes, Salome Gray is the mastermind behind the explosion, and we would have been under a massive attack right now if my men didn't catch her before the North could act," Vidar announced. "Moreover, there was more than one bomb."

63. LIES AND LEVERAGES

"*W*hat proof do you have?" Forrest asked, running his hand through his rich brown curls.

"We analysed the explosion, and it was triggered by fire blood magic." Vidar nodded at one of the Alphas present, and the man started handing the papers to his colleagues. "And guess which Coven Salome Gray belongs to?"

"She is from the White Tree Coven," Fenrir grunted.

"Don't be hasty and read the papers I prepared for you." Vidar smirked. "That's her mother's Coven. Her father comes from the Obsidian Circle Coven, and his bloodline is famous for fire-wielding. Fire blood magic, to be specific, which is a rare gift, may I add. Barely any other witches can wield fire like the Gray bloodline."

"And you found out all this in less than one day?" Gideon arched his brow suspiciously.

"We work fast in the South." A chuckle rumbled through the God of Vengeance's chest. "Please, keep in mind that we're only sharing this with you, hoping that you would understand the measures we have to take against the North. Considering your relationship—"

"That's very generous of you." Gideon did not let him finish. "Queen Savannah is my sister, and King Kai is—there." He cleared his throat. "If you plan to wage war against the North, the West will not take this kindly, whatever reason you have."

"It's bold of you to say this," one of the younger Alphas at the table growled, "considering you're currently in our territory."

"Is that a threat?" Gideon's eyes glowed golden as a warning.

"You are not at all like I imagined you." Vidar turned away and took a few steps to draw attention to the view of the destroyed city behind it. "They say you are wise and just, but it looks like you're playing favourites because of your little sister's involvement."

"My sister was brought up the same way I was, and this is how I know she would never stand by something like this. I suggest the South look for their enemy somewhere else. Possibly closer."

"We'll take your words into consideration when we decide how to respond to the North's aggression," Forrest promised.

"I think it's rude to speak about the North as if they committed a crime," Fenrir added. "We still have seen no solid proof of their guilt. Keeping your own army at your own border is not exactly a war crime."

"But blowing up civilians of the neighbouring country is." Vidar was getting more and more confident.

"A flag projected on a wall is also hardly proof." Astrea folded her hands over her chest. "If the Northerners were this proud of their action, they wouldn't deny it now!"

"They are not denying. They aren't responding," Forrest said quietly, but everyone heard him.

Vidar nodded, and one of his minions brought a box to the desk, removing the lid and making everyone gasp.

A chill went down Astrea's spine because there was a new shiny bomb inside the box. An explosive device similar to the ones she was taught to work with on the Firstborn island. Only that one was triggered by magic.

"I came here because I heard rumours about the other three countries preparing to attack us. My father was investigating this, and I am pretty sure this got him killed." Vidar used everyone's shock to his advantage. "I continued his work when I arrived, and my men found this device underneath the very building we are at."

Everyone exchanged concerned glances.

"We found and disarmed twelve more," the Asgardian exhaled heavily. "Sadly, we didn't get to them all in time, and for that I apologise."

"Moon Goddess, Vincent!" someone gasped. "You are our hero! No need to apologise."

"If he hadn't found it in time, we'd all be dead!" someone murmured.

"The damage was supposed to be much bigger!"

Every muscle in Astrea's body went rigid hearing these words. Vidar wasn't a hero. He was a monster who probably orchestrated all this, and now he twisted the narrative in his favour.

"How convenient!" Fenrir commented. "I still don't see how any of this proves it's the North's fault. Or Salome's, for that matter."

"I am getting to that." Vidar raised his chin high and clicked a button on his remote. "The North is implicated just as much as the East. And it all comes back to the witch. Although I am not surprised you try to save your lover, King Fenrir Vanargard."

Astrea growled as Nova was ready to pounce on their enemy.

"Apologies, *Luna*." Her mate offered a fake smile. "You are yet to learn who you chose to spend your life with. But here is the proof you've been asking for."

Images of Fenrir and Salome from their life back in Solace appeared one by one, and Astrea had to use all her willpower not to rip the screen off the wall. In some of the images, Salome had her arms wrapped around Fenrir's. In another, they were hugging, and many had them laughing together, looking like the cutest couple ever. Then, a video of the old woman from the square and her puppet show appeared as she told the same old story she believed in.

It was a disaster.

"So, your proof is that we know each other and some gossip from an old woman who lost her mind a long time ago?" Fenrir looked unbothered. "I never denied that Salome used to live and work in the East. This is how I know her character and doubt that she would accept a job which includes killing innocents."

"Unless you are the one who wants them dead." Vidar tilted his head with an arrogant smile playing on his lips. "She would do anything for you, won't she?" He cast a diminishing look at the witch.

For the first time since the beginning of this conversation, Salome lifted her head to look at her captor defiantly.

"A desperate mistress would do anything for you when a new plaything threatens her." Vidar locked eyes with Astrea, and her stomach churned.

"No!" Salome spoke. "That's a lie!"

"So, what is the truth?" The deity stared down at her. "Let's have a glance at how it all looks from here. Last year, King Fenrir sent you to be a spy at the Luna Trials."

He showed people a photo of Salome walking in the garden with Kai.

"I wasn't a spy!" The woman clenched her fists, her chains rattling. Her magic was undoubtedly blocked. "I was looking for an alliance, and the King knew it!"

"Exactly!" Vidar nodded eagerly. "Both Kings had to agree on the same plan."

"No!" Salome protested.

"Let him speak." Fenrir shook his head, and the witch bit her lip. Vidar would say what he wanted to say, anyway. They had to regroup.

"See, even now, she only listens to his orders. Would she do that if she was banned, as he claimed before?" He was gloating, moving to the next photo with a click. "When the Northerners had a civil war, Salome Gray brought her Coven and helped them change course, granting her the trust they all needed and the idea of destroying the only country in their way, the Southern Lycan Republic."

"Because what?" Astrea rolled her eyes. "Reasons? There is no motive!"

"Of course there is!" Vidar did not spare her a glance. "To ruin the strongest of the four countries on the continent is one of them. Besides, we all know that the North needs more land. They begged the West to give them some last year."

Gideon let out a low warning snarl.

"And the East is so poor it hurts to look at them." The God of Vengeance shrugged. "Their land is no good either. Who wants to live in the desert? Besides, they are literally just a bunch of rogues."

"Still. No. Proof," Fenrir growled loudly, slamming his fist on the desk.

"Oh, I am just getting there." Vidar was full of himself as he displayed the next image. "This is the report I prepared for you. The metal used for the bombs can only be found in the North. The crystals used to activate the magic are from Northern caves. Even the wire is produced there. If you wanted proof, there it is!"

They all needed a moment to process this, and Astrea glanced at Fenrir, who seemed calm. Yet she felt it wasn't exactly true.

Sounds of a commotion behind the doors distracted them all. The doors burst open, as one of the guards flew to the ground, and a scene of two more trying to hold back Warg unfolded before their eyes.

"Salome!" he shouted, and the woman on the ground flinched. She was the only one who couldn't see him.

"Command your barbarian to stop!" Vidar frowned at Fenrir.

"Warg, stop!" the Wolf God said, his voice unusually loud. The words made the first Lycan freeze, eyes begging his King for permission to fight.

"You are not helping her," the Wolf God explained, and he finally stopped struggling.

"As I was saying—" Vincent was about to continue with his lies, showing yet another image of Salome on the border, accompanied by the Northern army.

"It's all me," the girl whispered, but no one heard her, so she repeated. This time louder. "It's all me!"

The people in the room turned their attention to her, and she finally stood up, raising her head high.

"I am the only one at fault here! I used the token I got after the Luna Trials to move the army to the border. I planned to destroy the South and attack while it was weak. For me."

Fenrir closed his eyes. It was the end.

"Nonsense." Vidar angled his head to look at the witch with a cruel grin. "One little witch doesn't need this. But thank you for your heartfelt confession. Take her to the cell!"

"No!" Warg growled, and more warriors arrived to restrain him.

"On that note, I would like to ask our guests to leave." Vidar put his hands in his pockets, leaning on the glass wall as if he was the victor, proud of everything he had done.

"Not before you return my wife to me!" Gideon growled.

"Queen Riannon is our guest, and her safety is ensured as long as the West does not interfere in our matters," the deity explained.

"So, not only have you abducted her, but you are also blackmailing me?" the Westerner seethed.

"Of course not." Vidar shook his head. "Please, don't read this the wrong way and give us some privacy. We are almost at war."

Gideon stood up, clenching his fists so hard his knuckles turned white. Astrea followed him, knowing they would have to find her sister as soon as possible.

Fenrir was the only one who remained still.

"What are you waiting for?" Vidar raised a brow at him.

"I am waiting for the show. You like those, don't you?" he challenged his enemy.

"Very well." Vidar never refused an opportunity to show off. "I would like to address the Alpha Convocation. The matter is urgent, and our situation calls for a vote! We need a High Chancellor, even if a temporary one, to deal with the ones who attacked us! This cannot be left alone, and too many things seem shady! We need a leader, and our laws allow us to elect one within a Convocation gathering when we are on the brink of war."

Vidar spoke with more and more confidence. It showed that he had a lot of practice as a public speaker after millennia of ruling over the New Asgard. "I have gathered as much proof as possible in such a short time. I am the only one not allied with anyone here. Fresh blood. Blood ready to be spilled for our Republic. As the son of my father, I summon all of you today for an Urgent Vote to choose an Emergency High Chancellor to lead us during this time."

"Let me guess," Fenrir gritted his teeth, "you offer yourself as the candidate?"

"Yes, I do!" Vidar did not even bother pretending to be modest. "I believe I am the best choice right now, but I will let you all decide who will lead us during the dark times."

The room fell silent as everyone contemplated their next action.

"Joran is not here," someone remembered about Joran. "He'd offer himself as well, and he—"

"He is not present," Vidar reminded him. "Therefore, he'll have to miss this vote as a candidate."

"Let's go!" Fenrir grasped Astrea's hand and pulled her behind him, gesturing for Warg and Gideon to follow them.

"So," they heard Vidar's eager voice behind their backs as the door were closing, "shall we?"

64. SEVERED

*J*oran was storming through the halls in the direction of the Convocation Hall, knocking a man off his feet on his way and sending dozens of papers flying in all directions.

Usually, he would have stopped to fix his mistake and looked charming while he did it, but now... now, he did not care about his perfect reputation anymore and had more important things to do.

After all, he was out for blood!

He was ready to knock the doors out when they opened in his face, and fellow Alpha Convocation members started walking out, most avoiding his gaze as if they had done something wrong.

Instinctively, he already knew.

"Where have you been?" a member of his inner circle seethed and walked past him, hitting his shoulder on the way.

Joran couldn't care less. There was only one person he wanted to see now.

"Late as always!" Vidar sneered at him, making his fists clench in response. "Thanks to your incompetence, I am now officially the High Chancellor. And my first order was announcing the war against the Northern Lycan Kingdom."

Although that silent prick was clearly behind everything, he still wasn't the one who betrayed him.

"Congrats! You get to witness and hide in one more war!" Joran didn't grace him with as much as one look, walking into the hall and seeing his target still in his chair with his eyes closed.

Betrayal wasn't easy for Forrest Romero.

"You fucking traitor!" Joran was next to him in the blink of an eye, grasping his neck with enough force to make it hurt but not enough to kill him. Not yet.

Pinning him against the wall, he watched the Southern Lycan struggle against his grip.

"Did you think I wouldn't find out?" He lifted him so high that Forrest's legs did not touch the floor anymore, using almost his full strength.

He trusted that man. Not entirely, but even the drops of trust he gave him were priceless.

"Because of you—" the dragon couldn't finish that sentence. If he said that out loud, it would be real. "I lost Bjorn!"

"Just... because... you care about that one," Forrest gritted his teeth, his breathing laboured as he grew his claws and pierced the dragon's arm, struggling to get free, "doesn't mean... you are suddenly... a good person and in the... right!"

"The audacity!" the Serpent scoffed, throwing him across the room and watching the muscular body knock over chairs on its way. The dragon shook his hand, healing the claw wounds like it was nothing.

To his credit, Forrest was back on his legs in seconds. He had nothing to fight against him, but still took a fighting stance anyway.

This was going to be fun!

"Don't blame me when so many suffer because of your actions!"

"You'd better shut up while you still have your tongue!" Joran took a slow, lazy step towards him.

"Or what? You are going to kill me?" Forrest let out a low chuckle, narrowing his eyes. A bruise was already forming on his sharp caramel cheekbone, and his lower lip was bleeding.

Joran's jaw flexed. "You are going to die either way. I don't tolerate betrayal."

"Why?" Forrest arched his brow. "You betrayed your brother, didn't you? You aren't exactly a moral compass to judge me!"

"Don't compare us! We are not the same!"

"Yeah, I don't take children from their parents and don't turn them into my pawns! Seriously, Jor, you were nowhere to be found, and what was I supposed to do when a god approached me?! It wasn't exactly a request!"

"You could have warned me! You could have lied to him!"

"Lie to him and get killed for you?" Forrest shook his head. "And who will take care of the county, then? You? Him?"

Joran did not respond to that. He did not give a damn about the country, and they both knew it.

"There is always a way!" The Serpent's eyes glowed as he awakened the magic inside him, the ancient part that was the most powerful and did not require any stolen gifts or beads.

"For you... maybe," Forrest rubbed his swollen cheek, ready to fight until his last breath. "For someone like me... unlikely! I can't fight gods on my own! How long will a powerless Lycan like me last?!"

A smirk curled onto Joran's lips.

"Is it power that you want, Forrest?" He stepped towards the man, but Romero held his ground, brows furrowed. He knew he was encountering the most dangerous predator in his life, and if he tried to escape, it would only be worse. "I'll give you power!" The Dragon God's fingers clenched around Forrest's neck again as magic illuminated everything around them. Blinding and all-consuming force filled every cell of the Lycan's body, burning it and replacing it.

Changing it.

"Since I lost a Champion, I need a replacement!" The words were clearly a threat. "I will give you the most powerful gift, Forrest! Enjoy!"

"No!" The wolf tried to resist as much as he could, but it proved useless as immense pain overpowered him, subduing his whole being and breaking him.

Forrest's screams echoed through the halls and corridors, making people stop and wonder what was happening until a dazzling array of light illuminated everything around them. Time seemed to stand still for mere seconds as the burst of magical energy consumed everything and everyone.

And when it was over, no one could remember why they paused in their tracks and what happened mere seconds ago.

Joran's revenge was done.

ASTREA AND GIDEON reached the Archives when the flash of light made a chill crawl down the Dragonfly's spine. Gasping, she looked around, quickly realising that people had already forgotten about the occurrence and went on with their business as if nothing had happened at all.

She knew that trick and looked at the Western King at her side, who didn't seem to notice anything either, to confirm it. It was a typical reaction for a mortal, and only now had Astrea realised that she could see those little divine manipulations before but never really questioned them, assuming Joran wanted her to know when he used magic.

A part of her hoped that right now her Teacher and Vidar were kicking the life out of each other. This would have made things so much easier for them.

"What is it? Gideon caught her worried gaze.

"Nothing." She shook her head, thinking that Joran could take care of himself. She had to concentrate on finding her sister. "We need to look in the property section. Since Vidar uses his identity as a Lothgar family member, Riannon is likely hidden nearby in one of their residences. The Republic has stringent laws. Every document has to have a copy in the Archives. So, all we need is to find the registration forms on what belongs to them in the capital, and we will have a shot at finding her."

"Lead the way." Gideon nodded, following her. She could tell this was not easy on him, yet at the same time, he was holding up surprisingly well.

"Why do you think she didn't warn us?" The words slipped her tongue before she realised it.

"Riannon—" The King rubbed the bridge of his nose. "Ria is the Moon Goddess' Champion. There are things she doesn't tell, even me. Things that I don't need to know. She only reveals what is of use to the ones who listen, and if she didn't warn us, that means she either didn't know or—"

"She believes we didn't need to know," Astrea concluded. "Does it mean that she is safe?"

They finally found the section of shelves starting with L and turned that way, seeing rows and rows of documents.

"Not necessarily." A shadow ran over Gideon's face. "If she believes her death is for the greater good, she would go with it. Of that, I am sure. And while Riannon makes the world a better place, my task is to ensure that nothing bad happens to her. As you can see, I failed."

"You didn't fail!" She shot him a reproachful gaze. "I don't know if you noticed, but it's not exactly a level playing field here."

She was scanning the titles on the folders as she went. What they were looking for had to be somewhere here. In the meantime, Fenrir went to the underground level with Warg to get Salome out. Although they decided not to make a scene in front of the Alpha Convocation, there was no way they were leaving one of their own behind.

"I know," Gideon admitted. "And I know what you are, in case you are wondering."

"Can you tell me?" She let out a smothered chuckle that still echoed through the rooms with high dome ceilings. "I am not so sure myself what I am anymore."

"You'll figure it out soon," Gideon assured her and paused briefly, a perplexed expression painting his face. "Can you promise me something, Astrea?"

"What is it?" She had to move to the next row, as she still didn't find the correct folder.

"Save Riannon, please," he said, a noticeable quiver in his tone. "Our son... he won't survive without her."

Her body went rigid hearing this, and she met his gaze, sensing that there was more than what he was telling her.

"So pitiful." The snarky voice behind their backs made them turn on their heels and face Vidar, leaning against one of the tall white columns with his hands in his pockets. "Don't worry, the blonde Queen is safe and sound. She is my guest, after all."

A growl emerged through the halls.

"You got what you wanted," Gideon seethed. "Give me my wife back now!"

"That does not depend on me." The God of Vengeance pushed off the column and sauntered towards them, eyes fixated on Astrea.

Gideon stepped in front of her. "Don't put the responsibility on a woman."

"Boy," Vidar's eyes darkened, almost becoming black, "I am not talking to you."

"Too bad," the Western King bared his teeth, "because I am not going anywhere."

"Interesting." Vidar's lips curled into a smirk. "I wonder if you are simply stupid or don't know who you are talking to right now."

"Oh, I know." Gideon flexed his jaw. "I am talking to a piece of—"

"All right!" Astrea squeezed between them, trying to distance her brother-in-law from her mate. "Let's not go down that road, okay?"

Vidar and Gideon bore into each other's skulls with their glares for a few more moments before the God of Vengeance lazily shifted his gaze to her.

"As I was saying, the Queen's freedom is up to you, my love."

Astrea cringed at the words, but Riannon was more important.

"What do you want?" She pursed her lips, waiting for the worst. And the God of Vengeance did not disappoint.

"I just want you to make a choice," he taunted.

"Between you and Fenrir?" She arched a brow.

"No," he interrupted her, fixing the lapels on his coat. "Between the Queen of the Western Kingdom and that girl... Niki, was it?"

A shudder coursed through her body. Until now, she was sure Niki was safe in the penthouse with Bjorn, where they left them.

"Yeah." Vidar smirked, enjoying her reaction. This was precisely what he counted on. "It's your real sister versus a chosen one."

Gideon snarled, ready to charge at the man who would inevitably kill him, and Astrea grasped his hand, squeezing it as tight as she could to bring him back to his senses.

"What did you do to them? Where are they?" Her heart was racing.

"They are in my safe houses." Vidar pulled a bent folder from the inside pocket of his black cashmere coat. "And both the addresses are right here."

She stepped towards him, and he shook his head as a warning.

"Not so fast!" the deity sneered. "I've decided that when you are back in Asgard, you need a friend there too. And there is only one way for a mortal to get to Asgard—"

The colour drained from her face.

"Don't!" she warned him, instinctively growing her claws. If it had been anybody else, she would have torn him to pieces.

"Choose one to return to her life and one to join the gods!" Vidar grinned at her, maliciously enjoying all this.

"I will not choose!" Astrea pursed her lips. How could she? Both women were too important to her. Riannon was her sister by blood, but Niki... she spent years with her as the only family she had.

"Then I will kill both," Vidar promised, and she knew he would keep his word.

"Why would you want any of them in Asgard?" She gave him a withering glance.

"To help you with your choice, of course." He couldn't hold back his arrogance. "As well as with your life when you are finally where you belong – by my side."

"You mean to blackmail me?" she scoffed bitterly.

"We don't need to say that ugly word." The God of Vengeance waved the folder before them, and Gideon charged, trying to get to it, shifting into his royal Lycan form on his way to give himself a chance. Fenrir had already blessed him, and his magic was igniting inside. However, Vidar blocked his attack effortlessly and sent him flying across the room, knocking over dozens of shelves with documents on his way.

Astrea decided against angering the spiteful god more and kept standing, eyes locked with her divine mate.

"That was rude," he commented. "Now, do you have to be so stubborn? You can't avoid the inevitable! This was always how it was going to end, and you are lucky I am allowing you to take a friend with you."

"I'll go if you—"

"No!" he interrupted her, raising his hand. His tone changed to a much colder one. "The time you could have asked me anything is long gone! I am offering you the Asgardian crown and your divine status back, and you are still playing hard to get!"

She pursed her lips. Arguing with him was useless if this was what he was thinking.

"I am not playing at all," she tried to reason, but he wasn't interested in listening to her.

"Choose, Astrea! The Queen or the Firstborn." The words were soaked in venom. "I am counting. Five!"

The Dragonfly hectically tried to think of what to do. If she tried fighting him, both women would be dead. But he wasn't letting her save a life. He was making her the executor of one of her two closest people.

"Four!" Vidar lifted his chin higher, looking down at her. He was letting her know that her memories did not give her any advantage. Between the two, he was a god and she was a mortal. They were no equals.

"Three!"

Panic struck her. She loved Niki so much. She tried to save her all the time. Niki was so young. She still had to experience so much. The poor girl barely got any taste of life.

"Two!" The God of Vengeance flexed his fingers, ready to summon magic and destroy what was so dear to her.

Gideon was running towards them, but she knew it would be for the best if he didn't reach them in time.

Riannon was lucky to have him. Their love already was a source of so many modern legends. And their son... The family that Astrea hasn't had a chance to meet yet.

Right... Ria had a son. And she was a Queen of a nation. If she died, it would affect so many people.

Guilt prickled her for thinking about all this. Those were human lives!

"One!" Vidar's smile turned into a menacing one as he raised his hand.

"Riannon!" Astrea screamed, covering her face with her hands. The pain washed over her as tears streamed down her cheeks. "Let Riannon go!" she repeated the words, glaring at her mate. "Are you happy now?"

"Not really." Vidar stepped closer and cupped her face, running his finger over her wet cheek and then licking it slowly in front of her eyes. "But I will be soon."

He threw the folder at Gideon, and his eyes shifted back to his beautiful mate.

"Go!" Astrea said to the Lycan King. "I'll be fine."

Gideon hesitated. Leaving her alone was a horrible thing to do, but at the same time, it wasn't like he could have been of much help when deities were fighting.

"This one will be fine, but anger me again, and your wife will be not!" The deity's eyes threw daggers at him, and the Lycan clenched his fists so hard his knuckles turned white.

"I am almost done here, Astrea," Vidar said, pulling her closer. "The mortals are going to war, and they will end this world and destroy each other for me. Just the way the Moonrise Kingdom had already done once. Only with the weapons and powers they have now will it be quicker and more effective. At least a thousand years will have to pass for this realm to thrive again after I am done with them. Thanks to that, gods will replenish their powers, and I will rule them as their Saviour forever."

"Why are you telling me all this?" She scowled at him, trying to distance herself, but he did not let her. It was unbelievable how much she hated him, yet felt all the tingles and sparks of the mate bond simultaneously. It was the cruellest form of a curse and the sole reason for him pursuing her.

"I am tired of waiting," he confessed, studying her face. "I want to hear the words from you, but I don't want to waste any more of our time."

She swallowed the lump that formed in her throat.

"Therefore, I want to speed up your choice-making process too."

Astrea didn't realise what he was doing until it was too late. Vidar leaned down to her face, his palm curling around her neck and down to the back of her neck and shoulder.

Piercing pain rippled through her, and she screamed so loudly that Fenrir heard her underground, his heart hitching at the sound.

She finally grew her claws and slashed his face, making the God of Vengeance let go of her, shocked by her actions.

Blood dripped from his cheek to the floor as Astrea fell to her knees, feeling unwell.

"Too late!" the deity hissed, looking behind her. It took all of Astrea's strength to follow his gaze as searing agony coursed through her veins, draining her of her power simultaneously.

Through her blurry vision, she noticed a dull glow right next to her, moving hectically. She narrowed her eyes to see it better, gasping when she realised it was a small glowing dragonfly.

"What did you do?" she whispered, her fingers moving to her back to feel the scorched skin where her dragonfly tattoo used to be just a moment ago.

"It was about time," Vidar said coldly, watching her kneeling on the ground. She didn't even remember how she fell. "It's your last life, anyway. I decided to make it shorter to speed up your decision-making. After all, this dragonfly held you in this world, Astrea. Now, without Freyja's gift, you have days, if not hours. Your connection with the dragonfly is severed."

65. CHOICES WE MAKE

enrir and Warg were on their way to the underground cell, where Salome was detained until the Southern Alpha Convocation decided what they were going to do to her. By the local laws, she was under their full power. Although Fenrir hated leaving Astrea alone even for a moment, he also knew that Warg would get himself into trouble if he didn't see the witch.

"She'll be fine," he commented, watching his creation pacing over the small elevator space.

"You can make everything fine right now." The first Lycan looked at him with his brows furrowed, that half-begging, half-expectant expression on his tired face. "No offence, Rir, but you can destroy this building, free our friend, take Astrea, and we can all go home."

"I wish it was as easy as this," the Wolf God grunted. "If I do that, someone else will have to pay for these actions. We have already brought enough imbalance into this world, and although it always feels right at the moment, the feeling gets sour over time when I see the consequences. There has to be another way. This world can't take any more divine intervention anytime soon."

"When did you start caring about the world? I thought you were done with it!" Warg folded his large arms over his chest.

"When I saw a future for it," the deity admitted, adding, "and when I realised no one else gives a damn about any of it."

"All I am saying is we could have destroyed that place, taken Salome and Astrea and returned to Solace." The Lycan frowned. "You can keep it safe for a few hundred years. I am sure."

"And then what?" Fenrir's jaw tightened. "Neither Astrea nor Salome will live this long, and what do we do then? When the world around Solace ceases to exist, what will our children do?"

Warg stiffened, searching for a reply. "I guess what I am trying to tell you is that the world is not our responsibility. They were never kind to us."

"Well, that's on them," Fenrir countered. "What does it have to do with me and what I choose to do? Letting them die will make none of us feel better. Trust me, I have already been down that road once."

"Why don't the mortals save themselves for once?" The Lycan offered a disgruntled scoff.

"They did. So many times." Fenrir sighed and rubbed the bridge of his nose. "Gods were choosing their Champions for a reason, giving powers to those who were willing to make the necessary sacrifices. Those powers aren't really gifts, Warg. The price for them is higher than any benefit they bring to their owner. What goes around, comes around. This is why I don't want to abandon them now when I am partially at fault. We may not have started it, but Vidar wants to wipe this realm clean because of what Joran and I did during the Northern war. Blessing all those warriors was a mistake. I knew I should have walked away back then. But—"

"It felt right at the time—" Warg closed his eyes, realising it was the end of the argument. They would have to find another way.

"Yeah."

The elevator doors opened, and they walked into an immaculately clean white corridor. The Southern prison for high-profile captives was minimalistic and well-maintained, just like they expected. The two men showed their permission slip from one of the Southern Alphas to the guards and were led to the only door with markings on it. Fenrir recognised magical-blocking runes at once, knowing that Salome wouldn't be able to break out of there even if she tried.

One of the guards pressed a button, and a small window at the top of the door opened, revealing Salome sitting on the ground in a meditation pause. She didn't even flinch at the sounds.

"Sal." Warg rushed forward, but Fenrir held him in place.

Salome opened her eyes, immediately trying to blink away the tears that formed, seeing the two men.

"Guys!" She stood up, trying to straighten her creased dress and checking her hair on her way to the door.

Salome's thin fingers touched the edge of the window, and small bolts of electricity hit her, forcing her to wince from the pain.

"Careful!" Warg's claws elongated instantly, but once again, Fenrir placed his palm on his friend's shoulder, urging him to conduct himself properly.

Salome tried to meet the Wolf God's gaze, but he was checking the runes on the walls, occasionally eyeing the guards. She had so much to tell him, but... it did not look like he was interested.

"I am fine," she promised to the Lycan, whose chest was raising and falling at a dangerous rhythm. "They didn't hurt me, and I doubt they will."

"If as much as a hair falls down your head, I will make them regret it!" Warg let out a low growl. "And don't worry, I will die, but help you out of here. You are not staying here for long! I swear!"

Salome froze. If Fenrir said those words to her, she would have been the happiest woman alive.

But Warg was promising her something he couldn't deliver without endangering himself. She couldn't accept that. Not when she couldn't reciprocate his feelings. It wasn't right.

"Warg." The witch hugged herself, unable to look at him. "It's my fault. Everything that happened is on me. I made a mistake, and now I need to face the consequences."

"Hell no!" he replied. "We all make mistakes, it doesn't mean that you'll have to rot in here! I will blow this place up if I have to!"

The guards exchanged concerned looks, and their hands slowly moved towards the tranquilising smoke guns on their belts.

Fenrir swore under his breath, taking a bead off his bracelet. He crushed the ancient magic between his fingers, making sure the two werewolves froze before they could do anything.

"We have around ten minutes!" He avoided his friends' startled gazes. *So much for not interfering anymore.*

"Ok, so do I destroy the wall or—" Warg flexed his fingers, eager to free the woman whom he had been thinking about every day for the past fifteen years.

"No need." Fenrir shook his head and approached the wall, erasing one of the runes and disrupting the magical pattern that imprisoned Salome within. "We can go now!"

Warg couldn't contain his excitement, breaking the handle on the door. He walked inside, offering Salome his hand, but she stepped back.

Finally, Fenrir locked eyes with her, raising a questioning brow.

"I really can't," Salome confessed. "Just think about it. How will everything look if I escape?"

"It's already such a mess that I don't think anyone would care," the Wolf God retorted.

"On the contrary," the witch exhaled and took another step back, resolute on staying behind, "King Kai and Queen Savannah trusted me. I used their token to bring the Northern army to the border, thinking that you were going into a fight. The fight I caused when I set up you and Astrea. But when I tried to help, I only made matters worse. Now I see that the message I received was a trap. You didn't ask me for help, did you?"

Fenrir shook his head, and she bit her lip painfully, holding back tears.

"I should have known," she whispered.

"You can't win when you play against the gods," Fenrir told her, and she nodded.

"It explains why I lost." The witch forced a smile onto her lips.

"We have no time for this!" Warg rushed them. "We can talk about all this later. Let's go."

"You don't understand." She shook her head, finally locking her eyes with the first Lycan. "If I go now, the North or the East will be blamed for the explosion. I have to stay until the explosion is irrelevant and keep insisting it's all on me."

"They will execute you!" Warg wasn't having any of it.

"I don't think so." Salome tried to curl her lips, but her smile faltered. "Witches are precious cargo, and I am a member of my Coven. Killing me wouldn't benefit anyone."

"But they will never let you go!" The Lycan gritted his teeth. "You will not be able to come back home—"

"She doesn't want to come back," Fenrir said and Salome turned away from them both.

"Sal!" Now Warg was utterly shocked.

"I want to be where I am needed," Salome said. "There is no place for me in Solace anymore. No one is waiting for me there, and we don't have any sources in the South. Over time, I can be that source—"

"I am waiting for you," Warg whispered, slightly embarrassed that Fenrir was witnessing this conversation. "Salome, I—"

She pivoted and closed the distance between them.

"Don't say it." She grasped his hands and squeezed them tight. "Please, Warg, you are my best friend. Don't—"

The Lycan stared at her while his heart clenched painfully.

"Rir, we cannot leave her," he said.

"We cannot take her by force either," the Rogue King exhaled heavily. This was a surprise for him too.

"We will meet again," she said, brushing her palm over Warg's cheek. "Of that, I am sure."

"Come with us!" he pleaded.

"I am pretty sure that if I do, everything will only get worse," Salome confessed. "At least now Solace is safe."

"This is not right!" The Lycan looked at his creator again, and Fenrir's throat bobbed with emotion. He knew what Warg was going through very well. He knew what he wanted from him, but—

"It's her choice," he reminded his friend. "We have to accept it."

"But she is one of us!" Warg couldn't give up.

Salome smiled sadly, knowing that couldn't be further away from the truth.

One of the guards let out a whimper, and he knew they were out of time.

"Go!" she told them. "It's best if they don't see you here."

Warg looked at her, clenching his fists.

"Did I ever have a chance?" he asked her, some desperation in his voice that broke a piece of Fenrir's heart too.

Salome looked at him through tears, slowly shifting her gaze at the man she had spent years loving with all her heart.

"I am so sorry," she whispered to both of them.

A little pang in Fenrir's heart suddenly turned into a powerful stab, and he knew something was wrong with Astrea the moment it happened.

"I need to go!" he said, ready to leave, but before the guards woke up to witness everything, he took one of his bracelets off and threw it to Salome, who gazed at him with wide eyes. "For protection," he said with a nod and this time, he opened a portal.

He stepped into it, and Warg paused one more time, looking straight into the witch's eyes. He wanted to tell her so much, but she only smiled at him, shaking her head. Broken, the first Lycan followed his creator into the unknown.

Niki woke up tied to a chair, silver chains digging painfully into her flesh. Her vision was blurred, so she heard the two men before she saw them.

"Are you sure?" one of them asked, his voice echoing in what seemed like a large empty warehouse.

"Yeah. This signal means we have to end her now," another replied coldly.

"So young!" the first one sighed, spitting on the ground.

"Either her or us. Your choice," the second reasoned. "What will it be?"

"How do we do it?"

A wave of adrenaline rippled over Niki's body. Were they discussing her? The last thing she remembered was an ambush at the penthouse and the fight where Bjorn fought for her even though he didn't have to. She was their target from the very beginning. Not him.

Niki swallowed the lump in her throat, remembering how Darius' chest was pierced again and again by the assassins sent to get her. She couldn't forget how they dragged her out, leaving him lying there in the pool of his own blood.

A loud roar cut the silence of their surroundings, making the blood freeze in her veins.

"What the fuck is that?" one of the men asked before a soul-shuttering scream...

66. THE PROMISE

*N*iki had spent her life on the Firstborn island surrounded by all kinds of shifters, but she had never seen a monster of this kind. The warehouse she was being held in was dark, so the dull glow of the creature's eyes drew her gaze and a chill crawled down her spine. It wasn't directed at anyone in particular, but still gave such a menacing aura that Nikiah shrank in her chair.

Luckily, five men stood between her and the creature. There used to be more, judging by the blood dripping from the beast's mouth. *He reeked of death.*

Three werewolves, one werebear and a fox shifter, turned one by one, and every muscle in Niki's body strained. She could tell it wouldn't be enough.

Her captors launched their attack, charging at the enemy in turns.

Big mistake. The only chance they stood was if they worked in sync, which they did not. If Astrea was here, she would have rolled her eyes and called them morons.

A wolf lunged, snarling as he leapt at the beast, and the latter didn't even turn his head to look at it, raising his enormous paw with what looked like talons. They slashed the enemy's chest, throwing him away as if he was nothing.

The monster stepped into the light, and Niki's lips parted as she took it in. It resembled a white bear, but when it snarled, she saw rows of the sharpest fangs. The bloody talons also did not belong there, and neither did the spikes on the back.

What kind of monster was this?

Most of all, she was terrified to see enormous wings mounted on its back. They looked as if they belonged to a dragon, each wingtip bearing a sinister adornment – a curled spike that made him look demonic. Is that what he was? A demon?

This bear-like creature seemed to defy the laws of nature. He moved so fast, leaving dead bodies in his wake. The screams of her captors were ear-splitting as she tried to free herself from the silver chairs, afraid that she would be next.

She had to flee.

Luckily, the silver bindings weren't that tight, and after considering becoming the beast's dinner, she chose to break a few bones in her hand to squeeze it out of the chains. The small sacrifice seemed reasonable.

A fox covered in its own blood landed at her feet just as she freed herself ,breathless.

Niki realised the warehouse was too quiet as she watched the puddle of wine-red liquid growing on the ground. She was screwed.

Hot breath burned the skin on her back through the flimsy fabric of her top.

She could only hope these wouldn't be her last minutes, but chances were slim. Her hand wouldn't be able to regenerate in time, and if she shifted, this would slow her down.

Yet the creature didn't move. It smelled of blood and smoke.

And chestnuts... with a hint of wintergreen.

Slowly, cautious of her every move, Niki turned on her heels and locked her eyes with the creature, realising it did not see her. The dull glow was still there, but...

"It can't be!" she whispered. She knew Darius was a white werebear shifter from the North. He was Joran's Champion, and they said he grew some spikes during the war thanks to the blessing. But this... this was something completely else.

Not to mention she thought he had died in the penthouse. A thought she didn't let herself dwell on.

"Darius?" Her voice was barely a whisper, and yet it echoed through the empty warehouse.

The beast released a heavy breath as if a large boulder lifted off its chest.

The glow in his eyes died, and they became a greyish-white colour, just like the rest of him.

"Darius!" This time, she was sure it was him. It wasn't a question anymore, but she had so many others. "What—How?"

He shook his head, a million thoughts crowded his mind.

Bjorn had no idea how he looked, but he sure felt different as power surged through him. Darker and stickier than before.

He felt the wings, but for now, he wasn't sure how to use them properly. The talons came in handy during the fight. And so did the sharp teeth.

He must have looked hideous and was not even sure how to shift back. Her heart was racing in her chest. Bjorn could hear it. *He scared her to death.*

His whole body flinched when he felt her warm hands slowly wrapping around him. He must have been a spectacle, a real freak… but she didn't seem to care.

Strawberry.

When he found her scent after he awakened, he was so mad knowing she was surrounded by the men who hurt her. He didn't see her when they were defending themselves back at the penthouse, and she gave those assassins a good fight, but he knew those men harmed Niki when the scent of her blood hit his nostrils.

They hurt her, thus signing their own death certificates.

He closed his eyes, trying to sniff her. Did she have any actively bleeding wounds? Was she okay?

"Darius, give me a sign it's you, and I am not hugging a monster bear who will eat me for breakfast," she said, her face tucked into his fur.

"It's me." He didn't even realise how or when he'd shifted back, his hands sliding up her back and pulling her closer.

"You—"

She was going to say how terrifying and ugly he was. It didn't matter, though. She was fine now. He arrived on time and she was safe…

"You came." Niki tightened her hug, and Bjorn slowly lowered his head until his lips were touching her hair.

"Of course, I came for you, Strawberry." He planted a small kiss at the tip of her head and was about to do it again when she laced her arms around his neck and pulled him down to her, crashing her lips into his.

It was so unexpected. He didn't want to ruin this young girl, but neither could he resist her when she was this close, when her taste was now on his tongue.

He deepened the kiss and pressed her against his torso, only now realising he was naked. A little moan escaped her when she dug her nails into him, unable to control herself.

"Darius," she repeated his name when she desperately gasped for air before returning to what they were doing. And he completely lost it.

"Strawberry," he growled, "if you don't stop now, I won't be able to—"

"Then don't!" she breathed into his mouth, and he cursed the men who were now corpses around them. How... unromantic this scene was. He couldn't do that to her. This... this couldn't be her memory about him later on.

"Not... here, Strawberry," he shook his head, intoxicated by her closeness.

But fear was stronger. A deep primal fear born from his past wounds that she would reject him. That she would give herself to him and then realise how wrong she was.

"I don't care!" She drew her fingers over his bare back, not wishing to let him go. "Darius, I-I thought they'd killed you. I—"

"It would have been best for you if they did."

"Don't say that!" Niki furrowed her brows. "If you were as terrible as you try to portray. you wouldn't have bothered coming to save me!"

Bjorn's jaw ticked.

"Niki, I came to save you because—" He stopped himself in the middle of the sentence, knowing it was best not to finish it.

"Because, what?" Niki slid her palm over his chiselled chest. He caught her hand, pulling her close again, unable to keep the distance between them. As if they were two magnets.

"Because you are mine," he said and expected her to retort or at least say something snarky, to distance herself... anything, really. He'd been there before.

Niki felt a prickle of guilt because, for a moment, she was glad he couldn't see her flushed cheeks.

"You are not going to object?" he asked, and the Firstborn cupped his cheek, brushing her thumb over his scars.

"Why would I?" she whispered.

"Honestly?" The werebear was lost for words. "So many reasons come to my mind!"

"You know that Vincent is Vidar, right?" She sighed, and his whole body shuddered in response.

"Yes, of course."

"And Astrea is really Astraea, the one who is destined to become the Star Goddess." Niki's voice quivered.

Bjorn nodded.

"Vidar was there when they were taking me away." Niki traced the scar that went over one of his eyes, and he didn't flinch because he already knew those did not scare her. "He said that Astrea will have to choose between me and—"

He already knew the answer.

"Between me and her real sister." Darius did not see her, but he could tell she was sad by how the words vibrated in her throat. "He was confident Astrea would choose Riannon, and considering they were about to kill me, I guess he wasn't wrong."

"He is a manipulator," Bjorn assured her. "You shouldn't fall for his traps."

Niki smiled, pressing her cheek against his chest and listening to his heartbeat. Gods, she was happy he was alive.

"You don't get it." She drew a little circle on his skin with her finger. "I am not falling for anything. I just—I just realised something."

"What is it?"

"I love Astrea with all my heart," the woman confessed. "But if he made me choose between her and you... I don't think I would have chosen her either. Not anymore. And it's not because I don't love her—"

He was afraid to say anything. The world stood still as he waited for her to go on.

"It's just—I think—I think I love you so much that I can't imagine living without you. I'd choose you."

He locked her in his arms, face buried in her hair and heart racing. He had two mates, but it was the first time a woman he was in love with truly felt the same.

"Say something!" she muttered, tears running down her cheeks.

"Nikiah, I've belonged to you since the moment you let me touch you the first time." He brushed his fingers over her skin. "One contact mixed with your scent, and I was a gone man. I really tried not to fall in love with you. I did everything I could for us to go our different ways because, gods know, you deserve better—"

She interrupted him firmly. "But I want you!"

"And you have me. All of me. As long as you want me," he promised. "But right now, we need to go. This is not the place where your first time will happen."

"Darius, I don't care! As long as we are together!" Niki bit her lip, embarrassed to insist more. This was completely new territory for her.

"I know," Bjorn chuckled, taking her hand. "We are on the outskirts of the city, and I smelled a flower field nearby. That'll do."

Niki's heart was about to burst out of her chest when she laced her fingers with his. This was really happening, and she was ready to go wherever he took her.

However, Darius paused at the door, and she panicked, thinking he changed his mind.

"Can you do something for me?" he asked.

"Of course." Niki tried to sound confident.

"The field—I want to take you there on my back." She was watching him closely and only now noticed a slight tint on his cheeks.

The mighty bear was flustered.

He cleared his throat and added, "I am from the North. We have a tradition of bringing our one and only home on our beasts' backs. I don't have a home, but—"

"It would be my honour." Niki grinned, squeezing his hand tighter, barely able to contain her emotions.

He shifted before her eyes, and this time she studied him slowly, tracing her palm over his wings and every spike he had. She stroked his head, awakening the glow in his glassy eyes again.

He was a real monster now, but he knelt before her and she climbed on, finding a comfortable spot on his back between two large spikes.

And then Bjorn spread his wings...

FENRIR STORMED INTO THE ARCHIVES, noticing the broken bookshelves. People were trying to escape, and it took him some time to get through the crowd.

He found Astrea on her knees before a smirking Vidar, and his heart clenched painfully at the sight. A loud growl left his chest, rumbling through the spacious hall that was now empty.

"What the fuck did you do to her?" He wanted to pounce at him, but Warg held him back.

"Look!" He pointed at the dull glow in the distance, and Fenrir's lips parted in shock.

He was expecting many things, but this wasn't one of them.

A quick realisation made him ball his fists.

"You again!" Vidar chuckled. "My betrothed and I were catching up, but you can never leave us alone, can you? Always the third wheel in our relationship."

"You took her dragonfly away?" Fenrir seethed. "How?"

"It's been so long." The God of Vengeance looked smug. "The magic wore off, weakened. After all, she was using it all the time."

Astrea tried to steady her breathing on the floor. It felt like he'd ripped a part of her soul out with that dragonfly, and she still couldn't process what that meant.

"How weak and petty you must be to do something like this!" Fenrir snarled.

Footsteps echoed behind his back, signalling Devoss and Bash's arrival.

"Don't you get it?" Vidar's lips curled into a smirk. "Her human body is dying. Tick Tock."

"Bastard!" The wolf was ready to rip his head off. "Be a man for once and have a fight with me! The winner will—"

"I have no need to fight you, mutt!" Vidar gritted his teeth, his eyes emitting a red glow. "I am the ruler of Asgard, the immortal god in full power! You are scum under my feet! I have already won, and this is just the last piece of a puzzle."

Astrea stood up on wobbly feet, leaning against the column next to her. She felt weaker. Much weaker.

"Step away from her!" Fenrir was on the verge of exploding.

Vidar observed the two lovers with a sneer. They hadn't realised it was over for them yet, but here it was – his victory. At last.

"And if I do, what will happen?" He arched his brow dramatically, folding his arms over his chest. "How can you help her? She will only be immortal if she lives in Asgard and that's something you cannot offer, mutt."

Fenrir clenched his jaw, and his enemy threw his head back, laughing.

"I guess this is the real test," Vidar continued. "Do you love her enough to let me have her?"

"That's not for any of you to decide!" Astrea snarled, growing her claws to accelerate healing. Nova was working as fast as she could, but they still felt excruciating pain.

"On the contrary." The God of Vengeance gave her a look of disdain. "That's between me and him. You were always the collateral damage in our story."

"How romantic!" she fumed.

"Believe it or not, I never wanted to hurt you." Vidar's voice softened as he peered at her. "I wished for us to have a family one day. Just imagine what heirs you and I could have had—And now, if you stay with him, you will grow old in this mortal body and die. I have seen it before. It's not pretty."

"I'll survive!" Fury coursed through her body.

"No, you literally will not!" Vidar shook his head, pinching the bridge of his nose. "You will be reduced to worms in the ground, and you will never become the mighty goddess you were supposed to be."

"I don't care!" Astrea screamed, hating the fact she couldn't fight him right now.

"But what about the world?" her betrothed wondered nonchalantly. "Don't you care about it, too? You could have brought that balance back if only you had accepted my offer. I can make you my Queen, I can give your immortality back!"

"I don't—" She started saying, when Fenrir interrupted her.

"She agrees!"

Everyone snapped their heads at the Wolf God.

"Fenrir!" Warg was astonished by his side.

"What are you saying?" Tears stung Astrea's eyes.

He locked eyes with hers, eternal pain storming in his irises.

"We've lost, Astrea." He sighed heavily, forcing the words out of himself. "If you go with him, you will be safe."

"Screw safe!" she yelled. "Fenrir, I—"

"It's over!" he bellowed, turning away. "Take her, Vidar, save her—"

"Fenrir!" A sob escaped her as she covered her mouth with her palm, trying to breathe and not fall down. "Don't do this!"

"If you can't do it for you, do it for the people," he told her, barely looking at her.

No one dared to say another word. Fenrir's friends stared at him in shock, but he only clenched his fists so tight his knuckles turned white.

"Finally," Vidar commented, voice void of compassion. "At least you still have some sense to you."

"Fenrir!" Astrea whispered.

"Should I remind you I have your little friend?" Vidar seemed bored with the drama already. "If you don't go with me, her life in Asgard will be very sad."

Astrea's chest heaved as she closed her face with her hands.

It was over.

She looked at Fenrir again, and he offered her a sad smile.

"This is the only way," he whispered.

"My offer will expire soon." Vidar rushed her and wiped the tears off her face.

"Fine." Her voice was dry and hoarse.

The God of Vengeance shifted on his feet and angled his head at her.

"You accept?" He watched her every move intensely.

"I do." She straightened her back. "Take me back to Asgard. Make me your Queen but promise not to harm Niki."

Fenrir's lips twitched just for a second, but he didn't let any emotion slip onto his face.

"Is this what you want for me?" Astrea challenged the man she loved, but the wolf didn't even flinch.

"Fenrir, are you nuts?" Joran appeared out of nowhere. "What the fuck is going on here?"

The Serpent wanted to reach his Dragonfly, but his brother grabbed his arm and stopped him.

"Look!" He pointed at the dragonfly whose wings flapped weakly and erratically. "She is dying!"

"We will find a way! We will—" Joran frantically tried to come up with a solution.

"You are too late!" Vidar was already next to Astrea, taking her hand into his and bringing it to his lips.

Before anyone could do anything, flames devoured them both, taking them to Asgard.

Engulfed by flames, Astrea couldn't breathe, feeling every cell of her body burning. She wanted to scream, but it was impossible. Two strong hands were holding her, pressing her tight against a scorching torso.

She couldn't escape this.

However, everything was over in seconds and she lost her balance at once, landing on moonstone floors.

At first she wanted to stay there because of how cold the stone was, but her senses kicked back in sooner and she remembered she wasn't alone.

Vidar watched her, no emotions on his face.

She glanced around, not recognising the place.

"Wh-where are we?" she asked, getting up herself since he still hadn't offered her a hand.

"This is my new palace in the New Asgard," Vidar informed her. "You didn't get to see it, but everything was destroyed here and I had to rebuild the city from scratch."

If he wanted compassion or praise, she was not going to give it to him.

"These are your chambers." Vidar pretended not to notice her attitude. "The chambers of my Queen. Built with you in mind."

"But I was dead—"

"No, you never were," he countered. "For me, it was just a waiting game. You were always destined to end up here."

She shivered at the thought and remembered why she was here in the first place.

"So be it." She turned to face him. "The words of the gods are binding. Give me the divinity you promised."

He watched her, eyes roaming her face and body.

"No," he said, and her lips parted. Her reaction seemed to please him.

"No?" she gasped. "What do you mean no? You promised! The words are—"

"Binding, yes, I know," he confirmed. "But here is the thing: Today, when I made my last offer, I said that I would make you my Queen and give you immortality. Immortality is not exactly divinity, don't you think? And I intend to give you everything I promised *today*."

"You—" She let her eyes glow, allowing Nova to surface in a warning, but it only made the God of Vengeance chuckle.

"Cute!" He dismissed her challenge. "Don't get me wrong, Astrea, I can give you divinity. You just have to earn it first."

"Earn it how?" she seethed.

"By being a good little Queen," he smirked at her, "and following my orders. You need to earn my trust."

"Trust goes both ways, and you just tricked me!" She raised her voice, but he did not care. He was enjoying this. All of this.

"We will work on that," Vidar assured her. "And now, if you'll excuse me, I need to go. Get used to your new surroundings and... freshen up before dinner."

She shouted a curse, but he disappeared in flames, leaving her alone in this immaculate, cold room.

Astrea ran to the windows, to look out at the gleaming city, but did not allow herself to admire it for a long time. Then she ran to the doors and tried them, but they were locked.

She walked around the spacious room designed just for her until she saw herself in a tall golden mirror with an intricate frame.

Her hair was a mess. She still had dust smudged over her cheek from when she was helping the victims of an explosion. Deep, dark circles around her eyes reminded her she needed sleep badly.

And yet, a little smile curled onto her lips.

She'd made it.

Their plan was working.

67. THE SOURCE

a group of maids wearing pale pink dresses walked in and bowed before her. Astrea pursed her lips and gracefully acknowledged them with a nod. It was bizarre to be in this situation now, even though she was used to royal treatment in her first life.

"My Queen, we received an order to help you bathe," one of them mumbled, eyes on the floor. She noted they did not look overly confident.

Astrea remembered this place as more cheerful in her first life. Back then, the maids chirped, telling her all the latest gossip, laughing wholeheartedly as they brushed her hair. Now, everything was different. They looked as if they were scared to death.

What did Vidar do to them?

After a long day filled with disasters, a bath was not a bad idea. Besides, she had to kill time before she could act. However, there were things that had to be done first for the plan to work perfectly.

"I don't need company while bathing," Astrea announced, lifting her chin slightly to intimidate them.

"But, my Queen—" The maids hesitated to follow her orders.

"I am not even your Queen yet," she retorted, noticing how one maid nervously fiddled with her dress. These women definitely had a task from Vidar. "I want privacy. I will call you if I need you."

She sounded so confident that they didn't dare object.

"We will wait for you here." One of the women forced a little smile onto her lips.

"Fine." Astrea nodded and went in the direction pointed by the youngest-looking maid, waiting for them to close the doors behind her. She discovered a spacious white marble bathroom adorned with gold and moonstones. She'd forgotten how luxurious palaces were; it was strange that she felt so at ease here. As if centuries hadn't passed. As if she belonged here.

Not with Vidar, of course, but in general.

Remembering her main goal, she got out the Nightmare's horn she had with her and quickly hid it on a little table behind a bushy green plant and added some towels there for extra coverage. Done with the primary task, she stripped and dropped her clothes onto the cold floor. Stepping out of her garments, she slowly entered the spacious bath, which would be enough for two. Or three.

The thought of sharing it with Vidar made her shudder, and she inhaled before submerging herself to the very bottom of the bath. Astrea wanted to stay there for as long as her lungs allowed it.

The water felt divine, and she had to admit it was enjoyable to soak in the luxurious tub. The shadows in the room suddenly danced, which didn't surprise her. Someone was definitely in there, but when she returned to the surface, the room was empty.

From the corner of her eyes, she noticed the towels next to the plant lying not as neatly as she left them. One of the maids was probably already on her way to Vidar with the horn.

Astrea smirked and dove back underwater, allowing herself to glance at the beautiful beads on her wrist and a ring Fenrir had given her when they devised this plan.

"If he did this, then he would come for you soon," Fenrir said as they watched the buildings of the Southern capital burn before their eyes. So many skyscrapers had already collapsed in the cruel attack, but the Northern flag was still there to arouse more hatred and misunderstandings.

"Then we will let him have me," she announced coldly, her fingers gripping the balcony railing tightly as her beloved's head snapped in her direction.

"I hope you're not saying what I think you're saying." His words sounded like a warning, to which she only smiled, enjoying the possessive tones in his voice.

"I am," Astrea confirmed. "All we ever wanted was for him to leave us alone, but he will never do that. This is our last shot, Fenrir, and gods know, maybe we will lose again, but if I'm destined to die without even tasting a full lifetime of happiness with you, I want to, at least, go out fighting for what was right."

He stared at her for a few seconds with that discerning gaze of his, and she was afraid he would try to dismiss her offer.

"Then we fight," Fenrir stated dryly. He took no pleasure in this. "But I would rather die than let him have you."

"That is something I would prefer to avoid." Astrea gave him a stern glare but then took his large hand in hers, lacing their fingers together.

"Listen, I don't like it either, but—This may help us distract him. I am the only one who can get close enough to kill him. If you attack him now or challenge him for a duel in this realm, then he will disappear into Asgard, where you cannot enter. And everything will be lost for this world. Then he will return when we least expect it and—Well, you know how that goes. We need to beat him at his own game."

Fenrir grunted, hating all this already.

"I have Midnight's horn," she continued. "Riannon told me some riddle, and I now think that she meant the horn will be able to kill him. Midnight was my divine weapon, after all. Think about it. If he takes me to Asgard, if he feels like he won— Then I can try to kill him. I acquired skills in this life, Fenrir. I am confident I can do this."

"He will search for the horn," the wolf deity rubbed the bridge of his nose, already tired of this plan he hated so much. "He is not dumb."

"I will hide it!" Astrea insisted.

"You are going to let him have it," he interrupted, and now it was her turn to stare at him.

"Is it wise, though? This is the only thing I can use as a weapon against him." Astrea arched her brow as the flames of the burning city illuminated their faces.

"If you get your full power, you will not need any special weapons," he assured her, making her lips part. "All you need to do is get to the Source of Power in Asgard. Remember that each god is born from it, and when we die, our powers go back to their beginning. All divine sources are connected, so your power is somewhere there, waiting for you."

"Are you sure? It's been a while—"

"The Source goes through seven realms, helping to keep the balance. Your powers are in there, and only you can access them. If that power was a part of you once, it will want to reunite. This, and only this, is our best chance."

Astrea furrowed her brows.

"Maybe." She looked away. "But I still don't have my divinity. If I remember correctly, only gods can come close to a source."

"It's fine." He offered a reassuring smile. "Because there is another way."

"Another way and you are only saying it now?" Astrea tilted her head.

"It's not perfect," Fenrir confessed with a sigh. "The perfect way would be to take my divinity and—"

"Fenrir, it's out of the question. I will not take the divinity from you! You haven't stepped foot in Asgard for centuries. If you sacrifice your divinity, you will probably die, and then everything will be pointless. So, tell me the imperfect way, because I am not going into this if I know for sure I will lose you."

He muttered something under his breath and got a little velvet bag with moon and stars embroidered on it from his pocket. Pulling two strings, he produced a ring, and her lips parted for the first time because she recognised it instantly.

She had seen it in both of her lives.

"Selene's ring!" Astrea gasped. "The Moon Goddess—Mother—"

"So, you know what this is." He took her hand and locked eyes with her, seeking permission. "May I?"

"I never thought that the one ring you put on me would be my mother's," she giggled nervously as he slid the white gold down her finger.

"Trust me, if there was a choice, I would give you literally anything else but this. However, this is going to help you enter the Source."

Astrea looked at her mother's ring, still underwater. A crescent and a little star crafted out of diamonds. The ring of the Moon Goddess could be considered a divine weapon of sorts, but it was so much more than that. Each little gem in it had a particle of a divine soul encapsulated inside. Those were the souls of Selene's deceased husband and daughters. Souls of gods.

With their divinity.

Just a few specs of it, but if they calculated it right, this would allow her to be recognised as a deity by the Source of Power to enter it and get her divinity back.

Yes, the plan could have been better, but it was their only one.

Astrea bathed until her skin got all wrinkly and returned to the main room, glaring at the maids to make them stare at the floor again and hiding her hand with the ring and the bracelet from them. The Nightmare's horn was enough of a sacrifice for one day.

"One of you stole from me!" She folded her arms over her chest, piercing each woman before her with her angry gaze.

"My Queen!" They all fell to their knees simultaneously as if they rehearsed this. "We would never!"

"Give me back what you've taken, and I will spare you!" she hissed, but they didn't move.

"Please, understand!" The oldest maid in the room fell as low as she could, her face almost touching the floor. "We were told to discard the garments and everything you had from the mortal realm. We cannot disobey orders."

Astrea huffed an indifferent laugh but decided it was enough.

"Leave me!" she ordered.

"But—" This time, the youngest spoke. "We have orders to prepare you for the dinner. All-Father Vidar expects you to share a meal with him."

She felt bile rise in her throat.

"I can dress myself," she announced, and although the other women were reluctant at first, they left her alone, probably thinking it was a lucky escape.

"We will return in one hour to help you finish your preparations," the head maid said before closing the doors.

THE MAIDS WERE BACK as promised, probably staying pretty close in the first place, and assessed her look.

She chose a minimalistic silk chiffon white dress with a cape that adorned her shoulders with intricate embroidery and glimmering crystals. The sheer fabric was draped tightly over the corset, pushing her breasts up a notch. It was slightly more revealing than she usually preferred, but today, she would prefer Vidar to look at her chest and not her hands.

She hid the most valuable items in plain sight, adding white gold and silver diamond rings to her fingers and several bracelets to her wrists. The jewellery shimmered in the sunset, attracting attention, but blending well with what she managed to smuggle in.

"Maybe we should add a necklace?" one of the maids offered.

"Or a crown?" another chimed in.

"This is already more than I usually wear," Astrea cut them off. "Take me to him."

The maids passed her to two guards, and those guards led her through a labyrinth of a garden that she didn't recognise. After all, it had been so long. Nothing here reminded her of the past. It was as if Vidar tried to erase it. The main palace and a few buildings were the only remnants of what used to be.

"This way." Both warriors stopped and gestured for her to continue down a stone path.

Astrea did as she was told. After all, she had to scan as much of her surroundings as possible.

However, her lips parted in shock when she walked out onto a hill she had the most vivid memories of.

The scorched Earth and charred remnants of trees lay before her eyes as she took it all in. Once a vibrant and serene place, it was now a desolate and barren landscape that never recovered its former beauty. The Glowing Garden she loved so much and built with Fenrir's help, had been burnt to the ground.

She paused before the biggest tree trunk that stood lonely in the centre and looked like it was merely a piece of charcoal. Fenrir used to press her against this glowing willow, and they kissed until her head spun.

"All the preparations for the wedding ceremony are ready, Uncle," a tall and muscular man with long blonde hair informed Vidar as they stood on a cliff next to a table set for two. "Your bride will be happy."

Astrea did not move, hoping to hear more information from her hideout. The two Asgardians did not seem to notice her.

"My bride should be happy that I still want her after everything, Magnus," Vidar scoffed. "So far, she has been more trouble than she is worth."

Astrea rolled her eyes.

"And yet you waited for her for so long," the other Asgardian noted, patting his uncle's shoulder. "She must be really something, this future Queen of ours!"

"That she is." Vidar smirked. "The mate bond… it intensifies everything. I just can't resist having her by my side, but she will have to be punished before I allow her to wield any kind of power, so don't misunderstand what she is right now."

"What would that be?" Magnus' brows went up.

"My property," the God of Vengeance stated, and Astrea clenched her fists.

"But you are still marrying her—" His nephew clearly did not know what kind of man his uncle was.

"To seal the deal!" Vidar shook with laughter, watching his nephew's confused face. "You still have so much to learn."

"Then teach me," Magnus insisted, a small wrinkle appearing over the bridge of his nose.

"Astraea came with the power that should have made our rule so much easier," he explained. "When she died, that power was lost. Same as when my father, Odin, was killed by that mutt, his power vanished. There is nothing that could be done about the latter, but as for the Star Goddess' power—"

"You are planning to give her divinity," the young man gasped and Vidar burst out laughing again.

"Of course not!" He shook his head. "It will be a millennia of her behaving like an obedient little wife before I'd even consider it!"

"I am afraid I don't get it then." Magnus ran his hand through his silky hair.

"Don't worry, you are just like your father. Thor was the strongest god out there, but complicated plans were not his strong suit."

The nephew flinched as if he was slapped on his cheek.

"Astraea will not get any divinity as long as I can help it," Vidar stated. "So, she will not be getting her powers back. Those will go to me."

"H-how?" Magnus seemed as shocked as Astrea, who was still listening to every word.

"Easy. At the wedding ceremony, we will swear to share everything, binding words and all. Then, we will mix our blood in the final ritual. I will go to the Source of Power as soon as it's done. Alone."

Astrea covered her mouth, so as not to make any noises. Their plans were so similar.

"The powers in the Source would recognise her blood and—" The son of Thor stopped talking, pursing his lips.

"And come to me," Vidar sneered. "See? It's a good plan. I will have her powers and mine, becoming the most powerful ruler of Asgard to ever exist. I will wipe the mortal world clean, covering my actions with ongoing wars and restoring the balance, bringing prosperity back to Asgard. As for Astraea, she will be my reward for the hard work I did. And I intend to enjoy her to the fullest, mate bond and all."

They stood silently for a while, and Astrea used that time to tame her anger and get back in control. He was so smug, so confident. She wanted to push him off the cliff but knew that it wouldn't kill him, so she had to restrain herself.

Finally, she walked out from her hideout.

"Vidar!" she called his name, and both men turned to face her. Her mate's eyes grazed over her figure in the sheer dress, and his lips curled slowly upwards as he stretched his hand out to her, gesturing at the table.

"Ah, Astraea, welcome home. I've been waiting for you."

FENRIR WAS PACING around the penthouse's living room, constantly checking the clock. The elevator doors opened, and Gideon walked inside with his wife.

"It took you long enough." The Wolf God sounded impatient.

"Apologies." Gideon shrugged. "Despite the promises, they still did not want to give her up without a fight."

"What's the point of them being here?" Joran placed his foot on his knee as he sat on the sofa.

"No one is here accidentally," Fenrir assured him dryly. "Even you, Brother."

"Oh?" Joran lifted his brow up. "Now I am intrigued."

"You are going to like this one." Fenrir smirked. "See, the thing is—I want you to kill me."

68. ENEMIES

"*I* must say, you look so different." Vidar gestured for her to join him at the table right after Magnus bowed and left them alone. The God of Vengeance pretended to ignore the charred landscape around them while studying her face for a reaction to his statement.

She offered none and soon recognised the cruel glint in his eyes. He craved to see her pain over this. He still didn't think he punished her enough. It probably would never be enough for him.

"Back in the day, you used to have this… ethereal glow around you that is now gone. You've lost it completely."

His gaze was shamelessly wandering over her body, making her want to cower away from him, but she was used to handling herself in unpleasant situations. *He was the one not ready for her. Not the other way around.*

"Maybe you shouldn't have killed me if you liked it so much, then?" Astrea retaliated, brushing her fingers over the golden cutlery on the table before she took her seat. *Pure gold.* He wanted her to see the two contrasts, and now she knew him well enough to understand the hint. The ruler of New Asgard could make her life as barren as the garden they were in, or he could bathe her in silk and gold if she behaved.

She preferred neither.

"It was never my desire." His lips curled as if she had said something funny. His twisted nature enjoyed every minute of their encounter.

"And yet here we are." She offered him an unimpressed glance. "Centuries later. Same place. I have to say, the garden looks freshly burned, though. One would think life could find a way to restore itself since Ragnarok."

"I destroyed this place long before Ragnarok," Vidar admitted, admiring his work as if there was something to be proud of. "And many times after that. The first time I burned it was on the day my sword took your life. I couldn't stand seeing it anymore. It reminded me of you."

"How romantic," she scoffed, leaning back in her chair while he observed her every move.

"And then I burned it down every time I thought of you or saw a sprout of life here." Their eyes locked, and she knew there was no love in him. Not for her, not for anyone. He wasn't capable of it.

Gods were given powers that suited them most. He was a God of Vengeance because it was in his nature. There was no way around it.

"Did it help?" she asked, and he arched a brow at her.

"Did what help?"

"Destroying the Glowing Garden over and over. Did it help you feel better?"

"Only one thing could help me feel better." Vidar's tone got darker. "To get what is rightfully mine."

"And by that, you mean—?"

She wanted to roll her eyes badly, tired of him already.

She had to listen to him, though. That was the game, and she had to play it right.

"Everything!" Vidar slammed his fist against the table, causing the glass to clink. "I want to have the bride I was promised, the power and respect that were supposed to come with it. You and I were meant to rule the Seven Realms together. Our children were supposed to become the new generation of gods. I want to enjoy our mate bond and not feel like I am thrown into lava each time that mutt touches you!"

She felt the tiniest prickle of guilt. Was this why her mate became so crazy and obsessed? The bond definitely had its downsides for her too.

It didn't matter, though. Nothing excused what he had done. Not to mention, he was the one trying to salvage the mate bond. He was the one clinging to her despite so many rejections.

He was a child who still refused to hear no, and she was not sorry for him.

"You are the ruler of the New Asgard," Astrea commented, trying to stay civil. "Surely you have enough power and respect. Any woman could be yours. You don't need me."

Vidar's eyes flashed red again.

"You think I did not try to forget you existed?" His lips twisted into a menacing smirk. "So many women were in my bed I lost count centuries ago."

She swallowed uncomfortably.

"Maybe he just needed to take better notes," Nova snorted.

"And yet each time I went down to the mortal realm, each time I saw a glimpse of you, each time I touched you, kissed you—"

She shivered at the thought, and her reaction did not escape him, a frown deepening on his face.

"You were mine!" he snarled at her. "We were destined for each other. We belong together, and yet each time you met that mutt, you chose him. Every. Fucking. Time."

"Then, maybe we weren't destined for each other after all," she stated calmly, and his features hardened, making him resemble one of the ancient statues.

"Or maybe that son of Loki used sorcery to bind you to him!"

She pursed her lips, digesting what he had said. A part of her was still hoping he could be reasonable, but there was no chance if that was what he believed in.

"You know that's not true," she sighed. "Fenrir and I—It was written in the stars. Over and over."

Vidar furiously threw his glass at the remnants of the willow tree, breaking it into myriads of pieces.

"The stars wrote a sad story then!" he said through clenched teeth. "So many attempts and no happy ending. Don't you think it's time to try something new?"

He waited for her reply, and she knew it was best to say something to put him at ease, something to stroke his enormous ego.

She bit her lip, almost drawing blood. That was a hard challenge.

"Screw him," Nova hissed in her mind. *"At the moment, he needs us more than we need him. The wedding blood-sharing ritual has to be willing and mutual for it to work. He will have to play nice."*

"You're right," Astrea agreed, feeling her blood boiling.

"There is nothing new about this." She exhaled heavily. "We don't work. You've tested this many times and ended up killing me in every other life. So much for a happy ending."

Vidar's jaw ticked. "So what?"

His question caught her off guard.

"So what?" she repeated with a gasp. Even after everything, she was

surprised at how little her deaths meant to him. She could feel the trauma of her past lives within her bones. The tragedies that happened long ago marked her soul and almost destroyed Fenrir.

Vidar, on the other hand, seemed oblivious.

"Your little friend is at my mercy, Astrea. Do you really want to make her life that short?" The man before her smirked, knowing he had just won the argument. He had the leverage.

"I would like to see Niki, by the way." She tried to look calm when, in fact, her heart was racing with worry for her friend.

"I am afraid she doesn't want to see you," Vidar sneered. "The news you chose your real sister over her didn't sit well with that one. She has quite the temper."

Astrea's claws grew uncontrollably, and she dug them into the armrest, realising he was again playing with her. What if Niki didn't want to go with her when the time came? This could complicate their plan because Astrea couldn't leave her ward alone.

"That's another thing we need to talk about." Vidar cast her an irritated look. "We need to get rid of *that*."

"That?" She stared at him, puzzled at first. Slowly, she traced his gaze and realised he was staring at her, claws still digging into the chair.

"I don't want those mutt genes passed on to our children," he explained, pointing at her hands and causing Nova to growl. "That wolf has to go. You are my Queen, and I don't want that beast inside you."

"Nova is a part of me!" Astrea was appalled to hear this, even as a suggestion.

"A dirty and unnecessary part!" Vidar insisted. "You will not need the beast once we are married."

So, he wanted her as weak as possible. That was that.

"Just play along," Nova growled. *"It's not like we are going to marry him, anyway."*

"True." Astrea retracted her claws. *"I'd rather die again. Literally nothing else is worse than this man."*

"I will think about it," she said aloud and pursed her lips, wishing for the dinner to begin already so that the two of them didn't have to talk anymore.

"You didn't really think you'd be able to keep her," her mate said. "If you ever wanted to get your divinity, you'd have to say goodbye to her anyway. Werewolves can't be gods. It doesn't work like that. Besides, what's another wolf to you? Your constant rebirths ensured each wolf spirit was dissipated later. Surely you knew that."

She wanted to stab him with one of his fancy golden knives, but several servants appeared out of nowhere, pouring wine and removing domed lids from the golden dishes.

Astrea could feel how restless Nova was. They both refused to think about what her getting the divine powers back implied. The world needed her as Astraea, not just Astrea. But she needed Nova, her loyal companion.

"We'll figure something out," her wolf assured her. *"We always do."*

Astrea hated this. No matter what she did or how hard she and Fenrir tried, someone they loved would end up hurt.

One of the servants brought a tray of bread for her, and she waved him off.

"Please, help yourself to anything you like—" Vidar gestured at the food, encouraging her to eat and clearly hoping for a change of subject. "Divine food tastes different. I am sure you remember. It's been a while since you've been treated like the goddess that you are."

"You'd be surprised," Astrea's words were laced with venom as she forgot who she was talking to for just a mere moment. "Fenrir worshipped me whole just hours ago—"

The God of Vengeance's eyes glowed intense red, and he moved so fast she didn't have time to react before his palm wrapped around her neck, lifting her up in the air.

"You really shouldn't have said that!" he hissed as she struggled against his grip. A mortal against a god.

Now Astrea knew how he had managed to kill her so many times. If just a few words were enough to make him attack her…

However, she refused to be the victim again. He took too much from her. From everyone she loved.

Not to mention that she was a whole different person now.

Hectically, she scanned the space around them and kicked the table with a glass goblet balancing on the edge in less than a second. She caught it and, not wasting time, splashed it in Vidar's face, shocking him momentarily. His grip on her neck was still too tight, so she smashed the glass over the wooden edge and stabbed his hand with what was left of it, digging the glass as deep into his flesh as she could.

Vidar screamed, releasing his grip and letting her fall to the burnt ground, her beautiful white dress stained both with soot and his blood.

"You ungrateful bitch!" He raised his arm, a fire sword appearing in it.

She knew that sword. She remembered it all too well, along with the metallic taste of blood in her mouth it gifted her every encounter they had.

Astrea wanted to shove that sword up his arrogant ass and grabbed as many ashes as she could fit into her palm, ready to throw it in his face for a distraction.

"Stop!" a resounding female voice interrupted them as their heads snapped toward the Moon Goddess.

***

"Excuse me?" Joran stared at his brother, arrogance replaced by confusion on his face.

"You heard me," Fenrir taunted mercilessly. "Let's not pretend you weren't thinking about it, dreaming even."

The Serpent's jaw flexed, and he stood up, fists clenching.

"Even if I did, never in a million years would I imagine you of all the gods offering yourself on a silver platter like this."

"So?" Fenrir let out a dark chuckle. "Does it taste better when you lace it with betrayal, and I know nothing of it?"

Joran closed his eyes just for a moment, rubbing the bridge of his nose. "Is that what you think of me?"

"Can you blame me?" The Wolf God scoffed and stretched his neck, preparing for a fight. "I am shocked I still don't have a knife in my back, considering my generous offer. Do I need to turn and pretend I don't see it? Would that work for you?"

"I think I'll pass." Joran gritted his teeth and started walking towards the exit when Fenrir caught up with him and punched his jaw.

Hard.

The sound of cracking bones made Riannon flinch, and Gideon carefully tried to lead her as far away from the two divine siblings as possible. At the same time, Kara, Bash, Devoss and Warg watched them from different corners of the room, barely reacting to the show.

"Are you nuts?!" Joran seethed, spitting blood.

"Maybe I am just tired of letting you get away with everything. This was a long time coming." Fenrir circled him just like a predator would do with his prey.

"I am not playing this game! Not when Astrea—"

"You are not to speak her name!"

Another powerful blow, and Joran staggered, trying to keep his balance.

"I protected her for years!" The dragon wiped the blood away from his face. "Better than anyone ever before!"

"You tortured her more than Vidar did!" Fenrir growled, and that seemed to work because Joran charged at him, eyes glowing and claws elongating simultaneously.

"Take that back!" he yelled, trying to at least claw his brother, but the wolf dodged each time, angering him even more.

"It's the truth!" the wolf deity snarled, secretly locking his gaze with Kara, who nodded promptly, signalling to him that this was enough. "Even that psychopath didn't think of putting her in a silver pit!"

Fenrir froze just for a moment, and immediately, his sibling's sharp claws sliced through his chest. For a whole moment, Joran felt how close his brother's heart was to his fingertips, feeling the vibrations of its beats. So close... and so wrong.

He retracted his claws, stepping away. If Astrea saw him now, she would have attacked him herself. He knew that much.

The sound of something heavy hitting the floor brought him back to reality, and he turned on his heel to see Fenrir kneeling on the ground. His brother held his palm to his chest just where he'd been pierced moments ago. Dark blood, the colour of the finest wine, was soaking through his fingers, and Joran's lips parted in shock from the realisation that, for some reason, his brother was not regenerating.

The half-smile playing on his lips made his stomach churn.

"What have you done?" the Serpent whispered in horror as it dawned on him that Fenrir coughed blood, meaning something was fundamentally wrong with him.

Gideon Stormhold was about to move, but his wife stopped him, shaking her head.

They knew. They all knew.

"I can never leave her alone with that monster! Plan or no plan—" Fenrir confessed with a heavy sigh, and only then his friends charged towards him, catching him before he fell to the ground.

"You—" Joran's mind was frantically trying to understand what was happening.

Fenrir opened his palm to demonstrate the magical dust left after he'd activated one of his crystal beads.

"You stopped your own regeneration!" The dragon felt a surge of nausea, his head spinning. He guessed that part but still couldn't see the reason behind it. How would this help Astrea?

"I've done more than that," Fenrir chuckled. "I paused my immortality too."

"What kind of ability is that?" Joran felt panic coursing through his veins. He had never met someone with such power before.

"The one I took it from considered it a curse," his brother confessed. "Don't you worry. There was only one bead like that. It was a rare gift."

"We need to go!" Kara said, trying to sound firm, but her voice betrayed her, quivering by the end of the sentence. "I haven't done this for so long!"

"Done what?!" Joran demanded, angry that they treated him as if he was not there. The pool of blood next to his brother was getting bigger, and surely that wasn't a good sign.

Suddenly, his fingers burned as if he summoned fire, and the dragon realised, this time, the blood coating them was causing it.

His brother was dying, and it was his doing.

"Hurry up," Fenrir hissed from the pain as they carefully placed him on the ground. Riannon brought a little cushion to place under his head.

"What is this? What the hell are you all doing?" Joran felt he was about to shift right here in this room and demand answers. Fenrir looked so pale...

Bash turned away, not able to see his father like this. Devoss patted his shoulder gently while Warg knelt at his creator's side.

Kara towered over the Wolf God, a soft glow coating her.

Joran recognised this glow and did not flinch when two golden wings spread behind the woman's back. The Valkyrie stretched her hand to Fenrir.

"Rise, brave warrior, and join the ranks of the honoured. Your valour and courage have earned you a place among the chosen. Fear not, for your spirit shall be carried to the halls of glory, and I will be your guide."

"No!" The dragon stormed towards them to stop the madness, and this time, both Bash and Devoss stood in his way, restraining him. The only two in the room capable of holding him back.

"What are you doing? Stop this!" Joran bellowed, trying to shake them off.

"It has to be done, Uncle!" Bash tried to explain, but he did not listen because Fenrir took the Valkyrie's hand and rose... while his body remained breathless on the floor.

"You have about an hour in this world's time," Riannon told them. "After that time, no one will be able to reanimate him. Not even the bead he gave me would help. One hour is all you have."

"Then we'd better be quick." Fenrir's spirit nodded, still holding Kara's hand as the Valkyrie created a portal.

"Fenrir, don't be a fool!" Joran screamed. "You will not be able to come back from this! No woman is worth it!"

His wolf sibling locked eyes with him, a slow curl to his lips.

"I know you can't understand it, and that's okay. I forgive you for everything, Jor. Thanks for your help tonight."

This wasn't the answer Joran wanted to hear, so he tried to free himself, struggling against the other two deities as he watched his brother and the Valkyrie depart to Valhalla.

Someone let out a gut-wrenching scream that pierced everyone's ears and reverberated through the room. It took Joran some time to realise that he was the one screaming, his throat tightening painfully.

Riannon poured some potion over the breathless body's chest that stopped the bleeding but definitely did not bring Fenrir back to life.

"Why—" Joran asked in a hoarse voice when Bash and Devoss finally let him go, opening their own portals. Only Fenrir and Joran were banished from the divine realm.

"Because there was no other way for Father to return to Asgard," his nephew informed him out of pity.

"He had to be killed in a proper fight," Warg added, preparing to go with his friends. *"By an enemy."*

69. REPLACEMENT

*A*strea couldn't take her eyes off the woman before her, paralysed by all the memories coursing through her mind.

Her mother, the Moon Goddess, was still alive and well. And she was here in New Asgard, dressed in the finest silk and most exquisite diamonds. The contemporary silvery-white attire, adorned with her usual celestial embellishments to highlight her divine status, hinted that Selene was not facing any hardships. She was here as a guest of honour just like the last time, and this realisation made Astrea's stomach twist.

"Ah, Mother-in-law," Vidar sneered, slightly annoyed by her arrival yet respectful enough to let it slide. "We didn't expect you today. I was educating Astraea on the changes since her last time here."

His eyes slowly found his mate on the ground; her elegant white dress ripped in a few places from the fall, the delicate sheer fabric covered in dirt. It did not escape his gaze that she had a handful of ashes ready to be thrown at him, which annoyed him even more.

Why was this woman so stubborn? As if dirt on his face would make a difference. She had lost. She had to deal with this by now.

"Vidar, my boy!" A nervous smile graced Selene's lips. "I believe it's my duty to educate my daughter today. Something I failed to do properly in the past."

"Glad we agree on that." Vidar jerked his chin towards Astrea.

She didn't even look at her daughter, which caused a sense of betrayal and disappointment to settle in Astrea's chest. Had her mother been watching her misery all those years and did nothing?

Vidar dissipated the flames on his sword. He looked so smug that it made her sick.

"My love," he said coldly, offering his hand to Astrea. She ensured to give him the one with no bead bracelets on it and did not regret it when he roughly pulled her up and into his chest, moving her palm to his lips for a kiss. However, he changed his mind, as her skin was still covered in soot, much to her relief. She wanted as little physical contact with this man as possible.

"Children," Selene smiled at the couple as if she hadn't just witnessed them trying to murder each other, "I thought you'd spent the last centuries maturing, but you both are still too temperamental for your own good."

"I'm afraid there's still so much we need to teach Astraea." Vidar flexed his jaw.

"Well, tonight is definitely my turn. The wedding is tomorrow, and you still have many things to deal with." The Moon Goddess radiated artificial sweetness, and Astrea couldn't take it anymore.

Nothing had changed. Her own mother had watched her being tortured for centuries, and it never occurred to her to come to her daughter's aid.

"I am afraid I don't want to part with my betrothed, even for just a second," Vidar sneered, locking his arms tighter around her waist. "I missed her too much."

"But Astraea—" Selene was about to say something when the Dragonfly lost her temper.

"It's *Astrea* now. Your daughter *Astraea* died a long time ago, thanks to you and your choices." Their gazes met briefly before the Moon Goddess cast her eyes to the ground. "It's fine. I have nothing to say to this woman. I want to return to my room if that's all right."

Vidar's gaze lingered on her momentarily until a cruel smirk curled onto his lips.

"Now, my love, one conversation with your only remaining parent will not hurt." He gestured for Selene to come closer, enjoying that he had found yet another way to make his bride miserable.

"I really—" Astrea wanted to protest, but Vidar interrupted her.

"Your mother will be leaving us right after the wedding. She is a very busy woman and wants to give us space to… explore each other the way we should have done years ago. So, one last conversation on the way to your room wouldn't hurt. The guards will be with you at all times."

Four Asgardians stepped out of the shadows and bowed respectfully. At least two of them emitted divine auras, which was terrible news. The Dragonfly was a skilled warrior but still no match to them as a mortal.

Vidar took her wrist, ready to kiss it again, but just like last time, he remembered it wasn't clean and distanced himself to her relief.

"Your wedding dress is probably already waiting for you in your suite," he added. "I can't wait to see you wearing it at Valhalla tomorrow."

"Burn the dress," Nova scoffed.

"Noted!" Astrea wanted to say it out loud, but Selene draped her arm around hers and urged her away.

"Thank you for your understanding, Vidar!"

When Astrea glanced over her shoulder to see what her mate was doing, she saw Vidar storming away and the four guards following them closely.

"Let's go." Selene pulled her gently toward the exit, her tone lacking the previous sweetness. "I don't know what he was thinking about bringing you here!"

"The usual," she stated bluntly through clenched teeth. "You know, my wonderful mate and his desire to torture me for not loving him."

The Moon Goddess pursed her lips tightly and then let out a small sigh.

"It wasn't supposed to be like this," she said, her voice barely a whisper.

"It doesn't matter how it was supposed to be," Astrea seethed. "This is how it is now. This is how it's been for centuries. And I only have you, my mother, to thank for it!"

"Child," the Moon Goddess lowered her voice, "I know I made a mistake —"

"Mistake?" her daughter hissed, knowing the guards were too close to speak out loud. "A mistake would be a wedding dress in the wrong size! With your cursed mate bond, you bound me forever to the wrong man!"

Selene looked like she slapped her, but the Dragonfly did not regret a single word.

"Back then, I only wanted to protect you so that you wouldn't have faced the destiny of your siblings—"

"And the one you assigned to love and protect me has killed me dozens, if not hundreds of times!" Astrea countered.

"I chose wrong," Selene whispered. "I knew so little back then. If you think I haven't regretted it every single day since the day you died for the first time—"

"And yet you did nothing to help me!" Tears burned Astrea's eyes.

"I did what I could."

"Not enough, apparently!" The daughter locked eyes with her mother again, nothing but hatred in her eyes. She spoke with sarcasm, "Well, at least you came for the wedding! Maybe he won't kill me by the end of the ceremony! Fingers crossed!"

Selene dug her fingernails deeper into her flesh as if warning her. "He won't."

"This is useless," Astrea muttered and tried to free her hand, but Selene grasped her wrist, her gaze on the bracelets and the ring.

Something twisted in the pit of Astrea's stomach. How could she be so careless with this woman? Maybe her mother did not know what the bracelets were, but she surely recognised her own ring!

"Leave us!" Selene ordered the four men who followed them, and they stumbled, unsure whether they should listen to her.

"My apologies," the tallest of them bowed, "we follow only the orders of Vidar, the All-Father."

"He's not yet a father to be called that. Only one god had that name," the Moon Goddess replied calmly. "But if you insist, didn't the ruler of New Asgard tell you to make me feel at home when I arrived?"

"Yes, he did," the Asgardian replied, dipping his head in his shoulders.

"So, let me inform you that I would never be comfortable at my home with four strangers following me this closely. I understand you must do your job, but why don't you take twenty steps back? You will still be able to see us and perform your duties, but without disturbing me or my daughter."

The guardians exchanged glances and backed away synchronously, allowing the two women more space.

"We have a similar taste in jewellery." Selene returned her gaze to Astrea, and the latter yanked her hand away, ready to fight now if she had to.

"That's—"

"The mate bond wasn't a mistake." The Moon Goddess turned away to look at the sea beyond the cliff they were on as if nothing special was going on between them. "Don't get me wrong, I know that mating you to Vidar was one. But the mate bond, in general, can be a beautiful thing. It became a beautiful thing for so many."

Astrea rolled her eyes but said nothing. Before all this, before she met Fenrir and got her memories back, she had once dreamt of a mate, too. Now, she wanted to laugh at her past self.

"Your bond was the first one, and I thought you and Vidar would be a splendid match. I believed I planned all that so perfectly. An heir of Asgard and the future of Olympians—I almost believed it was written in the stars."

Astrea fidgeted with the ring on her finger, her nerves getting the better of her. She wanted to be done here as soon as possible.

"I forgot only one thing," Selene clasped her hands tightly together, interlocking her fingers as if that was supposed to give her strength, "to ask my daughter, the Star Goddess, for her thoughts."

"That you did."

"I was thousands of years old and truly believed I knew better. If I could turn back time—"

"But you can," Astrea let out a mocking laugh. "You did it for Riannon!"

"I love Riannon," Selene admitted. "She is the perfect Luna, one of the best she-wolves I have seen, but when I turned back time to bring her back just one year, it weakened me immensely. I wouldn't be able to repeat that any time soon. And I didn't do it for her alone. Not really... I did it for you and for the mortals in general. I brought Ria back because she started a chain reaction of changes that helped me to fix so much of Vidar's and Joran's work. Those boys—"

Astrea did not allow a single muscle on her face to flinch despite the waves of shock ripping through her body.

"You can't be serious!"

"I am. Freyja told me it was your last life, and I became desperate. I was always carefully choosing the families for you to be born in, but each time it was a wasted effort. This life, I was sure I thought of everything. I even gave you a twin to—"

She stopped talking but Astrea realised what she meant, memories of her sister Stella flooding her brain.

"No!" She rubbed her temples, not wishing for these dark thoughts to break her now when she needed to be strong. "You don't mean—You couldn't!"

"I am sorry." Selene watched tears rolling down her daughter's cheeks. "She was a sweet child, and I set her for the best new life possible after Vidar's monsters killed her. He thought she was you, and I thought that you would have a chance this time if he kept believing that."

"You let him kill Stella instead of me," she whispered what was the equivalent of a knife piercing her heart.

"There was no choice! Vidar tainted everything he touched. He weakened our realm, and his own is barely holding up. He took all the power and—"

"Listen to yourself!" Astrea raised her voice, desperation overwhelming her. "She was just a child! And you—you are a monster!"

Selene held her gaze with an unwavering determination.

"I am a mother," she corrected. "But I am a mother not only to you but to many others, and my life's goal is to take care of as many of you as I can. That's a burden I carry with me. I am not perfect, and I made my fair share of mistakes, but I am trying, Astra—Astrea. After what happened to you, I made it possible for mates to reject each other. I gave them a choice regardless of me connecting their souls. And I am sorry I cannot give this to you because you were first, and Vidar never died, making your bond unbreakable. You are still attached to him every time you are reborn. I wish I could break it, but it's impossible since he is a god too. Therefore, I made a deal with Joran. It cost me a mate bond I did not plan to create."

"Yeah, I heard." Astrea frowned. "You ruined quite a few lives doing so, you know."

"It all turned out well in the end. Besides, look at you. You are stronger than ever before, and you need this for what's coming. I only hope you will let me be by your side."

She contemplated for a few moments.

"I can't trust you. Not anymore. Probably not ever. You took so much from me; you let Fenrir and me suffer for so long just to prove a point. One conversation is not enough to mend what was broken."

"I know, and I understand." Selene nodded and then pulled her daughter into a hug roughly so that she didn't have time to push her away.

"What are you—" Astrea grunted, wishing to distance herself as soon as possible.

"Your friend is not here," Selene whispered quickly. "Vidar doesn't have her. He wants you to believe that he does to keep you compliant. She is still in the mortal realm and is reported to be by Fenrir's side.

Astrea froze.

"How do you—"

"It doesn't matter. What matters is that you need to get to the Source of Power behind the main palace. It will be heavily guarded at night, so choose a different time."

"I don't need your advice!"

"But you do. Vidar wants the wedding to go smoothly. Whatever happens, do not let him mix your blood. He... he doesn't love you. You cannot share your power with a man who has no feelings for you."

"Don't worry, I won't," her daughter promised, frustrated by the fresh revelations. She glanced at her mother with her brows furrowed, unsure whether she could believe her.

"I know you don't trust me, and I would never blame you for that," the

Moon Goddess confessed. "But I want you to know that I did anything possible to help you and will keep doing it. I will be on your side even if you never want to see me again. However much I crave your forgiveness, I need to see you happy more. Use my ring right, Astrea, and… be happy when all is done."

Astrea did not know how to respond. Her mother was always a sweet-talker, and yet it felt different now. She could feel her pain. She saw it in the woman's eyes.

However, trust had to be earned, and they couldn't reach that point with one conversation.

"I need to go," she said, and Selene withdrew from her with a reserved smile curving her lips.

"I will be there," she added. "Waiting."

This time, Astrea decided to stay silent, as she needed to think everything over.

SHE HAD to take another bath to clean herself up after the visit to the remnants of the Glowing Garden and was served dinner back in her room. Luckily, Vidar was too busy to keep her company.

The maids looked as terrified as before, which, she realised after carefully contemplating, was helpful to her.

Sleep wasn't an option, and she wanted to try escaping over the roofs like she usually did. Still, a quick observation session through her windows allowed her to notice several guards spying on her from different angles.

Usually, that number of men to kill wouldn't have bothered her, but this wouldn't be a fair fight since at least some of them were minor deities, thus much stronger than her mortal body. Again, she had a plan for that, too, but there would be only one shot at this. They would have officially lost if she got caught, and everything would be over for her, Fenrir, and the mortal realm.

The morning came faster than she realised, and the maids walked back in with covered trays to prepare her for the wedding ritual.

Astrea observed them with her arms folded over her chest, a mask of indifference on her face.

"Let us help you with your hair," the oldest woman suggested, and she nodded in agreement, allowing them to put a beautiful star crown halo into her hair. She pulled on the tight white undergarments they offered and let them rub lotions on her body, making her skin shimmer like diamonds.

"Just your bridal make-up is left," the same woman chirped with a wide smile on her face. "Allow us to—"

"Enough!" Astrea raised her hand to make them stop in their tracks. "It's getting tiring, and I already have a headache, thanks to you."

The women exchanged uncomfortable glances.

"I will do the makeup myself," Astrea announced, and they dropped to their knees again.

"Please, my Queen, we have precise instructions!"

"If something is not to Vidar's taste—"

She closed her eyes and pinched the bridge of her nose, showing them how much they irritated the future wife of their ruler.

A few moments more and they would be ready to agree to anything she proposed as long as it was remotely reasonable.

"Her!" She pointed to the youngest maid with blonde hair, who shook when she realised she had been chosen for a potentially deadly mission. "Does she know the instructions?"

They did not want to reply, disappointed with how things were developing.

"Does she?" Astrea made her voice sharper, trying to scare them more.

"Y-yes," the Head Maid finally admitted, looking at her colleague with pity.

"P-please, I—" the chosen maid stuttered. "Maybe it's best if you choose someone else to—"

"You stay to help me. Everyone else leaves!" Astrea commanded and Nova added a growl, making all the women rush out of the room.

All but one.

She waited for the doors to close and nodded at the vanity table, causing the little maid to get back to her feet.

"What are you waiting for? Do your job."

This wasn't her first time playing an arrogant, heartless asshole. Astrea watched the maid open the bottles of cosmetics and arrange the brushes as she crushed the first bead, activating the veil of silence in the room. From now on, no one would be able to hear what was going on here. Just like Fenrir taught her.

The girl was shaking like a leaf during a storm, and Astrea felt so guilty. She tried to never hurt the innocent; this time, though, she had to make an exception.

"What is your name?" she asked lazily. As if she wasn't really interested.

"Nora, m-my Queen." The maid tried to control her voice, but it still came out shaky. She picked the first brushes and exhaled sharply as if gathering all her strength and confidence, but when she turned to face Astrea, the woman was already there, towering over her.

"You are not a minor goddess, Nora, right?" The Dragonfly tilted her head, playing with another bead in her fingers.

"G-goddess? M-me? No." The girl shook her head, her dread palpable.

"Good." Astrea nodded and crushed the second bead, grasping the maid's hand. "If you play your cards right, Nora, you are going to survive this. I really hope that you do!"

VIDAR LOOKED at the sparkling white marble road leading to the Halls of Valhalla. It was time to go downstairs, as his bride was supposed to be on her way.

A young woman who looked like Niki, whom he failed to get as he had recently found out, stood beside him, dressed in mortal realm jeans and a black leather jacket. It had to do for now. He would have to figure something else for later, though, to keep his wife on a leash.

"Cover her face better," the God of Vengeance ordered. "I want Astraea to see her right before she walks in."

She was already supposed to be in the middle of the marble path. It was time, and everyone who mattered waited for them downstairs. Although it was predictable Astraea would be late.

"Any news from my bride?" he asked one of his loyal advisors.

"She was a bit stubborn in the morning," the man replied. "But it had been handled. She must be on her way. Any minute now."

He could wait a minute. Vidar had waited millennia for this.

Still, it was hard to believe he would get what was rightfully his after all this time. Doubt crept into his soul. *Wasn't it too good to be true?*

Then, at last, he saw the procession walking out of the Queen's part of the palace. Several maids dressed in pale golden dresses at the front and an equal amount at the back. Right between them, where she was supposed to be, walked his mate with her head cast down and covered with a thin veil.

For a moment there, Vidar was afraid it wasn't her, but when his man used a mirror to reflect sunshine on her face to bring her attention to them, she looked up. Primal fear was in her eyes when she saw him holding who she thought was Niki by the hair. He shook the woman in his grasp for a more dramatic effect and then threw her to the ground so that Astraea couldn't see her face.

His bride looked down again, clasping her hands at the front, which indicated his final victory. At last.

Vidar walked down the spiralling stairs straight into the main hall of Valhalla, making everyone stand in his presence as he took his position at the chancel. He had ruled over New Asgard for so long, but this day was incredibly satisfying. His right to rule, powers, and decisions had always been questioned.

Today would be the day that ended.

Once his blood mixed with Astraea's and he got her powers from the Source, no one would object to him ever again. Not to mention that the woman he craved more than anything would finally be at his mercy.

This was indeed too good to be true.

The doors opened, and the maids stepped aside, letting their Queen walk towards her future husband.

She was mesmerising in the silk dress he chose for her. It was too tight for her so that she wouldn't be able to have too much freedom of movement and also to make it easier to rip it off her body later when they were alone.

The veil covered her face, but it was her. Her sharp chin, plump rosy lips, her hair that looked like starlight... too short for his liking, but he would help her grow it back tonight so that it was easier to pull on during their first official night.

She was visibly shaking, and he was delighted.

That woman would be his victory. Once and for all.

She took too long to get to him, and he was growing tired. Too many important guests were watching him in his moment of triumph to let his irritation slip, though.

Finally, she was by his side after what seemed like eternity, and he grabbed her small, icy hand, drawing his thumb over her skin, causing a rush of goosebumps to appear. He liked her that way. Trembling and obedient.

"You look divine, my love," he said, leaning down to her to remove her veil.

"No," she whispered, her tone begging and eyes desperate. Beautiful brown eyes...

The realisation came crashing down on him like a thunderstorm on a tranquil day. Astraea's eyes were divine blue...

He yanked the woman closer to him, causing the magic concealing her face to dissipate and reveal the much plainer features of a young, terrified girl.

"Who are you?" he growled at her, tears streaming down her face.

"I did not want to!" she stammered. "She made me! I—It was some kind of spell! Please!"

"Where is she?" he asked menacingly, hand on his sword, ready to kill the imposter.

The Halls of Valhalla burst into waves of whispers just as the alarm bells of the Source started ringing loudly through the air.

Now he knew where she was.

Vidar pushed the girl to the ground, and she scrambled away on her knees in the dress that someone as low as her was not supposed to even touch, let alone wear.

However, he did not have time for this. He had a bride to drag here by her short silver hair.

She couldn't just let him be nice to her. She had to make this hard and ugly.

"Everyone, stay in your places!" Vidar announced. "My beautiful future wife decided to play one last game with me. Didn't she, Mother-In-Law?"

His glare landed on Selene, who nodded calmly in response.

"Olympian tradition," she lied on the spot. "You want a bride, you catch her."

"Consider it done!" Vidar gritted his teeth and was ready to leave when a loud growl made his blood freeze in his veins.

No, it couldn't be...

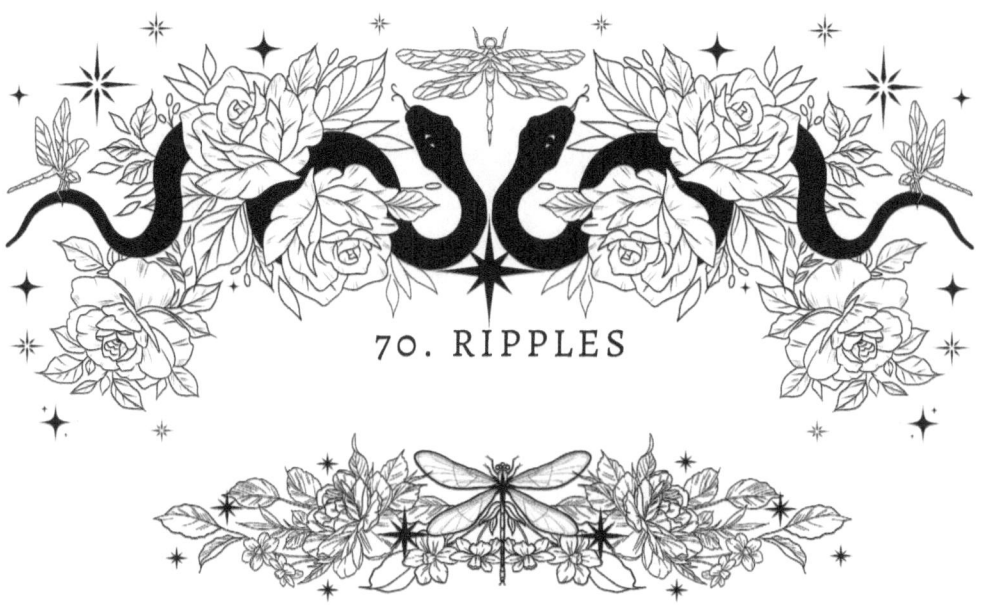

70. RIPPLES

*A*strea observed the guards stationed around the intricately arched domed building at the centre of the empty square for a few minutes, making sure she took note of each one. The stakes were incredibly high as she had only one chance to reach the Source nestled within. The path to it demanded crossing an empty yet heavily guarded space surrounded by towering walls. With no hiding spots available and a direct approach virtually impossible, she found herself at a distinct disadvantage against Asgardians, the majority of whom probably wielded some form of divine powers.

Fenrir gave her three rows of beads as any more might have raised suspicion, and maintaining a low profile was crucial to their plan. Each bead was priceless because these were her only defence against her adversaries.

"Start with the ones on the walls," Nova suggested. *"Then they can't hit you with anything nasty from up there."*

"I'm not sure it's a good idea," Astrea confessed. *"I won't be able to do it quietly, and if they notice me when I'm up there, it's possible I won't be able to get down at all. It's too risky."*

"Then let's do it the old-fashioned way!" Nova snarled, ready for a good fight. *"With a bang."*

It was almost the time for the wedding ritual when the guards saw a petite maid clad in a delicate golden gown strolling out from the central entrance to the square, holding a covered tray in her hands.

She had taken only a few steps when the warriors swiftly aimed their sharp spears and swords at her throat.

"Stay where you are!" one of the men ordered, and she froze, her visible trembling betraying her fear.

"I-I have the gifts prepared for the Temple of Freyja," she stuttered. "In honour of the newlyweds. It was an order of Selene, the Moon Goddess. Sh-she is the mother of the bride."

The men exchanged doubtful glances, causing the woman to swallow uncomfortably.

"You are in the wrong place." The warriors lowered their weapons and stepped aside, giving way to their leader, and Magnus sauntered towards her. "Freyja's Temple is that way."

He pointed toward the exit behind the dome on the opposite side of the courtyard, and the maid nodded respectfully, correcting her path.

"I'll be on my way then. Apologies for disturbing you," she murmured, speeding up.

Now she simply had to walk past the Source on her way to the indicated exit, all the while being observed by the guards trailing behind. Only a handful of them were stationed as sentinels for the dome building.

"Wait!" The voice of Thor's son echoed through the square. "What kind of maid doesn't know where Freyja's Temple is?"

The woman flinched but did not stop, knowing she had gotten caught and every step was essential now. The magic that changed her appearance rippled, letting her know she had mere seconds until her mask was completely gone.

"A new one?" Astrea suggested, hoping he would give her more time. Just a few feet more, and she would reach her goal.

"Isn't that dress for the maids who will take part in the wedding ceremony?" Magnus questioned further; his instincts kicking in at the worst possible time.

"I'm supposed to return for the procession as soon as I am done with this task," she kept lying through her teeth. "I follow orders from—"

"Slowly turn around and put the tray to the ground so that we can see your hands!" Magnus interjected as the warriors raised their weapons again, following their commander's lead.

Releasing the illusion, she allowed her hair to return to its silvery-white hue, and her features settled back into their natural state. Some of the men were still surprised to see the change.

"Now," Astrea sneered, removing the cover from the tray, brandishing two shiny daggers she'd stolen on her way here, "where would be the fun in that?"

"Seize her!" the captain of the guards shouted, and men charged at her from all angles, but Astrea had already crushed another bead on her wrist simultaneously, throwing the tray at the closest warrior and knocking him off his feet.

In a burst of energy, wisps of thick fog materialised, swirling and billowing around the square. The clouds expanded and exploded, their tendrils enveloping the area, allowing Astrea to disappear and even out her chances in the fight.

Her movements were like a dance of death as she manoeuvred swiftly through the clouds, striking her opponents with calculated accuracy, using beads where necessary.

A bulky warrior found her in the mist and lunged forward, his sword slashing through the air inches away from her. The Dragonfly sidestepped, narrowly avoiding the deadly blade. Just in time for another to appear behind her. She swung, bowing down in time to escape the second blow, and delivered a swift kick to the back of her attacker's knees, sending him crashing into the first guard. When the two men got back to their feet, she had already moved on and was nowhere to be seen.

Finally, the advantage was on her side. They had magic and heavy armour, she had Fenrir's beads, Joran's training and her speed.

They may have been stronger than her, but right now, she was the only werewolf here. She could count on Nova's senses as she navigated through the fog, staying mostly invisible to the men who were used to trusting their eyes over anything else.

She became a blur of motion, movements fluid and graceful as she masterfully took them out one after another on her way to her goal.

"Fire!" Nova warned her, and she barely managed to crush a protective bead, creating a shield around her. Flames hit it in seconds, trying to devour her, to no avail.

She was relatively safe, but her lungs burned thanks to the unbearably hot air, taking away from her strength.

"Run!" Nova suggested. *"I'll heal your lungs!"*

"Right!" Astrea agreed, knowing she had to move. A tall Asgardian appeared out of nowhere, and she wondered how she missed him when he threw his helmet at her, and she barely dodged it, recognising Magnus, the only remaining son of Thor.

"Give up," he grunted, annoyed she got this far, making his men look stupid.

He was a dangerous opponent. Not like the others at all. A god almost in the prime of his power, and a pure-blooded one at that.

"I knew your father," she said, watching pain and frustration wash over his face. Joran taught her well, indeed. If she couldn't overpower them, she had to get into their heads. "He would be ashamed of you," she spat, causing him to flinch.

She threw a dagger at him, which he barely avoided, letting her know she was on the right path.

He recovered quickly, lips curling into a smirk. "Why would he be ashamed? I am the defender of Asgard!"

"What Asgard?" she scoffed, twirling the remaining blade in her hands. "This is a faded memory of what it once was!"

"And whose fault is that?" he seethed, stepping closer. Another guard tried to knock her out from behind, and she deftly manoeuvred out of his reach, cutting his Achilles tendon on her way and making him fall to the ground in pain as she disappeared into the fog once again.

Only this time, Magnus followed her closely.

"Not mine!" Her voice echoed in his ears. "Vidar killed me long before that."

"Because you cheated on him!" the Asgardian spat.

"I was promised to him. Don't confuse it with me promising him anything. Those are two different things!" she corrected, quickly avoiding two more warriors in the fog. *There were so many of them! Too many!*

"He deserved justice!" Magnus roared, searching for her.

"You dare to lecture me about justice?" she let out a mocking laugh. "I was the goddess of stars *and* justice! He should have challenged Fenrir if justice was what he wanted! Fenrir would have accepted, and that would have been a fair fight. Instead, Vidar imprisoned him by making his trusted friend set up a trap and then tortured him while he was helpless. Some hero!"

Magnus was about to say something, but she appeared out of nowhere, hands sliding over his back and neck from behind and something cold and sharp poking at the artery in his throat.

The Asgardian struck her with his elbow so hard that even one of his soldiers would be on the ground from the blow, but Astrea took it in stride with a sharp hiss.

"Yield!" She gritted her teeth, not willing to give up. "This is a Nightmare's horn! Yield or die!"

"I will never yield—" he groaned, noticing the fog dissipating. The beads' magic only lasted for a limited amount of time.

The soldiers froze, seeing their commander taken hostage.

"This is a divine weapon!" she warned them. "Move and his blood is on your hands."

She knew they wouldn't. They had too much respect for him. She didn't observe them for nothing and knew he was their group's biggest weakness. They could sacrifice anyone else but him.

Unfortunately, Magnus had pride just like any other major god. It was his destiny, after all.

"I'd never—" He wanted to protest, but she pressed the horn a little deeper into his skin, drawing divine blood to the astonishment of everyone.

"If I have to kill you, they are next!" she said bluntly, not letting any emotions slip into her voice. He had to know that she meant it.

"Fine!" He dropped his sword to the ground. "Everyone stay in your places."

"Good little god," she whispered and felt his whole body go rigid. He definitely was not used to this.

Slowly, she took him with her to the domed building, pushing the main door with her foot, and was surprised that there were no guards inside.

The well was just within her reach, yet something felt really off.

"I am sorry," Magnus said, and for a second, she wasn't sure what he was talking about.

Right until it sunk in...

There was no glow. She did not feel anything special in this place.

"What—what is wrong with it?" she asked and heard him sigh.

"Vidar knows you too well, I guess. He predicted you would try this," Magnus admitted, and she shook her head in denial.

"He doesn't know me at all!" She clenched the horn tighter in her hand, pulling the tall man closer to the well.

He did not fight her anymore, letting her have a proper look at the empty old well.

"Impossible!" she muttered, frantically thinking of what could have happened to the source.

"He transferred it to another place centuries ago," Magnus replied to her silent question. "Several gods died helping him, but he couldn't let you—"

"—Gain my power," she finished for him. "I know. Because he wants it for himself, and he wants me weak so that he can use me any way he likes, and I can do nothing about it!"

He stiffened again.

"What?" Astrea let out a bitter laugh. "A noble Asgardian doesn't like to hear the truth? You know I am right!"

"He is the ruler," Magnus said, his voice darker than usual.

"A shitty ruler!" she exploded. "There had already been one 'All-Father' before him! Too afraid of three children who wanted nothing but his approval!"

"It wasn't like that—"

"It was exactly like that!" Astrea fought the tears burning her eyes. It was neither the place nor the time for emotions. "And your father, a noble warrior loved by so many, watched him abuse those children and said nothing against it! I bet he did not like it too, but just like you, he justified it."

"Jormungandr was his enemy!" Magnus roared. "They were equal rivals!"

"Compared to mighty Thor, he was just a kid back then!" The Dragonfly put him in place. "A strong, misguided youth who didn't know any better because he wasn't taught any better! And Fenrir—"

Emotions finally betrayed her, manifesting in a quiver in her voice.

"Fenrir did everything they asked! He followed every rule! He performed every task! He took all the humiliation! He deserved better—"

"My father had nothing to do with his chains. He made the first one weak on purpose so that—"

"He watched them torture him! He never said a word in his defence!" she screamed. "Just like you are watching and staying silent now! You know right from wrong! You know that a man like Vidar doesn't deserve to win! You—"

She pushed him away, tired of this game. If the Source was not here, then all of this was a waste of their effort.

Magnus couldn't bring himself to turn and face her.

"He'll be here soon," he informed her. "Vidar will—"

"A true ruler would make this place flourish." Astrea walked around the well as if to check there wasn't a drop of divine power inside. A part of her still couldn't believe it. "He would consider how to make his people happy. How to restore the lost balance without unnecessary sacrifices from any of the worlds. Because destroying the human realm will not benefit anyone, but Vidar doesn't care! All he cares about is power, which does not belong to him! Just like this place never belonged to him!"

"He won the battle with Fenrir." Magnus finally turned, and their eyes locked. She could tell that he wanted her to confirm the knowledge he had, but she was a cruel assassin and never lied if she absolutely did not have to. So, she offered the ugly truth.

"Won?" she scoffed. "He stabbed him in the back and used that moment to throw him out of here, closing the divine gates forever. Fenrir could never return after that. But there was no battle!"

"But then—"

"Then everything you ever knew was a lie?" She smiled sadly. "Welcome to the club."

Magnus stayed silent for a while, processing the new information.

"He will come for you and get you—" The warrior looked at her differently now. She could tell he felt guilty.

"He will try." Astrea sat on the edge of the well. "And I will fight him with everything I've got. If I am lucky, I will kill him with the horn. If I am not lucky, he will have to kill me."

The God of Strength watched her with pity, and she rolled her eyes.

"Trust me, that's better than a life with him," she confessed. "He is a sadist who has nothing good in him. There is nothing—"

A mighty roar echoed in the distance and she jumped to her feet, lips parted in shock.

"No," she whispered, recognising the sound at once. "He couldn't—"

Magnus looked out of the window, noticing his men ready to attack any moment.

"Go to the wedding!" he ordered and saw them confused by the unexpected order. "Make a formation around Valhalla and do nothing without my personal order. Whatever happens."

Even more questioning glances followed.

"Now!" he shouted at them, and the soldier bowed, quickly leaving the square.

Astrea furrowed her brows. "What do you think you are doing?"

"He is ready for this too." Magnus locked his eyes with her. "I am sure he has a plan for Fenrir's arrival as well."

She did not say anything, fingers counting the remaining few beads on her bracelet. She'd already spent most of them.

"This is all I can give you without breaking my oath to protect New Asgard." Magnus lowered his head.

Astrea stood up, hope still trembling in her chest.

"What are you—" she whispered, afraid to say the words out loud and end up being wrong.

"You will have just a few minutes." Magnus seemed serious. He exhaled heavily and added, "The Source is now in the cave where he killed you."

She sucked in a sharp breath, a myriad of thoughts crossing her mind.

It could have been a trap. He could have been lying.

"What are you waiting for?" Magnus asked, bringing her back to reality as another growl sounded somewhere far away.

Fenrir's growl. She couldn't have mistaken it for anything.

"Thanks." She nodded to her unexpected ally and shifted into her wolf form in seconds, giving Nova full control. If they had mere minutes, they had to give it their all.

Nova ran as fast as she could through the square and into the city, to the cliffs, finding the cave where it all happened.

It could have been a trap, but she had no other choice because finding the Source of Power was their best bet. She had to try even if she failed.

She was in the mountains in the blink of an eye, chest burning. Racing through puddles inside the cave, the memories of Fenrir chained in there danced in her head, mixed with the vivid recollection of her own death. For a moment, it seemed she couldn't breathe anymore, but it helped that Nova was in charge.

"A little more!" her wolf encouraged.

"I am fine!" Astrea assured her when they finally reached the cavity filled with light.

"Time for you to do what you were born to do," Nova said, pushing her to take the control back. Astrea shifted into her human form and walked towards the light, naked, embracing it.

The warm glow seemed so familiar. It caressed her skin as if it recognized her, as if she belonged with it. Something she hadn't felt in a while.

Before her was another well, rugged and uneven, hewn from ancient rocks and filled with a glowing substance that seemed to have a life of its own.

With each step, Astrea felt it grow stronger. Raw power, bigger than any deity, bigger than any realm. Vidar may have changed its location, but he couldn't subdue it or take from it what it was not willing to give.

It was the end and the beginning of each god. Primal power to which each of them bowed their heads.

"I don't want to take what's not mine," Astrea said loudly, knowing it had to be done. "I only need what was always mine. Please—"

The power rippled as if the Source was responding to her, and she knew what she had to do.

Slowly, Astrea climbed on its edge, ready to dive in.

This would solve all their problems, but one thought stopped her from jumping inside.

"Do it," Nova whispered, a subtle goodbye in her voice.

"I don't want to lose you." Astrea bit her lip. *"I have already lost Midnight. I can't lose you too."*

"If you don't do it, I am doomed anyway. He will kill us all," her wolf tried to reassure her. *"You are a goddess, Astrea. You are not a mere werewolf. This is what you were always supposed to be. You are supposed to fix everything, and I am willing to make that sacrifice."*

She knew Nova was right, even if it felt wrong. She would save so many lives. The mortal realm would get another chance under her defence… Fenrir and she would finally have a shot at happiness.

And yet, it felt like ripping a part of her soul.

"You were the best wolf anyone could ask for," she whispered, tears rolling down her cheeks.

"I know. I was a star in my own right!" Nova joked the way she always did when they were at their lowest.

"I'll miss you more than anything about my mortal life," Astrea promised.

"I know. I am quite unforgettable." Nova smiled in her mind. *"Do it, Astrea. And… be happy. For the two of us."*

Astrea let out a little sob, and her wolf used the moment to push through the controls, forcing her body to take that last step and fall into the Source of divine power…

Bjorn did not want to come back to this cursed place, but when he held Niki in his arms on that field, he could feel her worry even through all the happiness.

"I have to say goodbye to Astrea," she told him back then, and he gave her his word.

This woman accepted his monstrous self. The least he could do was grant her every wish.

"Fine," he said, cupping her cheek. He couldn't see her, but he knew how beautiful she was. He could feel those beautiful dimples on her cheeks, the fullness of her lips. "And when you are done, Strawberry, I will take you far away from here. No one can stop us."

She buried her face in his naked chest. And it was the best feeling.

He wished they had stayed there forever, especially when they were back in the elevator of that damn building, getting closer and closer to that abhorrent penthouse.

When they were almost on the top floor, he clenched her hand tighter in his.

"Something is wrong," he informed her, and he could feel how Niki immediately left her happy state, going back to her assassin self. Sometimes he forgot that his girl was a trained murder weapon.

"Whatever it is, we'll face it together," she said firmly, causing a slow smile to curl his lips. Bjorn had never been so proud of his woman before.

The elevator doors opened and a huge fireball froze in the air right before them, inches away from incinerating them both.

Bjorn instinctively pulled her behind himself and heard Joran cursing as he dissipated his weapon.

"Oh, it's just you!" he muttered, as if he hadn't almost killed them both.

"We shouldn't have come," Darius summed things up, but Niki let go of his hand, charging forward.

"What is going on?" she asked, her beautiful voice filled with worry.

"Astrea was taken to Asgard," Riannon replied, raw emotions colouring her tone. Now that he was blind, Bjorn picked up on these things with ease. They were all worried sick.

"What happened to Fenrir?" Niki gasped. "Is he dead?"

"Temporarily!" Joran cut her off, adding with less confidence, "Hopefully."

"Strawberry, we need to go!" Bjorn told her, hoping she loved him enough to leave all this behind. The air around them was getting thicker and harder to breathe.

"What—" Niki seemed lost in the situation. "How can we help?"

Bjorn cursed inwardly. He could feel Joran staring at him now.

"You should go," the Serpent said dryly, to his relief. He was really setting him free, and this opportunity had to be used.

"Nik, please," Bjorn begged her, knowing it was their last chance.

"When he comes back to life, can he save Astrea?" Niki asked, as if she hadn't heard him. *Did she have to be so noble at heart?*

"He is saving her now," Gideon explained. "At least we hope so."

His ear picked up something from a distance. A buzzing of sorts. A noise that he hadn't heard before.

"Something is coming," the bear shifter announced as the noise intensified. "So many of them—"

"We don't have much time," Riannon said. "He needs to get back soon or —"

"Don't you dare say it!" Joran interrupted her. "It's Fenrir. He... can survive anything."

The cacophony of strange sounds became more distinct, causing Bjorn to grow his claws out just in case. Eerie cries and screeches blended with guttural growls and piercing shrieks were coming closer and closer.

"Something is coming!" he repeated. "So many of them!"

Joran's power pulled him into the room roughly and he felt his fireball exploding in the elevator after all.

"We know!" the Serpent grunted. "We could see them!"

"Wh-what do you see?" Bjorn didn't really want to know the answer. He wanted to take his Strawberry and leave this place.

"Demons!" Niki replied. "Darius, there are so many of them!"

"We need to go!" He navigated himself through the room thanks to her scent.

"It's too late," Joran informed him.

"Darius!" Niki grasped his hand. "It's—Remember how you told me you hated being the bad guy?"

He wished he had never told her now. She was too young, too pure at heart.

"We can't leave them." She cupped his cheek. "Besides, there is a swarm of flying demons heading in our direction. We are not getting too far away. It's not the time to run. It's time to be a hero."

"Nik," he sighed, giving up. She was the first woman ever to see him that way and the only one that mattered to him. "Stay safe."

"I will need to try to restart his heart soon," Riannon said, her voice trembling. It was an unusual show of emotion from her that everyone in the room felt the heaviness of their situation.

"Then you do that." Joran stretched his neck, preparing for a fight. "I'll give you as much time as I can."

"Careful!" Gideon roared, and the glass wall shattered into millions of pieces, flying at them like tiny daggers.

So it began...

71. OUT OF TIME

*V*idar stormed out of the hall and froze at the tall gates, his loyal men following his every step, ready to kill for him if necessary.

An intense heat struck the God of Vengeance's face, making it difficult to breathe. His lungs felt like they were melting, and he found the reason for it instantly – a giant fire wolf glared at him from above.

"Impossible!" Vidar exclaimed, realising his worst nightmare was unfolding before him. "He was banned from Asgard forever! He can't just waltz in here and—"

His train of thought was broken when he saw a Valkyrie flying high in the sky. Her golden wings reflected the sun, causing him to blink.

Realising how his adversary had infiltrated his domain, Vidar swore under his breath at the inescapable loophole. If only there were any other surviving Valkyries able to seal the entrance to this realm for him, he could have prevented this. Sadly, none of them wanted to join him, so he killed them one by one. Some were even killed before Ragnarok started. A pang of regret struck him as he acknowledged that he should have dealt with Kara the same way. He should have eliminated her just like her sisters, but after finding out she was helping the rebels, he wanted to punish her. He found a twisted pleasure in witnessing his enemies suffering, firmly believing that Kara would eventually return, begging for his mercy. That was when he would kill her. Or make her his slave. It would have depended on his mood that day.

Yet she chose to oppose him and dared to bring that mutt into his home. Whispers rippled through the crowd.

"Is that Fenrir?"

"And a Valkyrie? What is happening?"

"I thought all the Valkyries were already dead!"

"This must be an illusion! Who is this?"

Fenrir lifted his head up to the Asgardian sky and let out a roar that shook the ground under everyone's feet. They had heard a similar roar before, and just the memory of what followed made everyone shiver.

They feared him. It was a primal, bone-chilling fear that made gods tremble in his presence.

"Shoot the Valkyrie!" Vidar ordered, annoyed by her presence, a reminder of his one and only weakness – the desire for revenge. His warriors hesitated, still paralysed with shock.

Flames flared up and covered the giant wolf as if devouring him whole, but the next moment, they dissipated, leaving a tall, dark figure of a man.

"There is no place like home!" Fenrir smirked at them, tilting his head. "I haven't seen you all in ages!"

A portal opened, and three men walked out of it, taking their places at Fenrir's side as Kara descended from the sky.

"Traitor!" Vidar threw at her, but she ignored him, spreading her wings wider, each golden feather as sharp as a dagger.

"That's a compliment, considering who is talking." Devoss brushed non-existent dust off the golden chains on his bright red leather jacket. "But there is no need for honeyed words. We will drink mead *after* we win."

"Win?" Vidar's jaw ticked. He couldn't believe the audacity of these people. "You must be kidding!"

"Jokes aside," Bash arched a brow, "this wedding looks dull. Feels like something important is missing. The bride, maybe?"

The silence in the square became deadly as a smile curled onto Fenrir's lips. His girl was on her way to the Source, just as they planned. He trusted her to reach it, and he would take care of everything else in the meantime.

"The last remaining son of Odin, I challenge you to combat! At this point only Death can settle our score!" Fenrir's words reverberated through the air as a wave.

"It's beneath me to fight you!" Vidar seethed, gaining the support of his closest warriors, who chuckled in response.

"My liege, allow me to deal with this abomination," one of them offered, stepping forward and materialising a large axe in his arms, but the next moment, something shining and powerful swept through the air, landing in Fenrir's hand.

A veil of dark clouds covered the sky, and lightning struck right between them as everyone gasped, seeing Odin's spear for the first time in millennia.

"You have no right to wield Gungnir!" Vidar bellowed.

"Why not?" Fenrir spun the weapon between his fingers. "I killed Odin in a fair fight. It's rightfully mine. Same as Asgard. You grabbed your father's helmet while his body wasn't even cold and ignored your siblings' battles to declare yourself the ruler, but guess what? That doesn't make you one."

"You count on usurping my throne?" Vidar grated out.

"Out of the two of us, you are the usurper! I did not want this place; I did not need it. I had only one wish, one desire, but you couldn't leave me and Astrea alone. Whatever happens here today is on you!"

"Astraea is mine!" the God of Vengeance seethed. "She was given to me! She, and everything she has, belongs to me!"

"She is not a thing to be given to anyone! She is a person, and she made her choice a long time ago. Refusing to listen to it doesn't make it any less true."

"Vidar will crush you!" Magnus interjected, walking through the milling crowd. "No Asgardian god would decline a challenge, and you are talking with the son of Odin!"

"I am counting on it," Fenrir sneered, happy for the sudden intervention. "After all, we don't need to repeat the past. How about we let the loss of one life decide the fate of the realm? Vidar's or mine. Only one of us will walk out of here alive, and that person will have everything."

"You have no chance!" Magnus commented and then made a gesture to his warriors. "Form a circle!"

The soldiers obeyed, pressing the crowd to make space and only letting Fenrir's people stay as close as them to be fair.

"I still haven't heard your leader accept my challenge."

Vidar scanned the space around him, swearing inwardly as he saw so many faces expecting him to do the honourable thing. He was in the prime of his power and trained at the same level as Fenrir was, if not better, but... he did not like to take risks. Fighting Fenrir was an enormous risk.

However, if he came up with an excuse now, it could ruin his reputation once and for all. Magnus cleared his throat as if to hint him it was time to respond and only now Vidar realised his nephew was not guarding the fake Source.

He had questions, but they would have to wait. Life in the mortal realm had to weaken Fenrir at least a little. Gods needed to be present here, close to the Source, to replenish their divine powers.

Vidar made his decision.

"I accept your challenge!" He raised his hand, summoning flames that ran through his skin and materialised in his fire sword. "After all, how can I deny your request to have your soul utterly destroyed? This time, there will be no banishment!"

"You are right," Fenrir agreed. "Only one of us walks out of here. Or neither of us. I am fine with both outcomes."

Vidar did not like this turn of events. He would have preferred to have more options.

"No one helps either of them!" Magnus announced loudly, rendering any alternative to a one-on-one battle implausible.

"Thank you, nephew," he locked his eyes with the God of Strength, "your help today will not be forgotten."

"Of course, Uncle." Magnus bowed his head respectfully. "I ought to have your back just as you did for my father and grandfather."

The words made a mocking snort escape Fenrir, and Vidar charged at him in a fit of raw anger. Minutes ago, he was at the top of the world, and now this mutt was in his way again.

The blade missed just two inches from the Wolf God's throat as he dodged the attack, not putting too much effort into this. The air between them crackled with tension as Vidar wielded the fire sword, trying to slash his rival in his vital points. One agile assault after another, he tried to gain superiority in the fight while Fenrir, with the spear in one hand and the other held behind his back as if to demonstrate that he did not need both hands, countered each blow with deft parries and expertly timed lashes.

Another sharp lunge, and all Vidar managed to cut was a strand of Fenrir's hair.

Anger simmered in his veins, and he couldn't control it anymore, the fire slowly taking control of him.

This wasn't right! From the very beginning, Fenrir wanted what he shouldn't have desired – a place in his home and possession of his woman! When Vidar won the first time, it felt so right, but he spent all those years alone in Asgard, not able to enjoy his mate.

This wasn't right! He was entitled to his revenge! He earned it! And they earned what he gave them! *He couldn't lose this stupid fight! Not now! Not ever!*

JORAN SHIFTED mid-flight on his way out of the window, taking a bunch of winged dark creatures along with him. Flames erupted from the dragon's mouth, followed by the smell of burnt flesh as he went through rows and rows of demons.

Bjorn managed to spread his wings before the shards of glass reached Niki, covering Riannon and Fenrir's body as well. In the meantime, Gideon, already in his enhanced royal form, caught two demons and ripped their heads off, throwing their bodies outside to clear the space.

"Strawberry, can you hide?" Bjorn asked, knowing they had mere seconds until the next wave.

"I can fight!" she retorted, slightly offended by the suggestion, and although this was not what he wanted to hear, he respected her choice.

"Stay safe!" He pulled her for a quick, sloppy kiss. "Please."

"Darius—" She wanted to tell him so much, but he had to retract his wings to be able to leave the room, and he couldn't hear her. Just like the Serpent, who was slaughtering big groups of ugly creatures in the sky, Bjorn fully shifted into his new form as he leapt out of the shattered penthouse.

Niki ran to her hidden stash of weapons and got her knives out, throwing one of them instantly at a demon who had reached the broken window, attempting to get inside. Another followed, and then one more. She was running out of knives quickly, and, to her astonishment, the three creatures she hit were not dead.

"Aim for the head!" Riannon told her, trying to detect any kind of rhythm in Fenrir's chest.

"Gotcha." Niki nodded and evaded a slash of sharp claws, getting her blade out of the demon in the meantime and piercing its temple with it swiftly, enjoying how the sharp silver-coated steel went through his skull. Just like a knife through butter.

Another two were standing up.

"If you see the future and know a trick for us to get out of this mess, this would be a great time to share!" she said to Riannon, who crushed a healing bead over Fenrir's body and started applying compressions to his chest, praying to whatever gods were listening for their plan to work.

There weren't too many reliable gods left, though.

Fenrir was not a mortal, so there was a chance that luck would be on their side. Mortal rules did not apply to him, and this was what they counted on. However, this chance was slim. Their time was almost up.

"I am afraid it doesn't work like that," Ria sighed, wishing she was able to fight instead of watching the man her sister loved lingering between life and death.

"I figured it was a longshot." Niki threw her last dagger, getting it right between a demon's eyes this time and watching him fall breathless. "Do you at least know what these are? Where do they come from?"

"They are—" Riannon was afraid to look at her pocket watch. "Wild vampires, I think. The lowest of their kind."

"Damn!" Nikiah whistled. "And I always thought vampires were hot. We had a couple on the Firstborn island. I wonder if they survived the sweep… Never mind, I am clearly dying today anyway, so who cares?"

"You are going to survive," Riannon muttered, blowing off a strand of hair that stuck to her forehead that covered with crystals of sweat. They were almost out of time. "You will live a very long life. I saw glimpses of it."

"Really?" Niki grinned at her, and Ria realised she shouldn't have said that. "Thanks for letting me know! That unties my hands right now!"

"No!" Riannon wanted to grab the girl's hand and warn her not to do anything stupid, but the Firstborn had already shifted into her wolf form and lunged at the new creature who got through their defenders.

"Come on, come on, come on!" Ria whispered, biting her lip nervously. She knew the outcome of today and that this burden would stay with her forever. Sometimes, her gift felt like a curse, but she already knew by trial and error that letting the knowledge she had out into the world was only making things worse.

The Queen of the West looked around. Niki's wolf sank her teeth into a demon's neck, decapitating it almost instantly. Gideon was holding three vampires back at the other end of the room, not letting those get to her. Outside, Bjorn and Joran were working in perfect sync. It was all going well.

Except for the fact that their time was running out, and Fenrir wasn't waking up.

"Come on!" she whispered. "You can wake up and then go back again. I am sure we can work something out!"

Something tall and weighty thudded before her, prompting Ria to lift her gaze to the repulsive creature towering over her. Its grey, wrinkled skin resembled that of a decaying corpse. Draped in torn rags that hung loosely from his muscular body, which still resembled a skeleton in some places, the monster bared his sharp, jagged teeth at her as his bat-like wings spread, preparing for an attack. They did not look like the majestic wings of a creature of the night. Instead, they were tattered and worn, with gaping holes scattered across them. His eyes gleamed red with bloodlust, convinced that he had, at long last, discovered his elusive prey.

Once upon a time, Riannon thought that wild vampires were a myth. Vampires, in general, were considered to be demons, and wild vampires were the ones who were lost to the curse of bloodlust. Not being able to control themselves in their beast form, they stayed in it forever, decaying and only living to hunt for blood. Similar to Lycans, who couldn't typically use their third form without going mad.

But she had never seen a wild vampire before, never heard of anyone actually seeing one.

This right now... was as unreal as it gets.

He was about to pounce at her, and Ria was still performing CPR on Fenrir. She had to keep going. She could swear she still heard a weak irregular rhythm inside as the power of the bead he used was wearing off.

Riannon heard Gideon's possessive growl as he noticed his wife in danger, yet the determined woman crushed another bead between her fingers and stretched her hand, emitting lightning and frying the vampire on the spot.

She was watching his still-convulsing body fall to the ground when the alarm clock on her watch rang, letting her know Fenrir had no more time to spare.

Not thinking twice, Riannon placed her hand on his chest... and charged it, hoping to hear anything resembling a strong heartbeat again.

Nothing.

"What's going on?" Joran shifted effortlessly, stepping into the room straight from the sky. Worry washed over his face despite him trying to hide it. There were hardly any demons left, and Bjorn was dealing with those.

"I have no time to speak," Ria brushed him off and sent another charge to the Wolf God's chest. "I am saving your brother. You will help if you deal with the demons."

Joran watched her with distrust. It all seemed surreal. How could his own brother trust these people instead of him?

The thought came and left. He knew how that happened...

Niki stood near a shattered window and watched Darius battling the beasts all by himself. There were four of them now, and in all honesty, Joran had left him too early. It was evident that the dragon bear hadn't yet mastered the art of using his wings effectively, unlike his adversaries, who faced no such challenge. Helplessly, she witnessed their relentless assaults, aware that she couldn't help him from her current vantage point.

Niki shifted back to her human form and pulled on an oversized shirt she found on the floor among shards of glass, not caring who it belonged to. She began scouring for her knives, discovering two embedded in the vampire corpses. With precision, she extracted them both and returned to the window.

"Here!" she shouted, trying to attract their attention. "Bring them here!"

Bjorn looked at her just for a second, and her heart clenched painfully. He would do no such thing.

"Stupid bear!" she muttered.

A demon landed on Bjorn's back, digging his claws into his flesh and ripping into one of his wings in the process, causing the bear to roar from the pain and lose balance. A second more, and the vampires would kill him.

Niki threw one of her daggers at the attacker and got him straight into the temple, making him fall off of her Darius.

She turned to the next one, aiming with precision, and killed off one more, allowing the dragon bear to grow his talons and slash at one, decapitating the third demon.

Only now Niki realised they had lost the fourth demon. Where was it?

Her eyes locked on Bjorn right when she heard Riannon screaming, "Niki, dodge!"

72. STARS BURN

Fenrir blocked another desperate attack from his nemesis, wondering what was taking Astrea so long and regretting he couldn't go searching for her.

The God of Vengeance was properly exhausted by now, but so was he. It really didn't help that he didn't have his full strength with his body kept between life and death in the mortal realm.

The spectacle had run its course, leaving no room for attributing Fenrir's potential victory to mere chance. Resolute he'd had enough, the wolf prepared to bring this to an end as he had little time left.

"I will avenge my father!" Vidar spat blood to the ground, acutely aware of his people's intense gazes in his direction. They looked disappointed, and he knew that with each missed blow, he was losing another bit of their respect. This realisation led him to a cascade of mistakes, so the glorious victory he had dreamed of for so long was slowly slipping from his grasp.

"You had centuries to do that," Fenrir reminded him, "but suddenly, you can't wait any longer?"

"Let's just say I wanted to see you suffer first!" The son of Odin narrowed his eyes, ready for his next move. Channelling his wrath, he waved his hand, conjuring a blazing wall of fire which engulfed the battlefield in a deadly inferno.

The Asgardians around them gasped; some even materialised their shields for protection, but Fenrir spun the spear in his hand, dissipating the flames with ease, to everyone's astonishment.

"You can't fight fire with fire! If your father could see what you've turned into, he would be so embarrassed right now!" a chuckle left the Alpha God's chest. "And that's me saying that. The man who hated Odin more than anyone else. At least I still had some respect for him. You—you are nothing but a disgrace."

Vidar let out an angry scream, lunging at him with another slash of his blade.

"Says a mutt who could only dine with us as a pet!"

"And just look how that worked out for you all!"

Fenrir intercepted the desperate attack with a smirk playing on his lips and kicked his adversary's leg, dislocating his knee and throwing him to the dirt without gracing his insult with a response. It was all in the past. He had moved on a long time ago.

Vidar was a good warrior. Great even, but not a match for him in a fair fight. The God of Vengeance's main advantage lay in the peak of his divine power that had grown all these years since he lived close to the Source. Fenrir was deprived of that, not to mention that his current state wasn't his strongest, but he was still ready to fight and win. He had centuries preparing for this exact moment. Devoss, Bash, Warg and Kara had helped him train for that battle, even when they were not sure if it would ever happen. Now, the centuries of dedication finally borne fruit.

Fenrir's eyes met with Devoss' just for a split second. The old fox was probably the best of his teachers, thanks to his brash tricks and cheating. He always kept the wolf on his toes, so when Vidar decided it wasn't beyond him to cheat either, he was prepared.

The ruler of New Asgard had to duck down to escape Fenrir's spear. Desperate, he dug his fingers into the Earth under his feet, whispering a quick spell. The ancient demon language was his last hope. Playing noble was not working out in his favour, and now it looked like he had nothing to lose.

The Earth trembled and groaned, fissures spreading like veins across the ground. The solid surface fractured, and the widening cracks moved towards Fenrir as a wave of deadly energy threatened to swallow him whole.

Dark ancient magic.

Demon magic.

He watched it with an arched brow, not a muscle flinching until it almost reached him. When it was near, he hit the ground with his spear, simultaneously throwing a few beads and creating another shattering wave of energy to oppose the destruction coming his way and subduing it before it could bring any damage to him.

Whispers and gasps rippled through the crowds.

"How did you—" Vidar gritted his teeth, knowing this was one of the best tricks up his sleeve. He couldn't fight the mutt with fire, he did not have any divine weapon to oppose his father's spear, and he clearly did not have superior fighting skills.

He'd started working with demons precisely for that reason. They were the only ones who could offer him something he didn't already have – a type of magic that could help kill all his enemies, no matter who they were. All he had to do in return was sacrifice a few people who'd wronged him. It was a mutually beneficial agreement. Even when they wanted to kill Astrea and take the essence from her dragonfly mark, it was still worth it. Or so he thought. Back then, he had no idea it was her last life. However, even if he'd known... he would probably still sacrifice his defiant mate. Power was better than anything anyway, and Hunters were always one step ahead of him. This was more important than having a stubborn woman.

Anger boiled in his chest. *He'd sacrificed so much for this. He was the higher being! A god! An heir of Odin! Brother of Thor and Baldur! He was not going to lose his kingdom to an abomination like Fenrir! And once again, he was ready to do what others couldn't to achieve his goal. This was why he was always the winner.*

Not thinking twice, Vidar threw his hand towards Kara, the spell igniting her wings, causing her to scream in pain. Fenrir snapped his head in his old friend's direction, and Vidar took the opportunity.

"Die!" he hissed, charging and aiming at his enemy's throat, but Fenrir was ready for that too, stepping aside and tripping him while knocking the sword out of his hand.

This time, the wolf ensured the spear's blade was at Vidar's throat, pinning him to the ground. The God of Vengeance tried moving away, which led to a slight cut on his neck because Fenrir did not budge. The blood unpleasantly trickled down to his chest from the fresh wound, letting him know his next move would be his last.

The spectators were quiet this time, paralysed by the realisation that their ruler had just lost the fight. None of them thought it was possible when the battle began, and now this was the result they faced.

"Kara, are you okay?" Fenrir asked without looking at her.

"Yeah," the Valkyrie responded while Bash helped her to put out the flames on her feathers. The woman hissed, and Fenrir snarled at the one who hurt her out of spite.

"Here!" He did not take his eyes off Vidar, knowing that it would be too risky now that he had won. He took a bead off his bracelet and crushed it between his fingers, throwing the green glowing energy at Kara to accelerate her healing.

"That was a dirty trick!" the Alpha God said, pressing the sharp spear tighter into the flesh of his enemy. "And was that demon magic right now?"

"All is fair when fighting an abomination!" Vidar tried to look brave, but his voice trembled, giving away his fear.

Amusement curled into Fenrir's lips.

"It still did not help you, did it?" he chuckled. "Now... yield!"

Vidar's eyes grew wide.

"Wh-what?" He must have been hearing things.

"I said yield and accept your defeat before everyone who has witnessed our fight today!" Fenrir demanded.

"I would never—"

The blade drew more blood, and Vidar gulped in panic, still desperately trying to hide his weakness and hoping for a miracle.

"Wh-why don't you just kill me? After everything I did to you—"

Fenrir gave him a withering glance.

"Because when I killed your father, it did not make me feel better," he admitted. "Yield, hand New Asgard to me and I will banish you to the mortal realm. This is your second chance and my last offer."

Vidar contemplated, but Fenrir moved the spear up his neck so that he could feel the vibrations of ancient magic. If he did not submit, it would be the end of him. His essence would be back in the Source in seconds.

Vidar, son of Odin, would cease to exist.

"I... yield!" Vidar forced the words out, and disappointed gasps mixed with shock erupted. "New Asgard is—"

The blade slid down his throat, and a shiver went down the God of Vengeance's spine. He lifted his eyes at Fenrir and furrowed his brows, watching the wolf deity breathing heavily.

Something was wrong with him.

"Finish... the sentence!" Fenrir ordered, his chest heaving.

Now Vidar saw he could barely stand on his feet.

Fenrir swore under his breath. He could barely hold it together in this realm. Something was changing rapidly, and he realised his time here was up. Riannon was already trying to bring him back.

However, he needed just a few more minutes...

"Say the words!" he growled.

"You are not really here, are you?" Vidar sneered at him. "Like your father, the Trickster, you tricked us into believing that you are, but you are somewhere in between. The spear helped you fight, but you are neither dead nor alive and I guess your body is calling."

Fenrir hated that he was getting weaker. The Queen of the West was making attempt after attempt to save his body back in the mortal realm. A few minutes more, and he would not be able to wield the spear. It was time to leave. He'd won the battle, and everyone present was his witness.

However, Asgardians could not be trusted and Astrea was still not here. He couldn't leave... not yet.

Their plan was different. He needed her to be here before he could leave safely.

"You're out of time!" The revelation widened Vidar's eyes.

"I have enough time to end you!" Fenrir seethed and prepared to do just that, but a wave of electricity ran through him, freezing him for just a second. That mere moment was enough for Vidar to roll away and scramble back to his feet.

"He can't fight now!" he screamed, pointing at Fenrir, who was now using the spear for support while another wave of electricity rippled through him. "Kill him now, and we are free of him forever! Help me defeat this monster! Together, we can do that! Attack him!"

Devoss, Bash, Warg and Kara exchanged glances and bared their weapons, stepping closer towards Fenrir as the Asgardians began to wield their powers.

Eyes glowed, magic of all shades crackled in the air. The gods and the mere citizens of Asgard were ready to kill the one they always took for the enemy.

"Cousin?" Bash raised his brow at Magnus expectantly, and the latter seemed shocked by the way he was addressed. After all, he was a mere infant during Ragnarok and barely remembered anyone from these times. "You look just like your father," Bash explained how he recognised him. "How about a helping hand?"

Magnus pressed his lips tight, torn between a desire to follow his heart and what he was taught. His people were still standing in a protective circle, the last obstacle between the Asgardians and Fenrir.

"I am sorry," the son of Thor muttered, "my warriors won't fight our own people. That's different. We gave an oath—"

"Yeah, sure." Bash rolled his eyes, losing interest quickly. "We know how noble everyone here is. There's no need to explain."

Magnus clenched his fists, looking down, and then waved his hand, signalling his warriors to break their formation and step aside.

Vidar finally came to his senses and materialised his fire blade into his hand, ready to impale a weakened Fenrir with it from the back. He was already inches away when a wall of blinding light formed right between them, throwing him back.

The radiant light engulfed everything and everyone, overwhelming and all-consuming. No one could see anything, lost and disoriented on the spot. All colours and forms were erased, leaving them all defenceless.

Vidar screamed in agony; the skin on his hands turned into charcoal, and his sword was lost once again.

"Didn't I tell you," Astraea smiled as she observed everyone helpless and at her mercy, "stars can burn. You should have listened."

They could not see her yet, but her sweet voice rang in their ears.

The light was gone in a flash, and the world slowly filled with colour again. Blinking, Vidar was searching for where her voice came from until he finally saw her at the top of the stairs. Right where he was expecting to see her earlier today, walking to the main hall of Valhalla as his bride.

The Goddess of Stars was back and more beautiful than ever before. Her long white hair cascading down to her knees in soft, perfect waves put forth an ethereal glow that he remembered so well. He'd dreamed of her like this, of wrapping those locks in his fist and making her his, again and again.

Vidar devoured her with his eyes, unable to resist his own mate in this form.

Her gleaming dress was made of thin shimmering starlight infused threads, woven into intricate patterns reminiscent of constellations. She was a vision, and he could stare at her forever if not for the stern glare full of hatred she was offering in return. Her eyes were different now from any of her lives. Full galaxies were swirling and storming inside, a reflection of her cosmic gift.

That brought him out of his stupor.

"You drank from the Source," he whispered, and the corners of her lips tilted up in amusement.

"I bathed in it," she admitted without so much as a hint of regret, her grin growing wider. "And I wasn't there alone."

NIKI GASPED, knowing that even her werewolf speed wasn't enough to dodge the demon whose jagged teeth were already too close to her.

She had been careless!

The impact happened so quickly that she had a hard time processing it. Her head hit the floor, and some of the glass pieces on the ground cut her flesh, eliciting a groan from her. Yet still, she didn't feel the teeth piercing her neck and draining her blood. The creature was so heavy she could barely move. It was surprisingly soft, and she wasn't sure what to make of it until the scent of wintergreen hit her nostrils.

"Darius!" The sound came out muffled when she realised that her dragon bear was the one on top of her. She pushed herself from under him and greedily gulped the air when her head finally got out.

He tried to move off her, but something was preventing him, and very quickly, she knew exactly what that was. Dark wings spread above them when she saw a demon with his mouth covered with blood. Pieces of fur and flesh were hanging off its teeth, making Niki feel nauseous.

The vampire's eyes focused on her now, and she tried to wriggle herself out, noticing one of her daggers nearby. The Firstborn stretched her hand but still couldn't reach it.

The deadly creature crawled over the massive bear's body towards her, clearly wishing to prolong its feast.

Niki grew her claws, since now it was her only weapon.

A wave of fire knocked the demon off Bjorn and sent it out of the window, its screeches piercing her ears.

Niki desperately looked around and saw Joran turning away from her to look at Riannon who was still trying to save Fenrir.

"Darius!" Niki whispered. "Please, send me a signal you are still alive."

He was so heavy and she was absolutely stuck underneath him, but all her thoughts were just prayers to have him alive and well again.

He'd saved her.

Even without his vision, he'd sensed she was in danger and sacrificed himself. No one had ever done anything like this for her.

"Darius, please!" She felt tears rolling down her cheeks.

From the corner of her eye, she saw a few more vampires flying their way. They were the last ones.

Niki peered at Joran, but he was busy. Gideon growled, standing before her, ready to take the blow. She knew his presence would not be enough if he was alone.

The creatures charged at him, and he took the first one, pinning it to the ground and breaking its neck. Two more were fast approaching and Niki tried to free herself again.

Sparks of magic flew before her eyes and dispatched the threats. For a second she believed it was Joran, but he was still in the same place.

"Are those the last of them?" Salome walked forward with Forrest following her. The witch held her hands ready for new spells.

"I think so, but keep an eye on the windows," Forrest replied and his eyes locked with Niki's. "This one is alive."

He walked towards her fast and pushed the bear off her, giving her a hand.

"Are you all right, love?" he asked, but Niki only shook her head, crawling towards Darius.

A sob escaped her when she finally saw his state. Forrest nodded understandingly and stepped away. He still had all this mess to deal with.

"Speak to me!" Niki demanded from the bear when he saw him opening and closing his eyes. He was still alive. "Darius, please!"

She hugged him and sobbed into his blood-stained white fur.

"Remember, we have so many plans!" she begged him. "We were going to go away to travel the world! And then we were going to choose the best place to spend our lives together. Darius, I can't do this without you. I need you!"

Two arms wrapped around her and she gasped seeing her bear in his human form again. She hoped that it would make a difference, but blood was gushing out of Bjorn's neck and she tried to apply pressure, knowing far too well that wounds like this didn't heal. Shifters were always going for each other's necks in battle for a reason.

"Strawberry—" His voice came out all broken and gurgling.

"Darius!" Niki cupped his face and gently touched his lips with hers. "Hold on, please. For me! I need you!"

He was silent just for a second, his grip on her weakening with each passing second.

"Straw... berry... I love you so much!" he breathed the words out. "But you don't need me."

"No!" she protested, her tears now spilling onto his face and breaking his heart.

"I've lived longer than I was supposed to." He forced the words out, his breathing laboured. "It was my destiny to die a long time ago. Gods... play with us as if we are toys. Deep inside... they don't care."

She could hear his struggling heartbeat.

"Niki," his fingers dug deeper into her flesh, "whatever you do, don't trust them. Keep away from them. Live your life. Be happy. Do… all the things we wanted to do."

"Darius, I only want to do them with you!" A loud sob escaped her when he could no longer hold her. She was suffocating here, drowning in her own tears. "No, Darius, no! We can fix this."

"You are the only thing I don't regret," Bjorn whispered, and his lips froze after he released his last breath.

"Joran!" Niki forgot about all the familiarities, calling for her Teacher. He was a god! He loved Darius. He had to save him again.

Only, when she turned to look for him, Jormungandr was missing.

"KILL THEM ALL!" Vidar shouted. "Don't you see? They planned it all along! Astraea set up this trap for us, but that doesn't mean we have to lose the war! She may be powerful, but she is just one goddess! We are Asgard!"

"Oh, dear mate," Astraea smirked as a thunderous sound echoed through the air, "haven't you heard me the first time? I am not alone."

She tilted her head, and everyone followed her gaze to see a magnificent creature emerging from a thick fog at the far end of the garden, its hooves crumpling beautiful flowers underneath. A silver mane with teal and lilac highlights glimmered in the setting sun as a pitch-black Nightmare unicorn made its way towards the group.

The formidable divine weapon of the Star Goddess, capable of slaying gods with its deadly horn. The only one of his kind.

"Impossible!" the God of Vengeance muttered. "I got rid of that thing!"

"Now," Astraea's resounding voice took on a commanding tone this time, "I believe Fenrir has just won a battle for the Asgardian throne. Shouldn't we—"

"Do you see?" Vidar interjected again, raising his voice even higher. "This was their plan all along! They are the usurpers! They want to destroy Asgard again! Help me kill that bitch!"

"Oh, no!" Astraea sighed, "I guess the romance is dead."

"If anyone touches a single hair on my daughter's head, they are going to pay with their life!" Selene made the crowd part for her, walking towards the centre of the commotion with her head held high. She wore a silver-plated armour with moons and stars embossed all over it, her pale blue hair in an intricate crown braid.

"See?" Vidar seethed. "The Olympians are behind this too! They betrayed us! They want to end us! We should kill them all while we still have a chance!"

Fenrir groaned, falling to one knee but still holding his spear. His team formed a tighter circle around him just in time because a single fire arrow flew in his direction.

Devoss dissipated it with his nine tails, which appeared and then vanished the second he no longer needed them. His eyes flashed dangerously silver.

"I wouldn't do that if I were you!" the fox warned them. "Or something may fly back at you. Something you wouldn't be able to catch. Trust me."

"Trust you? I am one of those who survived Ragnarok! I've seen what that wolf did to the All-Father! I've seen my children die in that war! And I have no place for traitors and abominations like you in my home!" One of the Asgardians stepped forward and launched his attack. A surge of dark energy lunged at the Wolf God, but Selene blocked it with a crescent shield which materialised in her grasp. The next moment, attacks exploded at every angle. Asgardians clearly tried to use their numbers against the group of rogue deities.

Enraged, Bash summoned lightning from the skies, striking down the ranks of haughty gods. This decision, however, made Asgardians feel threatened even more and drove them to double their effort.

Flashes of magic, smoke and starlight mixed into a picture of pure chaos as gods slaughtered each other.

As Midnight surged through the enemy ranks, scattering them in disarray, Astraea descended the stairs. She wanted to go to Fenrir, but she couldn't see where he was anymore, so she used Devoss' fluffy tails or Kara flying in the sky as her navigation points. Luckily, their gang was noticeable anywhere.

Every Asgardian on her way tried to kill her, and she quickly grew tired of blocking their relentless but useless attacks.

The star magic was both familiar and new to her. She remembered how to wield it, but controlling the intensity of the power swirling inside her was another matter.

A man darted ice shards at her, and she turned them into mist before his eyes, but when he charged at her with a blade, she had no choice but to dissipate him into stardust. Tiny specs of his soul glimmered in the lights of the battle as they flew into the sky, and the goddess swore under her breath. There was no need for all this, but Vidar managed to turn everyone against each other. That man was like poison, destroying everything he touched.

A blast of energy flew straight at her chest, but she managed to disperse it with a mere glance.

Someone's daggers, their divine weapons, followed – destroyed with a wave of a hand.

A stomp of water crushed over her, but she turned it into harmless steam.

They couldn't let her take a step without an attack, and she had had enough of it. She had to get to Fenrir, whatever it cost her.

Astraea felt the fire blade approaching with her skin and turned to glare at Vidar, who tried to kill her from behind like the coward he was.

"This is low even for you!" She arched her brow, mocking him as he paused, caught red-handed.

"It is my destiny to destroy the plague within Asgardian walls!" He still tried to play the hero, even though he was the only one to blame for all this mess.

"Oh, really?" Astraea let out a cold giggle. "Weren't you the one who forced me here in the first place?"

"I should have killed you all centuries ago!" Vidar's every word was laced with venom.

"Yes, you really should have," she agreed, sparks of magic tingling at the tips of her fingers, ready to burst any moment.

"Doesn't matter!" Her mate gritted his teeth, taking a battle stance. "You are all going to die today, anyway!"

"Interesting…" Her lips curled. "The stars tell me otherwise. Don't forget, Vidar, everything and everyone is made of stars. Even gods. Even you."

He lunged at his mate, but one glance of hers was enough to freeze him in the air, unable to move or breathe. She was in full control now, and he had never expected her to take a grasp of it all so fast.

He underestimated her, and now he was going to pay for it.

She felt it now – her raw power, which she had never had access to before. She could feel them all, every person on that battlefield. She could differentiate enemies from foes. She knew which stars took part in forming their bodies, how old they were and what happened to them. She could awaken those elements and submit them to her will.

That was the real power of the Star Goddess.

The only one she couldn't sense right now was Fenrir, which made her anxious. She had to move faster.

Astraea carelessly waved her hand, and Vidar's arm twisted at an unnatural angle, eliciting a loud scream from the God of Vengeance as his bones cracked.

"You wanted the power of the stars for yourself?" she taunted him. "I'll give you a taste. Be careful what you wish for, Vidar. Gods of Stars are not made. You have to be born this way!"

"Kill her!" he shouted right before she broke his leg, and a few of his remaining warriors charged at her with their divine weapons, surprising her by still following orders of that pathetic excuse of a deity.

Tired of it all, Astraea sucked in a sharp breath and raised her hands to the sky to channel more energy.

They were not listening to reason, so she couldn't waste her time on them anymore. Deep inside, her worry for Fenrir was growing.

Starlight magic laced around her fingers, forming and shaping into something bigger until a blazing inferno erupted from her palms, engulfing everything around in mere seconds. It felt like a flash, but everyone who pointed their swords at her friends dispersed into divine dust before they even realised what was happening.

There was no stopping the Starfire. Their last screams echoed through the air, alerting the survivors to put their weapons down and admit defeat. The all-consuming power swept through the space, paying attention to everyone on that battlefield. It burned the enemies, shattering their forces and scattering their ashes in the wind while sparing the rest from harm.

Magnus and his warriors froze on their spots when the unbearable glow reached them. Unable to see anything, they waited for their destiny to unfold. The screams of others were terrifying. Gods were dying like flies, and no one had the power strong enough to fight the Star Goddess. They simply were not ready for this. It was as if the Source itself helped her awaken her full potential, and Magnus thought maybe it was for the best. If recent events proved anything, it was the fact they needed a cleanse within their ranks.

Magnus couldn't be sure what the Starfire would do to him and his men when it touched their skin like a silk feather. The light brush radiated heat, ready to burn them to ashes, but gradually, the powerful presence left them alone, allowing them to breathe again.

"Kneel," the son of Thor ordered his soldiers, and they followed his lead. Magnus knew a warning when he saw one. So he unsheathed his sword and put it on the ground before him, standing on one knee next to it to demonstrate his acceptance and respect for the new ruler of Asgard, who had just spared their lives.

Astraea exhaled heavily and opened her eyes, done with the fight. So many emotions ran through her. She took part in many battles but had never possessed a power like this before. For a second there, she felt invincible.

Vidar was still hanging in the air before her, like a limp doll, exactly where she wanted him. New burns scorched his skin, and he stopped struggling.

"Just admit it," he said in a hoarse, broken voice. "You can't find it in you to kill me. After all, we are mates!"

She dropped him to the ground, and he chuckled darkly, trying to get up.

"I knew it!" he let out a nervous laugh. "You can't find it in you to kill me! You—"

A glowing purple and teal horn protruded from his chest as shock coursed through Vidar, leaving him unable to make any sounds as he processed what happened. He touched the blood gushing out of him with trembling hands, yet Midnight lifted his head together with the body of the helpless God of Vengeance, and then he threw him forcefully to the ground, finishing the dirty work for his creator.

Astraea watched her mate bleed out his divinity and knew that this would be a fatal wound. Vidar was done, but that did not bring her joy. She turned on her heels and searched for Fenrir, leaving her past tormentor behind.

Her heart was racing in her chest, but when she noticed a familiar tall figure behind Warg and Kara, she sprinted towards him.

Fenrir caught her in his arms effortlessly, spinning and pressing her as close towards his chest as he could.

"You did it," he whispered. "Astrea, you did it. I knew you could do it."

"*We* did it, Fenrir," she corrected, lifting her head to lock their eyes.

"You are as beautiful as the first day I laid my eyes on you." He smiled at her, but his smile did not reach his eyes, and she sensed that something was off. Why was he sad when everything played out so well for them?

They were in Asgard at last and had just won their battle, but something was off—something really important.

She distanced herself from her beloved, scanning him up and down. Fenrir was perfect – not a hair in the wrong place. His tunic had no creases, and the golden embroidery on it was like the one he wore the first time they met.

His eyes were the only thing giving away the pain that stormed inside him.

"What happened?" She was surprised to hear her own voice. It sounded so foreign now. "Fenrir!" She grasped him, nails digging into his flesh through the fabric. The looming sense of dread was overwhelming.

It did not help that everyone was silent. Their friends were not celebrating the victory. They already knew something she didn't.

Only now, she noticed a young woman standing behind her favourite Wolf God. The girl looked perfect, with radiating skin and raven black hair flowing down her slender shoulders. However, she tilted her head, and Astraea was taken aback when she saw the second half of her face – a landscape of scars and darkening grey skin. It was the face of the monster from legends. Her left eye was glowing white and missed the iris. Her lips on that half were black, forsaking their vibrant red colour.

Astraea knew who stood before her, and so did everyone else.

Hel, the Goddess of Death and the ruler of the Underworld.

"No," Astraea whispered, shaking her head. She must have come for the ones Astraea dispersed. Many men fell here today.

Then again, those deities would not be going to the Underworld. Their essence and divinity returned to the Source. Other than that, there was nothing left of them. Hel, however, was collecting souls.

"Astraea, it's all right." Fenrir placed his arms on her shoulders, drawing soothing circles with his thumbs. "We won. You are alive, and... I couldn't have asked for more."

"No!" she repeated, firmer this time, and glared at his sister, repeating, "No! You can't take him!"

"I wish I didn't have to." Hel offered her a sad smile. "I dreamed of a different destiny for you two, but he didn't return to the mortal realm in time. Now, he doesn't belong here or there. My brother belongs with me."

"No!" Tears streamed out of Astraea's eyes, and she wiped them angrily. She tried to push Fenrir away and stood before him to ensure the Goddess of Death kept her distance. "I will not let you take him!"

"No offence, but it's not for you to decide," Hel replied with the kind of confidence that let everyone know she was not used to objections. The sky darkened behind her, the last rays of sunshine disappearing.

Astrea flexed her fingers, and stars shone brightly, illuminating them all.

"You are a powerful goddess," Hel admitted. "And I have seen and enjoyed your wrath, but there are things even gods can't do. After all, we are all servants of the powers we were given. I can't change that, and neither can you."

"We overcame destiny before!" Astrea insisted. "We will do it again. You are not taking him! If you so much as try, you will have to fight me, and I swear that I—"

"Astrea," Fenrir took her hand and pulled her into his chest, kissing the top of her hand. "No, Astrea, I don't want you to fight. It's okay. It's fine!"

"No!" She hit his chest with her fist. Nothing here was fine. Her body contorted with a sob she had suppressed for so long. "I told you not to come here! I told you not to risk it! Why did you, Fenrir! Why?"

He closed her in his embrace, kissing her hair again and again.

"I love you so much. We deserve our time together! I can't—I can't lose you like this again." She clenched his tunic, inhaled his scent, looked into his dreamy eyes and then tucked her face back into his massive chest. Nothing seemed enough. Not when each moment was their last.

Her heart became an empty void, her soul aching. She could never recover from this.

"My love," Fenrir whispered, peppering her with kisses. "How I wish we had more time, but even like this, it was all worth it. Each fleeting moment with you—each second we spend together. I wouldn't change anything. You gave my life a purpose, you filled an empty heart with love, you were my everything! During the endless night, you were always my guiding star. All my life, I was waiting for you to appear—"

"Fenrir!" She grasped him tighter, unwilling to let go.

"We need to go," Hel urged them, and Astraea looked around, searching for support. Devoss averted his gaze, and Bash helplessly shrugged his shoulders, turning away. Selene stepped forward, but looking at her expression, Astraea knew she couldn't help them either.

"I am sure Hel will allow you to visit sometimes," her mother said. "Even if for a little, it's better than nothing."

"No!" Astrea said firmly, and Midnight came to her side, lowering his horn as a sign that he was ready to fight for her. "We didn't go through so much to not end up together!"

"Are you sure you want to fight me?" Hel formed dark energy around her hands, taking a battle stance.

Astrea did the same with her Star Fire when an ugly cackle interrupted them.

"I did it!" Vidar chuckled painfully on the ground, still bleeding his divine essence from his wound. "I was destined to kill Fenrir after all. I was destined to keep you apart! I succeeded!"

Hel turned with her dead side towards him, her empty eye gleaming menacingly.

"I don't know what you are so happy about," the Goddess of Death sneered. "Now you get to spend eternity in my Kingdom, where my main task is to devise the best punishment for you. I am currently choosing between Fenrir's lowest slave or a giant's pet on a leash. And that's just for the first century or two. I haven't gotten souls worthy of punishment for a while. I am a bit rusty!"

"Take him and leave Fenrir here!" Astraea suggested desperately. "This would be the worst punishment for him."

"I wish I could. I really do." Hel sighed. "But I have no choice."

"Then neither do I," Astraea blinked the tears away, and the Star Fire on her wrists intensified.

The two women were about to clash when two strong hands wrapped around Astraea's waist, pulling her back.

"Dragonfly, stop!"

JORAN LOOKED at Fenrir's lifeless body as Riannon struck him with bolts of lightning again and again, trying to restart his heart. He blocked out the entire world and the fighting to listen, too, hoping for that rhythm more than he hoped to return to Asgard.

"Come on, brother," he muttered under his breath. "You can't die like that! Not on a carpet in some… room! You were supposed to have a glorious return to Asgard, remember?"

Riannon charged his sibling again, his back arching as if he could feel something, but the next moment, Fenrir fell back to the floor, breathless and still.

"Again!" Joran ordered, and the Queen of the Western Kingdom gave him a stern glance.

"There is no use—" she said, pursing her lips.

"Do it again! Harder!" he ordered. "He is not a mortal. He needs more than that to—"

"Do you want me to fry him?" The woman shook her head, but the electricity was already playing between his fingers.

"If you don't save him, I will rip your head off!" the Serpent promised, and Gideon's growl followed immediately as the Lycan appeared next to his wife, baring his teeth at the deity.

"The worst thing you could do to me, you have already done," Riannon replied dryly, stunning him. As far as he remembered, he did nothing to her. Or at least he didn't do much.

"He is the love of your sister's life!" The Serpent tried to change his approach. He could definitely guilt-trip her into saving his brother.

"Do you think I don't know that?" She glared at him with hatred. "I like him! We all owe him! My husband was blessed by him! If I could, I would have brought him back, but, of the two of us, I am not the one who wields such power!"

His lips parted as he tried to process what she was saying. He had no power to bring the dead to life, either. At least not anymore. He'd wasted that bead on Bjorn months ago.

"What are you—" He stopped, finally getting what the she-wolf was trying to tell him.

Joran fell to his knees, looking at Fenrir's lifeless face.

If he was really dead, then it was all over. Hel would take him to the Underworld, and that would be where he would spend the rest of his existence. He would not be a god again. He would be just another soul... At best, Kara would allow him to enter the halls of Valhalla, but he and Astraea would never have the life they dreamed of.

The dead couldn't experience life...

Jormungandr closed his eyes, exhaling heavily and trying to sense his way back home. To his surprise, the way to Asgard was clear for him for the first time since Ragnarok.

A bitter chuckle escaped him. Fenrir succeeded and defeated Vidar.

Only why did it have to end this way? His brother deserved so much better.

"You told me once you saw my ending." Joran opened his eyes and looked at the Queen of the Western Kingdom, who was waiting patiently next to Fenrir's dead body. "What was it?"

"If you're asking me this, you already know the answer," she replied, confirming his suspicions.

She did not seek revenge on him because destiny had already taken care of it.

Joran had seconds to make the decision, so he looked around, his eyes drawn to Niki holding Bjorn in her arms. The girl's face was stained with tears as she rocked back and forth, whispering something to the bear's ear. They had fallen in love indeed... just like he wanted them to.

But he did not sense life in Bjorn anymore. That battle was lost.

Forrest and the witch stood over them, trying to console Niki, but Joran knew it wouldn't be this easy.

He had lost Bjorn again. He'd lost Astrea. He couldn't lose Fenrir, too.

He was okay with his brother hating him, but he did not want to imagine him in the Underworld. Just as he did not want to see Astrea tortured by the separation.

"Well played, witch!" He smiled at Riannon, and for the first time, the woman had nothing to retort. "Here, my gift to you. I know you will use it wisely."

He took a few portal beads off his bracelet and handed the rest to her. She hesitated before accepting it, but the gift was too valuable to reject it.

"I know you will use these wisely," he added, standing up and crushing the beads in his palm to activate them. A huge glowing portal to Asgard opened up before him. "See? I'm not that bad!" He winked at Riannon and stepped inside before he could hear her reply, walking out back into his home.

It was strange walking in Asgard again. Not to mention that it was only the second time he'd done it without sneaking around.

The portal took him to his siblings, and his heart clenched, seeing Astraea ready to fight his sister for Fenrir. If the Goddess of Stars and the Goddess of Death had a fight, it would result in another Ragnarok and they were still dealing with the consequences of the first one. She was in so much pain, so desperate... worse than when he'd chained her in the silver pit.

Fenrir tried to reassure her, ready to sacrifice himself as always. How did someone with such a good heart end up being born into their scheming family?

His brother noticed him first, and Joran gave him a sad, apologetic smile. Astraea was about to lunge at Hel, but Jormungandr caught her while his siblings watched him.

"Dragonfly, stop," he whispered. "This is not the solution!"

"Let go of me!" she yelled at him, realising who it was and trying to elbow him. Her star magic almost burned his skin when he added quickly, "I have a real solution! Just let me help you with this for once."

She stopped fighting him. Astraea was too desperate, ready to do anything. He had seen and used many people in such a state to recognise this look.

"Remember you once told me that I don't know what love is?" he reminded her, and she remained silent. "I finally know. I love you, Astrea. A lot. I loved Bjorn as if he was my son. I love my children even though I haven't seen them for centuries."

Her chest was heaving. She absolutely did not see where he was going with it.

"But most of all I love my brother," the Serpent confessed. "The one and only man who has never failed me. Not really. The one who tried to help me and whom I betrayed in the worst ways. I love you both in my own sick way, and I know you deserve your lifetime together. I want you to have it."

"What are you—" Fenrir stared at him, bewildered.

"Take my divinity," Joran suggested. "And you, Hel, take my life instead of Fenrir's."

"For the love of all things!" The Goddess of Death rubbed the bridge of her nose. "That's not how it works!"

"Then we'll make it work!" Joran pushed Astraea into his brother's arms and walked towards his sister. "Just think about it, Hel. This is what our family does. It's in our blood! One last trick. The universe needs to receive a god, and here I am. We have the same blood, the same lineage, and the same amount of divine power. The replacement will not affect the balance. It's just perfect!"

"Oh, Jor!" She sighed and looked at Fenrir, who wrapped his arms around Astraea. That woman would fight for him until she destroyed the Underworld and got him out. Maybe it was for the best.

"May I also add that if you agree to this, you will get the funnier and more handsome brother? I bet you get bored ruling the Underworld alone, and the righteous Baldur can hardly make you laugh!"

Hel rolled her eyes.

"Besides," Joran added quickly, "if someone can get it all, it's you. You were thrown down there and prevented from living your life. You never got a proper shot. Neither did Fenrir. And although we can't free you, we can—"

"Free him," Hel agreed. She knew full well Fenrir spent years serving Odin just for the chance to have them reunited. This was more than anyone else had ever done for her, and she was grateful to have a sibling like that.

"Jor," Fenrir called his brother, and the Serpent walked towards him and Astraea. "You really don't have to."

"I really do," the Serpent disagreed and hugged them both tightly, placing his forehead on Fenrir's. "Take care of each other, okay?"

"We will," Astraea promised, tears welling in her eyes again. She noticed sparks flying from Joran into the sky, meaning he was already dying slowly, committing his sacrifice for them.

She hugged him tightly, still clenching Fenrir with her free hand just in case. She used to think of her Teacher as a monster, but now she wasn't so sure about that anymore. Everything he did had paid off in the end and helped them to get here. She still couldn't believe he was actually doing this. Maybe she'd been wrong about him all along.

"Astrea, I will remember our kiss even in the afterlife," Joran mumbled, his lips grazing over her ear.

"Asshole!" Fenrir growled, feeling his brother's divinity and immortality slipping through the cells of his new body.

"Always." Joran smiled through tears, holding them both tightly.

"Thank you," Astraea whispered, grasping him tighter, when she realised he was already gone and only specs of his divine essence were flying around them. She caught a fistful of the gleaming dust, and she could not find it in her to let it go with the rest, keeping this little reminder of her Teacher for herself.

Fenrir wrapped his arms around Astraea, not willing to let go. Just a few seconds ago, he was ready to leave her to prevent the love of his life from fighting his sister. He'd accepted his loss and now he needed time to believe that this was actually happening.

Their enemies were dead, and they had eternity, together.

They stood like that for a while, no one daring to disturb them.

Vidar was still slowly dying on the ground when Bash found him.

"I can offer you a deal," the God of Vengeance hissed. "I can—"

"The only thing I need from you, I can get myself," Bash snorted and sent a lightning his way, finishing him off. Years of experience taught him to get rid of a problem at once.

Devoss walked towards Magnus to give him a few orders from the new rulers and although the latter did not seem too happy about one particular fox feeling comfortable in this realm, he obeyed, knowing Astraea trusted these people.

Midnight slowly walked to the couple that were still afraid to move and find out it was all a dream. Slowly, he nudged them with his muzzle, and they finally got distracted, peering at him.

"How did you …?" Fenrir had no words.

"When I jumped into the Source, I had Midnight's horn with me. We got out of it together," she explained with a grin. "And look at this!" She scratched behind the Nightmare's ear, and two wide wings materialised on his back. "He got an upgrade!"

"That thing can fly now?" Fenrir whistled.

"Well, not yet," Astraea admitted, "or we would have used it in the fight, but we are working on it."

"You are really something, do you know that?" He brushed his palm over her cheek.

"I know," she giggled. "You are a lucky man!"

"The luckiest man in the world!" Fenrir pulled her closer and crashed his lips into hers in a greedy kiss. The world around them faded away, leaving all their troubles behind.

For the first time, they didn't have to count minutes and seconds together. They had all the time in the world.

"So, what now?" Astraea broke the kiss to breathe in.

"Now?" Fenrir hugged her and turned to look at the nighttime Asgard, which would wake up to a new ruling dynasty in the morning. "Now, we live, Astraea."

73. EPILOGUE I

*H*e watched the love of his life brush her delicate fingers over the flower they grew together the other day and smiled when the petals emanated a soft glow, responding to the touch of a goddess. Astraea smiled and peered at him, catching his gaze.

"You could help, you know." She arched her brow at him.

"If I come closer to you, no more work will be done today," he promised, leaning against the glowing willow. His lips curled when he noticed the rosy tint on her cheeks.

"You could *help, you know*," she taunted him, repeating the same words with a completely different tone and meaning. A growl rumbled through Fenrir's chest, and she giggled, picking up the hem of her long silvery-white dress and charging into the garden maze.

He chased her, allowing her to think she'd escaped just for a few minutes, when, in fact, he knew exactly where she was the whole time. Her sweet scent and loud heartbeat told him everything he needed to know, so when he appeared out of nowhere and lifted her up in his arms, the scream of surprise was real, causing him to chuckle, spinning them until he fell into a flower bed with Astraea on top.

"I love you so much, wife." He grinned at her.

"Right back at you, husband." She brushed her lips over his, light like a feather, and immediately, he rolled them so that her glowing hair was scattered around the flowers and grass, and he was the one towering over her.

Their private ceremony happened just days ago, but it still felt surreal. Finally, no one could object to them being together.

"Asgard be damned, I missed you!" He couldn't take his gaze off her. Their eyes locked, electricity crackling between them.

"Then do something about it." She slid her hand under his shirt, getting a low, hungry snarl from him. The novelty of their reunion hadn't worn off yet, so they still couldn't imagine staying apart for long.

"That's exactly what I plan to do." Fenrir chuckled and leaned down to nip at her delicate neck, grazing his canines over her skin and parting her thighs at the same time. He nestled between them, sliding his hand up her leg and lifting her skirt. The Alpha God was already painfully hard for her, and just their clothes separated them from being one.

He would never get enough of this. He would never get enough of *her*.

"This is probably not the best place," she panted as the sweet scent of her arousal reached his nostrils.

"Too late," Fenrir muttered under his breath and crashed his lips over hers, unable to control himself anymore. A part of him was still afraid that it was a dream. What if he woke up, and she wasn't there?

His hand moved up her torso, grasping the fullness of her breast and kneading it greedily.

"You are mine," he growled into her ear, sliding his tongue down her neck.

"Yes!" Astraea breathed out, ripping buttons off his shirt because she couldn't wait anymore either. She reached for his belt, trying to unbuckle it, but Fenrir caught her wrist, then added her other to it and pinned them both above her head.

"Hasty little goddess," he chuckled, sliding his hand up her thigh and hooking her silk underwear with his fingers to move it aside. "Tsk! Didn't I tell you that you didn't need these anymore?"

"Why don't you rip them off me, then?" she taunted, licking her lips, and he sucked in a sharp breath, knowing she was playing with him.

"All in due time, Menace," he promised, drawing his finger across her lips to feel her wetness. She was so ready for him, so eager, but he wanted to see her scream first, so he drew a circle over her sensitive bud and watched her tremble.

"Fen…rir!" She already had trouble forming words.

"I know, my love." He offered a devilish smirk as he picked up speed, knowing exactly the kind of friction she loved. His goddess arched her back, and he inserted a digit in her, finding the little ridged spot inside that always brought her over the edge.

On instinct, Astraea tried to squeeze her thighs back together, but he held her in place until a loud moan escaped his wife when pleasure rippled through her body in powerful waves.

She tried to catch her breath when he pulled her dress down and off her shoulders, returning his attention to her breasts. Fenrir tugged a hard nipple between his fingers while inhaling the other, her sweet scent enveloping him.

"Fenrir," she called to him, and he stopped everything to lock eyes with her.

"Yes?"

"I love you so much!" Astraea confessed, eyes glistening with tears that she desperately tried to hold back. "If I ever had to lose you again, I wouldn't be able to take it."

"You will never know that loss again," he promised. "Until the last star fades from the sky, you and I will hold our hands together in our Glowing Garden."

She smiled, and he brushed his palm over her cheek.

"No more tears." He gave her a light kiss. "Not when we got to have our happy ending."

"Fine." She smiled and pushed him off, taking him by surprise and straddling him before he had time to object. Her nimble fingers freed his cock, and she stroked his length up and down a few times until she lined it at her entrance.

"Menace," Fenrir grunted, giving her all the control as she sunk onto him inch by inch. He grasped her waist to give her support and cupped one of her exposed breasts with his free hand.

Slowly, she rose again, torturing him, and then slammed back, eliciting a growl from him.

"Two can play this game." She rose again, and this time, he grasped her bottom, pushing her down and meeting her movement with his hips. Astraea threw her head back, unable to suppress a moan.

"You are so right about that," Fenrir grunted as they repeated it over and over.

She rode him slowly at first, breasts bouncing up and down, the light from the glowing plants around reflecting on her skin covered with beads of sweat. However, soon, he placed his large palms on her bottom, guiding her and rocking his hips to intensify their pleasure.

Astraea felt like she was soaring, so close to the edge she lost her rhythm, but Fenrir took it upon himself to continue the pace. He held her tight as he plunged into her again and again, her inner muscles clenching around him so tight he could only growl in response.

"Fenrir!" She exploded.

"Divine!" he snarled as he watched her come undone on top of him and stopped before he reached his peak, sitting up and still holding her in his arms as she needed rest. He was not done with her yet.

She draped her arms around him, trying to calm her racing heart as he drew soothing circles on her back.

"Why did you stop?" she asked, slightly confused.

"I want to ask you something," the wolf confessed.

"What is it?" The Goddess of Stars furrowed her brows, gazing at him through her lashes.

"Do you remember… last time in the mortal realm… you wanted me to—"

He stopped talking. *She'd just blurted it out in the heat of the moment and never mentioned it again. Maybe she'd changed her mind.* The last thing he wanted was to push her into doing something she did not want.

"I asked you to mark me." She nodded in understanding, her cheeks getting a more vibrant tint.

"If you've changed the way you feel about it," he started, but she interjected.

"I didn't. Fenrir, I wanted you to ask me, too." Her confession made him the happiest man alive. As if it was possible to be happier.

"Astraea." He straightened his back, trying to ignore the fact that he was still painfully hard and inside her clenching walls. "Would you—I want—I want to mark you. I want the whole world to see that you belong to me, but also, at the same time, I want you to mark me too, so that the whole world can see who claimed me."

"I thought you'd never ask!" she giggled and moved her thighs, causing him to close his eyes from the pleasure. He dug his fingers into her hair, pulling it back and making her arch her back for him, allowing full access to her beautiful neck.

Carefully and slowly, he brushed his lips over her collarbone, tasting it as Astraea dug her nails into his flesh. He started moving his hips, slamming his cock into her to the hilt. She moaned his name each time until she began screaming it, losing herself in all the sensations. They both were on the edge when he pierced her skin with his canines, unable to wait any longer. At the same time, she broke his skin with her nails, releasing her star magic inside. They both grunted, riding their release and allowing their marks to do their work.

Now Fenrir pounded into her as if there was no tomorrow, taking his pleasure as he watched another earth-shattering release cascade through his wife. His eyes shut closed when he felt her centre exploding and clenching around him so tight that his seed spilled inside, to the last drop, in just a few thrusts.

Astraea collapsed against his chest, and he slowly lay back on the grass, wrapping his arms around her, wishing to prolong this moment forever.

They stayed like this for quite some time, listening to each other's heartbeats and inhaling their mixed scent. Until a soft glow made them both open their eyes.

Astraea felt her marking spot tingling and touched it with the tips of her fingers.

"What does it look like?" she asked.

They weren't werewolves or Lycans, and now, only one of them was technically a wolf, so they marked each other with their divine powers, each choosing the shape and pattern for the other.

"It's a golden dragonfly surrounded by silver stars." He kissed the still sore flesh and smiled at her. "The first dragonfly you had gave us this chance. I thought... you would like a reminder of it."

"I love it!" She pulled him closer for a kiss and then told him, "Yours is a black wolf covered in flames with a star on his forehead. I wasn't sure about the star, but—"

"Are you kidding me?" he chuckled. "You could draw a whole constellation on me, and I would wear it with pride."

He found her lips again, and they both forgot how to breathe as he rolled her back to the flowers and towered over her, finally ripping off her underwear and preparing for the next round.

"Children, I hope you are decent." Selene's voice made Fenrir groan, his hands frozen somewhere in the middle of Astraea's thigh under her dress.

"If we pretend we didn't hear her, she would walk away." He locked eyes with his wife, who only giggled into the crook of his neck in response.

"It's time! Everyone is waiting for you!" the Moon Goddess insisted.

"I think I liked it more when she wasn't speaking to me," the Wolf God grunted, rolling his eyes.

"Just remember, she is leaving after the coronation," Astraea hissed, biting her lip and trying to hold back a laugh.

In the meantime, Selene grew impatient.

"The rituals won't perform themselves, and without them, Asgard will never recognise you as their King and Queen. Now, you may have gotten away with your private wedding, but this—"

"We are done here, Mother." Astraea walked out from behind thick bushes, glowing petals still entangled in her long hair and cheeks flushed. Fenrir followed her, shoving her torn lacy underwear into his pocket.

The Moon Goddess politely did not comment on any of that.

"I am taking Astraea, and Magnus will help you prepare," she informed them. "There is still so much to be done today."

"Is there a need to separate us?" Fenrir's jaw tightened. "It's not like it's a wedding, and I am not allowed to see the bride."

"No, but you still have different things to prepare and trust me, you can live a few hours without each other."

"Debatable," Fenrir grunted under his breath.

"I'll see you soon." Astraea stood on the tips of her toes and gave him a little kiss on the cheek. Two massive hands wrapped around her waist, pressing her against him as he covered her lips with his in a long, possessive kiss. Breaths mingled, fingers tangled in each other's hair. They were ready to forget about the whole world…

Until Selene cleared her throat loudly, bringing them back to reality from their bliss.

"Just a couple of hours, and you can do whatever you want," she insisted. "A few hours that would help you earn the respect of your people. Show them that not much is changing. Asgard is under new rulership, but they have nothing to fear."

"We will think about it, won't we?" Astraea lightly elbowed her husband.

"Sure." Fenrir rolled his eyes, remembering how much he hated politics.

After a few more minutes of passionate goodbyes, the Moon Goddess was finally able to drag her daughter away from her beloved.

"You two are like children with new toys," she complained.

"We value every minute together," Astraea corrected. "And fear spending any moment apart. We've lost too much time as it is."

"I know, and I am so sorry for my part in it. I just hope to earn your forgiveness one day."

"You are doing all the right things." Astraea smiled. "It's just… it will not happen in one day. But we appreciate your help during the fight and now. I know you are trying, Mother."

A shiver shot through Selene's body. She didn't think she would hear that word again, yet her daughter turned out to be kinder than she expected.

"I have something for you." The Moon Goddess stretched her gloved hand out and produced a small shining ball of energy.

"What is thi—" Astrea stopped talking because she recognised that aura. Her eyes darted back to her parent, and Selene's lips curled slightly.

"It took me a while to get her out of the Source, but the fragments were still there. I pieced them back together, and although she will still need a few years of healing, she is alive."

"Nova!" Astraea breathed out in relief, accepting the ball of magic.

Losing her wolf left a hollow in her soul, and she was so happy that she had something to fill it with.

Her wolf survived!

"Thank you!" The Goddess of Stars threw herself into her mother's arms, hugging her for the first time since... centuries ago. "Thank you so much for this!"

"Anytime, my sweet girl." The Moon Goddess tried to blink away the tears that threatened to escape her, too afraid to ruin the moment.

Astraea knelt and added a speck of her divine power to the ball of energy, slowly adding more and more until a beautiful glowing wolf looked at her from the grass.

"Nova!" She beamed at her old friend, who recognised her immediately and jumped into her arms. The goddess tucked her face into the soft silver fur, still not quite believing that it was real.

"In a decade or two, she will be ready to become someone's wolf again," Selene explained, "but for now, all she needs is your love and good care."

"And she will always have both." Astraea stroked her wolf's head, trying to mind link her and only hearing silence in response.

"Nova, do you hear me?" she asked again and again.

The wolf tilted her head in response as if she didn't understand what she was doing.

"Nova?" Astraea tried again, disappointed that their connection was lost.

"Don't worry, my girl," she hugged her wolf tighter, "you will stay with me, and I will take good care of you. Just like you did for me all these years. And when the time comes, I will pick the best human for you."

"I think I've earned the right to pick my human for myself. Fair and square," Nova's sarcastic voice rang in her head.

"Nova!" Astraea was happy, angry and shocked at the same time. "Don't you ever do that!"

"Oh, come on!" her wolf chuckled. "I wanted to see you cry for me. I earned that too, don't you think?"

"You—" She was about to scold her when love overwhelmed everything else, and she simply placed her forehead on her wolf's, closing her eyes and enjoying the return of her closest friend. *"Welcome home, Nova!"*

"We need to go," Selene urged them after a few minutes. "You still have a lot to prepare before the coronation."

Astraea hated that their reunion was disrupted, but Nova spoke up in her mother's defence.

"Just so that you know, she risked her life getting me out," the wolf confessed. *"Do you see her wearing gloves now? It's because her hands were badly burnt in the process. The scars will probably never heal because the Source itself gave them to her."*

The Moon Goddess caught her gaze and placed her hands into the pockets of her long, modern gown.

"Thank you for this, Mother." Astraea stood up and gave Selene another hug.

This time, it wasn't rushed or due to heightened emotions. This time, it was a choice, and at first, the Moon Goddess was so shocked that she froze in her daughter's embrace.

However, in just a few seconds, her arms wrapped tightly around the starry goddess' frame.

"Of course," Selene whispered. "I'll do whatever you need to be happy."

74. EPILOGUE II

"They still hate me, don't they?" Fenrir asked his wife as they were about to enter the main Hall of Asgard. As Asgardian traditions required, they both wore white and gold today, which made the wolf slightly uncomfortable. The fur on his cape added to his misery.

"Of course not!" Astraea looked into his eyes, a slight curl to her lips. "If it makes you feel any better, they hate both of us!"

"We can still abandon them and run away to the mortal realm," the wolf reminded her.

"They will ruin it within a century," she countered.

"Right…" Fenrir exhaled loudly. "So, ruling Asgard it is."

He laced his fingers with his wife's even though, according to customs, he was supposed to enter the ceremonial hall first, and she was to follow him.

"Together," he said, and Astraea smiled back at him.

"Together," she agreed, beaming at him.

The massive doors opened before them, and they started walking. Gasps rippled through the crowds who were there to witness the coronation. Before today, the supreme ruler of Asgard was always a man. Both Odin and Vidar allowed no one to walk next to them at official ceremonies.

This was the first message they were sending to their people as a couple: They would rule together, share the throne and the responsibilities equally, and support each other no matter what.

Regardless of what anyone thought about it.

The future King and Queen continued their steady stride, their gazes locked ahead as the hall was bathed in an ethereal light that streamed through tall, stained-glass windows. The light danced upon marble floors, casting hues of red, blue and gold and reflecting off Astraea's glowing hair and the golden elements of Fenrir's armour. The golden embroidery on their long brocade capes matched each other perfectly, telling their story of love, loss, pain, and reunion.

The ancient Asgardian music played, intertwined with the guests' whispers. However, once they reached the top of the steps on which two tall, intricate golden thrones stood and turned to face the crowd, everything and everyone went quiet.

Their regal presence commanded attention, and no one could deny it.

Selene and Magnus stepped to stand by their sides with Devoss and Kara next to them, holding the crowns.

"Today, we finally unite our realms." Magnus spoke in a voice that wouldn't tolerate any objections. "Fenrir, son of Loki, and his wife Astraea, daughter of Selene, accept the responsibility of ruling the divine realm as one."

"You are here to witness the momentous occasion, the beginning of the New Divine Era," the Moon Goddess added and turned to the royal couple. "It is with great pride and honour that we bestow upon you this sacred responsibility and ask you to lead us justly, wisely, and selflessly."

Fenrir and Astrea knelt, still holding hands, and lowered their heads. Magnus stepped behind Fenrir.

"I, Magnus, son of Thor and grandson of Odin, pronounce you, Fenrir, son of Loki, the new King and ruler of New Asgard. Do you accept the honour and the responsibility?"

"Yes," the wolf responded.

"I, Selene, the Goddess of the Moon, daughter of Hyperion and Theia, pronounce you, Astraea, my daughter, the new Queen and ruler of New Asgard. Do you accept the responsibility?"

"Yes," the Goddess of Stars answered firmly.

"Do you promise to put the needs of your people before your own, to rule with wisdom and fairness, to protect the sacred lands standing as a shield against any threat?" Magnus asked.

"We do," both replied in unison.

"Do you swear to seek knowledge and wisdom, continuously striving to grow and improve as leaders?" Selene's voice sounded majestic.

"We do." Again, Fenrir and Astrea did not hesitate.

"Do you promise to defend the Source and the balance between realms no matter the challenge?"

"We do." The couple stole a glance at each other.

"Then, we proclaim you the King and the Queen of Asgard," the God of Strength announced loudly, his voice echoing through the hall as others didn't even dare to breathe.

"Rule with honour, strength and dignity," Selene finished, and they both placed the crowns on the new King and Queen of New Asgard.

Fenrir stood first, then helped his wife to rise gracefully, and as they stood together, all those present knelt, acknowledging their royal status and bowing their heads in respect.

Fenrir inhaled sharply, knowing it was now time for the part he dreaded the most.

"I know you never wanted to see me as your ruler." His words made everyone tense and wary. They still expected consequences for the past, but the new King only laced his fingers with his wife's and smiled at her. "I never wanted to be a King either, but destiny kept bringing me here, so I am not the one to deny it anymore. If anyone was born to rule, it was my wife, Astraea. She has a rare moral compass inside that guides her and a strong desire to make any world she lives in better. As for me, I have the utmost desire to protect her and anything she values. Luckily for you, that now includes you too."

"We promise to honour the important traditions built through the centuries of our existence." Astraea took the lead. "But at the same time, we both recognise that change is required to move forward. Mistakes were made, and a looming threat is still upon us. We will face it together as the gods we were always supposed to be. We were always meant to keep the balance and to protect the mortals when they needed it. This is the course we will now be pursuing. So that when new legends of us are formed, we are proud of the tales attributed to our names."

"We ask you to join us on this course," Fenrir finished and glared around the room. He expected it to be quiet as always and was ready to intimidate them into submission if he had to because, clearly, there wouldn't be any other choice with haughty gods.

"I pledge my loyalty and trust in your reign," Magnus and Bash said in unison, startling him. Astraea squeezed his fingers, reminding him people still looked at him.

"I pledge my loyalty and trust in your reign," Kara, Warg and Devoss followed.

He nodded regally, thanking them for their support and ready to wrap this up, when suddenly…

"I pledge my loyalty and trust in your reign!"

"I pledge my loyalty and trust in your reign!"

"I pledge my loyalty and trust in your reign!"

God after god, they all bowed their heads and touched their hearts again, acknowledging him and his Queen on a whole new level.

All of them.

Not a single one objected.

"See," Astraea whispered as the pledges still rippled through the spacious marble hall, "I told you so."

Fenrir smiled at her, still shocked but finally feeling like he was in the right place.

As if he had always belonged here in Asgard.

He raised his hand, and Odin's spear appeared in it, forming from a flash of lightning. At the same time, a glowing wolf appeared by Astraea's side. Together, they turned and walked to their thrones and sat on them for the first time ever, Nova lifting her head proudly at her goddess' feet.

"See, it doesn't feel so bad," Astraea teased him, stroking her wolf's fur.

"Only because you are by my side, my love."

He took her hand once again and brought it to his lips.

The sound of neighing distracted them both as a dark shadow covered the light from the windows again and again. Something was flying above Valhalla.

"You really should have thought twice before giving that thing wings," Fenrir grunted.

"The Nightmare needed an upgrade," she said with a sweet smile. "Give Midnight a break."

The shadow flashed above them again, and people lifted their worried gazes to the skies, not sure what it was.

"All I am saying is they were already scared as it is. That thing—"

"He has a name!" Astraea arched her brow at her husband while Magnus and Devoss announced the beginning of coronation celebrations to the crowds. "It's about time you started using it. After all, he was crucial to us finding each other again."

"Fine," Fenrir exhaled heavily. "You shouldn't have given Midnight wings."

"But he looks so cute!" she argued. "Look at him!"

The shadow flew by the glass-stained windows, causing the glass to tremble and making people shy away from them.

"Yeah, sure," the wolf let out a chuckle and kissed her fingers again, "whatever you say, Menace."

WHEN THE CORONATION celebrations were coming to an end, and most Asgardians either left or were so drunk they couldn't speak properly, the gang of rogues gathered on the main balcony of the throne room, waiting for the sunrise together.

"And they call us barbarians," Devoss huffed, taking a sip of his wine. "They can't even make a good martini here. It's either mead or wine, and that's it. You guys are going to have so much work to do here!"

"Trust me, adding the martini is at the top of our list," Astraea teased him, but the fox pretended not to notice.

"Speaking of work," Fenrir interjected, "I have some for you. The East is now technically without a ruler."

"Yeah, Bash, good luck with that," the fox deity chuckled.

"Don't look at me." Bastian grinned at him, folding his hands over his chest. "I have already spoken to them both and told them I am going to travel and search for information about the Hunters."

"Warg! My man!" Devoss quickly switched to his other friend.

"Nope." The first Lycan shook his head, enjoying the irony.

"Kara!" The fox turned to glance at the last one left, the Valkyrie, but she let out a mocking laugh.

"I am the only one literally created to travel between realms. I am too precious to stay in just one," she pointed out.

"Then who—" The fox locked eyes with Fenrir, who gave him a devilish smirk, then peered at Astraea, who offered a reassuring smile.

"You are going to do just fine!" The wolf had a hard time holding back a laugh.

"And all the martinis will be yours," Astraea added.

"But... I am a terrible choice!" Devoss grumbled, trying to persuade them to reconsider.

"You are literally the only one with an experience of being a King." Fenrir was not going to let it go.

"Yeah, but my country was destroyed!" The fox looked at his friends pleadingly.

"And it wasn't your fault." Fenrir placed a hand on his shoulder, giving it a light squeeze.

"But—"

"You were always the one who was meant to bring the East back to life," the ruler of Asgard insisted.

"My brother would never tolerate this," the fox reminded him.

"Your brother will have to deal with it." Warg patted him on the back, making the fox deity cough from his strength.

"But—" Devoss still tried to object.

"You'll do great!" Kara ruffled his hair.

"Hey, watch it! Don't ruin the 'do'!" he yelled at her, and they all burst out laughing.

"Don't worry. You are still the prettiest of us all, even with your messy hair," Bash scoffed, leaning over the balcony rail.

"So, you leave me all the dirty work and everyone but Warg is leaving me?" Devoss sighed gulping his drink and tossing the goblet over the ledge. Someone yelped from below the balcony, and they all stepped away from the rails so as not to be seen.

"Actually, there is something I would like to discuss with you," the first Lycan said. "I have a request."

"Already?" Devoss whistled. "It's exactly as I remember. Everyone wants a piece of me."

"I want to be your ambassador in the South." Warg met his gaze, and everyone went silent. "We still need to get Salome out."

"Sure." The new King of the East nodded. "Bring her back home, but then you two stay with me forever. Got it?"

"Fine!" The first Lycan hit his shoulder in a friendly matter, almost knocking Devoss over.

They continued to sip their drinks and make jokes until a tranquil silence enveloped them, causing their collective gaze to shift towards the breathtaking Asgardian sunrise.

"It just occurred to me," Devoss turned to face his friends, "this is probably the last time we'll all be together like this. It's like the end of an era."

"No," Fenrir pulled Astraea closer and kissed the top of her head, "it's the beginning of a new one."

75. EPILOGUE III

When the royal couple of the West returned to their hidden home in the woods, Riannon dashed up the stairs. Her heart set on seeing the man she loved as much as Gideon, if not more.

She found her son sleeping peacefully in his bed with her Beta, Maya, sitting next to the crib while her own daughter, Danielle, was crawling on the prince's fluffy playmat surrounded by toys.

"Hi." Riannon smiled, her eyes on her beloved baby, who looked like a little angel. "How was he?"

"No episodes." Maya smiled understandingly, while Dani destroyed a building cube tower at her feet.

"Good," Ria let out a deep sigh of relief. She was sure the Moon Goddess would have sent her a vision if anything was wrong, but after Fenrir and Joran's bodies disappeared in front of her eyes, a faint but persistent doubt continued to gnaw at her soul. What if they didn't win? After all, she didn't have a single vision since they parted and did not know how her sister was doing.

They managed to leave the South unharmed, but the political situation between the countries left much to be desired. The North was accused of despicable things, and it was possible that soon they would have a choice to make. None of the options were good. They would either drop their biggest ally, The Northern Lycan Kingdom, or... would take their people to war. Probably the latter, if she was honest with herself. Gideon would never abandon his sister's Kingdom, and she personally felt safer allying with the Northerners, considering they could be trusted. The South turned out to be a bigger problem than she anticipated. Barely anyone there wanted peace, and from what she saw, it looked like they were ready for war.

However, all that left her thoughts when Rafael made a cute little noise and opened his eyes. Right now, she had to be a mother first.

"Mummy is here." Riannon smiled and played with the blonde curls on his head before picking him up. "I missed you so much!"

"He missed you too," Maya confirmed, "and we are almost out of milk, so... would you mind?"

"Of course not." The Queen's lips curled. She loved their little connection.

"Was it as bad as it looked on the news?" the Beta enquired sensing the unrest in Ria's mood.

"Yes and no. It's complicated." Riannon walked to her favourite armchair and settled in for a breastfeeding session. "We will have to have a long brief today. You will need to clear your week for strategizing and stuff."

"Got you." Maya nodded. "I will call the babysitters in. The Gamma and the Delta are already on the border."

"Good." Ria nodded, preoccupied by her thoughts. Luckily, her Beta was prepared for anything.

The unmistakable scent of a dirty nappy filled the air.

"Dani Again?" Maya sighed, rolling her eyes as she realised her baby needed yet another change. "I swear, sometimes this werewolf's sense of smell is a curse," she chuckled to herself as she scooped up Dani and walked from the room, leaving Riannon in peace with her son. When the Queen lifted her gaze, instead of her Beta she saw Gideon leaning on the door frame.

"How is Raf Raf doing?" he asked, trying not to display his concern in front of her. Her husband always did that. He stayed strong so that she had the space to fall apart if she needed to.

"Maya said he has been great," Riannon replied, undoing the buttons on her dress and offering her son a meal. The little lips found the breast in a second, latching on to it as his little hands entangled in her blonde locks. Rafael's sweet scent enveloped her, and if she could, she would have stayed like this forever, alone with the two most important men in her life.

Gideon watched his family with pride, not wishing to disturb them, and yet he couldn't help himself from saying, "You've never been more beautiful than now."

Ria chuckled, knowing exactly how she looked after their long flight: hair dishevelled, yesterday's makeup, circles under her eyes. Yet Gideon still looked at her as if what he was saying was true, and she loved him so much for it. Rafael made a displeased noise, not happy to have her attention anywhere else, and she returned her gaze to him.

"He is going to be one possessive Alpha," his father noted and then froze as his Beta Reid mind linked him. "Ria, I need to go. A few urgent decisions have to be made."

"I'll see you at the briefing, then." She nodded, knowing that he wouldn't have left her if it wasn't urgent, at the same time, trusting he would have told her what it was, if it required her presence. They had gotten that part of the King and Queen thing figured out.

"Love you both." Gideon quickly reached his wife and son, giving a soft kiss to each of them, and left the blue-hued room.

Taking a moment more, savouring their time together, as Riannon gently settled the blissed-out Rafael back into his crib, she felt a presence in the room.

Her sister's aura was so different now. She could sense the divine energy and wasn't sure how to behave.

"You should have told me." Astrea appeared right next to her. She was wearing a long, flowing silver dress with intricate bead patterns adorning it, and her hair was much longer than the last time they saw each other.

So different again. Ria smiled to herself, remembering how every time she saw her little sister, she was able to adapt and change from the innocent Astrid at the Luna Trials, to Astrea the assassin. Now, her sibling was a serene goddess who could alter the entire universe with a flick of her finger. The Queen of the West did not know how to respond given this change.

"You should have told me," Astrea repeated more firmly.

"You had a lot on your plate as it is," Riannon sighed, "besides, I already knew you cannot fix it."

Astraea pursed her lips. She knew that too. However painful that was, healing the child now would require turning back time and the gods had definitely overused their intervention opportunities. This was why she had never attempted to do something like this before. Once you alter one destiny, then, when you need to change another, you no longer have a choice to do so anymore.

"I won't leave it like this," she promised. "I couldn't! Perhaps, over time—"

"Astrea, please, I am not sure I am ready to talk about this."

"I am so sorry, Ria. I would never forgive myself... If I hadn't used that potion on you during the Luna Trials, it could have been different."

Riannon placed her palm on top of the goddess's hand, giving it a light squeeze.

"I don't blame you, little sister. The Moon Goddess told my wolf that there is no way to know what caused this. Sadly, we will never get the answers and even if we did, they wouldn't change a thing in Rafael's life. Maybe it was the potion, maybe it was Jormungandr's attack on me, or maybe it was our destiny all along. I personally prefer to blame Joran."

Ria let out a bitter laugh, but at the same time, tears rolled down her cheeks. She was about to wipe them when Astrea caught her wrist and pulled her into a tight hug.

"Even if my hands are tied to heal him now, I promise you, he will never be alone," she whispered.

"Will you stay?" Riannon asked, not wishing to let her sister go.

"I can't." Astrea bit her lip to suppress a sob. "The divine realm is a mess. Someone is hunting the gods, no-one is safe. The balance is almost broken, and unless we mend it from up there, all realms could crumble. It has already happened once in the past and it would be best not repeated. Not to mention these demons that have become active. I am really needed up there."

"And what about us, here, in Midgard?" Riannon rebutted.

"Fenrir blessed both your countries, the North and the West. You should withstand even if the South attacks."

"But what about the demons?" This time, the Western Queen distanced herself from her sister. "They attacked us! We barely managed to survive."

"We are working on that too, I promise." Astrea clenched her sister's hand. "I will never leave you alone. Not again."

"Then why does it feel like I am losing you all over again?" Riannon exclaimed, letting the question slip off her tongue. She was always more reserved than that, but something told her Astrea would know how she felt, anyway.

"You will never lose me." The goddess smiled. "And I have something for you."

Riannon felt a row of beads materialising around her wrist.

"Is that—" She couldn't believe this.

"They are mostly healing beads," Astraea told her. "For when my nephew needs them, or you... if you've wasted too much of your gift helping him."

"Thank you so much!" She did not know what else to say.

"I wish I could have done more for you now," the goddess admitted.

"You are not her anymore, are you? You are not Astrea." The words were like daggers to them both.

"I am, and I am not." The answer was the truth, a realisation they both had already harboured deep within. "You are family to me, Riannon, but I can't stay in the mortal realm for long. I have the memories of my first life back, and the rest is returning to me little by little. Now, I am both Astrea and Astraea, but no matter what, you will always be my sister, and I will always come to your aid. One day, the balance will be restored, and we will meet again."

"I will wait," Ria said, tucking her face in her sister's hair and wrapping her arms around her until she disappeared.

Riannon knew more about the rules of the divine world than any mortal, but still couldn't help but feel the loss.

Rafael's tiny arm twitched in his dream and Ria tensed, but when nothing followed, she breathed out in relief.

"It's all going to be okay, Raf Raf." She smiled at her son, knowing she needed to concentrate on him and his well-being now.

SALOME PLACED her hands on the wall to help herself stretch her back. In the limited space of her modern cell, she quickly realised that keeping herself busy and moving was important not to go crazy. The walls blocked her magic and there was literally nothing else to do in here but pace.

The sounds of steps made her alert, but she did not plan to show this to any who visited her cage.

"Hey."

Forrest Romero's voice made her turn on her heels slowly and raise a questioning brow at him. "It took you long enough!" She folded her hands over her chest.

"Getting a criminal out of prison during this chaos is not an easy matter," he retorted with a smirk, showing her a paper in his hands with the Southern seal and stamp, "but I did it, and now you are officially working for me, under probation."

"Yay," she said unenthusiastically. "Lucky me."

"We don't have to do this if you don't want to." He moved his fingers, ready to rip the document in two, and deep inside she felt he'd do it, if she didn't stop him.

"No need." She shrugged. "I guess working for you is better than staying here."

"You still have to be careful," he warned her. "Your new workplace is connected to your private quarters and you are not allowed anywhere else. Sorry, but this is the best I can do for now. We will work on better conditions over time."

"Fine." The witch decided not to argue. This was the best any of them could be expected to do right now.

Fenrir was gone, there was nothing for her in Solace anymore. Going back there would be too painful.

At the same time, with her new criminal reputation, going back to her Coven would also be a mistake. This was indeed the best she could do presently. Not to mention that hopefully, thanks to general Romero, she would have insider information to send to her friends.

Forrest took her away from the Alpha Convocation building, but she noted that they didn't drive for long, despite him covering her eyes on the way. She also had to wear the magic blocking cuffs. However, he handed her the key for those on their way down a lengthy corridor to her new abode, allowing her to remove the blindfold from her eyes.

"Where are we?" the witch asked, looking around and noting the old stone walls. It looked like a castle, but the South did not have many castles, as far as she remembered.

"It's probably best you don't know for now," the wolf general confessed. "Baby steps, okay?"

"Baby steps?" she scoffed. "Are you serious? For now? I saved your ass during a demon invasion, and you took me from one prison to another."

"And this is exactly why I am doing this." Forrest opened the massive wooden door before her with a badge, and she realised that the old look of the building was just a façade.

The room with tall ceilings was filled with all the equipment she could possibly need. Jars with rare ingredients, glass bottles for potions, test tubes for experiments, and anything else a witch could possibly have need of for her work, were here on massive wooden tables. It was a complete laboratory, and she was impressed by how prepared he had been.

Still, she wasn't going to show it.

"So, your surprise is more work for me?" She rolled her eyes at the general.

"No." Forrest shook his head, and now she was finally interested.

Salome followed his gaze and only now noticed a dark figure in the corner.

"What are you doing here?" she gasped as tears stung her eyes. She thought they agreed she would deal with all of this alone, but here he was.

"I am not officially here. Not yet," Warg informed her, pushing off the wall. She threw the handcuffs, the key and the binding from her eyes at Forrest before running to her friend.

He caught her in a tight embrace, and she felt so safe in his large arms. Safe and guilty.

Warg shouldn't have done it. He shouldn't have come here for her. Not when she wasn't offering anything in return.

"I am the ambassador from the Eastern Kingdom," he informed her with a slight curl to the corner of his lips. "It is my job to stay here now and improve the connection between our countries."

Salome smiled. "That's... amazing, Warg."

"Sorry, but we need to go now," Forrest informed them. "It was already trouble enough to bring you here today, but over time, we will work on letting you two see each other more often."

"You do know that no one actually attacked the South, right?" Salome furrowed her brows at Romero. "It was Vincent all along."

"Do you have proof of that by any chance?" Forrest tilted his head and watched the witch cast her eyes down. "I thought so. Until we get the proof, I am afraid my hands are tied. But I do hope for the support of the East in suppressing this war."

"And you've got it," Warg promised.

"I'll help too." Salome joined them. "Whatever it takes."

"Well then," Forrest went to the huge fridge installed into one of the walls and produced a bottle of champagne, "I think we should celebrate our new alliance then."

NIKI FINISHED UNPACKING and sat on the old couch, looking around. After Joran and Fenrir disappeared, she managed to slip into her Teacher's old bedroom and found his briefcase with a stack of fake documents, money and cards. Altogether, it was enough for a small house in the middle of nowhere. Including making her traces disappear for anyone who could have been of interest.

Just perfect for her because she wanted peace.

Forrest helped her to cremate Bjorn's body, and all she had now from that big, incredible love of hers was the urn with his ashes.

Better than nothing, but not nearly enough.

If only she didn't ask him to return... if only she thought of him more than of Astrea back then... *if only...*

An ethereal light illuminated the room, making her jump to her feet.

Astrea knew she couldn't count on a warm welcome, but the hate she saw in her friend's eyes was still unexpected.

"Nik—"

"Go away," Nikiah said and turned away as if she wasn't in the presence of a goddess.

"Niki, I am so sorry."

The words would never be enough because of what was taken from her. If anyone in the entire world knew what it was like, it was Astrea.

"I am sure you are." The Firstborn let out a bitter chuckle. "I still got visited second after your real sister, right?"

"Niki, it's not like that," Astrea tried to protest, but saw her friend clenching her fists harder.

"You know what his last words were?" The Firstborn turned to face her former mentor. "Do you even want to know?!"

The Goddess of Stars nodded.

"He said that gods cannot be trusted, and honestly, I now think that Darius knew exactly what he was talking about! You—you use us for as long as we are useful, and then you are done and move on. While us mortals have to gather up the pieces after your divine intervention."

"Niki, I came to—"

"You came to make yourself feel better, but you know what, you have others for that. It's not my job anymore!"

"I am sorry you lost him," Astrea said, locking their gazes. "I still think you would like to know that now he is finally at peace."

Nikiah's lips parted in shock.

"You saw him?"

"It will be a while until his soul is ready to "see" anyone, but he is in a peaceful place. He is not tortured anymore. Bjorn—Darius is happy now."

Niki didn't know why it hurt her even more than before now.

"I have something for you." Astrea broke the silence.

"I need nothing from you."

"It's not from me." The goddess stretched out her arms and an old blue wooden box appeared in her hands. "It belonged to him."

Niki recognised that box. It used to stand on a mantle in Darius' old room on the Firstborn island, and she was never allowed to touch it.

Finally, she would have something of his. Something to remember him by.

"Thank you." She took the box out of Astrea's hands and turned away not to let her see her teary eyes. Her anger faded slightly, but it didn't change anything.

"I just want you to know that if I could—"

"But you *can!*" Nikiah faced her again, fury rippling through her. "You are the most powerful goddess ever to exist. I did my homework. You can turn back time. Or you can give his soul a new host. You can do so many things, but you just brought me an old box of his old crap!"

"Niki, things are bad up there. We can't make big changes anymore."

"And why is that?" The Firstborn laughed through tears. "Oh yes! It's because your love and his brother entertained themselves with a mortal war, blessing everyone on their way and taking that opportunity from others. All of you are the same! And now I-I have to live my life alone with my memories of the life that could have been!"

She finally let out a loud sob and covered her eyes.

"You are not alone," Astrea said softly, taking a hesitant step towards her former student.

"No offence, but I don't want you in my life anymore!" Niki announced, and although it hurt like hell, Astrea stepped back, respecting her decision.

"I am not talking about me," she said, and Niki stopped crying, darting her gaze back at her ex-friend.

"What are you—"

"Don't you know yet?" Astrea tilted her head. "You are with child, Niki."

The werewolf's hands slid down to her stomach. She was sure it was all the stress eating, but now, when she touched her slightly rounded belly, it felt so different.

Darius's child. She would have *his* child. A piece of him was living in her. A piece of him will forever live in this world.

He wasn't entirely gone.

"Niki, I know you don't want to hear from me for now," Astrea used the opportunity, "but know that I will never leave you. Not really. I will not be able to visit for some time, but I will always look over you and your little one."

The Firstborn wasn't sure what to reply to that. Too many thoughts were in her head.

All this... it wasn't the end.

"As I have said," Astrea cleared her throat, "I will not be able to be here for at least a few years, so I want you to have this.

She touched the young woman's wrist, and a row of beads appeared on it.

"Use it for you and your son's protection," Astrea said, and slowly, Niki managed to offer her a nod. Those beads were priceless. Those beads meant protection.

She would have a son. His son. With silver hair and the strength of a bear.

"Thanks." The Firstborn brushed her fingers over the cold beads.

"Niki—"

"It's not that I don't want to forgive you," she said, interrupting the goddess. "I just can't. At least not now. Not soon. It would feel like betraying him."

"I understand." Her old mentor forced a little smile on her face. "You can call me anytime. I will come to help you, I swear. It's the truth because—"

"The words of the gods are binding," Nikiah finished for her. "But they also, always, have a double meaning. Leave me. At least for now."

This wasn't how Astrea wanted their last meeting to be, but she had to accept it.

"I hope to see you again," she added before disappearing.

Niki was finally alone, her hand still on her stomach. She cried for weeks and now, for the first time since Darius's death, her lips curled into a warm smile.

"Hello, my little cub."

Now that she thought about it, she would never be alone again.

BASTIAN HOPED TO LEAVE UNNOTICED. He hated long goodbyes, and knowing his friends, they would want to throw him another party. So, his plan was simple. Just portal to the mortal realm and be done with it.

"Going somewhere?" His father's voice startled him and he slowly turned on his feet.

"We really don't need to do this." He was by his parent's side for centuries, trying to repay him for what had been done to him.

Bash knew really well that he wasn't a product of love, yet his father tolerated him. Fenrir was to be admired.

"Let's agree to disagree." The ruler of Asgard arched his brow.

"I just want a taste of freedom and independence!" Bash let out a chuckle.

"You were always free. I hope you know that."

He knew, but … he had never really felt it before. The debt he placed on himself, the fault… they were too real, and the nicer Fenrir was to him, the worse he felt. Surely, he did not really think he was his son. When Astraea gave him children, they would be his real family and heirs.

Now, his job was done, and he had to leave to give them peace and let them be happy without any reminders of the past.

"Anyway," Fenrir cleared his throat, "I have something for you, Skoll."

"What is it?" He flinched hearing his old name, but tried to play it cool.

"You are going to look for the Hunters," his father reminded him, "I am not the one to prohibit you from doing anything. You know that. After all, you have long passed an age of needing to listen to me. However, I can't let my child go on such a quest without some additional... help."

"Please, don't make me take the mad flying horse!" he begged.

"I wish!" Fenrir rolled his eyes laughing heartily. "But Astraea would never part with that thing. However, I can easily part with something else in my possession."

He stretched his hand, and immediately, Odin's spear appeared in it.

"You can't!" Bash couldn't contain his astonishment.

"I absolutely can," his father insisted. "It is yours now. It's about time I create my own damn divine weapon, and I would feel better knowing that you had this one in your possession during your adventures. Use it at your will. You have my complete trust, Skoll."

The young wolf wrapped his fingers around the cold metal spear and felt electricity ripple through him as the power within acknowledged him as its new owner.

"Just... be careful when you pierce people with it," Fenrir warned him. "It may revive them and leave you with... complications. Just saying."

"I'll keep this in mind." Bash smirked. "Thanks."

His father placed a hand on his shoulder. "And now go, son. Write your own story."

ABOUT THE AUTHOR

Marissa Gilbert resides in the United Kingdom with her loving husband and three beautiful children. When she's not immersed in the magical world of writing, she finds solace in other forms of creative expression, such as painting and scrapbooking. She also enjoys creating aesthetically pleasing videos for her Instagram channel, showing glimpses of her life.

Marissa has authored several captivating books that form part of an enchanting series called "The Moonrise Kingdom." The titles include:

Book I. The Perfect Luna

Book II. The Luna Trials

Book III. The Alpha God's Luna.

Book IV. His Shadow Luna

Book V. The Forgotten Bond

These works transport readers to mystical realms where romance intertwines with elements of Greek and Norse mythology, setting the stage for unforgettable tales.

Currently, Marissa serialises her books on Inkitt app, where loyal readers embark on extraordinary adventures guided by her vivid imagination. This is also where you can get special editions of her books if you are a subscriber of the Moonrise Tier.

After the books are done on Inkitt, they are published on Amazon, Waterstones and Barnes & Nobles.

For those who wish to connect with Marissa Gilbert, she warmly invites readers to join her dedicated community on Facebook, named "Marissa Gilbert's Reading Circle." It is within this engaging space that book enthusiasts can come together, share thoughts, and delve into lively discussions surrounding the captivating worlds she has crafted. In addition to Facebook, Marissa also maintains a vibrant online presence on Instagram, TikTok, and

Threads under the username @marissagilbertauthor, where she keeps her readers enthralled with intriguing glimpses into her writing process and shares exciting updates about upcoming projects.

You can also find all important information and the latest book-related merchandise on her website www.marissagilbertauthor.co.uk

www.ingramcontent.com/pod-product-compliance
Lightning Source LLC
Chambersburg PA
CBHW030843030726
47495CB00005B/1340